Here's to the losers!

Alan G Boyer

DREAMS TO DIE FOR

ALAN G BOYES

Copyright © 2014 Alan G Boyes

The moral right of the author has been asserted.

Apart from any fair dealing for the purposes of research or private study, or criticism or review, as permitted under the Copyright, Designs and Patents Act 1988, this publication may only be reproduced, stored or transmitted, in any form or by any means, with the prior permission in writing of the publishers, or in the case of reprographic reproduction in accordance with the terms of licences issued by the Copyright Licensing Agency. Enquiries concerning reproduction outside those terms should be sent to the publishers.

This book is a work of fiction. Names, characters, businesses, places and events are either the product of the author's imagination or are used fictitiously and any resemblance to real persons, living or dead, is purely coincidental.

Matador
9 Priory Business Park
Kibworth Beauchamp
Leicestershire LE8 0RX, UK
Tel: (+44) 116 279 2299
Fax: (+44) 116 279 2277
Email: books@troubador.co.uk
Web: www.troubador.co.uk/matador

ISBN 978 1783061 600

British Library Cataloguing in Publication Data.
A catalogue record for this book is available from the British Library.

Typeset in Aldine401 BT Roman by Troubador Publishing Ltd
Printed and bound in the UK by TJ International, Padstow, Cornwall

Matador is an imprint of Troubador Publishing Ltd

Acknowledgements

Firstly, and most importantly, my thanks are to my family who have given me immense support and encouragement to fulfil my ambition of writing a novel. I must also thank those who inspired me to write this story: the numerous victims of crime that I had the privilege to meet and whose courage in overcoming adversity is humbling; and also to those perpetrators of crime who provided me with a brief insight into their own ambitions and motivations. My publishers have throughout given me invaluable help, expertise and advice and, lastly, to my springer spaniel whose antics, behaviour and character I have unashamedly drawn upon for certain passages in the book!

I must also thank the following for permitting their copyrighted work to be reproduced:

In Dreams
Words and Music by Roy Orbison
Copyright © 1963 (Renewed 1991) BARBARA ORBISON MUSIC COMPANY, ORBI-LEE MUSIC, R-KEY DARKUS MUSIC and SONY/ATV MUSIC PUBLISHING LLC
All Rights on behalf of SONY/ATV MUSIC PUBLISHING LLC Administered by SONY/ATV MUSIC PUBLISHING LLC, 8 Music Square West, Nashville, TN 37203
All Rights Reserved Used by Permission
Reproduced by Permission of Hal Leonard Corporation

Quoich Dam Scheme (Cross Section)
Reproduced by kind permission of *Water Power* magazine

"A candy-colored clown they call the sandman
Tiptoes to my room every night
Just to sprinkle stardust and to whisper
Go to sleep, everything is all right.
I close my eyes, then I drift away
Into the magic night. I softly say
A silent prayer like dreamers do.
Then I fall asleep to dream my dreams of you.
In dreams I walk with you. In dreams I talk to you.
In dreams you're mine. All of the time we're together
In dreams, In dreams.
But just before the dawn, I awake and find you gone.
I can't help it, I can't help it, if I cry."

'In Dreams' by Roy Orbison

QUOICH DAM SCHEME
Lochaber, Scottish Highlands

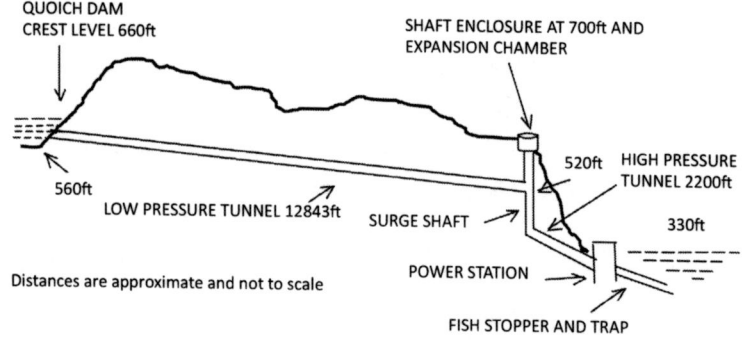

Reproduced by kind permission of *Water Power* magazine

1

Yasmin Hasan's family were Sunni, like Saddam Hussein, but her parents never liked nor openly supported the autocratic leader of Iraq. They never opposed him either. Her mother and father, and their parents before them, had been born and raised within Baghdad's ancient city walls and learnt that to survive and prosper it was necessary to adapt to the demands and turbulence of the changing ruling forces which had governed their lives. They had witnessed the bloodshed of the overthrow of the old King Faisal II and the murder of the royal family in 1958, dutifully turning out to join the gruesome parade of their bodies as they were dragged along the soiled and bloodstained streets of the new Republic. Ten years later they mingled with the crowds lining the same streets to cheer the success of the bloodless coup led by General Ahmed Hassan al-Bakr that brought to power the Arab Socialist Baa'th Party and some of his close army colleagues, including Saddam. Throughout their lifetimes Baghdad had never been a place for freedom of expression and democratic principles, and during Hussein's rule they had witnessed how even the slightest critical comment of the regime could lead to a whole family's sudden and permanent disappearance. Yasmin's family were more than content not to notice the abuses going on around them, preferring instead to take advantage of the benefits bestowed upon the minority Sunni population and to make certain that they at least appeared to be loyal citizens.

By comparison with most Middle Eastern children, Yasmin had experienced a happy childhood free of poverty, principally because of the reforms and economic progress made by Iraq under Saddam, which had enabled her father to establish a flourishing and profitable electrical business. Her parents had come from modest backgrounds and life for them was initially tough until Hussein took control and installed himself both as President and Prime Minister in July 1979. Saddam actively fostered the modernisation of the Iraqi economy and protected it by creating a strong, often brutal, security force to prevent the country from returning to factional warfare. It also served to ensure no one threatened to overthrow him. The revenues from the newly nationalised Iraqi oil industry, swollen by massive increases in the world prices, had provided social services and public health systems, including free hospitalisation, which were unprecedented among Middle Eastern countries. There was universal free schooling up to the highest education levels for both boys and girls and Yasmin was but one of hundreds of thousands of children who benefited from it, gaining an excellent degree in chemistry from Baghdad University before undertaking a postgraduate course at the University of Birmingham in England.

During her year in Britain, the crisis between Saddam and the West worsened and when she returned home she found a nervous populace, confused by the West's attitude towards an Arab country that had embraced very many western values, and a city wondering what its future may hold. Yasmin was determined to assist the country of her birth and she quickly obtained employment in a genetic research establishment on the outskirts of the city.

On the first day of the invasion in 2003, the 'Shock and Awe' targeted bombing of her native city blasted the laboratory where she worked to rubble. From then on life for Yasmin and her parents rapidly descended into a daily ordeal of avoiding the coalition bombs and missiles. Her father's business collapsed, initially not from high explosives, but simply because nobody wanted luxury goods any more. Prices were rocketing and money was needed to buy bread and other basic items that kept a person alive. When the Americans entered Baghdad and Hussein fled, Yasmin's parents did not celebrate but neither were they dismayed. They were not political and their prime concern now, like most of their countrymen, was how quickly the city, and particularly their business, could start functioning again. Anticipation turned to frustration and then to anger when over the weeks it became clear that the forces that had almost destroyed their city had no intention, nor the resources, to repair even the most basic infrastructure. Day upon day passed with no electricity, no water and little food. Roads were impassable, buildings dangerous and all the while the resentment towards their new rulers grew. The khaki-dressed soldiers were now seen as invaders and tension rose as the general population increased its protests.

Under Saddam there had been little terrorist activity as his security forces liquidated any such opposition with ruthless efficiency, but Yasmin noticed a dangerous change of attitude growing from those like her and her family who were forced to continue to live in ruined buildings and on broken streets. Saddam's own military forces slipped quietly back into civilian life or joined the swelling numbers of the various disaffected factions who quickly armed themselves with weapons from their own hastily deserted military compounds. The next few months were both terrible and frightening for Yasmin. She watched as bombs and mortars, from one side or the other, rained down upon the street where she lived. She witnessed several of her friends die in these attacks, their limbs twisted and torn by shards of red hot metal and saw the spattered trails of dark red blood drying on the white concrete walls acting as a daily reminder of where they had fallen.

"Why has this happened? What harm have we and our friends ever caused to Saddam or America to bring about this carnage?" She angrily questioned her father, after her oldest friend had her leg blown off from the blast of a car bomb. Her father could not answer. He did not understand either. He had believed the coalition forces would quickly restore order and provide safety as well as renewing the essential services, but it had not happened. He was a disillusioned and a deeply saddened man who often sat for hours in his empty shop gazing through tired eyes at the street outside and the destruction around him. Slowly Yasmin's fear and grief turned to anger and resentment.

Within a few months Haifa Street – Grenade Alley, as the Americans later nicknamed it – had suffered so many street bombings and helicopter attacks that hardly a building remained intact. Her father's shop was so severely damaged it had to be boarded up, and Yasmin and her family were confined to the small flat at the rear of the premises. The intensity of the attacks escalated and tragedy struck Yasmin's family in September 2004. The Shia-dominated new Iraq army, intent on driving out the Sunni population of the street, claimed that the area was occupied by insurgents and, bolstered by coalition forces, moved in to cleanse the street of its inhabitants. In the midst of a particularly fierce gun battle raging elsewhere along the dusty and now empty road, a trigger-happy American soldier suddenly burst through the Hasan's living room door, firing his machine gun in all directions. Yasmin witnessed her parents being propelled to the floor as the impact of a spray of high-powered bullets smashed and ripped into their flesh, leaving only a horrible crimson stain spreading across the sofa where a few moments earlier they had sat reading books in the dim light. Too late the soldier realised that the two corpses lying on the carpet were unarmed civilians. Yasmin came running through from the bathroom and screamed. The soldier ran. Cradling their bodies, the twenty seven year-old Yasmin screamed and vowed to avenge their deaths. Frustration and resentment instantly turned to hatred.

2

Cindy Crossland had not slept much, despite having every intention of doing so when retiring to bed the previous evening. Having set her digital alarm for 5:30am, a quick glance at the pale blue display informed her she could indulge in the comfort of her light summer duvet for a little over half an hour longer.

There had been times when this postponement to the daily routine would have been met with relief, excitement even, and on more than one occasion she would have turned over and put her arm out across Alan and gently woken him. But it wasn't going to happen this morning and neither had it yesterday – in fact, she had not done so for several months. Another long night of disturbed and fitful sleep had left her feeling tired, her brain having been ceaselessly active from trying to analyse and make sense of the different thoughts and images that had invaded it since she turned off the light seven hours earlier. Yet she knew why she found sleep difficult. It was the same reason why she could not now slip her hand across the bare back of the man whom she had once loved.

Cindy had achieved virtually every goal she had set for herself as a young girl: financial independence after a dazzlingly successful short career, a loyal and hardworking husband, a magnificent Cotswold home with a flat in London – what more did she want or need? But for some reason she simply wasn't happy, and hadn't been so for many months. She had lain awake at night for several weeks trying to work out a solution; she had even given up her job in the belief that such a radical change might help, but it hadn't. At times she felt her mind was near to exploding with the constant churning over the same issue, but she had reluctantly concluded there was no simple fix or easy answer to her anguish. She knew the problem. What she needed was the courage to do something about it. Several weeks previously she had insisted on separate bedrooms. Of course Alan had not liked that, but her restlessness at night often kept them both awake, and he had eventually acquiesced. Cindy had moved her clothes into the adjoining room where she now lay and, as she had done on many mornings, gazed up at the stucco ceiling cursing silently to herself for her cowardice.

There had never been a better opportunity than yesterday to explain to Alan just how she felt. They had returned a couple of days ago from Kalamata, having enjoyed a week in the Marni. She loved Greece and particularly the Southern Pelopponese, and they had once again relished the peace and quiet of the spectacular peninsula. The small, family run hotel in Agios Nikolaus was furnished in stark contrast to their Stillwood home but she had not missed the so-called necessities that she and Alan regarded as essential in England. They were content to tour gently around in the Group B hire car they had collected from the airport, stopping wherever and whenever they wished to soak up the atmosphere. They sipped lazily from their ice-cold drinks and spoke little as they enjoyed the freshly prepared fine food, and most evenings wandered down to the small harbour near their hotel where they watched the fiery sun set over the still water. The basic twin bedded apartment was comfortable and Cindy was grateful for the excuse not to round off an evening in a shared bed. The holiday break had gone as well as she might have anticipated and in fact she had been temporarily uplifted by it. *Perhaps things may get better*, she thought as the plane touched down at Birmingham International airport – but it was now Thursday and yesterday had proved somewhat of a disaster.

Alan had suggested that as a finale to their holiday break they should dine out at the nearby Buckland Manor. It was a particular favourite of Cindy's, and they talked and laughed their way through the fine cuisine reminiscing about past holidays. As they relaxed in the sumptuous leather sofas chatting amiably whilst they took coffee with brandy liqueurs, Alan had completely stunned her by suddenly changing the subject.

"Are you seeing someone else?"

Blunt. This was unlike Alan who usually avoided direct questions and answers – a character trait she increasingly disliked.

"Are you having an affair?" he became louder and more insistent.

"Certainly not, Alan. No. Of course not. Why on earth would

you ask that? Especially now when we've just had a lovely holiday and such a nice evening" she replied, somewhat taken aback.

"Because I can tell you haven't been yourself for quite some time and ..." he hesitated and then lowered his voice "... there is nothing physical between us anymore. That is not what we married for and surely not what we want. I need you Cindy. You know I love you dearly, but what else am I to think?"

Alan was clearly pained and Cindy quickly suggested that they finish their liqueurs and then continue the discussion at home. The hotel lounge was not the place for debating their sex life. The short drive back to Red Gables, a spacious, beautifully appointed Victorian house built of Cotswold stone and set in three acres in the hamlet of Stillwood, gave Cindy time to marshal her response and she hoped she could regain some control of the situation. She wasn't having an affair, and had never even been close to having one since their marriage – which now seemed a long five years ago – but she could hardly deny that the 'Millennium Madness' of their marriage of which they both joked about in happier times was no longer a laughing matter. She knew the marriage was in trouble, it was what kept her awake at night. Those heady days in the year 2000 had started in a crowded London coffee house when a stranger, awkwardly carrying his tray and trying to look for a spare seat, asked if he might sit across the table from her. Two months later, they were married; four years later she knew she had made the wrong decision, but still hoped. Now, five years since her wedding day, Cindy was finding she could no longer pretend nor disguise her feelings. She knew that someday soon she would have to face Alan and explain. But please, not now, not tonight.

"So, are you going to tell me what's wrong, then?" Alan enquired cautiously as he poured them both a brandy before he sat back in his favourite armchair. She noticed a slight quiver in his voice that revealed he was finding this a lot more difficult than she. He looked so vulnerable now, quite different from the assured and confident city bank executive. His eyes seemed more tired, the handsome facial appearance almost defeated by the anxiety he so clearly felt. He was only five years older than Cindy but his pained expression had caused deep lines to appear on his forehead and he now looked considerably nearer fifty than forty. She could not bring herself to answer his question, not at this moment. *Why should I, anyway*, she reasoned to herself. She had recently given up her job in the Cabinet Office and was starting out on a new venture in the hope that it might revive her spirits and provide a fresh stimulus to her life. She really didn't need an in depth discussion of her innermost feelings right now. Tomorrow she was going to London to meet an ex-colleague who had intrigued her by saying that he needed her advice on 'a delicate international matter', so answers to Alan's probing questions on the state of their marriage would have wait.

"Oh Alan, this is silly. I promise I am not having an affair. As you know I've been really busy for several years now and it's just that I'm a bit tired and jaded. The holiday was marvellous and I am sure that within a few weeks I will be back to my normal self again. I'll see the doctor if you like, maybe he can give me some magic pills – you never know what they might do!" She gave a fainthearted chuckle hoping it would lighten the mood.

"I'm also at a funny age, maybe that has something to do with it. Thirty-five isn't old I know but women can get a bit strange in their thirties, maybe that's it."

The latter seemed plausible to Alan, as virtually every male colleague had passed a comment at some time or other that seemed to confirm that women do, indeed, go 'funny'. It also crossed his mind that such comments had been made in relation to women of virtually any age, not just in their thirties.

"Well maybe it is then" said Alan slowly, thinking as he spoke. "But I want you to promise that you would tell me if there was ever anyone else. Will you do that?"

"Of course, Alan, but I assure you there most definitely isn't." Cindy spoke confidently, relieved at not having to lie.

"I know we have never wanted to start a family but perhaps that's what we need?" Alan gently posed the question causing Cindy to almost choke as she took too large a gulp of the brandy. A pram, nappies and shopping for baby clothes were definitely not what she needed and whilst she was aware her biological clock was ticking, she was determined it was not going to be stopped prematurely.

"Me? A mother? I don't think so Alan. No." This was very

definitely the truth and Cindy delivered it with such firmness that it was designed to put an immediate stop to further discussion of the subject. She went across to his armchair where he was seated and kissed him gently on the forehead.

"I still love you very much" she lied, "but if you don't mind I've got this meeting tomorrow and I do need to get in some undisturbed sleep. I think I'll go up to my room now".

Alan Crossland sighed, quickly poured himself another stiff brandy and then muttered "goodnight", but Cindy was already at the top of the stairs and heard nothing as she quickly hastened to the sanctuary of her own bedroom, oblivious at having made her worried husband even more anxious. For several months he had been aware that her feelings towards him had changed. It was obvious. Cindy no longer did those small, meaningful things around the house that partners do for each other in a happy, fulfilled relationship. Her language too had altered. She had started referring to *your* bedroom and *my* bedroom.

"It's our room" he suddenly yelled out, "not *my* room. It's *our* bedroom, and both of us should be using it." But his wife had already closed the door.

The nightly separation particularly angered him. Cindy seemed to be slowly excluding him from major aspects of her life, *their* life, which together they should share. He tried to analyse why she should be doing this to him. He had done nothing to deserve such unreasonable treatment. He had been good with money even though Cindy herself had received a high salary for many years in a lucrative career. He had never had a casual girlfriend let alone a mistress. He had not visited a lap dancing joint nor the superficially posh London night clubs where you can get anything, and anyone, at a price. He was confused. Cindy had told him that she wasn't having an affair and he believed her. Or did he? Was it perhaps that he wanted to believe her? He had loved everything about her from the very first time he saw her across the table at La Cramanche having a coffee, and recalled how he nervously asked if he might join her and how delighted he was when she agreed.

Thoughts turned over in his head, but there was one thing he resolved. Cindy had denied an affair. He had given her every opportunity and even though he would have been terribly upset if she had been seeing someone, he could have accepted it, but not if she had lied to him. He would continue to believe her, continue to try and make her happy, and hope she was right in saying that it was only a short-term blip but he would never forgive her if she was lying. He deserved better than that. He emptied his glass and started turning off the lights.

3

Cindy was still thinking about the previous evening when the sudden sound of her favourite radio station, blasting from the digital alarm clock, was a reminder that she could not stay in bed any longer. After a quick shower, she and Alan shared a breakfast of orange juice and croissants. Normally Alan would have his driver collect him from either Red Gables or, if he was staying in London, the luxury apartment he and Cindy owned in Shoreditch, but Alan had given him leave that extended beyond the duration of their Greek trip and so for today and tomorrow he was commuting. Cindy, too, was making the same journey for her meeting, and so they sat together on the smart Great Western Intercity to Paddington before taking the long walk across the station concourse and joined the hundreds of fellow commuters hurrying down the steps to the underground Circle line platform. They were fortunate and were able to stand together on the first train to arrive, though in the cramped conditions conversation was not attempted.

At Liverpool Street station it was only possible for Alan to half turn towards Cindy as he said 'goodbye' before he pushed his way forward to leave the carriage. Standing in the middle of a throng of fellow passengers, she could just glimpse Alan exiting the platform concourse and she reflected that they had not spoken more than two sentences to each other during the whole two hour journey. Alan had assiduously studied *The Financial Times* before turning his attention to the crosswords in *The Times* and *The Daily Telegraph*, whilst Cindy had read the latest Kathy Reich novel. Grabbing the handrail above her head to steady herself in readiness for the train to pull away from the station, she turned her mind to what her morning meeting was really all about. She had left the Cabinet Office six months earlier, so what could her friend Peter Knowles possibly want to discuss now? And more intriguingly, why? It certainly wasn't going to be what he had inferred, it never was. Peter was renowned for speaking in riddles.

The powerful electric motors whirred as the London Underground train 204 accelerated into the tunnel and had started to pick up speed when a blinding flash of light was followed almost instantaneously by an explosion that echoed and reverberated like a massive clap of thunder. The blast threw Cindy across the floor. Bodies tumbled over her. She instinctively raised her slender arms to shield herself as more people were hurled back and forth whilst the crippled train shuddered to a violent halt from the automatic emergency braking system.

Cindy, dazed and barely conscious, tried to focus but the swirling black dust stung her eyes forcing her to squint into the murky darkness. People were screaming, crying, shouting. Something heavy was lying across her. She pushed against it but the lifeless body refused to move. She tried to raise her head but her neck hurt. Someone nearby started to groan, obviously in pain. Smoke and fumes started to replace the filthy dust and an acrid, bitter, burning sensation pricked the back of her throat as she gulped the foul air. She started to panic as her lungs became slowly starved of the oxygen they needed, causing her to breathe harder and deeper. Terrified that her lungs seemed incapable of working, she cried out for help but her voice went unheard as it blended into the many other screams, cries and groans. She glimpsed fresh blood running fast across the bodies near to her. The carriage lights flickered, as if struggling themselves for survival, and were accompanied by a synchronised crackling noise like the rasping sound of breaking matchboxes before they uttered a final hissing screech and were no more. The silver-coloured carriage plunged into almost total darkness until a dim, emergency light came on and cast an eerie, yellow glow. The screams of its trapped and wounded occupants intensified.

Slowly the acrid smoke cleared easing the sour pain in her mouth and chest. The thick black dust began to settle. It clung to open wounds, much as small iron filings do when placed near a magnet. Warm, crimson blood turned a cold, dirty purple. Cindy tried to move her arms to wipe the soot away from her nose and eyes, but her strength had gone and she was unable to move. Loud, terrified voices were shouting.

"Get Out. "Get out" someone yelled from the opposite side of the train.

"No, no. Stay put. Everyone stay put. The current may not be switched off, we could be killed" screamed a woman near to Cindy, panic evident in her voice.

But over and over she heard people saying "Bomb, it's a bomb".

Cindy watched helplessly as some passengers managed painfully and slowly to get to their feet, groggily exploring themselves for injuries. She could see blood pouring from faces, arms and legs, some covered only by slithers of cloth that were moments earlier expensive tailored suits and dresses. Torn garments hung helplessly from the shattered limbs of blackened people whose faces were distinguishable only by the whites of their eyes. Larger pools of blood appeared, slowly filling the indentations of the tread pattern etched onto the rubberised floor. As the contours became overwhelmed, the warm, life-giving liquid spread out into small rivulets and formed macabre, crimson diagrams between the prone bodies of the injured. Cindy, her eyes focusing more clearly now, had to look away from those whose injuries were obviously severe and from which most of the thick, sticky blood had oozed. She tried to raise herself once more but gave up when she started to feel pain, first in her legs and then her arms but which slowly spread to her entire body. She tried to stay calm but the intensity of the pain kept interrupting her determination and she started to shake from the dangerous cocktail of panic and fear. She kept repeating to herself that she must try to remain conscious. She so wanted to stand, desperate to get away from the hell around her. She made one last abortive attempt to push away the lifeless body that was pinning down her leg before she let out a loud scream and passed out.

It was 8:50am on Thursday 7th July 2005, the day which became known as Britain's 7/7. A day of huge implications and consequences for the United Kingdom generally, but for Cindy it was the day that changed her life forever.

★ ★ ★

Alan Crossland reached the top of the crowded escalator, walked across the concourse and out into the bright, summer sunlight. The noise and bustle of the city never failed to excite and impress him. He loved its buzz, its people, its business and delighted at being a part of it. He had cut his teeth in banking during the later Thatcher years when employment within financial services stopped being a humdrum, boring existence and turned itself into a dynamic, progressive and world-leading industry which rewarded enterprise and risk taking. He had witnessed how under a Labour government the traditional virtues of 'a man's word is his bond' and 'uberrima fides' ('utmost good faith') had been slowly overtaken by the more ancient vices of greed and lust. Banking was at last freed of over restrictive regulation and now looked upon benignly by an administration anxious to boost its own exchequer from the additional taxes raised as the burgeoning profits of the financial corporations soared.

Although personally saddened at the diminishing integrity that was once prevalent within the financial world, where his own pocket was concerned Crossland was not so distraught as to try to impede its ongoing decline. He embraced the new radical monetarism that had severed the shackles from the city and which was why, if he were totally honest, he regarded London as the best capital in the world. It was where you could now make serious money.

He stood amongst the throng of pedestrians patiently waiting for the traffic lights to change. Absorbed in speculative thoughts as to where his fellow commuters might be headed for, or pondering the sort of jobs they might have, he only noticed that it was safe to cross when the mass of bodies surrounding him moved forward. Halfway across, a sharp noise, like a car backfire, momentarily caused a few to turn their heads in alarm, but seeing no imminent danger they quickly continued on their journey.

Four minutes later Crossland walked up the seven brown marble steps that marked the entrance to his bank, pushed through the large revolving glass door and took the lift to the executive suite on the third floor. Jane, his long serving and trusted secretary, welcomed him as he settled back into his comfortable black cloth and leather chair and immediately poured some freshly-ground coffee into his large, personal mug which he preferred to the bone china cups that had to be used whenever clients were present. Crossland switched on his computer and took a quick glance at the papers on his desk. How he hated being away for so long. Since his rise to chief executive, he had personally steered the Bank's principal activities away from traditional banking towards the new financial services products and into areas where the risk of taking on more lucrative ventures offered great rewards – occasionally even taking personal control of a few very special accounts of which no one else was aware. The profits, and with it his performance-enhanced salary, leaped. He enjoyed the wealth, and the risk-taking. It was in his blood.

"You're a natural" the old chief told him at his first appraisal, and he was.

He joined the little known Hannet-Mar International Bank in 1996 having gained a 2nd class business degree at Bristol University followed by a three year stint at a small accountancy firm during which time he gained distinctions in the external professional qualifications. He then set about climbing the ladder of commercial banking. Hannet-Mar ostensibly specialised in providing finance to mainly Middle Eastern clients for development projects in Arab countries, via a mix of funds, bonds and securities. In reality however, the bank was either investing in or underwriting real estate, mortgages and debt guarantees, some of which he ensured received his personal attention. The downside of having control of these few accounts was there was no one else to deal with them in his absence. His private clients knew that – some even insisted upon it – but it meant it was going to take him the rest of the day to get up to speed on them. As he took his first sip of the steaming, much needed caffeine, he started to browse through his emails and read a particularly long memo about a pipeline project in the United Arab Emirates which the bank were part financing, but he was unable to fully concentrate. The office, fully air-conditioned and triple-glazed, was usually very quiet given the general noise levels of the city, but a constant wail of sirens from emergency vehicles penetrated the sound protection and invaded the room with a continuous cacophony of irritating noise. The combined effect of so many sirens blasting forth sound waves of differing amplitudes and frequencies, with the only common factor being that they were clearly designed to alarm anyone near to them, was too distracting. He got up and looked out of his window and was shocked to see large numbers of ambulances and police vehicles dashing in different directions, each emblazoning a path through the traffic aided by their flashing lights and awful wailing.

The time was approaching 9:30am and Britain's full emergency major incident procedures were being implemented, and the necessary responses mobilised, for what was initially believed to be at least six separate terrorist attacks across London but which later was revealed as four. The London Underground network – on which a little over forty minutes earlier Alan and Cindy had travelled into work – was rapidly being shut down. As he stared out of the window, intrigued by the commotion, it did not occur to him that one destination for the emergency teams might be Liverpool Street Station.

He returned somewhat absentmindedly to his desk and to the remaining emails. One particularly caught his eye as it had purportedly been sent by Halima Chalthoum. He knew that name as an alias for Fadyar Masri, a young, but very intelligent young woman. She had been recommended to him two months previously by another trusted personal client with whom Crossland had enjoyed a very profitable long-term business relationship. Fadyar said she was exploring a number of business opportunities in the UK on behalf of a Consortium based in Dubai, and was hoping to attract more overseas partners in joint ventures. It was clear she had a lot of potential contacts and Crossland had invited her to Red Gables for dinner with him and Cindy. Momentarily his recollection of that May evening distracted him. The meeting had seemed to lighten Cindy's mood and everything went well. Whilst Cindy was preparing the meal, Fadyar and he were able to discuss all they wanted to, and by the time dinner had arrived they could all relax and enjoy each other's company. Thinking back, it was probably the last time he remembered Cindy as appearing really carefree and happy. He clicked the mouse and opened the email.

Dear Mr Crossland
    Further to our discussion, I am the UK representative of the Corniche

Consortium based in Dubai and we are now in a position to proceed with our UK investments. I should be obliged if you would open an account in the name of my company Chalthoum Universal Holdings in order that I may draw upon it as necessary. A Letter of Authority from Corniche Consortium is attached. Funds to the value £200,000 (two hundred thousand pounds sterling) will be deposited as soon as you let me know the account number and any other required info by your bank. Further funds will follow in due course.

I also enclose the various documents, in pdf format including a photograph also sent as an image file, which you require to satisfy UK legislation; the originals will be posted to you on receipt of your confirmation that all is in order.

As discussed, I require full online internet access to this account 24 hours a day every day with no limit on withdrawals or deposits. Please send initial passwords and account details separately to me c/o Box 4593GA, Baraha Street, Dubai

My esteemed regards and thanks

Halima Chalthoum

Having read it once quickly, he studied it more closely. No mention of a meeting, just the more ambiguous word 'discussion.' Good. It showed she was careful, like him. He enjoyed dealing with such clients, but for all Fadyar's charm and vivacity he realised that underneath the exterior there was a very committed and determined woman indeed, and the meaning of the deliberately chosen words was clear: 'I will not implicate you, so do not do anything to implicate me'. He accessed the JPEG file and looked at the picture. It bore no resemblance to Fadyar, but Crossland was not concerned. He could trust Fadyar to ensure that all the documentation would pass scrutiny should that ever be required.

The communication had been in Crossland's personal mailbox for over a week awaiting his return from Greece, and he decided to action it urgently. He printed off the email and enclosures, and thirty minutes later the account was opened and a reply sent. A small folder to retain the documents was put in his personal filing cabinet and he restricted access to the computer record by placing a special security digit upon it. Code G files were for his attention only and enabled him to have unrestricted rights over any data within the record itself. At this stage he was convinced no dangerous data existed, but using the code now might be useful in the future. His risk assessment was in fact wrong. The limited entries on the computer were already sufficient to place him in jeopardy and had he known he would certainly have exercised considerably more caution before acting on the apparently innocuous email from the professed Halima Chalthoum.

4

Cindy Crossland slowly became more aware of her surroundings and the strange sounds around her. She blinked her eyes rapidly, trying to rid them of the stinging soreness caused by the smoke. The gloom frightened her. She tried to move, to see where she was and what was holding her down. She attempted to shout, to call to anyone, but the only sound she made was a dry croaking groan. Almost immediately she started to cough, a rasping coarse cough which hurt not just her parched throat but somewhere deep inside her stomach. She, like everyone else, was gradually being coated with more layers of the foul-tasting black soot as the dust and dirt drifted slowly in the dank air. She was getting hot, very hot. She began to panic. *Where is the heat coming from? Why can't I breathe?*

"Help me. Can anyone help me please?" she managed to say the words but they were weak and indistinct. She struggled to shout, making more noise but her efforts seemed doomed against the onslaught of the din resounding within the stricken carriage.

"Try and remain still, your legs are trapped" a soft male voice spoke from somewhere to her left. Her eyes were beginning to adjust now to the dimness in the carriage. She noticed a mass of twisted metal by the door – at least she assumed it was the door. Her memory sluggishly struggled to recall what had happened and where she was. *Yes, a door* she recalled *I was standing by the door.*

"I must get up". She lifted her head in readiness to stand up.

"No, stay still. Don't move or you may hurt yourself more." That voice again, slightly louder now, more earnest.

"Me, do you mean me?" She tried to speak normally but her fear reduced her voice to only a rapid, frightened whisper "Not me, I have to get out. What's happened? I must get out. It's so hot."

"Yes, you. There has been a large explosion, probably a bomb. It seems you are trapped by your legs. The heat is only because the train is not moving; there is no fire." His voice was calm but authoritative. Cindy found it reassuring to know that this person, whoever he was, was nearby. She tried to move her legs a little, but it hurt and she screamed in pain.

"Believe me now, will you?" he chuckled. "Look, this isn't good. I don't know when anyone will come for us but for the moment our best option is to wait here and stay still. The rescue services will be here soon."

Her mind had cleared now. She recalled the horrors of torn limbs and the rivulets of blood she had witnessed before the lights finally went out. She had to get out of this hell.

"I must get out. Get out, get out – do you hear? Please just get me out."

"If I could, I would, but it's not possible. Please accept that and remain calm. That is the best thing to do for… " the man hesitated and nearly added 'for your survival' but stopped himself in time, "… us."

"The blood" she said. "I remember the blood, the bodies. Am I bleeding too?"

"I really don't know. You may have internal injuries as well as the problems with your legs. That is one reason why you should stay as still as you can."

She lay back in silence. She suddenly felt very tired and closed her eyes momentarily but she was now suffering increasing levels of pain.

"My bloody legs hurt." She said, cursing weakly.

"That's probably a good sign but I think you should try to stay awake" said the voice in her ear again. Cindy opened her eyes, but then shut them.

"Please try and stay awake." The voice was deep and warm, but insistent.

"I'll try" she said, but her thin voice was husky and the stranger was concerned she might lapse into unconsciousness.

"Tell me about yourself then. You must try to keep talking".

Cindy was not used to being told what to do but she now found reassurance in his voice. She suddenly felt very alone and she didn't want this man to go. She held up her arm and reached out, waving it about until she felt someone grasp her wrist. Relieved at the contact, she pulled her arm downwards until she could firmly clasp her hand around his.

Somewhat breathlessly, due to taking quick, short intakes of air to avoid deeply inhaling the stinging dust, Cindy began to talk. Normally she would have been reticent about revealing information about herself, especially to someone she had not known long, but she sensed this was different. She found his manner reassuringly trustworthy and she had no hesitation in summarising her life.

"I'm Cindy Crossland, aged thirty-five. Married Alan in 2000 but no children. As an infant I was a pupil at a small school near my home village of Fladbury in Worcestershire before attending The Alice Ottley School in Worcester from the age of eleven. I graduated with a degree in history from St Catherine's, Oxford. I joined the world of journalism working on a free local paper and was fortunate that one of the residents who received it happened to be a sub-editor on *The Sunday Times*. He seemed impressed with my writing and features, made contact with me and so I joined him. My father worked in oil exploration, and when he retired my parents moved to Dorset."

She paused to clear her throat, the stranger helping to steady her as she leaned her head forward.

"Go on Cindy, you're doing great", he gently encouraged her to prevent her slipping back to semi-consciousness.

"I quickly gained something of a reputation as an investigative reporter on the regular Insight columns which brought me into contact with politics and politicians. After a while I was given my own team and we specialised on the political topic of the moment, provided background, analysis and that sort of stuff. Then, out of the blue, the Blair government approached me – I supposed they had read some of my articles – and I served on a couple of governmental committees on things like freedom of information and media power. That sort of thing." She stopped. "I'm sorry, I don't think I can go on … I'm so very tired." Her eyelids started to close and her head slipped sideways.

"Yes you can. Go on. What did Blair want you to do?"

Cindy opened her eyes again and made a thin smile.

"You were listening then?"

"Yes, of course."

"I worked in the Cabinet Office press team alongside a great bunch of guys until last January, when I left to go freelance and write novels based on my political experience."

She could have added that she was one of the few insiders to be trusted by both Blair and his Chancellor Gordon Brown, and that whilst others found it difficult to sustain more than a year or so around the two ambitious men, she had no such problem and had greatly enjoyed being admired by both.

"And I'm now talking away about my life to a person I don't know and can hardly see in this darkness."

The man, still holding her hand, laughed.

Whilst the physical effort of speaking had been very hard, it had kept her awake and mentally alert. More importantly, it had somehow reassured her to know that someone was actually interested.

"And what of your hobbies? It doesn't sound as though you have much time for any?" He enquired, delicately trying to keep Cindy conscious by getting her to talk.

"Riding and sailing, but I think that's going to be a bit difficult right now", she rejoined and they both chuckled at the absurdity of it all.

"Where are you? Are you hurt?" She asked anxiously.

"No, I don't think I'm too bad. I seem to be able to move things but I think my face or head is cut and my ribs hurt, but I should be able to stand."

"Oh, that's good – if you know what I mean. How come you're next to me then?" She was curious why this man hadn't tried to escape from the wrecked carriage if he could stand.

"I got thrown around and ended up somewhere behind you. I heard you cry out, so got down on the floor to find out who it was and if I could help. You know the rest."

"Thank you. Thank you so much" Cindy blurted out and she started to cry once more.

Cindy and her companion did not know at the time that perhaps they were fortunate not to have been travelling on the Piccadilly line, which was also bombed that fateful morning. The large twin track tunnel of the Circle line had probably saved Cindy's life, and that of many others, as a significant part of the explosive force of the bomb had been able to dissipate across the wide cavity, thereby lessening its impact. The single track Piccadilly line did not allow the bomb blast to be vented and the force remained concentrated within the tunnel and carriages themselves, resulting in a greater number of casualties. The narrow tunnel also made rescue considerably more difficult but access was easier on the stretch of the Circle line where Cindy's train was attacked. The Emergency Response Unit (ERU) was soon able to set up lighting in the adjoining tunnel that normally transported passengers on the Hammersmith and City line. Some emergency arc lamps started to appear and an amplified voice was saying that rescue was at hand.

"Follow the lights and hold onto the rope" bellowed a loudspeaker.

Most of the passengers that could move with ease clambered cautiously and carefully over the bodies of others as best they could in order to escape, but some were not as considerate where they trod and several of those still lying on the floor groaned in agony as they were stepped on. As they left the stricken train, a small army of rescuers wearing their silver and red protective jackets marshalled the groggy, tottering victims away to the waiting medical staff who had set up an emergency centre at ground level, little more than thirty feet above the wreckage. The stranger shielded Cindy from the exodus and within minutes most of the carriage had emptied.

"Are you OK, mate?" a grimy-faced man with the word "RESCUE" written across his back shouted to Cindy's protector. "If so, get out quickly."

"I'm alright but this lady can't move and needs urgent attention."

"All in good time. Medic! One here trapped. One OK and coming out."

"You're not going are you?" Cindy was suddenly very nervous of being alone.

"Not if you don't want me to."

"Please stay a bit longer" and she squeezed his hand a little tighter.

"Look mate, there could be another bomb. Just go and follow the lights. We will have the lady out as soon as we can." The silver rescue jacket again.

"I'm staying, so you just carry on," said the stranger.

Cindy turned and said, "I am so sorry, you must go. It is obviously still very dangerous here."

"I'm going nowhere until I know you'll be safe, so let's just change the subject. Tell me about where you went riding. Did you have your own horse?" He encouraged her to think of more pleasant times.

She was just about to reply when the fire service and a doctor arrived and told Cindy they were going to get her out.

"Now you really do have to go, mate. We can't get your wife out with you in the way and holding her hand!"

For the first time Cindy laughed loudly and then instantly regretted it as pain shot through her stomach and chest.

"Quick", she said, in an urgent and panicked voice, "I don't even know your name. Do you have a pen or something? Please give me your phone number."

Knowing he didn't have much time he quickly found a felt tip pen in his jacket pocket and wrote the number on her arm. He spotted a scrap of paper on the floor, a blood stain traversing the page almost along its entire length but he tore a clean area and wrote the number down again. He folded the grubby note and gently placed it in the palm of her hand, before closing her fingers around it.

"Good luck, let me know how you get on. My name's Gordon by the way."

Another man appeared next to her, the word DOCTOR emblazoned on his luminous coat, and said something to Cindy but she wasn't listening. She was intent to watch Gordon leave the train and followed the shadow he made as he passed in front of the temporary lighting. The Doctor then shone a torch into her eyes and strapped something to her wrist. He performed a quick but thorough examination and gave her an injection. As he stepped aside the rescue crew started their work of cutting her free.

★ ★ ★

Alan Crossland had finished his emails and cleared his desk of most of the accumulated papers and files. The few folders and letters that remained would need time and care. It was 11am. He was troubled by the noisy clamour surrounding his office and deduced that there must be some kind of major incident happening but he did not investigate further, other than to glance out of his window from time to time. The unruffled working of his office was in stark contrast to the mayhem throughout the rest of the great city. The emergency services, aided by well-trained London Underground staff, were rapidly counting casualties and arranging for the speedy evacuation of the injured to the various hospitals.

Paradoxically, probably the only other calm office was now the control centre for the entire London Underground network. Their large computer indicator boards, colour coded like the original 1933 Harry Beck map that was still in use and imitated throughout the world, recorded that the operational status of all thirteen lines on the network was 'SUSPENDED', causing more than one manager in the centre to openly weep. Nor was the distress limited to the management. London Underground employees, many of whom had given years of dedicated service to 'The Tube' as it was affectionately referred to, regarded the outrage as an attack upon their trains, their lines and their passengers. They had never expected to witness the unique and complete shutdown of the entire system, something that even Nazi Germany failed to do during the London Blitz.

"What time will you and Mrs Crossland require the car, Sir?" Jack Donaldson, Crossland's burly driver, enquired.

Donaldson also held the title of 'personal security consultant' but in reality that was little more than a bodyguard, though he never carried a firearm. His sheer size made him an intimidating figure. He stood a little over six feet tall and weighed close to 240 pounds. His spiky ginger hair was short-cropped close to his scalp and his cavernous mouth was circumscribed by thick bulbous lips. His pale blue eyes, set in a deeply pockmarked face interrupted only by a crooked nose that had been on the receiving end of too many fists, constantly darted back and forth. His alert and piercing gaze was frightening in its intensity of penetration, and just looking at him made others nervous. He was superbly fit, despite his size, and since leaving the army and subsequent spells as a mercenary, Donaldson had made certain his physique was maintained by regular visits to the gym. Whenever Crossland travelled, the doughty driver at his side was a reassuring and necessary presence for a well-heeled banker of dubious repute and probity.

"What are you doing here, Jack? I told you to take a break until Monday" Crossland retorted somewhat exasperatedly.

He did not take kindly, when working on his private files, for his concentration to be interrupted by his secretary buzzing through his driver, especially when the man should be on holiday.

"I thought you would need the car to get home, seeing as those bastards seem to be blowing London to bits and the stations are likely to be closed."

"What? What did you say?"

A thousand images entered Crossland's mind as his brain struggled to absorb the realisation of what he had just been told and had been witnessing out of his window. Bombs, bloody bombs – that would explain it. He turned away from his desk, slowly rose from the comfort of his chair and walked to the window and stared at the assortment of vehicles below, their powerful engines rendered impotent as they were hopelessly trapped in the congestion. He stayed silent, trying to clear his mind but there was one recollection that kept repeating over and over in his head. The traffic lights, the backfire behind him, the startled, turned faces. He walked slowly to the chair and sat down. Crossland's face went suddenly ashen, the realisation of the possible horror etching itself into a facial expression of deep shock. He looked over to Donaldson.

"My God, Jack, I hope Cindy is OK. Tell me what you know. Quickly."

★ ★ ★

Alan Crossland spent a worrying few hours trying to trace what had happened to his wife but it was not until almost five hour hours later, at his fourth enquiry of the emergency call centre telephone number, that he received news that she had been admitted to Charing Cross Hospital that morning. Despite his pleas, the operator had no additional information to help remove his anxiety. An hour later he was at her bedside where she lay sleeping; worry turned to relief when the ward staff informed him that Cindy's injuries were not particularly serious. She had undergone a simple routine operation to reset her left leg which was now covered in a protective plaster cast, and she had suffered numerous cuts and bruises. Evidently her injuries would have been far worse had not a fellow passenger's full briefcase landed across her legs just as the blast threw her sideways and onto the floor. A split second later the back of the seat she had been leaning against was wrenched from its fixings and twisted around onto the lower half of her body, crushing the case. Cindy was due further X-rays on her ribs, probably the following day, and there was some fluid on the chest that was being kept under observation. Crossland drew up a rather uncomfortable plastic and chrome visitor chair and sat beside the bed. He gently held her hand and waited. Two hours later, Cindy started to regain consciousness and gave a thin smile.

"The Tube. Dust. What happened? Do you know?" she asked.

"There was a bomb, and you have a broken leg, cuts and bruises, but thank God, you have had a pretty miraculous escape. It could have been a lot worse." He kissed her gently and gave a broad grin. He kept telling her how much he loved her and how worried he had been.

"I'm alright, Alan, I'll be fine. Thanks. Thanks for coming, for being here." She spoke in a croaky voice, explained later to him by a nurse as the consequences of the toxic smoke and dust his wife had inhaled and swallowed. As he spoke quietly he noticed that she began to close her eyes again, the anaesthetic still partially having its effect. Alan used his index finger to gently clear her face of some long, loose blonde hairs and kissed her again before departing. He told her that he would stay for the next few days in their Shoreditch apartment in order to be close by and so he would be there whenever Cindy needed him.

★ ★ ★

The following morning Cindy awoke early and despite the previous day's ordeal, she was surprised that she felt reasonably well. She ached all over and had various items of medical monitoring equipment and plastic tubes attached to her – but if she had been inclined to complain of pain anywhere on her body she would only have mentioned the site of the injection tube on the top of her hand which was very sore. She wriggled her toes just to check that she wasn't paralysed and pronounced to herself that she had been a very fortunate woman not to have suffered more extensive injuries. As her thoughts of the preceding day gradually returned, she remembered the kind stranger on the train; the way he had kept her talking, and how calm and reassuring he had been. She blushed slightly when recalling that she had informed this man of much of her life history, but she couldn't remember all the details of the conversation and wondered just how much she had revealed.

"God, I hope not," she mumbled audibly as thoughts of things she might have told him raced around her brain. She remembered he had written his telephone number on her arm and she eagerly raised it up in order to read it. It wasn't there. *Where was it?* She tried her other arm but uttered an immediate low groan of disappointment. Both limbs had been cleaned, along with large parts of the rest of her body, by the surgical team at the hospital and the precious vital number had gone! The frightened loneliness she had experienced in the battered carriage twenty-four hours earlier returned, unwelcome and invasive, and the haunting memories made her physically shake. She needed to see this man again, or hear his voice, whoever he was, and in a slight panic she started talking rapidly to herself as she placed her arms closer to her face, desperate to see if there was any trace of ink remaining. Nothing, both arms had been scrubbed clean. Her mind flashed back to those horrible, final moments in the carriage and the scrap of paper the stranger put into her hand. She knew she had held onto it, recalling how tightly she had clutched her fingers around the crumpled ball as the doctor gave her an injection.

What happened to it? Where has it gone? she asked herself over and over again. She tried to change position to see what was on the small cabinet beside her but found it was difficult for her to move and so called out for a nurse.

"When I came in yesterday or whenever it was, I had a slip of paper, a telephone number, in my hand and it's most important that I find it. Do you know where it is? Can you help me find it? Please?" she blurted out the words, her normally careful delivery overtaken by the imperative of finding the note.

"There's nothing here my dear. In fact you were only identified by the smashed phone in your pocket. The police traced your name through that. I expect the rescue services gathered up all the handbags and briefcases and they will be returned sometime. None of that sort of stuff came in here."

Cindy was disappointed but managed to reply to the well-meaning nurse.

"Well, no, I don't suppose it would, everything was thrown about. It's marvellous that with so much to do they had time to check phones and things." She paused, wondering who had found the note or what had become of it. The realisation that she might never find out the identity of the kind stranger who helped her in the immediate aftermath of the explosion made her sad.

"Are you sure it's not there? Please, please look again," she implored. The nurse started to re-examine the cabinet but it was very apparent there was nothing of Cindy's except her smashed mobile in the drawer and a bag of clothes beside the bed itself.

"We have put what remained of your clothes in a bag but there's nothing in there either" said the nurse when she reappeared from sorting through the few belongings. Cindy said a meek "Thank you" and closed her eyes.

After a few minutes, she started to cry quietly to herself. Whoever he was, she knew this man was important to her. The only slight comfort was that she remembered his name.

Gordon. It was Gordon. Gordon, she repeated it over and over in her head. She did not want to forget his name, ever.

★ ★ ★

The day passed slowly and quietly for her. Alan visited a couple of times before going back to the apartment at eight-thirty in the evening. He had taken the bag and Cindy had given him a list of fresh clothes and toiletries she needed for the following day.

An hour after Alan had waved goodbye to Cindy, a bright-faced, cheery young nurse came by and closed the curtains around the bed.

"Hi! I'm Jacqui, night shift. I'll be recording various measurements for the chart and I can let you have some more pain killers, if you need them. Just ask. Actually, you look a lot better than you did last night. How do you feel now?"

"Not too bad thanks… my husband has visited a couple of times… but this tube hurts" said Cindy falteringly, whilst pointing to her hand.

"Yes, that one usually does. It will be taken out in a day or two, so not too long." The nurse started feeling inside her tunic pocket and then held up her hand saying, "I've got something for you. As you can imagine, virtually all of us here were drafted down to help in Casualty and the ER yesterday, and when you came in I was on the team to which you were allocated. You were asleep of course due to the drugs the rescue doctor gave you, but when you were examined you were still clenching a bit of paper. When I took it, I noticed it had a phone number on it and that you also had the same number written on your arm. Thought it must be important so rather than risk losing it in the chaos down in ER, I put it in my pocket and resolved to find you today, whichever ward you were on."

She passed Cindy the paper and said, "Bit of luck finding you here."

Cindy was so overjoyed, she was temporarily lost for words and burst into tears. After several seconds she blurted out, "You wonderful, wonderful girl. Thank you so much, I really thought I had lost it."

Nurse Jacqui smiled back. "All part of the National Health service. Well, don't lose it now, will you?" She picked up the pen she had used to record Cindy's blood pressure on the admission chart, and slipped back the bedclothes covering Cindy's broken leg. "Perhaps I should write it on your plaster?"

Alarmed, Cindy quickly replied "Oh God, no, don't do that.

But if you can put it on another piece of paper or something that won't get lost, that would be great – just in case."

The nurse turned and a wry smile spread across her lips. "I'll be back," and true to her word within two minutes she was. "Here" she said. "Sounds to me as if you might not want the number seen by too many people, so I've written it on this."

She handed Cindy a new tampon with Gordon's telephone number clearly written on the internal applicator. "That, hopefully, you can keep private," she said laughing.

5

Since he sold his own business in 1999, Gordon Truscott had extensively refurbished and extended his Scottish Highland home, Mealag Lodge, and its adjoining estate of open land and forestry. He had never totalled the cost involved but his accountant had mentioned to him once that it ran to several million pounds, though this did not elicit any concern or further interest on Gordon's part. The Lodge was substantial but it was not grand. It had been built in the early 1920's and whilst Gordon had spent a considerable sum improving, extending and furnishing it to his taste, he had spent more on developing the estate forestry and renovating the workers' own cottages. On part of the estate near to the lodge, Truscott had built nine high-quality chalets. These were generously spaced around a large clearing that had been made close to the southern shore of Loch Quoich. Three chalets were utilised to accommodate any casual staff or special visitors, and the remaining six were solely for 'guests' – as Gordon liked to regard those who attended the management courses he ran periodically. There were a further two buildings, both hidden by trees. One, which resembled a very large bungalow from the exterior, was a spacious purpose-made conference and training facility, with its own well-equipped kitchen / dining area, a lounge and various rooms including wash room facilities, ensuring it lacked nothing in its support for the delegates that studied within its walls. Affixed to the outside was an erratically shaped slab of wood, part of the Old Caledonian pine forest which Gordon had found one morning on the shore of the loch. It was about twenty inches in diameter and burnt into it was the name Ruraich – literally meaning "search for" in Gaelic, but used by Gordon to remind him of his first springer spaniel which he had named Rummage.

Sited next to the large Mealag Lodge, but at least thirty metres away from it, was a compact, but spacious, timber-framed bungalow. This was permanently occupied by Sandy and Margaret

MacLean, both of whom were indispensable to Gordon. Margaret was general housekeeper and cook, and Sandy attended to any maintenance whether to the lodge or the boats or anything else – plus he was a fully-accredited instructor in safety and first aid, a mountain rescue volunteer and an excellent fishing and shooting companion. Sandy and Margaret were now in their late thirties and were the only estate workers within the actual grounds of the lodge complex, the others having their own crofts or homes scattered amongst the adjoining two thousand acre estate which spread into the area known as Knoydart. Well to the rear of the MacLeans' bungalow, Gordon had built a private helipad. It had been cleverly positioned within a separate unevenly-shaped clearing, such that it was shielded by trees and therefore out of view from the large house itself and the bungalow, though not so distant as to be completely out of earshot. The entire Mealag complex was surrounded on three sides by high wire steel fencing that had been constructed within the forest to obscure it from view, leaving the only open aspect to the front where it bounded and faced the loch.

At 11:30am, Gordon was standing at Quoich dam having walked the two thirds of a mile from the lodge before clambering over the small, iron gate barring the entrance to the walkway at the southern (Mealag) end of the dam wall. He was wearing an unzipped, size thirty six camouflage jacket, deliberately loose-fitting over a cotton check shirt. Each leg of his matching multi-coloured green, black and brown trousers was tucked inside an expensive Aigle boot. His dark hair, worn just slightly on the long side, had a slightly unkempt look about it. Fractionally under two metres tall, weighing no more than 190 pounds and with a weathered, tanned complexion gained not from some Mediterranean resort but by regular exposure to every conceivable type of weather that only the Highlands can produce, he cut an imposing figure. A pair of high powered Zeiss field glasses, slung from his neck by a platted leather cord, swayed in sync with his movements.

It was the middle of July, a week after the London atrocities 650 miles away, though to Gordon those events now seemed of another time zone and another world. The sun was high, bright and intense, pushing the air temperature well into the seventies and the loch surface water was barely ruffled by the soft breeze. This caused an edge of sparkling, uneven light to run along the entire length of the dam wall as the strong sunlight caught the water lapping against the protective concrete slabs. He checked his Omega stainless steel all-weather watch. In the next half an hour or so he reckoned his new 'guests' would be travelling along the Kinloch Hourn road that passed alongside the north side of the loch and he had deliberately come to the dam early to witness their arrival, an event which usually provided a spectacle of some amusement. From his high vantage point by the dam he had a tremendous view of the narrow road opposite as it wound its way along the base of the glen and passed through Corach five miles or so away. A white transit van, travelling towards Kinloch Hourn, would be visible to him at least ten minutes before it would pass the far side of the dam, and he could follow its progress onwards for almost another mile before the driver would pull in at the lay-by almost opposite Mealag and allow his apprehensive passengers to alight.

Gordon chuckled at the thought but his attention was temporarily taken by a golden eagle soaring high above Gleouraich, the 3,400 feet mountain opposite. It was not uncommon to witness eagles around the Munros, as hill walkers have generically named all Scottish mountains that exceed a height of 3000 feet, and Gordon was always fascinated by the large bird's combination of power and grace. As he lowered the binoculars from his eyes he slowly turned his head to admire the vast empty spaces all around the loch. It was a view he had seen a thousand times and more, but it never failed to take his breath away.

Between the dam and the end of the road at Kinloch Hourn, the loch was flanked by eight Munros towering imperiously skywards. To his left on the southern shore, were the Sgurr Mor and Gairich mountains. The triangular Gairich was pointed and sharp, its gravel surface washed light grey by the thrashing rain that beat upon it virtually every day of the year. Several large, dark scars bore witness to the frequent cascading torrents of water that had scoured deep ravines into the triple faces of the mountain. Sgurr Mor in contrast was part of a massif, as its western flank joined with the eastern flank of Sgurr na Ciche over a mile from it. The broad roundness of its summit was quite unlike the pointed hat worn by Gairich. Huge boulders, some seemingly impossibly fixed as they jutted out at crazy angles, gave periodic shelter from the elements to those who tested their bravery and skill in making an ascent upon the mountain. Around the black rocky faces were areas of bright green where grass and mosses clung to the thin earth blown into the numerous shallow crevices. Directly opposite where Gordon stood was series after series of grey, ebony, and purple-coloured pinnacles, the high hills illuminated by the ever changing light and appearing to criss-cross over each other like a crowd of standing spectators striving for a better view of the loch below.

As he slowly turned his head, he refocused his eyes to study the loch. The dam had raised the water level by over one hundred feet and the enlarged canyon was nearly seven miles long and a significant contributor to hydro-electric energy supply. When he was first brought here by his parents, he was in awe at the sheer grandness of the mountains and the size of the dam. The whole panorama and setting both excited and scared him in the same moment, and that familiar adrenalin rush was now sweeping over him just as it had as a ten year old. He took several slow, deep gulps of the clear air and slowly closed his eyes. He wanted to savour the peace and the open space for a few moments more; to enjoy and listen to the silence and tranquillity that can never be found in a city and which certainly had been shattered so completely the previous week when he travelled on London Underground train 204. He opened his eyes three minutes later and glanced towards Corach, briefly catching sight of the van as it suddenly appeared and, just as quickly, vanished as it made its tortuous progress along the winding single track road. Gordon began to walk briskly back along the wall towards the south gate in order to take up his favoured vantage spot to witness his latest arrivals. Mealag Lodge was sited well back from a dog-legged, narrow bay on the southern shore of the loch, which made the house almost impossible to spot by those driving casually along the road on the far shore. It also afforded total obscurity of the dam wall from the house, yet permitted its occupants to enjoy the vastly superior, uninterrupted view down almost the entire length of the loch towards Kinloch

Hourn. Gordon was in his concealed position just as the van came to a halt in the lay-by. The six passengers got out, stretched their legs and arms, and then collected up their own cases and bags from the rear of the transit. They gathered round awaiting the driver to join them, speculating with each other as to where they were to be taken next. The van drove off. Unknown to the stranded passengers this would turn onto a short track about a mile farther on and from there be parked inside a large garage. The driver would covertly make his way back to the shore by foot and then use a boat to return to Mealag, but not before he was certain all the others on the van had got safely across the water.

Gordon picked up the field glasses and focused on the six bewildered souls. Two were existing directors of the board of a global insurance corporation and the remaining four all aspired to a position on it. Each felt they deserved the promotion. All they had been told by their chairman, in a letter marked 'PERSONAL' and received three days previously, was that they had been specially selected and invited to attend an 'Executive Development Course to include Team Building' in the Scottish Highlands and to present themselves at 10:30am on Monday 18th July outside Fort William rail station, where the driver of their onward transport would be holding a placard. The entire six, had they spoken truthfully to each other, groaned in dismay when they read the chairman's invitation.

"Another bloody course," uttered the deputy finance director whilst travelling on the overnight sleeper, a comment which found much empathy amongst his colleagues and accurately summed up the collective mood of the chairman's chosen few. They had received no guidance as to what to bring, wear or carry, and now they were alone in the middle of nowhere with instructions from the driver to make their way to Mealag Lodge.

"Where did he say that was?" called out the gruff voice of the compliance director, standing away from his colleagues.

"He didn't – merely pointed across the loch as he said the name."

"Great. Terrific. So what do we do now?"

This was the moment Gordon wanted to witness. He could see that two of the nervous men had chosen to wear suits for their

Scottish trip and each was carrying a suitcase. Three others were dressed smartly, but casually, and one was dressed in jeans and shirt with a rucksack on his back. He was busily changing his trainers for walking boots. After about five minutes of animated conversation, several hands pointed towards the dam wall a mile away. However, it was evident that the prospect of carrying a heavy bag a considerable distance, dressed in a suit, was not to everyone's liking and the sound of raised voices carried across the still water to be heard by Gordon, who laughed.

A further fifteen minutes went by and still the group was no nearer to resolving its dilemma, though a couple of delegates had begun to trudge wearily towards the dam. Everyone was tired from the ten hour rail journey to Fort William and had then undergone a most uncomfortable hour and half being bumped and swung around inside an old, noisy van, its seats – having lost their springing long ago – supplemented only by bare, thin foam mattresses. The dishevelled driver who had awaited them at the station, wearing an oil-stained dirty denim overall on top of faded brown corduroy trousers and a considerably worn chequered shirt, had been singularly gruff and unhelpful in his responses to their questions, and conversation with him had been almost non-existent. Indeed they felt he had driven deliberately fast around the bends in the road simply to make their journey even more disagreeable.

Gordon noticed the one with walking boots heading towards the loch. It was a steep downward slope from the road to the loch but easily manageable. The ground was completely barren, strewn fifty years ago with the waste rocks not used in the infill of the dam and which in several places had reached a height that prevented the water's edge from being visible from the road. Lodged amongst the boulders were various items of heavily-rusting ironwork, discarded and deliberately abandoned on site to keep the building costs at a minimum. Some were small, some very large but all were twisted or rotted beyond recognition, and had clearly emanated from some form of reinforcement pipework or broken machinery. Gordon noticed how easily the new visitor progressed on his perilous path downwards, avoiding the jagged, sharp splinters of reddish-brown rusted metal as he stepped purposefully around the obstacles which could seriously injure the unwary. When he came into sight of the shoreline, he turned and shouted to the others above him. Almost immediately three figures started to clamber down but the two others were still headed for the dam, their distance from the rest of the group preventing them hearing the shouts of their colleagues.

At the shore, a single wooden clinker boat had been tied to a small jetty little more than twelve metres in length but which was quite sufficient to permit more than just the one rowing boat to be tied up alongside. The thick landing stage planks had originally been stained a dark brown but now resembled a sombre grey matching its precast concrete supports, all of which had been firmly embedded deep within the loch floor making the structure extremely sturdy and able to withstand the violent storms of winter. On the cross bench of the boat, inside a polythene sleeve, was pinned a note on how to start the outboard and a map marking the precise location of Mealag Lodge. As the others reached the shore, the man with the boots picked up the note, read it and passed it to his grateful companions who gleefully slapped him on the back as one by one they stepped into the boat. As the last one sat down, someone started to row the boat away from the shore and quickly thereafter the raucous noise of the outboard cut through the air, causing an initial small spurt of blue smoke to curl along behind them until it dissipated in the breeze. Gordon saw that a lady was sitting in the stern and steering the boat, her right hand gripping the tiller on the outboard and her left resting easily on top of the port bulkhead. She began to make a turn towards the dam. The two visitors – still laboriously making their way along the road, lugging their heavy cases and frequently pausing to pass their burden from one hand to another – had heard the outboard and the boat was now in their view. They waved and started their descent to the shore. Gordon watched keenly as the man with the rucksack took up a position at the prow and peered into the diminishing depths of the crystal clear water, giving directions to the woman who was able to carefully navigate a clear passage.

Gordon was impressed with the care both had shown at ensuring the boat could be safely brought into shore and near to where their colleagues were waiting. Such team work and initiative would score highly when he completed their course report. She cut the outboard and lifted it from the water whilst one of the others dropped the anchor. The realisation by the two men in suits that to reach the boat would involve taking a few steps across the rocky terrain and into the cold loch could be seen in their faces as their initial joy turned to dismay. Gordon laughed out loud as he viewed their dilemma through the binoculars. They both removed their shoes and socks, but neither seemed too keen to damage their expensively-tailored suits. For a few moments they both hesitated. Then one slowly removed his trousers before gingerly stepping into the water. He quickly realised that keeping his balance on the slippery rocks below was no easy task at any time. To do so whilst carrying a suitcase and his shoes was well-nigh impossible. Clearly embarrassed and feeling very self-conscious of his brightly coloured underwear that had already attracted some sarcastic wolf whistles and ribald comments, he stepped back onto the firmer shore. Once he had regained his composure he stood up, looked around himself in an assured manner and then placed his removed clothes in his suitcase before picking it up again and hoisting it onto his shoulder, keeping one arm around it to ensure it did not fall as he entered the water for the second time. To shouts of encouragement from his rescuers he half-stumbled, half-slipped his way to the boat where eager hands hoisted him aboard and clapped as he sat down, relieved at not having fallen on his short but dangerous journey.

The second, an Armani-tailored executive, was not so fortunate. Emulating his colleague he gingerly took his first steps into the loch but the coldness of the water surprised him. He uttered an expletive so loud that even Gordon heard it, before the man lost his footing completely and he inelegantly performed a slow pirouette before crashing face down in the loch. The suitcase landed with a heavy splash next to him and immediately started to drift away from both the boat and its owner. Desperate to retrieve the case, the man swam after it, grabbed it by the handle and brought it back to the side of the boat where the amused makeshift crew had extended their hands in offers of assistance. The suitcase was lifted on board, streams of water leaking from it as surely as if it had been a sieve.

Turning their attention to their hapless colleague, they started to haul him up by his arms over the side of the boat. The laws of gravity quickly operated upon the weight of water within his soaked and unflatteringly long white boxer shorts, such that they slid gently down to his ankles. His semi-naked trunk was upended as he was pulled into the boat, causing his colleagues to roar with laughter. It was a very angry and red-faced executive that eventually regained his modesty as the anchor was weighed and the engine re-started. Twenty-five minutes later, Gordon met them all outside Mealag Lodge. It had, as usual, been an enjoyable and thoroughly entertaining morning witnessing the arrival of his guests.

Gordon Truscott did not need the income from the eight, one-week courses he hosted each year. There was always an element of team building on the course, but principally it was to acquaint rising stars of business with the experience and advice of successful people, usually entrepreneurs and executives from other organisations, from Britain or abroad, who were prepared to give of their time and who were prepared to make the journey. Few charged for their services apart from expenses and were pleased to impart their wisdom and knowledge to the next generation. Most helicoptered in, though some took a more scenic and leisurely route like the guests themselves. Gordon personally always took at least one of the daily sessions himself, and his courses had won a deserved reputation and admiration from those who had attended them.

He led his visitors to the clearing at the front of Mealag Lodge, pointed out the chalets which each had been allotted and took the wet suitcase from the man who had introduced himself as the compliance director.

"Get yourself dried off and I will have a tracksuit sent over to you in a few minutes. We will dry out your case and have its contents all ironed by tomorrow morning. Any non-clothes items will be dried and returned as they are ready." Gordon had little sympathy for someone whom he was already regarding as silly at best and probably incompetent at worst. He certainly had shown little common sense by wearing a suit for his journey and he recalled that this man had been the first to walk away from the group when they had alighted from the van. Gordon was not going to extend any fatuous sympathy for what had befallen him.

"We will meet at Ruraich in thirty minutes. Any questions?" Gordon asked. He wondered if anyone would ask where or what Ruraich was, but no one dared.

"Good. See you in half an hour."

All the guests found Ruraich without difficulty. In fact with the exception of the shivering compliance director whom they insisted went straightway to his chalet to get warm and dry, the group quickly split up and searched the immediate area, finding the training centre within a couple of minutes.

A small but excellent buffet had been prepared and was laid out on the table, alongside some bottles of white wine and fruit juices. Gordon sat amongst his new arrivals and over the informal lunch introduced himself fully and outlined the events, seminars and conferences to be held during their stay. Sandy MacLean joined them a few minutes later bringing forth astonished gasps from some of the visitors. Sandy had completely transformed his appearance from that of a poorly-dressed white van driver to a rather imposing figure, in tracksuit bottoms and short sleeved white shirt. Sandy went through all the safety procedures both at the Mealag complex and those that appertained to the more physically demanding, and potentially dangerous, external events. Gordon ended lunch by pointing out to them that their first task, that of arriving at Mealag Lodge, had not been an outstanding success and he counselled them to reflect upon the morning's events.

"If you fail to learn the lessons from today," he spoke softly but with authority, "you will not acquit yourselves well on this course or in business. Your very survival might be at stake at some point this week and you will then be required to deploy all your combined resources of skill, enterprise and initiative quickly and effectively. Many of you were dressed quite inappropriately for a trip to the Highlands and as a group you failed to show any team work or devise a suitable plan once you left the transit. In fact, within minutes your group had fragmented. Not an impressive start and if it had not been for one person's initiative in putting on his boots and searching the immediate area for a boat, and another person's skill at managing the boat and its outboard, I suspect that some of you would not have reached here until mid-afternoon... " and fixing a withering stare upon the two previously suited gentlemen Gordon remarked "... perhaps not at all! We shall meet again, here, at 7:00pm. Dinner will be taken in the main house at 7:30pm when we shall be joined by the Chief Executive of Bowden Chemicals Inc of Massachusetts."

"Is it a formal dinner?" enquired one of the insurance corporation's employees "I mean, er, dress-wise," he nervously added.

"Whatever you think is appropriate," replied Gordon, and he walked smartly out the door quickly followed by Sandy.

"There's always one" said Sandy as he and Gordon relaxed over a beer in Mealag's spacious kitchen.

"Yep" said Gordon laughing. "Arrivals never fail to amuse. Why companies employ prats in senior posts when they can't even make a decision on what to wear is beyond me."

They both liked organising and running the courses that were held at Mealag but for quite different reasons. Sandy could utilise his experience on the vigorous outdoor activities, which enabled him to visit the more remote parts of the estate and to keep his fitness level up, whilst Gordon enjoyed them because he was giving something back to a business world that had been extremely generous to him. The eight short breaks throughout the year also ensured that living at Mealag was generally enhanced, not diminished, as the fresh arrival of 'guests' removed any potential possibility of life becoming routine. The courses provided a stimulus not just to Gordon, Sandy and Margaret but to all the estate families who, in one way or other, were included and made a contribution – whether helping Sandy on the various outdoor exercises or in helping Margaret with the catering and cleaning.

6

As Gordon's guests were trying hard to mask their apprehension at the challenges that awaited them over the few days whilst seemingly enjoying the light lunch provided, a black Mercedes E300 saloon drew up outside a row of garages situated in a small cul-de-sac off the Rue Raspail southeast of Paris. The driver, Claude Carron, kept the engine running and thirty seconds later Fadyar Masri emerged from the rear of her apartment block, opened the passenger door and got inside. Carron quickly executed a three-point turn and turned left at the main road. They chatted about nothing of consequence for several minutes before Fadyar raised the subject that had been the reason for her coded call to meet Carron.

"Does London alter anything?" she demanded. "Why wasn't I informed?"

"Because you didn't need to know; I wasn't told either. Actually, I am picking up rumours that the London bombings were carried out by some dissidents angry at the Iraq War but I just don't know. Frankly no one else does either. It wasn't anyone we are aware of."

This temporarily stunned Fadyar.

"Amateurs!" She shouted. "Are you saying a bunch of amateurs did that?"

Carron thought a while and in a slow sombre tone said, "No Fadyar, I'm not, but whoever they were they gave their lives. Our turn will come."

Fadyar had no answer to that. It was true.

"OK." She paused whilst she tried to think of something useful to say but could not. "OK *Claude*". She sarcastically emphasised the controller's name knowing it to be false. No one knew real names, only the aliases given to each of them whilst training.

"Fadyar, we don't have much time. The less we see of each other the better, and driving around Paris is always an accident waiting to happen. So, you are to abandon your planned mission and await further instructions. It may be some while before you hear from me or anyone else." said Carron, gravely.

"But I've deposited some of the money, ready for when we need it." She tried to find an excuse, any excuse, to have her mission go ahead.

"Money isn't important," he mockingly reproved her. "That's one thing we are never short of. Leave it where it is, we might use it someday if we have business in the UK. Britain is now on maximum alert. Their security forces are going frantic, picking up anyone that moves or has connections with Pakistan or the Muslim community. The furore will gradually subside. Their guard will be down again and that is when we will strike."

There was little more Fadyar could say. She had to obey and so she accepted that she would continue being a loyal secretary to her fat boss in the clothing factory until Carron next called upon her.

"Drop me home then, will you?" she asked.

Carron duly obliged and stopped the vehicle on the main road, just long enough to allow Fadyar to hurry inside the main apartment block entrance before he pressed the accelerator and the powerful automatic swung back into the traffic and disappeared.

Fadyar climbed the two flights of stairs and opened her apartment front door, went into the lounge and slumped onto her sofa. She was dismayed at the prospect of just waiting, certainly for months and possibly for years – had she realised then just how frustrated she would become at the enforced postponement she would probably have packed her suitcase and returned to her home town of Baghdad. She recalled the joy and exhilaration she had felt when she had heard from Carron that she was to head up an attack on Manchester Airport but just as she was preparing her plans the London bombings had occurred, spoiling everything. She just hoped all the laborious and demanding training, both physical and mental, that she had received from the fundamentalists would not now be wasted. She understood the need for Jihad, but the burning resentment she felt towards the British and American forces was intensely personal. Her primary need was to avenge the cold blooded slaying of her parents.

***

Cindy Crossland took a few faltering and unsteady steps along the ward helped by the young nurse Jacqui. Cindy was determined to dispense with the crutches as soon as she was able and was making remarkable progress towards her goal. She had combed her hair whilst sitting up in bed but she was anxious to reach the bathroom where she could have the benefit of a large mirror. She needed to uplift her spirits. She had not yet been able to contact Gordon and, for a reason which she did not wish to properly analyse, the absence of hearing his voice, even just once more, had made her feel depressed. The young nurse left her at the door and twenty minutes later Cindy emerged, smiling broadly and looking radiant. Her shoulder length light brown hair, with blonde highlights, was now immaculately groomed and swayed softly as she hobbled on the shiny vinyl tiled floor. Her face, slightly flushed but still gentle and smooth, was complemented only by the faintest of make up around her lips and her grey-green eyes sparkled in the cold white fluorescent light of the ward. Cindy looked good, and she knew it. At five feet nine inches she was not overly tall, but she stood high enough to show her figure to best advantage. The swell of her breasts – moving rhythmically and in unison as she hobbled along – was sufficient that, even constrained by a less than flattering red dressing gown, Cindy was still able to look both attractive and slightly sensuous.

"You look great" the nurse said, "and home tomorrow then?"

Cindy viewed that prospect with mixed emotion. Of course she wanted to get home, out of this hospital and back to the Cotswolds, leaving behind her the awful events of last week. However, that meant living with Alan again and possibly never knowing anything more about Gordon. She had gone over and over her last real conversation with Alan. She had lied to him so as not to hurt his feelings but that had only made her feel worse. For how much longer could she go on living a lie and masking her lack of affection for him? Yet Alan had been wonderful to her during her hospitalisation, visiting two or three times a day, driving back to Stillwood to collect clothes and generally showing great concern for her well-being. Whilst she was hospitalised, she knew he had tried really hard to positively demonstrate his love and support for her, yet she disliked herself for finding his attentions irritating. She had even refused to be transferred to the private hospital Alan had proposed, not because she would not have welcomed a room to herself – she would – but she could not bring herself to agree with her husband's suggestion. It was yet another example of how much she had drifted away from him.

As Jacqui helped her back into her bedside chair, she whispered to Cindy, "Would you like the phone again?"

Jacqui had been marvellous, thought Cindy. She had never asked prying questions about the telephone number but intuitively knew that it represented something deeply personal and important to her patient.

"Please," said Cindy. "Thank you."

Cindy had been going over and over in her head just what she was actually going to say to Gordon if ever she did make contact and she was no nearer resolving that dilemma as she punched out the numbers. Her heart was beating noticeably hard and her mouth had gone dry. The ring tone seemed to her slower than usual, or perhaps it was just her imagination. One ring, two rings, three rings… Cindy let it ring on when suddenly a voice answered.

"Truscott," the voice was soft but firm. "Who's calling?"

"Is that… is that… Gordon?" Cindy found difficulty uttering the words through her parched mouth.

"Yes. Hello. Who is that?"

"Cindy Crossland. Do you remember? The woman on the train."

"How could I forget" Gordon laughed. "How are you, where are you speaking from?"

"I'm getting along fine, but still in hospital."

"Did you know I found out which hospital you were in and looked by, but you had someone with you so I left. I had to be in Scotland by Sunday so there wasn't much time to come round again. I'm so sorry to have missed you."

So much information and delivered so quickly that Cindy thought Gordon sounded really pleased that she had telephoned.

"That would have been Alan, my husband. I've got a busted leg, but its been reset and in plaster and I'm out of hospital tomorrow. I would really like us to meet up sometime so that I can thank you personally." Cindy blurted out the words she had so wanted to say ever since they were forced to part by the medics. She couldn't help herself even though it was quite out of character for her to be so open, especially with someone she hardly knew.

There was a slight pause before Gordon said, "That would be great, I'll look forward to it. How about you give me your mobile number now and I will catch up with you next week."

Cindy duly obliged. Almost as an afterthought she enquired whether Gordon was injured by the bombing, and was relieved that he had only suffered a couple of minor cuts and had some superficial bruising.

"Speak soon, then." and with that Gordon wished Cindy well and said goodbye.

As she put the receiver back into its cradle, Cindy's mind was in whirl, already excited that the stranger on the train had agreed to a meeting. She desperately hoped he meant it.

7

Alan came to visit Cindy as usual at 7pm and immediately noticed how much brighter and cheerier she was. She told him it was because she was going home the next day, which was adequate explanation for Alan who was just pleased that Cindy had apparently overcome the trauma of the blast in such a short time – as he had been warned by the medical staff that her anxiety and depression might last for several weeks at least.

"I'll get Jack to drive you home. The hospital staff say 10:30am would be fine as the doctor will have finished his round and will have discharged you by then."

"I'm happy to get a taxi, Alan. Don't bother Jack." Cindy did not view the prospect of a two and a half hour drive with Jack Donaldson with any sort of pleasure. She loathed the man whom she thought was nothing more than a middle-aged lout.

"You can't get in and out of taxis in your state, and beside which I have nothing for him to do tomorrow. He might as well earn his pay for once."

Cindy knew she was going to lose this discussion but decided to have one more attempt.

"How much do you really know about Jack, Alan? What is his background and how exactly did you meet up? You have never really told me and I find him quite creepy. He always seems to get just a little too close physically and lingers for just a second too long. In fact I find him almost threatening at times."

"Nonsense, Cindy, I'm sure I have explained all this to you before. Jack served in the first Gulf War, spent some time abroad in Africa and South America before briefly doing some work for the good guys when we went into Iraq. I'm not quite sure exactly what he did but he knows how to look after himself and he is an excellent driver. I first met him at some banker's do in the city when he was working for an American organisation, but he didn't like the people much so I offered him a job there and then.

Anyway, he's married now and settled down. I think you are a bit paranoid about him."

Had Alan Crossland bothered to investigate his driver's background he probably would have found out very little, but at least he would have tried to verify his suitability for the post. The absence of any adverse information about his driver did not however mean that he was an upstanding citizen. As a child, Jack was neglected by his single parent mother and drifted into petty crime and almost permanent truancy from his inner city comprehensive school which he left at the earliest opportunity to join the army. There he found the male companionship he had lacked as an adolescent but he gained little experience of relationships with women. On the couple of occasions he had dated a girl, his overeager and clumsy advances were quickly rebuffed and he ended up feeling humiliated and ridiculed. His frustration turned to anger and it was not long before he started using his physical superiority to enforce his will on any vulnerable female who would not respond to his overtures.

Sergeant Jack Donaldson had been accused, though it was never proved as there were no living witnesses, of the rape of two Kurdish women whilst he was serving in the Gulf. He finished his time with the British Army and gained an honourable discharge. As a mercenary in Mozambique, he was able to satisfy his predatory sexual needs almost whenever he wished as most tribal villages were devoid of any men to protect them and the remaining women were easy prey. Several women would have testified to Donaldson's brutality if only he had allowed them to live. He returned to Iraq in 2004, having gained a contract to assist in the protection of an oil installation taken over by the Americans, but when that got blown up by insurgents he found himself wandering around the streets of Baghdad. At that time the old city was in chaos and virtually lawless – just the sort of environment Jack Donaldson relished – and within two weeks of arriving he had obtained a military uniform that made him indistinguishable from the various, and numerous, coalition troops. Suitably camouflaged and anonymous, he set out to enjoy the second largest city in Western Asia.

One day he happened to be walking along a side street when he spotted a high school, deserted except for the playground where a group of three teenage girls were playing. As he watched them the thunderous rolling sound of bomb blast filled the air. The few pedestrians in the street ran for cover behind walls or in nearby buildings and the girls fell to the ground, protecting their heads with their bare arms. He seized his moment. The girls were clearly frightened by the proximity and loudness of the blast and when he motioned them with his rifle to go into the building, they thought he was going to shelter them and ran inside. The school had clearly been disused for several months and was filthy. Everything was covered in thick dry dust mixed with coarse sand and the place was littered with debris of every description. There were broken desks and chairs and various papers were strewn everywhere. Some boxes of equipment had been ransacked, the ropes once securing them cut, with anything of value long since gone. All the light bulbs had been taken and radiators had been ripped from the wall, leaving dried and dirty water stains from the broken pipes. Many of the windows had been smashed and glass shards littered the floor.

Once they were out of sight of the road Donaldson shouted at the frightened girls asking if any of them spoke English and one answered that she did. He then pulled his knife from his belt and pointed his rifle at her, ordering to tell the others that they must do exactly as they were told or their throat would be cut. The girl translated and one girl started to scream. Donaldson immediately hit her across the face with the butt of his rifle which sent her crashing into the wall, her mouth crimson with blood. Donaldson picked three chairs that were still intact, arranged them in a row facing him and then ordered the girls to sit facing him. The girls hesitantly did so. Donaldson gathered from his pocket some long heavy-duty nylon cable ties, used by the military as handcuffs, and secured each of the girl's wrists to their chair. Once he was satisfied their arms were pinned he used more ties to secure the chairs to each other and the end chair to an old radiator pipe. He slowly and deliberately waved the knife in front of their eyes, then walked up to each girl in turn and looked them up and down. He started to gently play with the small white buttons on one of the girl's dresses.

He became more agitated and excited as he imagined what secrets lay beneath the flimsy fabric within his fingers and he started to tear at the buttons ripping open the dress. The girl sat motionless, tears welling in her eyes but too frightened to cry out. Donaldson slowly removed his belt and dropped his trousers and then his strong arms wrenched her head down towards him.

The girls' ordeal lasted over three hours before his desires and appetite diminished. They had ceased to be of use to him and, battered and bleeding, the three naked bodies lay whimpering and groaning on the concrete floor, each barely conscious and curled up in the foetus position to await their next humiliation. Donaldson, now tired from his exertions and fully spent, stood over them. He raised his rifle and then brought the butt down fiercely on each of their heads before removing his long knife and slitting their throats. As their last moments of life drained away, turning the floor a horrible deep red, Donaldson casually opened the door and strolled out into the sunlight.

A few pedestrians had decided to brave the possibility of another bomb blast and were now scurrying along the street, staying low and cowering as they passed behind the shelter of the low wall that surrounded what a few hours earlier had been a large and impressive block of flats. Smoke was still rising from the damaged buildings and the area was now a mass of wailing and anguished people, clawing desperately at the rubble as they tried to find their loved ones. Very few glanced at Donaldson as he walked away from the school opposite, and those that did see him certainly had little interest in the sight of a soldier checking an empty building after a nearby bomb blast and his exit through the crowds did not arouse suspicion. A week later Donaldson bribed his way onto a flight out of Baghdad on an American cargo plane and eventually made his way back to the UK. At first life was dull for Donaldson who yearned for a meaningful and fulfilling relationship with a female partner, but whenever he thought he was on the point of achieving it he ended up being emotionally hurt. Gradually he drifted to the superficial contentment of surfing the pornographic websites on the internet until he hit on the idea of a Russian bride. He was amazed at just how many seemingly attractive women were willing to trade their body for a modest sum of money and a passport and it was not long before he found what he was looking for. Ludmilla was in her early twenties and obviously desperate to escape her homeland which made her an ideal target for someone like Donaldson. The pretty Muscovite would not let him down and in return the young Ludmilla would eventually get her passport, but at a price that would have little to do with money.

"Ok Alan. I'll be at reception at 10:30." Cindy was not going to argue any more. Anyway, her mind was once more turning to Gordon Truscott and she was rather hoping Alan would leave soon so that she could devote her thoughts solely to that alluring subject.

8

The 7th July bombings killed fifty-six people including the four bombers and injured a further 700, with over one hundred requiring overnight hospitalisation. It was the deadliest single act of terrorism in the UK since the blowing up of Pan Am flight 103 over Lockerbie, and more people were killed that July day than in any single bomb attack by the Provisional IRA. It was also the first suicide bombing in Western Europe.

Unsurprisingly, the most intense police investigation ever undertaken in the UK was mounted and over the years a number of persons thought to have helped the bombers in some way would be arrested. The identity of the bombers was quickly established, but it was for the Anti-Terrorist Unit (ATU) and Military Intelligence Section 5 (more commonly known as Britain's internal counter intelligence and security agency MI5) to undertake the laborious process of finding out who assisted the bombers in their deadly mission. The attack came at a time when the Metropolitan Police and the Government were already undertaking an urgent review of the UK's counter terrorism command and control processes, both for the capital city and nationwide. In due course these would result in radical organisational changes and even controversial legislation affecting civil liberties – but when the bombers struck, Assistant Commissioner Phillip Manders of the ATU had amongst his responsibilities that of heading up a small specialist task force dedicated to tracing any funds the terrorist bombers might have received to finance their suicide missions.

Nearing fifty, he regarded the various internal reviews as likely to lead to yet another disruptive reorganisation and, possibly, an even more unwelcome job posting. He had been contemplating early retirement if it was ever to become an option, something he would not have countenanced a few years previously, but the July terrorists had immediately changed his depressed mood. After a career that had been spent largely debating and planning the theoretical, there was now something practical to do. The bombings had given him the opportunity to really get stuck into something big and possibly make a name for himself along the way. This was now a real challenge for him, and he was more than ready to meet it.

"Follow the money, lad. Always follow the money and you'll get your reward." The words had been spoken to him by his chief when Manders was a young officer in the Metropolitan Police. This usually proved to be a wise and true maxim, but the July bombers were "clean skins" – the name given to criminals not previously known to the police. They lived and worked in Britain, and came from respectable, law abiding families. Once their identities were known, Manders' priority was to get a specialist team up and running which could begin the painstaking task of trying to identify and trace bank accounts and any suspicious financial transactions pertaining to the crime. It was going to take a very long time but his team was briefed and within twenty four hours of the bombs going off they had an enlarged office plus the extra desks and chairs for the additional resources provided to him. Communications equipment followed within hours. The powerful computers necessary for sifting and sorting the huge amounts of data were installed within two days and he was told that his budgetary limits were being increased. Suddenly, life for Manders had got an awful lot better.

★ ★ ★

Donaldson parked the sleek black Jaguar on the double yellow lines immediately outside the hospital entrance and walked briskly up the steps to meet Cindy. He wore his peaked cap and smart driver's uniform that added elegance to his military bearing. He saw Cindy, her left leg heavily plastered, standing by a small green suitcase and leaning upon an aluminium crutch under her left shoulder. Donaldson gave her a broad smile, exposing his almost flawless set of white even teeth.

"Good morning, Mrs Crossland. You are looking very well," he said with only the slightest of emphasis on the word 'very' as he picked up the case.

"Thank you, Jack. Yes, I'm fine but I'm not sure how I'll manage the steps, so perhaps we can walk down the ramp." Cindy started to walk towards the slope but it was not as easy as she thought it would be and, fearful of losing her footing, she flung her right arm out and held onto Donaldson's jacket. Donaldson immediately responded, his rapid reflexes borne of years of training sprang into action and, with a speed and agility which surprised Cindy, he dropped the case and thrust his left arm around her to steady her. His grip was firm and certain, but not hard. Still supporting her, he deftly picked up the case in his right hand and started to walk slowly down the ramp.

"I would have got you a wheelchair had you waited. There is no point in risking a fall."

Cindy knew she had been silly to attempt the walk which to her instant regret had given Donaldson the opportunity to get physically close to her.

"I think I can manage now, Jack, thanks." Cindy was steady and felt uncomfortable that Donaldson's arm was perhaps just a little too tight around her and that his hand was resting an inch or so higher than it needed to.

"Can't have you slipping. Alan would sack me if I let you go now and you fell". He was clearly enjoying this moment.

From the very first time that Crossland had introduced his wife to him, Donaldson had been longing to get to know her better and this was too good an opportunity to miss. He regarded Cindy Crossland as not only a very attractive woman but sexy as well, and Donaldson had often fantasised whilst making love to Ludmilla that it was actually Cindy moaning underneath him. How he would love his chimera to become reality! He thought about the sort of life they could have together, how hard he would work for her – the army had taught him how to be self-sufficient and practical – and his hopes were high that on the journey home he could ingratiate himself sufficiently to tempt her towards his deluded ambitions. Things could not have got off to a better start, with Mrs Crossland now physically close and apparently happy at having him hold her firmly.

Reluctantly Cindy allowed him to escort her to the car and he dutifully opened the front passenger door. Donaldson had ensured the front seat was fully set back to permit Cindy sufficient room for her plastered leg to remain straight.

"Can I get in the back?" Cindy asked. Donaldson pointed out to her that he had prepared the front passenger seat to permit her to get in easily and to sit comfortably for the journey. In fact, as Donaldson rightly commented, it was by no means certain that she would have even been able to sit with any degree of comfort in the rear of the saloon.

Cindy had a brief glance through the car window and nodded, but it came as an unpleasant surprise to her when she realised that for the next two or three hours she would be strapped into a seat next to a driver she intensely disliked. She eased herself onto the fine leather cushion, bottom first followed by her right leg, and then cursed when she couldn't manoeuvre her left foot above the door sill and into the foot well. Donaldson removed his cap, leant forward and bent down, his face brushing against the side of her hair. Carefully and very gently, he placed his left hand underneath the calf of her leg easing it upwards and into the car. As Cindy leaned backwards into the deep backrest Donaldson stood upright and took hold of the seat belt pulling it out a little.

"Can I give you a hand with this?" he enquired innocently.

Cindy thought she knew only too well what he was likely to do next if she agreed, and rapidly refused his offer, quickly grabbing hold of the tongue and pushing it firmly into the clasp. Donaldson closed the passenger door and walked briskly around the vehicle to take up his position behind the wheel.

Apart from a couple of occasions – when Cindy wrongly thought Donaldson deliberately put the automatic into 'PARK' for no other reason than to have an excuse to brush her right thigh with his hand – the journey passed by uneventfully and by one o'clock in the afternoon the fat tyres crunched the gravel drive as the car made its slow journey towards the front entrance of Red Gables. She had to endure his overlong assistance as he helped her from the car, much the same as at the hospital earlier, and despite his protestations that he ought to see her safely inside, curtly dismissed him as soon as she was at the door. The old familiar feelings of rejection welled up inside Donaldson and his face reddened but he controlled his emotions. Cindy Crossland was different. Cindy Crossland was worth waiting for.

"Not even a bloody cup of tea, the bitch," Donaldson muttered silently to himself as he returned to the car.

The night before Donaldson had lain awake, half dreaming and half imagining helping Cindy indoors and making sure she was perfectly comfortable. He had assumed that she would invite him in and offer him something to drink when they arrived at Red Gables, which would have been the perfect opportunity for the two of them to relax into conversation and get to know each other better. When it was clear that close contact with her was going to have to wait, Donaldson was more than disappointed, he was angered. *But it will happen,* he told himself. He was convinced that Cindy knew how attracted he was to her and misguidedly concluded that the real reason Cindy had been so dismissive at the door was because deep down she really did fancy him and was nervous about taking the plunge. He would be patient, give her more time. He had met a few women like that before and they had all given in eventually.

Although tired, Cindy knew she had to make a phone call to Peter, the ex-cabinet office colleague she had been due to meet on that fateful Thursday. She had been putting it off until now, not wanting a stream of visitors at her bedside, and she knew that whatever Peter wanted to see her about it was unlikely to be a subject suitable for discussion in an open hospital ward.

"Peter, its Cindy. Sorry we missed each other last week but given what happened I guess you may have had a few problems anyway."

"Lovely to hear from you, Cindy. Hope you or Alan weren't caught up in that shindig?"

"Actually, Peter I was. Got a broken leg and some other minor injuries as I was on one of the trains, the Liverpool Street to Aldgate one. I'm home now though, which is why I'm phoning."

"My God! How awful for you dear girl. I'm so very sorry. Wished I hadn't dragged you down here now. Anyhow, no need any more for us to meet just yet. I was being a bit mysterious by not telling you why I wanted you to come, bit of subterfuge really to make sure you made the trip. I feel dreadful now I know what's happened. Anyway, the real reason was to have a surprise glass of champagne with you and then off for a bite together to celebrate my promotion. Can't speak over the phone but I'm now at the FO and so we will have our little party another day. Superseded by events shall we say, but we must stay in touch. Let me know if I can ever be of help. You know – anything. Just ask."

Peter was one of those civil servants who always chose what he said very carefully and yet always managed to make his words sound relaxed and informal. This could be very disarming and many a person had let their guard down and revealed just a little too much when in his company. Cindy therefore knew he meant what he said, and that he would definitely contact her again sometime. She momentarily wondered why – as she had left Peter's world of high politics and its intrigues far behind – but he and his boyfriend Stephen, twenty years his junior, were both great fun to have around and she had really enjoyed the quite outrageous parties she had been to at the house they shared in Chelsea. *The Foreign Office will certainly be livelier with Peter around*, she thought.

It had been over a week since she had spoken to Gordon, and Cindy was finding it hard to concentrate. As the days passed, she had become more and more anxious that perhaps he had changed his mind and would not ring her mobile after all. She then wondered if he had lost the number and whether she should call him again, but decided that as this would be such a transparently false excuse it was likely to be very counter-productive. Either he did want to speak with her again or he didn't, she told herself. If he did he would not have lost the number; if he didn't call, there was little point in her chasing him. Despite her impeccable reasoning, this morning she had twice started dialling his number before aborting the call. Mrs Crookes, the cleaner, who normally came only twice a week, was now doing an extra three hours on Friday afternoons and would be arriving shortly and Cindy did not think it would be sensible to make a call to Gordon once she had arrived.

To take her mind off Gordon, Cindy decided to check her emails and logged on to her computer. Staring blankly at the small blue lights across the centre of the screen, indicating the normal start-up procedure of the operating system, a thought flashed into her brain. Impatiently she drummed her slim fingers on the desk beside her keyboard and wondered why computers were so slow to get going, yet so phenomenally quick at doing the really complex stuff. Her password prompt appeared and a few seconds later she had clicked the internet icon on the desktop screen. Selecting her preferred search engine, she typed in "Gordon Truscott" hoping she had spelled the surname correctly. *It was a chance*, she thought, *just a slim hope, that there might be some information about this man that fate had brought into her life.* As the search results rolled onto the screen, Cindy was amazed. There were at least fifty or more matches. Deeply curious, she rapidly scrolled through the list and read the summary of each until deciding to start with one of the more promising looking items.

Gordon Truscott. Born 16th February 1966. West Wickham, Kent. Attended Collington Road Primary School then Grovewood Comprehensive. Left school at 18, eight GCSE 'A' grades and 3 'Advanced Level' passes, again grade A. No university. At aged 16 started writing games programs for the Sinclair ZX Spectrum and, later, the BBC Acorn computers. Reputed to be one of the most prolific of early games programmers with several well known titles to his credit both under license to software houses and in specialist computer magazines of the day. Started own games software company, 'TrustSoft', on leaving school and later aged twenty-two founded Truscott Commercial Solutions dedicated to producing software for the emerging business PC market. In 1999 sold Truscott Commercial Solutions for a reputed £300M. Also sole owner of Truscott Enterprise Holdings the full extent of its activities are unclear, but thought to include property development.

Single, never married. Truscott avoids overt publicity and spends most of his time at one or other of his homes. These include a large shooting lodge, extensively renovated, built on his 2000 acre estate in a remote area of the Scottish Highlands. Other properties are known to include a London penthouse suite overlooking the Thames and a villa in Monemvasia, Southern Greece. Interested in the Arts and occasionally seen attending charity functions at which Truscott is usually unaccompanied.

Cindy bookmarked the web page in order that she might return to it quickly and then set about accessing the other web sites listed on her search results pages. She became immersed in reading everything about Gordon, time sped by, and after a little over three hours she concluded that most of the other articles were more about gossip and supposition than hard fact. A few females had been named but nothing of any substance was forthcoming that might hint at a long-term relationship.

She returned to the search screen and clicked 'images' and pressed the enter key. Almost instantly, the screen filled with pictures of Gordon. Some were of him casually dressed, some in black or white tie for a particular charity gala or some such. A few showed him accompanied by a female but his companion was either the host or fellow guest. The photographs however fulfilled Cindy's prime purpose of seeing exactly what Gordon looked like, as she had only faint recollections from the train. The clear images now showed him to be quite tall, probably a little over six feet with slightly waved brown hair, always – it seemed from the photographs – immaculately groomed. There was nothing particularly remarkable about his facial features, nothing to get overly excited about at all, but her heart was racing.

"I don't believe it… three hundred *million*… on the underground?" Cindy muttered absentmindedly to herself. Then, more audibly, "So that's what you look like", and she immediately hoped Mrs Crookes didn't hear downstairs.

She needn't have worried. Mrs Crookes was pushing the powerful, red vacuum cleaner across the deep sitting room carpet gathering up non-existent dirt, whilst listening through a headset to her favourite *Scissor Sisters* latest album. Cindy's expert fingers flashed across the keyboard and she paged back to the first text item. This time she studied the words in detail and the more she read and reread them, the greater her delight and anticipation of his promised phone call – the call that would change her life.

9

Alan Crossland had finished reading his emails when Jane opened his door and walked into his office. In her right hand, she was carrying a small DL-sized white envelope which she gave to her boss.

"I haven't opened it but it has just been delivered by the police."

"What? Did you say the police?" Crossland's raised, incredulous voice reverberated off the oak-panelled walls. "Since when have they been postmen?" He continued, as he took the envelope. Jane remained motionless, clearly curious as to what its contents might be but Crossland made no attempt to open it in her presence and said a mere "Thanks, Jane" in a tone that clearly implied 'goodbye'. Jane stiffened and slowly turned before she left the room, closing the heavy door quietly behind her.

Crossland carefully slit open the envelope and placed the letter onto the desk. It was obviously word-processed, despite the personalised salutation to 'Dear Alan' and informed Crossland that following the terrorist outrage of the 7th July, some bank accounts (not named or identified) had been frozen by the Bank of England in accordance with the powers entrusted to it by Parliament. Hannet-Mar was not one of the banks involved but Alan was reminded of his obligations in respect of the legislation and asked to report any suspicious transactions immediately to the Anti-Terrorist Unit. His cooperation was being sought and in this regard he could expect a visit from the ATU to whom every courtesy should be extended.

Bloody cheek, thought Alan. He knew full well the law and the obligations of all banks in respect of money laundering or indeed the possible financing of terrorism. He might not be too fussy over some of his personal clients but he knew all those people and they were certainly not terrorists.

Anyway, he thought, *I can only act once I know, or ought to know, or have reasonable grounds for suspicion. Until that arises, how can I assist the ATU?*

Nonetheless, he was shaken. This was the first time the ATU or any law enforcement agency was going to visit his bank, and Crossland suspected that the delicate phrasing within the letter 'to whom every courtesy should be extended' carried with it an implicit threat. He knew he had nothing to hide that would be of interest to the Anti-Terrorist Unit, but he was also certain the ATU were not just going to pay him a social call. He hoped that their investigations would not lead to an in-depth examination of his personal files which were likely to reveal some uncomfortable, if not illegal, commercial transactions between some rather murky characters and the bank. Hiding the odd bank account from the Financial Services Authority was both easy and relatively risk-free, but concealment from the ATU was not an option. He would have to disclose all his files if asked.

He buzzed his secretary's phone. "I'm not going to lunch today Jane and you can cancel any of this afternoon's appointments. Thanks."

He thought it would be prudent to undertake an immediate review of his personal files to make absolutely certain there was nothing he had overlooked. It did not take him long as he was very familiar with them, and by mid-afternoon he was nearly finished and apart from one was totally satisfied. Most involved investments and accounts lodged by or for various foreign multi-millionaires, mainly Russian, Middle Eastern or American, and he was feeling rather relieved. The one he had a slightly uneasy feeling about was the latest addition to his personal drawer, the Halima Chalthoum email on behalf of Corniche Consortium. As promised, all the paper documentation had arrived and appeared to check out. The funds had arrived, via a respected bank with branches throughout the Middle East, but he was none too sure whether there really was a properly constituted and functioning consortium. When he met Fadyar she was very reticent to talk about its intentions and changed the subject. Crossland was beginning to realise that he knew very little about Fadyar Masri other than she obviously wished to disguise her identity, at least to the extent of using a different name, and that she had been had been recommended by his old friend Kenneth Styles – at one time probably Crossland's most profitable personal client but who had sold everything up a year back and now enjoyed comfortable retirement in Sussex. He rang Kenneth's number and his wife Penny answered.

"Oh. Hello Penny, Alan Crossland. Just a quick call to see how you both are and to have a word with Ken about a mutual friend of ours."

A brief silence followed.

"Alan, you haven't heard then. I'm sorry I thought I sent out the funeral invitations to all our friends but Ken died several weeks ago," she replied faintly.

"What? No, surely not? Oh, Penny, I am so, so very sorry. I really didn't know. What happened? Did the fags get him?"

"No, Alan, nothing like that. He was driving back from the golf club when his car went off the road on that dangerous hill just outside Eastbourne. The strange thing was that he was well over the limit, nearly three times according to the police. But you know Ken, he never really drank much and only ever had one drink if he was driving. Everyone at the club said he only had one glass of wine after the match. We assumed he must have called into a pub on the way home as the accident occurred at three in the afternoon and he left the club, which is only half an hour from here, just after midday."

Alan Crossland was stunned. He had known Styles for twenty years and could vouch for his temperate habits. He didn't know what to say, other than to proffer more commiserations and to promise that he and Cindy would definitely be down before the end of summer. The news had visibly shaken him. He shook his head, his mouth went dry. Slowly he replaced the receiver. He thought he could hear his heart as it began to thump away inside him, slowly at first then rapidly as the wave of fear travelled from his brain to his stomach before rising upwards again and crashing into his chest. He shuddered and sweated. He was certain that whatever had befallen his friend, it was not likely to have been an alcohol-related road accident. Suicide perhaps? But that made little sense. Ken was a wealthy man enjoying a happy retirement with his wife whom he adored.

The more Crossland thought about Styles the more convinced he became that his friend's death was more likely to be related to his past employment. Crossland knew himself that consultancy in the Middle East rarely followed Western ethical standards. Styles was good, very good. He had brought to fruition the financing of some of the most prestigious and expensive projects in the Arab world and could personally bring together chief executives of multi-national organisations to sign up to deals. He had the skill to always remain on excellent terms with both sides in a negotiation even when, rarely, it went sour. Perhaps, unwittingly, he had upset someone or maybe he knew too much about a particular contract. Whatever it was, Crossland did not believe Styles had died in an accident. Another shiver ran down Crossland's spine. He had good reason to be fearful.

10

Gordon Truscott was a careful man. His father had died when he was just three years of age and his mother had struggled to keep a roof over their heads, often having to take on a part-time cleaning job in addition to her full-time work as an insurance clerk. She ensured that Gordon's childhood was happy and safe, and was delighted when he had shown considerable aptitude for the subjects taught to him at school. Gordon had not just gained knowledge and passed examinations, he had understood the merits of loyalty, devotion and particularly the virtues of hard work and the value of money. His meteoric and unexpected rise to untold wealth and fortune brought about initially by his quest to teach himself how to programme the earliest micro-computers had not distorted those core beliefs. In those early years of personal computing he wrote games programs for fun, until he started to receive ever more lucrative offers from the fledgling magazines that needed to satisfy the hungry appetites of their new, young readership. The money rolled in, and being astute he quickly formed a small company and began copyrighting his material. Annual licence fees earned him more in a week than most men earned in a year, and very soon he was able to expand into bespoke business software offering PC-based solutions to global companies with deep pockets.

His personal life contrasted sharply with that of his business persona. He had seen the struggle and sacrifice his mother had made and this had made him risk-averse when it came to personal relationships. For many years he had successfully eluded the tenacious clutches of several females, although that had not been difficult. He simply did not love them, nor even feel a strong emotional attachment, but he was slightly bewildered as to his feelings for the woman on the underground. He hardly knew her, yet she excited him. He felt an affinity and warmth towards her that he knew was totally irrational, but was also a powerful attraction. He had spent days, and some nights, thinking about her and whether he should honour his promise to phone her, apprehensive as to exactly where it might lead – but there was something very compelling about her. He had met women of all nationalities, sizes, shapes and status. Rich, powerful women and those from the poorest of countries, but they easily slipped from his mind. Cindy, though, was different.

She seemed to be invading his mind, persistently, almost to the exclusion of everything else. That didn't just make Cindy Crossland interesting, it made her dangerously alluring. She was clearly intelligent and well educated – the manner of her speech and choice of words even in those extreme conditions told him that – though he wished he had been able to see more of her face and features when he was close to her in the carriage. Most of the time however, it had been pitch black and impossible to see anything at short-range and even when the emergency lights were in place he had not been able to see much as there was frenzied activity going on around them and the doctor was attending to Cindy. He had hoped to see her in hospital but the brief glimpse he managed from the doors of the hospital ward revealed only that she had light brown hair.

Cindy had told him on the train she was married, but it was nonetheless a shock to see the man at her bedside. Gordon knew instantly by the body language and the concern etched into his face it was her husband, and that chance sighting was what had delayed Gordon from making the call. He needed to be absolutely certain that he was prepared to face the consequences and had spent the last few days on the losing side of an irrational debate with his conscience. He checked the time; four thirty in the afternoon. He took a deep breath, picked up the telephone and dialled her mobile.

The call itself was brief lasting little more than two minutes, but that belied the volume of information and words exchanged. Both spoke with gathering enthusiasm and speed, often the two of them speaking simultaneously yet both perfectly understanding what the other said, though Cindy carefully avoided letting slip anything that might have revealed she had been gleaning information about Gordon on the internet. At her suggestion, they agreed to meet for lunch the following Tuesday at the Bunch of Grapes in the small Worcestershire village of Meckerton as it was far enough away from Stillwood for her not to be recognised. Gordon did not offer to pick her up, and Cindy did not suggest it to him. It suited them both not to ask.

The next few days, Cindy could hardly contain her growing excitement and anticipation. She started doing things she hadn't done for years, such as loudly singing along to a favourite CD, the volume level on the amplifier turned up high. She skipped around the house, flitting from room to room for no apparent reason whilst lightly muttering to herself. She was happy again.

For the first time since the crash, Cindy felt like returning to the feature article she had been preparing prior to the bombing. Such articles were still something of a novelty for her, but she was enjoying undertaking the research and the discipline that imparting sufficient factual and interesting information within a relatively small number of words imposed. She had so far managed three articles, or rather two plus the one in preparation.

Her first since she left mainstream journalism had concerned the Black Country and how it became the beating heart of Britain's industrial revolution with great iron foundries that produced the massive engines and heavy engineering equipment that powered the nation to prosperity. Her second was a complete contrast, a walker's guide to the canals of Worcestershire.

Whilst researching that article, walking alongside a disused canal early one Sunday morning, the path widened until she came to an open space of common grassland dotted with some trees and large brambles. A small band of ten people stood facing each other in a large circle. Each had a dog sitting at their feet. The spectacle was so unexpected and surprising, Cindy stopped to look. After a brief moment, the dog owners started walking slowly clockwise around the circle having told their dogs to stay, which they all did for a few seconds. A young black Labrador was the first to break ranks and ran into the middle of the circle to loud shouts of "No" and "Get back". The clearly embarrassed owner fearing that her dog would be the sole transgressor, need not have been concerned. Seeing the Labrador running free and clearly enjoying itself, two – and then three – other dogs, all springer spaniels, joined in the revelry and began playfully chasing each other. Four owners were now frantically running into the circle themselves trying to catch, scold or even plead with their respective dog to come back but this only extended the game. Cindy thought the whole thing hilarious and laughed out loud. When order and calm had eventually been restored one of the circle, a grey-haired man of medium build (whose own dog Cindy noticed had not been one of the miscreants) called out in a broad Worcestershire accent to the reassembled group, "That wasn't very good was it? It wasn't even very funny despite it causing a great deal of mirth amongst the spectators." Everyone, including Cindy laughed.

"I couldn't help it," she shouted. "I hope I'm not in the way or putting them off."

"They're supposed to sit still even if they are being distracted, that's the whole point of the bloody exercise though you wouldn't believe it by looking at this lot." As he finished his sentence, he airily waved a long walking stick he was carrying in the general direction of the assembled group.

"Join us if you want," he called out.

Cindy spent the rest of the morning walking in and out of dogs that were supposed to sit still and ignore her, throwing dummies for them to retrieve, and when the dogs had been turned to face in the other direction, putting tennis balls behind bushes prior to the owner sending the dog to find them. Overall, she had been impressed with the dogs and even more with their dedicated owners. In the pub afterwards, she had learnt all about them.

They were members of a small gun dog club, though not all wanted to shoot or even go beating, their aim was just to achieve a really obedient dog. Whilst the club itself separately ran more formal and advanced training as the dogs progressed, a few members local to the particular area went out each Sunday for what they termed informal training. The group would meet up, give two or three hours training to the young dogs, principally in obedience and retrieving, then adjourn to the nearest pub. Cindy enjoyed herself enormously and she left with an open invitation to contact the grey-haired man, whom she now knew as Don, a qualified trainer of springer spaniels, to join them again.

Cindy turned on her computer to continue composing her

third feature, "Gun Dog Stories – by those who try to train them" gleaned of course, and written down in note form with permission, from Don and his friends.

Alan Crossland was feeling slightly more relaxed. Several days had passed and the ATU had not paid him a visit. The weekend was looming and having spent a week in the Shoreditch flat, he was looking forward to Red Gables and seeing Cindy. At 2:45pm, he said goodbye to Jane and stepped into the back of the car waiting outside the front door of his office building. He asked Jack to stop at Woodstock where he bought Cindy a large bunch of roses and was indoors just as the 6 o'clock news bulletin came on. Alan was not accustomed to buying flowers or surprise gifts as some husbands do for their wives, but a couple of colleagues had said that 'women like that sort of thing'. As he was desperate to make his wife happy, he had resolved to do everything he could to make her feel wanted and loved since her return from hospital. Cindy put her arms around his waist and briefly kissed him on the cheek as he passed her his present.

"Thank you, Alan, what a marvellous surprise. You. Buying flowers?" she said, jauntily. "What *have* you been up to?" she added with a mischievous note, overly exaggerating the word 'have'

"Not much really. The flat will need a bit of a tidy up. Sandra and Susie left it in a bit of a state; those oils make a real mess of the sheets, you know" he replied drily.

For a split second, Cindy was unsure if she heard him correctly. Then laughing loudly, she shook her head, causing her hair to move left then right before it fell gently back strand by strand to its original position. Alan thought she had enjoyed his quick repost to her question, but in fact Cindy was laughing at a vision of a naked Alan in bed with two blonde bimbos each rubbing scented oils onto the others bodies. She could not think of anything less likely or more grotesque, and in her current mood of elation, it made her laugh heartily.

A couple of hours later, Cindy was seated in a spacious armchair, a foot stall supporting both her legs, trying to work out the sudoku puzzle in *The Daily Telegraph*. Alan was on the sofa, reading a book.

"Shall I put the news on?" Cindy asked.

"Not for me. Not unless you want it. I've had a pretty tough week and I might get to bed soon." He hoped Cindy might, just might, take the hint and oblige tonight. A broken leg might stop Cindy walking far, but it wouldn't stop them making love.

"OK, I won't be long myself," Cindy was non-committal. "By the way, I'm thinking of getting out and about a little next week. The leg is coming along fine and I think I can manage quite a distance, so thought I might go and look in the shops or something. Haven't decided which day yet, probably Tuesday or Wednesday," she innocently remarked, using the excuse she had thought of, in case Alan phoned home on Tuesday and failed to get an answer. Mrs Crookes, the housekeeper, would also have to be told the same lie.

"Are you sure you're up to it, Cinders?" Alan asked, reminding Cindy that he only used that silly nickname when he wanted something. She now loathed it. It reminded her of when they first started to go out together.

Crossland continued with what he felt was a kind offer, "Tell me which day and I'll make sure Jack is around to ferry you about."

This was the very last thing Cindy wanted, and it took her off guard. Inwardly she cursed herself for not anticipating Alan's response and now had to think quickly or she would never convince him of her cover story. Maybe she could turn this to her advantage if she was bold.

"Absolutely not, Alan. I'm sorry, but that man has a problem and I find him quite threatening at times. On the way back from the hospital I felt he was deliberately putting the automatic into PARK as an excuse to touch my legs, and he brushed against me whenever he could as he helped me in and out of the car. He makes me shudder. No, Alan, I am quite capable of getting a taxi."

"I'm sure you're just being over-sensitive and looking for things that don't exist. The man's a driver, damn it, and a good one at that. It's sometimes safer to put the selector into PARK. Anyway, how do you help someone who can't walk in and out of a car without touching or brushing against them? But have it your way, use a taxi." Alan rose and came over and kissed her gently but fully on the lips. "Maybe see you later, goodnight."

Once he was upstairs Cindy exhaled a long, deep sigh. Tuesday couldn't come a moment too soon; Alan's closing remark already forgotten.

The weekend passed uneventfully and far too slowly for her. At times she snapped at Alan and had to apologise quickly, putting her bad temper down to her frustration at still having the leg in plaster. This was partly true, but she knew the real reason was that Alan intruded upon her thoughts of Gordon. However, Tuesday arrived at last.

Cindy woke a little before eight to find the mid-August sun already casting a square of golden light around the closed curtains. Brilliant rays speared into her bedroom and danced their way from wall to wall, illuminating the room in a soft yellow glow despite the curtains. She loved this room. It was not grand like the so-called master bedroom, though still large, and it provided a cosy and warm haven even on the coldest of nights. This morning was not one of those. The summer sun was hot, even at this hour, and she could feel the heat pushing its way into the room. As was usual she had slept naked, and turning the cover sheet to one side, she stepped out of bed and stretched her arms, looking at herself in the full length mirror. She anxiously examined her face, to check if any blemishes or spots had appeared overnight and she pulled her skin so tightly that it made her mouth contort into weird shapes. Relieved, she examined her eyes – no deep lines there, nor on her neck. Her breasts were still firm but perhaps ought to be just a shade larger; her tummy wasn't too bad she thought, still pretty flat, thanking the Almighty that she had never borne children; and her legs were definitely good, at least they both would be once the plaster was removed.

Turning round she studied her back. No spots. Bum could be a little firmer but it still had good shape. The five minute evaluation over, she didn't need to summarise the result. In many respects, she had been overly harsh on herself. She was a very attractive woman who looked considerably younger than her thirty-five years. She showered, put her cream silk dressing gown around her and made her way to the kitchen where she had a leisurely breakfast of natural orange juice, coffee and two slices of toast whilst watching a twenty-four hour news channel.

After breakfast, she had spent the morning trying on different outfits. She did not want to go over the top. She tried to imagine what Gordon might wear. Jeans? A summer suit perhaps? Surely not shorts? She wished she knew him better as then she could have dressed herself with more certainty, but she concluded that he definitely would not be in shorts nor so laid-back as to look even mildly scruffy. Probably smart casual, whatever that meant.

Eventually, and with the digital clock in the room reminding her that a decision had to be made, she decided on a very pale yellow summer dress with tan shoes and small handbag. She had visited her hairdresser the previous day and her usual stylist and colourist had, as always, earned their generous gratuity. The natural wave in her hair had been slightly accentuated, and the subtle blonde highlights merged smoothly with the flowing range of light browns, giving her hair an overall effortless but vibrant appearance. It rested naturally away from her face and hung softly around her ears, complementing the outfit and glowed in the sunshine that now flooded the room. Cindy knew she looked stunning but not in any way powerfully or overdressed. The only downside she thought was that her plastered leg was all too visible, but that didn't persuade her to wear trousers.

The taxi arrived exactly at the time she had asked, midday, which she estimated would mean a deliberate slightly late arrival at the pub. She had booked it with a company in Lower Dister, not the local Stillwood firm, and was pleased to see that they had remembered she needed a vehicle with plenty of leg room. The driver dropped her by the front entrance of the pub but before entering she glanced at the car park. Barely half-full, Cindy was able to look carefully at all the vehicles, expecting to see a really expensive model, perhaps a high-powered sports car or possibly even a limousine. There were none that really caught her eye, only the usual mixed assemblage one would expect, and she wondered anxiously if Gordon was either going to be late or perhaps may not come. She turned to face the door, drew a deep breath and turned the handle. Almost instantly, Gordon came across and introduced himself.

"Hello, I'm Gordon" and with a quick glance at her legs said "and you just have to be Cindy". He pointed to the large bay window on the far side of the room and asked if the table there would be suitable. Anywhere would have been acceptable to Cindy, though she noted that the place he had chosen was in a spacious area, well apart from other diners.

She was pleased to see that he was wearing light cream coloured slacks and a sports shirt, confirming the assumption she made in the morning. A few brown hairs could just be seen at the top of his chest and he was noticeably sun tanned. He wore his Omega watch on his right wrist from which she deduced, correctly, that he was probably left handed. He was slightly taller than the web page photographs of him suggested and his hair longer. She deliberately avoided any awkward shaking of hands and having exchanged the introductions made her way to the table.

The predominant conversation while waiting to order their meals and wine was, unsurprisingly, about Cindy: the exact nature of her injuries, how many days she was kept in hospital, how she was coping around the house and other small talk. She managed to reciprocate the questioning a couple of times and learnt that Gordon's cuts and bruises were very minor and of no consequence to him. He seemed willing to talk and she found conversation easy with him. They both quickly relaxed and by the main course they were chatting as if they had been friends for years. Gordon told her of Mealag Lodge and made her laugh as he described the scene of the executives rapid descent into chaos and farce within minutes of alighting from the Transit van.

"I should have liked to have seen that," said Cindy.

"Maybe you will sometime, if you would like to. It's usually pretty much the same on all of the courses, which is why I like to observe their arrival."

It was obvious that Gordon was not the sort of person to make such an apparent throw away invitation unless he meant it, and the muscles in her stomach involuntarily fluttered with excitement. Gordon could indeed have told her more such stories but the two of them were so enjoying listening to each other and making comments that no single subject dominated their time. As the coffee was being served, either deliberately or inadvertently, (Cindy was not sure which) Gordon let it be known that he had never married and there was no one in his life.

In addition to his home in the Highlands, Gordon had mentioned he had sold his business a while back but still had a property company and a London apartment. They quickly discovered their common interest in Southern Greece, though Gordon did not tell her that he owned an extremely large villa in Monemvasia. She thought that slightly curious but assumed it was probably because he did not want to appear to be immodest or showing off. Cindy deliberately did not mention her husband Alan; neither did Gordon.

They were so absorbed with each other that it was 3:30pm before Cindy glanced at the ostentatiously ornate wall clock mounted high above the original black iron fireplace, and suggested that perhaps they ought to leave as she couldn't face another coffee. Gordon offered to drop her home, but she declined saying untruthfully that the cab firm was only a few minutes away and started keying on her mobile before he could interject. Gordon called for the bill which he insisted on paying despite Cindy's pleas that she wanted to thank him for being of such comfort when she was injured. Gordon remarked how much he had really enjoyed their meeting and, somewhat awkwardly and hesitatingly, enquired if they could meet up again soon. Cindy's heart leapt and she accepted the invitation a little too quickly, but she didn't care.

"I have the plaster removed in a couple of weeks and then I should be able to drive, but I can make lunch again next Tuesday here, same time, if that's OK."

"Agreed then," he said and then continued, "it has been really great to meet up and I'm so pleased your leg is pretty much healed. I shall look forward to next week very much."

The taxi finally arrived and as they stood, Gordon took her arm and led her to the waiting car. He made no attempt to kiss her but just lightly squeezed her hand as she settled into her seat.

"Thanks again," he said as he shut the door.

"And you too, Gordon. Take care, bye" and with that she gave a quick wave out of the window and was gone.

Gordon opened the door of an ordinary saloon car and as he sat behind the wheel gave a long, soft whistle through his teeth. He thought that Cindy Crossland was one hell of an attractive woman and he knew that he was about to embark on an adventure, but to where it would lead he had no idea. Cindy spent the journey home regretting she had suggested meeting again seven days later. She wished she had said tomorrow.

The next few days passed slowly and uneventfully for both Cindy and Gordon. She sent him a short text message thanking him for the meal and saying again how much she had enjoyed it, and he responded with a brief 'Ditto. See you next week. G'.

11

In marked contrast to his wife, Alan Crossland was enduring some mounting difficulties. The three officers comprising the financial investigation team of the Anti-Terrorist Unit had paid a visit and asked to go through the bank's records. Alan knew that it was not a request, but merely politeness that they posed the question. They indicated they might be two or three days, which caused Alan to gulp deeply before he offered them the exclusive use of the interview room. Their first request was to ask for a printout of all the bank's open accounts, of whatever type, detailing account holder(s), numbers and summary balance of financial information for each. The second request was to obtain the same information for all accounts closed in the past twelve months. They asked if the same data could also be supplied on optical disks or tapes and suggested that whilst that was being gathered perhaps he might like to discuss any particular problem accounts or concerns he may have regarding any of his clients or overseas banks that conduct business with the Hannet-Mar. Thus began almost a day of questioning and probing, which at its conclusion left Alan exhausted and irritated. He hoped he had not shown it.

The requested data, copied across to commercial tape drives, was obtained late afternoon and the ATU decided to continue their work the next morning. They arrived in an unmarked car along with a marked police van, which did nothing to dispel Crossland's anxiety. They unloaded several computers, printers and associated equipment, and set them up in the interview room. At 4pm, one of the officers produced a printout of thirty two accounts and asked if he might have full computer access for these accounts plus a look at the paper files. Alan said stiffly that he was sorry but it was not possible to give anyone unfettered access to the bank's own computer systems, but if it helped he would make a senior member of staff available to sit with them. The member of staff would access the full computerised record of any account they wished and they could ask for the detail they required. This satisfied the ATU and Alan asked Glen Simmons, who was one of the brightest young managers at the bank and regarded by Alan as something akin to a computer whiz-kid, to undertake whatever was needed in the quickest possible time. Simmons was a wise and sensible choice and by mid-morning on the third day the list had been reduced to seven accounts, all of which were marked as Code G, and for which Alan was sole keeper of the paper files. The ATU senior officer and Alan then met to discuss the files. The officer asked to see certain documents for himself and every so often jotted down some notes which were then handed to another officer who disappeared into the interview room before returning. Alan found the whole experience quite unnerving. They had finished with four files when the officer asked for the Chalthoum Universal Holding file. Again he made some notes which were passed to the interview room.

"I see this is a recent account with two deposits made, one as recently as a week ago" the officer remarked casually, but it was a question, not just a statement of fact, that invited comment from the bank manager. Alan knew of the subsequent deposit when a further £100,000 had been deposited by Halima Chalthoum through the El-Hamisra Bank of Cairo, the same bank but a different branch as before, and was able to respond in positive terms.

"Yes, it is. I hope it turns out profitable for all concerned," Alan said blandly, giving a typical banker's reply.

"When did you meet with Halima Chalthoum? I see the original email refers to a discussion."

"Actually, I haven't seen her. She telephoned me and I was initially very reluctant to take such instructions from someone I didn't know so I turned down her initial approach. She then said I had been recommended to her by a friend of mine and asked what I would need by way of verification and certification as it was impossible for her to fly to London. I told her, but stressed that I would need to make very detailed enquiries before I could agree to open an account. The next I knew I received the email." Alan was beginning to sweat despite the air conditioning.

"That is highly unusual isn't it?" asked the officer.

"Well, er, no, not necessarily. As you will see from the file, there are certified photographs – even an Affidavit if I remember correctly – plus impeccable references, one from that long-standing friend whom I would trust implicitly. Ms Chalthoum represents a very important consortium. You can see their impressive prospectus is also in the file."

The officer did not respond directly but asked another question. "I see you opened the account and actioned the email on the 7th July. Why that particular day? Why not earlier?"

Bloody hell, of all days thought Alan, as he recognised the date of the London bombings.

"I had only just returned from holiday and that was my first day back." He lowered his voice adding sombrely, "in fact my wife was quite seriously hurt by the Liverpool Street bomb, suffered a broken leg and other bits and pieces. We travelled to London together but I got off at Liverpool Street." If Alan thought this might invoke some sympathy and introduce a slightly less formal note in their discussion, he was mistaken.

"Yes, I suppose you would get off there. I'm sorry to hear about your wife; I hope she recovers soon. Sadly others, of course, lost their life. I presume the bank logs all phone calls and retains a recording of them?"

Crossland smiled. "You must appreciate we are a very traditional, rather old fashioned bank and that, sadly, extends into our use of what I would call hi-tech equipment like that. So, no, we don't have automated recording but you will be pleased to hear that the Board have agreed to install a system next year."

The officer fiddled with the papers. "I think that will be fine, perhaps we should go onto the next one. Oh, one last question. Why is the Chalthoum file marked Code G? I can appreciate why the others are, their size and political sensitivity etc but this Chalthoum case just looks pretty ordinary. Other than the highly unusual circumstances of not knowing the client, it would appear this case has little to merit your personal involvement." The question caught Alan slightly off guard and he stumbled over his words.

"It is. Well it isn't, but might be. I will probably remove the code if the account amounts to very little but I thought this might be a promising new client and really only marked it G so that I could monitor its early development, especially, as we said earlier, since I hadn't met Ms Chalthoum."

The officer closed the file saying nothing and the remaining accounts were discussed until they had concluded them all. He then stood up, thanked Alan and walked into the interview room. "Anything turn up?" he enquired.

"No," answered a young man in civilian dress from one of the computer stations.

The officer however was not convinced that all was in order at the bank and had noticed that Crossland had seemed ill at ease during certain aspects of the interview. He also regarded some of the bank procedures as less than transparent, especially in relation to Crossland's own files, and would ask the other agencies for some help to ensure that each and every transaction on the manager's personal accounts would be monitored very closely indeed.

"We're finished then," he said. "When we get back, I want all those code G accounts fed into the Watch system. If anything moves on those, I want to know. Continue running checks against every name we have from the last lot of files and let Five know the names as well, particularly that Halima Chalthoum woman. Maybe the gooks will find something we can't, if not get our overseas friends to help."

12

The police investigation had kept Alan Crossland in London all week, which frustrated him; he had not been able to get home just at the time that he felt he should be helping Cindy and seeing a lot more of her. Her incapacity meant that she had not been able to continue her feature writing and research as much she had hoped, and Alan could sense from his telephone calls to her that she was once again becoming somewhat tetchy.

Remembering that when they first went out together Cindy had always said how much she loved surprises, Alan decided that a quiet weekend away in the Lake District would not only cheer her up, but could be just the right fillip for their relationship and he booked a two night stay in the Corinth Suite at the luxury Watersbeck Manor hotel. The Victorian rooms were spacious and furnished to the standard expected of a five star hotel and the food Michelin rated. Prior to booking, Alan had carefully ensured that the suite was equipped with a king size double bed as he desperately wanted the weekend to bring Cindy and he closer together in every respect. He had needs and it had been several months since the two of them had been close physically, and he was becoming increasingly unhappy at the lack of any sort of personal affection being shown to him, but he was particularly disgruntled at the absence of sex.

He could not understand Cindy. She continually denied any sort of affair, yet up until fairly recent times they had enjoyed a reasonable, if not exciting or adventurous, sex life which usually left them both satisfied such that he believed Cindy needed the physical side of their relationship almost as much as he did. It troubled him that apparently this was now not so and he therefore remained suspicious of his wife's apparent mood swings. The weekend should be likely to clarify things.

On Friday afternoon whilst Donaldson was chauffeuring Crossland home, Alan mentioned that he was taking Cindy away for the weekend and that he had decided to take Monday off.

"No need therefore Jack to pick me up until Tuesday."

"Going anywhere special? It isn't Mrs Crossland's birthday is it or your anniversary?" enquired Donaldson, as always taking great care to refer to Cindy only as Mrs Crossland.

"Lake District, Jack. A couple of days away will do us both good. Cindy has been a little down lately, the leg and all that, and I thought it would cheer her up."

Crossland's comments merely confirmed to the perceptive Donaldson that his employer's wife needed some excitement, and he thought to himself that he knew exactly what she needed to boost her spirits. He only needed the right opportunity to prove it.

"Let's hope so. Please give my regards to her."

Cindy was less than overjoyed at going away for the weekend, but did not want to hurt Alan's feelings and found herself saying that it was a wonderful surprise and what a thoughtful husband he was. Her mind was elsewhere. She had been thinking of Gordon and the arrival of his so-called guests at Loch Quoich – and when her husband mentioned the trip to the Lake District her mind could only focus on the following Tuesday, when she would be lunching again at the Bunch of Grapes. *How can I be expected to be at ease with Alan in such circumstances?* she thought. In fact, the deceit was starting to make her feel more miserable, but she knew she could not, would not, let that change her mind about seeing Gordon.

The next morning Alan drove them in the Jaguar, and they arrived at the hotel just in time for a light lunch. The porter had taken their small overnight cases and, after finishing their meal, Alan and Cindy went to the Corinth Suite. Alan was delighted. The room offered spectacular views across the Lake and was in an elevated but totally private and separate location, yet only a short distance under a covered walkway from the main hotel. He opened the large double glazed patio doors and stepped out onto the balcony. The weather was still very warm and he thought this a perfect place where later in the day he could sit quietly with Cindy over drinks and watch the sun set over the water.

However, Cindy's deep misgivings about the trip intensified when she saw the large double bed and she was on the verge of complaining about it to Alan. She weighed her options. Whilst she might not really want Alan any more, she had told him she would try harder. She had nothing to gain by continually upsetting him and she also had to be realistic. Gordon was hardly likely to want to get over involved, and if ever things got really messy with her and Alan she reasoned that Gordon would make his excuses and exit from her life pretty rapidly – after all, he had remained single up to now and with his wealth he would never lack for female company. This was not the time for impetuous gestures, so she said nothing. She continued to admire the view and after a brief rest they drove around the twisted lanes and went sightseeing. They took dinner early, at seven thirty, as Alan was quite insistent that as it was such a lovely evening it would be good to take drinks on the patio and watch the sun go down. So, after an excellent meal, they changed into more casual clothes before walking out on the balcony. Alan poured them both a glass of an excellent Pinot Grigio and they sat in the comfortable wicker armchairs. They spoke now and then, but their main attention was divided between looking at the reddening sky and the respective books they were reading.

As the light faded, Alan switched on the soft, unobtrusive balcony lights and dimmed them using the remote control that was handily placed on one of tables. The hotel had a menu-driven cabled music system which could be operated from any room in the suite and he turned it on from the illuminated green panel brightly glowing in the centre of wall next to the patio doors. He scrolled through the options and selected 'classical', placing an asterisk against eight of Cindy's most loved pieces.

For the next hour and a half, they just sat back in their chairs, enjoyed the music and intermittently continued to read their books. It was going as well as Alan could have hoped. The wine had helped Cindy to be noticeably more relaxed and he observed how she frequently shut her eyes for quite long spells, seemingly totally absorbed in the music. Looking over at her reclining in the chair, in slacks and blouse with a thin jumper draped around her arms, he thought she still looked fantastic and admired how well she had kept her figure.

Cindy would have liked to retire to bed and sleep much earlier, but had deliberately not done so. The more tired she could claim to be the better, and with any luck the glasses of wine might affect Alan to the extent of perhaps leading to a postponement of what he had so obviously arranged this trip to achieve. However, at eleven o'clock her eyelids started to drop and she told Alan that she was going to take a shower and go to bed. Alan rose from his chair and having turned off the balcony lights, followed her into the room closing the large doors behind him.

As he heard the sound of the spray, he reflected upon the many times they had undressed and showered together, each gently stroking and caressing the other under the warm foaming water, but tonight Cindy had precluded any such delights by shutting herself behind the locked door of the spacious, marbled en-suite. Several minutes later she came out, her pink face glowing even in the subdued light of the bedroom, wearing her silk dressing gown over the multi-coloured, patterned pyjamas which she had deliberately chosen to wear in the hope of perhaps postponing the ordeal she was about to face in a few moments time. She walked quickly across the room, took off the robe, and slipped between the sheets. She gripped the lightweight duvet that rested easily on the huge bed and pulled it around her before turning her body so that her back faced Alan's side of the bed.

He quickly undressed and washed, and came out of the bathroom naked. He turned off the music and slowly slid his expectant body into the bed positioning it as close to Cindy as he could manage before placing his arm around her. She could feel him rising against her lower back and swore silently to herself. She did not want this, really did not – but what was she to do? She turned herself over to face him.

"It's been a lovely day, Alan, thank you," giving him a brief kiss on the cheek before quickly turning away.

Alan however started gently kissing the nape of her neck and running his fingers through her silky hair. He followed this by sliding his hand inside her pyjama top and gently cupped her right breast. Cindy made a plea that she was very tired but her whispered words vanished unheeded. It was clear that Alan was not listening and any words from her were unwanted and would be ignored. She knew then that if her marriage was not to end here and now, there was only one thing to do. She turned onto her back and pretended to enjoy their lovemaking.

A short while after another excellent evening dinner on the Sunday, Cindy complained of having an upset stomach and made several visits to the bathroom before retiring to bed prior to the onset of dusk. Alan was fussing over her, offering her an assortment of the various medications he always carried as a precaution against the most common ailments and Cindy took an antacid tablet. Having successfully feigned her illness, she was easily able to ward off any suggestion of physical contact from her husband and hoped to enjoy an uninterrupted night's sleep. Alan, however, could not sleep, slightly troubled at Cindy's apparent illness.

As the hours passed without her waking to visit the bathroom again, he began to be more and more convinced he had been deceived and that Cindy's illness was mere subterfuge. He was hurt and angry. Without thinking, he grabbed at the sleeping Cindy and pulled her onto her back.

She stirred and still half asleep murmured, "what... what are you doing Alan?" but he ignored her question. He quickly wrenched her pyjamas down her thighs and threw his body onto hers. She struggled but he held her arms above her head and his weight firmly pinned her thighs. As she tried even harder to get free she started to roll her body from side to side but her plastered leg inhibited her movement and her husband's superior strength prevented her from getting away. Alan was inflamed now, the rhythm of her movements only making him more excited, his blood pumping so hard through his bluish tinged veins that they swelled and protruded from their imprisoning flesh like thick strands of string and he thrust his swollen penis hard between her open thighs.

"No, Alan, no – I won't do this" she shouted and moved her leg to try and get free but he continued to move on top of her and with each quickening jerk of his body pushed ever harder and deeper. Sweat started to drip from his flushed, hot face. He had control now and knew her resistance was futile. Holding her shoulders, he pulled her towards him synchronising his movements with hers.

"Come on Cindy... come on... come on baby" he urged, panting breathlessly into her ear, his words subconsciously synchronised to the rhythm of his own body.

Cindy knew her position was hopeless. She gave up resisting him, and lay still whilst he pumped away until he climaxed a minute later.

"You're wonderful, wonderful," he repeated. "Thank you, thank you. That was so good," he blurted over and over and went to kiss her on the mouth but Cindy turned her face away.

"Then you had better remember it. That's the last time you're going to fuck me, Alan. Now get off me and take me home tomorrow." Cindy spoke slowly, deliberately, determinedly, and pushed him away from her.

They spoke little on the return journey. Alan had made a fulsome apology but Cindy was having none of it. He tried to introduce some topics of conversation about the scenery or the traffic on the motorway but she was disinterested and made only cursory replies. When they had unpacked, she sat in an arm chair in the lounge and watched the television specially choosing a programme she knew Alan disliked. At 10pm she rose and, saying nothing to Alan, went to her bedroom where she had a contented and undisturbed night's sleep dreaming of Gordon.

13

On Tuesday morning, she heard Alan moving about the house as he prepared for work but did not get up to see him off. By the time she had breakfasted Donaldson and Alan were nearing London. The weather had turned, and a grey overcast sky heralded the possibility of rain. Cindy wore a pair of dark, tailored trousers and a close-fitting, vivid orange jumper that emphasised her figure. She had applied ever so slightly more make-up than usual and spent a great deal of time accentuating her pale green eyes with the skilful application of various shades of eye liner and mascara. Even in the gloomy morning light, her face looked fresh and her complexion radiated a warm natural glow that contrasted with the subtle smokiness of her eyes, sparkling invitingly and promisingly.

As she entered the pub, the effect upon Gordon was both startling and exciting. He was immediately appreciative of the efforts his lunch companion had made to impress him and he stopped walking towards her, took a pace backwards still gazing admiringly upon her and said simply, "Wow, you look terrific". Then taking her hand, he guided her to the table. As they sat down, he brought out of his pocket a small box, wrapped in gift paper.

"For you," he said, and laughed as he did so. Cindy wondered what on earth it could be. Surely not a ring or expensive jewellery – he didn't know her well enough for that sort of thing and anyway she wasn't certain he was an expensive gifts type man, despite his wealth.

"For me? Can I open it now?" Cindy was eager and her fingers nervously picked at the paper not waiting for his response.

"Of course," he replied. The paper fell away to reveal a small, dark red, velvet-covered box which she carefully opened. Inside all she could see was cotton wool but a small slip of pale lilac-coloured card was loose inside the lid. In neat script, written with a black fountain pen, were written the words:

To the Lady on Train 204
7 July 2005

It was unsigned. Cindy delved carefully into the box and parted the cotton wool protective packaging. She squealed with delight. It was a gold brooch of the logo for Liverpool Street underground station. Beautifully crafted enamel work reproduced exactly the different authentic colours, including the unique logo with a yellow bar, depicting the Circle line.

A small tear ran down her cheek as she looked up at him.

"It's wonderful", she said. "Thank you Gordon, so much, it is so very kind of you."

"I'm glad you like it," he answered. "Now, let's order shall we?"

★ ★ ★

Lunch was unhurried and the conversation relaxed. Cindy felt completely at ease. In fact she was immersed in everything Gordon was saying to her and totally absorbed by his presence. He likewise was interested in listening to Cindy and quite overwhelmed when she laughed as her broad, open smile seemingly lit up her face and caused her eyes to sparkle with even greater intensity. At one point, Cindy asked Gordon to tell her more about himself and of the business he had sold. He was usually very reticent about revealing his background, let alone his business interests, but felt that Cindy was different from any other woman he had met. He already regarded her as one of the very few persons whom he could trust and confirmed to her everything she had read on the internet, though he said he sold the software business for 360 million. Gordon added that his main property company had numerous investments across the world and that its portfolio was worth an estimated 200 million such had been the rapid rise in real estate values across the globe. He also had, what he termed, a small private company that managed only the properties which he maintained solely for his personal occupation and use.

"Can you guess what I miss most?" he asked.

Cindy was so relaxed she started to speak impulsively, all her natural reserve gone, "No idea, Gordon. Is there anything you could miss? Not much I should think. That is a heap of assets you are sitting on. Oh, I don't know – the buzz of running your software business and seeing it grow from nothing."

Gordon was impressed; that was a large void in his life but it was not his main loss.

"Near. Not bad. No, it's actually being a programmer. I loved those early days on the Spectrum and the BBC computers. They were real home computers, and more advanced than anything any other country had, but became another example where Britain led the world but failed to develop the products and technology. Eventually that competitive advantage slipped away and others moved in. We could have had our own Microsoft, you know." He paused. "Sorry, this must be boring you. Its programming I really miss."

Cindy wasn't at all bored, she was enthralled. Gordon had opened up to her and she felt, rightly, he had not spoken like this to anyone before.

"But you've developed many other interests, like Mealag and so on," she said reassuringly.

"Yes, but that gives a different pleasure. As for the property company, I am actually in negotiations at the moment to sell it, the whole lot. I shall keep the properties I own in my own private company; Mealag Lodge, the London apartment and I also own a villa in Greece but what do I want with any others? I have no one to share even those with, and life can be quite lonely sometimes, even for me. The property boom will not go on for ever, and I have made two fortunes. For goodness sake, how many fortunes does a man need?"

Cindy was aware the conversation was becoming very personal and quite intense. She was unsure whether to press further but couldn't resist a little more probing. Smiling, and slightly tossing her head back to sway her hair, she said, "I'm sure you must have had dozens of opportunities not to be alone."

"Well, not dozens, but I can't deny that there have been some! Of course there have been one or two people who have come into my life briefly over the years but things never worked out, and I'm not the type for one or even two night stands. Anyway, this is quite enough about me. What about you? I know very, very little about the real you, only your work and background; the stuff we spoke of on the train."

"I can hardly remember what I said now, but as for the personal stuff… " Cindy's speech tailed off and she took a deep breath trying to decide exactly how much she should say.

"If you would rather not, then let's change the subject. When does the plaster on your leg come off?" Gordon thoughtfully tried to lighten the suddenly sombre moment, acutely aware that Cindy may not wish to explain, yet, why it was she had wanted to meet up again.

"No, no I want to tell you. I do. My teenage and college years were pretty ordinary. I wasn't a rebel and I didn't sleep around. I had two or three boyfriends, none serious. I met Alan in a London coffee bar one lunch time in 1999 and we married in 2000. No children. God, said like that, it isn't much is it?" she ended, slightly relieved.

"Do you think it is too little, then?" This was Gordon at his best. Disarming, yet in a few softly spoken words asking the question to get to the real issue, rather as a top barrister would when discussing a complex brief with the client and his solicitor.

Cindy also realised the importance of the question. Gordon up to now had just been a kind, seemingly rather ordinary man in many ways, but the flash of intellect behind the question revealed another side, a really sharp brain and someone who would not be fooled.

"Is the cup half full or half empty?" Cindy asked rhetorically. "Mine is half empty… " She paused and Gordon knew better than to interrupt. "Alan thinks the world of me and is very kind. He works hard and we have all the money we need, though not of course in your league! We have a good lifestyle, home and interests. But, for me, things are not working out and the really sad part is that I don't want them to. I have known for quite a while that I can never be really happy with Alan."

There, I've said it she thought. *This is where Gordon makes for the door.* But he remained seated in the chair.

"I think we need another glass of wine and a change of subject," he said, and called over the waiter.

Their conversation soon returned to the easy discourse of earlier in the meal with laughter and genial banter emanating from their table and, as if on cue, the sun finally appeared from behind broken clouds, adding its own change of mood as the warmth and brightness flooded their table. When it was time to leave, Cindy telephoned for her taxi and Gordon suggested they wait in the car park. As they made their way to the exit, he tenderly placed his arm around her waist to steady her as she walked.

"There is something I think I need to say to you Cindy. Firstly, I shall be away now, out of the country for at least three months tying up the deal on the property company, and sorting out a few other things. I was hoping to postpone it until the plaster had been removed from your leg but the financiers and lawyers are all set up, so regrettably I have to go. It's probably a good thing in one way that I am away for a while because you are becoming increasingly important to me. I'm not good at saying these sorts of things, but I should very much want to know you better and see you more often. In fact I should like to invite you to Mealag when I get back, but – and it's a big 'but' Cindy – you have to want it too. You are married and Alan sounds a thoroughly good husband, you are very fortunate in that. My experience, little as it is, says that a loyal, loving husband is hard to find. Clearly to continue seeing me has big risks for you. There are very few risks for me and in the end this may not work out for either of us. I am not certain that it is right for us to keep meeting, but I know I want to and I really want you to reflect on what might happen if we do go on seeing each other. Sooner or later someone, or all of us, is likely to get hurt and I do not want to take that risk unless you do as well. Please use the time to think about it and if you want to come to Mealag, phone me in three months' time. It will be near to Christmas then and I can think of nothing better than Christmas with you at Mealag. Don't give me an answer now, as I will not accept it."

Cindy had listened to him in silence as a thousand thoughts and images flooded into her mind. She was excited, nervous, confused and emotional all at the same time. For the second time that day, a small uncontrolled tear slipped slowly down her cheek before she gently wiped it away. She knew he was right. If she carried on seeing Gordon, she was willingly embarking on an affair which, as she knew from her working days in London and some of her friends, was likely to have unpredictable results.

After what seemed to her an eternity as she struggled to find the right words to convey how she felt, she finally managed to speak. Quietly and trying to restrain her welling emotions, she looked into his eyes.

"I know what you are saying. I'll do that Gordon. You are so understanding and thoughtful, but perhaps my answer *should* be given now. You are becoming very important to me as well you know, and I'm not sure that what you have just said, wonderful as it sounds, isn't just a long excuse to say goodbye. If it is, please be honest now and tell me. I couldn't bear to wait three months and then find out this was some kind of charade."

"What? Absolutely, positively not, I promise. One, I am not the kind of person to say something I don't mean; and two, you can trust me totally."

Cindy turned to directly face Gordon and clasped both her hands around his.

"OK."

The taxi arrived at that moment, sweeping around in a semi-circle so that the car was facing the exit as it drew up beside them as they separated. Gordon quickly cupped his hands around Cindy's face and lightly kissed her on the forehead and then went to help her into the car.

"Hope your trip goes well." Cindy was holding back a few small tears but just managed to say the words before she shut the door and waved goodbye. She would certainly consider carefully all that Gordon had said, would think of little else over the next twelve weeks, but she knew *now* that she would make the call and spend Christmas at Mealag Lodge.

14

"Have you seen the Lanasse order, I can't see it anywhere." Monsieur Henri Pethane, the fat boss, was searching his desk, rifling through the various scattered files and papers whilst talking to Fadyar at the same time. She knew exactly where it was: In the filing cabinet where she had put it an hour ago but said she would have a good look round. She spent ten minutes apparently searching through files before going to the cabinet. Saying nothing she withdrew the file, slowly closed the drawer and placed the paper on his desk. The routine drudgery of the office was making her sullen, and she desperately yearned to be told of a new mission where at last she could get out of this dump and seek retribution for her parent's murder still vividly etched in her mind.

On that fateful day, Yasmin had hurried out of the centre of Baghdad, keeping to roads that she hoped would be safe, though a nearby bomb blast and distant automatic weapons fire caused her to jump over a partly demolished wall and take shelter. Others in the street did likewise, scrambling over the bricks as quickly as they could manage. Yasmin noticed their frightened eyes. Dark, like her own, they appeared to be stuck into their hollow, dusty faces but were also, like hers, cold and defiant. A few machine gun shots could be heard periodically and she and the others waited several hours before the gunfire stopped.

During this time she struck up a conversation with a young man next to her and told him of the death of her parents a few hours earlier. He, too, had his own horror story but he had joined up with a small militia dedicated to confronting the Americans and to force them out of the city. However, in a recent fire fight he had become separated from his group and was trying to work his way back to their headquarters. He offered to take Yasmin with him and later that evening she met his commander. He realised that with no military training Yasmin would be a liability not a help but she still might be useful to the cause and so she was passed along a trail that led her to ultimately join a group with close links to Al-Qaeda and whose first indoctrination of her was to tell her that Yasmin Hasan was now dead; henceforth she was Fadyar Masri. She excelled in her training, from map reading to communications, from survival techniques to combat and her knowledge and fluency in English quickly singled her out for overseas service. Fadyar longed to go to America, the country who had sent the murderous soldier to her home and who had inflicted her parents' savage death, but her instructors told her that she may be sent anywhere in the world.

"The imperialist American infidels commit their acts of brutality wherever they tread. Our Holy War is global."

There would be opportunities for her to deploy her special skills and these would ensure that her dream of killing Americans would be fulfilled. Prior to that happening, she was to live an apparently normal life in France and await orders. Although provided with excellent forged papers, she had been able to persuade the factory owner to take her on at a cheaper than usual salary, with no perks or pension, and paid in cash only – thereby ensuring there would be no official record of her employment. Casual labour was a common practice in France and hard-pressed small businesses were only too keen on ways to avoid taxes and state bureaucracy by employing unregistered immigrants, especially those who were, or claimed to be, Algerian.

She knew her Islamic controllers would test her in a minor operation before she would be granted her wish to plan and carry out a major mission, and when her tutors thought she was ready she was given specific instructions regarding the opening of an account at the Hannet-Mar International Bank in London. This was a bank that had many contacts in the Middle East and a new account with links to Dubai, provided it seemed authentic, was unlikely to arouse suspicion. However, there was a risk the bank might not wish to create a new account unless the manager, Crossland, could be convinced of the bona-fides of the client.

She was told of a Mr Kenneth Styles, a friend of the English bank manager and who was a businessman with extensive interests in Dubai, and her mission was to get to know Styles and use him to effect an introduction to Crossland. Fadyar executed the plan perfectly. She ascertained when Styles was next attending a conference in Dubai and took a short holiday from work. She posed as an agent for a consortium and deliberately became acquainted with him. Styles was clearly impressed by the good looking, dark skinned and very westernised woman, and easily flattered. Once she was satisfied from her meeting with Crossland that he would be prepared to set up an account, Fadyar set about removing the connection between her and Styles. On false, but seemingly perfect, papers that would pass any computer scan or database search, it was only a few weeks later that Fadyar emailed Crossland, by which time Styles was dead.

She knew approximately where he lived from their cosy conversations in Dubai, and once she had located his address it was easy to monitor him covertly. Styles was a man of habit and that is always a weakness. Fadyar had been given the name of an operative who could organise and carry out the next stage for her, and in a coded message passed on the details. Driving home after his regular visit to the golf club, a simple interception on a quiet country road by a large 4x4 and two cars, forced him to stop. His car was moved to the side of the road where he was first made to sign a forged affidavit and then made to drink mouthfuls of whisky until he passed out. Styles' car was then driven farther along the road to a spot where it straightened out for hundred yards or so before turning a long and increasingly sharp left bend that clung to the side of a hill.

Keeping in touch by mobile phone, the drivers of the other two vehicles quickly took up position and, pretending to have stalled their engines whilst performing a three point turn, blocked each approach to the bend at a point which made certain that what was happening at the sharp turn remained out of sight of any other motorists, irrespective of their direction of travel. The bull bars on the 4x4 driven by the third man ensured that Styles, now belted into the driver's seat, and his car rolled over the hill, and as it did so the cars blocking the road quickly sped on their way. The whole operation had been carried out with ruthless efficiency and was over in less than thirty seconds. There was no immediate trace of any accident having occurred and no suspicions were raised in the minds of the other road users. Apart from a brief confirmatory message to Fadyar, enclosing the affidavit, she never heard from the operatives again.

As she sat in the office, she yearned to be in action again. She had proved herself and now needed the opportunity to put into practice all her specialist training. She just had to get out of this hell hole in France if she possibly could, but how and when? She decided that she would wait six months, and if no assignment had been given her by that time she would look herself for opportunities to go it alone. Despite the assurances she had been given by her controllers, she was not prepared to just sit around, almost moribund, for what might prove to be months or even years. If Carron was right that the London bombings were the work of a group acting alone, then she was more than capable of following their lead.

15

The weeks were also passing far too slowly for Cindy. Not that she had little to do, nor was she any longer inhibited by her leg. The plaster had been removed, the physiotherapy exercises determinedly undertaken, ensuring that her wasted muscles were quickly restored to full strength, and she had rapidly regained her normal fitness. She was thrilled at being able to drive again and in itself that provided her with a sense of freedom whether she sat behind the wheel or not. It was a great comfort for her to know that she could escape Red Gables whenever she wanted, but having finished the magazine article, she was now busy spending a great deal of her time writing a novel loosely based on her experience working on the fringes of government and rubbing shoulders alongside such notables as Alastair Campbell and Jonathan Powell – a novel which she would dearly love to complete. Her friends in the Orchard Gun Dog Club had kept in touch with her and she knew that they were hoping to be invited by the organisers to give a demonstration of their skills at the forthcoming Autumn Show at Lanthorne. Cindy had never been to a Game Fair or Show and during a rest from her writing telephoned Don to confirm whether the club were going.

"Absolutely, both days. We're now busy practising a couple of evenings a week, but the light fades so rapidly that we shall be doing the next two weekends as well. That's all the time we have left. In fact we are at Tony's farm tonight, up at Farrington. Why not come along? Five thirty start if you can make it?"

Cindy jumped at the chance and at 4:30pm she had changed into a pair of faded jeans and a thick jumper to ward of the chill air that was now prevalent most evenings and put her boots and wax cotton jacket into the cargo area of her Accord Estate. Even though the cost of fuel was not an issue for her, she took careful note of the odometer reading so she could claim the tax back as a freelance journalist working on a story.

When she arrived, she was warmly greeted by the members.

What particularly impressed Cindy about the dog club was how genuinely egalitarian it was. The educational background, financial status or chosen career mattered not a jot. There was a mix of persons from landed gentry and estate owners to unemployed youngsters, and no one cared and nobody was made to feel inferior. She found this attitude totally refreshing, so different from her experience of London and even, she had to concede to herself, from life in the Cotswolds. Everyone's focus was solely on the dogs. After two and a half hours or so, the sun had set and the early September light started to fade rapidly until the point was reached where the training had to cease. The group adjourned to Tony's farm, enjoyed hot drinks and chatted excitedly about the forthcoming show. Someone asked who was going to be the club's compere. The group needed someone to stand in the centre of the ring with the microphone to inform the spectators of what was going on and to generally introduce the dogs and describe the tests they would be demonstrating. A lady named Pamela had done this previously, but this year she had a young dog and felt she could not demonstrate and compere. Don turned to Cindy.

"What about you, Cindy? You know all the dogs' names and their breeds. You know the exercises and tests, could you do it?" Cindy was dumbstruck, not knowing quite what to say. Everyone round the large pine table started saying that it was a great idea, and implored her to say yes.

A young lad, no more than seventeen who was training an excellently bred black Labrador, and who lived in a council house in Lower Dister shouted out, "Maybe Cindy don't wanna do it. I know I wouldn't. I ain't got the guts. Don't let this lot talk you into it Cindy if you don't wanna."

Cindy thought that very kind and thoughtful and told him so, but she was thrilled at being asked.

"If you're all sure I can do it, really sure. After all I've not known you that long, but you have all made me very welcome and so, yes!" she exclaimed excitedly. "I'm really honoured to be asked but I'm not even a member and even worse, I don't have a dog."

"No problem" said Don. You don't need to own a dog to be a member and we can grant you honorary member status."

Cindy did not think that fair and so, after a few more minutes, she handed over a ten pound note for her membership and a further twenty pounds for one of the club's brown jumpers emblazoned with O.G.D.C. on the back in large gold lettering. Before leaving Tony's farm, she took detailed notes about the dogs, their respective owners and the tests that each would be demonstrating. At home the next day, she typed out her notes onto small individual pieces of paper before laminating them to make the waterproof crib sheets she might need.

There were just two practice sessions remaining prior to the show and these took the form of full dress rehearsals, including Cindy providing the narrative. She was determined to look the part and chose to wear her moleskin trousers and placed a rather fetching dull green hat at a slightly jaunty angle upon her head that complemented her appearance perfectly. She had tied her hair, swept back, with matching olive-coloured ribbon and the overall effect was both elegant yet casual. Even the brown club jumper, the like of which Cindy had never worn before and which she would never have considered wearing only a few months ago, looked good, fitted well and closely hugged the curves of her figure. A wax jacket and boots completed the transformation. Everyone was impressed with her.

She introduced the dogs perfectly, faultlessly describing each by breed, age and gender. She eloquently described the exercises and training techniques, explaining why these were so important for gun dogs but also emphasising that any dog would benefit from the thorough obedience training so necessary in a working dog. When a dog did something wrong or broke ranks, Cindy was able to add an impromptu narrative, often humorous, that showed her skill at keeping the continuity whilst order was being restored.

The club were providing two demonstrations on both the Saturday and Sunday. Special car park permits had been provided that enabled presenters to park their vehicles close to the show ring and Cindy was amazed just how many exhibitors, let alone paying visitors, thronged the stalls and activity centres. She soaked in the atmosphere and marvelled at how her life was changing. The days of claustrophobic city meetings, the endless hours of political intrigue and spin and the boredom of life with Alan were gone. This was truly a breath of fresh air, liberating and uplifting, genuine and honest. She had not told Alan where she was going when she left Red Gables on Saturday morning and to disguise her movements even more she wore only jeans and an old jacket, changing into her gun dog clothes at Tony's where several members were meeting up to minimise the number of vehicles making the trip. In fact, she was hardly speaking to Alan these days. It was obvious he was terribly upset and confused but her love for him had gone. She knew that sooner or later she must face Alan and tell him that they would have to part but she was not ready for that yet. She did not even want to think about it. The last thing she needed was another argument and bitterness to spoil the current happiness of her life. Alan interfered with that enough just by being her husband, and she unfairly resented him for it.

The whole experience at Lanthorne for her was nothing but joy. The dogs did much as expected. Most behaved well, but the odd one or two caused some laughter from within the crowd of several hundred standing around the ring perimeter, as they broke ranks or decided to cock their leg instead of fetching the dummy. As Pippa, a normally very well behaved female springer suddenly broke ranks to pick up a dummy that was not meant for her, Cindy overheard one very rustic looking elderly gentleman, leaning over the white wooden railing which he was using for support, say in a broad Gloucestershire accent, "Them spaniels do that, them buggers they are, and she's a good bitch. Showin' off that's all, too clever by 'arf," making Cindy smile as that was precisely what Pippa's owner had said only a few nights previously, though then with the addition of a few more earthy expletives.

After a hearty supper at Tony's on Sunday night, they all said their goodbyes and particularly thanked Cindy. Her colleagues thought the shows had been all they could have hoped for and they proclaimed Cindy a star act. After a mock election, she was formally booked for next season before the discussion moved on to the Weston Park Game Fair, held at the end of September. It was the last major game fair of the year within reasonable travelling distance of the gun dog club members, and whilst they were not participating it was evidently a show they all tried to visit if they could for end of season bargains. They asked if Cindy would come along with them and were delighted when she agreed.

The next few weeks Cindy spent around the house and gardens, keeping busy and her mind occupied. Despite her lack of feeling towards Alan, she loved Red Gables. She had devoted a lot of time to the planting of the garden with her choices of bushes and perennials, bulbs and fruit trees. Many of these were now fully established and the garden looked colourful and interesting throughout most of the year. It was also what she termed "low maintenance". The total plot exceeded a little over three acres in size, but its upkeep now did not take up so much time as to be intrusive, as she and Alan employed a gardener to mow the grass, edge the borders and prune the bushes and hedges. Weeds had been controlled by the prolific use of bark chips and only minimal intervention was needed to keep the gardens looking their best.

She had also decided to go out more, visit various acquaintances in the neighbouring villages or invite them round for coffee. The meetings provided a ready excuse to be out of the house and catch up on the village gossip, and through them she made a couple of good female friends, who were excellent shopping companions in Cheltenham or Oxford. She also joined an exclusive Ladies Only gym, not that she needed to lose weight but because she was keen to get fitter. Her training sessions with the gun dog club had necessitated a lot of walking and standing, and there had been times when she had become aware of just how much stamina members seemed to have. On more than one occasion, when walking up a steep hillside, she had gratefully accepted the offer of a springer that she could take hold of by its slip lead. The eager dog, typical of the breed, pulled her along, thereby easing the strain on her lungs and legs.

Alan would occasionally come down midweek, but it was the weekends that Cindy dreaded most. Try as she might, she could not find it within herself to be totally relaxed in Alan's company, and she kept inventing new excuses to go out or force herself to appear interested in whatever conversation they were having. She would try to write more of her latest novel, but the solitude it entailed paradoxically made it harder to concentrate as when she was alone she kept thinking of Gordon, and conjured up pictures in her mind of how Mealag must look in the snow of winter. Fortunately the gun dog meetings, formal and impromptu, carried on at various times and were an increasing source of material for not just one feature but several. Her agent had been able to secure an excellent publishing deal for them in a high-priced monthly glossy magazine aimed at A and B class readers but of the type who liked to read about the countryside and all aspects of country life rather than enact it, and whose interest in rural pastimes did not extend to getting their shoes, let alone boots, muddy.

By late October, Alan had almost exhausted himself trying to please Cindy and was seriously worried that she might have permanently drifted away from him and that her love, or at least close affection, might not return. On several weekends he had mentioned to her that he should like to discuss their relationship and feelings for each other, but Cindy had always avoided it and also failed to give any indication of when she might be ready to talk to him. He felt quite helpless, utterly bereft of any ideas that might rescue his failing marriage. The calamity of their weekend away in the Lake District still haunted him, but Cindy had not at any time referred to it nor used it as an excuse. He still loved his wife, but it was obvious this was not reciprocated. He tried not to show his anger and frustration when Cindy pointed out to him, as she usually did, that of course she was happy.

"Look at the work I've done in the garden," she would tell him. "And don't I still cook you your favourite meals when we're together?"

Alan acknowledged this was all true, but he also silently believed such protestations were a sham designed to avoid the real issues. Yet Alan had to face the fact that he had no evidence Cindy was embarking on an affair. Her attitude had been the same for months. During this troubled time, there had been no strange phone calls where the caller suddenly puts down the receiver. There were no evenings when Cindy was out late. She always said where she was going and who she was with and so on. He had seen the draft articles she had written on the gun dog club, and Cindy seemingly spoke quite openly about the people she met there, just as she had about the gym or anything else.

Frustratingly, reluctantly and sadly, he had to accept the position. He wasn't happy about it, but he needed Cindy and would always love her, even if she would not share his bed and satisfy his needs. He was in his mid-thirties, had a successful and lucrative career and he needed physical affection. He had been patient but something had to change if Cindy was to continue to work out her hang-ups month after month without any apparent resolution in sight.

After a couple of large glasses of whisky, he broached the delicate subject in as light hearted a manner as he could muster. Alan put his crossword down onto the glass coffee table, and in a slightly jocular tone, his anxiety making his speech more clipped than usual, spoke to Cindy.

"Cinders, I know what you've said about being happy here and all that, and of course you do know that I love you so much, but I can't really be expected to sleep alone for the rest of my life. I need physical affection. You surely understand that. I should have thought... you would also want that in your life." The last few haltingly spoken words trailed slowly across the space between them.

"Oh Alan, you're not on this again are you? Look, I'm really very happy and when I'm not you will be the first to know. But if you're saying that you want to try and find someone else that can give you the affection you need, then I understand. You deserve better than me Alan. I'm sorry but I really don't think I can give you what you want anymore." *This was at least honest*, she thought, *and no more than she had said after their last physical encounter.* Alan started to explain that he didn't want to find anyone else but Cindy rose from her chair cutting him off mid-sentence.

"Coffee or another whisky?" she enquired, but didn't stay in the lounge long enough to hear his answer. The whisky, allied to Crossland's inner tensions, seemed to be having more than its usual affect. Alan began to get quite angry and when Cindy returned, he raised his voice at her.

"Then we must consider a divorce, Cindy. We cannot go on like this." Cindy had not expected this, and with her relationship with Gordon still to get to first base, she was not going to say anything she might regret. She still liked Red Gables, and her current life with Alan had a lot to commend it. She knew a lot of women would be deeply envious of her creature comforts and the life she led. This was not the time to be impulsive and throw it all away. That moment, should it come, would be when it suited her and when she was absolutely certain she could improve upon the life she had now.

"Why on earth would we want to do that? Look at what we have both achieved over the years. We make a good team, you and me. I know the sex thing with me is a bit strange at the moment – and you hardly helped that, remember – but I can't really explain how I feel at the moment. I'm sure it will sort itself out, but if you have someone else in mind then tell me. I would understand."

This was disingenuous. Cindy knew it. Alan knew it, but there was nothing he could say other than to repeat his love for Cindy. He rose and poured another whisky.

16

The weekend discussion had, however, alerted Cindy to the tricky situation with which she was going to be faced at Christmas. There was, of course, the problem of what she was going to tell Alan, but additionally there was always the possibility that even if Gordon and she got together over the festive season all might not work out well, or continue as she was hoping. Ideally, she had to find a plausible excuse to placate Alan which would permit a continued life back at Red Gables if needed. She knew that simply not telling her husband the truth would be difficult and she began to lose confidence. Whatever she came up with was going to be hard to carry off convincingly and whatever she ultimately decided it was almost inevitable that her relationship with Alan would deteriorate further.

She thought of little else over the next few days and wished she had a brother or sister living the other side of the world that she could say she was visiting and whom she could rely upon to cover for her. There were few friends she knew well enough to ask such favours from and, anyway, she thought that to ask one's friends to lie for you, whilst you conduct an illicit affair, would be a particularly shitty thing to do. Whilst sitting at her computer one day she thought of Peter and his boyfriend, Stephen. Alan had only met Peter and Stephen once, at a party, and Cindy gained the impression that they were not overly impressed by him. Peter was extrovert and Alan was a naturally reserved, quiet person who did not seem able to relax amongst the strange guests at the party. Cindy went alone to their future invites. Her work had brought her into frequent contact with Peter, whom she regarded as a most dear and trusted friend. At the very least he would provide some advice to her, but could she trust him enough to lie for her at Christmas?

Despite her misgivings, she phoned Peter's personal mobile and was relieved when he answered. Pleasantries over, she asked if he had a few moments to talk.

"Of course, my dear. For you, anytime."

"Peter, this is a simply dreadful thing to ask but are you and Stephen going away at Christmas? Have you made any plans?"

"Why? Do you want us to join you sometime over Yuletide or do you wish to join us in Portugal? You will always be welcome."

"No, it's not that, Peter. I have problem. I need to be away at Christmas and probably New Year, but I will not be with Alan. In short, I may need some sort of cover and wondered if I could possibly say I was coming to you, or some such. I really don't know quite what to do; I can't seem to think straight on this. It's an awful thing to ask of you, but this means so much to me."

"Oooooh. I see" Peter slowly exhaled. "Well, this is your business Cindy, so I won't ask, but we go back a long way and you will always be a friend. It could be tricky though," he was thinking hard as he spoke. "I know" he said. "Say you have been invited to spend Christmas with me and Stephen. You have absolutely no details or other information as it's a mystery – you must stick to that as Alan is bound to pressure you for information – but you understand we are hosting a sort of a special gathering for the old backroom people from Number 10. All I've told you is that we won't be staying in London and to bring your passport. If Alan phones me, and I doubt it will happen but it just might, I will confirm only what I have just told you. Once Christmas is upon us, Stephen and I will be gone and out of contact so there will be no way Alan can check on your whereabouts. Give me a call after your holiday and I can then tell you all about what happened in Portugal. "

"Peter, thanks, thanks so much. Are you sure you don't mind? I feel really bad at having to ask."

"My darling Cindy, for you to ask it must be important and what else are friends for? I shall always be your friend, but should Alan ever find out about my involvement in this it will in all probability cause him a great deal of understandable resentment and anger. To be brief, it is likely to end our mutual friendship. Perhaps sometime you will tell me the reason you ask this of me. Until then, say no more."

Cindy was overwhelmed. *It was not perfect, and still had a lot of risks, but it might just be enough,* she thought. Cindy delayed mentioning Christmas knowing that sooner rather than later Alan would bring the subject up in conversation. She didn't have to wait long and the following week he asked what they should do.

"Is it the usual Christmas this year, with the parents staying with us or should we go there?" he enquired. Cindy rejoined that it was up to him as she had already told him she was going to spend Christmas with Peter and Stephen, but she was unaware of the exact whereabouts as Peter wanted it to be a surprise. Alan was dumbstruck. He knew she hadn't mentioned any such thing, and after saying so a heated argument broke out.

"Are you saying I can't go, then?" Cindy indignantly shouted. "Or is it that you want to come to? You didn't say so when I mentioned it a month or so ago, but if you do then say so and I will ask Peter if partners are invited – but you know you didn't like him and I doubt you'll enjoy spending several days at Christmas in his and Stephen's company, to say nothing of their gay friends."

"Bugger you Cindy. I either come with you, somewhere God knows where, doing God knows what, with people I profoundly dislike or I spend Christmas alone. Some choice! Thanks."

"I take from that you won't be coming then" she swiftly retorted. "I'm sorry if this has upset you, Alan, but it sounded fun. I knew it wouldn't be your scene but I thought it might snap me out of things a bit." The carrot of her returning from her Christmas break in an improved mood was cynically dangled like a poisoned chalice being offered to a man dying of thirst.

Alan gave up arguing, defeated again though now he felt a rising anger within him. He visualised the embarrassing conversations he would have with his parents and friends when he would tell them through a false smile that Cindy was holidaying with past work colleagues at Christmas. They would of course nod their heads and say how wonderful, but in reality he knew they would think that something a little odd was going on with the Crosslands. It would be humiliating.

"You know, just lately you treat like me shit. I work bloody hard at the bank, and there are all sorts of pressures at the moment that I never bother you with, but which I have to deal with during the week. All I ask is that at weekends and holidays we can spend some quality time together."

"I'm truly sorry, Alan" said Cindy, deliberately lowering and softening her voice. She meant it, but she knew she couldn't help herself. She had fallen out of love, and since she had met Gordon she rather resented Alan's presence. It was as if he was an impediment now to her future. Gordon excited her, made her feel alive, and although they had spent only two brief lunches together she wanted to know and experience everything about him. If that hurt Alan so be it. She had a life and only she was going to live it. She waited a few moments before speaking again in a firmer, more authoritative tone.

"I'm going away at Christmas, Alan. Get over it." Her mind was focussed on Gordon now, and whilst she had desperately wanted to phone or text him since he had been away she had refrained from doing so as per their agreement. Now, however, she felt an uncontrollable urge to be near him. She went to her room, picked up her mobile and sent Gordon a text message.

miss you. Looking forward to xmas.
x

It made her feel better, closer to him and she felt sure he would reply even though he would be back in the country in the next few days. She was surprised and delighted when five minutes later she received the small bleep on her phone telling her a message had arrived. It was from Gordon and said simply,

me 2. Back next Monday.
G xx

She lay down on her bed and gradually went to sleep, with thoughts of Gordon and Mealag once more on her mind.

17

Assistant Commissioner Manders was not satisfied that his team's investigation into tracing possible contacts of the London bombers was proceeding as he had hoped. Sure, the ATU had some spectacular early successes, but the shooting by police of the innocent Jean Charles De Menezes in the wake of the bombings had taken up valuable time and had been at the very least a distraction into his own specialised area of tracing suspects via business and bank records, accounts and the like. It was one of his team that had visited the banks in July and they had frankly got very little of worth. He reviewed the outstanding areas still under investigation, and for the umpteenth time read over the information on each of them again. Every time he reviewed the progress reports and files, he puzzled over just one – the Hannet-Mar International Bank and the account of Chalthoum Universal Holdings with its links to the Corniche Consortium opened by Halima Chalthoum.

Apart from the two deposits there had been no activity on the accounts. That in itself was not particularly unusual, but it hardly smacked of some dynamic consortium ready to fill their boots during the current Dubai boom times. Also, the amounts were pretty small yet the bank's chief executive seemed convinced the account was worth his personal attention as he was clearly expecting it to expand. Then there was the very close proximity to the 7th July, possibly indicating that friends or relatives of the bombers might be about to receive some compensation for their loss, but even that theory hardly stood up to what the ATU already knew. The bombers' families were as shocked and surprised as anyone could be that their loved ones had committed such horrendous acts of violence against innocent commuters.

None of it made any sense to Manders, which was precisely why he was becoming more interested by it. In his twenty two years of experience in the Metropolitan Police Force, his nose had become ever more sensitive to the smell of criminality and there was a slightly pungent whiff emanating around the Hannet-Mar account. Whilst he was not convinced the account was genuine, he had scant reason to believe it was linked to terrorism. More likely would be a dodgy business deal, possibly involving the bank manager himself, but obtaining a rational explanation for his unease would not be easy. All he had to do was find it. That was his job – looking into seemingly innocuous crevices, examining for cracks in apparently pristine paperwork, shedding light on the concealed. Checking, rechecking, data mining, cross-referencing. It was boring, hard grind and very unglamorous. But he loved it, because whilst other units stole the headlines and appeared in front of TV cameras, Manders knew that often these public success stories were down to the men and women of his team. Unseen and unsung, they had proved vital in the detection of those wishing to harm the country he served.

Manders picked up his phone and asked Bill Ritson, the lead officer of the Hannet-Mar Bank investigation, to join him. Over a lengthy chat and two cups of coffee, they reviewed what they knew.

"I don't like it," said Manders. "Something isn't right but what it has to do with 7/7, Christ knows. Everything apparently checks out, yet only partially, like the PO Box in Dubai. We know it was genuine but strangely it was closed immediately after Crossland's confirmatory letters arrived. Didn't Crossland tell you, Bill, that he had received excellent references including an Affidavit or some such? Presumably you've had them checked them out?"

"Well of course, Sir. I personally read them and noted down the details. We didn't retain copies but most were from organisations and companies from abroad. All seem reasonably bona fide but who knows what goes on over there. There were a couple of references regarding the woman Halima Chalthoum. There were at least a couple from business acquaintances in Dubai claiming to have known her for many years and vouching for her in quite glowing terms and the affidavit was from a friend of Crossland. I think he said it was from someone whom he would trust with his life or something a bit OTT like that, and from memory the document itself said all the right things. Pretty formal, but impressive I seem to recall."

He began searching through the paperwork. "Here's the name, Kenneth Styles. He runs his own consultancy firm, unimaginatively called Styles Project Consultancy, and acted for various organisations mainly based in, or with connections to, Dubai. Lives in Sussex when he's back in the UK. Of course, quite what exactly his services are I don't know. He may just be a fixer of sorts between various parties or he may be a hands-on specialist. Do you think we should give him a tap?"

Manders stroked his chin, a sign he was deep in thought and not wanting to be disturbed. After two minutes, he replied to Ritson's question and said that interviewing Styles could be tricky. If Styles complained to Crossland, the whole investigation could get messy, meaning it might come to lawyers – and whilst the ATU could, he felt, justify pretty much anything they did or wanted to do under UK Anti-Terrorism legislation, this case didn't warrant the use of the heavy hand, at least not yet.

"I don't want the local boys handling this, Bill, but tell them you'll be on their patch making very discreet enquiries. See what you can turn up on Styles and his known associates."

"I have to ask what sort of priority you want me to give this, Sir. Sorry to ask but we are already at full stretch."

"Understood, yes I know. Well, let's say do what you can when you can. Something within a month would be good."

Manders was therefore surprised when within an hour, Ritson put his head around the door.

"Styles is dead. Died 4th June when he drove his car off the road, apparently drunk. We're getting coroner's stuff and the Sussex reports here A.S.A.P. The web page of the local paper has a quote from the widow saying she can't understand how it was that her husband was over the limit – apparently he was only a moderate drinker and never drank if he was driving."

"Maybe so, maybe not. She wouldn't be the first wife of a drunk driver to say her husband never touched a drop. His death is probably just pure coincidence but keep on it, Bill. Same priority."

The information was intriguing, certainly, but until more actual evidence and some hard facts were obtained, at this stage the assistant commissioner could not justify an increase in resources to undertake more rapid investigations. Manders decided to wait and see what turned up, but smiled as he recalled his old mentor's favourite phrase. It was strange how often 'following the money' led to unexpected results.

18

Alan Crossland spent the remainder of the weekend thinking about his life. The thing with his wife was now causing him pain and anxiety. His sleep was being affected and he was finding it more difficult to concentrate at work. The more he reflected, the more hurt and resentful he became.

He simply could hardly believe this nonsense story of a Christmas mystery gathering – who would attend that? Who would wish to if you couldn't take partners at Christmas? Partners had to be invited, so why didn't Cindy ask him to whatever it was she was actually going to? All sorts of uncertainties entered his mind and he seriously considered phoning Peter Knowles. He was sure he had his number somewhere but then he thought what precisely should he say? Is my wife coming to your Christmas party? That would make him look silly or, worse, bloody stupid if the whole thing really did turn out to be genuine. Cindy had shown no signs of having an affair or even of occasionally seeing someone else. He regularly rang home during the week, deliberately usually in the evenings at various times, and pretty much always found Cindy at home. When she wasn't he would call again and she would then be home and give some very plausible explanation that could be verified if he really wished it. He had not noticed any other giveaway signs, such as a new wardrobe of clothes or different hairstyle and make up that might justify his doubts. If Cindy wasn't having an affair something else surely had to be going on in her life, and leaving him alone at Christmas meant that whatever it was had to be taken seriously.

He could no longer pretend, nor hope, that his marriage would survive. He held his head in his hands and closed his eyes, trying to think rationally. He decided that whatever his wife was doing, it was probably occurring during the day as he knew Cindy was often out either allegedly at the gym or for lunches or seeing her friends.

God forbid that she has joined some quasi-religious bunch of nutters, he thought, *though if true that would at least offer some kind of explanation for her recent mood change.* More thoughts, more doubts. His head was spinning trying to make sense of all the possibilities. Maybe there *was* someone else, someone local whom she could meet, but Crossland concluded that the Cotswold villages were a hotbed of gossip and the chances of a clandestine affair remaining unnoticed for long were virtually non-existent. Everyone knew about everyone else either directly or indirectly, with news of local scandals usually being imparted at the tedious pre-lunch drinks gatherings which each Sunday rotated around the houses in the village – but still the nagging doubts lingered. He thought more about his plight until finally determining a course of action that might, at least partially, resolve his dilemma. Knowing what needed to be done, he firstly would have a chat with his friend and driver Jack Donaldson who was just the man for the task. He would talk to him first thing tomorrow.

"Jack, sit down. I need you to do something for me. Strictly between us, and I mean that, things are not going well between Cindy and me, and I am really not sure why. I want you to do a bit of checking up, very discreetly of course, on what she gets up to during the week."

Jack was thoughtful and feigned surprise, but confirmation of his perception that all was not as it should be for Cindy Crossland was news indeed. He wondered just what the attractive wife of his employer was up to, and his mind instantly started to consider what opportunities might be offered by this assignment beyond just the favour of his boss.

"I am really sorry to hear that, sir. Thought you two were joined at the hip but sure thing, OK, but I will need to hire some non-descript cars and such like. Do you think she is seeing someone else?"

"Money is no problem, Jack. Just get what you want and I'll pay you back in cash. Here's five hundred to be going on with. If anyone asks, you're on holiday."

Jack was shrewd enough to realise that by paying in cash Crossland was not going to have a paper trail that might lead back to him – a further indication that this could become quite a lucrative, as well as pleasurable, assignment.

"I'll have to start soon, Christmas is only a bit over three weeks away. How long do you want me to tail her for? Jack asked.

"I suggest you start now, straight away, and for two weeks maximum. I know what she is doing at Christmas."

"Oh," said Jack, surprise in voice, his round face slightly flushing. "What's that then, or shouldn't I ask?"

"It doesn't matter Jack, but I'm okay about that. It's the life we have at home that really bugs me. Do you know she hasn't slept with me for months, goes off to a separate bedroom?"

"Jesus! That's serious." Donaldson was now definitely as interested as Crossland to find out what activities Cindy was getting up to in the sleepy limestone villages. He could not imagine that she was the type to do without sex for long, and in that respect she fitted into his stereotyped view of all women. He firmly believed that every woman secretly wanted sex as often as they could get it, and these days with as many different blokes as they could lay their hands on. *Who knows,* he thought, *she may be getting to the point where he might be able to help her get some stability into her life as well as physical fulfilment.* He felt sure he could make her happy if only she would allow him to get close to her.

Four hours later, Donaldson had hired a small Peugeot from a firm in Stratford, loaded his digital camera with a new battery back and was driving through Stillwood. The long drive at Red Gables deprived him of any view of what cars may be parked on the drive and Stillwood was not exactly a village where one could park up unnoticed for very long. It was always busy with tourists, but the long road through the village centre did have a number of bays into which, if he was lucky, he could park the car. These would afford some sort of anonymity. He could pass as a bored husband waiting for his wife to return from a shopping spree, and several bays afforded a reasonable view of the entrance to Red Gables. Whilst he waited, he also thought he would hire another car of different make and colour and from a different supplier. If this job was going to entail a lot of hanging about in public places, different cars would make recognition that much more difficult for the curious.

After an hour, he saw Cindy's Honda emerge. He started his car and tailed her at a discreet distance. She went to the gym, met no one in the large car park and came out an hour later, again alone. She then went home. For the next several days Donaldson followed Cindy around, alternating vehicles. She was totally unaware that she was being spied on and failed to recognise Donaldson or either of the cars. On one occasion a large cock pheasant suddenly ran across the country road totally oblivious to the oncoming danger of Cindy's car bearing down upon him. She performed an emergency stop, skidded to a halt and missed the stupid bird by inches. Donaldson, following, was forced to stop behind Cindy and to prevent her recognising him he leant down as if reaching for the glove compartment, but the experience ensured that subsequently he left an even greater distance between his car and hers.

The more he observed her, the more Donaldson was convinced she was definitely not seeing anyone else. She seemed to be doing exactly what she presumably had told Crossland: going to the gym, attending gun dog meetings, shopping, taking lunches with friends and other pretty mundane stuff. Donaldson couldn't help but be impressed with her though. She always looked fabulous, and when she put on, or took off, her coat at the gym car park, her figure stretched her sweat shirt, revealing just how shapely she was. He really wished he could find some excuse to speak with her alone but for that he would need her husband's permission. By the middle of the following week, he could wait no more.

"Alan, its Jack. This is going nowhere, as I said to you on Monday. Are you absolutely sure no one is seeing her at the house? I really need to make an impromptu visit but if she is at home I need some excuse to say hello. I can tell her I was just passing, doing a bit of shopping in the village as you have given me a few days off or something like that. Might ask her out for lunch, eh?" he chuckled.

"You and Cindy as a lunch date! You must be joking. You won't get anywhere there. But, yes, why not go round and say I asked you to call as I am missing some urgent papers and must have left them at home. Ask Cindy to give them to you. There are a few papers in fact that are in the study, in a file headed Sun Union Inc of America.

Ask her to get those. It will at least enable you to see if there are signs of anyone else having called, or even if they are there!"

Cindy was in jubilant mood when Donaldson pressed the brass bell push adjacent to the front door. She had just finalised arrangements for her Christmas trip to see Gordon. He had wanted to meet her somewhere and then travel up together, but she was having none of that. She wanted to experience the drive for herself and also particularly wished to have him meet her at the loch he had described to her. The long range weather forecast was for cold days and little snow, but Gordon had insisted that if snow did indeed arrive, at Mealag or en route, they would phone each other and he would meet her in his 4x4. If the weather remained fair, Cindy planned to arrive midday on Saturday, Christmas Eve. This would necessitate an overnight stop for her somewhere around Glasgow on the Friday evening and Gordon recommended a good hotel that overlooked Loch Lomond.

She was all set to go now and was finding it hard to constrain her impatience. She had bought all her presents for her friends and family, and for Alan. A feeling of guilt had made her buy a much dearer present for Alan than she would normally, but she knew it was what he would like, an original painting by Anna Baker. For Gordon she had deliberately decided not to go overboard and anyway, she reasoned, what on earth could she buy for someone who can afford anything he wished. So she came away from the jewellers with an attractive pair of gold cufflinks. The present also had the very necessary advantage of being easily concealed whether at home in the interim period pending her travel and also within her luggage. Nonetheless, she took the additional precaution of not affixing a label to the wrapping – if discovered the gift could be for anyone. She was in such high spirits, that she was skipping around the kitchen in time to the beat of an old pop song playing on her new digital radio, when the three tone chimes alerted her to a visitor waiting at the porch.

"Why Jack, it's you. I didn't recognise the car. Is everything all right?" Cindy's normally cautious reserve with Donaldson was subsumed by her mounting excitement at soon setting off to see Gordon.

"I'm fine Mrs Crossland, may I come in?" and as he spoke Donaldson walked forward into the large entrance hall, almost forcing Cindy to step out of the way before turning to face her.

"How is the leg, now?" he asked in a well-meaning tone. "I must say Mrs Crossland you are looking very well, better than last time we met."

"Don't keep calling me Mrs Crossland, it sounds so formal and we have known each other for quite a while now. Cindy will be fine. And yes thank you, Jack, the leg is fine, I've forgotten about it now, seems so long ago. I'm not sure I really thanked you enough for your kindness that day when you brought me home."

Jack felt a stirring within him. What exactly was she saying? It sounded as if she might be willing to thank him some more. Why the sudden change of attitude to him? This wasn't like Cindy Crossland at all and it unnerved him slightly. He felt he needed to take great care in how he responded to her enticing, possibly coded, comment.

"It was nothing, really. I was pleased to do it and anyway it really is part of the job. If I can help you or Alan, especially after the terrible experience you had, then everyone gains" and he chuckled to lighten the moment.

"I've just poured a coffee for myself, would you like one?" She turned and made her way through to the kitchen.

Donaldson's heart was now racing. Christian name terms, coffee, and wondering if she had thanked him enough. Such things would excite any man, but for a lecherous ex-mercenary they were a delight to hear.

"What exactly did you want Jack, anyway?" She turned her head toward him as she asked. Donaldson postponed answering her second question, fearing that once he had the papers it might provide Cindy with an early justification to terminate his visit.

"That would be great, thanks. No sugar, but some milk please. I'll give you a hand bringing it in." Donaldson followed her through the hallway into the kitchen, glancing into the other rooms along the way. No signs of other cups or plates, absolutely nothing that suggested any visitor had called in or was likely to. Cindy wasn't made up, dressed only in blue jeans and a big, sloppy T-shirt. Even her hair was pretty straight. But she still looked good, very good indeed.

Over coffee, they chatted about nothing in particular and Donaldson eventually asked for the papers which Cindy got for him. He could hardly take his eyes off her, and found it hard to stop mentally undressing her. He began to sweat but he knew this was not the time for him to be impulsive. She had to make the first real move which he felt sure she would.

"What are you and Alan doing for Christmas?" Donaldson asked, innocently.

She hesitated, briefly, but noticeably. "Well, it's a bit strange this year. I'm off to see some old work colleagues who are having a sort of get together, reunion type thing, and Alan is seeing his folks, I think." She hoped it sounded authentic.

Donaldson passed no comment. Her response was exactly as Crossland had told him. They finished their drinks and as Cindy made to tidy away the mugs she leant forward to pick them off the low table, Donaldson not missing the opportunity to look down the front of her T-shirt. As she carried them through to the kitchen, Donaldson followed. When she bent down to place the dirty crockery in the dishwasher, his soft voice broke the sudden silence of the room.

"You know, Cindy. If I can be of any help to you at any time, all you need do is ask. I mean, there would be no need for me to tell Alan, if you didn't want me to. You can trust me absolutely."

It was Cindy's turn to be cautious. *Did he know something? Had Alan spoken to him or was this a clumsy but genuine attempt at making a pass?*

"Thanks for the offer, Jack. I'm sure I can, I'll keep it in mind."

Rapidly struggling to think of what to reply, she instantly regretted her ambiguous response. To Donaldson, her words were not capable of any misinterpretation. They were a green light.

"I do mean it, Cindy. I've always admired you and wanted to get to know you better. You always look fantastic, but I bet Alan has never told you just how good you look – especially in those jeans."

Donaldson spoke the words smoothly, unable to resist making

such a comment and as he did so he ran his hand softly over her bottom.

"You and I could have some fun."

Cindy was taken aback and she was in no mood for this nonsense. Standing up quickly she said, "I don't think so, only in your dreams, Jack. I'm minded to call Alan about what you have just said… "

Donaldson, hurt and angry, smartly interrupted her. "But you won't though. Firstly, I would deny it and I'm pretty sure Mr Crossland would believe me, and secondly, if you did succeed in getting me sacked you would then be beholden to him. I don't think you would want that."

Cindy cursed silently. She knew he was right. Donaldson was certainly astute. She felt she should be enraged at him for coming on strong and touching her but there was nothing to be gained by creating a scene and having Alan involved.

"Just go, Jack. Now. Just get out." Cindy went to the front door and opened it wide, waiting for Donaldson to catch up. He was unhappy and disappointed but was determined not to quarrel with her. At the very least he knew he had given her plenty to think about and he had also surprised himself. Cindy Crossland was the first woman for whom he had managed to successfully control his lust and temper, but then he had never before had the same depth of feeling as he had about Cindy.

"OK. When you change your mind, let me know." The implied certainty within his statement sounded almost threatening, though the latter was unintended. He opened the car door, and as he nonchalantly threw Crossland's papers onto the rear seat he turned to say 'goodbye', but Cindy had already closed the door. She fleetingly thought again about telephoning Alan but again dismissed the idea. Her adrenaline was still running high from thinking of Gordon and she wasn't going to let another row with Alan spoil her euphoria. In any event, it would have mattered little had she phoned her husband. Unknown to her, he needed Donaldson and Donaldson knew he was safe in his job.

★ ★ ★

Alan Crossland sat in his London flat and went over Donaldson's brief report, at the end of which he told Donaldson to continue making periodic checks on Cindy after Christmas. Nothing made sense to him except that something was very seriously wrong with his marriage. He felt both anger and a deep sadness. He still loved Cindy but was very resentful of the way she had treated him in recent months, and there seemed little prospect that would change. Christmas was looming and that made him even more depressed. Being alone was bad at any time, but at Christmas and New Year it was going to be simply awful.

He decided he had let Cindy control events for too long and that however painful for him he must start rebuilding his own life. He logged onto his computer and scoured the internet – after about thirty minutes he had found a hotel where he could stay over the festive period that claimed to cater for both couples and singles. Almost on impulse he booked himself into a room, and he surprised himself that such a simple action immediately lightened his mood. He would have to apologise to his parents of course, but they would understand. Buoyed by his new found enthusiasm he resolved to see a solicitor as soon as possible, not that he wanted a divorce, but to receive some advice on how he might be placed if matters continued to deteriorate between him and Cindy.

The next morning he walked into the offices of Gardner, Kline and Jacobson, a large city firm, that catered for every conceivable type of litigation, but which also specialised in Family Law and Divorce. As he walked through the entrance lobby, he was taken aback at the superb standard of décor and furnishings. The lobby oozed wealth and it was obvious little expense had been spared. He sat on a deep red leather sofa whilst the receptionist glanced down a pre-printed list of expected visitors and made a phone call to notify the secretary to Mrs Avril Hennington of Alan's arrival. Within minutes he was being escorted to the partner's well-appointed, but rather small, office by a leggy blonde of about twenty-five whose initial greeting to him sounded deeply false and rather too rehearsed.

Crossland outlined his situation to the solicitor stressing he did not want a divorce but just some initial advice. Hennington, a rather plain woman of about fifty with dark hair and dressed in a navy-blue suit, started by telling Crossland that how she acted was dependent upon him. He had to be really sure if in the future he wanted a divorce or not. She explained that she would always protect her client's interests to the best of her ability, but that task was sometimes made a lot more difficult if a client was unsure what precisely he wished to achieve or gave conflicting instructions as time passed.

"You must understand, Mr Crossland, that either of these aspects can regrettably be the cause of a significant increase in the estimated costs, though of course I will always do my best to achieve a satisfactory outcome for you," a statement by which she disarmingly and carefully introduced the fee structure into the ensuing conversation.

After an hour and a half, Crossland left. Hennington would keep a small file of the meeting, pending further formal instructions and her secretary could conveniently arrange to take payment for today's meeting now, if Crossland would prefer. He came away a very displeased man. Evidently the starting point of settling the financial aspects with Cindy would be a 50/50 split of their joint assets. Hennington had said she would argue on his behalf that any financial settlement should be made on the basis of need rather than strict equity and thought that a 60/40 split in favour of Crossland might be possible, but she was by no means certain. The detail could be attended to later when, and if, any such paperwork was needed. She understood that he had earned more money, a lot more, than Cindy and she also understood that Crossland had been generous to Cindy over the years but the fact remained that the courts were likely to split the finances equally and would certainly take a hard look at the variation in private pension that both might receive upon retirement.

"Mortality tables are increasingly used by the courts these days, and given that women live longer than men, it is open to the court to decide that any settlement reflects those facts." Hennington's words slipped off her tongue but their effect was not lost on her client.

"In other words, she gets more," Crossland said testily. He was not expecting such a downbeat assessment. It seemed to him that Cindy could do what she liked and would receive a substantial financial benefit even if she was the sole cause of the marriage break up. Hennington provided scant comfort when she explained that the courts like to take responsibility for the marriage break-up out of any of the proceedings. Crossland did blame Cindy and that was not going to change. Why should he have to bear an equal settlement? It also appeared that as there was, as yet, insufficient evidence (actually none, as his solicitor sharply pointed out) of any adulterous affair on Cindy's part, she might even have the audacity to contest any divorce Crossland sought to obtain on grounds of her unreasonable behaviour, even though eventually the divorce could be obtained on grounds that the marriage had irretrievably broken down.

"Mr Crossland, my advice at this stage is that divorce proceedings initiated by you may be costly should your wife wish to contest them, and you have little to gain anyway. I am not sure you really want a divorce nor are you happy at the likely financial settlement provisions should a divorce petition be served. If you can persuade your wife to jointly enlist the services of an organisation such as Relate, at this stage they may be more help than I and a lot less expensive."

The words of the experienced lawyer echoed in his head. He knew he would never go to any marriage guidance outfit, and neither would Cindy, so dismissed the sensible advice out of hand. Yet again, it seemed to Crossland that Cindy was holding all the cards. His best hope seemed to be to wait until, if and when, she wanted a divorce, then at least she might be more amenable on the finances. Why, he reasoned, should she benefit – when she has had a good job and career, still has relatively high earnings from her writing and therefore can still contribute to her pension – just because he, Crossland, had worked his balls off and made a great deal more money? He returned to his office in a foul mood, his remaining level of affection for Cindy slipping away rapidly by the minute. He thought the situation was grossly unfair even if it was cynically endorsed by the courts under the umbrella disguise of equity.

19

Cindy left Red Gables at midday on Friday, leaving her plenty of time to drive to the hotel at Loch Lomond. She hadn't heard from Alan since Wednesday and could not bring herself to phone him. Instead she left his Christmas present and card on the dining table with a separate note, hastily scribbled in black felt tip.

> *Have a good time*
> *C x.*

It wasn't much but felt she had to say something. There had been no present from Alan but she presumed that he had intended to give it to her that Friday evening when he returned from London, which was indeed his intention – but when he arrived home to find her gone, he simply left it on her bed, feeling he had made some sort of pertinent gesture by placing it there. He did not linger long at Red Gables, quickly packing a case and then driving off to Wales, wondering what his Christmas at the Asterhays Country Park Hotel would be like.

On their first night away, it was probably Alan that fared the better of the separated couple. Cindy had dinner at the amazing restaurant that was right on the shoreline of the loch, though being dark it was difficult for Cindy to appreciate the fantastic location in which it was set, and afterward returned to her room and watched the television until she retired to bed.

Whilst Cindy was seeing an episode of *Have I Got News For You* at nine o'clock on the new LCD television, Alan was starting to relax and meet more of his fellow guests who like him wore a small identity badge. He was quite amazed at how many apparently divorced or single women there were, and most were much younger than he had anticipated. Of course there were some who were in their mid-fifties and beyond, but also some a great deal younger. All seemed to have a made a determined effort to look their best. After circulating amongst them for over an hour, it suddenly dawned on him that everyone was doing the same as he was – getting to talk to as many other guests as possible and to fix upon a shortlist of those in whose company one might want to spend if not the week, at least a few days. He had already compiled a short list of three and he found himself drifting back towards the first on the list, a slim blonde-haired woman whom he presumed to be about forty or just under, named Anna. As Alan approached, she detached herself from a small group with which she was in conversation and came to meet him, smiling.

"Why don't we sit at that table over there, and get away from all this?" she said, pointing at a small, round table in the corner of the large room. Its Alan, isn't it? I'm Anna, as if you needed reminding with this thing pinned on!" she laughed as she fiddled with her badge, before removing it and placing it in her small handbag.

Alan felt a little awkward. It had been years since he had engaged in anything like this, and he felt rather out of practice. He needn't have worried as it was Anna who spoke as they sat at the table.

"This is my first time at a singles event since my divorce three years ago. Just could not pluck up the courage before, but life must go on; or so my friends tell me. What about you Alan, are you divorced?"

"It's going through," he rushed the words out of his lips without thinking. "My wife seems to be finding other interests these days." It wasn't a lie but it was misleading.

"I see. That's hard. Well, good luck. I suggest no more talk of those things. We are here to enjoy ourselves and I vote we start now." She raised her glass and said, "Happy Christmas". The ice well and truly broken, Alan and Anna did indeed start to enjoy themselves. By 11:30pm, the bar was still busy but Alan was getting a little tired and he suspected that Anna, whose consumption of wine had considerably exceeded his own, might also be feeling weary. They had chatted and laughed almost non-stop for over two hours and clearly enjoyed each other's company, and Alan felt as though a great burden was lifting from his shoulders.

"Shall we have a final coffee?" Alan thought this was a good way to signal that he was ready to leave.

"That would be lovely. How about we take it in one of the rooms? Yours or mine?"

Alan gulped. He had not expected this and was unsure how he should respond. He felt lost for words and it was several seconds before he replied, "I didn't ask for that reason Anna. I mean, I'm not used to doing this kind of thing."

"Are you saying I am then!" she exclaimed, but laughed as she said it. "I told you I have lived as a semi-recluse for the past three years and was pressurised by friends to take this break here. Oh, come on Alan. We're not bloody teenagers, let's enjoy ourselves. No strings and all that."

Fifteen minutes later they had joined together the two single beds in Anna's room and slipped between the crisp sheets, the steaming cups forgotten on the table.

20

The first shafts of dim grey light of the December dawn were slowly revealing huge shadowy shapes on the far side of the loch as Cindy helped herself to an orange juice and croissant at the self-service breakfast bar. She sat at a table immediately adjacent to the panoramic glass frontage of the restaurant that allowed unrestricted views across Loch Lomond. She had never visited Scotland and was hoping that her first views of it would be favourable and she was not disappointed. She watched, fascinated, as the layer of mist that hung over the loch quickly dissipated as the light brightened and the weak warmth of the early morning sun struck the water. The sky changed from being a leaden dark grey canopy to an umbrella of the palest cyan, providing a perfect contrast to the deep green of the acres of spruce trees that partly covered the massive rock faces of Ben Lomond and its neighbouring peaks opposite, their tops dazzling from a dusting of fresh snow. Cindy took several minutes simply looking at the view, stunned by its breathtaking range of colours and grandeur.

By the time she had started her second juice and helped herself to perhaps too much bacon and eggs, convinced that she needed additional sustenance for the drive ahead, the loch had become a mirror image of its surroundings. The water was the colour of the pale sky, its smooth glass surface reflecting in perfect detail the vivid yellows and browns of the past summer's dead bracken amid the myriad of colours that painted the shoreline grasses and the green mountain slopes with their beautiful frosted hats. Occasionally she spotted the tell-tale sign of a fish, swimming fast and trailing the tiniest of wakes as its dorsal fin cut through the water – or sometimes she noticed a series of small ringlets, which expanded slowly as though a small stone had been thrown into the water, revealing the presence of a trout below.

She could not have wished for a better start to her day, and in buoyant mood she was soon driving north, quickly passing by the twenty-four miles of Loch Lomond. The route emailed to her by Gordon was exceptionally simple:

Stay on the A82, through Fort William, until Invergarry. Then take the A87 until the left turn, unclassified road, for Kinloch Hourn. Stop at the large dam.

It couldn't have been easier and Cindy was able to take full advantage of viewing the vast landscapes that were presented to her at every turn, whilst also enjoying the luxury of driving without traffic on a superbly maintained smooth road – a marked contrast from the potholed suspension testers she had often encountered. Each scenic view seemed to be better than any of its predecessors and Cindy was quite overwhelmed by them long before she reached Glencoe.

Gordon had told her to look out for Buachaille Etive Mor, the mountain on her left that would mark her entrance to Glencoe and, almost opposite on her right, the edge of Rannoch Moor and the Seventeenth Century *Kings House Hotel*, but she didn't need his guidance. As soon as she saw the road stretch ahead into the distance for several miles, as it traversed the length of a deep glen flanked by huge mountains, she was filled with awe. She knew that before her lay Glencoe, the site of the worst and bloodiest treachery to take place in the Highlands. The few cars upon the road appeared small and vulnerable as they weaved their way amongst some of the highest and most foreboding peaks of Scotland, and it thrilled her to know that in a few moments she would be driving through the sombre pass. Even in sunlight, the glen was intimidating and Cindy shivered slightly as she drove onwards, nervously excited by Glencoe's mix of myth, massacre, legend and sheer scale.

Once through the Glen she felt a slight relief but also a fresh wave of anticipation. It was a little before 11am and, having made good time, she was nearing Fort William. Gordon had asked Cindy to phone him when she arrived at the town so that he could estimate the time he needed to be at the dam to meet her. Sat in the lay-by on the shore of Loch Linnhe, watching grey seals laze on a cluster of rocks near to the shore, Cindy had little appreciation of the level of anxiety that had been rising in Gordon since he first woke. It had been several months since they last met, and apart from text messages and emails, they had not been in contact. Gordon had found it hard to sit still, even for a moment, worrying that perhaps at the last moment Cindy would change her mind about coming. He let out a huge sigh of relief when his hall telephone rang. They spoke briefly, not wanting to waste time, and arranged the time for Gordon to wait at the small parking area by Quoich Dam. As soon as he replaced the receiver, he rushed to tell his housekeeper the good news.

Cindy drove towards the dam, passing through the tiny hamlet of Corach, and noticing that the road was exactly as she had imagined it from Gordon's previous descriptions and from his tales of watching the arrival of his guests. She correctly assumed that Gordon would be at his favourite vantage spot on the southern shore watching for sight of her blue Honda. As the narrow road twisted and turned she wondered just how long it would be before the dam came into view, her anticipation rising at every bend. She realised she had to be very close when to her left, nestling between the barren trees, she passed a red brick box-shaped building. There was a sign in white lettering upon a navy background erected on its access road stating 'Quoich Power Station'. She turned a sharp right-hand bend and audibly gasped as the entire dam came into view, its huge structure completely spanning the wide glen in front of her. The road ahead climbed gently uphill for about two miles until it was level with the top of the dam wall, occasionally twisting around the few remaining granite foothills not blasted completely away and levelled by the construction engineers. As she drove onward, she guessed Gordon could see her now, and strained her eyes as she tried to glimpse him. In fact, Gordon had spotted her well before she had reached the power station and had already crossed the dam wall to await her arrival. Whilst Cindy was searching the south end of the dam, Gordon was leaning against the north gate adjacent to the road. Five minutes later, she turned the car onto the rough stone parking area, excitedly waving to Gordon as she did so. Without turning off the engine, she rushed out of the car to greet him whilst Gordon came over to her. He was dressed in a wax jacket over a thick white roll neck sweater, mole skin trousers and a rather incongruous black beaver hat. It wasn't at all as she had expected him to be dressed and it made her giggle. They hugged each other briefly and then kissed each other firmly on the lips, but not for overly long as they were both bursting to speak.

"I honestly didn't know if you would come, you know. I really thought you might have backed off. I'm just so pleased to see you, I can hardly believe it's you and you're here!" Gordon for once sounded slightly less than in total control of his emotions.

"Of course I would come. We've waited months for this. I couldn't have done that to you anyway. Oh Gordon, this is just so… so bloody, bloody marvellous." Cindy did not know quite what to say either and her words were instinctive and spontaneous. They hugged and kissed each other again, and it was some minutes before Gordon realised that Cindy was still wearing only her jeans and jumper and without any kind of jacket.

"Cindy, you must be frozen. Let's get in the car and I'll show you where to park up and get your stuff out."

"Not yet, Gordon, please not just yet." She turned off her engine then made her way to the back of her car, opening the boot.

"I'll put on my jacket, gloves and hat. See I remembered what you said. Please let's stay here a few minutes. I need to remember this moment, this view, you and me, and I want to make certain I have taken it all in."

Gordon held out the coat for her and she slid her arms into the sleeves and zipped up the front. She placed a simple, dark blue, woollen hat onto her head and produced a matching coloured glove from each of the jacket pockets.

"There now, do I look ok?" she twirled around.

"Fantastic, but you still may soon get cold as it is only just above freezing today and several layers are needed if we are to stay out for any length of time."

They locked arms behind their respective backs whilst Cindy slowly turned her head, taking in every aspect of the view and firing a barrage of questions at Gordon. He answered them as accurately as he was able to, given the brevity of time Cindy allowed before asking him another, until he eventually said, "Tell you what. I'll give you a brief answer and a more complete version over dinner or later this afternoon. How's that?"

"Agreed," she said.

Fifteen minutes later, Cindy did start to feel the cold and they got into the car. They had driven just over a mile when Gordon pointed out a barely noticeable small track leading off to the right and which immediately swung behind a large mound of rocks into the crevices of which had sprung tufts of coarse grass. The track was surprisingly smooth, having been layered with small rock chippings, and from the highway seemed to almost immediately disappear somewhere into the lower slope of the mountain. Cindy drove along it and in fifty metres came into cleared area where there were two enormous, separate garages, each with a different coloured door. She stopped the car, as instructed, in front of the one with the green door.

Both garages had tiled gable roofs and were built of block but then faced with the natural rock stone hewn from the hill to hide (and protect) the unsightly brick work. There were no windows. Gordon got out of the car and pulled back two sizeable black bolts before unlocking the padlock that retained the two ends of a length of thick chain that had been wrapped between the handles of the garages double doors. As the doors were pulled apart the warning, intermittent shrill sound of an audible alarm pierced the air. Gordon quickly punched some numbers into the keypad to disarm the security system and prevent the main alarm from being automatically triggered. He switched on the fluorescent lighting and beckoned Cindy to drive in. She parked alongside an old Land Rover, proudly wearing its battle scars of skirmishes with the local terrain and whose mud spattered windshield could not possibly have permitted much vision. The remaining space was largely unused except for an old white van parked by the far wall, one or two minor pieces of machinery, a trailer in an equally battered state to that of the Land Rover and some small items scattered on the shelves. A few poles and stakes along with rolls of fencing wire were in the far corner and several large plastic fuel containers, placed against the near wall, completed the inventory.

"By the time we get your stuff out here, Sandy will be over and we can get moving. One thing, very important, both these garages have double doors that share the same alarm system and spare padlock keys hang in the kitchen lobby cupboard at Mealag. Can you give me an important date, it doesn't have to your birthday!" he quipped.

Cindy obliged giving him 24 12 05 and Gordon pressed a number of buttons on the alarm key pad before turning to her saying, "You might need to come here and get your car, so remember to key in that code number to stop the alarm, else we will have everyone at Mealag and the local police force down at Invergarry or beyond racing up here."

"You surely don't get any crime here, do you Gordon?" she asked.

"Fortunately not yet, but we might. People visit the Highlands from all over, especially the big cities. Some come to fish, some to find work in summer, many to simply walk the hills. I doubt they are all fine, honest folk. Sadly, even Fort William and Fort Augustus are not without the occasional opportunist thief. We also have many sightseeing tourists in the summer of course, but a few at other times of the year. Once that alarm goes off, the local nick can just block the turn off at Invergarry whilst they investigate. No one could get far, but why put temptation in anyone's way? That's why the exterior alarm is also very visible and has a notice that says it is directly wired to the police."

Cindy had barely observed that as she had driven in, too busy making sure she parked the car in the right place, but wondered just how expensive the equipment had to be to justify the cost of installing its own dedicated power supply and telephone link in these remote parts.

"So, can I ask what's in the adjoining garage?" Cindy enquired.

"At the moment it has my Range Rover and Volvo in it, though I often keep one or other at the house. Also the launch trailers and some other more expensive gear, and we can keep a boat or two in there if we need to. We can launch the boats from the shore a couple of miles from here where the road skirts the edge of the loch and where there's no bank or boulders. You'll see, I'll explain it all later."

The steady, rhythmic crunch of gravel of Sandy MacLean's footsteps forewarned Cindy of his impending arrival and when he came into view he waved and called out. "Welcome to the Highlands, Mrs Crossland."

"Cindy. Please call me Cindy, and thank you."

After a few more brief pleasantries, Cindy pulled on her gum boots whilst Gordon and Sandy took hold of her bags and coats.

"Thought you might have had more than this?" Gordon mischievously teased.

"Why? Because I'm a woman I suppose," Cindy laughed back. "Actually, I took on board what you told me about your executives last summer with some of them coming laden down with suitcases."

Sandy laughed. "Aye, they make a rare sight sometimes. That they do."

Gordon reset the alarm and locked the garage before following the other two back along the track. They crossed over the road and easily stepped down the slope to the waiting boat below, bobbing gently alongside the small wooden jetty.

Cindy could only just make out what she thought was Mealag in the distance at the far shore. In fact what she could see was the edge of one of the chalets within the complex. Having been built on the eastern edge of a bay, Mealag Lodge would not become visible until she was two thirds of the way across. She could hardly believe what she was now doing. Here she was, in a boat, crossing a loch in one of the most remote parts of the Highlands on a cold winter's day – and not just any winter's day, but Christmas Eve! She looked around her in total amazement. The huge loch stretched out to the west, but she realised that as the distant shoreline occasionally disappeared from view, the loch must also penetrate to the north and south between some mighty Munros. She looked up at the lofty white peaks surrounding her.

"The snow line starts at about 2000 feet," Gordon shouted above the noise of the outboard. Cindy nodded but continued to stare all about her. To the east, a mile away, was the dam. In itself a massive structure, man-made and faced with large concrete slabs, it fitted in well with the scale of its surroundings but not their beauty. Sticking out from the centre of the dam was a thirty metre straight, steel walkway closely railed at either edge for safety which led to the dam's plain concrete valve tower that was perched on four, ugly thick steel legs that disappeared into the depths of the loch. The whole thing resembled an oversize observation post protecting a concentration camp wall. Despite all its blandness, Cindy's eyes kept returning to the dam.

"I'm looking forward to learning more about the dam, Gordon. Remember you promised. It's just colossal, isn't it? It looks so much larger now we are on the water than when you drive up to it, and it looked huge then."

As Sandy turned the boat slightly to port, Cindy saw Mealag for the first time. Her eyes lit up. She could see how the deep bay had obscured the lodge from the road opposite, but she could now make out the full complex. Mealag was to her left, about fifty yards from the shore, and through the trees behind the lodge, were two separate buildings. One was Sandy and Margaret's bungalow and she remembered that the larger one was the Training Centre, Ruraich.

On the other side of the substantial lawn and garden area, well back from the loch, in two staggered rows and with plenty of space between each, were the nine separate lodge type chalets. She wondered which three were for the favoured or special visitors. Almost instantly, she felt a sense of unease. Had Gordon planned, albeit no doubt only for the start of her stay, that she should be given one these lodges? *Surely not*, she thought, and quickly reassured herself that any awkwardness or embarrassment she was feeling at the prospect of even being asked the question of which chalet she would prefer was unlikely to arise, as Mealag itself had a number of separate bedrooms if either she or Gordon wished to be coy. She was so absorbed in her thoughts and subsequent sense of relief at the conclusion she reached, that she let out a quite audible giggle. The harder she tried to quell her laugh, the more she chuckled.

"Are you going to share the joke?" asked Gordon, which made her laugh all the more.

"No, definitely not. At least not yet," she teased.

"Probably saw the reflection of that daft hat you're wearing Gordon." Sandy responded just as he drew the boat alongside a much larger landing stage than the one on the opposite shore. Made from heavy wooden railway sleepers and a thick reinforced steel frame that protruded thirty metres into the loch, this had been designed to provide a safe mooring for several boats. A shingle pathway traversed the lawn and directly into the complex where it divided into separate walkways to the chalets, lodge and beyond to the MacLeans bungalow and Ruraich.

The main house, Mealag Lodge, was far larger than Cindy had imagined and its name rather belied its impressive appearance. This was no ordinary A-frame type lodge of the type erected for the guests, but an extremely grand traditional stone house. Although of a unique design based upon more traditional shooting lodges, it had gables on three of its sides. The front of the house faced down and across the loch. The lounge had double floor-to-ceiling triple glazed patio doors and the room immediately above had another, slightly smaller, set of patio doors that led to a balustrade balcony which afforded a spectacular view. Cindy realised that this must be the main bedroom and her heart started to beat more rapidly. A thin stream of bluish smoke rose gently from one of the three chimneys and curled into the air. The closer she studied the house the more rooms she counted, and she wondered just why Gordon would need such a large home when he lived alone. As they passed a row of finely clipped miniature hedging to their left, Gordon said to Cindy that they would use the 'Tradesman's Entrance', as he jokingly put it.

This was located at the side of the house and the plain entrance door was in marked contrast to the large main front oak doors. She followed as Gordon entered a lobby area, slab-floored and brightly lit. Various jackets hung from pegs on the near wall and an assortment of muddy and well-worn boots and wellingtons were kept untidily on the floor, though a few remained in the purpose-built boot racks. A whole shelf had been devoted to a wide range of moccasin type house shoes of various colours and a few pairs of conventional slippers. A large double stainless steel sink was immediately below the window and an assortment of clean towels hung close by. In the corner opposite to the entrance door was a small bathroom where one could shower and change without firstly having to go through the main house. Various cupboards and shelves filled most of the remaining spaces on the sparkling tiled walls, apart from two large steel fireproof gun cabinets that were fixed close to an inner door that led through to the kitchen.

"This is the boot room, or lobby as we call it, so get your boots and jacket off and put them wherever you want, and take a pair of the moccasins – there's bound to be a size that fits!" said Gordon. "Then we'll go through and meet Margaret."

Margaret was in the kitchen and warmly welcomed Cindy giving her a hug and small kiss on the side of her cheek. "You must be frozen, my dear, the chill can get right through you on that water. Sit down and I'll get us all a hot drink and some soup."

As with most things that Margaret MacLean undertook, contained in her offer of immediate refreshment was a great deal of understatement. Piping hot drinks were served at the large, centrally placed, pine table and Cindy was offered the choice of two soups plus bread from any of the three types of crusty loaves. This was followed by a simple serving of various hams, cheeses and homemade chutneys.

Cindy looked around her and was now able to appreciate the size of the kitchen and the quality of the fitments. It had been fitted out with a range of appliances that might be seen in exclusive luxury hotels, and under Margaret MacLean's stewardship was clearly capable of providing excellent cuisine. Near to the lobby door, a large cooking range stood against one wall with a steaming kettle simmering gently on one of the hot plates. There seemed to be several ovens and cooking hobs sited in various places, and at differing heights, and numerous electronic gadgets were sitting atop the granite worktops. Behind two half-height swing-doors was a recessed area that contained the fridges, freezers and drinks chiller.

After twenty minutes, Cindy felt completely reinvigorated and was keen to see the rest of the house but Gordon suggested he show her around after she had unpacked and changed. She was unaware that Sandy had removed her cases until she asked for them and Gordon started to lead her out of the kitchen. As he escorted her, Gordon did mention the location of some of the important rooms though she simply could not assimilate them all. She did, though, make a mental note every time he said there was a bathroom. Cindy had learnt from experience in other people's homes how embarrassing it can be gently trying to open a door to see what's behind it, when looking urgently for a toilet. She followed Gordon upstairs and saw that her cases had been diplomatically put down on the corridor carpet and not outside any particular room. Gordon picked up the cases, one in each hand, and opened a door. He started to speak but a little hesitantly at first.

"If you're agreeable, Cindy, this is the main bedroom of the house but, er… ", his speech faltered and Cindy smiled widely – her ruddy cheeks, fresh from the warmth of the house and the bracing journey, glowing from the light streaming in the window.

"If you're going to say it's already occupied that will suit me fine," she paused, "as long as the occupant isn't likely to object to my cold feet."

She jested with him. Every woman he had ever known seemed to suffer from that problem, but he did not tell Cindy that. Instead he laughed, hugged her gently and gave her a long, soft kiss before bringing the cases into the bedroom and leaving Cindy to arrange her clothes in the wardrobes and drawers he suggested.

She went over to the window. The house faced northwest and the setting winter sun cast a pale yellow glow on Loch Quoich and the mountains on the far shore. The bedroom was almost as stunning as the view. It had been fitted out with the most amazingly expensive, tasteful furnishings and was huge. Original paintings, mainly of the Highlands, hung from the fabric-lined walls and the super king-size bed was sumptuously covered. Two separate dressing areas led to a sizeable en-suite bathroom. She noticed the deep bath and its futuristic taps, plus a matching double shower decorated with wonderfully designed tiles on the sides and splashback. Cindy lay back on the bed, her mind simply blown away by the day. It was everything and more she had dreamt about the night before at the hotel, and this was only the beginning.

Cindy changed into a different pair of jeans and sweater, then eagerly accepted Gordon's earlier offer of being shown around the house. In some rooms the art was contemporary whilst in others it was modern or fine. Watercolours and sculptures were tastefully placed to supplement the décor rather than overwhelm it. An estate agent would describe Mealag as possessing a 100% 'wow factor'. Superior design consultants had been employed on every aspect of the house, but it was clear that Gordon had not given them free reign and had been very much part of their team rather than a remote client. Most of the downstairs rooms showed aged, but gleaming dark wood polished floors onto which were laid an assortment of Persian carpets and rugs, whilst the upstairs bedrooms and Gordon's computer room had fully-fitted carpets. There were two dining areas in addition to the kitchen. One was clearly for more formal dinners and set at the side of the house. Not only could this room comfortably seat fourteen around the splendid oval table, but leading off was a sitting room where easy sofas and chairs allowed guests to relax comfortably between or after courses. The other was a small dining room, adjoining the kitchen / bar used to make snacks and serve refreshments for those guests enjoying the cinema or snooker facilities. On the way to the gym and pool, Gordon pointed out the laundry room but it was the large, indoor pool that took Cindy's breath away. She was over-awed, and was sorely tempted to strip off and dive in. The cinema room was housed adjacent to the gym but its neat, red chairs had been carefully stacked against the walls to permit a full-sized snooker table to occupy the centre of the floor.

"Have you ever played?" enquired Gordon.

"No, never, but I'd like to have a go another day, maybe?"

Gordon smiled. "I expect that can be arranged!"

Lighting throughout the house was controlled by a variety of sophisticated switches and there were electronic systems that also controlled the heating, in-built music and televisions. Data outlets had been installed in nearly every room, large or small. As she went around the house what really impressed Cindy was that despite its size and the obvious expensive furnishings throughout, it was still very much a home. No room, with the possible exception of the main dining room, was overly tidy to the point of not looking lived in. Ornaments were not always in the correct place and the normal household accumulation of miscellaneous items that get put aside here or there was much in evidence. This was not an impersonal baronial type home where she might be frightened to break anything or leave a dirty fingermark on the light switch. She could relax here.

They finished in the drawing room – a truly magnificent room which she estimated to be about thirty-five feet long and almost as wide. The large glass patio doors that she saw from the path did indeed afford a wonderful view of the loch, now darkened to almost black as the last light faded. An ornate white and grey stone fireplace was the central feature of the room and housed a well burning log fire, the flames providing a welcome, intimate feel to the room and which supplemented the background heating system supplied by the two ranges in the main kitchen. Double, eighty-piece crystal chandeliers hung from the ceiling but were not switched on. Obscured side lighting glowed discreetly upon the walls which coupled with the lights illuminating the various pictures provided a soft ambient glow. A Christmas tree with a few presents already placed underneath its spreading branches and lit by numerous single white miniature bulbs was placed in a corner. To Cindy it was like being in Wonderland, and she struggled to really believe this was really happening to her. It was just so perfect.

Their tour over they sat on one of the large sofas and started to talk about Mealag and Gordon's background. He added little to what she already knew. He started out writing various games programs but his big break came when he wrote a program based around owning an imaginary oil tanker. Evidently, the object was to send the tanker to various ports, buying and selling oil and overcoming hazards on the way and over time to enlarge ownership from a single vessel to a fleet of twenty tankers or other cargo carrying vessels. The program was quite sophisticated as to how the end user had to use the information held at the various ports and thereby select the most economical routes to the ports and what to purchase or sell. The speed of the ships and associated fuel running costs had to be factored in as well as the risks of sailing the slowest yet safest route versus the quickest more dangerous route. Various sub routines about the company's accounts and profitability added to the game's complexity. Random perils like storms or engine failure would occur to add to the game's authenticity. The program was so successful it resulted in Gordon being approached by an executive of a real international oil company who astounded Gordon by telling him that the program was more sophisticated than anything they had on their main frame computers, and invited

Gordon to join his company and head up a team to write bespoke programs for use on their new PC's. Gordon's career took off, and within a short time, had his own business and a large team of analysts and programmers working for him on many varied commercial applications.

As the company expanded, he found he was spending so much of his time running it that he was not able to continue with the aspect he most cherished – namely that of programming. Neither was he able to simply enjoy the opportunities afforded by his wealth. Leisure time was minimal, travel was always related to his work, and living out of a suitcase as he journeyed between continental hotels seemed a total waste of his young life, so he disposed of his shares and went into property development in a big way. Again, he built up a multi-million pound organisation and had just sold it for the same reasons as he sold the software company, plus he feared a collapse in property values. He told Cindy he had retained ownership of a number of overseas and UK properties as part of the portfolio within his own private investment company, but otherwise he was now, as he put it, unemployed. This was not strictly true as he explained that the Mealag Estate was, of course, a business and operated on broadly commercial lines, but he could afford to be a little more lenient than his normal strict assessment of businesses performance when studying the financial statements of the estate. He also now had time to indulge, just for fun, in playing around on his various computers.

21

Later that evening, Margaret prepared a meal for them both and then left for the night returning to her bungalow. Cindy and Gordon spent an enjoyable evening relating stories to each other of their past and of their hobbies and could not stop looking and smiling at each other. They were both very happy and having finished their last glass of wine, Cindy jumped up from the sofa.

"Race you to the shower" she shouted excitedly, and started to run out of the door along the hallway and up the stairs to the bedroom, chased by Gordon.

As Cindy entered the room, she kicked off her moccasins and turned to face him. He took her in his arms and kissed her whilst slipping his hands down her back. She lifted her arms so they were outstretched above her head and Gordon gently removed her sweater and let it fall to the floor. Repeatedly kissing her quickly and softly on her face, neck and lips much as a butterfly flutters from flower to flower, his fingers skilfully detached the small fastenings of her bra. He bent down and kissed first her left nipple then her right, and felt them instantly swell under his tongue. His hands again searched her back, sending shivers of delight through her spine, and he pulled her against him so she would feel the urgency within him. She undid the zip on her jeans and removed the rest of her clothes in one movement, whilst Gordon quickly undressed himself. As she lay on the bed she whispered to him to come closer, and put her arms around him as he lay beside her.

Her mind was filled with the images and sounds of the day. Glencoe, the dam, the echoing sound of the outboard, the rush of water from the boat's bow wave; one after the other, over and over, and over again, the excitements of the day came back to her until her mind closed out. She was no longer the independent woman she thought she was. She needed Gordon and needed him now. She turned herself over to lie on top of him and began by covering his face with short, strong kisses, gradually working her way down his body. She could feel his flesh jerk as she reached between his legs and opened her mouth, taking him in. He moaned and squeezed her breast but could do little more. The gentle rhythmic pressure of her lips and tongue were now acting in unison with her hands, making him powerless to move except in reflex movements of his hips. He tried to stop her, to turn her over on her back, but the exquisite delight at what she was doing to him was so intense, he stopped resisting and raised his hips higher to urge her to take more of him into her mouth. The harder and faster she sucked, the louder he groaned until he exploded in a series of uncontrolled spasms. She slowly released the grip of her lips and lay beside him, both panting rapidly. Gordon had exceeded any previously experienced delights at oral sex and he stared into her eyes, almost disbelieving at what he had just enjoyed. Cindy noticed his slightly quizzical look.

"Before you ask. No, that's not something I'm used to either!" she laughed. "Anyway, I'm going to have that shower and then you can get your own back," she giggled as she ran naked into the cubicle. They showered together, enjoying the sensuousness of touching their warm, wet bodies and lingered over their frequent embraces under the soft spray. They were drying each other when Gordon suddenly put his arms around Cindy, lifted her up and carried her to the bed where he dropped her onto her back. She smiled and held out her arms but he ignored them.

He knelt between her legs and gently brushed his hand over the soft mound of hair, whilst licking her nipples. They were full now, hard and erect, sensitive to any touch and he cupped her firm, round breasts to his lips. Whilst not large they felt full and heavy and he delighted in their smoothness. Cindy began to moan softly, and her thighs were straining to engulf him. He lowered his head. His eager tongue first traced the outline of her opening then, probing, he gradually increased the pressure until her slit opened. He pushed his tongue just slightly deeper into her, and with short rapid movements of his tongue, her moans grew louder. She was breathing heavily, her legs straining to be let loose, and as he sucked at her pearl he could feel her hips raise.

"Harder, harder" she cried out a few times, but Gordon did not obey. "Now, Gordon, now!" but he wanted them both to wait, to heighten still further their shared ecstasy. He slowly eased the pressure of his lips and just flicked his tongue occasionally as he began to remove his face from between her legs.

"Don't stop. Don't stop now. Please Gordon, don't stop," she pleaded but again he ignored her.

Instead of entering her he took her hands in his and placed them around his engorged penis. Then he knelt slightly forward until its tip just touched her opening. He felt her straining to take him in. She urgently wanted him now and she pulled his cock hard against her jerking it back and forth, round and round, in an effort to satisfy her desperate hunger.

"Gordon, come nearer, nearer" but every time she pushed herself onto him he backed away slightly. He knew she was coming now, deep, slow and uncontrollably. Her body had taken her over completely and was writhing up and down, synchronised to the rhythm of her rubbing him against her. A wave came across her and she yelled for him to give her what she wanted. She was still yelling when she climaxed and as she did Gordon squeezed her nipples a little harder.

"You bastard, you bloody bastard," Cindy panted, swearing in-between taking breaths.

They continued to gently caress each other for several minutes, and when Gordon felt they had both recovered sufficiently he whispered, "Now, Cindy, this is for real."

He entered her. As he slid easily into her wetness, she gave a long sigh feeling his warmth and size. He nestled his mouth over her right nipple sucking hard. It was more than she could bear.

"No, no, I can't, it's too soon" but it was a half-hearted protest. Anyway Gordon wasn't listening. He slowly increased his thrusts until she was wide open with her legs wrapped around his back. He moved carefully and deliberately, waiting for the reflex responses that would tell him she was ready. Slowly, they came. He felt the contractions deep within her, clenching his penis and then releasing it in firm spasms. He quickened and her clenches grew stronger, sending her mind uncontrollably wild with delight. This was no act. It was for real, as he had said, and she was about to enter the unknown, out of control and screaming loudly, "Oh, my God! Fuck me! *Fuck me now, you bastard!*"

Her spasms were rapid, her breathing loud and heavy. He climaxed with her, filling her with his warm liquid as their mouths became united.

Gordon slowly rolled away, breathing hard next to her. Tears filled her eyes and she started to cry. Gordon understood and let her relieve the emotion of the moment as best she could. He wiped away the tears with his hand and held her in his arms.

"Thank you," he said simply. "Thank you for being so wonderful."

They lay together, not moving, for several minutes, and it was Cindy that eventually broke the silence after her senses had returned to something approaching normality – though she could hardly speak through her own breathlessness.

"I'm really sorry," she said. "I have never, never cried out like that. I… er… don't. It just isn't me. I thought it was made up for movies," she laughed.

"Apparently not always," said Gordon drily. "Anyway don't apologise, you were fantastic. All I want is for you to be happy."

They both woke early on Christmas Day and Cindy immediately went to the window and looked out at the loch. She had hoped it might be snowing but was disappointed. Low white clouds were being driven across the sides of the mountains, whose tops had disappeared under a heavy, leaden sky that was reflected in the grey colour of the loch. It was a complete contrast to when she arrived but was still attractive to her. Gordon joined her and remarked that rarely were two days the same. The vista was ever changing with the seasons and there was always something different to see. The varying light and cloud formations resulted in great changes to the appearance of the landscape, not just daily, but often hour to hour or even minute by minute. He pointed out some deer, just below the snow line, herded together for warmth behind a knoll on the mountain opposite, and the circling buzzard high above them. Cindy was spellbound. At that moment she thought it magical, like a fairy story come true, and she remained fixated on the view until Gordon had dressed and asked Cindy what she would like for breakfast. She stepped back from the window and put her arms around him.

"You" she whispered, looking up at his smiling face.

An hour later, they both made their way downstairs. Mrs MacLean had already prepared the Christmas venison, and after a quick bite Gordon showed Cindy around the grounds. As was his custom Gordon had invited his estate workers and families to pre-lunch drinks in Ruraich on Christmas morning, and at eleven o'clock a slightly nervous Cindy was introduced to them as they arrived. It was not long before she found herself chatting away and acting the perfect hostess. She made sure that everyone's glass was refilled and that a steady supply of the various canopies prepared by Margaret was proffered whenever she saw that someone's plate was empty.

After everybody had left, Cindy and Gordon returned to the house and changed for a very late Christmas lunch. Margaret had beautifully prepared the grand dining table and the four of them spent most of the afternoon enjoying the splendid roast dinner and sumptuous food.

"I think you excelled yourself this year, Margaret" her husband's words only slightly slurred as he finished his second cognac.

"Indeed, Margaret," said Gordon. "I echo what Sandy says. It was tremendous. Thank you."

"Ach, it was nothing, a real pleasure it was. Visitors are rare enough here and to have someone at Christmas time… well, what better incentive could I have?"

Before anyone could respond Margaret stood up. "Come along Sandy, time for us to go. Cindy and Gordon will be wanting some time on their own now. Just leave everything where it is Gordon, I'll see to it in the morning."

She turned to Cindy and winked, causing Cindy's already ruddy cheeks to redden still further.

Some considerable while elapsed as Gordon and Cindy relaxed in the drawing room leisurely unwrapping their presents. He was thrilled with his cufflinks and she received several gifts including an expensive diamond necklace. It suited her perfectly and she wore it that evening. Whilst they were both relaxing in front of the large open fire piled high with a mixture of wood and peat, the telephone rang and Gordon answered it in the hall. Several minutes later he returned.

"That" he said, "was a good friend of mine, Dean Assiter, from Washington, with his Christmas greetings. He mentioned that he's coming over in September for some meeting in London and I've invited him to stay on if he can for a week or so and come here. He thought it a great idea and will try to clear it with his security people. If it all works out OK he'll bring Paulette."

"Security people? Paulette? Is that the Assiter who is the US Secretary of State?" enquired Cindy, the name familiar from her Downing Street days.

"The very same. I met him years ago at an international symposium aimed at addressing the technology imbalance between the rich and poor countries, and remained friends ever since. Good guy. Not a hot head and, unusually for a US politician, is not in Washington for what he can get out of it."

Cindy was impressed.

"You'll like Paulette. Only met her once, but she's a hell of an attractive woman. Ex French model and twenty years or so younger than Dean, who I think has just turned fifty. I'm not sure if Paulette came before his divorce or after. She likes the outdoor life so it should be a great time. It will be something for us to look forward to."

"You'll still want me in September, will you? You might have found someone else by then." Cindy cheekily retorted.

"I doubt that, but here's hoping!" he laughed, and Cindy picked up a cushion and hit him with it. For a few minutes they rained mock blows on each other as he picked up his own cushion to retaliate, before lying back, laughing.

After a few moments Gordon sounded a lot more serious. "You know, I admire guys like Dean. Since 9/11, they live under an almost permanent threat and I believe the pressure on them can be quite intense at times. I do hope his security people don't veto the trip. Probably wise if you don't mention his visit to anyone. Even his personal calls go through a scrambler."

Gordon was right to have been concerned. Within a month,

both the United States and the British security people had surveyed Mealag, vetted the staff and interviewed Gordon himself. As far as he could ascertain from the little he gleaned from his own interview, Gordon was reasonably sure that everything from a security aspect was deemed satisfactory, and that in February, Assiter or an aide would ring to confirm.

22

The weather had changed again on Boxing Day morning, and thin sunshine danced over the almost still water of the loch. Looking out of the bedroom window, Cindy noticed the deer had gone, and the buzzard was nowhere to be seen but a thin layer of fresh snow had fallen overnight onto the mountains and a heavy ground frost glistened on the lawn in front of the house – though the edges of the loch were free of ice. Later that morning, suitably attired for the bitterly cold conditions, the two set out and walked towards the dam wall. As they strolled past what appeared to be a small bay, Gordon remarked, "It will get a lot colder in a month or so. I've known the loch to freeze over in the shallower parts, especially during January and February." He then he pointed to the crusted, cracked and dry surface of the ground ahead. "Its very tempting to walk straight across and take the direct route to the dam, but never do it. Despite appearances, the peat surface is not hard and will give way at some point."

"How deep is the peat?" enquired Cindy

"I've no idea, but deep enough to drown anyone. The close proximity of the dam means this shore is very steeply shelved and the peat, which before the dam was reasonably firm, now remains totally sodden. Shortly after I moved here, and knowing nothing about this particular area, I got trapped in the bog and had it not been for a passing angler giving me a rod to hold onto, I might never have made it out. As it was I lost both boots and socks, but it was a frightening experience."

Cindy laughed. "I'm sure it was, I'm sorry I shouldn't laugh but the thought of you being hauled out of the mucky water, minus your boots and socks, is quite amusing. Bit like that executive you told me about!"

Access to the pathway above the dam was achieved by climbing over a metre-high, padlocked gate which, whilst of mild inconvenience to anglers and walkers, seemed to be locked only as a token of establishing the authority of the Hydro-Board and to prevent access by motor cycles. Iron railings, the same height as the gate, bounded each side of the footway to prevent anyone from accidentally falling down either slope of the dam wall, an occurrence that would result in almost certain death from being plunged into the deep, cold water or from hitting the rearward, rock slope of the dam and being propelled into the numerous boulders haphazardly strewn about at ground level. At the centre of the path, they stopped opposite the unattractive valve tower and Gordon started to explain some details about the dam.

"Firstly, the dam is over 1000 feet long, over 100 feet high and its base is almost 350 feet thick. Construction commenced in 1955, at a time of economic austerity, and completed in 1962. The method of building was pretty simple in that crushed rock rubble was compacted around a concrete core. It was a cheap, but strong, method. All the rock required was on site, but it was essential to ensure that no water could ever flow over the top as this would dangerously weaken the structure. If it did the water would permeate through from the unprotected rear of the dam, disturbing and eventually collapsing the integrity of the crushed rubble core, so a side slipway was built for those moments when the loch water exceeded its maximum design height." He paused briefly to allow Cindy to absorb what he had said then raised his arm and pointed.

"Can you see that the loch-facing slope is completely covered with concrete slabs which have been protected from the elements by thick bituminised paint? Each of those is a massive twenty feet square and twelve inches thick. They act as a membrane to prevent any water seeping into the rock-fill core of the dam which would be disastrous. If the dam hadn't been built with a slipway the rear slope would have needed slabs as well, but the slipway was a far, far cheaper option, especially back then." Cindy looked over the railings at the rear slope, the rough rock face clearly visible.

"I see now what you mean" she said returning to him. "So what's that, out in the water? Looks like some lookout post."

"The valve tower. It is a vitally important part of the functioning of the dam as it controls the flow of water through the dam's own turbine, which is right below where we are standing now, and it also ensures that sufficient water flows to other lochs below. There has to be a controlled flow of water at all times."

"How much water is there in the loch?" Cindy asked

"Everyone asks me that, and I really don't know! It seems difficult to find two reliable sources that agree. I think that's due to the irregular shape and depth of the loch – it has several tongues leading from it that penetrate deep into the mountains – so I suspect calculations would only ever be very approximate. I've heard mention of about 3800 million gallons, but that could be considerably out either way. What is known is that it provides over sixty thousand horsepower of energy from two 22 megawatt alternators; one housed inside the dam and the other at the power station further down the glen towards Corach. You would have seen that on your way here."

Cindy nodded.

"From the dam, water is led to the power station by a low-pressure tunnel, almost 13,000 feet long, and horseshoe in section, with a diameter of eleven and a half feet. There are no side stream intakes. The low-pressure tunnel terminates at the base of a surge chamber. From the base of the chamber, the water plummets down a vertical high-pressure shaft, 158ft deep and thence into a high-pressure tunnel about 2200ft long, to the main inlet valve. There are one or two more bits and pieces but essentially that's it."

"My word, Gordon, you're like a bloody encyclopaedia! What does all that mean in plain English?" Cindy smiled as she mildly reproved him.

"Sorry, I didn't mean it to sound like that. Virtually all the visitors that come here ask the same questions and over time I think I've learnt most of the answers off by heart, so I suppose it does sound a bit technical." Gordon explained.

"No need to apologise, silly! I was only pulling your leg. I am really interested. Do go on, please, it sounds fascinating."

Gordon looked at her and smiled. "As you insist! In simple terms the pressure of the water in the loch is sufficient to power the turbine built into the dam, but to spin the turbine down the road the water has to be carried by tunnel. It travels firstly along a long, low-pressure tunnel gradually increasing speed and then physically drops down into a high pressure shaft and tunnel through which it flows at an enormous rate thereby creating sufficient pressure at the turbine head. As the water pressure can fluctuate dangerously high, threatening to explode the tunnel itself, a surge shaft and expansion chamber are incorporated in the design to act as a sort of relief valve. Come on! Let's take a look at that now and you'll appreciate what I'm saying. We'll get to it by taking the easier route and walk along the road first, but the shortest route of course is straight over the hill in front of us. We'll come back that way."

They took a quick look at the intake housing and concrete slipway as they ambled across the dam wall to the north gate, then crossed onto the road and walked just over a mile before turning off and began to climb a small, almost unnoticeable, track. It was hard going as the angle was steep, but at the top the land had been levelled and facing them was a circular enclosure of steel pronged railings about forty feet in diameter. Standing on its own, atop a grass and rock-covered hill, the gleaming protective railings looked quite incongruous. Cindy was struck by how very quiet it was, and how magnificent the loch below them appeared. From this vantage point, she gained a greater appreciation of its size. To the west the loch disappeared into the distance towards Kinloch Hourn. To the east she could see far down the glen to the Quoich power station, then the small loch created by the river Garry and beyond to the much larger Loch Garry itself. Gordon explained how the waters of Quoich were used for the generation of hydro-electricity several times over. Firstly at Quoich dam and the power station, then at the Garry power station and from there into the string of lochs that formed the Caledonian Canal linking Inverness on the east coast to Fort William on the west. Cindy peered over the circle of railings, not sure what to expect. She was surprised to see a large black hole filling the entire enclosure, but as her eyes became accustomed to the darkness she could make out that the diameter lessened considerably about half way down into a much smaller shaft.

"What's that?" she asked.

"The top area is the expansion chamber and this sits above the surge shaft. If you look really carefully and adjust your eyes, at the bottom you can see small waves as the water passes through to the high-pressure shaft. Remember what I said at the dam about the surge chamber being needed to relieve pressure as the main inlet is opened and water rushes into the tunnel. If it wasn't for this expansion chamber, there would be a terrific, pressurised explosion of water within the tunnels. It would be really dangerous. When the pressure builds water is ejected here and despite the surge chamber a huge spout of water can still be thrown out high into the air at times."

Cindy was fascinated. Other than the steel guard rail fence that encircled the chamber, the huge hole was entirely open – as of course it had to be. On the way back to the dam, halfway down the mountain, Gordon pointed out the entrance to a maintenance tunnel that led to the surge shaft. Affixed to the heavy wrought iron gate securing the access was a large 'DANGER' safety notice, and a heavy chain and padlock completed the security.

"You can't see anything in there, its pitch black, and is only used occasionally when the surge shaft needs inspecting. I can't recall ever noticing anyone doing that, but I suppose they do."

Slowly, they made their way back to Mealag and enjoyed the hot lunch that Margaret had ready. Cindy was still rather dazed by the whole experience. It was not only the size of the dam and the grandness of the scenery that made it difficult for her to think clearly, she was beginning to wonder where all this was leading. Would she, did she, have a future with Gordon and if so could she spend a large part of it here, in this remote wilderness? She was starting to hope that the answer might be yes to all the questions, and her feelings were given added impetus when the following day she made a point of staying indoors whilst Gordon and Sandy took a 4x4 and drove into the estate to help the workers repair a fence.

Cindy had been telling Margaret about her background and early life and Margaret had been narrating stories of her childhood on a Hebridean island. They had been chatting for a while when Margaret put down her preparation knife and turned to Cindy. "You mean a lot to Gordon. Did you know?" It was asked more in the nature of an enquiry than a statement.

"Do I? Do I really?"

"Aye, young lady, you most definitely do. You must be very special. You are the first lady friend he has ever brought to Mealag – not that I think he has had many anyway, don't misunderstand me. But he obviously could do pretty much what he wants, yet I have never known him so excited since he met you. He spent one evening telling us both about your experience after that awful bombing on the train, and every time he came back from lunching with you he has been keen to talk to us about it. His folks have died, you know, so I think he views me as a sort of surrogate mother!" She laughed as she said it but before Cindy could say anything she continued, "I suppose I am in a sort of way, I wouldn't like to see him hurt by anyone."

Cindy understood the message. "I shan't hurt him, Margaret, he means a lot to me too. In fact, I am a bit overwhelmed by what's happening."

"That'll be fine then, I'm sure you will both be very happy. Gordon is a good man."

When Cindy later recounted the conversation in her head she realised that she had virtually sealed her future and answered the questions of the previous day. There was only one problem. She was married to Alan and he still loved her.

The remaining days passed quickly with Gordon showing Cindy around the estate and the area generally. A number of vehicles were kept at or nearby to Mealag itself, mainly agricultural but also a very powerful 4x4, and one morning he drove Cindy on the narrow track that wound through the mountains behind Mealag until it reached the single carriageway C-class road bordering another large loch, Loch Arkaig. They drove along the water's edge, eventually leaving the loch and road behind them, travelling cross-country heading northwards towards the sea. After a few more miles, it seemed to Cindy as if they were literally in the middle of a wilderness where no one had ventured, probably for years. It was indeed very remote. The ground became rougher until after three miles Gordon turned right and took Cindy through the spectacular mountains of Knoydart, where the barely passable trail swung round and linked up to the Mealag track that they had first ventured out onto in the morning. On another day, they crossed the dam and picked up Gordon's Range Rover from the garages opposite and undertook the much more comfortable drive to Mallaig, a picturesque fishing port, passing Glenfinnan and its famous viaduct and memorial. They enjoyed every moment together, whether getting battered by ferocious winds and thoroughly soaked by torrential rain, or simply enjoying a quiet drink cuddled up to each other on the sofa after a tiring walk. One luxury Cindy particularly enjoyed was coming back to Mealag after an exhausting day and going straight to the swimming pool; stripping off completely naked, showering and then relaxing in the warm water. Gordon sometimes joined her. When he did, they usually spent longer in the shower room than the pool.

As New Year approached it snowed heavily, once again utterly transforming the grandeur of the mountains. The whiteness was dazzlingly bright and Cindy needed to borrow some dark glasses to study the loch. The branches of the pine and spruce were weighed down, and every now and then some snow would fall off, leaving a trail of perfectly white dust lingering in the cold air before it slowly and silently settled on the crystal carpet. In whichever direction she looked, Cindy felt she was viewing her very own picture postcard, and the emotion caused her eyes to moisten as she was overcome by the almost magical setting she was experiencing. If she did not know before why Gordon so loved Mealag, she did now.

Hogmanay was a riot of fun and laughter. The estate workers were again invited, and after a sufficient quantity of whisky and food had been consumed, an impromptu ceilidh started. Cindy was amazed at how talented some of the workers were. One wrote wonderful romantic poetry and spoke it beautifully. Several played the fiddle and the lively music of marches, jigs and airs filled the rooms of the large house as they danced away the hours. A particularly fine violinist gave a long virtuoso performance, listened to in silence by the admiring throng, of both Highland reels and the music of Gow and Scott Skinner of the Scottish east coast. Others simply told folk stories with yet another man being such a good comic and mimic many in his audience found difficulty remaining on their chairs. Margaret had a fine singing voice which was perfect for the poignant, haunting melodies of the Hebridean folk songs she sang, accompanied at times by the violinist. Whenever there was a pause and everyone was resting, Gordon would play recordings of Count John McCormack, the world famous Irish tenor who was much revered in the Highlands for his renderings of traditional ballads. It was nearly 5am before people started to crash out on the floor. A few hours later however, and after cooking some bacon butties for themselves, they started up again.

Cindy had so enjoyed her stay that she hardly noticed how quickly the days passed, but all too soon it was time to goodbye. Tears filled her eyes. The night before, she and Gordon had made love after talking quite seriously to each other for the first time. They both wanted the relationship to continue and hoped they might be able to share their lives together, but Gordon emphasised that any divorce must be a decision for Cindy alone; it was not for him to influence her. He also insisted that she should not make any commitments now but to wait until she had returned home, spending some time away from him to pause and reflect upon her situation, before deciding and planning her future. Whatever she chose to do, Gordon promised she would always have his love and support.

23

There was a distinct chill in the atmosphere that had little to do with the weather when Cindy arrived back at Red Gables. She had been away longer than had Alan and on the first weekend back together, he hardly spoke to her. He was no longer interested in her mystery holiday and chose to ignore the subject altogether. This wasn't because he had experienced a wonderful time himself. He had enjoyed the break and the companionship and delights of Anna's body, but they both knew that nothing more permanent would come of it. It had suited Anna and given her back the confidence she needed to perhaps now go on and find a new long-term partner or husband. Alan had managed to forget his mounting pressures at the bank and at home, but he was still finding it very hard to come to terms with the probable break-up with Cindy. She had of course asked after Alan's parents and was quite shocked when he explained where he spent Christmas, though he was careful not to mention Anna, and Cindy decided that if she asked more questions it might prompt Alan to ask a few of his own. A mutually observed silence on detail suited them both. They spent the next few weeks much as they had before Christmas. Cindy managed to see Gordon for lunch a couple of times and continued her gym, gun dogs and other activities. She became increasingly convinced that she needed to be with Gordon but divorce seemed such a drastic solution that she had not yet sought any legal advice. To his credit Gordon had not raised again the subject of her living with him – keeping firmly to what he had said at Mealag that it was entirely a matter for her.

Cindy was not even cheered, and only cursorily complimentary, when an excited Alan phoned her one evening to say that one of his personal deals had really paid off. Several years ago, he had purchased a large volume of shares in some far eastern venture and the company, whose shares had not been exciting, recently leapt in value. No one quite knew why at first, but it emerged that a

Chinese conglomerate were interested in taking the company over on the expectation that some oil rights the firm held would yield big profits. He had made over a million pounds and was jubilant. If anything, his new found affluence made him increasingly resentful of Cindy's behaviour. Despite what Donaldson had said about there being no evidence of an affair, he was convinced that Cindy was not just going through some weird "woman thing" as colleagues suggested. The more hurt and resentful he became at her behaviour and lack of affection towards him, the more determined he was that she would not get half the combined assets if they divorced, especially now he had invested the Chinese money in some rather obscure offshore accounts. He had seen his solicitor again and she explained that both parties would have to declare their assets and also make a declaration as to whether they intended to live with anyone.

"Most people say 'no' to that, whatever their real intentions," she explained. "After all, anyone can change their mind after six months or so and the courts are not likely to disturb an agreed settlement if one party is then financially better off than another."

Cindy was denying an affair anyway, and still lived at Red Gables and stayed there at night. Not only had Donaldson confirmed that, but Alan had made a point every now and then of driving to Stillwood midweek and arriving late, around midnight, half hoping to find the house empty. Cindy had always been home.

★ ★ ★

In early March Cindy received a telephone call from her friend Peter who had agreed to provide her cover story at Christmas. He wanted to meet her and suggested either London or Stillwood. It was highly unusual for Peter to suggest meeting Cindy alone, and even more strange to offer to visit Red Gables. Normally he would invite people to parties or see them with his boyfriend Stephen, and a perplexed Cindy wondered what he wanted. She chose to meet at Red Gables, but lunch at the nearby excellent Black Pheasant Hotel. Peter arrived, immaculately dressed in a grey, but heavily pinstriped suit, a rather flamboyant slightly patterned pale green shirt and a quite outrageous scarlet tie that matched the handkerchief which flopped from the top breast pocket of his suit. Shiny black shoes, a long furled umbrella in his right hand and a large bouquet of flowers in the other, completed his appearance.

"My dear, how simply lovely to see you," he gushed as he offered Cindy the flowers and turned his cheek for her to kiss, which she did before hugging him and inviting him in. They chatted for almost an hour about old times and colleagues, and not once did Peter ask about Christmas. In fact, he didn't ask about anything that would justify him travelling especially to see her, and she was becoming more curious as to why he had called her. As they left in his car for the hotel, Cindy felt she had to ask the purpose of his visit, but Peter was in full flow reciting a very crude joke he had heard recently in a London gay bar. Although it made Cindy blush, she had to admit it was very funny and she made a point of trying to remember it as she knew of a couple of her female friends who would certainly approve of its vulgarity.

The joke distracted her thoughts and soon they sat inside the sumptuous restaurant and were ordering lunch when Peter turned to her.

"Did you know my darling that you have appeared on our radar, so to speak?" Peter asked innocently.

"No, what are you talking about Peter? A rather bewildered Cindy replied.

"Gordon Truscott is a name that's familiar to you I believe?" He slightly raised his eyebrows as he started to talk more quietly, almost in a hushed voice but with more formality.

"What is this about Peter? How do you know Gordon?" As she asked the question, it dawned on her that Peter was now at the Foreign Office and this must have something to do with Assiter's visit to Mealag in September.

"Oh, wait a minute. I think I know. The American visitor." Cindy had not spent a large part of her working life in the Cabinet Office not to be discreet with names when it was called for, and the hotel was a very public place.

"Indeed, my dear. He's looking forward to it very much I'm told. We don't want any, shall we say, mishaps or accidents, so there has been an exhaustive threat analysis, you know the sort of thing, and of course your name has come up."

"How the bloody hell was that, Peter? I've told no one of Gordon."

"Well darling, it is our job to know these things, or if not ours those scruffy boys who occupy that ghastly building over the river. They really needn't have bothered to tail Truscott since the American told his people you and he would likely be around in September."

"What tail, what have you been up to and why are you telling me all this?" Cindy was becoming concerned, not because she had something to hide, but because of all the apparent mystery.

"OK, Cindy. Sit back and I'll tell you, but I emphasise I am here as a friend, and only as a friend, and we have not spoken. Understood?" Cindy nodded.

"The American visitor carries a certain profile, shall we say, where it would not be in the UK interest if anything befell him or he was unhappy with his visits here, including his personal trips. His own country too, has similar concerns for his well-being, probably more than we do, and always insist on having some of their people close by, even when the American is on holiday. When we were told of his September trip, we of course carried out the necessary checks. Truscott is pretty familiar to us, tycoons get noticed and a distant eye kept on what they are up to. His people on the estate all appear to be exactly what they are, good honest folk and all that. Truscott though has money – lots of it – that could give him potential influence if he was minded to use it for purposes of which we may disapprove. Ally that to his contacts across the world and you can see, my dear, how careful poor Peter must be as I have to sign off this recreational visit."

"Yes, I understand all that, Peter, but where do I fit in and why have lunch with me today?" Cindy was struggling to understand.

"Oh, don't be so impatient, you naughty girl," Peter said in mock reproof of her interruption. He could be quite incorrigible at times. "Before passing over their report the scruffy lot decided to make certain of one or two things, and that entailed them undertaking rather a lot of covert surveillance. The photos were very good though."

"Peter, I know we are in a public place but frankly you are talking in riddles. What exactly are trying to tell me? What have you found out?" Cindy's heart was racing and her mind in a spin. "If Five had found out that Gordon was up to no good, you sure as hell would not come and tell me. So what is going on?" Her voice slightly raised, Cindy was becoming mildly irate. She suddenly recalled her lunch companion's reference to photos and, more nervously, asked "And what photos, Peter? What or who are they of? Can you tell me?"

Peter Knowles replied smoothly in a manner totally befitting his Foreign Office status. "My dear, you're in them and, as always, looking marvellous. Remember when you picked up your friend at Oxford Station last month and after lunch went to that rather chic hotel round the back of Magdelene College for the afternoon? Also, that trip out to Meckerton to have lunch with some lady friends before you spent the afternoon at the Cheltenham Hilton where Truscott was staying?" He stopped allowing several seconds of silence to pass between them.

Cindy did not know what to say. She had no idea she was being followed, let alone photographed going into hotels with Gordon. In an instant Peter had just turned loving and precious moments into something that seemed rather tawdry. She started to cry. Peter immediately offered her his handkerchief which she used to lightly dab away the tears.

"You are real bastards, you know. She hesitated fearing the answer to her next question. "There weren't... weren't any pictures of us in the hotel, were there?"

"No, no, my dear you have it all wrong. I'm here personally – when I shouldn't be – as your friend, as there is more that you need to know. The British security surveillance people are really quite good you know, and they noticed that the good guys were not the only ones following you to Meckerton and then onto Cheltenham. A small blue car, driven by a pretty fit looking chap, was also on your tail so to speak". He smiled benignly. "You had already been flagged up by the system of course, so everyone knew who you were, and your security clearance given your previous job, but they still had to be sure. All our people wanted was to make certain that it was Truscott you met. He had been followed all the way down the motorway from bloody Scotland, would you believe! The gooks on your tail naturally took a note of the blue car details, hire car it was, and rented by a bloke named Donaldson. Works with your husband, we think his driver, so presumably you know him?"

Cindy sighed deeply. "Yes. He's Alan's driver and anything else Alan wants him to be."

"I'm here to tell you all this as I deduced, I guess accurately, that Truscott was the reason for your call to me at Christmas, and as a friend thought you may like to know about Donaldson. I was slightly worried until he was checked out that he may have been some kind of stalker, but of course it would have been difficult for me to make a complaint to the local police without a lot of questions being asked."

"I'm very grateful, Peter, so sorry about losing it a bit earlier."

"No matter, my dear, but please do be careful. I'm not sure what Donaldson is up to. When the boys realised he was tailing you they asked Uniform to stop him for a few moments on some excuse just to see what he did afterwards. They pulled him in at Cleeve. By the time he got going again, he turned round and went back home which strongly suggests he had no idea where Truscott was, nor if you were going to see him. Actually, of course, he may not even know of him."

"Yes, I see" said Cindy, still thinking of Donaldson tailing her and wondering if he was doing so on Alan's instructions or, more sinister, on his own account.

"Actually, I'm rather surprised at your husband employing Donaldson. Technically he's clean but he's only just the right side of that line, so to speak. He was always in trouble at the various schools he attended, got into bar brawls and such as a teenager, and then joined the army. They appeared to have some doubt about his conduct but nothing was ever proven and after that he joined the rather dubious profession of a mercenary, and so on. Not the sort of chap I would expect Alan to have as a chauffeur."

"Yes, Peter, I know most of that. I find him odious; in fact the bloke gives me the creeps."

They had finished their lunch and were enjoying the coffee by the time Peter had finished explaining the reason for his visit. He looked across at Cindy and said, "Very slight change of subject – are you happy?"

"Oh yes Peter, very much so, but obviously there is a lot I need to start sorting out and Alan is hurting. He doesn't know of Gordon, or that anyone else is in my life, so cannot understand why things have gone wrong between us."

"My dear, yes, I do sympathise. It must be awful for you both. We all strive for absolute pleasure, but if we get close to it I find it invariably results in pain to others, usually those that love and cherish us. Life can be so cruel at times. I knew I couldn't do without Stephen from the moment our eyes met, but his partner at that time was so mortified. Simply dreadful, you know. My advice for what it is worth is to sort things out quickly and don't look back. Less pain all round in the long run. Anyway, back to business. The Scottish place itself is almost a natural fortress so few problems there when the American drops by, but for our lads' sake I do hope he doesn't like mountaineering! I hope you all have a wonderfully happy time together. Do let me know, won't you darling?"

Cindy, of course, agreed. Peter refused the offer of more drinks when they arrived back at Red Gables and stayed in his car. As he lowered the electric window, he called for Cindy to come closer.

"One final thing, my dear. In September, there will be several of our people and some of the Americans nearby. Almost certainly he will have a couple of his Special Forces chaps by his side most of the time, possibly in and around the house. I just thought you may like to know that you will not be on your own."

Cindy thanked Peter again and waved him goodbye. She went upstairs and sat on her bed prior to changing. She stared up at the ceiling, trying to make sense of the morning and thinking hard about what the future had in store for a life with Gordon Truscott. How many other Assiter's did he know? If the US Secretary of State's visit was anything to go by, living with Gordon was likely to be a very bumpy or very exciting journey or both. The thought of being followed by Donaldson and photographed by the Covert Surveillance Unit (CSU) still upset her. It had been at the Hilton in Cheltenham when Gordon had confirmed to Cindy that Assiter was definitely going to stay at Mealag after coming to Britain to meet the Prime Minister, along with several senior political figures in Her Majesty's Government and Official Opposition. The press releases would say that after his three day meeting Assiter would be flying back to Washington, but actually he would arrive at Mealag on Tuesday 12th September and stay for about ten days, probably leaving on Friday 22nd. His journey to and from Mealag would be by unmarked helicopter, courtesy of the British government.

24

Assistant Commissioner Manders occupied a large office within the complex of New Scotland Yard, though it appeared to be much smaller owing to the numerous filing cabinets that were positioned around the walls. Manders desk itself took up about a third of the remaining space, and the addition of his sumptuous chair and two other leather faced chairs for visitors plus a small oval table, did not leave a great deal of actual floor space. The desk however was impressively clear, belying his workload, as he did not believe in disorder. Whatever landed on it was dealt with or delegated, the latter he closely supervised, and for that he needed to ensure he always had sufficient time to review his subordinates' reports. Detective Chief Superintendent Bill Ritson was updating his boss on what was now referred to as the Hannet-Mar case.

"I think Styles' wife was right to be suspicious of her husband's death. The local nick weren't too bright about investigating the crash. It seems they took the view that it was a simple traffic accident, and as the toxicology report showed Styles to be well over the limit, end of story. They pretty much ignored looking for evidence that could explain his drinking or the time lag from when he left the golf club and the time of death."

"Are you saying that this was a crime made to look like suicide?" Manders asked cautiously, adding "Sussex could still be right that it was a simple case of drunk driving."

"I'm saying I don't know, but there are some disturbing features and we still have more to do. We looked at the crash scene. The bend on the road has crash barriers, positioned to prevent vehicles going over the edge no matter which direction of travel. Styles was allegedly coming down the hill, approaching the left hand bend. To miss the barrier, he would have had to deliberately steer the car onto the right hand side of the road risking oncoming traffic and then ensure the car missed the start of the barrier. Even drunk it's hard to think he wouldn't have braked and turned the wheel hard at some point, especially as he knew the road so well. Our conclusion is that Styles was either so drunk he momentarily blacked out and was just terribly unlucky to miss the barrier, or other factors prevented him from turning the steering wheel. Frankly, the odds favour the latter. I think we can rule out suicide."

"So there's more?" Manders listened but wanted all the details before commenting.

"Yes, and this is where it gets really interesting. I visited his wife. She is a bit angry at Sussex not taking her seriously, but more upset by her husband being branded a drunk. After I had shown interest in learning more facts about her husband, she seemed genuine in wanting to help, hoping I could reopen the case. I couldn't promise that of course, reminding her that the purpose of my visit was essentially to seek her help in tracing some of her husband's ex-business acquaintances. Crossland's name came up and a number of other UK nationals, plus a few overseas people whom she said Styles had mentioned, but like most wives she didn't take too much notice of the names so couldn't remember them all."

Ritson paused to take a sip of his coffee and helped himself to a bourbon biscuit. He carried on with his report, accompanied by the crunching sounds as he chewed – noted, but not commented upon, by Manders who rather frowned on such things.

"She said she could not recall the name of Halima Chalthoum but then came up with a bonus. Evidently, at most of the overseas conferences Styles attended the customary delegate photo-shoot. The photograph taken was always accompanied with a list of attendees and who they represented etc. Usually some high-ranking potentate would be an honoured guest at the gala dinner and, of course, everyone wanted to be in the obligatory picture. Styles always kept his presentation copy, probably to impress the wife or the golf club crowd. We are now going through all of them for the past two years, but on a quick scan of them there is no mention of Halima Chalthoum, nor Chalthoum Universal Holdings, nor the Corniche outfit. You can imagine there are a lot of names, and it will take us a while to get them all checked out as a lot are foreign nationals."

Manders was thoughtful. He could order more resources be

placed at Ritson's disposal, but did the facts justify it? His DCS had done a good job, it might yield some result, but it was still looking extremely thin and there was no discernible connection with the Styles case and 7/7.

"What about the bank account? Still dormant?" Manders asked.

"Affirmative."

"Mmmm. Tell you what, Bill. You can have Deakin for a month. Concentrate everything you can on the preceding nine months, say, from end October 2004 to July 2005. Go over all those in the conference pictures who are standing, or sat, up to three persons away from Styles. If he met and hung around with this woman, whoever she is, at a conference then with luck she won't be far away from him for the group photo. These photo sessions get set up pretty quickly as they get in the way of the dinner or meetings. The photographer won't reorganise and shuffle too many people around as it's too much trouble and takes too long. See if we can match any of the photos. Also, crosscheck the names from previous lists of the conferences and investigate any new females. My guess is that if Styles did have a contact who he recommended to Crossland, she would only have come on the scene around late 2004 or early 2005."

Ritson was pleased with the extra resource, and one thing which always impressed him was how Manders could quickly and easily assimilate facts and distil them down to a particular line of enquiry that usually paid off. He left the room, keen to get started.

25

Fadyar Masri came out of the shower, quickly dried herself and wrapped the towel around her long dark hair and then over her head. She had enjoyed the luxury of being able to stay in her comfortable single bed this Saturday morning far longer than she could on a weekday, but she was not in any better spirit. She looked at her watch. 9am. Frustrated and displeased, she pushed hard on the digits on her mobile with her left index finger. Easter was only a couple of weeks away and she wanted to know just how much longer she had to endure waiting around. She had decided that Easter was her limit. If nothing was forthcoming by then, she would try to return to Iraq and carry on the struggle there. The emergency number she used was bound to elicit a response from someone.

"Bonjour," a male voice answered.

Speaking in French, Fadyar used her code word and said her grocery delivery was overdue and she needed to speak to someone urgently about it. She was told it would be made at 12am and to be certain she was ready. At exactly midday, Carron swung his Mercedes in front of the block of flats and Fadyar jumped into the passenger seat a fraction before Carron floored the accelerator. He was angry with her.

"I told you to be patient. This is not an emergency, what do you think you're playing at?"

"It is an emergency, Claude, because I am not going to wait around here, doing that crap job. After Easter, I shall go home."

"Not an option, Fadyar. We have discussed this. Anyway, let's not argue. Sit back and listen, I have some news which might interest you."

"Tell me." Fadyar remained sullen as she slid back the electric adjustment on her seat to give herself a more relaxed position.

"We are minded to change our approach, or at least amend it. In addition to our usual ways of waging Holy War on the enemies of Islam, we believe that kidnapping of high level officials or politicians within Europe and America might bring more immediate results, and so we are currently investigating a number of such people. I have a list here of six names, against which is a code word. You will see that the code word is that of a male relative: Father, Brother, Grandfather and so on, and you will also note that we have deliberately not included the President of the US or the Prime Minister of Britain. They are too well protected. Their subordinates however are likely to be a little more vulnerable. That is what we are looking into. Memorise the names now. I shall not let you keep the paper and you must not write them down when you get back. There are three Americans and three European. To help you memorise them, the American code names are suffixed with the words 'In Law'; the European ones are not."

He passed over the paper, and for the next fifteen minutes she read the names and repeated them to herself until she was satisfied she had committed them to memory. She looked over at Carron.

"How long before any of this gets firmed up? This better not be some elaborate ploy to keep me at that factory, otherwise I will get really mad."

He ignored her petulant remark.

"We already have a lot of information on all those on the list, and our special people have been asked to provide more details on them. Your skills will be needed to bring off such a wonderful venture, once identified, so please be patient. I don't think it will be long, but I honestly do not know when."

"Ok Claude, two months max. Absolutely final. Two months. Final. Do you hear me?"

He didn't answer.

As he headed back to her flat, Fadyar asked, "If I undertake such a mission, I presume I shall lead it and also it will be for me to determine if the kidnap can be accomplished. I may have no choice but to take other options." Carron understood what she meant. Kidnapping was fraught with risk, especially in a foreign country, and it was quite possible that Fadyar may have to resort to assassination if the kidnap was impossible.

"Your role will be to plan and effect the kidnap, removing the target away from the immediate area. We will provide the necessary support by which onward transmission could be achieved." He paused, taking in a deep breath. "However, if none of that is possible then survival of the target is not an alternative option."

Fadyar smiled thinly at Carron's wry phrasing; for once she was impressed by the man.

26

Red Gables had become an increasingly unhappy home. Cindy and Alan rarely spoke at weekends and when they did arguments between them seemed to break out over the most trivial of matters. Even Alan's phone calls midweek had started to tail off and, as there seemed little for them to talk about, had been no more than cursory. One evening when the two of them had spent the evening in virtual silence watching the television, Alan suggested they go somewhere at Easter.

"Rome would be good. What do you think?" he tried to sound cheerful as he asked, though expecting a refusal.

"I thought I told you Alan, I'll be away as I need some time to myself." Cindy was going to Monemvasia with Gordon but had deliberately withheld telling Alan she would be away at Easter, afraid of his reaction. Alan was furious. It was bad enough that his wife was going away, but her insistence that she had mentioned it – when she hadn't – was downright maddening.

"Why do you always lie to me over these things? You said the same sort of thing at Christmas. You know damn well you haven't mentioned it before. What are you hiding Cindy? What have I done to deserve this?" he pleaded, rather than questioned her.

"I'm sorry Alan, you have forgotten and it is pointless to continue arguing the point. I can't keep telling you" and with that Cindy stood up and walked out of the room.

The endless arguments were also now having an effect on Cindy. She realised she could not go on much longer pretending to Alan that her attitude was just a short term thing – it wasn't going to change. She genuinely did not wish to hurt Alan but she knew she was causing him pain, which made her feel wretched, and that was only going to be exaggerated further the more involved with Gordon she became. She had lost her love for Alan and that was a fact. She had to consider very carefully what she should do. Gordon was terribly important to her, and she wanted to be with him, but she was still nervous of abandoning one full-time relationship and immediately committing to another. She was convinced that Alan would be angry, very angry indeed, if he knew of Gordon. Alan had already shown how possessive he was by setting Donaldson to spy on her. God knows what he and Donaldson might do if they ever found out about Gordon – probably come up to Mealag and there would be an awful scene. She resolved that on no account could she risk that but it was clear neither Alan nor her were able to co-exist in harmony. She needed to plan and manage her future such that any potentially disagreeable aspects for her were kept to a minimum. Before she finally dropped off to sleep she knew what her next steps would be.

The next morning, she flicked through Yellow Pages searching for a solicitor in Worcester. She chose Worcester as she certainly did not want to be seen either entering or leaving a solicitor in Stillwood, or anywhere else that was local. Worcester was a forty-five minute drive away and would be far more discreet. A few days later she had seen the solicitor, a pleasant, rotund man in his fifties, and after an hour it had been agreed that Cindy would file for divorce. She rang Alan at their London flat that evening and curtly told him she wanted a divorce and that he would be receiving a letter from her solicitors shortly. As expected, he became almost apoplectic once the initial shock had worn off. He ranted and raged at her, then pleaded with her but it was to no avail. Alan wished he could spare the time to come to Red Gables straightaway, but he was still working on some important papers at the flat for an early meeting the following day.

"Do nothing Cindy until I can get down there Friday, we can talk about this nonsense then," he shouted down the telephone.

"It's too late, Alan. I am really sorry it has come to this, but we can't go on arguing like we did last weekend and anyway I'm not sure that I love you any longer. My feelings have changed towards you."

"And that's it then, is it? You just walk away saying your feelings have changed. What about my feelings? They haven't changed. I still love you."

Cindy gritted her teeth. Her solicitor had warned that this was not going to be easy and it certainly wasn't.

Before she had time to respond, Alan demanded, "Well who is it then? There has to be someone else, so tell me. It's not that awful hotel owner in the village who's always pestering you to test out his beds, is it?"

"Of course not Alan, he's just pathetic. Do you really think I would ever – could ever – go with someone like that? What do you take me for? There isn't anybody else. Absolutely no one."

"I don't believe you. If it's not him, it will be someone else – but think what you are giving up Cinders, all that we've achieved and just as things are going really well for us financially. We could do anything. We could move away if that would help. Anything."

The pain and desperation in Alan's voice was too much for Cindy.

"I'm so sorry, Alan. Really. I appreciate what you're saying and feeling, but this is for the best. You will receive a letter from my solicitors Mapley, Townsend shortly."

She put the phone down. It rang almost immediately. She lifted up the receiver and immediately placed it back down on the cradle before lifting it off once more to prevent it ringing again. Cindy was slightly unnerved by the exchange. Again, she had lied to Alan, as she had to her solicitor, about there being no one else in her life. Of course there was, but Cindy was justifying her denial of an affair on the basis that her feelings for Alan had changed *before* she met Gordon and, in any event, it was still too early for her to be 100% certain that Gordon meant everything he had said. She gathered her kit into her sports bag and left for the gym where she could work out her tensions.

When Alan came home on Friday, Cindy had already met Gordon at Heathrow and flown to Athens, where they collected a pre-ordered hire car for their drive to Monemvasia. Propped up against the kettle in the kitchen Alan found the brief message she had left for him inside an envelope.

I'm going away for a couple of weeks. I've put plenty of your favourite food in the fridge and freezer. Cleaner paid. Don't forget your appointment at the dentist next week. Sorry. xx

Cindy and Gordon arrived at the villa an hour before the low sun was due to disappear behind the mountains. The sea shone a vivid orange as the bright setting sun started to turn from glorious gold to a deepening scarlet. The villa stood on its own, built high on a hill just outside the village, and it was everything that Mealag was not. It was furnished sparsely, with modern decor and inexpensive abstract paintings throughout. Certainly the Italian marble floor tiles looked expensive, as did the fixtures and fittings but Gordon had managed to ensure that authentic Greek styling had not been lost. There were two outdoor pools, one on the same level as the villa itself and another on the large garden terrace farther down the hill. The villa was on two floors. Upstairs were three bedrooms, two comfortably held twin single beds, the third just one single bed. All the bedrooms had their own en-suite bathroom. Downstairs there was a bathroom and a large kitchen / dining area. A separate lounge led to a tiled balcony. A large vase had been placed on the dining table and smaller vases had been placed in each of the bedrooms and bathrooms, all filled with gloriously scented, beautiful flowers. The lawns were a lush green and cut short, with the gardens that supplied the flowers a riot of colour from the mass of well-tended blooms.

Within half an hour of their arrival, Gordon had completed showing Cindy over the villa, and as they relaxed on the terrace their attention was drawn by the sound of a vehicle as it drew up alongside the hire car. A tall, well-built, swarthy looking man with jet black wavy hair and typically Greek facial features got out and came over to where they were sitting.

Gordon stood up, and smiling broadly extended both his arms in an effusive welcoming gesture. "Dimitrius, how are you? Let me introduce you to Cindy."

"Gordon, it is so wonderful to see you again, and this is the lovely Cindy you have told me about. Yes?" Dimitrius spoke impeccable English but with a slightly Americanised accent and, as he neared them, Cindy couldn't fail to notice just how handsome the man was.

Dimitrius went over to Cindy and placed his strong hands just behind Cindy's shoulders and drawing her slightly towards him, kissed her gently on both cheeks. The introductions over, the three sat in the easy chairs sipping ice-cold drinks quickly retrieved from the well-stocked fridge.

"Mama and Papa send you their greetings, and insisted I come over to make certain all is well at your villa. They will of course see you soon but if there is anything you need now, I am to arrange it."

Gordon explained to Cindy that Dimitrius's parents looked after the villa.

"As always everything is perfect, my friend. Please thank your parents, there is nothing we need."

"OK, then. I will leave you. You will be wanting to take a swim before the sun goes down," said Dimitrius. "See you around I hope, especially the lovely Cindy!"

When he had gone Cindy smiled broadly and said, "That's some fit guy. Bit like you really!" and then laughed.

"Yes, he owns the most popular restaurant in Monemvasia, couples and single female tourists pack the place out every night in the season. The food is good but I suspect that he is the main attraction, certainly with the ladies."

Gordon and Cindy had taken the holiday to simply unwind and do a little sightseeing, and mainly spent their time relaxing at the villa or on the deserted sandy coves that dotted the coastline. Even in August, the area did not become busy and at Easter there were only few tourists. After a couple of days, whilst they were both by the lower pool, Cindy told Gordon that she had instructed a solicitor and of her discussions with Alan. Gordon listened to her intently and then turned to her and asked, "Why didn't you tell Alan about me?"

"He doesn't need to know. I fell out of love with him before I met you."

"That may well be true, but seeing me cannot help your situation with Alan. Even if you cannot bring yourself to live with me, at least not yet which I respect, we both know that sooner or later the truth is likely to come out."

"I would just prefer to be divorced before we live together. That's all. Then it will be none of Alan's business who I see or what I do."

A slight frown appeared on Gordon's brow and his expression turned serious.

"Cindy, it seems you want things both ways. I will support you whatever you do, but I will not deceive Alan if he ever confronts me. I will not lie and deny you and I don't really understand why you should deny me, but that is your choice. You must realise, though, that if news of our relationship leaks out, as it well might as the press and paparazzi are often doing articles on me, Alan could get very angry indeed, understandably so. It would, I agree, be bad enough for him to hear it from you, but it will be far worse if he learns it from the media. How will you feel then? You need to be prepared for that, and possibly seeing photographs of us in the tabloid newspapers. I am resolved to seeing our relationship through to wherever it leads – but are you? If you are not, then for your own sake, please consider what it is you do want."

He was right, of course. Cindy hadn't quite appreciated the fact that he was a sort of celebrity, and she had not considered that the press might well turn up anywhere in the hope of getting a story. She knew how they operated from her own experience of working in press and public relations inside the Cabinet Office, and as a self-employed feature writer. An involuntary shiver ran down her back.

"Yes, I do see. Thanks," she was thoughtful for a few moments. Then she abruptly stood up, stripped off her bikini, discarding it behind her as she ran to the pool. At the blue tiled edge, she turned and said, "I'm not ever, ever, going to stop seeing you. We will be together one day, I promise, but let me do it my way."

Then she dived in, closely followed a few moments later by Gordon.

The final three days of their holiday were spent on the stunningly beautiful island of Elafonissos, which Cindy had never previously visited on her trips to the Marni. As they lazed on one of the deserted golden beaches, Gordon reflected more upon their conversation and became increasingly concerned about Cindy remaining at Red Gables with her husband. They both agreed there would be more arguments, probably more heated than ever now that she had involved solicitors, but Cindy resolutely declined to live with Gordon even though she loved him and knew that he wanted her to live at Mealag as soon as possible.

"No Gordon, if I move in with you straightaway it will only antagonise Alan with possible unpredictable consequences. I've told you, I prefer to wait a little longer before moving in. Alan needs firstly to come to terms with the fact that our marriage is over."

"Then I think you should leave him Cindy. Surely that's best for you and for Alan? Why not rent a cottage or something?"

The idea was so simple she wondered why she hadn't thought of it before. Not only would it bring home to Alan that the marriage was over, but it would give her time to settle the divorce and to ensure that her feelings and emotions had some time to settle before she plunged herself into another full-time relationship.

"I suppose I could, though it would probably have to be a flat." She replied, still half thinking.

"Why? When you get back, find yourself a cottage. You can decide what and where, and I will buy it through the property company. You can rent it from the company, if it makes you feel better. When you leave to live with me, I can either keep hold of it or sell it." Cindy was momentarily taken aback but knew this was a perfect solution for her.

"That would be wonderful, Gordon. Are you really sure?" Cindy was thrilled at his suggestion. "You could even visit!"

"That's settled then. When we get back, you must find somewhere you like, tell me the details and I will do the rest."

27

Detective Chief Superintendent Bill Ritson was once more reporting to his boss Assistant Commissioner Manders. Ritson and his team had spent a great deal of their time going through the delegate lists and studying the photographs. None of the known names, including that of Halima Chalthoum, had appeared on the lists and the extra resource that Manders had given Ritson had only one more week to help on the Hannet-Mar investigation.

"As I said, Sir, not very promising. What we have done is try to trace and verify the new female names that appeared on the lists in 2004, but there are forty-one. We have been able to quickly eliminate twenty-three of those as easily traceable through UK, European or US agencies, leaving eighteen. We have crosschecked those eighteen against the names of the companies they claim to represent and twelve are apparently legit. However, we have not yet been able to contact all the relevant personnel people to obtain verification of their employment. Seven of the eighteen appear to be self-employed consultants – in those cases, if we followed them up, we would be contacting the people themselves so have held back on those."

"What about the photographs of this Chalthoum woman on the bank's file? Didn't you say Crossland had certified copies and an affidavit?" Manders' recollection of detail astounded Ritson; it also embarrassed him as he had forgotten about them.

"Well Sir, I took the view that to revisit Crossland might alert him, if he was involved," but it sounded unconvincing and Manders was not impressed.

"Look Bill. We now know enough about 7/7 to rule out Crossland of any involvement in that but I think that we may have turned up something else which Crossland is either into up to his neck or he's being used as a patsy. If he is involved, we need to know damn quickly, but even if he is an innocent dupe, he is the only one that allegedly has a photo which ought to match with a photo in the Styles collection."

"But if there is no likeness, we aren't any further forward." Ritson was getting a bit confused as to where this was going.

"Christ Bill, use your bloody head. Go round to Crossland and ask to take away the picture he claims is of Halima Chalthoum. At the same, time get him to look at the delegate photos. Assuming he denies any likeness and continues to deny meeting any of the women in those photos, then get the lab boys to compare Crossland's picture with the few remaining photos you have from the filtered delegate photos. They can compare them digitally. Even if the woman has changed her hair, there's a good chance they will match something up and then we have her real name. We will also then have a lot to make Crossland sweat about."

Manders was in full flow now and before Ritson could interrupt he continued, "If it all goes belly up, and nothing matches, we drop this until and unless money moves from the account."

Ritson didn't argue, though still somewhat puzzled and next morning he was in Alan Crossland's office. Crossland was trying to appear calm but inwardly he was becoming increasingly concerned at the continuing interest being shown by the ATU in the dormant account of Chalthoum Universal holdings. Ritson asked for the photograph of Halima Chalthoum and Crossland passed it over.

"I will take this back with me and return it by courier this afternoon, Mr Crossland. Thank you very much." Ritson carefully placed the photograph between several sheets of paper in his own file, placed it in his brief-case, and from it took out a large manila folder containing several enlarged photographs of individual delegates who could either not be contacted or traced at this time.

"Perhaps you could now look at these photographs, Mr Crossland. Is there anyone here you know or have met?" Ritson asked calmly.

"Presumably you want me to see if Halima Chalthoum is here? I have said before I have never met the woman, so to recognise her I shall need her photo back." Crossland felt confident in his story and was becoming slightly impatient, thinking Ritson was being silly, trying to trip him up in such a clumsy way.

"Mr Crossland, if you please, Sir, I want you to answer a simple question. Do you recognise any of the persons in these photographs?" and he pushed the folder nearer to Crossland.

Crossland was now irritated, wondering where all this was leading to, but he took out photographs and began examining them one by one. When he came to the fifth one, his heart stopped. It was unmistakeably that of Fadyar Masri. His mind swirled. Should he say he recognised the photo? No, he reasoned, he couldn't do that. This was the Anti-Terrorist Unit for Christ's sake. He could be locked up for years just for knowing a bloody suspected terrorist, let alone opening an account for her. He sipped his coffee, trying to appear natural, and turned over the page. When he was finished, his composure regained, Crossland handed back the photographs.

"Sorry Chief Superintendent, I don't think I can help."

Ritson had closely observed Crossland. He noticed the over eagerness to first sip his drink and then to quickly turn over photograph number five.

"Please, we want you to be very sure. Have another look." Ritson was applying pressure and Crossland was not amused.

"Well, if you insist," he said tetchily.

Having gone through them again, he handed them back to Ritson. Ritson pocketed them in his file and said in a firm voice, "I need you to be very clear on this Mr Crossland. Are you absolutely certain you have never met nor seen anyone in those photographs? Take your time."

"No need to. I've told you before. No." his reply was firm, but impatient.

Twenty-four hours later Ritson was again in Manders office and speaking to his superior. "Crossland said he didn't recognise anyone in the Styles photos and I gave him every opportunity to study them carefully. He seemed a bit edgy, slight hesitation at number Five, but if he was hiding anything he carried it off pretty well".

Ritson paused, expecting some comment but as Manders only raised his eyebrows, he continued. "The computer lads say there is no match on the Halima photograph to any of the filtered Styles ones, so it seems as though we have drawn a blank. The whole thing is bloody odd, though. I mean, setting up an account where none of the names can be traced and the holder has never made an appearance; where Styles acquaintance doesn't appear in any of his photos, and where the money is still dormant."

This time Manders did respond. "Well, Bill, it still remains a possibility that the woman that met Styles *is* in the photos. Your guys have not analysed every mug shot in the conference pictures, so she still might be there, but it's not worth much more time on this unless something else turns up. If the money moves, let me know. Meanwhile, if you have some time, why not go back to basics? Check out Crossland's known associates, relatives, that sort of thing. You never know, it might turn up something."

28

Alan Crossland was once more mingling with the guests in the large lounge at the Asterhays Hotel. He had decided to book himself in for Easter and rather hoped Anna would join him, but she declined. The pressures of recent weeks were beginning to make him feel edgy. He found it hard to concentrate and was also finding it difficult to get to sleep at night without the help of a couple of stiff glasses of whisky and paracetomol, and he thought that a few days away might help his general well-being. Besides, he reasoned, Christmas had turned out better than he hoped, and who knows – he might find another Anna.

As he surveyed the large ballroom, his mind started wandering back to the last meeting he had with the ATU. What were they onto? Was Fadyar really implicated in some terrorist plot? He went over and over the evening he and Cindy spent with Fadyar at Red Gables, almost a year ago. There was nothing about Fadyar that alarmed him. She was very amiable, polite and cultured. In fact, she was pleasant company and whilst she was quite clear on her requirements of the business aspects, at no time was she overbearing about them. Conversation had been easy and there was no hint that the woman might be involved in anything remotely connected with terrorism. True, the setting up of the account was rather unusual, but it was certainly not unique – and if that smooth detective really had any evidence of wrongdoing on his part, he sure as hell would have made it known by now. No, Crossland reasoned, probably the cop is just wanting to make a name for himself and being overzealous.

His thoughts then turned to Cindy. It really pained him that they were breaking up. He had brought Mapley Townsend's letter with him to the hotel, crumpled into a ball and thrown in his bag at the last minute before he left home. Mrs Crookes had placed his letters on the kitchen unit, as usual, and the letter from Cindy's solicitor was on the top. It was the only one he opened, though he quickly flicked through the others to see if there might be something else of importance, half hoping there would be a letter from Cindy. Negative. The solicitor had written only in the briefest terms adding to the angst Crossland was feeling, and he had shed a few tears as he read the letter. He wondered why his marriage and all his hopes, their hopes, were now cruelly reduced to no more than twenty-five cold words.

"Hi." A voice was nearby, but Alan did not hear it. His mind was preoccupied with Cindy and he was wondering where she was and what she might be doing. He wanted to believe Donaldson's ongoing reports and Cindy's own denial as it gave him more of a chance to rescue the situation, but his gut instinct and knowledge of Cindy made him doubt her. As his thoughts meandered over past events, he recalled yet again the meeting with Fadyar which sent a shiver down his spine. The sudden realisation that Cindy was at Red Gables when Fadyar came to dinner, and its possible implications for him with the ATU, made the nerves in his stomach tighten. He had denied meeting Fadyar, but if ever the police interviewed Cindy he would be in real trouble. In better times she may have been persuaded to cover for him, but he knew that wasn't going to happen now. Cindy would hang him out to dry, especially if she wanted to spend her life with someone else. The thought made him angry.

"The bloody bitch would do that, I know it," he muttered almost silently to himself. His mind raced ahead and images of him being interrogated again by the police flashed before his eyes.

"Hi, my name is Chloe. You seem a million miles away." The voice again, only louder this time; obviously someone trying to make an introduction to another lonely soul in the crowd.

"*Hello, I'm Chloe,*" a woman shouted and Crossland turned. She was standing right next to him. "You don't seem very interested in any of us, are we that bad?"

Crossland chuckled, pleased to break away from his thoughts. He apologised and introduced himself.

"In case you didn't hear, I'm Chloe. I'm twenty-eight, single, no children and I smoke. Cannabis if I can get hold of it, otherwise Dunhill." She smiled at him.

"OK, that's a pretty good start. I'm forty-one, not yet divorced but soon will be, no children and I don't smoke." Crossland continued the style set by Chloe.

"The 'not yet divorced but soon will be'. Is that the 'bloody bitch' you were muttering about?" Chloe jauntily enquired.

"Oh God, did I really say that? Hope I didn't say anything else, otherwise this might be a brief hello and goodbye!"

Chloe laughed. Alan noticed that her hair was a slightly darker colour than Cindy's, a glossy reddish-brown, straight and cut quite short, hanging only as far as her chin. Physically she was very slim and petite, her head barely reaching to the top of his shoulders. They sat down and spent the rest of the evening talking about themselves and also looking around the room, making up wild suggestions about their fellow guests and guessing what sort of persons they might be. The more outrageous they were in their fictional descriptions of their fellow guests, the louder they laughed. By the time the evening had drawn to a close, Chloe and Alan had decided that at least one of the other guests was a psychopath as he twitched his shoulder as he spoke; the lady wearing a rather boring dress with what appeared to be arrows patterned across it just had to be an escaped convict, and the tall man drably dressed in a blue suit standing alone in the corner was a police constable as he was eyeing everyone up and down. They had marked three married men who were at the hotel with their female secretaries, and at least two lesbian couples. The latter observation was not far from the truth, though they had identified the wrong people – and there were three. Alan, having gained confidence from his experience at Christmas, spoke quietly to Chloe at the end of the evening.

"It would be great if we could have a coffee in my room or yours if you prefer, but if you are tired I understand."

"Your room sounds good to me," and with that they walked slowly over to the lifts and Chloe pressed the illuminated square button to call the lift.

"Same as mine really" Chloe commented upon the room as she entered it. She picked up the kettle and filled it with water before placing it on its stand.

"Just going to take a quick shower" she said as she plugged the kettle into the brass-plated socket on the wall nearby before calling out, "Mine is black, no sugar."

Alan realised he had just been ordered to make the coffee and walked over to the cups whilst Chloe closed the bathroom door behind her. The low-wattage kettle seemed to take an age to boil and the water was still not hot enough when, true to her word, Chloe reappeared after no more than five minutes. Her short hair was wet and she was dressed only in a towel.

"Not ready yet, then" she said. Then giggled, "The coffee, not you, I meant!"

Alan was fascinated by her. She was fresh, young and carefree, all the things he had lost over the years, and he was already becoming quite attracted to her.

"Only be another minute or so. Why do hotel kettles take so long?"

She didn't answer him directly.

"Bring it over then when you can," and she dropped the towel and walked over to the bed. Alan glanced at her. She had a good figure but was certainly slim. Her breasts were small and pert and her tiny round bottom sat below an impressively narrow waist. By the time his eyes had wandered to her legs, she was already climbing into bed. The kettle eventually boiled and he made the drinks, taking hers over to her.

"Better have a shower myself, I suppose?" It was more of a question than a statement.

Chloe glanced up at him, her eyes sparkling in the light from the room, and flamboyantly threw back the duvet.

"The coffee will get cold if you do".

Alan looked at her lying invitingly on the bed, any thoughts of a shower instantly forgotten, and rapidly removed his clothes. He stroked his fingers through her wet hair and she placed her arm around the back of his head, pulling his face towards hers. She kissed him hard on the lips, before placing her hand between his legs. He started to climb on top of her but she pushed him back.

"Not yet, be patient!" her voice soft and sexy in his ear.

She grabbed her cup from the bedside table and swilled a large sip of the steaming hot liquid around the inside of her mouth several times before quickly swallowing. Instantly she leant over him plunging her mouth onto his male hardness. Alan gasped aloud, the searing heat further inflaming his desire and his hands fumbled to find her breasts. As he cupped them in his hands, she turned her face and took another swig of the coffee before again placing her hot mouth onto him. The exquisite sensations were almost too much to bear. He released her breasts and lay back.

"God, that's so good Chloe. So good." Alan had not experienced such heightened pleasure as this; Cindy had never been keen to experiment sexually and it had disappeared entirely from their lovemaking years ago. Chloe leant forward. Once more she refilled her mouth; once more her lips took him in. She started sucking, gently at first then harder and harder in rhythm to the strokes she was making with her clasped fingers. Alan started raising his thighs, urging her not to stop.

"Harder Chloe, harder," he cried out to her. Chloe's sensitive, moist lips detected his moment was almost due, the further swelling of him telling her he was near. Taking one quick last gulp of the coffee she opened her mouth and took him deeper into her throat. Tightening her fingers and rapidly squeezing her lips, she kept swallowing hard as Alan thrust his hips skyward.

Lying back on the bed, he seriously studied her nakedness for the first time. There were no faded sun tan markings, and even her arms looked white. In fact she looked small, vulnerable and pale but Alan realised that Chloe was anything but a timid, young girl. The freshness of her complexion, her deep brown eyes and reddish close-cropped hair made her appear even younger than her age, but this innocent looking girl had just given him the most exquisite pleasure of the kind Cindy had denied him for too long. He was elated.

"That was fantastic, Chloe. Just fantastic"

"Bet you're glad you came then!" she laughed, pleased with the double entendre.

"Thank you for having me!" Alan responded in like terms, and they chuckled before giving each other a close hug.

Alan spent the rest of the night enjoying every aspect of Chloe's smooth, glowing body. He lost count how many times he had been inside her even if he didn't finally climax again until the early hours, or how often he had used his fingers and tongue on her. He wasn't counting and neither was she, they had both escaped from whatever it was that made them come to the Asterhays and remained inseparable for the remainder of their stay. They were both saddened when they had to depart the hotel, but eagerly swapped mobile phone numbers, agreeing to stay in contact and meet up as soon as they could – possibly in London or, more probably, at her flat in Surrey.

29

Three weeks after Easter, the man known to Fadyar as Claude Carron lunched by arrangement in a small restaurant in Mennecy, just off the main A6 due south of Paris. He sat and waited. A few minutes later he was joined by a middle-aged, white woman dressed in a smart black suit. He ordered a bottle of the house red wine. A little later they were eating their meals, all the while chatting about nothing in particular. A casual observer would think them office colleagues. Without changing her voice, the woman suddenly said to Carron.

"Are you sure you have a contact that is suitable? This is an important operation for us."

"I believe so, but of course you haven't yet told me precisely what it is" Carron coolly replied.

"You wouldn't expect me to Claude. All I will say is that we have certain information about the movements of one of our relatives that has come from our London office. Someone who speaks fluent English would be needed. The full details will be passed only to the person you nominate, and I remind you that person is to receive every assistance from you thereafter."

Carron was pleased and smiled. An operation in the UK was just perfect for Fadyar. She had all the attributes and spoke fluent English; and she was becoming very restless. This would be her chance for glory or martyrdom.

"This will be an ideal operation for whom I have in mind. Indeed I would say the person I am thinking of will be eminently suitable, believe me."

"Then it is settled. Please pass me a contact number. We shall not meet again after this Claude."

Carron wrote down Fadyar's mobile telephone number on a spare serviette and the nameless woman slipped it into her handbag. They finished their meals and paid the bill. On the way out, Carron walked with the woman to her car. At the door, she turned and looked in the handbag for her keys and said, "You must now be very careful, Carron. You will be told the date of our operation in time for you to leave France. If anything goes wrong, you must not be captured."

She opened the door and sat behind the wheel, put the key in the ignition and lowered the window. She then leaned her head out slightly and said goodbye, and with a wave of her hand drove out of the car park. Her job was almost finished as far as this operation was concerned. She did not need, nor want, to know whom Carron would choose to carry out the mission. It was a rule that information exchange was to be kept to an absolute minimum to protect each other and to safeguard their organisation. What one didn't know, one couldn't reveal under interrogation. Two hours later Carron's lunch time companion was on a scheduled flight to Ankara.

Fadyar left the office that evening, and was walking along the Rue Chabonais in the midst of the usual throng of scurrying commuters and languid tourists when she heard the distinctive dual tones of her second mobile phone informing her she had a text message. She knew it had to be important. No one other than Carron was aware of its number. As soon as she was inside her flat, she excitedly accessed her message. It was headed 'Wednesday', which told her that the message had been written in Code 4 – Wednesday being the fourth day of the week. She retrieved her codebook from the small fireproof safe in the corner of her bedroom cupboard and turned to page four. An average observer would not have realised that seven of the sheets of paper inside the notebook represented codes. The codes had not been placed on adjoining pages but scattered at random throughout the book, and each page of the thirty page book was individually numbered but not in sequence. Anyone glancing at the book would wonder what on earth the various letters and numbers referred to and, even if a page was more closely scrutinised, it was only a one in four and a half chance that they would be looking at one of the real codes. She set about deciphering the garbled text on the small screen before her and an hour later looked at what she had written down.

Mother and Father in Law will visit UK 12 to 22 September. They will be looked after by friends, but hope to meet up with you. You should have enough funds in your London account for your expenses. Your three cousins in Birmingham may also wish to see them, phone 0701502488 on arrival. Good luck. NH

Fadyar was so thrilled she shouted out, "Yes! Yes! Yes!" She remembered that 'Father in Law' was the American Secretary of State, Dean Assiter, and 'friends' clearly related to him being guarded by some protection officers. She was going to be given three associates to help in the operation. Her supervisors at the training camp had told her that it was understood any operation took weeks if not months of planning, and once set and agreed the leader of the group, Fadyar in this case, was in sole charge of timescale, logistics and method, though in this case the timeframe for her mission seemed already determined. There was no mention of where she was to hand Assiter over to those who would be keeping him in captivity, assuming her kidnapping of him was a success. It appeared her masters would leave that to her or possibly provide details later.

Elated, she turned on her laptop and spent the next couple of hours browsing the internet, learning about Dean Assiter and researching location NH 0701502488 where Assiter and his wife were going to be in September for ten days. She very quickly assimilated all she needed to know about her target, which in reality turned out to be remarkably little and, having downloaded a few pictures of him and his attractive wife, turned her attention to the grid reference. It surprised her that according to the UK Ordnance Survey website the location was in the North of Scotland and that she would require the Landranger series of 1:50000 maps, numbers 33, 34, 40 and 41. Combined, these maps would provide her the necessary detail of both the general area and precise location of her assignment, though an even greater detailed series of maps were available if she needed them. Fadyar picked up the mobile and, deliberately not encoded, typed *'Great'* and sent the innocuous message to a different number. There was no going back now. The next morning she would hand in her notice to Pethane and leave her crap, stifling job one week later.

As soon as she had sent her acknowledgement, Fadyar removed the sim card from her mobile phone, placed it in her study room guillotine and cut it in half. She then went for a walk and crossed the river Seigne by her favourite bridge, the pedestrian only Passarelle des Arts – or Pont des Arts as she and most Parisians refer to it. Darkness had fallen, and although beautiful by day, the bridge – with its own illumination, and that of the city and of the nearby Louvre – was simply stunning at night. She never hurried across this bridge, never tired of the panoramic vista, never wished to think of the day she might leave it behind. The enemies of Islam may be infidels, but they too can create beautiful cities. Tonight she ambled more slowly than usual, her light steps muffled by the wooden planks that were laid across the bridge, and paused frequently to look down at the river, much like any tourist. The lattice steel side barriers were not high, ideal in enabling her to drop the sim card pieces and the phone into the water at different intervals without arousing suspicion.

Fadyar slept easily that night. She had been chosen. The next seven days passed slowly and well before she finally left the factory, she had finished going through the contents of her flat and identifying any items she would need for her initial, fact-finding visit to the United Kingdom. Although there was plenty of time between now and September, it was her responsibility to plan and execute the mission and she was determined to ensure that every detail had been considered and properly evaluated. There was a further reason for making an early visit to the UK. She had no idea with whom she would be working and she had to be certain that they would be reliable and have the necessary skills for what she would demand of them. She knew that they would have received specialist training in handling weapons and were, like her, dedicated to the cause, but the last thing she wanted was to work with fools or hotheads. If they did not come up to her expectations, they would be changed. They also had to be unquestioningly loyal to her. She was in charge and gave the instructions, and she would expect those to be obeyed. In due course, she would inform her comrades of the precise mission and detail their own particular role in it. Every bit as much as her, it would be vital that her team became familiar with all aspects of the assignment long before they were required to implement it.

She decided to pack virtually all her clothes, plus the contents from her small safe. The latter included her French passport and identity card, plus her codebooks and various papers, including the authorisation documents for the Chalthoum bank account should she require access to it. She pre-purchased her cross channel ferry ticket using the internet and paid for it on her own Visa card, booking an open-dated return journey within the next month. This would lessen any suspicion from British Immigration that she might be contemplating staying in the UK and anyway there was little to gain by remaining in Britain until September, which was four months away. She loaded her blue Peugeot 205 with her two suitcases and made a final look around her flat to check she had missed nothing.

Driving carefully through the eastern suburbs of Paris, she joined the E15 motorway and headed northwest. The drive to Calais was uneventful and boring. She arrived at the ferry terminal stiff and tired just after 7:30pm. The ship was not due to depart for another two hours, giving her time to take a quick meal, but the prospect of eating the food at the dockside cafe did not appeal so she made a short journey into town where she found a small family-run restaurant and enjoyed a homemade chicken fricassee. An hour later, she drove back to the terminal and joined the queue of cars waiting to board.

Fadyar had used her fake passport once before, when she visited Crossland. That visit had suited her well. Her cover story, if apprehended, was that she was on a courier mission personally delivering some papers – the address of which was fictitious, but in reality that trip had been a test of the identification provided for her in order to establish a normal life in France. If her passport and other documentation had failed, the punishment meted out by the French or British authorities would not be severe as the documents she was carrying were quite innocuous and her organisation would learn from her arrest. Fadyar herself also had to prove to her superiors that she could, and would, successfully carry out instructions given to her. Both Fadyar and her identity documents passed the test.

As she drove slowly towards the brightly-lit car deck deep in the bowel of the ship, she was in a relaxed mood listening to the radio. She lowered the volume as she presented her pre-printed booking and passport. The girl sitting in the booth gave Fadyar a cursory look, punched some keys on her keyboard and waited a few seconds before handing back the passport with her boarding card. She put the car in first gear and moved forward. She was waved through at the customs and police checkpoint for European Union travellers and proceeded to drive onto the ship – her little car anonymous and insignificant amongst all the other vehicles swallowed up into the cavernous belly of the vessel. Once the ferry was underway, she was able to exchange her remaining Euros for Sterling. Added to those she had exchanged the previous week, her bag now held in excess of a thousand pounds. She had left the Hannet-Mar account untouched. She would only use that if it became an absolutely necessary, meanwhile she would use her own funds and reimburse herself later.

Driving off the ferry two hours later, she entered the lane marked for EU visitors. Her passport was looked at by the immigration control officer whilst another scanned underneath her car with a circular mirror placed at the end of a long pole. As he returned the passport to her the officer asked a couple of routine questions.

"What is the purpose of your visit to Britain?"

"I'm taking a holiday."

"And how long do you intend to stay?"

Fadyar smiled at him, her white teeth prominent against the dark skin of her face. She looked directly into his eyes, "That depends on your British weather! I have an open return ticket for up to a month, so can come back earlier if it rains a lot!"

The few checks on her and her car completed, the officer wished her an enjoyable vacation and she drove carefully out of the port, remembering to drive on the left, and soon joined the A2 stopping overnight at the first hotel she saw. Within half an hour she was asleep, with Assiter very much on her mind. The next morning she turned off the trunk road and drove towards Canterbury, stopping on the outskirts of town at a small shopping complex of ten retail outlets that included an electrical store. She purchased a cheap pay-as-you-go mobile phone, and as soon as she had activated it and was satisfied it was working properly, drove back to the A2 and resumed her journey. At lunchtime she used her new phone to call an international number she had memorised from her training. A recorded voicemail message asked her in English but with a noticeable Arab accent to select the language she wanted to use. She chose English and waited.

"Yes" a male voice

"Fadyar" another wait. Fadyar's heart beat a little quicker.

"Please tell me your date of birth". She did.

"Your mother's name, please"

"Halima"

"Finally, what relative are you seeking information upon?"

The question both surprised and impressed Fadyar. She knew that the person at the end of the telephone would not have a clue what relevance the questions had, only that they were to be asked if and when a Fadyar called the number.

"My Father-in-Law. Can you help?"

"Not personally, but I will get someone to call you. As you have not set your phone to mask its number on outgoing calls, I have it. Keep it switched on."

The line went dead. Fadyar wished she had checked the phone defaults before making the call and made a mental note to alter the privacy setting at the earliest opportunity. Twenty-five minutes had elapsed when the ring tones finally sounded.

"Hello?" said Fadyar.

"I understand you need to speak with us so we can all meet up," said a male voice, speaking in English but with a Birmingham accent.

"Yes."

"We have been told of you, but did not expect you so soon."

"Can you make it this evening?" enquired Fadyar.

"No problem, just say where."

"OK. I will see you all this evening. Be ready. I will meet you at 7pm at the Corley services M6 heading towards Birmingham. I am driving a blue Peugeot 205, French plates. Introduce yourself as The Ferrymen."

"Will do. See you then." The male voice rang off.

Sharid Bagheri, Nasra Khan and Mawdud Mattar had arrived at the service station early, and Khan parked their Ford Mondeo so that they had a good view of the entrance. The men were all unmarried in their late twenties or early thirties whose parents had legally immigrated to the United Kingdom in the late 1960's and early 1970's. Sharid Bagheri lived with a white English partner, but Khan and Mattar lived alone. All had been born in Britain and all were therefore full UK nationals. None had been in serious trouble with the police and they all lived near to each other in and around the Handsworth district of Birmingham, where they regularly attended the local mosque. Sharid Bagheri and Nasra Khan had employment in different restaurants and Mawdud Mattar worked as supervisor in a factory manufacturing steel panels. Bagheri was the first to spot Fadyar. Noting where she stopped, Khan started the Mondeo and pulled into a bay next to the Peugeot. Bagheri got out and introduced himself as the Ferrymen.

Satisfied all was well, Fadyar and the others walked into the service station and having purchased three fruit juices and a coke, sat at a table near the far wall. Bagheri, Khan and Mattar gave Fadyar their names and more generally introduced themselves. Fadyar, speaking quietly, but not whispering, had some urgent questions she wanted answered.

"Can you all drive, have a licence and so on?" They all had.

"Good. Has anyone a UK bank account?"

Bagheri spoke first. "I have one in my own name, but we have all been provided with another account that could be used if you wish it to channel funds."

"Even better. I will take details later. Can you all take time off work, say ten days from next week and a fortnight in September?"

Khan said that he could manage both quite easily but Mattar said the fortnight might be difficult, a week was more likely in September. Bagheri said he was already working a week's notice at the restaurant so it was likely to be easier to remain unemployed, but that his girlfriend might present a difficulty.

"Mawdud, the week in September will be OK. You will just not go back. It is doubtful if any of us will return to work after our glorious mission is accomplished. Sharid, who is this girlfriend? I need to know more."

"She is a nice white girl I've known for over a year. She is not one of us of course, and as such cannot be involved. I realise that is a problem."

Fadyar remained silent whilst the three looked at her to respond. She was weighing up the risks of Bagheri inventing some excuse to end the relationship, or of leaving the status quo but trying not to arouse the girl's suspicions. More than a minute passed before Fadyar was ready to speak again.

"Sharid. This is not a good beginning. You have gone against our teaching and the instructions you would have received at the camp. Let this be the last time. If I order you to ditch the girl, she may well become difficult and I cannot afford to be side-tracked. Nor am I prepared to take unnecessary risks by having her more permanently removed, at least not yet. How will she react if you go away? Will she want to come or make a fuss?"

"I am so sorry. I can use the excuse that I need to go away to find a job and that will satisfy her. She is not very bright."

"That's obvious. She has to be pretty thick to shack up with you!" quipped Khan, easing the growing tension. Fadyar looked intently at Bagheri.

"OK then, but you must inform me if there is any hint of a problem with her. I will not have your dick compromising our operation, you understand? You are both expendable." Fadyar was asserting her authority and it was not only Bagheri that had a shiver running down his spine. They all knew now that Fadyar would be a ruthless leader.

The conversation moved onto more minor matters. None of the group asked Fadyar about the mission knowing from their training in Pakistan that they would be given information only when needed.

"Now, where am I to stay for a few days?" asked Fadyar. "I can use a hotel but would prefer a house we can use as a base."

Khan offered Fadyar his flat. It had two bedrooms in which he had frequently entertained one or more of his own casual female friends overnight, or had offered a room to a male friend who, living at home with strict Muslim parents, needed somewhere overnight to take a girl. Fadyar would be largely ignored by any neighbours thinking she was just another of Khan's many conquests. Although not overjoyed at the likelihood of being regarded as Khan's latest bedtime companion, Fadyar had to admit to herself that it was probably an ideal place for her to stay as she would not arouse suspicion.

"Good, thank you. I cannot leave the car here so I suggest we go now. I will follow you and park it close to Nasra's flat until you can find me a garage. One final thing, I shall meet you all together as little as possible. I shall pass instructions via Nasra, but it does not mean he is second-in-command. I shall inform you of whom I will choose as my deputy only when we go on our mission."

Later that evening, she and Nasra were sat around his small dining table. He confirmed that he and his two friends had each been provided with a bank account to be used only for emergencies or for a mission. The accounts were not large, but each contained about £5,000. Fadyar started writing out a list of things she wanted done. It also served as an aide memoir and check list for her.

- *Close two accounts and withdraw the cash.*
- *Book two medium-sized hire cars.*
- *Take two days to journey to Scotland, finding somewhere en route to stay.*
- *Ensure warm and waterproof clothes, boots – Scotland can be cold and wet*
- *Laptop computer, with internet access, 12v car adaptor, USB drive – NO details to be put onto hard drive*
- *Good digital camera. (She had brought her own, but hoped one of the three would possess a better one.)*
- *Hand held telescope, plus binoculars*
- *Passport, identity, insurance documents, driving licences etc*
- *Fadyar to obtain two copies of all the OS maps.*
- *New pay-as-you-go mobile phone for second car. Only used for assignment – NOTHING else.*
- *Weapons, explosives for September. Not needed on reconnaissance mission.*

She also carefully reflected on the three men on whose actions her life may at some point depend. They were all now joined with her on the mission and the fate of them all depended on how well they could work together. She had been harsh on them, deliberately so, at the outset, but it was obvious they were true patriots, intelligent and could be trusted. Her assignment had got off to a good start, but it had a great deal further to go.

30

Gordon was true to his word. Within three weeks of returning from the villa, Cindy had located a reasonably sized two bedroom detached cottage on the outskirts of Grimley, a small Worcestershire village. It boasted a fully equipped interior, was beautifully decorated and had a large double garage. The latter was essential so that when Gordon visited he could park his vehicle away from prying eyes. She was sure that Alan would do all he could to find out where she had moved to, and was determined not to make it easy for him or his poodle, Donaldson. She sent Gordon the property particulars from the estate agents, and his company completed the purchase quickly and without complication. Using the money Gordon had placed in her account, Cindy began to thoroughly indulge herself buying everything she required to completely furnish the rooms and add to the already high level of fixtures and fittings. As she expected, Alan was dismayed when she rang him at their London apartment to say that she would be leaving him at the end of April, but after the initial shock he calmed and they agreed to meet at Red Gables to discuss any remaining issues between them before she left.

Cindy had poured herself a large whisky and soda whilst waiting for him and, as she expected, Alan arrived on time. She had prepared a meal for them both and afterwards sat in the lounge on separate sofas facing each other. The conversation started amicably enough but Alan's initial pleasant demeanour changed to acrimony when she refused to say where she would be living – yet Cindy detected there was something about Alan's anger that was not quite as she had anticipated. It subsided much sooner than she believed it would. In a restrained, measured voice Alan enquired what he should do with any of Cindy's mail that got delivered.

"I have arranged with the post office to have it redirected to my friend Mary in the village. She will forward it to me. Alan, please do not embarrass yourself by asking her where I live as she will not tell you. I have also printed off from the computer some adhesive labels with Mary's name and address on them and, if you are agreeable, Mrs Crookes will forward any mail that slips through. Assuming of course you will be keeping her on here. If not, perhaps you could do it? That would be kind."

Alan agreed. An hour later they had finished their discussion which after the early exchanges had remained totally amiable and constructive, quite different from what she feared. Cindy was quite astounded when, remarkably, it was Alan who rose first from his chair, bade her a pleasant "goodnight" and smartly walked out of the lounge, leaving her wondering what had brought about his unexpected change of attitude.

It did not take Donaldson long to find out where Cindy was moving to. Acting under Alan's instructions, he had kept a discreet watch on her movements and as, almost daily, Cindy was making the trip to Grimley to oversee the arrival of furniture or tradesmen, the task of ascertaining her future whereabouts was an easy one. Armed with the cottage address, Alan charged Donaldson to trace its ownership as it was clear from his driver's description that it was unlikely his wife could afford to purchase it outright. Alan was certain that there was a new man in Cindy's life and perhaps the cottage might disclose who it was, but he was disappointed to learn that it was in fact owned by a private investment company called 'Lochside Fund Management'. He had tried to make enquiries of that but it was unknown to Companies House; investigations he made through Hannet-Mar's own banking systems had also produced no result. More in desperation than hope he and Donaldson accessed the internet one afternoon and typed the name into the search engine. There was little, except for a small news item in a past copy of *The Financial Times*.

Mr Gordon Truscott, the entrepreneur and self-made multi-millionaire from computer software and, later, property investment, has today completed the sale of virtually the entire portfolio of Truscott Enterprise Holdings for a sum reputed to be in excess of £200M to an unknown buyer, but which is believed to be the Kuwait Investment Corporation. Truscott Enterprise Holdings still retain Truscott's private, offshore, property company Lochside Fund Management and it is unclear what his intentions are with regard to this company.

Alan was disappointed. Out of curiosity he followed the link to articles about Gordon Truscott but they did not interest him overmuch. He switched of his computer and turned to Donaldson. "She's obviously renting it. There is no way she could have met this Truscott chap, beside which he is clearly way out of Cindy's league." He paused then chuckled, "Anyway, he certainly wouldn't be interested in her. A man with at least £200 million or more in spare cash could afford a bit better than a thirty-six year-old married woman – no need of that when he could be spending his time on exotic islands surrounded by numerous women half her age!"

"Too bloody right. With that kind of money I know I would," said Donaldson enviously.

As Alan Crossland was deceiving himself over Gordon Truscott, Fadyar, Nasra, Sharid and Mawdud were sat in Nasra's flat, several Ordnance Survey maps scattered on the table before them. Fadyar took a slip of paper from her pocket and looked at the reference she had written upon it: NH0701502488.

The British Grid Referencing System is based on the Ordnance Survey Great Britain 1936 (OSGB™) datum and can be used to accurately pinpoint any location in Great Britain and its outlying islands. To provide a unique map reference, Great Britain is first divided into a series of 500km squares starting at the southwest corner of the country. Each of these 500km squares is allocated a single reference letter; either S, T N, H or O. Each 500km square is then subdivided into 25 squares, 100km by 100km. Every 100km square is allocated a reference letter A to Z, omitting I, starting with A in the north-west corner of the parent 500km square. In this way, each 100km square can be referred to by a unique two letter reference, with the first letter referring to the parent 500km square, and the second letter referring to a particular 100km square within it. After the two unique grid letters, a further two sets of figures of three or more numerals (up to six can be used) are given for the east and then the north directions, further and further refining the small squared area. In this way, even a particular building can be pinpointed on a sufficiently detailed map.

Her fellow conspirators looked at her expectantly. She picked up two sharp pencils and placed one in each hand. Slowly and deliberately, her left hand started to map the east co-ordinate whilst at the same time her right hand followed the north co-ordinate until both pencil points met.

"There it is! There it is! Look, it's called Mealag Lodge. That is where we will carry out our glorious mission!" she could barely contain her excitement. Her heart pounded, the palms of her hands became suddenly damp with sweat and her brow perspired. The others stared, open-mouthed, looking at her in anguished astonishment. It was Mawdud that spoke first.

"Fadyar, are you sure, really sure? This is in the middle of nowhere, what possible value can it be to attack it?"

"That is where you are wrong, my brothers. This place will be receiving a very important visitor in September. You do not need to know who that is yet, but our mission is to capture him and hold him hostage. Only as an absolute last resort, if our mission is certain of failure, are we to kill him. Whatever, the outcome will be glorious and we will have done our duty and caused our enemies in the West immeasurable harm."

Sharid still could not believe Fadyar had correctly identified the location.

"Fadyar, my dear sister in arms, I do not want to appear difficult especially as I know I have already angered you but there are no roads to this place. Would it not be wise to recheck the location? Are you certain there has been no mistake because this place is so remote I'm wondering if it has been abandoned long ago?"

"Sharid, you have no need to keep apologising over the girl. Your contribution to us will be vital, but I will do as you ask."

Fadyar bent over the spread-eagled map, again using the pencils as long, slender pointers.

"There, you see, no mistake. Mealag Lodge it is. I suspected something like this when I realised from the NH part of the map reference that the location would be somewhere in the north of Scotland – that is why next week we are all going on a very busy trip, to learn how we can accomplish our task. It will clearly not be easy, but there has to be a way, there always is. All we have to do is find it."

31

Alan Crossland returned to his office after a discussion with his solicitor, Avril Hennington. Cindy was apparently seeking a divorce on the grounds of his alleged unreasonable behaviour. This had made Crossland furious.

"I will not agree to that, it's absolutely outrageous. The unreasonable behaviour is not mine, but hers."

The solicitor carefully explained to Crossland his options, whilst stressing that he did not have to agree to anything in the proceedings he felt was inaccurate.

"The issues could get complicated, Mr Crossland. We could cross petition, but you have no evidence that your wife has committed adultery so any cross petition would be on similar grounds to hers. You could both mutually say you can no longer live together and so on. The law may insist on a cooling-off period, but as you are both mature people and the marriage is a relatively long one compared to some these days, that may not happen. However, if both parties fail to agree, the proceedings will become expensive and protracted."

"But she has left home, surely that means something." Crossland pleaded.

"Certainly that is evidence that you both cannot live together, but the proceedings are so far couched in the briefest of terms. It is open to your wife to change or modify those. She might, for example, retort that she has been forced to leave home because of your unreasonable behaviour. I have known cases where a wife has argued successfully that her husband's anger made her fear for her future safety. The courts are very sympathetic to women who allege such things and unreasonable behaviour is a vague term that frankly can be applied to almost anything, for example like frequent changing of the television channels or insisting on staying up until the early hours."

"This is utterly, utterly wrong. I would say it's bloody barmy.

What you are telling me is that having treated me like shit for God knows how long, refusing me anything physical, she can suddenly take herself off, do as she wants, lie if she wants to and she will get away with it."

"Not quite, but a lot of men feel that the divorce laws are unfairly biased in the woman's favour and in many respects I agree with that assessment. All that you have just said, and the way you put it, confirms to me that the two of you can no longer harmoniously live together. However, I suggest we return to the main issues. It appears that the marriage is over, do you agree?"

"Yes."

"Then, bearing in mind the possible expense of contested proceedings, do you want the divorce as quickly as possible?"

"Yes."

"Is it important to you to be awarded the divorce or not? There is little shame these days in adultery cases, so think carefully. Does it matter if your wife obtains the divorce if we cannot get anything through quickly on grounds of mutual consent?"

"Put that way, I suppose not," Crossland reluctantly answered.

"Turning to the finances, I have explained before that in my opinion your joint net assets will be divided whoever obtains the divorce on whatever grounds. We can make an offer, of course I will negotiate as best I can, but your wife has employed an experienced solicitor who can be rather feisty and I am sure she will not be advised to agree to anything that is less than reasonable."

"Yes, yes. I know. This is a load of bollocks you know. I end up paying for her having an early mid-life crisis and going on a good time frolic."

Avril Hennington ignored the outburst. She had heard far worse many times previously.

"Then we are agreed? I will do my best to minimise costs, the divorce will proceed and we will not contest it. I will try and wrap up the finances as soon as practicable."

"Agreed."

"Good." Leaning across the table the solicitor held out a typed piece of paper. "In that case, here is a list of all the financial information I shall need and a form for your completion. I know it is extensive, but it is needed. Also, please ensure that original supporting documentation, by way of bank statements and so on, as mentioned on the paper, are not destroyed in case they are required."

Seated in his office chair, Crossland read the paper thoroughly. He was not amused, but he was no longer in the mood to care overmuch. Cindy was ceasing to be part of his life and, in any event, he was now enjoying his friendship with Chloe. He had not told his solicitor of that, deliberately, but Chloe was another reason why Crossland wanted the divorce and financial settlement agreed without further delay.

A little over a week later, Cindy received a letter and enclosure from her solicitor and could hardly believe what she was reading. As a result of a telephone discussion instigated by Avril Hennington and made to Mapley Townsend, the outstanding aspects had been discussed and the enclosed note from Alan's solicitor confirmed in summary the terms of an outline agreement. Alan would not contest the divorce and subject to satisfactory disclosure, he would make an offer to Cindy of £750,000 plus half the sale proceeds of the London flat provided he could keep Red Gables and the rest of his capital assets. Cindy could retain all her capital assets. Personal pension provision was to be the sole responsibility of each party. Cindy's own solicitor pointed out that this was an initial offer and that his recommendation was to explore further as negotiation might bring forth improved terms especially in regard to the pension disparity that there would undoubtedly be when they had both retired. However, he carefully pointed out that the proposals did provide a not ungenerous settlement in the circumstances. He also pointed out to Cindy that if the offer was not acceptable, Alan had reserved the right to cross petition and to raise other procedural points, all of which would delay matters and significantly escalate costs.

Cindy didn't need to think carefully. The offer was a good one and any "further negotiation" – as her solicitor had put it – would almost certainly antagonise Alan, and lead to endless protracted and bitter arguments, with the main beneficiaries being the lawyers. She would accept straightaway, but wondered what had made Alan so conciliatory. For a long time, he had been distraught, angry and upset, though just lately he had not got quite so uptight. Now, apparently, was his sudden acceptance of the divorce and a reasonable settlement, which intrigued her. Maybe Alan had finally accepted the marriage was over, or possibly he had more money than she knew of. Perhaps, even, he had found another woman! Cindy decided not to spend any more time on idle speculation. She didn't really care what had brought about Alan's change of attitude, she would have enough money to live quite comfortably for the rest of her life and even if things didn't work out with Gordon, she had her writing to fall back on. Above all, she was relieved that Alan was apparently not complicating matters. She could now look forward to improving her cottage, and to what she hoped would be a glorious summer with Gordon. The proposed settlement terms also confirmed to her one important thing – Alan had to be unaware of Gordon, as if Alan ever got close to the truth about her relationship she knew he would then get very irate and difficult.

32

Assistant Commissioner Phillip Manders was holding his regular monthly progress review with his immediate subordinates and Bill Ritson had reported on virtually all of the cases for which he was responsible, but there was one small aspect he felt he should bring to the attention of his boss.

"There has been an interesting development on the Hannet-Mar / Crossland case, Sir. The money still hasn't moved, but I did do a bit of checking along the lines you mentioned. Crossland's relatives are all legit – nothing there to cause us any alarm – but it would appear that his wife is known to some very high-ranking people. Part of her computer records are so highly classified that even we can't access the details."

"What!" shouted Manders. "We're the bloody ATU. We can look at anything, anywhere. What do you mean? What's going on?"

"Well, we were of that opinion too, Sir, so of course have checked it out and actually there is one classification of computer record that we are barred from. It's not mentioned in our manuals anywhere, but it is coded as SR12. Haven't a clue what that stands for, but anyhow, shall I tell you what we've found out?"

"OK, OK, get on with it then, but if its important I'm not going to let this go." Manders' ire was rising, something his doctor had told him to control only a few weeks earlier when he had his six monthly check-up for hypertension.

"Well, it isn't much. As I say, we used that secret software program that draws together data from all State computer records across the varying systems… "

"Eyeball… " interrupted Manders, "the one nobody knows we have."

"That's the one. Well, the data it came back with on the screen was virtually blank apart, of course, from the name of Mrs Cindy Crossland. The surname is how it came up on our regular cross check of names, and her address matches that of Alan Crossland.

Her date and place of birth, car registration details from DVLA, National Insurance number was shown and… "

"Get to the point Bill, I don't want to know if she is a fucking pensioner!" Manders blood pressure had clearly not abated and he was beginning to flush around the cheeks on his face. Ritson ignored the interruption.

"… and her security classification was in place of what was supposed to be the data from any of the geeks files." Manders let out a low, but clearly audible whistle and sat back in his chair taking in deep breaths. He waved his hand for his detective chief superintendent to continue.

"She has been cleared by Five" said Ritson, making reference to Great Britain's famous MI5 counter espionage organisation.

"Her clearance is high, level seven." He paused, deliberately knowing it would add emphasis to his next statement.

"What is even more intriguing is that Six have also cleared her to that level." The reference to Great Britain's foreign counter intelligence agency made Manders sit bolt upright in his chair.

"There is only one other note on the data record, in the comments box, and I'll read it if I may, Sir?"

Manders nodded.

"A Mr Jack Donaldson was noted on one occasion as following the subject by car. This aspect has been thoroughly investigated and no action required and assessed as no threat to the subject."

"We ran the name of Jack Donaldson through our systems, and came up with over a thousand possible matches. However, only one lives within a radius of twenty-five miles of the Crossland's and, this is another really intriguing aspect, he turns out to be none other than Mr Crossland's chauffeur."

Ritson was proud of the way he had presented the sparse facts, like an accomplished angler delicately casting a fly to attract his quarry. He just hoped that he had hooked Manders into finding out more.

"Well, I'm buggered. But you're wrong about Donaldson being the interesting bit. Probably nothing strange in her husband's driver being spotted driving behind her. I expect there was a pretty innocent explanation. But in any event Bill, that cannot be why the computer record is protected. What has Mrs Crossland done to be cleared by both intelligence services? Do you know?"

Ritson cursed under his breath. He was so keen to dramatise his presentation for effect that he had made a fundamental mistake of not reciting everything his team had found out. His lure had crashed onto the water and he now had to come clean with an impatient Manders.

"Mrs Crossland is ex-Cabinet Office, Press and PR, and now is a freelance journalist and writer. Her experience in government might explain why she has been cleared to a high level by some agencies, but all I can ascertain about SR12 is that all enquiries have to go through to the Foreign Office. That seems strange. As far as I can ascertain she has never worked in the FO nor be high enough in Cabinet Office to merit that level of attention by them unless, perhaps, she was or is some kind of agent. I thought I should await your instructions before proceeding further with that line of enquiry"

Manders rose from his chair and started pacing around the large floor. After a minute he sat back in his chair and leaned forward towards Ritson.

"This is bloody odd. We think that Crossland may wittingly or unwittingly be channelling funds to terrorists whilst his wife is cleared by both security organisations and has some highly important connection to the Foreign Office. I want this looked into, but do not, emphasis not, approach the Foreign Office. In fact, I will take over the file temporarily and raise the matter with the commissioner himself. He moves in circles that we can only dream of, and he might shed more light on this SR12 classification. The other aspect might be Donaldson, and whether he was actually tailing Mrs Crossland for a reason or simply following her down the road. Perhaps they had both just left somewhere. Anyhow, we can leave that Bill. If the security guys are satisfied, it will not be that important."

The Chief Commissioner, Sir Neil Roberts, an Old Etonian with a first in Classics from Balliol College Oxford had risen rapidly through the ranks, fast-tracked from the moment he entered the Police Academy. Now forty-eight he was less than a year into what would be his final appointment, and they came no higher in his chosen profession than chief commissioner. He was already well paid, but looking forward a few years he was expecting to make serious money from his final year salary inflation proof pension scheme, plus lucrative part-time consultancies and private company board appointments. The recent terrorist outrage, fortunately occurring on someone else's watch, and the threat of more, could have derailed lesser men's careers in the inevitable reshuffle at the top that occurs after such monumental events, but Sir Neil Roberts was not going to let that happen to him. He realised very early in his career that the greatest value of delegation was that it usually ensured he could never be held personally accountable when things went wrong. Getting one's own hands dirty was not something that appealed to him, and he disliked it when, as now, one of his assistant chief commissioners made a special visit to see him, albeit by appointment. It usually meant that they needed Sir Neil's personal authority for something.

Manders decided not to waste his Chief's time with the peripheral issues of the Styles death or Donaldson, and in ten minutes had outlined some chosen facts. He ended by asking if Roberts could, and would, access the concealed pages from the computer record of Cindy Crossland. Roberts had listened patiently, sitting perfectly still and upright in his large chair, and never nodding his head or making any other gesture or mannerism that might indicate how he was thinking. This lack of emotion and absence of feedback frustrated and irritated Manders whose animated manner displayed a quite different personality. The cold Roberts gave nothing away until he had to.

"Phillip." Having listened to what Manders had to say Roberts cordially addressed his subordinate who hated being addressed by his full Christian name, especially by his boss whom Manders was convinced only used it to sound pompous.

"You have no actual evidence, yet, with which to confront Mr Crossland and really, all you have are a lot of loose ends that you may eventually tie into a knot – though what you expect that to retain is problematic."

Manders' loathing of tortured metaphors exceeded that of not being called simply 'Phil', and he was sure his disdain slightly showed in his facial expression. Roberts raised his voice.

"Is that not right?" he said accusingly but continued before Manders could reply.

"As it happens I believe I can personally access SR12 cases, but I am not minded to do so at this point in time on this matter." He paused. "As you may be aware, the relationship between the government and myself has become a little strained of late and I really would have to have solid grounds to poke my nose into SR12 cases. The system will log my access of the computer record and if I were to be approached to explain my personal interest in the file, I can say little other than I did so out of curiosity. From what you have told me it seems that, if anything, the wife's classification from both Five and Six in itself implies, does it not, that her husband's probity is likely to be beyond question? She would not have got that clearance if there was the slightest suspicion about her husband."

Manders was not happy at the way the chief had turned the whole basis of the interview on its head, but knew when to retreat gracefully in defeat.

"As you wish, Sir." Manders rose to leave, but Roberts waved at him to stay seated.

"Phillip, stay a while. As you know, I am a great admirer and supporter of you and your crew at ATU, and that will always continue as long as I am at the helm." Manders inwardly groaned as he anticipated having to listen to a lecture from his sailing fanatic boss interspersed with nautical imagery.

"Your work in helping to clear up the London attacks last year was outstanding and you have saved this country from numerous other threats. Politically, however, we have a government whose main focus is conducting the war on terror overseas but obsessed with reducing domestic crimes, like burglary. Our very success here in thwarting the major threats to our security at home can lead to complacency in some quarters and the ATU is an expensive part of my ship. I get somewhat tired of the politicians in Whitehall who make incomprehensible comparisons, such as equating how many extra coppers on the beat we could have if we reduced our specialist task forces and technical departments. I just wanted you to know, I have to chart our passage through very choppy waters these days. I back you and Ritson. He is a good man. If you are suspicious then follow it through as best you can and come back to me when you have something more tangible."

Manders was genuinely surprised and appreciative of Roberts candour though not his pompous manner and his maritime analogies. He had never known the man to talk in such personal terms and could only wonder how much pressure he was under.

33

Fadyar Masri, Nasra Khan, Mawdud Mattar and Sharid Bagheri had taken almost eleven hours driving the 440 mile journey to Lochaber region of the Highlands of Scotland. Masri and Khan had hired a Renault, Mattar and Bagheri a 4x4 Freelander, but from different small garages who leased out very few cars. Both had been paid for in cash. Unlike Cindy Crossland, none of the four had taken much interest in the grandness of the mountain glens or of the glittering beauty of the lochs. The nearby church bell was striking eight o'clock when the group finally reached Spean Bridge on a wet Sunday evening. Fadyar and Khan pulled onto the forecourt of the local hotel where they had booked a room using false names, and waved goodbye to Mattar and Bagheri who continued along the road. They next met the following morning at 10am in the car park of the Eagles Rest Hotel, situated two miles from the tiny hamlet of Corach and near to Loch Quoich. Fadyar went over to Mattar, sitting behind the wheel of the Freelander. She was pleased to see that he and Bagheri were dressed as typical tourists, prepared for bad weather. An assortment of waterproof jackets, boots and hats cluttered the cargo area, whilst on the backseats were rucksacks, and thick woollen sweaters.

"Firstly, we are going to drive the length of this road, to Kinloch Hourn. Drive slowly as might a tourist. Sharid, you will make notes of anything of interest, whilst Mawdud drives. You should particularly make an accurate grid reference of every track that leads off this road as the Ordnance Survey maps may not have plotted them all, or some may have changed over time. I will be ahead of you on the road; don't follow me too closely. Wait about ten minutes before you leave here. If you see we have stopped, then join us." Fadyar then walked back to Khan and got in.

"Drive slowly, Nasra. I don't want to miss anything."

True to his word they took nearly an hour on the journey to the dam, with Khan repeatedly having to stop while Fadyar briefly took photographs or made notes.

As the rear face of the huge dam came into view, Khan gasped. "In the name of Allah, that is enormous. I wasn't expecting anything that size."

"Nor me," uttered an equally shocked Fadyar.

As they reached the dam they parked at the same spot Cindy had the previous Christmas, on the large area of flattened earth and rubble immediately adjacent to the bland building which houses the dam's recording equipment and a variety of switchgear controls for the shaft intake. For a full five minutes, neither said a word as they studied the dam and its surroundings.

It was Khan who broke the silence. "Our target cannot be far away, look at this". As he spoke, he passed the folded map to Fadyar.

"You are right, Nasra. That is why I am taking so long to study the dam. The lodge is on the far shore, probably over there I expect," she pointed her finger towards where the loch disappeared into a hidden bay. "We will see all that later, but this dam will be very crucial to our planning. It appears to be the only crossing point to the far shore, but is certainly not wide enough for a vehicle and I noticed as we passed it also has a small iron gate at both ends."

The Freelander arrived, parked next to them and they all got out of their vehicles. Bagheri placed the high powered binoculars to his eyes and slowly turned so that he covered every aspect of the dam.

"They have to get in by boat, Fadyar, but I've looked and can't see boats anywhere."

"The lodge must have at least two access options. The weather here can be appalling and crossing by boat would be highly dangerous in such conditions. There has to be a way in from another road." As she spoke, Fadyar looked carefully at the map and rested the tip of her index finger, much like a pointer, an inch away from the dam.

"Can you see that small road, the one next to Loch Arkaig? Even though no road is shown off it, there has to be a forest trail or track that leads into Mealag Lodge. A helipad has also been built somewhere within the grounds – I learnt that from the internet – so the materials needed for that must have required access by road."

"How wealthy is the target?" Bagheri inquired.

"I can tell you our target is not the wealthy owner." Fadyar didn't elaborate, and changed the subject.

"My guess is that if we carry on down this road towards Kinloch Hourn, in a mile or two the lodge will come into view. Nasra and I will stop there. You two will drive on as though you do not know us, and continue with your note taking. I want a thorough report on Kinloch Hourn. There are people there and it has access to the sea, so there must be some kind of anchorage or harbour. I shall visit there tomorrow, whilst you two will go back to the main road and find the road to Loch Arkaig and also confirm if there is a way from there into the Lodge. If you need to hire an even more powerful 4x4 then hire one the following day. OK let's move. I'll see you back here when you've completed your reconnaissance of Kinloch Hourn."

When the Mealag complex came into view, Fadyar asked Khan to stop the car. There was no immediate place to do so on the road, but he saw a passing place on the right and reversed into it so that they could look out of the front windscreen across the loch. Fadyar produced her small pocket telescope from her pocket. It was a cheap four section scope that extended to 35cm, but it provided remarkably clear images up to twenty five times magnification, and she preferred its simplicity to that of binoculars which always seemed to give her difficulty in focusing upon an object. She smiled as she thought of Bagheri's expensive binoculars that albeit provided sharper images but at less than half the magnification of her telescope and at ten times the cost. They could see the landing stage and part of one of the chalets, but not the lodge itself. She and Khan independently jotted down some notes. They casually got out of the car and strolled along the road pretending to take in the scenery and within a few steps noticed the trodden down grass that signified the pathway to shore. They walked down and found a single wooden boat tied up at a small jetty. The boat was without oars or an outboard.

"Well, that's how they cross." Khan's habit of saying the obvious sometimes annoyed Fadyar, but not today. She was puzzling out why there were no oars.

"Let's walk up behind where we left the car, there's a track that leads off from the lay-by. Maybe they leave the oars out of sight." She shouted back to Khan as she had already commenced the walk. They quickly found the garages and Fadyar made a specific entry in her notebook of the thick iron chain and cross bolts that secured the doors. She also observed an overhead telephone wire secured to the right top corner of the garages and followed it back to the British Telecom pole.

"I doubt that is for a land phone, or at least not only a phone. There's a notice that says this place is alarmed, and I guess it connects automatically to both the lodge and the police station, probably at Fort Augustus. If either alarm gets triggered, a simple road block could easily be set up where this road meets the main road and would prevent any escape. The lodge will have its own security system, probably a lot more sophisticated than this but almost certainly linked to the police, and that Arkaig road is similar to this one; it's really one long road leading to a dead end and easily blocked."

"We could disable the alarm," Khan suggested.

"Possibly, but that would require time and tools. It looks a simple enough system, but I suspect it may have one or two additions that could make it tamper-proof. Unfortunately, we do not have the luxury of being able to test that."

Fadyar was realising that this mission was certainly not going to be easy. In fact, it was already becoming far more difficult than even she imagined when she had first identified the lodge on the Ordnance Survey map back in Birmingham, but she was determined not to let her dismay be noticed by Khan.

"There is only one thing for it. Where there is water, there are always boats. We must hire a boat. I need to get a really good look at Mealag Lodge. The glimpse of it from here, and that cottage or bungalow – whatever it is – that we can see, doesn't help us much. The map shows quite a large area of various buildings over there. Before we hire a boat, we will need to buy a couple of cheap fly fishing rods and at least look like we have a reason to be on the water. No one will travel up and down these lochs without a purpose."

Fadyar and Khan returned to the stony parking area next to the switchgear building. Carrying their rucksacks, they climbed over the gate and crossed the dam appearing to be walkers out for a hike. Khan silently counted his footsteps and told Fadyar that the dam was over 300 metres in length. She had also been closely taking mental notes as they walked.

"What's worse, Nasra, is that as it is so narrow and straight, it affords no cover at all along its length. Your head and shoulders are visible to everyone around the loch and to anyone driving up the road towards the dam from Corach. The walkway itself is a killing zone. A single person placed at one of the gates could hold off an army wanting to cross."

Fadyar decided they should try and walk towards Mealag Lodge. She carefully noted where a pathway had been worn and they followed it. Her trained eye took in where it deviated from an apparently obvious straight line to keep well away from the water's edge.

"Write down 'soft at edge', Nasra, while I take a look around with my scope. We must appear to be tourists at all times. Remember that."

Stepping carefully well away from the peat bog, they continued their walk towards Mealag. A large knoll almost blocked their path as it sloped down close to the shore-line, which was itself littered with numerous pieces of wood, rope and other detritus swept to the water's edge by the high wind of a recent storm. Behind the barren rocky outcrop stood a dense forest of tall pine trees standing proudly against the skyline.

"It's got to be round the corner," whispered Fadyar. "Go carefully. I'll lead."

Khan nervously followed a few paces behind his leader. Suddenly Fadyar stepped abruptly back, almost colliding with Khan.

"There's a boundary deer fence at the edge of the trees, but it doesn't quite reach the shore and then it looks completely open. I don't think the entrance is sealed off." She spoke quickly, her excitement growing, as they sheltered once more behind the rock.

She was amazed that there were no notices prohibiting walkers, no strong high fence, in fact nothing that prevented access; it was too easy, much too easy. Had she known it, non-motorised access rights can be exercised over most of Scotland, from urban parks and path networks, to the hills and forests, lochs and rivers and so 'KEEP OUT' notices would have been of little legal effect. Not only did Gordon Truscott know that, but he would never have been permitted to scar the landscape by building ugly, visible, security fences even if he had wished to, which he certainly didn't.

Fadyar once more edged to the front of the knoll and peered around it. She discovered that there were actually two mesh fences, one on each side of the complex marking out its boundary but there was nothing that inhibited anyone from walking along the broad and expansive shore-line that fronted the lodge and chalets. Fadyar realised that the openness of the location also worked to her disadvantage. The main house, Mealag Lodge, was still out of view to her and she correctly deduced it was sited well back but almost adjacent to the forest behind the knoll. She looked across the loch, anxious to check if anyone else had parked their car or was walking along the road. It was clear, so she had time to consider her next move without attracting any unwelcome attention from sightseeing tourists. Somehow she had to get an uninterrupted view of the Lodge. She looked up at the knoll but it would be a dangerous climb and, anyway, the trees would almost certainly prevent her seeing the Lodge. She puzzled about her dilemma for a few minutes and then decided to be bold.

"We will walk past, then stop and take a few photographs of the dam. Then I will turn and we will pretend to take a few photographs of each other with the lodge and general area behind us. Actually, we shall try to take pictures of as much of the complex as possible, but quickly. We must be quick. We will then hold hands to look like a couple in love and walk on well past the lodge and continue wandering around the loch for about half an hour, before coming back so that we get an appreciation of the layout from the other direction."

Fadyar's elaborate subterfuge and concern were unnecessary. Only Margaret MacLean was at the lodge itself and she was busy in the kitchen whilst her husband was helping to remove a dead tree several miles away on the estate. There was nothing to inhibit her and Khan taking their time, but they were still able to take all the photographs she wanted.

The following days were spent gathering information. Kinloch Hourn had sea access and offered a potential escape route, but it was a small community and any dubious activity by outsiders would be noticed and reported. As it was, Mattar and Bagheri almost aroused suspicion when they asked at Kinloch Hourn if it was possible to hire a boat as they wished to go fishing near the dam at Loch Quoich. The boat owner explained that the dam was almost seven miles away and assured them that there was no need to travel that far in order to get a good day's fishing. Nonetheless, Mattar and Bagheri said that they really wanted to fish the whole length of the loch and so, after some discussion, they were sold an extra gallon of fuel at an exorbitant price. The bemused boat owner, thinking the two improbable looking fishermen were even more stupid than the average tourist levied an additional surcharge for the extra wear and tear on the outboard. That trip had however provided a wealth of photographs of small inlets around the loch where a boat could safely reach the shore, plus some more photographs of Mealag.

The four had determined that a larger 4x4, more suited to rugged off-road driving, would be needed to explore the apparently rougher terrain around the Loch Arkaig area – and so hired another vehicle. The alternative access to Mealag had to be land based and therefore near to Loch Arkaig, and they had observed a small track off to the right from the unclassified road marked on the map, which seemed to go at least partway towards the large house. As it turned out, the map was accurate and the track petered out to nothing after a few tortuous miles, leaving the group dismayed, frustrated and physically bruised at having to return along the rock strewn, ground, none the wiser.

Farther along the Arkaig road, they quickly found another track, this time definitely not marked on the OS map, which passed through a thick forest and which seemed an altogether more promising prospect in their search for a possible entry and exit route to Mealag. Although rough, the soil had been heavily compacted indicating that heavy machinery or vehicles had regularly passed over it and two distinct parallel tracks had been formed where the grass had been worn away. Attempts had been made to level the very worse bumps and troughs, as spasmodic small areas of compacted, crushed stone could be seen where it had been used to make the route more easily passable. A deer fence had been erected and threaded through the first line of trees on both sides of the track and two miles from where it joined the Arkaig road, a small clearing had been made. Here, double steel and wire-mesh padlocked gates marked the eastern boundary entrance to the Mealag Lodge complex and blocked the way ahead. Much higher and thicker gauge fencing depicting the side boundaries was fixed at the side of each gate and disappeared into the forest, eventually re-appearing where Nasra and Fadyar took their photographs at the shore of Loch Quoich just over a mile away.

Satisfied that they had at least found one alternative access, Fadyar and her team returned to the Loch Arkaig road. Like the Quoich dam road from Invergarry, this was a single carriageway and driving upon it was very slow due to the numerous humps and bends. The Arkaig road did not meet the sea, or at least not directly, as after a few miles from the recently discovered track it ended at a gated path that quickly deteriorated to just rutted, barren earth and projecting rocks that led for miles through the largely uninhabited area of Knoydart. Fadyar had read that those living in these parts did not welcome tourist motor vehicles but, whether true or not, at the very least their large four wheel drive vehicle would be conspicuous and its occupants observed, so they decided to turn around and head back.

They had used a stopwatch to get accurate timings of running and walking across the dam wall, as well as ascertaining the journey time by boat from the bay at Mealag to the small jetty below the road. Road distances were carefully measured, but more importantly the time it took to drive along them was scrupulously logged. Suitable places on the far shore near to Mealag were very discreetly examined as to their suitability for mooring or beaching a boat. They had visited several places on the coast nearby, such as Glenelg and Sandaig, in the hope that a road or track might be found through the mountains and ruled out ever being able to drive a vehicle from Kinloch Hourn through to Knoydart.

Crucially, they had also discovered that because of the

mountainous terrain the signal for their mobile phones was non-existent around the lodge and the dam, but was normal by the sea at Kinloch Hourn. The communications problem deeply troubled Fadyar. The mission was fraught with difficulties and to have any chance of success she knew that she would need to be able to communicate with her team at all times. The challenges Fadyar faced were formidable. She had no doubt that she could succeed with an assassination attempt, but capturing Assiter alive and escaping safely would be very difficult indeed. Still, she was determined to do her best and obey orders. She had all the raw data needed. It was now her responsibility as leader to devise a workable plan with reasonable chances of success, and if possible an alternative, if the original idea failed. At the conclusion of their week in the Scottish Highlands, the four terrorists had all the physical information they needed in order to prepare for their September attack, but it would be a daunting challenge.

34

Jack Donaldson learned that Crossland and his wife had agreed the terms of their divorce whilst driving his boss back to Red Gables. Crossland, seated comfortably on the sumptuous black leather rear seat, seemed quite relaxed about telling his driver of his personal matters. He told Donaldson that there was no longer any need to continue his intermittent surveillance of Cindy.

"I'm upset, of course, Jack. Still don't know what brought about her change of attitude but life moves on. The quicker she is part of my history, the better." Crossland sounded as if he had certainly become more confident and forward looking compared with the worried and morose figure he had been for the last few months.

Donaldson said little, but he was thinking a lot. There was something about Cindy Crossland's change of attitude towards her husband that still puzzled him. He had known them both for many years. Cindy had always been the outward going one of the pair, almost dazzling by comparison to Alan. It was Cindy that used to love sailing and horse riding, have a glamorous job in the Press Office of the Government, loved meeting people and enjoying parties. She even looked forward to the ritualistic pre-lunch Sunday drinks of the Stillwood crowd, only too eager when it was the Crossland's time to host to turn it into an open-house weekend party at Red Gables, that started on the Saturday afternoon and lasted late into Sunday evening. A mere two hours of topping up wine glasses on a Sunday morning wasn't Cindy's idea of fun. All were invited to her famed gatherings and she enjoyed nothing more than guests bringing along their own friends, especially if they were foreign as she could speak fluent French, German and Russian. And she was attractive. So much so that most of the men found excuses to gravitate in her direction as often as they deemed they would be safe from the admonition of their wives or mistresses.

Yet she had turned her back on that life and was apparently settling down alone in a reasonably sized, but not large, cottage in Grimley, going to coffee mornings, charity functions and genteel ladies lunches. True she retained an apparent liking for holidays, but her relatively new interest of gun dogs – when she herself didn't possess a dog or shotgun – totally baffled him. *No, it simply didn't add up,* he thought. He determined that he was going to find the answer, even if her husband had given up trying. What had he to lose? He still fancied his chances with her and if she were alone she would be missing male company. Why shouldn't they have some fun together? Alternatively, if she did have something to hide that he could find out about, she might be willing to reach a mutually acceptable agreement for it to remain a secret. Either way, Donaldson's interest in Cindy was far from diminished at hearing of her impending divorce.

He suddenly became aware that Crossland was still talking to him, saying something about a woman named Chloe.

"Sorry Sir, concentrating on the road. I didn't quite catch that last bit." He leaned back over his left shoulder as he spoke in order that Crossland might speak up.

"I was saying, Jack, that I recently met a woman named Chloe. She's quite a bit younger and we're getting on really well, so there was no point in trying to hang onto Cindy."

"Does she know? Mrs Crossland I mean? Does she know about this Chloe?" Donaldson was not simply a thuggish ex-mercenary. He was sharp, with a quick brain which he had needed to use on several occasions to survive some very dangerous situations.

"No, Jack. I haven't told her. Prefer her not to know just yet. Not until everything is finalised."

The chauffeur nodded, saying nothing, but logging another piece of information that might be useful sometime. *Perhaps,* Donaldson thought, *this might be an opportune time to raise the subject of his pay, especially as Crossland seemed in a good frame of mind and had now imparted some very personal information.* He explained that his own domestic situation had become somewhat expensive lately but did not tell Crossland that the long suffering Russian wife had finally sought the advice of a support group for East European immigrants. They had ensured that Donaldson had finally paid her in cash for the pleasures he had experienced and the pain he had inflicted. In return, they would not inform the Domestic Violence Unit of the local police.

"I know you have always paid the expenses, Sir, of my trips to keep watch on Mrs Crossland, but that has entailed some very long hours and has frequently been quite tiring. Perhaps sometime, I don't wish to trouble you now, you could consider the whole matter of my remuneration as it must be nearly two years since it was last reviewed."

Crossland's reply was not to Donaldson's liking.

"Well, Jack, to be honest, I think the bank pays you pretty well for what we might term your official duties. You have though been a great help to me personally and of course that is not strictly the bank's business so I think something in the way of a special bonus is called for. I tell you what, I'm going to order one of the new Mercs soon – you know the latest S class – they are really good. You can have this Jag. It's worth a few thousand and we'll call it quits. Your bank salary always increases at the rate of inflation so you have that protection. Also, you must be one of the very few drivers, if any, that is in receipt of a bank-subsidised mortgage plus an excellent pension scheme. All in all, I don't think you can grumble."

"OK Sir, thank you." Donaldson was so angry he could hardly get the few words out of his mouth. He didn't want the fucking Jaguar. What was he supposed to do with that? He couldn't afford to insure it, let alone pay the cost of pouring petrol down its greedy throat. He surmised, correctly, that the bank had probably written down its value to zero in its books, so the cost to Crossland or his bloody bank was nothing. All Donaldson would be able to do would be to hawk it round various dealers, or try and sell it privately for a measly few thousand quid. Three year old excessive-mileage luxury saloon cars were not renowned for fetching high second hand prices. The conversation marked a turning point for him. Henceforth, he would have a much more formal relationship with his boss and the next time Crossland needed a personal favour he would extract a high price, in cash, up front.

★ ★ ★

The months of May to August had been utter bliss for Cindy and Gordon. They had holidayed at the villa again and also taken short breaks in Rome and Milan. Cindy had wanted to see the Papal

Basilica of St Peter for many years and was spellbound by its grandeur, architecture and frescos. They also visited the Sistine Chapel within the Apostolic Palace, where Cindy marvelled at the beauty of the paintings by Perugino, Botticelli and Ghirlandaio and was moved to tears at the unparalleled magnificence of the Michelangelo ceiling. In Milan, Gordon escorted her to the famed La Scala opera house for a performance of Tosca, with Cecilia Bartoli in the lead role and the orchestra under the baton of Daniel Barenbohm – the theatre's recently appointed principal conductor.

When they were not abroad, Gordon had found time to visit the cottage at Grimley a couple of times and Cindy had made a brief visit to Mealag. She had never felt such happiness. She was totally at ease within herself and everyday was an excitement for her. The cottage was proving to be the perfect base. It was near to the M5 motorway, making road travel easy, and the more she discovered about the city of Worcester the more she admired the way in which it had blended a modern pedestrian-only shopping centre alongside the old architectural and historically important buildings, none more so than the divine cathedral itself.

The brightly coloured spring and summer bulbs in her garden seemed to match her own bourgeoning joy as they rose strongly upwards before bursting into full bloom. The well-cut lawns provided her with a private resting place on warm afternoons, and the colours of the flowers and lush, fine grass contrasted pleasingly with the white stonewash of the cottage.

Gordon, too, was elated. He was pleased at Cindy's divorce and that she and her husband had settled matters amicably. He had never before contemplated marriage, but he was now thinking more and more about when would be the right time to mention it. Margaret MacLean was in no doubt that before the year ended he would be engaged to Cindy, and was already speculating to her husband as to where the marriage would take place. She looked upon Gordon as the surrogate son she could never have borne, cancer in her early twenties necessitating major surgery that removed her womb and other internal organs. She had noticed how much in love Gordon was, and it gave her great pleasure to welcome Cindy whenever she made the long journey to Mealag.

Cindy and Gordon would not have been quite so ecstatically happy had they known that in June, when Gordon had stayed at Cindy's cottage, his arrival had been noted by Jack Donaldson sitting in his newly acquired second-hand blue and gold Subaru Imprezza. Donaldson had not really expected to find out anything new when he undertook one of his random surveillance trips out to Grimley to see if Cindy was at home. It was a Friday evening and he had already driven Crossland from his London Office to Red Gables, collected his car and instead of eating at home had decided to have a meal in the Dog and Whistle at Drakes Broughton en route to Cindy's cottage. He arrived a little before ten in the evening and stopped his car half way along a horseshoe curved cul-de-sac. The frontage of her cottage was in sight, about fifty metres farther along the road. He saw instantly that Cindy was home as the lights shone brightly against the darkening sky. He wondered what she was doing, how she would be dressed. His thoughts recalled how she had looked when he had visited Red Gables and how she had provocatively and deliberately leant over the table to tease him, only then to humiliate him when he responded.

"One day", he muttered to himself. "One day".

He had been stationary for about ten minutes when a car swept around the bend, travelling quite fast. It passed him so quickly that he was taken by surprise, but he noticed that it was a large silver Volvo estate. Almost immediately, the trio of rear braking lights glowed red and the driver stopped on Cindy's driveway leaving the engine running. Within a few seconds, the electric garage door swung upwards. The car moved slowly forward and the garage door started to close behind it. Donaldson instinctively knew the driver would be male, even though he had failed to make out any features of the person behind the steering wheel, as no woman he had ever known would drive a large estate at such a speed. He pondered what to do next, whether he should walk past the cottage or stay in his car. The open lounge windows might enable him to get a good view of the visitor, but what if he was recognised? Before he had decided, Cindy began closing the curtains just as he glimpsed the silhouette of a man at the back of the room. He couldn't recall Crossland ever implying or mentioning to him that Cindy had any living relatives, distant or near, in the various conversations the two had had over the years. No, Donaldson reasoned, this had to be someone new in her life, perhaps the reason for her changing attitude towards her husband that has led to the divorce.

As he waited, any lingering doubts Donaldson had about the nature of Cindy's visitor vanished the moment the lounge light went out half an hour later and a single upstairs bedroom light went on. He watched intently, looking to see if he could make out any shadows behind the curtains, but their thick lining thwarted his voyeurism. Donaldson started the car and returned home, determined to find out more about Cindy Crossland's new lover. The next morning he hired a small Fiat and drove to Grimley. The cottage windows were open, the curtains drawn back. He drove to the end of the road and slowly executed a three-point turn outside Cindy's cottage. He saw nothing. Disappointed, he left the cul-de-sac and parked half a mile away and waited.

An hour later he gave up and returned home, but in the afternoon he revisited the cul-de-sac. Cindy was kneeling in the front garden removing the dying and dead blooms from the flowers, and he thought how good she looked even when dressed in her old gardening clothes. There was no sign of the man and Donaldson wondered if he had left early that Saturday morning, if so why? Perhaps he was married, a salesman perhaps, who had to get back to the wife and kids at the weekend, but could use some excuse about being held up during the week. His thoughts ran riot, but none came close to the truth.

As he watched her, Cindy stood up, her gardening finished, and she opened up the garage door by pressing a remote control taken from her pocket. The Volvo was still there! Not a salesman then for a quick stopover on a Friday night. His Saturday vigil gleaned no further information but Donaldson was not dismayed, knowing he would visit again on Sunday morning. He was pleased that his tactic of regularly switching cars and parking in slightly different places had been successful in ensuring his visits had not aroused the suspicion of Cindy's neighbours. Nonetheless, he thought he should only visit twice on Sunday, first in the morning and at about ten in the evening. He never made the evening trip.

35

Alan Crossland was also really enjoying life and had returned to the office after a hectic weekend with Chloe. He actually disliked the fact that the divorce with Cindy might take some months to finalise, but it no longer played on his mind as it once did. Sure, he was still sad that he had lost Cindy, particularly as he did not know the reason why she had changed so much from the woman he married. It had caused him to seriously reflect upon their life together and wondered if he might somehow, however unwittingly, be partly to blame. He had always thought that Cindy enjoyed their marriage. He had given her freedom to work where and when she pleased, and never sought to control either her career or her hobbies. They had mutual interests, such as sailing and riding, and Cindy had always said how much she loved Red Gables and living in the Cotswolds. He wasn't a gregarious man, had no expensive tastes and also looked forward at the weekend to joining Cindy, even when she insisted on having the local crowd round. He had tried, in every way possible he thought, to be a loyal, hardworking, supportive husband. The only thing he wondered that might perhaps be levelled against him was that he wasn't adventurous or exciting enough for her, but she had never given the slightest hint that was true. It was, though, the only aspect of their lives where he felt he could be criticised. There had been a couple of occasions when Cindy had wanted to come to the London flat and spend the weekend in town, going to the opera or a West End show, and he had preferred to get out of London and away from all its noise and people to the calm and tranquillity of their home. He was determined not to make the same mistake in his new relationship with Chloe.

"Cindy was past, forget her and move on. Change your life, don't repeat it" he kept saying to himself.

There was little chance of an easy going life when he spent time with Chloe. He had almost forgotten just how active a twenty-eight year old woman could be, and Alan was often reminded all too painfully of the thirteen year age gap between them. In early May, soon after they had returned from the hotel, they were talking one evening about their hobbies and interests and Chloe revealed she enjoyed the occasional game of tennis. Alan, keen to impress his young conquest, mentioned that he had played it quite a bit at university – whereas the truth was that one drunken evening he and several others decided to hit a few balls at each other on the College all weather court.

Chloe immediately arranged for a game at a local club and Alan, desperate to look the part, had made a special trip to the shops to purchase white shirts and tennis shoes, plus a very expensive racket which differed considerably in size, shape and construction from any he had previously used. Chloe started gently enough and Alan was quite pleased how hard he seemed to be hitting the ball with his new racket. Slowly however, Alan was beginning to realise that the rallies were getting longer and that it was he, not Chloe, doing the running. His new shoes were beginning to cause a painful blister on each foot and his wrist and arm was starting to ache. Sweat began to trickle into his eyes as he threw the ball and looked up to serve, adding to the already considerable difficulty he had at mastering that aspect of the game.

Chloe by contrast, was able to accurately aim what Alan considered to be rather ferocious serves. If by some good fortune he managed to hit a return over the net to start a rally, it was he, and not Chloe, who watched the ball bounce speedily into an empty part of the court. Try as he might to place a shot in a position that she could not reach, Chloe seemed able to have plenty of time to reach the ball and hit it back venomously. After forty minutes, Chloe suggested they stop.

"If only because I don't want you worn out for tonight!" she teased.

It wasn't just on the tennis court where Alan found himself wishing he was at least a stone lighter and ten years younger. Chloe, seemed to live life at breakneck speed. She had a full-time job working as a history teacher at a public school for girls and seemed to enjoy a host of activities. She was definitely not a stay at home person, and both she and Alan rarely spent an evening either in his flat or hers. She loved going to the cinema at least once a week, the theatre or a show once a month. In addition to tennis she loved swimming, horse riding and badminton and wished she lived in the country as she liked trekking. Alan was thoroughly happy in her company. She was enlivening and he walked tall with pride whenever he accompanied her. Whilst his physical age and lack of fitness would sometimes become apparent, mentally he felt young again. Chloe had suggested he needed a new wardrobe and she came with him to ensure that he chose wisely. He found himself wearing brighter coloured clothes, in modern styles that he would never have considered when he was living with Cindy. His new bespoke office suits, too, were slightly more flamboyant in design and the size of the pin stripe. 'Firenze' was how his obsequious tailor described the Italian style, but his standard of dress still reflected the correct image of an executive city banker. Chloe had made suggestions about his hair styling and suggested he might try out a place she knew of in Chelsea. Much to his surprise he enjoyed the new look created for him, though was aghast at its cost.

Alan Crossland had become very much aware that Chloe was now an intrinsic part of his life and he was pretty certain the feelings he felt towards her were mutual. In fact, Chloe was very much in love, but was trying hard not to show it too much. She had been very badly hurt once and had vowed never again to go out with a married man so she was initially apprehensive when Alan had said at the hotel he was not yet divorced, lest it lead to another heartbreak or betrayal. Alan had quickly put those fears to rest when he showed her the papers from his solicitor and she relaxed more as they grew closer. She found Alan a welcome change from going out with young, single twenty-year-olds whose idea of a good time seemed limited to going to a pub, having a few drinks and then expecting to bed her. They lacked manners, grace and kindness, and she found them remarkably immature. It was for those reasons she had put aside her reservations when Tom, older than her by seven years and married, had first asked her out. Tom, like Alan, did treat a woman properly. He knew how to listen and be interested. He showed kindness and consideration, and was particularly sensitive to her needs of exactly when and how to make love to her, not just a rapid fumbling and quick bang. Their relationship had not worked out, not because Tom had deceived her, he hadn't, but just as she and Tom were seriously talking of living together, his wife was involved in a head-on collision whilst driving her car. At that moment, Chloe sensed the accident would end her relationship with Tom, and so it proved. His wife had a long period of hospitalisation and subsequent convalescence, and Chloe and Tom's liaisons became fewer and fewer. When Tom's wife came home, still limping and suffering some permanent disability in her right arm, Tom told Chloe that he had to remain and look after his wife. She suspected he would, but it had hurt. She now felt that with Alan there was really something good happening for her, for them both, and that she could put the pain behind her.

The change Chloe brought about in Alan's life gave him new-found assurance which permeated into his banking business. He became more proactive at work, suggesting to the board new plans and fresh initiatives. He wanted the bank to be modern, progressive and ambitious, not dull, dour and stolid. He was consumed by the idea of change, at home and office, and where better to start than a review of his own personal portfolio. His clients had served him well over the years, but perhaps this was now the time when he should write to the account holders notifying them of his intention to delegate their day-to-day control to others. Some of the investments might appear a little risky but none involved any criminal activity to his knowledge, and the initial up-front fees that he had received personally had long since been dwarfed by the returns they had provided to the bank and the clients. The only personal case that troubled him was that of the Chalthoum Universal Holdings account.

When he had met Fadyar at his home, she had led him to believe that the consortium or Chalthoum would be investing significant sums as had been the case with other Dubai based organisations. As it was, only a paltry £300,000 had been lodged at the bank and that, he reasoned, did not merit his personal attention; for a discreet but important commercial bank for wealthy Middle Eastern clients, probably not that of his staff either. He realised, however, he must be careful. The police were certainly suspicious of the account, and indeed he himself had serious misgivings once he had been shown Fadyar's photograph and learnt of Styles' death. The two were probably not related but it worried him nonetheless. He was also fully aware that somehow he had got into a position with the ATU whereby he had denied any knowledge of Fadyar and he could really do with the police getting off his back. He asked his secretary to get Detective Chief Superintendent Ritson on the phone.

"Ritson," a barking voice rasped into the earpiece. The officer sounded impatient before Alan Crossland had uttered a word.

"Good morning Chief Superintendent, how are you?" Crossland thought he should be pleasant and duplicate the introductions his secretary would have already made on his behalf.

"Well, thank you Sir. But busy." Ritson had moderated his tone but not the speed of his delivery. Crossland was not going to be rushed, what he had to say had to be carefully put.

"The bank will soon be undertaking a review of its activities, and one purpose will be to identify inactive or non-profitable accounts. I know you were interested a while back in Halima Chalthoum of Chalthoum Universal Holdings and the Dubai based Consortium she represents. I feel that account may not pass our review. As you are aware, there is only a modest sum by our standards in the account and it certainly has been disappointing to us that it has not been… " he paused slightly, "… more heavily subscribed, shall we say. The bank is still waiting to learn the specifics of quite how we can assist the account holder with regard to the proposed investment, and after this length of time I am not optimistic that it is ever likely to be an attractive proposition for us."

"In simple terms, Sir, what does 'may not pass your review' actually mean in plain English? Ritson asked, his voice having slowed considerably.

"Well, er, we might well decide to inform the client of our intention to close the account, and that unless we hear to the contrary within a specified period we would return the final settlement balance to the Egyptian bank that sent the funds to us. I am informing you out of courtesy of what the bank is likely to propose, as I thought you might like to know." Crossland could be smooth when it was required of him.

"Wasn't this account marked only for your attention, Mr Crossland? I seem to remember that it was for some reason though I can't recall quite what that reason was."

Crossland knew that Ritson was probing to see if he gave the same answer as he had done several months before when Ritson interviewed him.

"It was and is still. However, as I believe I said to you when you visited us, it was only marked for my personal attention as it was a new account and, having not met with the account holder, I wished to keep it under review especially as I was hoping it would be a highly profitable account for us. Perhaps you would like more time, Chief Superintendent? We can put off the review for a week or so if it helps." Crossland began to rather enjoy the exchange with Ritson buoyed by his newly acquired general confidence.

"That's very kind of you, Sir, but I shall not need more time. I must advise that we would very much prefer you to take absolutely no action on that account, none whatsoever."

"Well, I can imagine there is no point in my asking you to explain your reasons, but I do have the bank's interests to consider. I trust I can remove my own personal code on it?"

"I understand that Sir, but I have the nation's security to consider. I am requesting you do nothing with that account, but if you disagree I can insist upon it and legally force you to comply. I am not concerned if it remains marked for your attention only, provided no one takes any action upon it."

"Chief Superintendent, there will be no need for legal measures or anything like that. The whole purpose of this call was to ask your opinion. Now I have it, you have my word we will not take any action on the account." Crossland remained pleasant and calm despite Ritson's rather high-handed threat.

"Thank you, Sir, I appreciate your co-operation."

Crossland smiled as he put down the phone, satisfied with the outcome of his call. He would have been delighted had he known of Ritson's reaction once the conversation had ended. The detective stormed into Manders' office and explained what had transpired.

"I actually had to say thank you to the bastard," Ritson exclaimed to his boss. "But he's no bloody terrorist. He's a typically smooth wanker banker. That's what he is!"

Manders laughed loudly, "Crossland has really got to you, hasn't he? Clever though, he's turned the tables on us in a way. Yep. Clever… very neat. He now knows we are continuing to monitor the account, and by implication the persons associated with it, but has distanced himself from the enquiry. I tend to agree with your assessment of him Bill, but if he were to be involved with these fanatics or was being used by them, albeit unwittingly, he's someone we must keep on our radar. Was that telephone call really just out of courtesy, or was it to find out if we are still watching him and his bank? I have a feeling that the Chalthoum account is causing him more angst than we know. Why? That's what I want to find out. Why?"

36

In Paris, the morning June sunshine was causing the city temperature to rise rapidly, and a thin layer of smog from the emissions of thousands of vehicle exhausts hung languidly over the streets in the still air. Having eaten a simple breakfast of half a grapefruit and a slice of toast washed down with two mugs of very sweet black coffee, Fadyar Masri was ready once more to use her apartment as a planning centre. She pushed all her lounge chairs and occasional tables to the walls, clearing the largest area she could of her carpeted floor. Spread out were photographs, maps, notes and various diagrams. Before she contemplated even starting to draft out the detail, she wanted to know exactly what information she had. The most trivial piece of data could be vital and she needed to ensure that her plan would not omit something of importance that had lain unread on the floor. One by one she examined the photographs and placed them so it was possible to get a full panoramic view of all sides of the loch near to Mealag Lodge. When she had absorbed one set of photographs, she would remove them to be replaced by another. She moved other pictures in position to show areas such as Kinloch Hourn and the dam itself. There were nearly two dozen photographs of the latter, taken at every angle from both sides of the dam plus others that members of her group had taken as they walked across the dam towards Mealag. There were photographs of tracks and paths including several of the large garages, the padlock and chains that held them, and the external bell of the alarm system that guarded them. All the access points to Mealag had been photographed whether from Loch Quoich or Loch Arkaig. It surprised her that there were fifteen pictures just of Mealag Lodge and the complex, as she hadn't realised they had been able to take so many, and she was also impressed with the clarity and detail of all the pictures. Her initial fears at the dam of not being able to get close enough to the lodge had been unfounded as the sharp images before her proved.

Three hours had elapsed and Fadyar was suddenly very aware of the scorching sun searing through her cotton blouse and onto her shoulders. She stood up, her back painful and stiff from being bent over for so long, and stretched her arms upwards to relieve the pressure. She fully closed the window blinds and the room darkened, but was still bright enough for her to see everything clearly. She reached into the fridge and pulled the ring on a cola can. Holding it to her lips, she poured the cold liquid into her mouth swallowing quickly. Refreshed, she returned to the assortment of information strewn across the floor and took hold of the pile of maps. She had purchased some additional maps when in Scotland, two each of numbers 413 and 414 of the Ordnance Survey Explorer series. Scaled at 1:25000, these were twice as detailed as the Landranger maps. From her needlework basket, she cut a length of strong black cotton and spent the next hour and half carefully laying the thread along roads and tracks before measuring its length against the scale imprinted on the map. She compared the distances calculated in this way with those she and her compatriots had taken in the car or estimated by foot. She made a definitive note of the longer of the two measurements, thereby never underestimating journey times nor distances. Fadyar Masri was determined that this mission was going to succeed. The death of her parents had left her with a burning ambition for revenge, the flames of which could only be quenched by a retaliatory act of such daring that it would shock those who sent their soldiers to kill innocent Iraqi citizens like her mother and father. Failure was not an option and she was quite prepared to die proving it. She therefore needed to anticipate and understand every foreseeable difficulty that might arise, and find a way of neutralising any threat to the mission. She worked the next three days carefully compiling options and strategies until she was satisfied she had as near-perfect plan as she could devise.

The following day was spent building in options at key points in the plan, and the day after Fadyar worked on producing the list of equipment she would need. She was exhausted. Her brain was aching and her body was rebelling against having received only very spasmodic and totally inadequate replenishment of vital nutrients.

The strain of such intense reading had reddened the white sclera surrounding her soft brown eyes and her heart continually thumped hard into the wall of her chest. She knew she needed to rest and spent two days trying to relax, not touching any of the material gathered from the reconnaissance trip, but she had no control over her mind which whirred incessantly with details of the plan. The following week she meticulously checked and reviewed every aspect about her plan, making certain that everything that could be thought of had been. Satisfied, she left a coded message for Carron to visit her at the flat after dark, giving him a choice of three dates.

37

The Secretary of State is the chief executive officer of the United States Department of State, the most senior of all federal executive departments, and, after the President and Vice President, is the third-highest official of the federal government. Dean Assiter was a man who wielded considerable power and influence around the world, not just in Washington. He was the President's chief adviser on U.S. foreign policy and personally negotiated, interpreted and, when the need arose, terminated treaties and agreements. US foreign trade missions and overseas intelligence assets reported to him. He was a familiar face at international conferences (he had first met Gordon Truscott at a world poverty meeting) and was responsible for the administration and management of foreign embassies and consulate offices. All the inter-departmental activities of the U.S. Government overseas were known to him and he was responsible for giving them direction and ensuring their effective co-ordination. Such was his stature within the US Administration that he reported directly to the President.

It was well after 6pm on a sultry midsummer evening in Washington DC, and Dean Assiter had been behind his desk since seven that morning. He would have liked, just for once, to have been able to go home after an eleven hour working day and enjoy a drink on his patio, or stroll along the mighty Potomac. Instead, it seemed as if he would yet again be stuck in his office breathing artificially cooled, regurgitated air for a couple more hours. Whilst he never minded working long hours, indeed they had been the norm since taking office, he felt he had more important things to deal with than discuss his September holiday arrangements, and he was becoming impatient.

Seated before him in the large, oblong room were three special advisers who together had found it necessary to approach the Secretary of State's chief of staff in order to get the top man to see them, as their several requests through more normal channels had been largely ignored. Assiter had hitherto put off any meeting but, pressed by his own department's chief of staff, had finally conceded to the request and scheduled a half hour meeting commencing at 5:30pm. Forty minutes had now elapsed and his usually mild and affable demeanour, that belied nerves of steel and a brain as sharp as a rapier's blade, was close to changing.

"Look, guys, let me sum up. You all want me to take, at the US taxpayers expense, at least four Special Forces as protection to Scotland, in addition to the two already scheduled. Yet you say Truscott's place is easy to defend and has minimal risk of attack. We're going in by chopper right to the door and the Brits will also have some of their people around, all armed. Is that right so far?"

Three heads nodded their agreement. Assiter continued.

"You need to understand this is supposed to be a holiday, a goddamn break away from all this crap here." He waved his arm across the top of the magnificent mahogany desk, indicating the sheaves of papers stacked neatly upon it. "It's not a trip to Baghdad for Christ's sake. You also say I shouldn't go out fishing or walking in the mountains since even if you had an army you couldn't guarantee me safe from sniper fire, so whether you have two SF's or six seems to make little difference to my overall safety as the whole goddamn point of this trip is to go fishing, hunting and so on."

The middle of the trio in front of Assiter had gradually taken on the mantle as spokesperson for them all.

"Secretary of State, as you have heard this afternoon the CIA, FBI and the Executive Protection Agency are all agreed that more SF's would be better for your overall protection, in the unlikely event that some threat did exist."

Pointing to the man on his left the spokesperson continued, "Roger, here, has told you the CIA assessment is that Great Britain has become the European hub of Islamic militancy due to its relaxed immigration stance over many years, especially in relation to immigrants coming into their country from states like Pakistan. A second important factor is the rise of home-grown militant fanaticism, whipped up by the religious teachers who exploit the disenchantment of many adolescent young men who have grown up poor and out of work in the ethnic communities of their parents. The UK's own 7/7 on the London Underground last year sent shock waves through Downing Street when it was realised that the perpetrators were all resident British nationals. Turning to your holiday itself, if you go fishing in a small boat in the middle of one of their Scottish lakes, or lochs, or whatever they're termed, you can be picked off anywhere from the surrounding hills by someone with a rifle equipped with a telescopic sight. It is simply too damned dangerous, Sir."

Assiter was quick to respond. "If I cannot fish and shoot, what is the point in going? None. I repeat gentlemen, I *am* going and I *am* going to fish and hunt. So, extra men will be superfluous; they will not protect me more. You tell me there are only three ways into the Lodge: One, over a dam which has a single track across the top for 300 yards and can be easily defended at the lodge end. The second would entail any attackers negotiating some of the roughest, most remote mountain tracks in the Highlands – and then they face a locked gate built into a high wire fence, where doubtless there will be a patrol. Lastly, the only other access is from the water itself. Anyone crossing directly and trying to storm the house from the shore-front will be easily visible for at least fifteen minutes, or they somehow land themselves miles away, unseen, from a boat; carry their assault gear through a thick forest, only to be faced with another high steel mesh fence that will be patrolled. Most rooms in the house are alarmed and the only two roads that could be used can be sealed off quickly and are dead-ended. If your two guys and the Brits can't defend these access points, only God can save me. I'm very sorry gentlemen, I thank you for your concern which is appreciated, but the answer is no. I will take two Special Forces, that's all. You have confirmed to me that only very few people within the British government, and within our own Administration, know of my plans and that we will be supplying disinformation to the press and media via releases and misleading TV newsreels and so on which will purport to show my departure to the US after the three day meetings and will also confirm my arrival back here in Washington. I think that is sufficient. Any final questions?"

"Can we please ask you to wear one of our protective vests at all times when you are fishing or out walking?" One of the aides implored.

"I'll take it and try to remember to wear it, but if it interferes with my fishing I shall throw it away." Assiter's dogmatic tone stifled any further discussion on that subject but the aide did ask another question.

"The Brits have insisted, as they always do, that our SF's are unarmed; a request they know we routinely ignore but which could aid them politically if there was an incident. I presume, Sir, you will be happy for us to follow normal procedure?"

Assiter replied quickly, "Yep, that's fine and the only concession I will make. The guys looking after me may be armed with semi-automatic weapons and a single hand gun each. Nothing else, understood?" Three heads nodded. "You may use my personal baggage if you need to."

"No need, Sir. Our embassy there has adequate provisions of material."

"OK then. Apart from me thanking you for your concern and advice which is appreciated, that, gentlemen, seems to be it. There is no more to say".

Turning to his chief of staff who had remained silent throughout, he concluded the meeting. "Draw up a minute of this discussion and I'll sign it. Thank you all again."

Assiter rose from his chair, grabbed his jacket from its hanger and walked to the door with the advisers, hopeful of making it home before eight. As his secretary held the door open for the others to walk through, his green telephone rang. He took a deep sigh, returned to the desk and lifted the receiver.

"Good evening, Mr President."

38

Fadyar opened the door of her flat. She had hidden away all the plans and photographs that the previous week had littered her floor and the furniture had been returned to its normal place. On this occasion Carron was not displeased to be visiting, though he was a little out of breath. He had parked his car over a mile away and then walked through a maze of small side streets before turning back on his route to ensure he was not being followed. Satisfied, he made his way to Fadyar's flat and was glad of the glass of peach juice she offered on his arrival.

"Here's to success, Fadyar, whatever your mission is." Carron raised his glass and gave the toast.

"Indeed, yes. To success". They lightly clinked the glasses together and drank a little.

"Claude, I have to tell you something of what I am planning as there are some aspects that trouble me. Are you happy about that, or would you prefer to contact someone else asking them to speak with me?"

"My role Fadyar is to assist you in certain ways if I can be of help. Please keep details to an absolute minimum, but what is it you want?"

Fadyar then outlined the terrain and the lodge where her target would be staying, carefully not revealing its whereabouts nor any information about Assiter. She said she had a good plan, with inbuilt contingencies for the target's removal, but the location presented innumerable difficulties.

"An outright assault on the house would end in certain failure. Reason one: it would be hard to even get to the location without being seen. Reason two: once there, the target's security forces would be a major obstacle and there will be little chance of a surprise element. Long before we could reach the house the alarm would be triggered and those inside would be alerted."

"So, are you planning an external attack? Surely that carries more risk?" Carron's surprise registered in his voice.

"I don't think so. Firstly, not all those guarding my friend at the house will necessarily leave when he does, and anyway I need to ensure we have a rapid departure from the scene. The lodge itself does not have that. My target likes the outdoor life – fishing or shooting, and he may even just go for a walk. It is a very scenic area and I am hopeful that makes a quick exit easier with various options open to me."

Fadyar continued before Carron could comment, "I need to know from you Claude whether resources will be available to take the suspect off my hands quickly. Whilst initially we can use a vehicle for our escape, the roads are very few and will be easily blocked long before we can travel far. It will be impossible to get the subject a long way away by road. That leaves boat, helicopter or small plane. I favour the latter. Where he is taken after that is not my concern."

"OK. Others will probably have already considered that aspect. As I understand it, your mission is limited to making the initial capture and removal. I presume you have made a note of the various options and details I can take?"

"Yes." She handed him a sealed envelope on which she had crudely applied melted candlewax onto the flap. Fadyar was not happy about giving out any sort of note but she had little option, as for her plan to succeed she needed to be certain of the additional support. Besides, she knew Carron would not dare open it but merely pass it on.

"I also have a list of equipment we shall need, plus some instructions I should like implemented please." She passed Carron a slip of paper, which he studied, whist Fadyar kept talking. "I shall require some items here but most will need to be given to our brothers in Birmingham. On the note is a code-word I have agreed with them for when you contact them with any shipments. Remember, any stuff you get must work in the UK, I'm particularly referring to the two-way radios." Carron's eyes widened as he read.

"I, er, I don't know if we can supply all this Fadyar, but I will try. You have been very specific on some items and may have to accept substitutes. Your instructions are clear enough."

"Actually Claude, I think you will find you can obtain them. We used the weapons at the camp and were told these would be fairly standard issue for high profile operations."

Carron managed to hide his irritation at the mild rebuke. "Well, I will of course try anyway. What items did you want delivered here?"

"The sniper rifle and some ammunition. As you can see, I have given you a choice but it must be one of those."

Carron read the list again. Fadyar had specified the Heckler & Koch HK417 with 0.308 ammunition, the AWSM or Arctic Warfare Super Magnum with 0.50 ammunition or the Barrett M95 with 0.50 ammunition. All had to have sound-stifling silencers and 10X scopes. Her preference was for either the British-made AWSM or the American Barrett, both fitted with Schmidt and Bender PM11 scopes to provide the necessary magnification.

All the sniper rifles she listed had a Minute Of Angle (MOA) of 1 or better. The most common way of describing the accuracy of a sniper rifle is to measure the average diameter of a circle that may be drawn around a group of bullet holes in the target. Several groups of five or three rounds are fired and then every group is measured. The average group diameter is calculated and expressed in MOA. 1MOA is roughly equivalent to 1 inch group diameter at 100 yards or to 2 inches at 200 yards etc. So a rifle that shoots to 1MOA accuracy could place five bullets in a circle of no more than three inches in diameter at 300 yards. The American Barrett and the British AWSM, when loaded with the right ammunition, could shoot 0.5 MOA (or better) meaning 1 inch grouping at 200 yards, or 2 inch grouping at 400 yards. They were incredibly accurate weapons up to and well beyond 800 yards.

Fadyar needed the rifle early to fine-tune it, and she reassured Carron that she would be happy to conceal it on the car when she travelled over to England in September. Carron thought that an unnecessary risk but Fadyar assured him that controls on cars were lax at the ports, especially when a large vehicle ferry was in need of being loading or unloaded. She laughed and said, "The British cannot even find the Sangatte refugees that use the ferries!" Carron smiled. It was certainly true what she said, he just hoped that her confidence was not misplaced. He continued reading down the list.

"I'll put in the order but this will cost and if you require a plane or boat we are talking serious money Fadyar, at least 100,000 euros."

"Yes, I realise that, but my task is to capture the target; it is for others to notify me at the appropriate time how I am to hand that person over. When I was sent to Europe, I was tasked with setting up a special account for such situations. If you cannot get the money through your channels, I will ensure you receive it, but you will understand that the funds will have to pass through many hands before reaching you. I assume you have a secret account known only to our friends at the Yemeni Bank? I may not be able to fund everything from my special account – my team will incur considerable expenditure and I may need some funds of my own to draw upon quickly, it's all in the note." Fadyar sounded commanding, her confidence growing as she talked more about the operation and the equipment.

"Yes. I'm aware of the existence of the accounts, Fadyar. No problem."

"OK then. I think we're done. I shall not move the funds until the last moment to minimise any risk of them being noted and tracked, just in case. No, wait. There is something else. I want no harm to befall the English bank manager and his wife, either before or after the operation, whatever its outcome."

Carron looked at her enquiringly and raised his eyebrows.

"There is simply no need. If I fail, I will be dead or captured. If I succeed, I will be long gone. He will have enough trouble on his hands with the British authorities and identifying me after the event is only likely to add to his problems. He will not affect us in any way."

"That's true," conceded Carron. "I will ensure nothing happens to them."

After consuming some biscuits and cheese, and another glass of the fruit juice, Carron bid Fadyar farewell. As he was walking out and into the fresher, but still warm air, he turned slowly and faced her. "We have known each other a long time, my dear sister. I shall pray for your success and safe return. Praise be to Allah."

As she closed the door behind him, a slight tear dropped from her eye. She had grown to like him.

39

Jack Donaldson returned from his customary weekend five mile run, hardly having raised a sweat. He took pride in keeping his body fit and in good condition, and the early morning exercise on Saturday's and Sunday's supplemented his weekday workouts at the London gym. Usually he took great interest in the ever-changing flora and fauna as he ran into the woodland and along footpaths, but today his mind was preoccupied with Cindy and her unknown friend in the Volvo. As his feet pounded the uneven surface of the country trails, his speculation of what Cindy and her friend had spent the night doing grew in intensity, the rising anger making him run faster and faster. Had he bothered to set his stopwatch, he would have recorded his quickest ever time. After a quick shower and light breakfast, he drove to Grimley, arriving close to Cindy Crossland's cottage at just before 9am. He had only just switched off the car engine when the garage door opened.

Cindy and Gordon were dressed very casually in country clothes despite the warmness of the weather, and were busy putting boots and waterproof jackets into the cargo area of the estate. Two minutes later the couple drove out of the garage, closing it by remote control as they left. As the door latch locked into position, several loud bleeps from the setting house alarm disturbed the otherwise peaceful cul-de-sac, the security system being mentally noted by Donaldson. He was reasonably certain where she and her lover were going and he decided not to follow close behind, nor even keep them in sight. Sunday morning in summer was favoured by Cindy to meet up with her gun dog friends at the disused canal and Donaldson assumed that her male friend must be someone from the group. The canal was little more than five miles away so Donaldson drove slowly, arriving a few minutes after Cindy. He could see the Volvo parked alongside others on the scrubland verge and drove past, pulling into a vacant area. He got out of the car and briskly walked back. His military training quickly identified an area where he was able to remain unobserved behind a cluster of very large and dense gorse bushes, but which afforded him a good view of Cindy and the dogs. He was taken by surprise when he witnessed Cindy's companion shaking hands with everyone, and he could quite distinctly hear the stranger saying how pleased he was to meet the small crowd of handlers. The man looked a little familiar to Donaldson but he couldn't place him. Puzzled, Donaldson lying prone on his stomach, inched himself forward to a nearer bush, straining to get a better view of the mystery boyfriend.

The dog training had already started and a small group was standing reasonably near to where Donaldson was hidden, with a second group some distance away. Despite his wealth and large circle of contacts -- obligatory for successful executives in the business world – Gordon had never found it easy to make friends. Usually his perceived status had been a barrier to familiarity with people outside of his work, as all too often the persons he met were either intimidated and stayed almost silent, or would keep making silly references to his wealth and success making Gordon embarrassed and quickly bored. Last night, he had talked to Cindy of his apprehension of going to the gun dog meeting the following day, but she had assured him no one would be the slightest bit interested in who or what he was, provided he liked dogs.

"Anyway, you had a springer once didn't you – isn't that why you named the teaching area Ruraich?"

"Yes," said Gordon, "that was some time ago. A liver and white English springer bitch but she was only a pet, not a fully trained working dog, but a lovely temperament. I became so attached to her that when she died of old age I couldn't quite bring myself to have another one, although I've promised myself that someday I'll get another."

Having effected the introductions at the first group, Cindy started leading Gordon over to the others. Her clear voice carried across the still air to Donaldson.

"Don, this is Gordon. Gordon, let me introduce you to Don our leader and trainer." The two shook hands.

"We're very pleased to meet you Gordon and welcome. Join in whenever you want or just watch, but we usually could do with a hand throwing the dummies or some such. Cindy will help you out."

As Don walked away almost immediately, Cindy turned to Gordon, "See, told you they wouldn't make a comment. Gun dog people are only interested in the dogs, not the social standing of their owners."

The startling revelation as to the identity of Cindy's new lover struck Donaldson like a bullet between the eyes. "Gordon? Bloody hell! She actually *has* pulled fuckin' Truscott, the fuckin' tycoon. That's who it is. How the fuck's she's managed that?" he said excitably to himself. "Christ, no wonder she doesn't want that poor sod Crossland."

His objective of seeking precise information about Cindy had been achieved beyond his wildest imagination, but it was a very irate Donaldson that went home. There he looked up all he could about Gordon Truscott, and his Scottish home, Mealag Lodge. He was not able to find an exact address but he had the general area, Knoydart, so sometime he would obtain a detailed map and find it on that. His thoughts turned again to Cindy and the recent images he had of her and Truscott. He had always felt slightly uncertain as to why she had decided to move out of Red Gables and to the cottage at Grimley, but it was now clear to him that it was solely as a well-planned subterfuge to deceive her husband until her divorce came through.

She certainly wouldn't want him to know she was shagging a multimillionaire. That might reduce her husband's pay-out to her, he thought. He expected that Cindy would leave the cottage and move in with Truscott as soon as she could, leaving Donaldson's own deluded hopes and prospects of making out with Cindy in tatters. He thumped the table again and again.

"No better than a fucking whore," he angrily shouted, but no one heard his foul-mouthed outburst. His house had been empty of other occupants since Ludmilla had departed with her foreign friends. His anger did not abate and he flew into an uncontrollable rage – the sort he felt before he attacked the girls in Iraq, but this time there was no early release and the resentment against Cindy burned within him.

40

The weather in Lochaber, Highland Region, on Tuesday 1st August, was terrible. Driven by a storm force Atlantic weather system, rain was lashing down onto the hundreds of tourists in Fort William who had flocked into the town and were scurrying in and out of the shops along the pedestrian-only high street. Stooping low against the ferocious wind, and struggling to stay upright, most were quite unsuitably dressed in the flimsy, lightweight showerproof jackets that were adequate for an English summer, but not a Highland one. The sky was an unremitting dark grey, below which a seemingly endless procession of billowing thick clouds were being propelled just above the town's rooftops. The gloom was more akin to late dusk than mid-morning and the dipped headlights of the cars travelling along the shoreline of Loch Linnhe shone brightly onto the wet, glossy, road. Standing at his second-floor office window, and looking down onto the scene below, was Chief Inspector Keith Maythorp, the Central Region Area Commander of the Scottish Police Northern Constabulary. He was chairing the formal monthly progress meeting with his two immediate subordinates, Area Inspector John Curry (like Maythorp based at Fort William) and Colin MacRae based at Portree, Isle of Skye. Whilst a formal meeting, the three men had known, worked and been friends with each other for over twenty years and none had any aspirations of moving home to take a promotion. The trio recognised the abilities of each other and held a shared belief that living and working in the Highlands was far too precious to be put at risk by petty jealousies and office politics. It made for a comfortable working relationship.

Maythorp's command covered a huge geographical area, but had a very sparse population. Crime was generally low, and the main activity for the law enforcers revolved around speeding traffic offences and vehicle accidents in the summer – mostly caused by frustrated motorists unsuccessfully attempting to overtake caravans

– or climbers getting into difficulty on the high peaks in winter. There was the odd burglary or vandalism, usually to fund an increasing number of locals who had a drug habit, which broke the monotony, and the odd spot of poaching, but generally there was little trouble. He had a total officer force of only one hundred and two, and that included nearly twenty special constables. Averaged out, he had one officer for every fifty square miles. The monthly review was normally routine and so it was surprising that today there had just been a quite heated discussion over one agenda item, and Maythorp was taking time out to let tempers cool. Northern HQ was based in Inverness, only about seventy-five miles northeast of Fort William, but a world away from Maythorp's patch in policing priorities and requirements. Inverness suffered in proportionate terms from the same problems as any city in the United Kingdom and Maythorp was frequently under pressure to justify his low detection and prosecution figures, particularly those in relation to drink or drug-related motoring offences. When Maythorp had told his two lieutenants of the contents of a memo he had received from the chief constable at HQ, virtually implying that the three of them had taken their eye off the ball, Curry and MacRae had exploded.

"What does he want us to do, put a sniffer dog up the exhaust pipe of every lorry going through the Great Glen? Or perhaps Colin here should get the tourists to turn out their pockets before they go across the Skye bridge?" Curry's normal Highland accent became even more accentuated when excited, and the sarcastic tone of his response had led him to emphasise almost every vowel. Colin MacRae himself was not pleased either.

"The tourist board are always on at us not to be too hard on motorists, lest it impacts on the number of returning visitors, yet HQ say hammer them because of stupid bloody targets. This job isn't about policing anymore, it's about politics and saving the arse of some prick in London or Edinburgh. I haven't spent my entire career serving this community just to end it by ticking boxes. Bollocks to them, I say. Ignore it Keith." MacRae never lost an opportunity to remind his boss that after thirty-five years in the force he would be retiring at the end of the year, the proximity of which gave him the confidence to pretty much say what he liked without regard to his future job performance assessment.

The discussion had raged for about ten minutes when Maythorp called a halt to it, rose from his chair and absentmindedly looked out of the window whilst he thought about what to decide. It was also giving time for everyone to calm down.

"HQ's memo doesn't actually demand a reply, so I will not be sending one," he said before turning to his secretary.

"Record in the minutes that we had a lengthy discussion and that Inspectors MacRae and Curry will review the appropriateness of our enforcement strategies in the light of the quarterly results at the end of next month." Curry and MacRae smiled. They could have a considerably worse boss than Keith Maythorp and for that reason were extremely loyal to him. Maythorp then sat down and picked up the agenda.

"Finally, gentlemen, under A.O.B there is only one item to discuss. HQ has forwarded to me an advisory note they had received from the Foreign Office in London." He started to read it through quickly again whilst summarising for his audience.

"It seems as if next month some people – not named – are going to spend a few days up at Quoich, at the Truscott place. Yes, September. Arriving and departing by chopper. The FO is providing security and our services are unlikely to be required. That's really all it says." He placed the communique on his desk and looked up before continuing.

"It looks as if HQ has been informed only as a courtesy seeing as the Foreign Office is sending some protection officers up there. Naturally, HQ has passed this onto us. Any comment?"

MacRae was the first to respond.

"Mmmm, must be a foreign rock band or celebrity going there on holiday. Can't be a politician, otherwise the Met and ATU would be swarming all over the place as well as the Geeks. I guess their people will all be armed?"

Maythorp picked up the note and read it quickly.

"Doesn't say, but it would be unusual if they weren't. Assume yes," replied Maythorp, "but aren't we in danger of making a lot of assumptions here? I mean, why are we assuming this is just a couple of people or a pop group, and what about Truscott? Will he be there?

The room fell silent whilst all three considered what the Commander had said. It was Curry that spoke first.

"Good point. I suppose it's possible the place has been hired by the FO itself for an out of the way, private meeting of some sort away from any press, perhaps between ministers of different countries. Truscott wouldn't need to be there for that."

"If that were the case, and it was going to be a pretty large gathering, surely we would need to have been told more, maybe even assist with resourcing. This must be small beer – strange we've been told anything at all. But if it's nothing very much, maybe something would go to HQ beforehand but I wouldn't have expected that to happen until the day of the meeting, or at least much nearer to it. My money would be it's a FO course" added MacRae. "Anyway, what are we expected to do?

"Yes. What about us? Are we asked to do anything?" enquired Curry. "It's a goddamn awful place to get to if anything goes belly up."

Maythorp quickly scanned his eyes over the memo from HQ.

"No nothing else, which in itself is a bit odd. I should have thought we would be asked to increase patrols or something if it was really important but this note makes no mention of anything at all like that, although the phrase that our services are 'unlikely to be required' is pretty vague."

"Can't be much then. Probably some Hollywood film producer and a young actress or his secretary!" jested MacRae

"Not everyone's like you, Colin," said Curry, referencing a very public affair that MacRae had many years back.

"OK lads. Let's get back to what, if anything, we should do." Maythorp restored a little formality. "Who are our trained marksmen?"

"Johnstone and Greaves. We also have a number of certified firearm officers – I think six, but can check." Curry responded.

"Find out if they are on duty between 12th and 22nd September, that's when this will be happening." Maythorp again.

"Gosh, that long!" exclaimed MacRae, "Why did I think this was only something that was going to last a day or two?"

"I probably should have said earlier, sorry," replied Maythorp.

"Well, I think that explains why HQ has sent us the advice, doesn't it?" said Curry. "That's quite a long time for FO people to be up there; its gotta be some hell of a meeting or a very long course. Do you want me to check on Johnstone and Greaves now, Keith?"

"Yes, do. We're not that pushed. Let's grab a coffee."

Curry left the room and returned three minutes later.

"Johnstone will be on leave, abroad we think. Greaves is around. Convenient, as he is based at Fort Augustus. What have you got in mind, Keith?"

"Firstly, have a confidential word with Greaves. Tell him what we know; there's no reason to hide it from him but he should keep it to himself. I agree, this could just be that the FO itself is sending up some of their bright young things on a team building exercise, doesn't have to be anything more than that, but I don't want a lot of off-duty officers suddenly going up there at the weekend to see if they spot some celebrity or other. Then, agree with him not to take any leave over that period and ensure he remains contactable 24/7." Maythorp was thinking as he spoke, and Curry and MacRae were busy taking down notes.

"How often do we routinely patrol along that Kinloch Hourn road, John? Any idea?"

Curry hesitated. "Not often that's for sure. Once a week would be tops."

"Make it at least once a day for the duration, commencing the 13th. No need to go on the 12th or 22nd, that leaves nine days. Make sure Greaves, with his weapon, and an armed officer are the only ones on board. Use a marked 4x4. I want it to look like normal patrols. I'll sign the necessary authorisations from here and give them to you before you leave the building. If they drive slowly, and take in the views they can be out on that road for several hours."

"You're taking this very seriously aren't you Keith? It's only a routine notification." MacRae could not disguise the surprise in his voice.

"Yes and no. Sure it is a routine notification. If we obviously overreact, bloody HQ will be sending me emails about it until

Christmas, but if, just if, anything went tits up over there and we hadn't taken any action at all, everyone would look for a bloody scapegoat and that's not going to be any of us. HQ would say it was a gross dereliction of duty having notified us. All balls of course, but I'm not having mine squeezed."

The two subordinates winced at the analogy but appreciated that Maythorp was covering everyone's back, not just his.

41

Claude Carron lived alone and in a shadowy world. He was known to only a few people and had independent means. Those that had contact with him never asked him questions about himself and they did not stay long in his company. Meetings were short, conversation sparse. He possessed a small list of telephone numbers and names, against each of which was a description of their specialism. These contacts would have been amazed to learn that he was controlling all the Western European operations for Abu al-Mazan, a terrorist group with links to Al Qaeda, but which had nothing to do with the London atrocity. Whilst he was always careful to give the impression that he was but a small cog in a big wheel, even to those like Fadyar, it was in fact a well-concealed lie. His was the authority Fadyar had unwittingly sought and Carron was not going to deny her.

He had virtually recommended her when he met with the intelligence courier in the restaurant and he felt his own reputation was now on the line. Having left Fadyar, he had swiftly set up a series of brief meetings and also commenced the procurement of her requirements. Equipment should not be problem and, as everyone had a price, there should be no difficulty either in obtaining a pilot and small, fast plane to be on standby for ten days. He then spent a rather nervous week before receiving the contact numbers for Fadyar to use when she was in the UK, and confirmation that all her needs would be satisfied.

One evening, well after dark, the bell at Fadyar's flat gave three short rings followed by one longer ring. She went to the door, put the safety chain into position and turned the handle. The door swung open a few inches. Fadyar was passed two aluminium cases; one square, the other large and oblong. She closed the door and took her parcels into the lounge where she carefully opened the clasps. One was a box of ammunition; the other held the jacketed weapon which she had specifically asked for, the British made

AWSM. She thought it ironic that most of the weapons used against the British and Americans were either captured or bought on the black market to be used against the very people that manufactured them. It was true of the AWSM and Barrett, used in Iraq and Afghanistan, and also true of the Israeli-made Galatz used in their ongoing battle for survival. Even Fadyar was astonished at the amount of discarded military hardware in Middle and Far Eastern conflicts that provided ever increasing numbers of insurgents to be supplied with high-spec, accurate fire power. Fadyar wasted no time in testing her rifle.

The next day, driving into the French countryside, she went deep into the Forlesques Forestière, many miles out of sight and earshot of anyone, and set about familiarising herself again with the bolt action rifle. She liked the AWSM and fully understood why the British military liked it too. It had originally been designed as a long range sniper rifle that combined high manoeuvrability and low weight when using 0.338 calibre Lapua Magnum ammunition, but had even greater power and range when used with 0.50 BMG bullets. In addition to less weight, the AWSM had less recoil, muzzle flash, smoke and report than some comparable rifles. Its twenty-seven inch fluted stainless steel barrel offered a superb compromise between velocity and precision on the one hand, and weight and length on the other. She suspended a few targets from some low-hanging branches, carefully ensuring that the trees behind were of sufficient girth to withstand the shock of a bullet's impact, and placed some others on the ground. Fadyar found it comfortable and easy to handle and three hours later she was back in her flat, having fully tested and calibrated the rifle and its accessories.

The following morning she rose late (for her) at 9:30am showered, and wearing only a thin nightdress to cover her body, slowly made her way to the small, bright kitchen. On the wall hanging above the refrigerator was a monthly calendar and she placed a large cross over the previous day, the 10th August.

"Another day gone, another day nearer", she muttered to herself. Subsequent days were not marked except for items such as reminders to pay bills or renew her car licence, being careful not to identify any date to do with her assignment. She wondered how she would spend the next thirty days before she made the trip to Scotland.

Fadyar had deliberately decided to make the ferry crossing on Saturday 9th September. The ferries would be laden with tourists, the car decks fully filled with vehicles bulging to their rooftops with the paraphernalia of family holidays. The port authorities, customs and immigration would be tired, overworked and under pressure to keep the exit lanes open and to clear the traffic before the next ship arrived. Examination of people, cars and their contents would be cursory at worst; in all probability everyone would simply be waved through. The officials would use what time they had to check the contents of heavy goods vehicles and commercial vans, not cars.

She only had one remaining task to carry out from France; to take out the funds necessary to finance the mission, or rather to reimburse those who had financed it to date. She did not know, nor want to know, quite why the group of which she was a dedicated member operated on this basis of refunding, rather than simply outright purchase, but it certainly obscured the money trail. It meant that in the event of a compromised or aborted mission where equipment had to be jettisoned, it was unlikely that the finance for it could be traced back to all members of the cell, like hers, who were appointed to carry it out, or to those like Carron and his superiors who had authorised it. She studied the calendar carefully, flicking the sheets between August and September whilst calculating timescales for the money to move in and out of accounts in different banks across the world. She put a small circle in the top left corner of Thursday 7th September. As she did so, some muscles deep inside her stomach fluttered uncontrollably and for the first time the adrenalin within her body reached a level that made her feel slightly sick.

There was little for her to do until the time came to pass the instructions to the banks and she decided that a trip to Languedoc Roussillon, to enjoy the hot weather, warm sea and generally chill out, was what she needed. It should take her mind off things, at least a little. She finished her breakfast, packed a small suitcase and by midday had cleared the Paris suburbs and was travelling at a steady 100kmh on the A71 motorway heading south. Fadyar stopped overnight at a small, cheap pension and the next day travelled to Port-Leucate. There she found a reasonable hotel that provided a comfortable, though basic room, with a balcony from which she could view the coastline a few kilometres away, and which served surprisingly excellent breakfasts. As she unpacked her small case, she carefully took from it a small photograph of her parents, taken in 2003 standing in front of their shop, kissed it lightly on the glass and placed it next to a day calendar on the table beside her bed. At the resort itself, she went rollerblading along the superb promenade, sailed, and even visited the fun park and mini golf course. She took in the local culture with a visit to the 15th century fort at Salses-le-Chateau but the majority of her days were spent, at least in considerable part, sunbathing in her white bikini, fully aware of how attractively it contrasted against her dark olive skin and long black hair.

A quarter of a kilometre from the bustling centre she was able park her car easily on the road that ran for many miles alongside the glorious beach. A short, ten minute stroll on the golden, fine sand always enabled her to escape from the crowds and noisy families to a place where she could enjoy peace and relative privacy, occasionally seeking the shade of her own parasol or taking a short, lazy swim in the warm blue waters of the Mediterranean. During her stay, she frequented many of the resort's excellent restaurants and bars and found that she did not lack for company if she did not wish to dine alone, often being joined at the table by a hopeful, young buck who at the end of the evening left disappointed as they went their separate ways. Every night, as she switched off her light she turned over the calendar counting down the days and fell asleep dreaming of her mission.

42

Alan Crossland was sitting in the lounge at Red Gables. He picked up the telephone and quickly punched in the numbers on the keypad. He rarely came back to the house nowadays, even at weekends, preferring to stay with Chloe at her flat in Coulsdon. He had never suggested to her that she come to Stillwood out of respect for Cindy and, anyway, Chloe had not been at ease with staying overnight in Alan's flat in London for the same reason. Whenever it was necessary for him to stay in town in order to be in the office very early the next morning, Alan did so alone and he was seriously thinking that he would shortly sell Red Gables and move to Surrey, or at least somewhere a lot nearer to Chloe, to a house that held no memories. He was just about to replace the receiver thinking no one would answer when Cindy came on the line.

"Cindy, how are you? It's Alan." He was cautious. It was months since they had spoken and he wasn't confident that she would be pleased to talk to him.

"Alan! Good to hear from you. To what do I owe this call? No problems I hope?" Cindy sounded quite pleased which encouraged him.

"Well, I expect you've received the final papers, and bill through, from your solicitors. God! Don't those sharks make a fortune doing nothing! I wish I'd done law instead of accountancy. Anyhow, what I'm trying to say is… er, can we meet or can you come round to Red Gables sometime? I know this is out of the blue and all that, but I really would appreciate it. I shan't go funny on you, or anything like that. It's just that, well, um, I've got a few things I really would like to tell you."

Cindy was surprised in more ways than one. Despite the rather rambling sentences, Alan sounded a lot more relaxed than when they last spoke and he also sounded very sincere. It also happened that Alan had phoned at quite a convenient time. She would shortly be going to Mealag for several weeks and so if she was to meet up with Alan it had to be soon. She glanced at her watch; it was just past 7pm.

"No time like the present, what are you doing at the moment, Alan?"

"Now? Nothing at all, apart from sitting on the sofa at the house. Can we meet up now then?" It was Alan's turn to be taken aback.

"I'll do better than that. I'll grab a coat and come over. I've eaten, so if you haven't I suggest you grab a bite whilst I'm on my way. OK?"

"Um, yes. That's wonderful, see you soon then. Bye – and thanks."

Cindy did a little more than just taking a coat. She had a quick wash, changed into a pair of smart white shorts and sneakers, donned a bright orange tee shirt, applied a little make-up, combed her hair and was in her car fifteen minutes later, arriving at Red Gables just as the hall clock struck eight-thirty. As Alan opened the door, Cindy couldn't believe the change in Alan's appearance. His hairstyle was totally different and had clearly been very professionally styled, his skin was more toned and he was wearing a multi-coloured shirt, tan slacks and brown moccasin type shoes.

"My God Alan, you look fantastic. What a transformation! I can't believe it's really you. The new hairstyle has taken years off you and you look so well. Good for you." She leant forward and kissed him on the cheek as she went inside.

Making her way to the lounge, she sat on the armchair opposite the sofa. Alan poured her a drink of her favourite Pinot Grigio and himself a red Merlot, and they settled back to a few minutes of meaningless pleasantries and superficial conversation before Alan started telling Cindy what was on his mind.

"As you know the divorce is all but through, and I have been giving some thought to what I now need to do with my life. I was hoping to remain here at Red Gables, but for a number of reasons I think I really would like to sell it. I wouldn't do that without telling you, no matter what has happened in the past, as I know this house meant a lot to you."

Cindy appreciated his frankness.

"You always have been kind, Alan. Thank you for the thought but I shan't need it. You sell it as it must be difficult for you here. I'm not surprised you want somewhere else." Cindy deliberately did not ask where he might live as she did not wish to pry, and anyway it was now none of her business.

"Yes, I do find it difficult here. Too many memories of you, I'm afraid." He tried to smile and chuckle, but Cindy could tell it was a strain for him. "I have no particular place in mind at the moment, but I think I'll move away from this area – probably to the south-east. After all, it was you that persuaded me to come to the Cotswolds, remember?"

"Yes, all that seems a long time ago now but we both have some good memories," Cindy wistfully replied.

Alan poured himself another large glass of the wine and several minutes later, buoyed a little by the alcohol, started to tell Cindy all about Chloe.

"That's marvellous Alan, good for you. She sounds a lovely person, and she has certainly succeeded in improving your looks!"

They both laughed as they relaxed more in each other's company and, having such a lot in common, chatted easily together. They caught up on the news of past friends, a few of whom had either continued seeing only Cindy whilst others remained in contact solely with Alan, and brought each other up to date on a host of matters in which they had shared an interest.

Cindy did not mention Gordon but after Alan had finished his third large glass of the Merlot and Cindy her second Pinot, Alan said, "And what about you, Cindy? I've told you about me, anything happening in your life?"

Cindy knew he would ask the question at some time, and had spent some time thinking of how she should respond. "Well, as you ask, yes Alan. There is a new person in my life. However, I absolutely promise you he was not in my life prior to my feelings changing towards you. To this day I genuinely do not know why I changed, it was totally my fault not yours, but I had anguished for over a year before I met anyone else. That is the truth, and it is important you understand that, for your sake more than mine."

"Does this friend have a name, Cindy?"

"Oh, that's not important. What is important is that you accept that I first met him on the day of the tube bombing. I was trapped, as you know, for quite a while and he stayed with me until the rescue services cut me out of the wreckage. He was a complete stranger at that time."

"So… so… you did start the affair whilst we were together… living here? That story you made up at Christmas… ", he paused, "and Easter. All a lie I suppose." Alan was clearly upset and Cindy did not want to hurt him further.

"No, we just kept in touch by phone occasionally, but when I left I did start seeing him a bit then. Even now, I don't see him often." She lied and it was not convincing. Even though she had succeeded in telling Alan what he wanted to hear, he didn't believe it.

"Oh well. I wish you the best and hope something works out. You are still very attractive, Cindy, you won't have any problem getting fixed up with someone. Just make sure they look after you. Whatever my faults, I have always tried to be kind and to treat you well."

Cindy felt the tears welling up behind her eyes. What Alan said was true, he *had* always been kind. Cindy tried to laugh off her mixed feelings of sentimentality and angst at how she had treated him.

"Stop it, Alan. All this nostalgia is too much for me. How about we have another drink and a change of subject?"

"OK, I'll get them, but while I'm doing that just take a last look around the house – if there is anything that you want take it now, or I'll arrange for it to be stored or delivered, whatever you decide. I've got everything out of the attic, its upstairs in the fourth bedroom."

Cindy went around the house. There was nothing she had seen upstairs that she particularly wanted, but as she entered the dining room two china ornaments of working breed springer spaniels caught her eye – a present from Alan when he was trying so hard to please her.

"Can I take these Alan? You gave them to me, remember? I always loved them."

"Of course. They're yours anyway." Alan was pleased she had taken them, for they reminded him of unhappier times. "Are you still involved with the dogs? Don't tell me you have got your own!" he chuckled.

"Yes I still enjoy the club but no, I haven't got a dog."

As soon as they had finished their drinks, Cindy said it was time for her to go and Alan rose from his chair. Not long ago he probably would have asked her to stay, but now the thought did not enter his head. He accompanied her to the door.

"No goodbye's Cindy, please. Just au revoir. And thank you. We did have a lot of good times, shared some laughs and for me you will always be the girl in the coffee shop!" Alan softly wrapped both arms around her waist and kissed her briefly on the lips. She didn't object and the kiss was fleeting.

"OK then; au revoir it is. Good luck Alan. I really hope things work out for you."

She got into her car, pressed the switch to wind down the electric window and waved as she drove around the large semi-circular driveway. Alan remained standing in the porch, waving back. He was surprised at how much his feelings had changed towards Cindy. She could no longer hurt him, his emotions were controlled and calm – almost, but not quite, indifferent. It was obvious to him that she had lied over the affair, though somewhat perversely he did believe her story that it had started after the fateful journey to London. He was sure she had told the truth over that, but she had still not provided any explanation of her indifferent attitude to him that started way before 7/7. Her confession to the affair made him somewhat angry. He wished she could have been honest sooner and saved him the hurt and torment of wondering whilst they were still living together, but maybe, he said to himself, that's what people do in these situations – lie until they are either found out or they themselves can't stand the strain. He shrugged his shoulders. He considered it a little odd that she did not wish to reveal her boyfriend's name, though in all other respects it had been a pleasant, cordial evening. He was glad he had suggested that they meet for a last time, but he was already looking forward to seeing Chloe tomorrow.

A few days later, Donaldson was driving Alan to a banking conference in Leeds. Alan was simply a delegate, going more for reasons of finding an excuse to have a day out of the office than in the expectation of learning anything useful and certainly not with a view to contributing to the discussions. He was seated in the ample, comfortable front passenger seat and had been chatting to his driver for quite a while when Crossland said, "Cindy came round the other night to Red Gables, we had a very pleasant evening. She seems pretty relaxed now the divorce and everything is wrapped up."

"Really, that's good. What brought that about?" Donaldson enquired.

"Oh, I'm thinking of selling Red Gables and moving to the southeast. Thought I would ask her if there was anything she wanted etc and really to say goodbye. Of course, if I do move, I'll make it worthwhile for you to come too."

Before Donaldson had time to reply Crossland quickly added, "Don't get the wrong idea Jack, nothing happened between us. It wasn't one of those final fucks for old-times type of things!"

"Well it wouldn't be, would it? Now she's getting laid by this Truscott bloke." The words came out before Donaldson had given them any thought, and he instantly regretted saying them.

"What? What did you say? Truscott? The millionaire who has that property company that owns the cottage at Grimley?" Crossland paused slightly before shouting, *"Him?"*

Crossland was dumfounded and Donaldson spent the next quarter of an hour providing some excuse as to how he didn't think his boss would want to know given Chloe and his divorce. He explained he had seen the two of them together in Cindy's car and, out of curiosity, had followed them back to Grimley where Truscott stayed the weekend. It was several minutes before Crossland spoke, his mind trying to unscramble the plethora of recollections along with dates to try and make sense of what he had just been told. Once he had recovered from the initial shock, he became angry; very angry indeed.

"She bloody deceived me. Not just about him, but she even got me to pay her three quarters of a million plus half the flat! Bloody money-grabbing bitch."

His ire came from the deep hurt he felt. He could scarcely believe that Cindy could be so duplicitous towards him. She appeared so pleasant and friendly the evening they spent together, whilst all the time she was hiding this enormous secret from him. She should have been honest with him. He deserved to be told. He had a right to know when he was her husband and they were living together, and he certainly should have been told before he agreed the financial settlement. He felt deceived, betrayed, tricked.

"Turn the car round, Jack. Fuck the conference. I'm going home"

43

Fadyar Masri returned to Paris, refreshed and invigorated by her holiday. The journey back was tiring and she relaxed in her bath, letting the hot water soothe away the ache between her shoulders and at the base of her spine caused by driving such a long way in a small car. She had been unable to take her mind completely off her assignment whilst away, but it had helped her unwind and had also ensured that everything about the operation had been firmly committed to memory. She was ready. Tomorrow morning, she would send the necessary instructions to the banks.

She rose at 7:30am and an hour later was sitting at her laptop, typed in her password and waited for the desktop icons to appear. She was calm and unhurried. She accessed the internet and then the online banking service for Hannet-Mar International Bank. She keyed in her bank logonid, then her password and was presented with a final security screen. The bank's computer had randomly selected that she had to infill the first, third and fourth digits of another password, the other four digits being blanked out. She typed them in and 'Welcome Halima Chalthoum" appeared in large, bold lettering in the centre of the screen alongside, in smaller print, her account number. Listed below were a range of services that she could select. Fadyar marvelled at the technology. The infidels sure were good at developing technology that made life easy for everyone including their enemies. She double-clicked her mouse against the service marked 'Withdrawals', and a few moments later the screen appeared and she commenced filling in the required fields. She needed a sum that would cover all of Carron's expenses, plus reimburse the Birmingham accounts and also give her some money to draw upon and exchange for sterling. There were bound to be some losses on exchange and currency rates, plus charges from some banks and she had calculated that she should therefore withdraw 150,000 pounds sterling.

She carefully entered the name of an Egyptian bank, its

international sort code and the account number into which the money would be initially credited. She completed the remainder of the screen and pressed the 'enter' key. A copy of the screen she had just input appeared with a message saying to key 'enter' again if all the details were correct. She carefully re-read the completed boxes and pressed the key. Nothing happened for a few moments, then another screen appeared telling her the transaction had been successful and asked if there was any other service she would like. She declined and logged out of the bank's system. She was unsure just how quickly the funds would be credited into the Egyptian account but she logged onto their system anyway. Having navigated through all the screens and passwords that were similar to those of Hannet-Mar, she was disappointed to find that the account did not record them as being received. She tried again a quarter of an hour later and obtained the same negative response. She started to get nervous. She had understood from the banks that such transactions were immediate, and she really hoped that information was correct as she had not planned for a lengthy delay. She became agitated when she thought that perhaps they would not be credited until the next day since that would seriously affect her timetable. *Surely, she thought, there is not going to be a problem so early in the mission.*

She waited, nervously tapping a pencil hard onto a pad beside the computer such that the point penetrated the paper before breaking off. She carried on banging the broken end ever harder into the paper, whilst she feverishly kept logging onto the Egyptian system. After an hour she had become quite dispirited, and out of habit pressed the enter key again to view the account screen, following the 'Welcome Halima' message. Her eyes lit up and euphoria swept over her. There it was, a seemingly huge sum of Egyptian pounds and a few piasters, such was the exchange rate. The delay, unknown to Fadyar, was not that the transfer had not taken place. It had, but it took an hour for the web site to be automatically updated. She navigated to the withdrawal section of the system and this time completed the screens for 75,000 Egyptian Pounds, equivalent to 10,000 euros, to be transferred to the Yemeni Bank. She did not however exit the system when asked if there was any other service she wanted. She answered in the affirmative and selected again the withdrawal facility. She now entered the details of the Banque Privee del Solegit SA that was based just outside of Geneva and transferred to it the remaining money. The Swiss account was particularly important as she knew it was the major vehicle by which the Abu Al-Mazan terrorist group concealed the bulk of their funds, not just for Fadyar's mission but for all their activities throughout Western Europe. As with most Swiss bank accounts where anonymity of ownership was a pre-requisite, the account itself was in the name of corporation registered in the Cayman Islands which in turn was owned by a Panamanian Trust. The trust had purportedly been set up by two apparently wealthy individuals, both from Lithuania – though any country where individuals are likely to be difficult to be traced would have sufficed. The persons themselves knew nothing of the Trust, their stolen passports being used to set it up without their knowledge.

Fadyar again suffered anguish and nervous fatigue from the even longer delay in receiving confirmation of the transaction from the Yemeni bank, but the Swiss transaction went through quickly. Eventually she saw the details on the Yemeni system and immediately transferred that to an account in Dubai. This was her own account, in her real name of Yasmin Hasan, but which had been set up to allow a Fadyar Masri to access and withdraw funds on demand – and it was as Fadyar that she had logged onto the Dubai bank. Becoming weary from staring at what had become a succession of soporific screens, she stood up and made herself a coffee. Her eyes were grateful to be removed from the brightness and slowly adjusted to the ambient light in the room. Refreshed and stimulated from the intake of caffeine and the fifteen minute break it afforded her, she returned to the desk and sat back on the fully adjustable chair before embarking upon the final part of the deception. She successfully entered the passwords and other security details, and using the name of Fadyar Masri electronically transferred a sum roughly equivalent to 10,000 euros to a French bank account in the name of Yasmin Hasan. Thirty minutes later, it appeared on her account as credited. In just over three hours, sitting behind a desk using an ordinary laptop computer she had transferred 150,000 English Pounds half way around the world, into different currencies and back again into Euros. In the note she gave to Carron were instructions for drawing upon the Swiss bank accounts and for that bank to credit her fellow conspirators in Birmingham. That would take longer than a few hours, but the money would be received well before it was needed. Carron, or whoever, would have the cash to finance the expensive items of the mission.

It had all taken place so smoothly, and Fadyar wished now she had transferred the money the following day. She had not done so in order to give herself a day's contingency, whereby if there had been a problem she might have been able to resolve it in time for her planned trip on the Saturday to still go ahead. As it was, she would now spend almost the entire day nervously twiddling her fingers. She also realised that if, just if, the transactions came to the attention of any authorities in the countries involved or were reported to them by any of the banks, there were twenty-four hours to trace her. She did not think such an outcome would happen, being confident that enquiries into the Swiss account would come to nothing, but the theoretical possibilities for her own account were a concern.

Prior to shutting down her computer she had one more task to perform. Fadyar was aware that virtually all internet sites, especially the interactive ones such as online banking, download a small program known as a cookie onto the user's computer without the user knowing. In the main, these cookies are harmless and help to speed up the user's navigation through the various screens, pre-filling as many as possible to save the user time and to minimise errors. Some cookies therefore hold data about the user, and their computer, which can subsequently be accessed by other programs as well as the programs they were originally set up for. Fadyar had set her computer to block such access, but in case any had managed to by-pass the system she now commenced removing all cookies and the automatic log of her internet browsing history from her hard disk using a disk clean-up facility. Tomorrow she would totally erase the disk but she would not do that now in case she needed the computer again.

44

Cindy ached to be with Gordon, she knew she loved him, wanted him, but completely severing her relationship with Alan had always sent a slight shiver of apprehension down her spine whenever she thought about it. It was such a big step to take, but the meeting with her ex-husband at Red Gables the previous evening had stripped away from her any excuse at delaying her decision. Alan had found someone else, and was lost to her forever. The divorce had been finalised much quicker than she had anticipated, and there was now little reason for her to stay in Worcestershire. It seemed that just at the point when she had completed the furnishings and decorated the cottage to her style, the raison d'être for living in it had disappeared. This was a disappointment but she needed to be with Gordon permanently at his loch side home, experiencing the wonders and excitement of the vast natural wilderness and challenge of the Scottish Highlands, rather than the amiable, unruffled pleasures of rural Middle England. Her thoughts strayed once more to Mealag. She yearned for the gale-driven sleet smacking into her cheeks, the blue black clouds racing between the hills, the angry waters of the loch crashing into the dam wall, the thunderous sound of the deer stampeding across the thick white snow, as well as the calm, crystal clear days where one could watch the soaring eagles and predatory buzzards. She wondered if the vivid images captured in her mind were really an indulgent metaphor of her future life with Gordon; unpredictable, exhilarating and tumultuous. Mealag beckoned, and she responded. She packed a case and within an hour she was driving north on the M6 motorway.

Several hours later as she sat in the large lounge overlooking the loch, she spoke to Gordon about when she might move in permanently.

"Whenever, it cannot be soon enough for me. I miss you terribly when we're not together so why not now, what's to stop you?"

"Well, it can't happen quite like that!" Cindy's voice rose with excitement, not anger. "There's all the cottage to sort out and my things are there, but if you are happy to leave the cottage empty and re-let it later then that's great." She leant across the sofa and kissed him. "In fact, it's wonderful. Oh, I do so love you, you lovely man. Thank you for rescuing me"

"That's settled then. We have a few weeks before Dean and Paulette arrive, so in a couple of days I'll get the company to start the re-letting process on the cottage. We can arrange from here a removal van for your stuff and we'll fly down the day before. I've never asked, have you ever been on a helicopter or private jet? Would you like it?"

Things were being decided so quickly Cindy was a little stunned. "Mmmm, yes, I guess so. I mean, you know I'm OK with flying but I've never been in anything other than a commercial airliner. Sounds like it might be fun, but how do we get the large items into here, Gordon? Not by small plane or helicopter, that's for sure!"

"No, silly. There are two ways really. In the garages by the dam there is a much larger boat and that will take items up to the size of a single wardrobe and the like. Anything really difficult can come in a container from the Arkaig road, then into the estate at the rear of Mealag. We use a tractor pulling a large, very large, trailer. It's slow but certain, and as long as one uses plenty of foam packaging and makes certain the load is secure, very effective. So, leave all that to me. You bring everything you want. There's an excellent removal firm based in Fort Augustus that I've used several times. They can get any contents you want from the cottage to here. They know Mealag well and can use all the equipment we have on the estate to move stuff into here, so we can leave it to them to advise what method we need to use. So, you have no reason to delay moving in."

Cindy decided to tease Gordon, "Well, I must check with my other male friends. I have several offers to consider and now that I am a young single girl again I may wish to take my time playing the field." She laughed as she said it.

"You wish! Young single girl indeed! Perhaps you need some

encouragement to make up your mind." Gordon leant across, held her close and kissed her passionately on the lips.

The following week, the cottage had been cleared. Gordon had arranged a private plane to fly them from Inverness to Staverton Airport, near Cheltenham, where a hire car awaited them and they spent a couple of days preparing for the removers to arrive. Everything went smoothly, watched over closely by Cindy and Gordon. They returned to Mealag arriving a day before the removers who, of necessity, had stopped overnight. They determined that the tractor approach would be easier, not because there were any really large items, but the volume could all be loaded safely onto the trailer and the move completed in one transit from the Arkaig road, whereas several boat trips would be necessary from the Kinloch Hourn road. Cindy spent the following weeks improving her loch fly fishing and becoming familiar with handling a shooting rifle for the deer stalking. The latter was not an activity that greatly interested her, apart from having a day out on the hills, as she did not relish the prospect of killing such a large beast and so she was quite willing to be patient whilst the formalities of her obtaining a gun licence were processed. Trout she could kill, and probably salmon – though she had yet to catch one – but she felt there was a fundamental difference between taking the life of a fish to that of a magnificent stag. She eventually obtained her shotgun licence, and the separate firearms certificate needed for the rifle, and had been surprised at how thorough the police were in their investigations prior to granting the licence.

Unknown to Cindy and Gordon, much of the delay in issuing the certificate arose as Officer Greaves scrutinised every firearm licence application and Cindy's application form gave rise to more than just idle curiosity on his part. Only a week or so earlier, he had been briefed on the September assignment of keeping an eye on Mealag and now he had a firearms check to carry out. He reported to his superiors as to how he should proceed and was told to undertake the usual checks but that if he could, he should try to discreetly ascertain if Truscott was going to be at Mealag in mid-September. Routinely undertaking the searches for Cindy Crossland, he came across the same protected computer record as had Bill Ritson several months previously but, unlike Ritson's boss, Greaves's superior instantly wanted the matter dropped. Whatever was going on at Mealag, or going to go on, one thing was clear to Central Division Area Commander Keith Maythorp; shotgun certificate applications in an area such as the Highlands were almost as common place and routine as the issuing of parking tickets in a city. Truscott himself possessed a licence as did a number of his estate workers. Maythorp was astute enough in the art of self-preservation to realise that to withhold or even delay the licence, especially for someone who had obviously been vetted and cleared by the security services to an extremely high level, was not likely to earn him favour at HQ or anywhere else. Truscott moved in wealthy and influential circles and Maythorp was not going to raise any questions.

As the issuing officer, Greaves however was entitled to visit the place where Cindy's guns were going to be stored in order to be satisfied that all was in accordance with the regulations and conditions appertaining to the issue of the certificate. He knew it would be, for he had been to Mealag on a couple of occasions and each time the storage arrangements were impeccable. On his own volition, however, he decided to visit again as Maggie MacLean's scones were absolutely delicious and it was probably the only way he was likely to find out a little more about what was happening in September. He came away disappointed, though not with the quality of the housekeepers baking.

Gordon's twin large steel cabinets that held the various sporting firearms were sited in the lobby near the kitchen. One cabinet had within it a separate locked compartment for the ammunition. There were several shotguns and three sporting rifles. One was a Browning 0.375 with Schmidt and Bender scope and there were two general purpose RPA 0.308 hunting rifles both equipped with 2 x Weaver scopes, one of which Gordon had earmarked for Cindy. Although he could afford to purchase any gun he wished, he was not interested in expensive status symbols, albeit ones that claimed extreme accuracy and many useful add-ons. He regarded a gun as no more than a tool, and he had been delighted with his rifles which he found accurate enough, easy and light to handle. As the three of them drank their coffee and enjoyed the scones, Greaves commented that he was obliged to point out the close proximity of the ammunition to the guns. "However, I know that Sandy and some of the others on the estate also have secure cabinets, so all you will do is tell me that he will put the ammunition next door and that you will have his guns, so I'll say no more about it," recognising it would be futile to make it into an issue, and changed the subject. "I suppose you'll be needing the certificate so you can both get in some good sport later in the summer? I'll make sure it all goes through in time."

"Possibly. It will likely depend on whether any of our friends can come. I don't believe in fixed arrangements," Gordon replied smoothly.

Having visited Gordon and met Cindy, for whom he had an instant liking (reporting back to his colleagues that Truscott had got a real beauty up at the Lodge), Greaves issued the certificate.

45

Chloe's school, in common with most English private schools, had at least a week longer summer vacation than did the state schools and would reopen its doors to students on Tuesday, 12 September. Chloe, along with the other members of staff, was required to return to duty on Friday 8th to help with the preparations, meet any new teachers and to familiarise herself with her allotted classroom and any last-minute changes to the curriculum. Thursday morning, therefore, was the last opportunity of the summer recess she and Crossland had of a taking an extra few minutes in bed – and she wanted to end her holiday with something special for him, especially as he had seemed a little on edge of late. She had woken early and made two cups of steaming hot coffee, plus some toast and marmalade and taken them to him in bed. Forty minutes of rapturous pleasure later, and completely spent, he started munching rapidly on the cold toast and finished the small remainder of his coffee that Chloe had not used. He hurried around the room seeking to find a clean shirt and underclothes, but he was totally untroubled at being well behind his normal schedule.

Donaldson had waited impatiently outside Chloe's flat, having guessed the reason for the delay. Both the Crosslands had now become a source of considerable irritation to him, and jealousy at their respective love affairs only added to his mounting disillusionment. He wished he could strike back at them in some way: Alan Crossland for his meanness, increasingly erratic work hours and at his boss's apparent ease at being able to bed incredibly attractive females; and with Cindy for teasing and leading him on before making him feel inadequate and foolish. When Alan Crossland finally appeared, Donaldson offered none of the usual pleasantries and instead gruffly told him that the delay in leaving the flat would mean the traffic would be worse, and so it proved. Crossland eventually decided to get out of the car and walk. Having to rush through the crowds, he arrived at the Hannet-Mar an hour later than normal at 9:30am, slightly flushed and out of breath.

He glanced at the post, which had already been opened by Jane and sorted into a small pile with the most urgent on top, and then checked his diary. He was pleased. He had no major appointments other than a short meeting scheduled for 11:30am where he was to present a junior member of staff a congratulatory letter and cheque for passing her recent Accountancy examinations. The substantial part of his day could be spent catching up on some matters that were overdue his attention and he settled back in his chair and opened a file. Two hours later, his secretary knocked on the door and entered Crossland's office.

"Miss Kelly Palmer is outside. Shall I send her in?"

"Yes please, thanks." Crossland rose to welcome the young woman, moved around his desk, extended his hand and smiled broadly.

"Do come in Kelly, would you like some coffee?" They shook hands and Crossland pointed for her to sit in one of the four comfortable armchairs surrounding a circular smoke-glass table.

"Thank you, Sir, I would."

Crossland looked up at Jane, still waiting at the door, and nodded affirmatively. A cafetière and two china cups and saucers quickly arrived, along with a large plate of assorted expensive biscuits and chocolates. Crossland noticed how smart Kelly Palmer looked in her dark, tailored suit and cream blouse, enough of the top buttons open to arouse interest but insufficient to reveal any cleavage, well cut hair, understated make up and he detected only the faintest hint of perfume. *She will go far* he thought, *still only twenty-two, knows how to dress and obviously very bright as her rapid progress in the examinations proved.* Crossland then congratulated her and formally passed over his personally addressed and signed letter that enclosed the £2,000 cheque. He then asked how she liked the bank and what her aspirations were, the type of questions that all chief executives are good at asking, but rarely bother to remember the replies. Towards the end of the conversation, Kelly noticed that his computer was not turned on.

"I see, Sir, you have not logged on yet so you will not have seen my note to you this morning."

"Oh, Kelly, what was that about?"

"An account in the name of Chalthoum Universal Holdings. The system threw up an automated alert message at about ten this morning that a withdrawal of £150,000 had been made online. It popped up on my screen. Everything seemed to be in order, but as you had at one time controlled the account, and there was a note in the comments section of the screen to notify you of all developments, I thought I should email you."

Kelly's words stunned Crossland. He tried desperately not to show how really shaken he was.

"Thank you, Kelly. Yes, thank you," he muttered barely audibly, his mind in turmoil. Fortunately the meeting with Kelly Palmer was scheduled for only twenty minutes, and whilst he may have been prepared to extend it a little in more propitious circumstances, it was now certain he would keep to his timetable. He closed the door when Kelly departed and sat at his desk, quickly turning on his computer and accessing the account. He was calmer now, having convinced himself that this eventuality was precisely why he had distanced himself from the Chalthoum case. He had removed his direct involvement and played down its importance.

"So, a transaction has occurred on a small beer case." He mused quietly to himself. "Nothing to get excited about," but the perspiration upon his forehead revealed his nervousness.

He picked up the telephone and asked Jane to put him through to Ritson at the ATU and then replaced the receiver. A few moments later, Jane buzzed his intercom.

"Ritson is evidently tied up, do you want anyone else or shall I leave a message?"

"Leave a message, Jane, please. Ask him to contact me as soon as possible. Thanks"

Ten minutes later, his phone rang and it was Ritson.

"Good morning, Sir. I understand you would like a word?" Ritson sounded calm and polite and Crossland relaxed back into his chair.

"Chief Superintendent, good morning. Thank you for calling back. It's really in the nature of a courtesy call. You remember, I'm sure, the Chalthoum account? Well, following on from our previous conversation, I removed it from my own personal attention accounts and, frankly, had forgotten all about it. However, this morning one of my junior staff received an automated alert on her screen that it had been the subject of a large online withdrawal and naturally she brought it immediately to my attention. Slightly regrettably, she did so by email, and being rather busy I have only just got round to reading it. I thought you may like to know."

"That's very considerate of you, Sir, I appreciate you informing us. Can you provide any more details about the transaction?" Ritson smoothly asked.

Crossland told him all he knew from the computer record and offered to email Ritson a copy of the screens, but he declined. The details provided by Crossland matched exactly those of which Ritson was first informed at 10:45am and had immediately resulted in a flurry of activity within the ATU.

"Two questions, Sir, if I may at this time. Does your computer system keep a log of the computer id that carried out the transaction, and do you have the name of the Egyptian bank's account holder?"

"Good grief Chief Superintendent, I honestly couldn't tell you the answer to the first question. I will ask one of our computer boffins to talk to you if you like, I'm sure he'll know the answer. As to the second, I am sorry the answer is we do not have that on the record, though again I am happy to ask my staff to try and find it out."

"Thank you Sir. May I suggest I send over one of my people this afternoon and perhaps your computer guy and mine can put their heads together. My chap's name will be Doug Ongles – funny name, likes to be called Dongle. Something to do with computers I'm told!" He laughed, as did Crossland.

Immediately after replacing the receiver, Crossland asked his own computer expert to come to his office. "Glen, the police are coming round again this afternoon and sending one of their computer guys. Give them every co-operation, but note what they say and keep a copy yourself of anything they want to take back. Let me know how it goes."

In 2006, although the United Kingdom government (through

HM Treasury and the Bank of England) purportedly monitored suspect bank accounts, its experience and resources were vastly inferior to those of the United States Office of Foreign Assets Control (OFAC) an agency of the US Department of the Treasury that came under the auspices of the Under Secretary of the Treasury for Terrorism and Financial Intelligence. Its founding went back to 1950, under another name, but it formally became OFAC in 1962, and over the years had been highly successful in tracing and monitoring the funds of drug barons and, latterly, terrorists. The British and American organisations shared intelligence reasonably openly with each other and, in return for HM Treasury willingness to unquestioningly freeze assets of an OFAC identified suspect, OFAC would help its smaller counterpart when asked to monitor specific accounts, even those held at UK banks. Ritson had passed a request for monitoring of the Chalthoum account at Hannet-Mar International Bank to HM Treasury shortly after his first meeting with Alan Crossland back in 2005 and at 10:15am UK time on the 7th September 2006 OFAC reported the withdrawal to HM Treasury. They passed the information onto New Scotland Yard ATU at 10:35am and ten minutes later Ritson was reading the details. He immediately went to see a jubilant Assistant Commissioner Manders.

"I told you, Bill, always follow the money. We now need to be really careful. If there is anything going on, I don't want it spooked too early. I need to know a lot more before we get heavy as its still not certain that this is anything other than a normal transaction, but I feel this is a breakthrough and worth pursuing. Take two lads from John and get Chris to deal with anything urgent that crops up on your other stuff. Put your whole team on this and keep me fully updated 24/7. I have a feeling we may be about to get lucky."

Ritson was delighted at the extra resources. He would need them. He was in the process of gathering his team together for a briefing when Crossland phoned, but his information provided nothing new. Nonetheless, the mere fact that the bank manager had called at all showed that he was nervous about the account, a thought he pondered over as he returned to chair the briefing. He outlined the facts, gave out copies of all the documentation the ATU had gathered from Crossland, and from the latest printout from OFAC. He brought his team, which even with the additional help numbered only twelve including himself and the computer expert Dongle, up to the same level of knowledge regarding all aspects of the case, including the mystery surrounding the death of Kenneth Styles. He asked for their input, collectively and individually, before going to a portable whiteboard that had been rather precariously perched across two chairs – its screw fixings having loosened, resulting in it falling from the wall months previously – to write down a summary of the immediate actions to be taken:

OFAC to be asked to trace if similar funds transferred from Egypt, if so where and details.

Recirculate names of Chalthoum Universal Holdings / Corniche Consortium and Halima Chalthoum to all trusted Financial Regulatory Authorities.

Alert HM Treasury and Bank of England to monitor significant deposits from the Middle East being placed in private British accounts.

Notify all British banks to report all amounts in excess of £50,000 credited to private accounts from any overseas banks.

Dongle to visit Hannet-Mar, investigate system.

Ensure both MI5 and MI6 representatives within ATU briefed.

Highlighted in red and circled was GET NAME OF EGYPT ACCOUNT.

★ ★ ★

Ritson allotted the tasks to his various Heads of Section and glanced at his watch. It was 1pm. Several hours had slipped by since the money left British shores and he knew that if he was to be successful, speed was of the essence. The liaison between MI5, MI6 and the Metropolitan Police International Counter Terrorism branch (of which the ATU was part) was born of necessity, but since the London outrage of 7/7 working relationships had improved considerably and there was now much greater co-operation and the sharing of intelligence. The ATU had a dedicated liaison officer within both security services and Ritson himself undertook to talk with them. He was in a difficult position. He still only had suspicions and there was no additional evidence that could justify devoting the amount of resources Manders had given him for very long. He had to come up with some tangible results very soon or the investigation would be scaled down. He had another concern which he had not shared with his team, realising that in all probability they would be thinking along the same lines. If the money was for onward transmission from Egypt, he hoped it would be one large sum rather than several smaller sums. With the millions of financial transactions around the world every day, even a sum as large as £150,000 was pretty small and therefore would take the agencies powerful computers time to isolate and identify. If the sum was split and sent in smaller units to many different banks, it could be totally impossible to trace before an incident might occur. A certain amount of luck might be needed, but even more critical was that Ritson needed time.

Things did not start well. Within an hour he had learnt that there were considerable translation problems with the Egyptian authorities, plus jurisdiction issues. Eventually, the Egyptians had managed to find someone who spoke good English and so the translators that Ritson had called for had to be sent away. The Egyptians then said that whilst they would wish to help the UK if possible, they could not just divulge their account holder's details unless good reason was provided. Ritson did not want, nor could even if he wished, allege it was in connection with a possible terrorist threat, but after some considerable time and further lengthy discussion, the Egyptians said they would refer the British request to their Interior Ministry for a decision. Ritson now desperately hoped that OFAC could identify a similar transfer from the Egyptian bank. If so, more information regarding names would be available. He waited most of the afternoon, impatiently sitting at his desk whilst others did likewise. All they needed was something, anything, more tangible to give them a lead that would then cause them to spring into action.

It was Dongle that provided it when he returned to the office a little after 4:30pm. He went directly to Ritson. "There isn't a lot, but you will find it interesting. The bank's systems are rubbish, and they don't retain much unfortunately. They do use cookies but whoever logged on had a blocker, and as the cookie was pretty basic and not important to their online banking system, it didn't function."

"Don't give me this jargon about stuff that doesn't work, just tell me what you found out. Is it helpful or not?" Ritson really didn't have time for a computer lesson.

"OK. The logon holder is Halima Chalthoum. You probably know that. To access an on line account the user has to give a logon id, password and input three digits the bank's computer randomly requests from a stored memorable name. The account id is her customer number, 7348754, not the bank account number. The password for the account is corn1che – note it has got a figure '1' in it instead of the letter 'I'. But, here is the interesting bit, her seven digit memorable word, is 1nf1del again the number '1' instead of the letter 'I' but an interesting word isn't it?

"Bloody shit" whispered Ritson "anything else?"

"Yes, hopefully, but I have to run some stuff from here before I can confirm. Computers use things called IP addresses, and there are static addresses and dynamic addresses. These are governed by all sorts of international and other protocols that… "

"Stop it, Dongle," Ritson cut him short. "I don't want to know. Just go and do what you need to do. Please."

Dongle was, for sure, an expert guy on computers but like most highly specialised technical people, he could never resist trying to explain his science to others. Dongle shrugged his shoulders, turned and walked lazily away to his own desk. There he powered up his own system and within a few minutes his fingers were typing furiously at the keyboard as numerous brightly coloured screens flashed before his eyes. Every now and again he would pause, lean back into his chair and subconsciously run his fingers through his overlong crop of black hair and study the screen intently, sometimes scribbling a note on his desk pad before resuming his typing. He was using all his skills to glean information from a number of sources that he felt would be helpful. Amongst the sites he accessed were the Internet Corporation For Assigned Names and Numbers (ICANN) based in California and the Réseaux IP Européens Network Coordination Centre (RIPE NCC) whose headquarters were in Amsterdam. ICANN's tasks include responsibility for Internet Protocol (IP) address space allocation, protocol identifier assignment, generic and country code top level domain name system management, and root server system management functions. More generically, ICANN is responsible for managing the assignment of domain names and IP addresses. RIPE NCC acts as the Regional Internet Registry for Europe, the Middle East and parts of Central Asia. Somewhere, deep in the caverns of their collective databases, would be information on the specific whereabouts of the computer that had made the withdrawal.

Dongle was so absorbed in his work that he failed to notice that most of his colleagues on the other ATU teams had left for home when at 8:15pm he picked up his desk pad and went over to Ritson.

"Not as much as I had hoped for boss, sorry. But whoever made those transactions did so from France. That much is certain. I was hoping to narrow it down to area. There is some possibility it might be Paris, but I wouldn't want you to take that as anywhere near certain."

"France! How do you know that?" Ritson was astounded, but quickly decided not to let Dongle answer.

"No, on second thoughts don't tell me. Good work, Dongle. This job is all about putting together pieces of a jigsaw and you have just given us a very large piece indeed."

Ritson was certainly pleased. He was thinking he could now get the French Sûreté Nationale or, more accurately since its reorganisation, the National Police, involved and interested. Ritson also quietly hoped that any threat, if indeed there was one, would not be being planned to take place on British soil. It was a frustrating three additional hours before Ritson was finally able to confer with his equivalent in the French Anti-Terrorist department. When he first called, there had only been a lowly junior officer on duty, the rest of the department having left the building and gone home. The duty officer had eventually managed to impress upon his superior that there was a serious matter that required his immediate recall to the office. Ritson carefully explained all he knew and left the French to carry out their own urgent investigations, both forces promising to co-operate and share any relevant information.

It was now nearly midnight and as there had not been any further information from OFAC regarding the possible onward transmission of the funds from the Egyptian bank, Ritson decided to send his men home. He and they were exhausted. They had spent most of the long day trying to brief agencies and obtain hard information, but their endeavour had yielded scant results. As he put on his jacket, the telex machine clattered into action. He saw immediately it was from OFAC and his pulse quickened. He ripped the page from the tractor feed before it had completely finished, but he had already read the text as the paper clicked its way through the machine.

TRANSFER OF EQUIVALENT ONE HUNDRED AND FORTY THOUSAND GBP STERLING FROM AL KENEMESSAN BANK TO BANQUE PRIVEE DEL SOLEGIT SA GENEVA MADE AT APPROX 1100 HRS 7 SEPTEMBER. SECONDS LATER TEN THOUSAND EURO (SEVENTY FIVE THOUSAND EGYPT POUNDS) TRANSFERRED FROM AL KENEMESSAN BANK TO YEMENI BANK ADEN. SIMILAR AMOUNT THEN TRANSFERRED FROM YEMENI BANK TO DUBAI (NO DETAILS). DETAILS OF ACCOUNT HOLDERS AND NUMBERS BEING INVESTIGATED.

Ritson knew the Swiss bank would not release details of its account holders unless he could obtain a court order from a Swiss judge. That took a great deal of time and would probably be a complete waste of time, since the judiciary demanded such high-level of proof of wrongdoing that almost invariably no disclosure order was granted. Further, he knew from bitter experience that the principal drawback of seeking to use the Swiss legal system to prize information from their secretive banks, was that any action almost always resulted in the account holder being made aware of the enquiry – thereby enabling the miscreant to slip quietly away and go to ground, often withdrawing the money before a freeze order was implemented. Ritson cursed. This was going to be a tough case to break open, but the involvement of the Swiss banking system within a convoluted chain of banking transactions had confirmed one thing to him: whatever purpose the Hannet-Mar funds were ultimately to be used for, it certainly would not be legal. He turned his attention back to the printout and considered the significance of the second transaction. Was it relevant? Or had OFAC included it only because the timing was so obviously suspicious? The absence of hard information meant there was little he could do and he certainly wasn't going to get anywhere at nearly 2:00am Aden time. He placed the telex on his desk and went home.

46

Fadyar Masri spent Thursday preparing for her trip to Britain. She visited her local bank and withdrew €6,000, immediately exchanging a thousand of them over the counter for English pounds. She ordered a further £3,000 sterling; the funds to be taken from her account. The bank clerk promised her currency would be ready for her collection by 11am the following day. Much to her surprise, the bank clerk raised no comment and simply put the slip into a basket that was placed next to him. She was certain that £4,000 plus the €5,000 in her pocket would be ample for any expenditure she would require. After dark, she carefully started to prepare her lethal luggage. She fully dismantled her rifle, inserting the barrel inside foam pipe insulation, the sort one uses to prevent domestic pipes freezing in winter. She then placed the covered barrel inside a long aluminium tube, ostensibly a fishing rod carrier. The bolt and box magazine were carefully wrapped in aluminium foil and placed inside larger plastic boxes that contained an assortment of fishing equipment, purchased on her previous trip to Britain. Metal fly boxes and packets of various odd-shaped lures and spinners surrounded the metallic parts of the rifle. She packed her suitcases and started to load her car, making sure it was obvious to anyone that she was going fishing. She collapsed the back seat to accommodate a couple of the several long, tube rod holders, both of which held a rod, though one also contained the smaller length barrel concealed by its foam covering. Anyone cursorily examining the rod holder would see the fishing rod and not notice the rifle barrel at the base of the long tube. She made certain the carrier tubes were placed on the floor of the enlarged cargo carrying area and piled on top of them were her suitcases, various coats, boots plus various items of assorted luggage. Placed on the assemblage for her holiday trip was a third rod carrier containing a three section, ten foot fly-fishing rod. It would take several minutes to unload the car and she guessed that she would only be asked to do that if the car had to pass through an X-ray machine. If it did, and she was asked to pull over and have the car searched, she thought there was a good probability that the tubes would be sufficient to allay any fears of the busy customs officials. Having loaded her car, she returned to her flat. It was nearly midnight and she sent a coded text message to Carron saying she was on schedule and that she would be leaving Paris tomorrow morning. She knew that over the coming weekend her flat would be cleared of most of the remaining personal belongings – leaving only items that would confuse or delay the police – and thoroughly cleaned before a letter ending the tenancy and enclosing a cheque for one month's rent would be sent to the managing agents. By Monday morning all trace of Fadyar Masri would have disappeared from the flat.

She woke early on Friday 8th September. The wind had got up to storm force at about 5:00am and the heavy rain had begun half an hour later. The sharp sound of the heavy droplets hitting the windows reminded Fadyar of small calibre automatic fire and, half asleep, she sat bolt upright in bed, her dream of the loch and the dam summarily disrupted. She shivered, not from cold but from fear. The shudder went through her body before her brain slowly disassociated itself from her mission and the rapid firing, and eventually made sense of the noise hitting the glass. She dressed slowly and poured herself a fruit juice. She did not want to eat. She turned on the television to see a twenty-four hour news service but there was nothing of interest to her. Had she been watching a few hours later she would have learned of a Taliban suicide car bombing near the US embassy in Kabul. As it was she quickly became bored and switched off the set, preferring to listen to her small radio. She had one final task to perform before she left that morning.

She put on a thin pair of rubber surgical gloves, found a small screwdriver and carefully removed the casing from her desktop computer. This gained her easy access to the four securing screws of her hard drive, and five minutes later the small, heavy unit was in her hand. Once she had successfully carried out the currency transfers, she had taken the precaution of overwriting all the non-critical files using a free downloadable utility program from the internet, but she also knew that the only absolute guarantee of the disk not being read, even when overwritten, was to destroy the disk itself. She removed the central small bolt holding the disk assembly together, and as the two halves came apart she saw the shiny silver disk. Using a pair of pliers, she lifted it away from its spindle and placed it on the table before thoroughly scratching it and bending it almost in half. She reassembled the unit, minus its disk, and put it back in place in the computer. She leant down to the bottom drawer of her desk, took out an identical hard drive and wrapped it in a plastic supermarket bag before hiding it behind the kitchen refrigerator. This drive contained thousands of images and pages of text downloaded from various internet sites, which had been saved on the disk either as word processed documents or bitmap files. These had been password protected by the software's own highly powerful encryption program which ensured far more effective security than the computers log on screen password. The task had taken her several months but it had given her some sort of purpose whilst she was waiting to be given a mission, and now the 120 gigabyte drive was 85% full of rubbish and had never contained any of her personal information. Fadyar was taking no chances. If, and when, the disk came into the possession of anyone else, it would take them a considerable time to realise and discover what was wrong as they could not afford to miss something really important amongst the dross. The delay might give her a few critical extra hours. One could never be too careful in this business. At 10:30am, she slipped on a lightweight anorak, put the now useless and damaged disk into her pocket and ran to her garage to avoid getting soaked. As she drove to her bank the sky began to lighten and the brightness raised her spirits. She put the radio on and turned up the volume, singing along to one of the latest hit records. By the time she reached the bank and parked her car on a meter opposite, the wind and rain had stopped and she removed her anorak before crossing the road. The currency was ready for her and she placed it carefully inside a second wallet which she then hid amongst one of her suitcases in the boot. She drove steadily to Calais stopping on route for a very leisurely and lengthy lunch, finally arriving at a cheap travel hotel outside the port in early evening. After dinner, she dropped the disk into the murky water as she strolled along the Quai du Rhone.

The following morning, feeling a little apprehensive, she drove her car the short distance to the terminal and joined the queue for the ferry. She retrieved the internet obtained ticket from her handbag. The printout gave details of her name, Fadyar Masri, her make and model of car plus registration number, and confirmed her place on the outbound 8:20am ferry to Dover on Saturday 9th September 2006. Her stomach muscles tightened as she read the inbound details of 23rd September 2006, departing Dover 2:30pm local time. Whatever happened, she knew she would not make the return journey and fleetingly she became distracted, wondering just where she would be when the quoted sailing left the famous white cliffs astern. The sound of a car engine starting close by quickly alerted Fadyar that she should move forward in the queue. She watched as each driver ahead of her, in turn, presented their tickets to a bored-looking woman wearing a bright yellow plastic waistcoat sitting high up in a grubby booth. When she reached the kiosk, the woman stuck her hand out of the window and took Fadyar's ticket without saying a word and checked it against a list of names on a computer screen. In silence, she handed Fadyar a boarding pass and returned the ticket. Fadyar drove on and was quickly at the rear of another queue, again making slow progress forwards. She knew this would be the passport control and when she was level to the officer, she smiled at him.

"Bonjour," she held out her passport and boarding card as she spoke. The officer smiled back. He took a brief look at her papers then at her face and, wishing her a good holiday, waved her through. Ten minutes later, she was marshalled onto the vast platform of the vehicle deck. The crossing of the English Channel was uneventful and Fadyar was able to relax by reading a paperback she purchased on the ferry. Dover was really busy, much as she had hoped and anticipated. Ranks of cars and heavy goods vehicles thronged the huge concourse waiting to embark whilst those arriving in the UK, like Fadyar, gradually followed the signs to exit the terminal. She entered one of the four designated lanes of slow moving traffic marked 'Cars Only' for European Union passport holders and proceeded towards the border control point. She was waved through. No one examined her ticket, passport or vehicle, and a little before 11am British Summer Time, Fadyar had cleared the port of Dover and was driving steadily towards Birmingham. She pressed the automatic search button on her radio and a few seconds later was tapping her fingers in rhythm to the music.

47

Friday had not been good for Detective Superintendent Ritson of the ATU of the Metropolitan Police. His team had diligently pursued what enquiries they could but were hampered by a distinct lack of any hard facts or evidence. Indeed, they had very few leads and still did not know whether they were chasing ghosts and simply wasting their own and everyone else's time. The Egyptian Interior Ministry had, after lengthy deliberation, simply referred the ATU back to the Hannet-Mar Bank in London stating that, in their opinion, all the information the ATU required could be obtained on their own door step. The telex machine remained stubbornly silent and Ritson concluded that OFAC had not been able to trace any more details than those that had come through late the previous evening. He decided to talk things over with his superior Assistant Commissioner Manders.

"You really believe there is a plot, Bill?"

"Yes Sir, I do. Very much so." Ritson replied assertively.

"So do I. It's the little things that make it certain, the Dubai connection for one. The money being transferred to several different banks in a single day – why do that? Why not just transfer it from London to Switzerland? Why lose so much on exchanging good currency for bad and then back again, if it's not to obscure the identity of those wanting the funds?" Manders became more pensive and absentmindedly began scratching his chin. "I think there is a plot alright, but seemingly in France."

"Not necessarily. I would back Dongle that the transactions were made from a computer in France, but let's not lose sight of the fact that the money was originally in England," Ritson reminded his boss.

"That means nothing. These bastards will put money wherever they want to, probably concealing their identities along the way. I think it could be just an accident that they chose England, unless of course the manager is suspect. If so, that would explain why it was deposited with the Hannet–Mar. That small sum transferred to Yemen, then to Dubai, interests me though. What use is that to a supposed large consortium? What on earth is it for? You know my motto, *always follow the money.*"

Ritson successfully managed to conceal his groan at the umpteenth repetition of what had become more like a mantra than a motto.

"Did you have anything in mind, Sir?" Ritson enquired.

"Yes, I think so. The last time I saw the commissioner on this case he virtually booted me out. I'm going to try again. He has influence in high places and, after 7/7 last year, he won't be too keen to ignore me if I put this to him in a certain way. We need details of that Dubai account, and hopefully he is going to get it for us."

A short time later, Manders was seated before the Commissioner Sir Neil Roberts and quickly outlined what ATU now knew and suspected.

"Is this that SR12 case you spoke to me about some time ago?" Roberts tersely questioned Manders.

"Yes, Sir. The same."

"Well, my answer is also still the same. I'm not poking my nose into it on this collection of suppositions." Manders could tell that Roberts was irked even though he had not been asked on this occasion to look into Cindy Crossland's file.

"Actually Sir, I quite understand that and it never occurred to me to ask you to access that file again – at least not yet. No, it is this Dubai connection and the bank account there that troubles me. You see, if it is subsequently established that it does form part of the financing of a terrorist cell, I am just anxious that any plot that may be in the offing is not carried out against British subjects. Britain has a lot of close connections to Dubai, not just commercial. Politically, I believe our government has excellent relations with the Constitutional Monarchy of Dubai and, more widely, the whole of the United Arab Emirates. All are very positively disposed towards the British, so co-operation between agencies ought not to be a problem. What little we do know of this Hannet–Mar money is that there is certainly a Dubai connection. That is a fact. I should not like us to pass up such an obvious link only to find out later the money was used against our national interests, when perhaps enquiries at high-level could either confirm or rule out such a threat at an early stage." Manders gave a deliberately long and reasoned argument, delivering the words slowly and with clarity. "I was thinking that an approach by a senior Treasury official to his counterpart in Dubai might bring forth some answers."

Roberts saw the trap. If this turned out to be a plot and he had obstructed an enquiry which might have prevented it, his already difficult relationship with the government would be impossible and he would have to resign. On the other hand, he could not use his position unless he was certain there was reasonable cause. Treasury ministers are close to the Prime Minister and so whatever he decided carried a certain amount of risk.

"OK. Give me the details in a typed-up, formal note referring to this conversation and precise details of what information you want from Dubai. I will do my best."

"I have already taken the liberty of doing that, Commissioner. Thank you." Manders withdrew an unsealed envelope from his jacket and passed it over. Roberts laughed.

"And if I had refused, did you have another one for me?" Roberts asked.

"No Sir, of course not," Manders lied.

When he returned to his own office he took out the second envelope and shredded it. Sir Neil Roberts wasted no time. He made an immediate, brief phone call to the Financial Services Secretary, whose remit included national and international financial crime, and then arranged for a courier to deliver the note by hand. At 6pm a formal request for assistance was sent by the British Treasury to the Financial Administration Bureau of the Dubai government. There was little more that Manders and Ritson could do but wait. They were still waiting at 9pm when they decided to go home and leave the duty officers to notify them if any information was forthcoming.

Ritson carried out his normal summer Saturday routine of helping his wife with the shopping in the morning before mowing the lawn in the afternoon, but all the time his mind was elsewhere. He had become increasingly frustrated and worried as the day passed, with still no word from the office. It was the fifth anniversary of 9/11 and he was desperately concerned lest his enquiries were being made too late to stop another terrorist outrage to mark the occasion. He kept telling himself that the money was being moved far too late for it to be anything to do with a 9/11 follow-up, but the worry remained until he fell asleep several hours later. It was not until 2:30pm on Sunday that Ritson's mobile sprang into life and he was informed that a telex from Dubai had been sent to the Treasury, a copy of which was being forwarded to the ATU. A quick check on the news channel told him that no atrocity had been carried out abroad overnight and he was soon heading towards New Scotland Yard.

Manders was already in his office reading the copy telex when Ritson came in. "This is what we wanted, Bill. This is it. I suggest you call in the team and get cracking." Manders rubbed his hands and spoke with obvious glee. There is nothing a seasoned detective likes better than being on the chase of a suspect, and for Manders the remoteness of high-level promotion had denied him that frontline opportunity for too long. Many times he had wondered if he had not sacrificed the very best part of the job – the part he was good at and liked – for the Queen's shilling, but he had never been allowed to dwell on these thoughts for too long by his status conscious wife and an extravagant lifestyle. As he passed Ritson the paper, Manders quipped, "There's a lot to be said for the way the Dubai and some other governments in the UAE go about things; if they want something they just go and get it!"

ON LINE TRANSFER OF 75000 (SEVENTY FIVE THOUSAND) EGP INTO DUBAI CFB ACCOUNT 65660981 OF ACCOUNT HOLDER YASMIN HASAN MADE 7 SEPTEMBER BY HALIMA CHALTHOUM. SAME DAY 50000 (FIFTY THOUSAND) AED WITHDRAWN BY FADYAR MASRI TO BANQUE GRECORIALE, PARIS ACCOUNT 32356239.

Ritson was stunned. He read the telex over again.

'This *has* to mean something… but what?' he pondered quietly to himself. Who were Yasmin Hasan and Fadyar Masri and what was their connection to Halima Chalthoum? He went to his whiteboard and wrote in the details beside the relevant action point. There was no need now to seek OFAC's assistance, and he was at the point of sending a message withdrawing his request when the telex clicked into life again. It was from OFAC, confirming the Egyptian account holder being one Halima Chalthoum and also giving details of the transfer of 75,000 Egyptian Pounds to the Aden Bank in the Yemen. All he was missing was the information regarding the Swiss account, but he knew he was not likely to get any information from that source. He had already asked OFAC and the British Treasury to monitor transactions from the Banque Privee del Solegit SA, but unless a large sum was moved that corresponded to about €140,000 it was not a line of enquiry that he was expecting would yield a positive result.

At 5pm on a dull, warm September Sunday afternoon, Ritson stood before his team, bringing everyone up to speed with the telex information. "No one goes to these lengths to transfer out of England a large sum of money, pass it through several Middle Eastern banks, bring a much smaller sum back into France, deposit the balance in a private Swiss Account – all within the space of a few hours – unless they want to obscure the audit trail. This is deliberate. It has been planned. It's all happened on the same day. I want to know why. Why transfer it on the 7th September? We have the list of all significant events for the next month. Double-check them. Renew security advice to the organisers. Above all, I want to know about Fadyar Masri, Yasmin Hasan and Halima Chalthoum. I would proffer a guess these are not their real names, but they have to exist and live somewhere. I will be speaking with our French colleagues seeking their help in tracing these people, but our own boys at MI5 and MI6 need to be very much in the picture and working on this now".

As he spoke he looked towards the two liaison officers whose role was to keep Britain's secret security services updated. They both nodded. Ritson moved across to the wall where the moveable panel whiteboard had been repaired and now hung on sliders alongside two others. The first board was full of scribbled notes and he pulled across a second clean panel and added some more details before setting his men to work on the tasks. He then called over Doug Ongles.

"Dongle, I'm becoming more and more convinced that to counter terrorism we need computers. Everything we have got on this case so far is because of computers, or at least what people like you can do with them. You have free reign on this case if you need greater authority for any systems that you wish to, what do you say, interrogate? Is that it? Anyway, speak to me if you have any problems otherwise do whatever you want, but I need more information on those names."

Dongle visibly swelled with pride, his expertise finally being recognised instead of being regarded as playing second fiddle to the virtues of 'good, old fashioned policing' that he had grown tired of hearing about. He spoke deferentially to his senior officer.

"No problem, Sir, but it's now after seven. No one is going to be around at this time of evening on a Sunday – even Five and Six will have only the duty people at work. Sure, I can start a few searches of databases but, just a suggestion, there's a full week coming up and I can see this job for all of us being twelve hour days and possibly some working shifts. Only a thought, but it might be better to make a real crack at this tomorrow morning, early."

It was actually a constructive point and Ritson admired Dongle for making it. Only a computer nerd would have the gall to suggest it. Dongle did not have aspirations for high office nor a managerial promotion. He loved his keyboard and his computers and never wanted to be taken away from them, which gave him a freedom to express what others might only think. It had been simply hell for him when, at the age of sixteen, he had spent three months at a Young Offenders Institution for hacking into the computer systems of several major corporations, even though he did no actual damage. His conviction, however, was principally because he had managed to infiltrate the computer system of the Rosworth Observatory. Although only ever used for the genuine purpose of astronomy, for some perverse reason it was still owned and operated by the Ministry of Defence, who did not view kindly his action of moving the seventy-six metre telescope five degrees west of where it should have been pointing. The Government did not wish to publicise the inadequacies of their own system, so settled instead to pressure the commercial organisations to pursue a prosecution based on his exploits in the private sector.

"You're right, Dongle. Good suggestion." Then in a louder voice, he shouted out across the room. "Dongle thinks you lot would prefer to go home now and work your bol… " he broke off, remembering there were two female officers on his team "… work your socks off all next week, so let's pack up here. See you all tomorrow. Early."

As the team gradually gathered up their belongings and filed out past his office, he noticed the two female officers on his team walking across the room, giggling. One, Sergeant Jean Hill, put her head around his door and said, "Glad you said 'socks' Sir. I don't know anyone here capable of working anything else off."

He laughed, the stress of the day relieved and he went home happier than when he arrived. Tomorrow would be a Monday morning he would actually look forward to.

On the weekend that Ritson was worrying about the money transfers, Cindy and Gordon were preparing Mealag Lodge for the visit of Dean and Paulette Assiter who had confirmed that they would be arriving on Tuesday as planned. Gordon had insisted that Mrs MacLean prepare one of the grander guest chalets used when Gordon entertained a number of friends for several days, even though he was hoping Assiter and his wife would stay in one of the guest rooms at Mealag. These chalets were in fact quite large A-frame dwellings, and Gordon had made certain that they were comfortable, but he was anxious that if Assiter or his wife wanted real privacy then they had an alternative to Mealag. The principal guest room at Mealag was lavishly equipped and furnished, and Cindy was absolutely certain she knew where the American and his model French wife would sleep. Cindy was delighted that Gordon involved her so much in the preparations for the visit. He asked her opinion on virtually everything: the rooms, the meals, the sorts of entertainment and activities they could undertake – it was obvious that Gordon was relishing having a woman's opinion other than Mrs MacLean to rely on. During their joint discussions of how to entertain the Assiters, Cindy suggested that perhaps one day, she and Paulette might go to Inverness, unless it was clear that Paulette was the type that always wanted the outdoor life.

"Do you think she would find going into town interesting?" Gordon enquired.

"Absolutely Gordon, of course. There are some really excellent shops there and Inverness is a great place just to mooch about in. There's a lot to see and do. Don't forget, Assiter's wife is very young and she might find life at Mealag somewhat of a culture shock, especially as she has only recently given up international modelling. I expect she may welcome the sight of a few good boutiques and chic restaurants, as would I."

"That's settled then, if Paulette agrees. Another good idea of yours, Cindy, thanks." Gordon made a mental note to suggest it early into Assiter's stay.

48

Fadyar Masri reached Birmingham in mid-afternoon on Saturday and immediately made contact with Nasra Khan. She quickly parked her car in a lock up garage and transferred her cases and belongings to a hired Vauxhall car, the rental agreement having been taken out by Sharid Bagheri. That car, too, was well concealed in a rented garage. The following morning Fadyar, Bagheri, Khan and Mawdud Mattar would be making the journey to Scotland, and Saturday evening provided her with an opportunity to check that the deadly supplies she had ordered had been delivered and ready for use. She checked off the items from her list:

- *plentiful supply of grenades*
- *pouches and ammunition for the Walthur P99 handguns*
- *four correct sized camouflage combat jackets*
- *four two-way radios UK military specification with IP54 and IP55 protection; built in scrambler; minimum 7km range, plus lightweight headsets. Each to have a UT110 rolling scrambler for private, secure conversations and a scanning channel to detect other radios in the area.*
- *Three automatic sub-machine guns, CAR-15 SMG's, with the four and a quarter inch flash moderator fitted.*
- *Various additional maps, night scopes and goggles.*

Everything was exactly as she had asked. In fact the sub machine guns had a specification well in excess of the model she had requested. She was thrilled, but the CAR-15s added considerably to the group's fire power and were short-barrelled and easy to use, as she wanted. Currency was plentiful and Khan, Mattar and Bagheri each confirmed their bank accounts had been topped up from Switzerland. Finally, Khan reported that they had hired a fully equipped camper van for three weeks. The van had been deliberately chosen as the particular model had a space beneath a side sofa that could hide someone and its blacked out windows in the rear also offered the occupants some sort of protection from them not being visible should it ever be attacked. Mattar had been charged by Fadyar to organise the transport once in the Highlands. Their earlier trip had revealed just how conspicuous tourists were just by the types of vehicle and registration plates they carried. Mattar said that awaiting them tomorrow evening or Monday morning at MacGregor & Berry's garage in Fort William was a second-hand green, Land Rover Defender 110. He had ordered, and paid the deposit for it, online. He was confident that the powerful 2.5 Turbo diesel, five seat version, would more than meet their needs and be capable of traversing the roughest of off-road conditions. The vehicle was only a few months old and had originally been registered in Inverness so carried local plates, which hopefully would attract limited attention. There were only a few thousand miles recorded on the odometer and there was no reason why the vehicle should not be in A1 condition. Completing her final check of all the equipment, Fadyar congratulated them.

"You have done well, my brothers. Now I can reveal to you my plan. Come. Let us sit at the table so we can all see the papers"

The three men leaned forward across the table, expectantly, as Fadyar spread the maps and her blueprint before them. In fact she had two principal plans depending on the circumstances, but the key point of both was, she emphasised, adaptability. She stressed that whilst she was satisfied with the reconnaissance and the information gained from the previous trip, it was simply impossible to devise a single plan that covered every eventuality as she would be unaware of precisely what security arrangements would be in place to protect Assiter until his actual arrival. The group spent several hours discussing every detail of the plans, asking questions, making suggestions, learning their precise role, what they had to do, how they were to do it.

At the end of the evening, Fadyar spoke to them. "We are ready. Our mission will bring glory to our people, revenge for all those murdered by the invading, imperialist infidels. Sharid will be my deputy and he will ensure that if for whatever reason I am unable to continue command, or carry out the mission, it will still succeed."

She went to bed, tired but not totally happy. It was the second anniversary of that awful day when her parents had been murdered and the horrible recollections came flooding back to her in a series of vivid images, as if she was watching a movie in slow motion. Before going to sleep she said several more prayers than usual.

The following morning the group rose early and spent Sunday driving leisurely to Scotland, stopping frequently on the journey. Bagheri drove the Vauxhall, with Mattar as a passenger and Khan drove the large camper accompanied by his tense, but focused, leader. Mattar was able to collect the Land Rover, paying the balance in cash, and drove along the A82 to meet up with his companions a little while later in the small public car park at the rear of the shops in Spean Bridge, the supermarket providing all the provisions that Fadyar and her conspirators would need for the next few days. They all knew what they were to do next. Bagheri took the Vauxhall and Mattar the Land Rover. Khan drove the camper van with Fadyar as passenger. He headed along the A82, past a very grey Loch Lochy, and onwards to Invergarry where he turned left on the A87. However, he did not make the second left turn a mile later that would have taken them along the Kinloch Hourn road via Corach and the dam. Instead, he stayed on the A87 for another twenty-one miles and having filled the camper with diesel from the petrol station sited at the junction, turned left at Shiel and climbed into the hills and forest of Ratagan along an unclassified road. The view was awesome as they climbed higher and Khan expertly handled the camper around the tight and twisty bends.

After the summit, the road became easier and Khan was able to increase speed as they gradually dropped down towards the strait that divides the Isle of Skye from the mainland. The stretch of water, known as the Sound of Sleat, is a frequent passage for sharks, whales and a host of other marine life, plus British and NATO submarines, and all are often seen as they make their journey through the narrow channel but, as Khan approached, the surface of the sea was totally flat and undisturbed.

At the coast, he headed left once more before finally stopping at the large car park, seemingly constructed almost on and only a little above the rock strewn beach, at the pretty village of Glenelg.

They parked the camper at the far side of the car park, well away from the tourists who usually wished to stop and loiter, looking either at the view of Skye or at the Memorial to the Fallen proudly standing at the centre of the coastal edge of the car park. The road beyond Glenelg follows the coastline and continues for several miles around the massive mountain Beinn Sgritheall, meeting the waters of Loch Hourn and finishing only a few miles short of Kinloch Hourn village. When Fadyar had first visited the area, she cursed how unlucky they were that the Glenelg road had not been continued to meet the Corach road at Kinloch Hourn – but it was obvious why it had not been constructed. Sheer massive cliffs formed a promontory at the mouth of Kinloch Hourn, making any linking of the roads completely uneconomic. She also lamented the fact that Loch Quoich itself had no navigable outlet to the sea, either at the Straits or at Loch Hourn, despite reaching almost to the village. Because a couple of miles or so of rock had not been blasted away she had been forced to devise a much slower escape route, one that relied upon the camper van now parked at Glenelg.

The car park was not empty. Glenelg is a tourist destination not just because of its commanding position across the narrows from Skye, nor due to its famous Bernera military barracks of 1725. Nearby, along the coast at Sandaig a few miles to the south-west, was the site of 'Camusfearna' where Gavin Maxwell had lived with the otters he made famous in *'Ring of Bright Water'*, and within a mile of the village were two of the best preserved 1st and 2nd Century dwellings of the ancient Picts – Dun Telve and Dun Troddan. Visitors arrived for many reasons and, as usual, several vehicles were scattered across the tarmac, all facing towards the Straits and the Isle of Skye and all immaculately parked within the neat, white lines that marked an approved space. The occupants of the camper were not interested in looking at marine life, nor ancient monuments. Once they had stopped, the two fundamentalists got out and made a deliberate effort to be noticed. They walked around, stretching their arms above their heads and casually walking over to the memorial. They looked at the small row of terraced houses, and then lingered a while on the road opposite a row of clean, colour-washed cottages. Fadyar and Khan waited, hoping that someone local would come along. A quarter of an hour passed, then half an hour, and the light was rapidly fading causing the mountains on Skye to glow a vivid orange that reflected onto the calm sea. At last a small, plump woman came out of one of the terraced houses and went to walk along the road.

"Excuse me," said a relieved Fadyar. "We have come a long way and I was wondering if it is permitted to leave our van on the car park," she pointed to the camper, "over there?"

"O aye. Nay problem. Ach, I know it says no overnight parking but folks do it all the time and old John, who is supposed to check these things, usually turns a blind eye. Anyway, leave a note inside the screen that says you're staying with me a wee while. Morag's the name."

Fadyar smiled at Morag.

"Are you sure? That's very kind. We have some friends we hope to see and they have a four wheel drive vehicle that can go where our van can't. They are also renting a cottage but it's a bit of a way from here, so we may leave the camper for a few days and then come back to it. Sort of come and go." Fadyar did not allow any time for conversation to be developed about the supposed friends and changed the subject before Morag could interject.

"This is a really lovely area, isn't it? We hope to be up here about a fortnight and do plenty of walking in the mountains so we may not see you much, but thank you again."

After a few more exchanges, to reinforce her apparent integrity, Fadyar wrote a fictitious mobile number on a piece of paper and handed it to the woman. "I know these things don't always work in the hills around here but if there is a problem with the van, do please phone me or leave a message. I will get here as quickly as I can."

Fadyar was in her element and the chat went exactly as she had hoped for. She knew that they could leave the camper van and it would be perfectly safe, watched over by Morag, who reassured her again that the parking would be 'Nay bother'. Khan and Fadyar returned to the van where they spent a surprisingly comfortable night after a good meal cooked on the camper's stove. Tomorrow's supper would be eaten in the self-catering cottage they had rented at Kinloch Hourn.

Bagheri drove from Spean Bridge straight to the Eagles Rest Hotel at Corach where he and Mattar had reserved a room with twin single beds. They had given false, English sounding names that belied their ancestry, but had credit cards that backed their deception. After unpacking and a brief rest, Mattar was anxious that the sparkling clean Land Rover was itself too noticeable, but he was also impatient at wanting to test out his new toy and its two or four wheel drive options. He suggested that he take the vehicle for a drive.

"Whenever have you seen a clean Land Rover, especially if we are supposedly local?" Mattar rhetorically asked his companion as he gave him a wave before heading out of the hotel car park.

He headed back towards Spean Bridge, then along the A86 Newtonmore road. He had not travelled this particular road before and was awe struck when after a few miles he parked next to another large dam. This dam, at the head of Loch Laggan, was quite different in construction from the one at Quoich. Whereas the Quoich dam was huge this was only moderate in size, but the Laggan dam was equally, if not more, impressive. Built before Quoich, it was of a more expensive form of construction having a weather protected rear face as well as an impervious front slope – features which permitted a slimmer design. Along the length of the top of the dam were thirty-six arches through which water over-spilled when the level rose too high, sending it spectacularly cascading down into a gorge one hundred feet below. It also had four huge independently operated siphons which passed through the wall of the dam, each being automatically triggered by successive increases of the water pressure as the loch level rose. When functioning, these created a massive water spout churning out hundreds of gallons of water a second into the gorge. There was no power station, the dam being used solely to ensure that an adequate supply of water could be fed through miles of tunnel to yet another loch, Loch Triegg. At the opposite end of that loch, water was continuously being drained at a staggering rate by a second tunnel through the mountains, emerging immediately above the aluminium production plant at Fort William. The processes required enormous volumes of water for power and cooling, and three huge pipes carried the water as it accelerated down the mountain slope directly into the works.

Bagheri was fascinated as he stopped and studied the elegant dam, before turning back towards Spean Bridge.

He turned onto a very narrow road marked 'Fersit' that meandered through a large, dark forest of tall conifers, hoping to find some suitable rough land on which to dirty and test his vehicle. In places, the road had grassy unkempt earth banks at its edges that provided the ideal mud splash to despoil the clean Land Rover. He also found a forestry road that clearly had not been used for several months and he soon became accustomed to handling his vehicle in rough terrain. The light was fading fast as he cleared the forest and he suddenly had to brake hard as he found himself rapidly approaching the base of yet another dam, this one very small, only a few yards ahead. The crudely finished back slope of the dirty brown, rock-fill dam, no more than thirty metres in length by twenty high, looked shabby and forgotten. Tufts of grass hung limply from the joints where the rocks had been piled on top of each other and mosses covered most of the area of the block work. The forest was behind him, dark and shadowy with only the tiniest glimpse of light arcing down through an occasional dead branch.

In the other direction was a level field, if you could call it that, of long coarse grass, not bright or even green but a dirty yellow, and through it ran what appeared to be a broad and deep dried up river bed. Regular, heavy winter rains swelled the loch each year to the point where the side-spill overflow was almost in constant daily use, frequently relieving the pressure on the dam of several thousand gallons of water an hour. Smooth white, brown and grey boulders were strewn along the length of watercourse, evidence of the forces created by the winter torrents that had long ago washed away all traces of the thin earth leaving only the cleansed stones and bed-rocks to remain exposed.

Mattar looked around. The place was desolate, bleak and unattractive, abandoned and forgotten by man and neglected by nature. There were no noises to be heard; no birds singing, no babbling of water, not even the sound of a breeze to rustle the trees. The totally eerie silence seemed to predicate foreboding. Mattar felt a chill run down his back. He decided to walk the short distance along the dried track that led towards the deserted, tiny dam, to view what lay beyond, expecting there would be little of interest. When he reached the top he immediately recoiled in shock. A mere few feet from him lay the vast, and deep, Loch Triegg. He shuddered at the realisation that so much water was held back by what he considered to be only a small, almost inconsequential, deserted dam. He had never felt so alone and vulnerable in his life. Shaken, he turned and ran down towards his Land Rover, jumped in and drove fast to escape from the frightening place as quickly as possible. He arrived at the hotel forty minutes later and was met by Bagheri.

"Looks like you had a good trip, I see you got some mud." Bagheri laughed.

Still unnerved by his experience at the Triegg dam, Mattar lied. "Yes, great time. Vehicle's good." He hoped the rest of the mission would not be as scary.

★ ★ ★

Cindy and Gordon, with Sandy MacLean's assistance, checked the boats and brought all three across to the jetty at Mealag. Sandy serviced two outboards and generally ensured that everything on them was in order. He particularly made certain that the small padlocks holding the outboard to the security chain had not corroded and were working properly as Sandy had once lost an outboard when the padlock hasp had rusted through unnoticed. When the skeg struck a large branch floating just beneath the water, the motor reared up and released itself from its mountings before sinking into the loch. The third, larger boat had an inboard engine and was used for the ferrying of moderately sized goods or simply to cruise the loch in comfort. Gordon had checked over his fishing tackle, wiped his spare rods, carefully re-varnished the whipping that secured the snake guides and re-greased all the reels. The fly lines had been stretched by tying one end to a drain pipe at the lodge and the other to a tree in the grounds to ensure that they would cast straight and true, and not be slowed by them retaining the crookedness and kinks that come from being wound tight around a reel for several months.

As well as the rods, Gordon had also cleaned his guns and made certain that they, like his fishing gear, were in fine working order.

He had even checked the two sporting rifles he kept in the garages, the gun cabinet containing them disguised as a wooden box. They had not been used for at least two years, but Gordon had protected them well and they were still very serviceable. He knew that technically he should not keep them in the garages, even though it would take an immense effort for anyone to break into them, but he had been grateful on occasions for them being handily placed on the far side of the loch. A couple of times whilst fishing, he had seen some deer on the hill, had changed his mind and decided to go shooting instead. It was easier to get a gun from the garages than go all the way back to Mealag.

Cindy had helped Margaret MacLean in the kitchen and around the house, finalising the preparations for their guests and making certain that four of the smaller chalets were ready for the security people. Gordon had been informed that there would be four British and two American police, though Cindy had said that she doubted any of them would simply be officers, more likely they would be Special Protection forces. Sufficient food and supplies had been brought in to feed an army, but Mealag was used to catering for large numbers of people. The police, or whatever they were, could eat at Ruraich, and the freezers there were stocked high with ready meals that could easily be microwaved to provide hot sustenance at irregular hours, should that be necessary.

By Sunday evening, Cindy and Gordon were satisfied that everything was in order for their important visitors the following Tuesday. They relaxed listening to a live recording by the Greek star *Yanni* of his sell-out concert performed at the Acropolis, whilst they each sipped a glass of Gordon's favourite whisky – an eighteen year-old single malt from a small Scottish distillery. As they settled back, enjoying the soft, warm glow of the amber liquid, excitedly anticipating the arrival of the American Secretary of State and his wife, four sinister subversives were closing in with thoughts of how they would wrest the U.S politician from them.

49

Monday 11th September was another day of preparation for some; for others, it was a day of frenetic activity and escalating concern.

At 8:10am Ritson and his enlarged team were busy at their desks. Everyone realised that time was of the essence and there was a high level of noise and chatter as officers spoke earnestly on telephones or to each other. Dongle was sitting alone at his computer, staring intently at the monitor as screens of information flashed before him. Other detectives seemed equally absorbed as they scurried across the room to check some detail or other with a colleague. Sergeant Hill, in marked contrast to her mirth of the previous evening, was seriously studying the whiteboard hoping that within the cryptic jottings and scraps of information there might be a clue to a vital aspect which everyone had missed. Ritson's phone rang immediately he had replaced the receiver from a previous call. His French counterpart, Pierre Dervisais, greeted him in English.

"Good Morning Chief Superintendent, I am sorry to convey to you some rather disappointing news. I can confirm that a Fadyar Masri certainly has a bank account at the Banque Grecoriale. We have visited the bank and are currently checking the account and all transactions, but so far it appears to be satisfactory. There are no withdrawals to other named persons, so no leads there I am afraid. We have however ascertained from the account that the suspect has a credit card and we are currently checking all those transactions but the only one of any interest appears to be for petrol. Of course, the suspect is probably using different names – until we know those it will be impossible to trace anything for them."

"Yes, I understand. Do you have an address for her?" Ritson enquired.

"Indeed, we got that from the bank. Fadyar Masri does not appear on our national register of persons, strongly indicating she is an illegal immigrant. If so, she no doubt was careful for that reason, let alone any other, to pay mostly in cash. Money probably earned locally. Sadly, we French regard avoidance of tax and state regulations as something of a national hobby and it is very common place for employers, even quite large ones, to pay their staff cash and only retain minimal records."

Ritson knew of the reputation the French had at flouting governmental, particularly financial and taxation, laws. It seemed to be something everyone took for granted across the Channel – rather akin to a French politician taking a mistress, or two, which merits little or no media coverage in France, unlike the UK.

"Anyway, we have visited Masri's apartment. It is nothing exceptional but it has been thoroughly cleaned, quite a professional job as we have found no fingerprints and it would appear that many of the suspect's items are missing. We have taken into our possession a computer, which doesn't appear to be working, and that will of course be examined by our technicians. There are some miscellaneous items like a kettle and so on but none have any prints on them. We are in the process of making a more detailed search and examination of the flat, but to be frank it looks as though she has left. We can keep it under surveillance but I doubt anything will materialise."

"I see. Thank you." It was another small piece of information.

"We have not yet disturbed the carpets and fixtures in the flat. It is leased by a highly respectable property company in Paris and we are contacting them regarding the ultimate owners, but if this person is part of some sort of terror group that will yield nothing. We may get a name, only to waste hours trying to trace someone who died many years ago. We plan to instruct the forensic team to go through the property, room by room, dismantling everything. It will take time of course but is the only way we are likely to find out more."

Ritson agreed, he had been down that route himself many times. It would be the same with the car, assuming Masri had one but he thought he had better ask. "Do you know if she had a car?"

"She did, a blue Peugeot 205, according to the neighbours. They can't really help with the registration number, but I can tell you that no car is registered on our national database, nor with any

French insurance company, in any of the names you supplied. You may wish to note that our registrations are in the format of *nnnn LL dd*, or *nnn LLL dd* where *nnnn* is a 2, 3 or 4 digit number and *LLL* is a 2 or 3 letter group and *dd* is the department or district (as you would call it) where the car is registered. The neighbours say the last two numbers are 75. That is Paris department. One person is certain that there were only three letters beginning with a 'P'. If correct that would indicate Paris registration in either 2003 or 2004 and there will only be three numbers preceding it. It is a crazy system Chief Superintendent, long overdue for change. You are ahead of us in your vehicle registration systems, if not in rugby!"

Ritson did not rise to the bait, but chuckled.

"You have been extremely kind and obviously very busy. I am very grateful." Ritson was actually quite impressed with the amount of work the French police had managed to do in such a short space of time. They must have dedicated considerable resources to the matter, perhaps fearing that any outrage might be going to be conducted on their soil. When he put the receiver down, he went over to the white board and wrote

Blue Peugeot 205 reg: nnn – Pxx – 75 . Masri left flat. No trace of her on French databases.

He then went over to his two liaison officers who were his contacts with MI5 and MI6, and briefed them on what he had just learnt. "Look," he told them. "There is something going down here and I need you guys to get the departments really involved. We haven't heard a thing from Five or Six, yet they have the most sophisticated stuff in the world. I need their help and I want it now."

His anxiety showed in his voice but it made no difference to their answer. Officer Greg Kingsley answered for MI5. "Sir, Five are fully aware of our enquiries, but with respect they will not and cannot deploy more resources until either the level of threat is raised or unless they receive specific instruction from the commissioner himself. In practice both would occur at the same time. The same will be true for Jack here, and Six." Kingsley referred to the MI6 contact.

"OK, OK. Understood." Ritson responded quickly, an indication of his growing impatience. He walked away thinking whether he yet had enough to escalate the enquiry, and decided that he did not. There was still nothing to confirm an actual plot, only suspicious financial transactions. There was no indication of where any attack (if one was being planned) would take place and there was no information at all on any of the names, other than the bank account in London and the recent overseas transactions. Everything else relied a lot on supposition. But in his guts he knew this was for real, and it was his job to turn emotion into evidence. He needed his specially trained team to turn up something very quickly indeed, for there was no point in Manders approaching the chief commissioner until some hard facts emerged.

★ ★ ★

The olive green Agusta Westland AW101 Merlin helicopter based at RAF Benson in South Oxfordshire landed on the helipad at Mealag Lodge at precisely 2:30pm, exactly the time Gordon had been told it would. Two passengers alighted. Numerous black luggage bags were passed down to them, which they quickly removed from the vicinity of the helicopter. Two minutes later, they stood away and one waved to the pilot. The blades of the helicopter, still spinning slowly, gradually increased speed until with a sudden roar the helicopter became airborne and was gone, disappearing over the trees. The noise of the rotors had been so loud the two men had not heard Gordon drive up behind them seated at the wheel of a quad bike onto which had been hitched an open trailer. The two turned towards the lodge, saw Gordon and came over.

"Hi. I'm Chuck Drew and the good looking one is Josh Atkins." The slightly taller CIA protection officer held out his hand. "Guess your Gordon Truscott"

"That's me. Good to see you and welcome to Mealag. I hope you enjoy your stay. If you want to put your bags on the trailer and hop on, I'll give you a lift."

Atkins answered in a deep Southern American accent, more of a drawl than an intonation. "That's mighty decent of you, Gordon.

Thanks. My, this is some place you have here – saw it from the chopper. Too out of the way for me; I like big cities."

It was true he had seen it from the helicopter, but he had also studied numerous aerial photographs and a whole dossier of information about Mealag before he flew over the Scottish mountains and he knew its layout and perimeters every bit as well as its owner.

Gordon took them to their chalet and they were pleased that it overlooked Mealag and also gave them a pretty good sighting across the loch. Two hours after the Americans had unpacked the Merlin returned, having picked up the four British protection officers. Gordon went through the same routine for them as he had for the CIA agents and left them to introduce themselves to each other. Gordon said that Ruraich would be placed at their sole disposal and he left the six officers chatting away to each other around the large table in the training room. It was an ideal operations room, equipped with whiteboards, large tables, data and communication links and superb lighting. A little while later, all six took a close look around the immediate vicinity of Mealag and at the dam. When they returned they made some decisions.

Drew said that he and Atkins would have to stay close at all times to Assiter, and that meant they would accompany him even if he decided to go fishing or was simply out for a walk. They would sleep when Assiter slept. The four British officers would remain in the close vicinity of Mealag Lodge, providing 24-hour cover. One would be stationed at the dam wall gate on the south (lodge) side of the loch; the second would primarily guard the access gate from the Arkaig track, and patrol the surrounding area; whilst the third would cover the grounds of the lodge to the shore, the clearing and helipad. The officer stationed at the dam would make an occasional reconnaissance stroll along the shoreline, as far as the large knoll, before returning to his station. Anyone seeking to cross the dam itself would still be visible. They would stagger the commencement of each of their shifts thereby allowing rotation of duties and sufficient sleep. The officers agreed that two other security measures were essential. All exterior lighting was to be left switched on after dusk and that they were to be notified of all proposed movements of every occupant of the house. At 6pm Atkins walked across to Mealag and asked if everyone, including the MacLeans, could meet for a short briefing an hour later.

After the introductions and pleasantries, the American, Chuck – who seemed to be taking the lead in the meeting – started to outline the security team's plan for protecting Assiter.

"Firstly, we really don't want this to be intrusive. We'll try and stay out of your hair as much as we can, but it is important that we know your movements and plans well in advance. If that is not possible, and if ever you go off to do something we don't know about, you must – emphasise *must* – write it big on this board first. Complete as many columns as you can."

He pointed to one of the white boards fixed to the far wall that already contained a grid with a row for each day of Assiter's stay. The grid contained four columns: who; where; time out; time due in.

"Now, I don't want to scare you people by what I am going to say next, but please listen up. The threat level assessment for this assignment is deemed low. Not by us, but by our superiors back in Washington. That means they don't expect anything much to happen, but that is a hell of a lot different from saying no risk at all. Frankly, I would put the level higher, 'cos I would need a team ten times what we have here to fully protect the Secretary of State and sure as hell I would not let him out on that pond. It's too exposed and too damned dangerous. If we encounter an incident, we do not want dead heroes. Keep indoors, your head down. Do not, repeat *not*, get involved. Stay calm. We can get people here quickly if we have to. Any attackers will wish to escape, not be trapped inside this house. Remember that. I gather that panic alarms have been installed throughout the bedrooms, lounge, kitchen of the main house and also in our huts and at Ruraich here. They are on a separate circuit, being wired independently of the main alarm system. Use them if you see or hear anything suspicious or are worried. Do NOT hesitate. The alarm could save not just your life. We will test all the alarms, and lighting, later today. Finally, all landline telephone communication to the main house or any of the huts will be re-routed and intercepted before it rings here. You may answer the telephone as normal, but remember it is being monitored and every call will be being traced. Any questions?"

Cindy looked blankly at Gordon. The MacLeans looked at each other. There really was nothing to say or ask, but Cindy was not alone in feeling a certain unease that she could not explain.

"OK then. Just go about your normal routines. Our guy arrives tomorrow at 11:30am. Have a great time."

The irony of his final statement in the light of his preceding comments brought a wry smile to Gordon's face. As they left the room, Cindy smiled and whispered to Gordon, "Didn't you just love his reference to the chalets as huts?" They both laughed.

50

Ritson was impatient for information, spending much of his time walking around his team checking on their progress but learning nothing of consequence. He had put out a bulletin asking all UK police forces to look out for the foreign registered blue Peugeot 205, but that had so far yielded nothing.

In mid-afternoon his telephone rang and it was once again Pierre Dervisais, his French counterpart. "Some more news, my friend. Fadyar Masri travelled to the UK on Saturday 9th September on the 8:20am ferry to Dover and has a return ticket for 23rd September departing Dover 2:30pm local time. Her car registration number is 969-PX-75. No passengers."

"That's terrific, Pierre. Thanks."

"Don't get too excited, Chief Superintendent. The car registration actually belongs to a Citroen and is certainly false for the Peugeot. The plate properly belongs to someone whom we have checked out. It will not provide any more leads for us."

"Pierre, it's the most I've got. So thanks."

Ritson gathered his team. "Circulate this number, absolute priority. If the vehicle is spotted, do not apprehend but report to us immediately. Also, get hold of all the near motorway and garage CCTV films to see if we can pick this vehicle up anywhere. We need to know where it went."

He updated the board. Half an hour later Dongle came to see him. "I've got something, boss. That car. On the 3rd May 2005 it went through a Gatso speed camera coming into Woodstock, Oxfordshire at about 6pm. It's recorded in the untraced driver file."

"Dongle, you are a bloody marvel. How on earth did you think to look there?"

"Well, everyone else can poke around into the main databases – I look where others don't."

Ritson hurried to his desk. May 2005. Two months before 7/7.

Two months before the bank account. He pulled the Crossland file from the grey, steel sliding drawer, slamming it back into the cabinet so hard that the sound temporarily silenced the room and caused his colleagues to turn around.

"Sorry".

The general murmur resumed.

He read the notes again. Crossland had consistently denied meeting anyone in connection with the Chalthoum file, but it must have been very close to May when some sort of initial contact was made.

"Someone get me a road map of the UK," he shouted across the room and within a few seconds one was handed to him. He quickly leafed through the pages and found Woodstock. Following the A44 road, he quickly came to Stillwood. He got up quickly, gathering the file under his arm and ordering a car to take him immediately to the Hannet-Mar bank. He bounded up the steps and, flashing his warrant card, demanded to speak to Crossland immediately. Within a minute, he was seated opposite a rather nervous looking bank manager.

"I am going to be very blunt, Mr Crossland. You could be in a great deal of trouble and for reasons I cannot disclose I do not have much time, so I want some straight answers to some straight questions."

Crossland's heart pounded. He had become rapidly fearful of what lay ahead for him, but he knew he did not have to be bullied.

"Chief Superintendent, please! You cannot just barge in here and demand answers. Am I suspected of something? If so please tell me, as I shall obviously wish to ring my solicitor."

"Sir, I can and will arrest you if you do not cooperate. I have the powers invested in me under the Prevention of Terrorism legislation, but actually I do not suspect you of being a terrorist. If I did, you would already be behind bars. I would however like some answers."

"I will see how this goes," said Crossland. "I have nothing to hide, so ask away."

"When did you first have any contact with Halima Chalthoum?"

Crossland called his secretary to locate the paper file, while he himself tapped away at the keyboard. As he studied the screen, the file was brought in brought in by Kelly Palmer.

"Well, the computer does not give an exact date," Crossland then read a few of the paper documents, "and neither does the paper file. From memory I think it was around April last year."

"I put it to you, Sir, that you did meet this woman – or someone who claimed to be her – and I have good reason to believe that you met her at your home Red Gables in Stillwood at about 7pm on the 3rd May last year."

Crossland was shaken. He had denied seeing Halima several times and if he backtracked now it would finish him. At the very least Ritson would certainly press charges of wasting police time and in all probability would add aiding and abetting terrorists, if that indeed was what Halima was. He resolved to brazen it out.

"Good God, man. You cannot go around accusing people like that. Have you witnesses? I strongly suspect not."

Ritson studied the file before him and froze. He stared for several seconds at the Styles photographs of the conference delegates. Listed half way down was the name of Fadyar Masri. *SHIT,* he said to himself, cursing silently at not remembering the name earlier. Without doubt there was now a connection that might be just sufficient to get his superiors really interested. Regaining his composure, he put the photograph of Fadyar Masri in front of Crossland.

"What about this woman, Sir. Have you ever met her?"

"Chief Superintendent Ritson, you asked me the very same question months ago. The answer is still the same. No."

"What about Mrs Crossland, Sir. Is it possible she could have met with either of these women?" Although quietly spoken, the question exploded into the room setting off alarm bells in Alan Crossland. Crossland reeled from its impact.

"Er, no, I doubt that. No. How could she?"

"Perhaps you could ask her to give me a ring Sir, just for the record."

"I'm sorry. We are divorced and I no longer have any contact with her. I cannot even tell you where she is living." Crossland replied.

"I'm sorry to learn that, Sir. We can probably trace her quite quickly, but perhaps you could write down the name of the solicitor she used."

Crossland obliged, passing Ritson the note.

"Thank you. My enquiries into the true identities of Halima Chalthoum and Fadyar Masri will be continuing. In the meantime, I must ask that you hand your passport in at any police station within twenty-four hours, and that you give me an undertaking not to leave the country. Indeed, I strongly urge you not to try. When my enquiries are concluded you will be informed."

"What! Chief Superintendent, please go now before I lose my patience. I have done nothing wrong and I shall seek to have your conduct thoroughly investigated. I shall not be leaving the country anyway, and my solicitor will be in touch with you regarding the passport and this whole matter. I think you have behaved quite disgracefully."

Crossland rang through to his secretary saying Ritson was leaving. Neither shook hands.

After Ritson left, Crossland poured himself a stiff whisky. He was sweating. Ritson's enquiries could be ruinous for him and he wished he had never taken Styles' advice and opened an account for Chalthoum Universal, but it was too late for regrets. His nerves steadied by the swift intake of alcohol, he began to think more rationally. Ritson could not have much on him as he was not under arrest, but he was being leaned on very hard indeed. The police were still very active on the case and that meant that Halima, or Fadyar as he knew her, was linked to some sort of terrorism. Crossland recalled that his friend Styles had died in rather mysterious circumstances, but he still found it difficult to believe that terrorists would be involved in staging a road traffic accident, and he dismissed it as absurd that the gentle, attractive woman that visited him and Cindy could in any way be implicated in his death. That idea was fanciful. There was, however, one very worrying aspect to Ritson's interview and Crossland left the office early, determined to speak to the only man whom he thought might be able to help him, Jack Donaldson.

Ritson stormed back into his office shouting for his team to gather round. "Why didn't one of you lot link Fadyar Masri with the delegate photographs of Kenneth Styles? Her soddin' name is on them for Christ's sake."

The faces at the desk looked up at him, much as a naughty children look at parents when they know they have done something wrong. Someone said, "We didn't put every bloody one of those names on the computer, because we had no reason to. Remember?"

"We fucked up. I'm as much to blame as you, I didn't remember either but we have lost valuable time. From here on in, everyone must sharpen up."

Ritson was angry with himself more than with the team and what he said was merely the product of his frustration. He gave instructions for Cindy Crossland to be traced and went over to the incident board that had brief details of what was known about the persons forming the subject of the investigation. On it were the names of Halima Chalthoum, Fadyar Masri, Yasmin Hasan, and Alan Crossland. As he studied it, he realised that very few details were present under the names of Chalthoum and Hasan, but there was good deal of information under Crossland and, particularly, Masri. Ritson stroked his chin, thinking hard.

"Are we certain that the photograph of Chalthoum is not also that of Masri?"

"Affirmative. The labs boys ruled it out." An unknown voice somewhere behind him called out. Ritson had studied them himself in Crossland's office that afternoon and it was pretty obvious they were of two different people.

"Of course, it doesn't mean they *are* different people, just that one used a different photograph," contributed one of his bright female officers.

"Well, it cannot be Masri's. Her photo must be genuine as it was taken by the conference photographer, so if there is a false one it has to be that of Chalthoum." Another, different voice spoke.

"That's assuming that the person claiming to be Masri at the conference was actually Masri." The female officer again.

"Bloody hell, just get me some answers!" Ritson's brain was swimming in a thick fog of confusion, "Not more bloody ifs and maybe's. Look, work on the assumption that the conference picture is actually that of Fadyar Masri."

Ritson returned to his desk, thinking. He had some clues, some detail, but he was really struggling to put it together. He went to see Manders, but returned disappointed. Certainly Manders was pleased with the results they had obtained and he agreed that something was in the offing, but he had nothing specific which he or the commissioner could use to seek an emergency meeting of the Joint Terrorism Analysis Centre (JTAC), and raise the national threat alert. Ritson also doubted that Manders could convene an emergency meeting of the newly formed Counter Terrorism Command (CTC) SO15, that had resulted from the merger of the previous anti-terrorism agencies, and which Manders himself now headed, without the approval of the JTAC. Ritson had to be satisfied with Manders' promise that he would have an off the record chat with the security agencies about using their resources regarding Fadyar Masri, but he would not ask for a hunt across a wide list of names until he was more certain of their actual involvement.

51

After taking breakfast in their room at the Eagles Rest Hotel, Mattar drove to Glenelg. Khan and Fadyar were standing at the memorial as he drew up alongside the camper. The three made a deliberate effort to be noticed as they loaded Mattar's Land Rover, and as they left the car park Fadyar ebulliently waved to Morag. The single track road climbed steadily around Mount Ratagan until, near the summit, Mattar pulled into the view point car park where Bagheri was waiting in the Vauxhall. Fadyar and Khan gathered their belongings and took over the Vauxhall as Bagheri jumped into the Land Rover. Khan, in the Vauxhall, drove away first followed fifteen minutes later by Mattar. It took them an hour and a half to reach the dam and both vehicles were parked facing the loch. Fadyar raised her telescope to her right eye and surveyed the far shore. It was a little after midday.

"No sign of any security forces," she reported, factually. "We'll go on. See you at the cottage."

Mattar and Bagheri stayed at the dam five minutes longer than their fellow conspirators in the Vauxhall, then they also set off for Kinloch Hourn. Fadyar and Khan collected the keys to their rented cottage which was situated near to the end of the road, and set back from the tiny harbour that sheltered a few small boats. They unloaded their bags and walked to the boat house where a few months earlier they had hired the clinker built boat and outboard, ostensibly for fishing on Loch Quoich. A burly, ruddy-faced man, with an unruly mop of white curly hair answered the door. He vaguely recognised Khan who was able to negotiate a small discount on the daily rate for booking the boat for ten days, delighting the owner. As the man closed the door, he chuckled loudly at the stupidity of tourists wasting all their holiday time fishing for a few measly trout. Kinloch Hourn was literally many miles from anywhere, tourists were few. Those who did venture to the end of the road faced a long drive back and so there was seldom any demand for a fishing boat at that end of Loch Quoich. Any that did would only want to hire it for a few hours, not several days, and he would gladly have rented the boat out at half price for a ten day period had he been asked. They rejoined the others at the cottage and as they ate a sandwich they heard the unmistakeable repetitive drumming as a helicopter's rotors thumped away huge swathes of air.

"Merlin," said Fadyar. She had heard hundreds of Merlin helicopters in Iraq and the sound sent a quiver of excitement through her. "His protection is arriving."

As is to be expected, information about the British Government Communication Headquarters (GCHQ) is limited. Over the years, its precise activities of intelligence monitoring of communications and other electronic signals, intercepted at listening stations in the UK and overseas, has given rise to more speculation than fact. The listening stations themselves are believed to include GCHQ Cheltenham, Composite Signals Organisation (CSO) Morwenstow, CSO Ascension Island and Ayios Nikolaous on Cyprus. RAF Menwith Hill, situated just outside Harrogate, North Yorkshire is one of the world's largest communications monitoring stations and, despite its name, is operated by the National Security Agency (NSA) of the United States. In return for allowing the US use of its old RAF base, Britain receives and shares communications intelligence with its US partner under a formal UKUSA agreement. CSO Morwenstow and RAF Menwith Hill work closely together and are probably the most important communication monitoring stations in the world. CSO Morwenstow, based near Bude, North Cornwall, comprises twenty-one satellite ground antennas of various sizes (three have a diameter in excess of thirty metres), and can cover the frequency bands used by orbiting satellites. CSO Morwenstow can monitor communications across the Atlantic Ocean, the African and Indian Oceans as well as over the Middle East and mainland Europe. RAF Menwith Hill, along with smaller stations based in Australasia, covers the South Americas and Pacific Ocean. It occupies a 560 acre site on which is a vast variety of satellite dishes, masts and radomes, often likened to large golf balls, which are constructed in the mass polygon shapes to disguise the direction of the satellite dish within.

Both locations employ American NSA and British GCHQ staff and their operations are so secret that the British and American governments refuse to release information about virtually anything of the sites' activities.

The Anti-Terrorist Unit liaison officer's first request for information, in 2005, on the names of Halima Chalthoum, Chalthoum Universal Holdings and Corniche Consortium was sent to GCHQ Cheltenham who checked their databases and reported back in the negative. The second request did not make it as far as an operator's terminal. Communications monitoring was a twenty-four hour, seven day a week operation and the hugely expensive computers, not to mention the optical storage data costs, were manned by equally costly personnel who had specific priorities. In short, ATU liaison could ask once; next time, it had to be prioritised by the Joint Analysis Committee. Despite Ritson and Manders both sensing that some plot or atrocity was being planned, there was little they could do. Manders' off the record chat with GCHQ had got nowhere and he was discussing with Ritson what to do next.

"You and I both know something is in the wind. We have to do something," Ritson implored the assistant commissioner.

"I agree Bill, but… I just don't know what." Manders sounded deflated.

"I've an idea, boss, but it's a bit of a stretch. Crossland's wife has left him and moved. She had been renting a cottage, but she's gone, we don't know for how long. It may only be a day or so. The local lads have been round, all looks OK, but the neighbours say she has been away quite a while – whatever that means – 'weeks' is the best they could come up with. One of the neighbours said she disappeared at about the same time that someone in a car parked up the road a few times. The neighbour thought it was a bit suspicious, but didn't report it. No vehicle make or identity of course, never is, but it appears that this person, whoever he or she was, has not returned since. Suppose we surmise that Crossland and his wife did entertain Chalthoum, or at least that his wife knew he did and could testify to it. The last acquaintance of Masri, whom we suspect is also Chalthoum, was Styles and he was killed or had a suspicious accident. Maybe, we could get people interested if we thought a murder or kidnap might have been committed. It would be a bit of a flyer, but it might attract interest especially given the Crossland woman's security clearance."

Manders thought about it. This was not for the commissioner as he would quickly see through this charade and rule it out, but it was worth a try elsewhere. He would modify Ritson's idea but the basis was the same. He picked up the phone.

"John. Phil of ATU. Sorry to bother you, but I need your guys help. The liaison officers have already been in touch, but when they first made the approach last year it was, frankly, premature and understandably they were shown the door when they came knocking yesterday with more names. Unfortunately, I don't have quite enough, yet, to convene the CTC, but my experience as head of the ATU leaves me in no doubt that something big is about to go down. However, it appears that a totally innocent woman has gone missing. She may be in serious threat of her life as she can identify one of our principal suspects in this plot, which I stress I am sure exists. I want to avoid her death and for that I need your help to give me all you can on a couple of names. Will you do it?"

John Walters was command head of Middle East section at GCHQ, which had replaced the Russian section many years previously as being the busiest and largest department within the secret establishment. He also sat on the Joint Terrorism Analysis Centre. He knew that Manders did not have enough to justify a formal approach, but he also respected Manders and had been impressed by how accurate his hunches had been in the past.

"I'll do it, but I can't do it as a special request. The best I can do is to put the names into the schedule for tomorrow. If something more urgent crops up it will be put down the pecking order, but I will make sure it is at least on the routine list. Now, Phil, give me the details."

"Fadyar Masri is one name, believed to live outside of Paris, but almost certainly now in the UK and also a Yasmin Hasan. She may have a Dubai connection as she has a bank account there. That's it". There was little point in repeating all the names, which could well be counter-productive. A routine request was far less likely to get actioned if it contained numerous names.

★ ★ ★

Alan Crossland was frightened. After Ritson's interrogation he had called Chloe saying he would be home late, and then summoned Donaldson to drive him to his London flat, which – like Red Gables – was still stubbornly refusing to sell despite the booming property market.

"What am I to do, Jack? What the bloody hell do I do now?" Crossland had spent the previous twenty minutes explaining about the Chalthoum account and now looked to his driver for help. Donaldson didn't answer him. Still smarting from not getting a substantial salary rise, and being fobbed off with a second-hand car that fetched only just over seven thousand measly quid, he was in no mood to bring solace to his employer. He decided to let Crossland suffer a little longer.

"The cops haven't interviewed you under caution and not arrested you. So they can't have much."

"Not yet, no. But they are bloody persistent, and I know they don't believe I never met the woman." A slight note of exasperation was creeping into his voice.

"Did you ever meet up with this Chalthoum woman at any other time? You didn't screw her did you?" Donaldson smirked as he looked towards Crossland.

"Oh for pity's sake, Jack, we're not all like you. No, I never met her again."

"So only the ex Mrs Crossland knows you met her and only she can state that?"

"As far as I am aware, yes. I certainly did not tell anyone and Cindy would have no reason to. I sometimes used to bring home prospective clients of the bank, so it wasn't something unusual, though not common." Crossland was becoming impatient at the questioning but Donaldson wasn't ready to end it.

"Do you think the ex Mrs Crossland would lie to protect you? Suppose you contacted her and asked her to deny that Chalthoum came to the house? I should have thought she owed you a favour," Donaldson went for the jugular. He knew that repeatedly referring to Cindy as his ex-wife, plus the oblique reference of her deception over the divorce settlement and the link that made to the new love of her life, would inflame Crossland.

"Bloody bitch. I am not asking her anything. Besides, she two-timed me acting all sweetness and light and then shafted me good and proper. She repeatedly deceived and lied to me Jack. Why should I believe anything she says now? It's just too risky. I could go to jail here, probably for several years if it turns out there is some criminal or terrorist connection. Even if I get charged with a minor offence I would be ruined at the bank, probably serve a prison sentence – and I can't see Chloe waiting around for long. She is young and attractive. She won't have any trouble replacing me."

"I thought you said the police asked where the ex Mrs Crossland was?"

"Jack, just call her Mrs Crossland or Cindy, please. You're beginning to sound as though she's dead."

Crossland's words hung in the air, Donaldson cleverly remaining silent for nearly a minute. Then, slowly, he spoke in a quiet soft voice.

"That's looking to be your only hope, isn't it? If Mrs Crossland couldn't give evidence, the police do not have a case against you, at least not a terrorist one."

"Some hope of that Jack! But I wish the bloody cow was dead, no more than she deserves for the way she has treated and used me. Bloody bitch."

"Well, it isn't going to happen naturally is it? Staging an accident or a professional hit will cost many thousands," Donaldson took full advantage of his chance.

"What? What are you saying Jack? That Cindy could suffer some sort of fatal accident as you put it? Are you saying have her killed?" Alan Crossland was shocked at his own words.

"I'm not saying anything. All I am doing is pointing out is that the police will trace her and if she is alive, she will testify that this Chalthoum woman came to your house. Mrs Crossland is flush with money, so one couldn't bribe her to keep her mouth shut, and anyway you say she wouldn't lie for you for old-time sake. I am simply stating the hard facts."

Donaldson was pleased at the way he had worked in the provocation that Cindy no longer needed money, it would again remind Crossland with whom she was now living and he suspected that still angered him every bit as the divorce settlement itself. Crossland held his head in his hands and closed his eyes. His brain was reeling, trying to make sense of it all.

'How did I get here?' He asked himself over and over.

Several minutes passed and slowly Crossland lifted his head and looked straight at Donaldson and in a soft voice muttered, "I wouldn't know where to start looking for someone who does that kind of thing."

Donaldson had a quick response ready. "I'm still in touch with a few blokes from the old days that might be interested, army types. They were pretty good at that sort of thing in Iraq and Africa."

Crossland let the words swirl around his brain. After a minute he spoke again to Donaldson, "Who? Can you introduce them to me?"

"You do not want to meet them, do you? You're in enough shit. I might be able to arrange it so that nothing can be traced back to you, so the less you know the better. The guys I'm thinking of will want about a hundred grand with fifty up front, they won't do it for less."

"A hundred grand! You must be joking."

Donaldson decided it was time to reel in his played-out fish. "In that case, come up with another solution. Is your career and a future life with Chloe not worth 100K? I thought you said you'd recently struck it rich?"

Alan sat, once more head in hands, thinking.

"Oh my God, Jack. What do I have to do then?"

"Give me the fifty in cash tomorrow. I'll meet you at the Italian place in Covent Garden. Get me off your payroll from last month with a year's salary and, if anyone says they have seen us this month tell them I took the dismissal badly and you were trying to help me out a bit. I will give you an account into which the money for the hit can go. It's not traceable but make sure all your money isn't either. After tomorrow, you and I must not meet for a very long time; you understand that, don't you? If you want me to do your dirty work, I'll do it as you've been good to me but it means the end for us." Donaldson's sweet compliment to his boss carried the sickly odour of blood money.

"Do you really mean that Jack? Can you find someone to do it? What about you? You must have something for doing all this; say twenty-five for yourself with the upfront cash. You would be entitled to the salary in lieu anyway, as it was part of the deal we made when I hired you. Just make sure it gets done, and done very soon, before the police get to her."

Donaldson could not stop laughing as he walked towards his hotel. He would not only fuck that prick-tease bitch before he killed her, but he had also screwed her ex-husband out of £125,000 plus a year's salary. He deserved a night in Soho. The next morning, Donaldson carefully packed the boot of his car with all the gear he would need, including his camouflage jacket and trousers plus his trusted army weapons and hunting knives. In the afternoon he met Crossland, banked the cash in an offshore account under another name and headed up the M6 motorway. By late evening, he was only a few miles from Loch Quoich.

52

Sandy and Margaret MacLean were up and about very early on the Tuesday morning to buy fresh vegetables and stock up on other consumable supplies in Fort Augustus. Margaret had insisted these should not be purchased until the last minute, and she and her husband had taken one of the boats across the loch shortly after dawn. The noise of the outboard awakened Cindy from her slumbering thoughts of the arrival of the US Secretary of State and his wife, imagined images which had scarcely left her mind as she dozed fitfully through the night. As Cindy and Gordon settled down to their breakfast in the kitchen, there was a loud knock on the rear door and the CIA Agent Atkins came in.

"Sorry to disturb you folks but the MacLeans left a while back without putting details on the white board at Ruraich. I know this is a real pain folks, but we must know when you plan to go out, and get back, and where you are going. Can you remind them, please?"

Gordon rested his cup back on the table and spoke quietly, "Sorry officer, they would have simply forgotten but I will remind them. Put on your board that they expect to return at 10am from Fort Augustus. Reason – shopping."

"That's mighty decent of you, Sir. Thanks," and with that Atkins left.

Cindy turned to Gordon.

"My word, they take it seriously don't they? Dean hasn't even arrived yet!"

"True, but their duty has started so they would take some flak if anything happened, even now."

The MacLeans returned slightly later than Gordon had estimated but had unloaded all their goods well before Assiter was due to fly into Mealag. After a gentle prompt from Gordon, Sandy wrote up the time of their arrival on the board at Ruraich.

At exactly 11:30am the Merlin touched down on the helipad. Two CIA protection officers leaped out of the helicopter whilst the rotors were still running and, crouching to avoid the down blast, ran to meet Chuck Drew who was waiting at the edge of the clearing with Cindy and Gordon. A few inaudible words were spoken into the ear of Drew who nodded his head. The protection officers returned to the helicopter and instructed the pilot to cut the engine. A minute later out walked Dean Assiter and his wife Paulette Brazeau, to be welcomed by Gordon and Cindy. The initial introductions were soon over and the four sat at the large kitchen table talking excitedly and drinking a cup of steaming fresh coffee that Cindy poured for them from the newly installed and very expensive machine she had recently persuaded Gordon they needed.

Assiter looked younger than how Cindy remembered him from his appearances on the television, but Gordon thought he had aged quite considerably since they last met. Aged now fifty-one, he reached high office after a long and distinguished career in both Washington and Capitol Hill. His receding, naturally waved, dark hair showed only a few signs of greyness, but it would not be many years before his loss of hair would become quite marked, especially if the pressures of the job he had held for the past three years did not diminish. He stood at only five feet ten and had a small oval face with pale grey eyes which were sharp and bright. He spoke in a slow, measured, deliberate manner – the mark of a man who knew the worth of being careful and precise in what he said, but it was without a heavy American drawl, his accent being almost lost amid carefully constructed phrases. Yet, for all the caution he took over his words he certainly did not lack charisma, nor humour. He quickly had everyone at the table laughing heartily as he told very funny anecdotes of political events and the people who featured in them. Cindy could appreciate why he and Gordon had become solid friends. They shared the same values and the same outlook on life, albeit in quite different circumstances.

Paulette was stunningly beautiful in the way of most top models. Tall and elegant with the slim firm body and long legs that Cindy had always wished for, she moved with an effortless grace and poise that others could only envy. Aged thirty, there were no lines on her oval face and her dark brown eyes contrasted with her flawless pale complexion. Cindy could tell that Paulette had applied very little make-up, certainly less than her, and it was not hard to imagine just how fantastic Paulette must look when professionally modelling.

"I do less now, of course, since marrying Dean," Paulette explained to Cindy whilst the two men were engrossed in a discussion about fishing, "and of course I am getting older. The trend these days is for younger and younger models with slimmer bodies and I cannot compete with that!" Paulette spoke flawless English but with an unmistakeably French accent.

"But you too, Cindy, look so wonderful. Gordon is very lucky to have found you. I never did hear how that came about, do tell me, please. It has to be an interesting story as Dean tells me that Gordon has never been serious on anyone before and certainly that is true for as long as I have known him. It was a wonderful surprise to us when he told us about you."

The two women chatted and laughed over the story of Cindy and Gordon's romance rising from the despairing depths of the tragic events on the train to the soaring delights of Mealag, Greece and Rome. Gordon and Dean could not stop talking about fishing and deer stalking. The two women separated from their respective partners after lunch, going for a swim and a sauna, whilst the men inspected the fishing tackle and boats. Dean tested out several rods by making a few casts with each from the bank of the loch until he had chosen three to his liking. It was clear from that very first afternoon together that whilst occasionally all four of them would agree to undertake a common activity, the likelihood would be that Dean and Gordon would do their own thing leaving Paulette and Cindy to do whatever suited them. It was natural and obvious this would happen, but it added to the concerns of the protection team. Whilst principally employed to ensure the safety of the Secretary of State, they could not simply ignore that of his high-profile wife. To the CIA men there was a lot to be said for the maxim of 'safety in numbers'. Had their charges adhered to it, they would not have exposed themselves to the imminent danger that would engulf them when the protecting forces were too thinly deployed.

53

The terrorists' cell met up at Corach at 9:30am. Fadyar and Khan had breakfasted at the cottage, before driving to the hotel where the others had eaten. As the four assembled in the car park, Fadyar noticed that a few of the guests were gathered on the lawn and inspecting a number of shotguns.

"What's that all about?" she asked Bagheri.

"They have a small clay pigeon shoot and guests can use it any time, for a fee of course, plus no doubt a good tip to the instructor. Pity we have other things to do, we could show them how to do it!"

Fadyar smiled, but made a careful mental note to listen out for the shots when she returned to the dam as she would be interested to learn just how far the sound carried around the hills. She informed the others that she and Khan had not stopped at the dam on the way to the hotel, merely driven slowly past, but she had not seen any sign of security people even though she had been looking through her telescope. They put their kit in the back of the Land Rover and once they were all seated, Mattar pulled out of the forecourt onto the highway heading, once more, for the dam.

Fadyar started to brief them. "We need to find out how many security people there are and where they are deployed. That is our first task. I am certain that one will be stationed at that walkway across the dam, if not today as soon as Assiter arrives. The dam provides the easiest and most accessible route by foot to Mealag Lodge; it just has to be guarded. They will also protect the rear gate, the Arkaig entrance, though the four metre high perimeter deer fence may be generally patrolled rather than place a single person at the gate itself. Assiter will have some people with him 24/7 wherever he goes; I don't know how many but let's presume four – how many more will they have? We must find that out." She spoke clearly and calmly as their Land Rover neared the dam.

"Park it sideways on to the loch. If anyone is on the dam wall opposite they will not be able to read the number and we will appear to be tourists."

Mattar did as he was instructed, driving slowly past the dam wall and parking on the wasteland next to the building that housed the switchgear and shaft intake controls. They had an excellent view of the far side of the dam wall and it was obvious that no guard had yet been posted there, so Fadyar ordered them to drive on and pull over by the track leading to the garages where they parked out of sight. Fadyar asked Khan to check if any boats were tied up at the small jetty and to take some field glasses and report back with what he could see going on at Mealag.

"Be careful, Nasra. Don't make it too obvious. You're a tourist just looking at the hills and the loch, remember."

Khan returned ten minutes later.

"I couldn't see any people. There is one boat here, small outboard. Two are tied up at the lodge. One is another clinker built boat with outboard for fishing the loch, and the second boat is a larger inboard cabin cruiser, probably for water-skiing or just travelling around in a bit more style."

Fadyar nodded, deep in thought, her gaze fixed upon the large expanse of water before them.

"Nasra. You and Sharid put on your gear and take the fishing stuff. Remember the polaroids so you not only look the part, but also to stop you being dazzled by the reflections off the water. There's a reasonable breeze coming over the hill behind us so you can cast easily and at least it will appear you know something about fishing. Walk up and down the shoreline, separately, between here and the dam, fishing as you go. Have a rest now and then tie on a new fly and all that. Look convincing, but all the time observe what is happening at the dam wall and the lodge. Note anything of interest, especially numbers of people over there if you see any. We will pick you up here in about two hours, maybe a bit more. I need to go to the cottage and change into some camouflage gear. After that Mawdud and I will be going to Arkaig."

They left Khan and Bagheri, changed at the cottage and drove back to the dam, stopping briefly once more on the rough ground. As Mattar switched off the engine a helicopter suddenly appeared, flying only a matter of feet above the loch. It seemed to be coming straight towards them, the downdraught from the blades creating a cloud of fine spray trailing like mist on the calm loch. As it roared over their heads, the spray mixed with an upsurge of dust and sand, like mini whirlwinds, causing the Land Rover to became covered in a dirty, sticky brown film such that it was impossible to see out of the windows or front screen until Mattar put the washers on and depressed the switches to lower the electronically operated windows. The helicopter turned sharply and throttled back. The roar became little more than a gentle throbbing hum as it hovered briefly above Mealag Lodge before disappearing behind the trees.

"Phew," said Mattar. "That's what I would call low flying."

"Assiter," said Fadyar curtly. "Our target has arrived. Good of his pilot to add some more muck to the jeep. I don't think Nasra and Sharid will be too happy, though."

Mattar smiled at the image of his two friends having to take cover as the helicopter flew over them. On the way to Loch Arkaig, Mattar asked Fadyar how she expected to get close to the gated fence entrance without arousing suspicion.

"We can't risk going to the gate but we can travel part way. If they have people on the track, we will have to bluff it out saying we are just out for a walk, but it's a small risk. Why would security people be outside a perimeter fence?"

"So why go, then Fadyar? You're losing me on this one."

"Firstly, two are less suspicious in a car than four. The same logic applies to fishing the shore. This is not a busy place, ever. Two people, fishing a distance apart from each other around the loch-shore, is reasonably normal, four is not. So we have to disappear and we might as well take a look at Arkaig and see what's about. You never know what we might see. Maybe they have a tank in the forest!"

"Surely not," said a very worried sounding Mattar.

"Oh, silly. Of course they won't, just a joke!" Fadyar threw her head back, giggling with nervous excitement. "Come on, start the engine. Let's go."

Fadyar and Mattar drove slowly around the twisting, narrow road that hugged the southern shore of Loch Lochy. A large bird, startled by the noise of the engine, took off from the water's edge and almost flew into the vehicle. They watched it fly up to a nearby tree and rest on a high branch. Fadyar paid it particular interest.

"A heron, Mattar. Did you notice its distinctive bill and the way it trails its feet behind itself as it flies."

"I didn't know you were interested in nature and all that stuff, Fadyar." Mattar was curious and invited Fadyar to say more.

"Life is strange, my brother. We are about to fulfil our destiny and when we came earlier in the year I initially took very little notice of the mountains and the wildlife and so on, but as we spent some time here I began to appreciate just what a beautiful place this is. Not just at the dam, but all around us. So, when I went home I got out a couple of books and read up about it and also the wildlife and birds. That is why I say life is strange. We came to do our work, our struggle against the infidel, our Jihad, yet that seems out of place here, which has remained like this for centuries. It is almost timeless, peaceful and full of wonderful, natural things. When we have succeeded, this place will never be the same again and some will regard it with horror and revulsion – just as we abhor the crimes and desecration committed in our homeland."

They remained in silence for several minutes until Mattar turned the 4x4 sharply left and drove along the Loch Arkaig road, stopping a few yards short of the Mealag estate track.

"So what now?" Mattar asked.

"Drive on the track for two miles, then stop and park. Try not to rev the engine too much. My notes say the track is two and three quarter miles long, so we should be ok."

A little while later, they had driven deep into the forest, parked and were walking slowly and very quietly towards the perimeter fence. Stopping every few yards, they listened for noises or voices but heard none. Eventually they reached the final bend before the fence and gate would come into view. Fadyar beckoned Mattar to stay down whilst she slowly made her way further forwards, crouching low and seeking to make the best use of the trees to conceal her approach. A small cleared area had been cut into the forest around the fenced enclosure and she lay down behind a tree and began rubbing the dark, damp earth across her brown face giving her a blotched appearance. Her dull green camouflage trousers and jacket perfectly blended into the scrubland beneath the trees, and in the half light of the forest she was almost impossible to detect. She peeped out from behind the tall trunk. No one! She lay motionless for several minutes trying to pick up sounds or make out any movement, but she saw and heard nothing. She inched her way forward on her stomach, staying on the grass but she was very aware indeed that if anyone now came to the gate she would be visible, but she desperately wanted more information on what was happening at the lodge. Surely there must be some security people somewhere? She looked around her. Still there was no sign of anyone. In mild panic she thought that perhaps they had after all been deployed outside the fence, and would soon come by on their patrol. Her heart beat more rapidly and she knew she should not linger much longer when suddenly she heard some voices. They were not close, but she heard them clearly enough. American voices!

"Those mother fuckers better not forget to use that board again, Chuck."

"I've told Truscott and he will tell the MacLeans. For Christ's sake Josh, give 'em a break, no harm's been done and it's just that they ain't used to doing things our way yet. Anyhow, suggest we get our stuff and have another short briefing with the Brits now our man's arrived, then get our own asses out where they should be."

Fadyar listened intently and having heard all she needed to, withdrew slowly and silently. She signalled to Mattar to go back to the Land Rover and minutes later they were travelling back along the Arkaig road whilst Fadyar cleaned her face with some tissues. She looked again at her notes, hastily scribbled the moment she got back into the vehicle lest she forget anything. Making their way slowly back to collect Khan and Bagheri, Fadyar looked out of the passenger window. She still could not see anyone guarding the dam but some security tape had now been attached to the north gate. When all four were reunited and the fishing rods dismantled and stowed, it was obvious that Khan was really excited and keen to show them what was in the plastic bag he was carrying.

"I got two fish! Look Fadyar – our dinner!!"

They all congratulated Khan and looked at the two trout, both reasonable loch fish weighing in at about twelve ounces each.

"Well done, Nasra. Let us pray our mission is as successful" said Fadyar, then more seriously remarked, "I suggest we don't say anything about what we have found out until we reach the cottage where we can relax and have some good, strong coffee."

An hour later, the four were sat around a square pine table beneath a small ground floor window, from which, in the distance, it was just possible to make out the western most point of Loch Quoich.

"Ok, Sharid. You first," Bagheri was being asked to begin the debriefing. He sipped at his sweet drink and then spoke, "We were very fortunate this morning we were not discovered at the garages. Two persons, middle-aged probably around fifty, male and female returned by car at 10:15am and unloaded shopping at the roadside by the jetty before parking in the garages. Literally only a minute or so after you left for the cottage, otherwise we would have been discovered on the track. They took themselves and the shopping across the loch by the boat moored at the jetty, so all three boats are now at Mealag Lodge."

Fadyar remained impassive. There was no merit in wasting nervous energy on what might have been; just as supposition should never be confused with fact.

"That would be the MacLeans. Makes sense and it fits with what I heard at the gate. Carry on, Sharid, anymore?"

"Better that Nasra tell you, as he was first to notice it."

Khan started to address them.

"I was fishing reasonably near the dam at 1pm. Sharid was not in sight having walked well beyond the garage track to avoid us being seen close together too often. I detected a slight movement on the opposite bank, well… er… not on the bank itself, but skirting the trees and bushes. It was obviously someone who knew or who had been told of the dangerous bog over there. Couldn't make out who it was with just my sun glasses and I did not want to raise my field glasses for obvious reasons."

Fadyar impatiently interrupted, "Nasra, please, just the facts. We don't want a minute by minute account."

"Sorry. Well, whoever it was walked across the dam, then a few minutes later walked back taking up position close to the south gate. We thought a guard would be placed there, but he is not easily visible as you drive by on the road. I had a walk along to check if I could see him but couldn't. On the way back up the road I noticed the tape on the north gate so stopped and hid behind that inlet building and got my glasses onto him. It's a British special forces or protection officer armed with a sub-machine gun. He seems to have some sort of seat or bench in the bushes there so he can see out, but it's very difficult for him to be seen which I thought was strange. I should have thought if they wanted to deter an attack he ought to be visible."

"Nasra. You really are quite naïve at times. Do you know the range of my rifle? Do you know how far it is across the dam?"

"The dam is just over 300 feet across, we measured it."

"Yes, one hundred yards give or take. My rifle is accurate for a kill up to a mile away. At half a mile it is so accurate I could hit a spot on a target's face. I do not blame the officer for concealing himself as best he can."

Despite his coloured skin, Khan still flushed and feeling very foolish, apologised.

"No matter my brave soldier, you caught a fish! No two!"

Fadyar had not meant to humiliate him especially in front of the others. She had grown to like all her colleagues, but she seemed to have more in common with Khan and she valued his company. Fadyar then briefed the others on her findings from the visit to Arkaig.

"To sum up: We have at least two CIA one named Chuck who seems to be the senior agent, another named Josh. We know of one British officer sited near the south gate on the dam wall. There will be others. Almost certainly one will now be posted near or at the Arkaig entrance. We also know that in addition to the estate owner, Truscott, there are two others, Mr and Mrs MacLean, whom we can now safely assume are employees of Truscott as they went shopping today. Mrs MacLean will be the housekeeper and cook; her husband will help on the estate and manage the boats and things like that. We should look out for him and Truscott. Both will be used to rifles and shotguns, and there will be some at the lodge, further ruling out an assault on the house itself." Fadyar paused to finish her coffee before pouring everyone another. "We didn't see the larger boat earlier in the year so it is new to us, but I am not concerned as it is essentially a pleasure craft. Also, at the dam, there were no sounds of the shots from the clay pigeon shoot, a fact which pleasantly surprised me – though the wind may have been a factor, as it was blowing towards the hotel from Kinloch Hourn, not towards the dam."

The three males seated at the table marvelled at Fadyar's attention to detail, their eyes wide in admiration as she reeled off specifics they had either not noticed or forgotten. It inspired them and they had the greatest confidence in their leader and their mission. They were determined not to fail her.

"Tomorrow morning we will meet at the cottage and load our boat. At 10:30am Sharid and Mattar will drive along the Corach road and also on the Coille Mhorgil track that ends about half a mile from the surge shaft and access tunnel. I want you to drive anywhere on those roads, at random, as I want us to test out our two-way radios so have them on at all times. Walk up and around the hills. Have the scrambler on for our talk and the scanning channel open to see if we can detect the British and CIA communications. Keep as much talk as you can to meaningless numbers – 1, 2, 3 and so on – but answer my questions properly if I ask. Nasra and I will be in the boat, ostensibly fishing, but really we need to test out the range of the equipment and find out where any blind spots are. We shall use channel 12 for the first hour and if we have not made contact we shall then switch to channel 1 at 11:30am. I believe the equipment will function properly, but if we have not made contact by mid-day we shall make our way back to the cottage and find out what is wrong. Finally on the radios introduce yourselves by a fruit. I shall be an Apple; Sharid a fig; Nasra an orange and Mawdud a melon. Understood?"

They nodded. It had been a busy day and Fadyar did not feel like a meal at Fort Augustus or at the hotel. In fact, she offered to cook the trout for her and Khan leaving Bagheri and Mattar to return to their more sumptuous dinner at the hotel.

The trout was delicious, wrapped in foil with a little added salt it had been cooked simply in its own juices and was surprisingly satisfying for their hungry appetites when served with a few vegetables. Nasra and Fadyar spent the remainder of the evening watching television – the satellite channels offering a multiplicity of choice that neither was used to – and they joyously flicked from one programme to another, anxious not to miss anything before finally retiring to bed shortly after 10:30pm. The two had shared a bedroom for many nights earlier in the year and now more in September, but Khan had never made any suggestion to Fadyar that they join the two single beds. In fact he had been meticulous in covering himself whenever he entered or left the bathroom and always changed out of sight of Fadyar, gaining her respect.

Fadyar lay in bed, trying to sleep, but kept thinking of the day's events, and her mind inevitably wandered onto the mission itself. She wished she had more detailed information, more facts, less uncertainty. She recalled the calmness and beauty of the heron flying effortlessly upward, oblivious of the defilement that was about to unleash on the tranquil lochs and impressive mountains. The enormity of what lay ahead for them filled her thoughts and she shook involuntarily. She wasn't frightened, but leadership could be so lonely and there were times when she needed reassurance just as much as did her brave soldiers. She remembered how her father's calm, encouraging but authoritative words "You can do it, Fadyar; you *can* do it" gradually instilled in her the confidence to succeed as a young, bright schoolgirl. She had often recalled his words in times of stress and she was convinced they helped her through the difficult times as she studied at university. She would never forget his tears of pride as he watched her graduation ceremony and the look of joy in both his and her mother's face as she set out for Britain on a postgraduate course.

"Britain will be good for you, my daughter. Enjoy." Her father's parting words. And she did. She made many friends, had a couple of relationships and thought how fortunate the British were to live in a country without fear – a place where it was possible to mix freely with others of a different race or religion, if she wished to. *No longer,* she thought. *The British threw it all away when they invaded my homeland, cruelly and without mercy.* She shuddered again. *This is why I am here,* she said to herself, *to avenge my mother and father and to give to their murderers the justice they deserve.*

Her feelings of loneliness and isolation returned. She turned on her small bedside lamp and sat upright to try and quell the shaking, but to no avail.

"Nasra. Nasra are you awake?" she called out.

"Yes Fadyar, what's wrong?" Khan replied.

"Nasra, come here. Please. I need you." She slipped off her night dress and pulled back the sheets. For too long she had devoted herself totally to the cause of the Holy War, even spurning the advances of one of the most handsome instructors at the Pakistan training camp. Now she was putting that training into effect, and the mission – her destiny – was underway. The harsh years of self-denial were over, but Assiter was now consuming every minute of her day and occupying her dreams at night such that she had become saturated with a heady mix of emotion and responsibility. She was thrilled yet nervous; excited yet worried; focused yet uncertain and the trembling that rose from deep within her body was now in need of urgent physical release.

Khan slowly walked across the room and lay on the bed next to her.

"Are you sure you want this, Fadyar? Really sure?"

"Yes," she whispered softly. "Come here."

54

It was nearing 9pm when Donaldson arrived at the southern shore of Loch Ness, stopped in the small town of Fort Augustus and booked a room for three nights at one of the cheaper bed and breakfast guest-houses. Unlike some of his overseas campaigns, which had proved fraught and dangerous, he viewed the killing of Cindy Crossland, and if necessary her boyfriend, as a relatively simple task. The few shops were still open for tourists and at the newsagents he was able to purchase a detailed Ordnance Survey map of the area.

Returning to his lodgings, he spread out the map to finally check the location and surroundings of Mealag Lodge. Hitherto he relied upon only his motoring atlas and a small print out of the area he downloaded from the internet, and was anxious to check the entry points. He studied the map for several minutes before he saw a cluster of small grey areas and the words 'Mealag Lodge' printed by them. He looked again, disbelievingly. He put his face nearer to the map thinking his eyes were deceiving him and recoiled in shock when he still could not find any road or track marked on the map that led to the lodge. He rubbed his hands through his spiky red hair and mopped his brow with the sleeve of his shirt. He studied the map again, noting that the dam offered a form of access provided it had a pathway along the top of the wall, however he knew from experience that dams varied significantly in design and it was by no means certain that entry could be gained that way. Such setbacks might have made less confident men a little apprehensive, but Donaldson was not like other men. This was a man who had trekked through the wilds of Africa, pursued by savages and hungry animals; a man who had crossed the enemy ridden desert sands of the Middle-East, only surviving in that hostile and arid environment by eating the insects that crawled over him; a man who has never countenanced failure in the face of adversity. Yes, easy access to a target was a bonus but difficulties would not stop him. The Donaldsons of the world thrived on challenges and of overcoming the odds. Cindy Crossland was still a soft target. Where she was shacked up did not alter that and Donaldson resolved to go up to the dam early the following morning so that he could see for himself just what the location was really like.

★ ★ ★

John Walters of GCHQ personally inserted the names of Yasmin Hasan and Fadyar Masri on the Tuesday list, knowing that they would soon appear on one of the dozens of analysts' specialist computer screens deep inside the Cheltenham complex. These were not mere keyboard operatives, punching in a name and waiting for something to happen. These highly paid experts had at their disposal millions of pounds worth of hardware and software and were trained in when and how to use it. Sophisticated data mining tools scoured the databases of the intelligence and security services, transport organisations, and even personnel records from selected companies, creating links between supposedly unrelated items. The size of the stored intercepts from Morwenstow and Menwith listening stations was enormous, with even seemingly innocent messages that contained a key word, phrase or name being logged and retained for years. Further software tools could be used to drill down further into the relationships between the data items and the links that bound them, yielding still more information for even deeper analysis. Complex algorithms were used to score the results and to indicate either fresh lines of enquiry or to suggest alternative actions. If any results linked to other data or messages, the detail of those could similarly be summoned and examined. Shortly after 10am, the chess game screensaver cleared in front of the operator seated at desk 17, Unit 5, and the name of Fadyar Masri appeared, followed by the initial results of trawling the numerous databases.

02 May 2005 Travelled to UK by car ferry 1400hrs Calais – Dover
05 May 2005 Travelled to France by car ferry 1100hrs Dover – Calais
02 June 2005 Travelled to UK by car ferry 1400hrs Calais – Dover

05 June 2005 Travelled to France by car ferry 1100hrs Dover – Calais
… … … … searching
… … … … No More – Options Follow

The options screen then appeared and the operator chose 'internet'

… … … … searching

The screen saver came on and the operator resumed his game of chess until a while later it cleared and the following appeared:

IP number
"0100663296";"0117440511";"FR";"France";"Paris";"Central"

Then another option: *Search for suspect internet traffic?* The operator clicked on *YES*.

During the next hour, the operator had completed his game of chess, which he won, and commenced another. The millions of suspect internet transactions, clandestinely copied and retained by GCHQ, were searched to see if they contained within them the name of either Fadyar or Masri. As it appeared this particular enquiry would take a long time, he turned to an adjacent computer and started his initial searches on the next item on the list before him. Eventually the internet traffic screen appeared.

No suspect traffic. No obscene material. General browsing. Online banking services, refer for authority to interrogate.

He declined to seek authority for the bank details. He knew how long the authority took to obtain and that was multiplied a hundred fold for the actual search time. Instead, he continued accessing various menu options and undertaking more enquiries, until early afternoon when he selected the *Telephone* option. Again, the screensaver appeared and he had another lengthy wait before some words appeared on the monitor.

One intercept message ref U10/3645/06/08/dft sent to UNIFONE mobile

+3797984765876 originator unknown. Message in code, classified low grade. Not actioned.

The operator accessed the file given by the reference number, but it contained no other information except the coded message which was the only reason it was still on file. It had been classified as low priority by a reviewing intelligence officer who made the decision to file it pending other potentially dubious intercept traffic from the same source being received, but as none had been forthcoming it remained stored away amongst the millions of other intercepts that are not pursued. The operator then turned his attention to Yasmin Hasan and went through the same laborious processes, again punctuated by lengthy delays. Despite the analyst's efforts, the hugely expensive computers at his disposal could only reveal the following.

Yasmin Hasan born 1977 Baghdad. Graduated 2001 Baghdad University – Chemistry. Attended Birmingham UK University 2002 one year postgraduate course. Returned Baghdad 2003. Lived with parents in Haifa Street. Parents killed September 9 2004 by shrapnel from bomb blast. Yasmin Hasan body not recovered, presumed dead in same incident.

He filed the details, compiled his report and sent it to Waters, who in turn forwarded it to the ATU. Ritson quickly copied it to his staff before addressing a meeting of his entire team.

"Our first priority must be to decipher the message, leave that to me. I will go back to GCHQ on it. Then let's get some detail on that phone number. Johnson, get onto Unifone and ask them to run a check against all the names and see if that phone was replaced and if so its number. If it you come up with anything, let me know and we'll see if we can't get our intelligence friends to tell us where it is. Kramer, I want you to check out both universities. Get dates, photos, as much detail as you can. Laycock, see if you can get the military to give us the names of the dead parents and some more detail on what happened on September 9. Do a check on the parents in case they were known militants etc." Ritson barked out his orders in quick succession to his Heads of Section and within minutes the office was buzzing with activity after a relatively peaceful afternoon.

It was Dongle who first came to Ritson with some information. "That IP number on the GCHQ stuff, Sir, it's the same computer as that of Halima Chalthoum."

"Are you sure, Dongle?" Ritson was puzzled.

"Absolutely. I obtained the IP address – that's different from an IP number – from Crossland's bank. By means of an algorithm, an IP number is turned into an IP address. The simplest piece of software can read another computer's IP address and retain it. That's one of the ways these paedophiles get caught out, plus of course they don't know how to delete data from their hard drive properly. Using the algorithm, the IP number from GCHQ matches the IP address obtained from the bank."

"Yes, quite Dongle. Thanks," Ritson spoke rapidly to his subordinate trying to mask his lack of understanding. "That's a great help. So Chalthoum and Masri are definitely the same person?" He asked the question but was really thinking aloud.

"Well Sir, probably, but all I can say for sure is that they use the same computer."

"Chalthoum, Masri, Hasan… three names, but almost certainly the same person; with Hasan being the real one." Ritson once more spoke audibly to himself.

"Probably, Sir, but not definite. We still need more proof. Computers are often used by more than one person."

Dongle brought Ritson's racing thoughts to a sharp and unwelcome end, and two hours later the two weary policemen went home along with most of the day teams. The night staff would work on with the tasks and Ritson hoped that when he returned to the office the following morning something more positive may have been learnt. He spent a restless night. The weather was warm and intermittent thunder rumbled across the sky keeping him awake. His brain was still actively going over and over the facts of what he now firmly believed was some sort of plot, but he knew he was missing the really vital details he needed before setting into action the entire resources of Counter Terrorism Command. He was also aware of the fact that time was running out. The intercept message from GCHQ had really alarmed him as he did not know what it contained, but the fact that it was in code was ominous.

Six hundred miles away, Fadyar Masri had fallen asleep, her head resting on the chest of her new lover, his powerful arms gently entwined around her smooth, supple frame. For once her dreams were not of martyrdom, not Assiter, not even of her parents. She slept deeply and contentedly whilst the Anti-Terrorist Unit slowly but steadily worked through the night to hunt her down.

55

An experienced observer of the Corach road might have been slightly querulous at the amount of traffic upon it so early on a Wednesday September morning. Tourists are not normally seen on the road until well after 10am but an hour earlier several vehicles were travelling along the unclassified highway. Donaldson was the first on the road. He had breakfasted at 7:30am and was out of the guest-house in less than thirty minutes. He drove quickly towards the dam, noticing in his rear view mirror a Land Rover pulling out from the Eagles Rest Hotel car park and also heading in the direction of the dam. At 9am, a brightly coloured blue and yellow checked 4x4 took the Kinloch Hourn turn just outside Fort Augustus and was several miles behind Donaldson, and Mattar who was driving the Land Rover. Senior Firearms Officer Greaves was in the front passenger seat of the Police 4x4, his automatic weapon close to hand. The vehicle was being driven by another officer, armed only with a hand gun holstered at his side. Donaldson pulled up at the dam and looked for Mealag Lodge. He saw nothing and drove on, stopping in a designated passing place when he glimpsed the Mealag Lodge complex. Such passing places were frequent along the narrow Kinloch Hourn road, not only to allow following traffic overtake safely but also to permit motorists coming towards each other from opposite directions to pass. Donaldson was always cautious and he was fully aware the Land Rover would not be far behind. He quickly got out of the car, crossed over the road and pretended to relieve himself against the rocky outcrop that ran along that side of the road.

The Land Rover passed, and Mattar and Bagheri chuckled as they saw Donaldson. He started to return to the car but on looking left he noticed the flash of the chequered police vehicle rounding a bend in the distance. He waited until he could hear from the noise of the engine that it was near and he then repeated his deception as Greaves and his colleague passed. The two officers, like the two terrorists, took no interest in Donaldson and drove on. Once they were clear, Donaldson returned to his car and looked through his field glasses. He could see a couple of people moving about but could not make them out properly. He waited until the reason for the activity became clear from the loading of one of the smaller boats with rods and nets. He remained in his car, watching, for a further five minutes and then decided that he should move the car lest the police vehicle make a return trip and wonder why he was still parked in the passing place.

He drove to Kinloch Hourn, passing the police coming towards him. At the harbour he turned his car round and started to return to the dam. Out of the corner of his eye he glimpsed the Land Rover that had pulled out behind him at the hotel and watched four people loading their fishing gear into a boat. He had never fished, but he noticed how similar some of the tubular fishing rod holders being put in the boat were to some rifle carriers he had seen used, but the thought was fleeting. He arrived back and deliberately decided not to use the passing place, instead pulling off the road where he had an excellent view of the loch. On the water were two boats, not far from each other and he assumed both were from Mealag Lodge. He peered through his binoculars and instantly recognised Gordon Truscott, but he had no idea who the other three men were. They were all dressed in fishing anoraks or waistcoats and to Donaldson they simply looked like four guys out for a day's sport.

Donaldson cursed. All his assumptions had been based on Cindy and Truscott being alone, apart from a cleaner or home help, but more people was without doubt a complication. He knew from his map that Truscott's home was within an assortment of buildings and he wondered if the people fishing were staying or whether they were just local friends out with the millionaire for the day. Donaldson weighed whether to abort his plans now, but two thoughts made him continue. Firstly, Crossland had paid him well and the honour amongst mercenaries was that you did the job, no matter what the difficulties, once you had the money. Secondly, he really wanted Cindy Crossland. He had fancied her for years and after she teased and humiliated him he was going to make her finally deliver what she owed him. There would be no going back, no change of plan until the fire raging within him consumed Mrs ex bloody Crossland. Donaldson quickly re-focussed his mind on Mealag and the problem of its access. The OS map was certainly correct. There were no roads to it and a car would certainly not be able to cross the dam wall, indeed he needed to check out whether even a person could. He started his car and drove the short distance to the dam, parking on the waste ground. He began to walk the fifty or so yards towards the gate but as he approached he saw the railings were wrapped with blue and white plastic tape with the words "POLICE – DO NOT CROSS" repeated along its entire length. Donaldson assumed this was merely to stop tourists crossing the top of the dam and was about to ignore the tape and climb over when a voice, amplified from some sort of speaker, called out from the far side of the wall.

"Can't you read? Do not cross. If you do you will be arrested."

Donaldson shot back from the gate like a startled rabbit. He was dumbfounded. What on earth was going on? He strained to see who had called out but could see no one, an aspect that caused him to be even more curious. He returned to the car and decided it would be prudent to drive a short distance away before deciding what action to take next. He could not understand why a guard was placed at the far entrance to the dam and not at the road entrance. It didn't seem logical to Donaldson, though the guard obviously had a very clear view along the length of the wall to the roadside gate. He also puzzled over the events of the morning: The police 4x4; the guard at the dam; the unexpectedly large number of people at Mealag. He deduced these meant only one thing: Truscott was entertaining some very important people – but who, and for how long, and was Cindy Crossland even with them or was she perhaps somewhere else? He had to know. It was obvious there had to be another way into Mealag. He once again studied his Ordnance Survey map but he could find no markings indicating even a track but he worked out that vehicular access had somehow to come via the Loch Arkaig road which went within a few miles of the rear of the Mealag Estate. He decided to drive there and see for himself.

Fadyar finished loading the boat with the fishing gear and jackets she and Khan needed and bade a brief farewell to Mattar and Bagheri as they left the cottage and climbed into the Land Rover. Each wore a miniature headset linked to a two-way radio, the earphones and microphone so small they were barely noticeable. A short distance from the shore Fadyar spoke.

"Apple calling. One, two, three, … "

"Fig receiving, level 10."

"Apple here. OK out"

Fadyar looked at the time and then calculated the distance to the dam. The outboard was only small and it was going to take at least another hour before they would get close to Mealag. The loch was calm and the weather mild, though not warm enough for them to remove their sweaters, and Fadyar leant back and looked at the hills. Several minutes had passed when she had a call on her radio.

"Melon here. One, two… "

"Apple, receiving level 6. Where are you?"

"Melon. Just past the garage."

Fadyar was impressed with Mattar for not saying a word like "Dam" or "Mealag", which would have blown their location.

"Apple. OK, out"

After signing off, Fadyar estimated the distance between her and Mattar to be at least seven miles. That was an excellent range for a radio, albeit across open water. A voice on the radio talked to her again.

"Fig. Two friends ahead of you."

"Apple. OK. Out"

"Did you hear that?" Fadyar asked Khan.

"Yes, I guess there's a boat out somewhere."

Eventually the Mealag boats came into view and Khan slowed his outboard.

"Perhaps we should do some fishing," he suggested calmly, "time to put our jackets on and get the rods out."

They stopped the engine and lowered the anchor before unpacking the rods. It took several minutes for them to attach the lines and reels, during which time the CIA agents moved their position to that of directly in line between Fadyar's boat and Assiter's.

"They're good," said Fadyar. "We must be at least a mile away but they've blocked off Assiter from any possible threat we might pose."

Fadyar and Khan continued to fish, casting their short lines gently onto the rippled surface of the loch but all the while observing the boat ahead of them, hoping it would move away just sufficiently for her to get a good view of her quarry – but it continued to mask the boat ahead of it. After a quarter of an hour, satisfied that she and Khan would be regarded as tourists, Fadyar bent down in the boat and retrieved her telescope. Still in a crouched position, she rose just enough for her to look through the small lens.

"Raise the anchor and quickly move to our left. I want to take them off guard," she commanded. A few moments later, before the agents' boat had been able to respond, she said to Khan, "Well done, Nasra. Truscott and Assiter are definitely in the far boat, the security guys are in the other. I am amazed he is not better protected. If I had my scope attached to the rifle I could probably kill him from here, if that were our mission. Why do they allow him to be so vulnerable?"

Khan did not answer straightaway, thinking of what Fadyar had just said. Suddenly the answer occurred to him, "Because he has forbidden it. Think of it Fadyar. He is up here on holiday. What sort of holiday could he have in this mountainous wilderness if he was completely surrounded by special forces and confined to the house. Surely, the pleasure of holidaying here is to get out and about to fish, shoot, walk. Enjoy the peace and quiet, away from the high life and politics of Washington. Even a ring of twenty guards around him on the water wouldn't protect him from a sniper on the hill."

Not for the first time, Fadyar was impressed by Khan.

"Then he is either very brave or very foolish, Nasra. Given his position in the US government, I doubt he is the latter."

They fished for a while longer but Fadyar remained thoughtful. She had planned for an assault on Assiter away from Mealag, but a kidnap by boat was seemingly impossible. Even if she could get off two rounds from her rifle, she would have to fire at long range. She might, with luck, kill the first agent she fired at, but the second would almost certainly have time to take cover and send an immediate radio message for help. Assiter and Truscott, in the other boat, would make haste for the safety of Mealag or the garages, both about fifteen minutes away with the outboard at full throttle, and from there trigger an alarm. There would simply not be enough time to overcome the second agent who would have a sub-machine gun and also catch up with Assiter and kidnap him. Any attack of Assiter on the loch would mean first positioning her boat between him and either Mealag lodge or the garages, at least blocking one line of escape, but it still would be impracticable to capture him on the water. His protection would always place themselves between him and Fadyar giving Assiter time to race away in whichever direction was safest.

"Today has confirmed what I anticipated" she said. "We need to take Assiter on land, where we can get much closer to him and his protectors. That way there will be no easy escape for him."

Khan raised his dark eyebrows, expecting Fadyar to explain precisely how she expected to achieve her ambition but his leader did not enlighten him. Instead she issued further instructions, "Steer over to the lodge side of the loch. Give them a very wide berth, I don't want them getting suspicious and, as we go, resume the radio testing."

Half an hour later, Khan had manoeuvred close to the far shore and was keeping parallel to it, leaving a distance of no more than ten metres between it and the boat.

"Stop now and drop the anchor" said Fadyar "We should start fishing. After half an hour we will move slowly towards the lodge, stop again and so on." Fadyar's orders were now rapid and succinct. Gradually the two spoof anglers edged nearer the dam, eventually passing Assiter. As the distance between them lengthened, and the potential risk to Assiter diminished, even his guards stopped repositioning their boat, satisfied that the occupants on the far shore were simply out for a day's fishing and, anyway, at nearly two miles away and almost out of sight, represented no threat. Once Fadyar was certain the agents could not easily see her through high powered lenses, she told Khan to quickly pull the boat into the shore. The boat scraped on the small rocky pebbles making a sound like the breaking of wooden boxes but apart from a little less paint the boat was quite undamaged. Fadyar jumped out and quickly pushed the boat back into deeper water.

"Come back when you see me," she shouted before she quickly disappeared into the trees, leaving Khan to resume going up and down the loch for short distances, pretending to be fishing over a good spot.

Fadyar walked carefully through the rows of tall conifers that were almost ready for logging and onward transportation to the nearby pulp and paper mill outside Fort William. Her feet sank into the thick, soft, bed of rotting pine needles that had built up on the forest floor over many years, muffling any sound from her cautious steps. At the boundary fence of Mealag Lodge she crouched low, straining her eyes through the natural gloom for signs of any patrolling guards but saw none. She was on high alert, her senses taut. She listened. No sound. Where were the other guards? She considered going past the fence but as that would entail her being in full view of anyone in the lodge she decided that was a risk she could not take. Suddenly she heard the crunch of footsteps on the gravel path, ahead of her, just inside the fence. She waited, tense, hardly daring to breathe. Slowly she slid herself backwards further into the forest and stood up behind a tree, concealing herself from whoever was walking the path. She realised that her green fishing anorak was not a good camouflage against the brown trunk and quickly laid it out on the ground, burying it in a thin layer of dead leaves and needles. A few moments later, a guard walked by, upright and rather formally, along the inside of the fence. *Definitely not CIA,* she thought. *British. Had to be. There was none of the swagger that would mark out the American enforcers.* The officer stopped at the shore and switched on his radio. A small flashing orange light immediately appeared next to the Channel 4 selector button on Fadyar's radio indicating another communication in the vicinity. She had no reason to listen in, knowing full well where it was emanating from.

"Mike 1. Mike 1. Are you receiving me? Over."

A brief silence, then Mike 1 answered, "Loud and clear. All quiet at the dam. I'll be there in a few minutes."

Another silence.

"Ok Mike 1. Thanks. Out." The officer pressed a switch on his radio and placed it back into its pouch before resuming his patrol walking slowly towards the jetty.

Fadyar was elated, this was more than she dared hope for. She had only gone onto the shore just in case she might find something that might be useful and had now learned that there were two guards who almost certainly from their accent were British special protection officers, one in the grounds and one at the dam. She surmised, almost accurately but not exactly so, that two or three British police would alternate shifts and patrols to ensure twenty-four hour coverage of the house itself. This would necessitate at least one of the guards resting up in one of the chalets, so her team would face opposition from a probable total of five security personnel including the Americans. She fancied those odds, though she would have staked slightly less had she known that there were actually four British Police not three, the patrol at the dam being handed over. Whatever, she would have surprise on her side and her team were all trained to work together, unlike the British and Americans.

Just as she thought of leaving a woman's voice called out.

"Would you like a cup of something? We're having one. The sun's still warm so we can sit over by the jetty."

"My mate's coming over. That will be great. Two teas, both with milk and sugar. Thanks."

Fadyar remained until she heard the soft rattle of crockery being carried on a tray signifying that the promised tea was being brought over to the heavy teak table near the jetty. Fadyar moved herself slowly around the tree and saw that two women were walking across the lawn. She instantly recognised the tall, model figure of Assiter's wife but Fadyar strained to get a better view of the other woman. The voice had seemed a little familiar but the woman had not spoken much and Fadyar had managed only a brief sighting of her face through the trees despite moving her position. Once the police had joined the two women, Fadyar sidled her way back through the forest to the shore. Assiter's boat was far in the distance and it was easy for Khan to pick her up unnoticed.

As soon as she was in the boat she asked him about the communication testing.

"It went fantastically well, Fadyar. Sharid even climbed half way up the mountain opposite and there was no problem at all. We should be able to talk to each other most of the time, there's a good signal along the entire road."

56

Dean and Gordon had spent a thoroughly enjoyable and relaxing day fishing the loch. They had caught only three fish between them, but were not disappointed. For a start, they had profited from the private wager made with their protectors of five pounds per fish caught and landed, and they greatly enjoyed taunting the CIA men that had it not been for the other boat fishing close to the shore – which was a known 'hot' spot – they might have relieved them of an even larger sum. More importantly, the day had allowed Assiter and Truscott to discuss a host of topics, some seriously political, others merely flippant, but some very personal. It became clear early on in the day that Assiter greatly yearned to enjoy a more routine domestic life and that many years of dedication in Washington, plus the social engagements and functions he and Paulette had to attend as a necessary part of the job, had left him feeling weary and tired.

"You know, Gordon, I wish I could have more days like this one. Free of work, feeling the fresh air on my cheeks and just the exhilaration of being in the wild, open spaces."

"Then do it Dean. You've served your country so well for many years; you deserve some time of your own with Paulette."

"She thinks like you, Gordon. Paulette wants me to give up and retire and is always suggesting places to move to, like San Diego or even Aspen. Perhaps I will because I have never seen her as happy as the last two days here at Mealag. She seems to worry about me in Washington and, of course, I never get to see her enough. Also, Washington is one of those places where you are forever meeting people, but make few friends. Paulette misses not having a close friend. You must have noticed how Cindy and Paulette have found an immediate rapport and already are not just friends, but confidants and soul mates?

"I have" said Gordon, "and I'm particularly pleased for Cindy. It hasn't been easy for her in many ways. The split with her husband caused some of her friends to shun her a bit, or at least she felt that they did even if they were actually only allowing her some space. She has really enjoyed the fact that you both have accepted her so readily."

"You two seem to be getting along just real fine," remarked Assiter. He paused. "Very fine indeed, I should say."

The comment was not lost on Gordon who turned to Assiter and said, "Dean. Please not a word, not even to Paulette, but I am going to propose to Cindy at the end of the month with a view to a Christmas wedding."

"My, my! Good for you. You both, I mean. Oh, shucks, I don't know what I'm saying 'cept congratulations buddy boy. Paulette and I wouldn't miss that for the world. We'll be over, or go wherever. That is, if we're invited".

For once Assiter's normally calm and reserved manner had deserted him, and he slapped Truscott hard on the back before pouring them both a stiff measure of the malt from his hip flask.

"Here's to you both, Gordon. I know you will both be so happy. I'd call it a perfect match. It's clear just how much Cindy loves you. In fact, Paulette says Cindy talks in such glowing terms about you that she is wondering if she hasn't married the wrong man!"

As Gordon and Assiter were confiding in each other, Paulette and Cindy were enjoying the luxury of the heated indoor pool, also talking of their respective partners. Paulette had answered Cindy's oblique question regarding the age difference that existed between Assiter and his young wife by saying that she had never known such a kind and thoughtful man. Certainly there were times when Assiter was tired, but that was more because of the long hours and stress of his job than any physical weakness. Paulette asked Cindy about her marriage to Alan and wondered why they broke up.

"I really don't know, but I blame myself not Alan. There was no one else in either of our lives at the time when I simply found life was not fulfilling any more. I needed a change of direction, something different but I didn't know what. Then there was the bomb on the underground. I met Gordon and I was deeply attracted. I think it was as simple as that, but I feel guilty as it hurt Alan at the time."

"Do you think you will marry Gordon?" Paulette asked.

"He has to ask first!" Cindy laughed. "Then I will think about it for… I don't know how long, but probably will keep him guessing for at least a minute before I say yes."

The two laughed and chatted a little while longer before Cindy suggested that as it was still warm outside, they should make the most of the remainder of the afternoon and have a drink down by the jetty.

"I'll ask the policemen if they want something too," said Cindy.

★ ★ ★

It was early afternoon and Donaldson was driving along the Arkaig road, looking for any telltale vehicle tracks that might indicate access to Mealag Lodge. A forestry track appeared on his right and he turned into it. He did not think he could take his car over the bumpy and rough ground, so parked it just out sight of the road and started to walk. After about a mile, realising the track had started to go away from Mealag and towards Loch Lochy, he retraced his steps back to the car. Making sure he was not observed, he drove slowly along the road until he saw another track. He was certain that this was the other way into Mealag he had been searching for, simply by the number of tyre marks and deep ruts which, hardened by the recent dry weather, had been sculpted into the ground by numerous 4x4 vehicles and other heavier, mechanised machinery. Once again, he found a convenient place to park his car and set off to find Mealag Lodge. Donaldson was fit, always had been, and the walk of several miles was no effort and he was not even out of breath when he sighted the steel fence and large gate. Donaldson worked his way forward slowly using the trees as cover. He noticed a guard nearby was carrying a semi-automatic weapon, but this only instilled in the mercenary a greater curiosity. What was going on here that merited armed police to guard all the entrances? Had Crossland lost his bottle and warned them of his plot to have his ex-wife killed? The thought seemed ludicrous and Donaldson quickly dismissed it, but it was certainly a fact that something strange was going on in the house only a few metres from him, and he was now desperately keen to find out what it was. He also needed confirmation that Cindy was here. Donaldson waited. The police radio bleeped and a few moments later the guard turned and walked towards the lodge, permitting Donaldson to break cover. He carefully moved right up to the gate, where he had a clear view of the guard walking briskly over the large area of lawn that sloped away toward Loch Quoich before disappearing into the distance.

Donaldson wasted no time. This was his opportunity to quickly skirt around the sides of the fence and view what he could of the buildings and the lodge itself. Crouching low, he crept back into the trees but stayed close to the fence which had been erected within the forest, about thirty metres behind the nearest buildings. He passed by the rear of the MacLean's bungalow and peered through the large, open squares created by the interlocking wires of the mesh. The woodland continued into the distance and it was difficult for him to get a clear view of anything except the lodge itself. He made a few mental notes of salient details that might come in useful before continuing to work his way along the perimeter. Once he was past the rear of Mealag, the trees suddenly thinned and a large, modern, single storey building adjoined to the Lodge came into view. Two small stainless-steel chimneys protruded from the roof of the brick extension which Donaldson immediately recognised were designed to carry away steam and air, not smoke. He estimated the building to be at least fifty feet long and forty feet wide. Clever design and siting had allowed it to have been built into the forest such that it was totally concealed from anyone approaching the front entrance to the main house. Jutting deep into the forest to the rear of Mealag had necessitated the boundary fence being only a matter of few feet away from the building, and Donaldson had to withdraw slightly and shelter behind a large tree trunk in order to be certain of remaining hidden. The swimming pool had several floor to ceiling large glass sliding panel windows, with blinds at either side that been left open. There was no reason to close them. The windows faced the tall trees of the forest which itself obscured any dazzling rays of the sun. The pool was not overlooked, its occupants never expecting anyone to make their way surreptitiously through the forest – but even if some lost ramblers did come innocently by, the thick wire fence would stop them from straying into the grounds.

Donaldson wasn't a lost hiker and neither were his intentions harmless. The lights were on in the pool area and he could just make out the two silhouetted figures of Cindy and Paulette, at the far end of the pool, sitting talking to each other. He stared, transfixed. Cindy was wearing a scarlet red bikini and Paulette, a pale lemon coloured all-in-one swimsuit.

After a few minutes the two women stood up and ambled along the side of the pool directly opposite Donaldson. His lecherous eyes followed them, his head gradually turning from right to left much as it would had he been watching a slow motion tennis match, his excitement and anticipation growing as he visualised himself waiting for them in the changing area. He remained at the fence, thinking and trying to work out who Cindy's friend might be. She was clearly an attractive woman, perhaps a famous film star, which might explain the police crawling everywhere. He continued his idle speculation whilst he waited, hoping that Cindy might return to the pool, but it was cut short a few minutes later when the pool lights were switched off.

With no reason to linger he very slowly edged his way back, listening and looking. Donaldson had long passed the visible protection offered by the swimming pool and was once more crawling through the forest several feet behind the fence when he heard faint female voices some distance from the house. He neared the wire. There was some activity at the jetty, but he couldn't quite make out what was going on. He saw two men together with Cindy and another woman – her pool companion – seated at the table near the loch. He studied Cindy Crossland for several moments. She was dressed in faded blue denim jeans and wore a cream-coloured lightweight jacket. The clothes were hardly flattering but to Donaldson Cindy looked as ravishing as ever, his thoughts still very much on what he had just seen in the pool. The woman beside her was also very good-looking too, and he thought that with a little luck and opportunism on his part he might be able to include her in his plans.

The other aspects of interest at the water's edge were the two officers. Both carried a sub-machine gun hung from a shoulder strap and he assumed that the same would be true of the one at the dam gate. The fact that armed security was present at Mealag would have deterred most men, but not Donaldson. He had faced worse odds and succeeded. Only wimps overestimated the opposition's strength and under played the value of surprise – he, like the four terrorists who unknown to him were also nearby, did neither. He pondered over whether the guards were really firearms trained police or specialised protection officers. Neither made much sense to him. Why would armed police be present to guard Truscott? Or for that matter the woman at the pool? Yet he knew of no private security organisation that would openly flout the ban on them using automatic weapons, so the police had to be genuine. Then there was the DO NOT CROSS tape at the gate. That was clearly visible and would be seen by passing police vehicles, so if that was fake it would surely have been removed. Satisfied the men must be part of a police protection squad Donaldson realised that they added a huge level of risk to what he wanted to do, but he loved a challenge. This assignment was beginning to get his adrenalin running fast and high, just as it used to do in Iraq and Africa. He had missed that excitement. The sweet smell of danger and the euphoria of overcoming the odds exhilarated him and he was glad to have the chance to experience it all once more, but he would first need to modify his plans a little. He rapidly completed his survey of Mealag, worked his way back through the forest and drove to Fort William. Two hours later, he had signed a rental agreement for three days hire of a four wheel drive, all-terrain vehicle and, at a specialised outdoor adventure shop, purchased some more appropriately coloured camouflage clothing as he had felt a little too conspicuous at times dressed in simple dark clothes and jeans. The multi green, black and dark browns of his new jacket and trousers would blend better with the shrubbery and forest that surrounded Mealag.

57

"Come on! Come on! I need some answers." Ritson's impatience at his team's lack of progress had become exasperation, and he was walking around the ATU office exhorting his men to even greater effort. He had arrived at 7:30am to find that his request to GCHQ to decode the message had been refused on the same grounds of 'Low Priority' as had earned it that dubious status previously – namely GCHQ needed more intercept material or other corroborative intelligence before they would set about deciphering the message. His MI5 liaison man, Kingsley, had provided all the information held by the ATU and Manders had counter-signed the request, but precious hours during the night had been lost. As the day passed bits and pieces of information had come into the ATU office but nothing of any great substance. There was little that would provide Ritson with sufficient cause to trigger a full scale alert or even that could justify making another approach to Manders. The Unifone number had been discontinued by the network provider through lack of usage and they did not have details of any subscriber by the names of Chalthoum, Masri or Hasan. The military were looking into the Hasan family and the parents death, but had said in an email that it would be unlikely that any separate file would be kept as deaths from bomb blasts were so numerous that only some of the names of the victims were known and recorded 'when circumstances permitted it' – whatever that meant. Hundreds, probably thousands, of civilian casualties had simply not been counted, or identified and therefore not included in any official figures. To the outside world they never existed, let alone died. Only their relatives knew the truth and they had no one they could tell.

The University of Birmingham had been quite helpful. They had traced Yasmin Hasan and confirmed that she left in May 2003 having completed her post graduate course and had a forwarding address of a shop in Haifa Street, Baghdad. The university did however have a photograph of Yasmin Hasan, plus various documents relating to her Visa, and a facsimile of each had been sent to the ATU and were currently being verified. A computer analysis of the photograph was not required to confirm that Fadyar Masri was definitely the same person and Ritson was even more certain that Halima Chalthoum was also Hasan and Masri, despite not having a photograph, nor Crossland's statement, to prove it.

Two officers had spent all day trying to retrieve as much footage as they could from numerous CCTV cameras from Dover and trying to ascertain which direction Masri had travelled. By 5:30pm all they had was that she had driven out of Dover and taken the A2 and then the M2 towards London. It was tiring work, looking at countless tapes for the foreign Peugeot 205 and progress was slow. They were also still interrogating the data from the very latest surveillance cameras deployed on the motorway network leading from London, but so far these had not assisted the ATU enquiries. The new digital cameras, with optical character recognition of vehicle registration plates, represented a considerable advance over the old analogue ones, but as their number increased, so did their downside. The cameras collect data like a vacuum cleaner collects dust. Every day, the huge amount of data is automatically searched for non-taxed, stolen or other vehicles of interest to the police, before it is offloaded and stored onto optical disks. The ATU officers had discovered this permitted the data to be searched extremely easily, but not necessarily quickly, given the massive volumes. Additionally, they were searching motorway by motorway without any certainty of the general direction in which the suspect's vehicle had headed or even which road it was on. If they were required to include non-motorway roads in their search, they would need a lot more time – examining every optical disk in the database would be an enormous undertaking.

The French National Police had been in touch with Ritson again. Pierre Dervisais told him that Fadyar Masri had been very clever in that she had removed the entire hard drive from the computer, but made it look as though it was still in situ. That subterfuge had been discovered relatively quickly. It was, however, embarrassing that his team had not realised the disk was physically absent until they had taken the computer back to their office for detailed testing. This dispirited them, but later they had become prematurely encouraged when the forensic search team returned jubilantly brandishing what was assumed to be the missing and vital piece of hardware. The disk was apparently nearly full with thousands of separate files each individually password protected. The police diligently set about unlocking the encryption of each file or, in many cases, tried to simply by-pass it with sophisticated software of their own in order to view the documents and images. It was a laborious and extremely slow process. Every file was discovered to contain nothing more sinister than copies of publicly available material from the internet. When the French officers realised what Masri had done they were furious. One was so enraged he threw his chair onto the floor; another banged on his desk several times; and several shouts of "merde!" filled the air for nearly an hour.

"There can be only one conclusion, my friend. The suspect made a deliberate and professional attempt to slow us down which I regret to say succeeded."

It was evident Dervisais was still angry at the waste of time and resources of his team.

"As I told you previously the property agency to which Masri paid the rent is quite legitimate, so we also made investigations to ascertain more information about the actual owners of the flat," he continued. "The main leaseholder paid a standing order each month to a Cayman Islands corporation which was no more than a shell subsidiary of a Panamanian Trust. This had been set up using names taken from stolen passports. As soon as any money was received into the Cayman Islands company, it was immediately transferred to a bank in Yemen. There is nothing on any documentation, if you can call scraps of paper that, about our suspect, nor on the ultimate owner's identity. Masri's own bank account showed nothing that wasn't already known. We have made enquiries of the service suppliers at the flat – the electricity supply company along with the other suppliers also received their money via a monthly standing order. I am sorry we could not get more."

Ritson thanked him, but was disappointed. Dervisais' efforts had yielded quite a lot of periphery information that corroborated the ATU suspicions that some sort of terrorist plot was well underway, but revealed very little about Masri's intentions or provided the hard, factual intelligence Ritson so earnestly needed. The detective chief superintendent could only wait and hope that the information now passed to him by the French was sufficient for his liaison staff to get GCHQ to decipher the message.

One hour passed, then two. Nothing. No more information was forthcoming. Two hours of vital time, two hours nearer whatever Fadyar Masri was plotting for it to reach fruition. Frustrated and bad-tempered, Ritson went home having posted notice of a full review meeting of everyone in his team for 4pm the following day. He had decided his enlarged team could not sustain their efforts for much longer unless some real and more tangible results were forthcoming, and the only hope of that lay in the yet to be deciphered message. There were also other matters that required his team's attention that had nothing to do with this investigation. Those might be just as important, just as critical to the UK's well-being and safety as Ritson believed the Masri case to be, and he could not ignore those pressures for much longer. He set himself a deadline of Thursday afternoon. Unless he had more hard evidence by then, the Masri file would have to remain in abeyance pending further developments.

★ ★ ★

Senior firearms officer Greaves had travelled the Kinloch Hourn road three times from end to end during the day. He had observed Donaldson's car and thought it totally unsuitable for a holiday in the highlands, but he was used to seeing tourists make real fools of themselves. Many did not even possess a pair of boots nor a waterproof jacket and returned home to tell their relatives that they got thoroughly soaked several times, as if it was someone else's fault. Where did they think all the water in the lochs came from? In his view there were only two kinds of vehicles for the Highlands – large estates and 4x4's, like the vehicle he saw parked at the cottage by Kinloch Hourn. Despite its local registration number, he had not recognised the Land Rover and gave it little consideration when he first passed by in early morning. Greaves paid it more attention in the afternoon when he spotted the three boats out fishing. He watched their occupants, his trained eyes observing small details casual onlookers would miss. It was immediately obvious to him that only one person knew how to cast a line properly. The rest were very poor and could only be beginners. *If Truscott was the practised angler, then who were the others,* he asked himself. The security agents for certain would be in the craft nearer to Truscott, but the very sloppy casting and poor technique in the handling of the third boat strongly suggested tourists, yet the only vehicle he had seen from where its crew might have come from was the locally registered one, now parked at the cottage. Local people would know how to fish and how to handle a boat, though it was just possible the Land Rover did belong to someone fairly new in the area, possibly having moved to the Highlands to escape the rat race.

Out of curiosity he typed in the registration number for it to be checked and watched the small screen in the centre of the fascia console of his own vehicle. It revealed that the Land Rover Defender was registered to the garage at Fort William and Greaves interest waned slightly. He knew that David, the proprietor, often hired out vehicles even those he might eventually sell, which would explain everything.

"More tourists", Greaves mumbled to himself.

Meticulously, he noted the result of his vehicle enquiry in his log book. Several hours later, when the first dark clouds raced across the tops of the mountains heralding the onset of dusk, Greaves was on his way home and passed by Eagles Rest Hotel and was surprised to see David's Land Rover parked there, since he had assumed it was being used by the tourists who had hired the tiny cottage at Kinloch Hourn. Greaves drove past the hotel and stopped, wanting to clarify his thoughts. Something niggled in his brain. He knew the tourists' blue boat must have been hired from Kinloch Hourn as those hired out by Eagles Rest hotel were all painted light grey and had two bright red stripes along each side. *Why would tourists obtain a boat from Kinloch Hourn and use the outboard to travel miles up the loch before starting to fish when the hotel boats were nearer and superior?*

Were the strangers staying at the Hotel or the cottage? He decided he would investigate the cottage and its occupants tomorrow, assuming the Land Rover was not parked outside. After a boring day travelling up and down between Corach and Kinloch Hourn, Greaves was looking forward to an evening meal with his wife and speculating about the antics of crazy tourists were not going to disturb that.

Margaret MacLean had prepared a superb roast beef dinner and the conversation around the table turned to what the holidaymakers would like to do the following day. Gordon and Dean had already agreed their chosen activity, but neither said anything until Cindy had made her suggestions. As none of these seemed to elicit any favourable reaction, albeit not direct opposition, from either Assiter or Truscott, she realised that the two men had probably already discussed the subject.

"Well, you two. Seeing as my suggestions do not appear to have your support, what would you really like to be doing?"

Gordon looked a little sheepish as he turned to his American guest.

"The weather for the next few days seems set fair, cloudy with a few sunny intervals but no major rain. Looks ideal for a spot of stalking and walking the hills, might even get a stag. If not tomorrow, then Friday. How does that grab you, Dean?" Gordon asked slowly.

Before Assiter could reply, Cindy screwed up her napkin and flung it across the table at Gordon, laughing. "You bastards!" she exclaimed smiling, "You two have cooked this up on the boat today. Don't lie. I'm right, aren't I?"

Cindy's joyful face radiated merriment and everyone at the table laughed along with her. It was Assiter who spoke first, "Well, ya see Cindy. Gordon and I may have spoken a little, but nothing was firmly agreed. We definitely wanted to hear what you and Paulette had to say first. Promise."

After a few further lighthearted exchanges it was settled that for the next two days Gordon and Dean would be on the hill, stalking. Cindy and Paulette would travel to Inverness for some shopping on the Thursday, and probably go for a walk around the dam and fish the loch themselves on Friday.

The four plotters were seated in the small lounge of the cottage, reviewing the day. Fadyar was still jubilant at discovering that there were at most only six security agents; two American and four British. She had also observed the marked patrol vehicle on the road, conspicuously and deliberately travelling up and down. The communication equipment worked really well and their tests confirmed that it was capable of receiving the transmissions from the British police radios. The CIA agents' transmission frequency was unknown, but Fadyar presumed this was due to the fact that as they were literally in the same boat there had been absolutely no need for them to be used. She was satisfied that if and when they were operated, her own equipment would be able to eavesdrop. She would have been overjoyed had she known that an elementary, but crucially vital, aspect of Assiter's protection had been overlooked. The American equipment brought into Britain courtesy of the diplomatic bag (in reality a crate accompanying Assiter on his cross Atlantic flight) did function, but used illegal UK frequencies which unsurprisingly the British radios were not manufactured to detect. As such the Americans were capable only of radio communication with each other and not with the British, something they would only discover later when the two forces desperately needed to talk with each other.

"First thing tomorrow, I need to make a phone call from the public telephone box down at the harbour to confirm the final aspect of our mission and to ensure that everything will be ready for us when we need it. Then I want you to put me back on the bank where I was today" Fadyar told Khan. "No one goes there and I shall never be discovered. I need to observe more, at close quarters, and in any event I can get a complete view from there of the mountains to the north of the Kinloch Hourn road. If Assiter and Truscott are going to go walking, or some such, then that is probably where they'll go. They may simply drive somewhere on the estate, but I doubt that as it looks to be mainly forest. My guess is that they will be happy to remain around here. I can observe everything from the Mealag side of the loch far better than I can from the boat, and if I can arrive there early enough I may learn some information that may prove helpful."

The others nodded.

"What shall we do then?" enquired Mattar.

"You and Sharid must take the Land Rover and drive along that very small track that is our first choice escape route. We have to be 100% certain that we can get through and we did not fully test that out last time. After that, make sure the camper van is still safely parked and drive it away for an hour or so. Be a tourist. Moving the van will be good as it will remove any suspicion of it. Nasra and I will not meet you at the hotel in the morning but we'll rendezvous with you in the evening, say 7pm hours at the cottage."

Later, when Khan and Fadyar lay in bed, Khan turned to her and said, "Fadyar, how many days do you think it will be before we can execute our plan? We have been here several days, although Assiter has only been here a couple, but do you share my anxiety that as each day passes, it could be our last. We could be discovered any time."

Fadyar knew exactly what he felt as she shared the same unease, but she could not allow frustration to compromise a good plan. She had to wait for the right moment. If circumstances were not favourable tomorrow, they would be the following day or the day after that. Neither was she comfortable about openly sharing her anxieties with Khan. Naked and sleeping with him was a special type of reassurance for her, but baring her soul was not going to happen. She put her arm around him and pulled him closer.

"Nasra, we have a good plan and I am totally confident it will work but we must remain patient. We have been so careful to cover our tracks and not provide any clues that I am sure the authorities do not yet suspect us. This mission is what we have trained for. We have been so honoured to be chosen to serve Allah. Is this not what we have dreamt of? Do not worry my dear brother, nothing will stop us. We will succeed and Fadyar will keep you safe."

58

The weather forecast as provided by Gordon Truscott the previous evening was not as yet, correct. It was cloudy and overcast on Thursday morning with intermittent squally showers mixed with an almost constant heavy drizzle that quickly soaked everything it touched. No one at Mealag Lodge was in any great hurry to venture forth and the conversation at breakfast was prolonged whilst everyone waited in hope for the weather to clear. There were no such qualms about the weather from either Donaldson or from Fadyar Masri and her associates. All had set out early.

Margaret MacLean, who disliked using the new machine Cindy had persuaded Gordon to purchase, made some fresh coffee, replacing the filled kettle on its usual spot on the hot-plate of the Aga stove. As she poured the boiling water into the cafetière Gordon called out to her. "Will this rain and mizzle hang around all day, Margaret? You know more about Highland weather than any of us, give us your view."

"Ach well, there's no real telling but I think it might clear soon enough," she less than confidently replied.

"That's it then. We'll go on the hill as planned. What are you girls doing, still going shopping?" Gordon turned to Paulette as he spoke.

"Might as well, Cindy, what do you think? We can still make a whole day of it and I should like to see Inverness and some of those Scottish woollens you told me about." Paulette was keen to experience several hours looking around the foreign shops, something she had been unable to do in London where she and her husband were kept closeted and out of sight apart from the organised, dutiful and specially scrutinised photo opportunities for the world's media; appearances which bored them even more than their hosts.

The kitchen clock showed a few minutes past ten as Assiter and Gordon began loading the boat with the rifles, ammunition and the most vital supplies for the day which included a flask of hot, black coffee, some bacon rolls and a bottle of single malt whisky. Sandy MacLean joined them at the boat, also carrying his rifle. "I'll take the girls over and see you by the road," he said "They're just coming."

Cindy and Paulette appeared just as Chuck Drew and Josh Atkins came out of Ruraich and walked towards the group. The special agents were both wearing waterproof clothing and carrying their weapons which were further protected from the weather by bright yellow nylon covers.

"Juss a quick word if ya please, 'fore ya go. Is the plan still the same given the weather and all that?" Drew asked.

"Yes," said Gordon. "No change and we'll also be going to the hill tomorrow unless the weather gets much worse. If it does we will put on the board what we are all doing, but otherwise everything is still the same. Cindy and Paulette are off to Inverness now and tomorrow they hope to go over the dam and walk up the mountain over there to see the surge shaft and tunnel. If time permits they may just fish around the shore close to the house."

"My, you British are real hardy folk. Me, I'm glad to stay indoors when it rains, but not you guys! OK, let's get in Josh."

Sandy MacLean then spoke. "Chuck, just remembered. It's Margaret's day off tomorrow and she and I will be going over to her sister's at Glenelg for the day, so we won't be around. I'll try not to forget to put it on the board later, but you may want to put it on yourself."

"Sure thing. Are we in for a good day's hunting?" asked Drew.

"Maybe. It all depends where the deer are. Weather has been a bit warm lately, so they may be too high up."

"Don't be a pessimist, Sandy" exclaimed Assiter, "I'm sure we'll have some sport."

At precisely 10:15am the small boats were started up and made their leisurely passage across the loch. Fadyar Masri, hidden in the same bushes where she had spent part of the previous day, watched them leave. She might have been expected to be rejoicing at the information she had just gleaned, a worthy reward for rising early, but instead she was extremely angry with herself. She withdrew to a safe distance where she could not be heard and called on the radio.

"Melon are you receiving? This is Apple. Over." No answer.

"Apple calling. Fig are you receiving? Over." The radio remained stubbornly silent.

"Apple calling. Come in Orange. Over." She knew that Khan would answer as she could see him, still fishing from the boat, near the loch's edge.

"Orange here. Loud and clear. Over"

"Can you move out and try to get either Fig or Melon to answer. If you do, tell them to go home immediately. Then come back to pick me up. Over."

"OK, Apple. Out" Khan signed off and almost immediately Fadyar heard his outboard start up.

She continued to look through her telescope until the Mealag boats arrived at the jetty below the road. Truscott, Assiter and MacLean unloaded their gear and began walking at a forty-five degree angle across the slope of Gleouraich mountain. Halfway to the summit the shooting party changed direction, going behind the hill but still climbing upwards. They waved to Cindy and Paulette as the two women passed below them on the road, warm and dry in the Volvo.

An hour later, Khan returned and Fadyar jumped into his boat. He had not been able to raise either Mattar or Bagheri on the radio, both of whom were obviously well out of range. Khan had even tried his mobile as he noticed he actually got a signal at one point, but as he dialled the signal disappeared again.

"Why did you want them back, Fadyar. Is anything wrong?" asked Khan.

"No, far from it. It was just that when I saw where our target was headed, I thought that if we could get everything in place, we might have been able to try to capture him today. As I expected he went up the hill." Khan's eyes opened wide but before he could comment Fadyar continued, "Visibility is poor across the loch, so the guard at the dam would not have a good view of what was happening until too late. If only I had known they were definitely going to the hills today, we could have done it. I know we could have. It's probably too late now, our chance today has gone."

"Well, Sharid and Mawdud will hopefully have been able to test the escape route so it's not a wasted day, Fadyar" Khan tried his best to placate her.

Fadyar was still cross with herself and frustrated by what she perceived as a wasted opportunity, but by the time they had reached the cottage the grandness of the scenery and the stillness of the loch had calmed her.

On the long trip back, Fadyar propped herself against the stern of the boat and rested her arms along its back and side. The rain slowly eased to a fine mist and then ceased altogether. The cloud lightened, teasingly suggesting that the sun might soon break through, and instead of focusing on her mission she found herself absorbed by the natural world around her. As she expectantly watched the surface of the loch for a telltale ring of a trout rising to take an unsuspecting fly, she observed a black-throated diver land on the water. It swiftly performed a half somersault then swam submerged, reappearing a short while later several metres away from where it first dived beneath the cold water, with a fish in its bill. She studied the mountains, now mostly concealed by billowing clouds of pure white gossamer. As the cloud raced sideways every so often a break appeared and she could see the illuminated summits rising imperiously through the mist. A pair of buzzards, probably startled by the noise of the outboard, took off from their high perch amongst the tall forest spruce trees and circled above the loch before flying into the distance and disappearing from view. She was so engrossed that Khan had to shout at her to get her attention.

"That police 4x4 is travelling along the road again. See him? He seems to turn up at any time, I can't detect a particular schedule" remarked Khan, an observation already made by Fadyar the previous day.

"Yes, he does, and that adds a slight level of uncertainty. He looks local police but must have been given a special patrol. I cannot believe the British have so many officers they can afford for one of them to travel up and down this road several times each day without good reason."

59

At about the same time as Fadyar was enjoying the scenery, Detective Chief Superintendent Bill Ritson was handed a sealed white envelope by the Intelligence Services liaison officer. Ritson slit it open and read the deciphered message. It was the breakthrough he so desperately needed.

case log: 003487AL87
decodmsg: 567-32459(FR)-STxy
140906-08.38

Mother and Father in Law will visit UK 12 to 22 September. They will be looked after by friends, but hope to meet up with you. You should have enough funds in your London account for your expenses. Your three cousins in Birmingham may also wish to see them, phone 0701502488 on arrival. Good luck. NH

Ritson immediately went to the photocopier and obtained six copies of the message. One he would retain, one he would pass to each of his three most able subordinates, one for Deputy Commissioner Manders and one for the Commissioner himself. The adrenalin rushed through his body, a potent mix of alarm and excitement. Alarm because of the dates mentioned, but excitement at finally obtaining the deciphered message that surely was evidence of some sort of plot. He briefed his three officers.

"I want every aspect of this message investigated. Who are Mother and Father in Law? Who is on a visit to the UK? I want us to check again the names of all VIP's, dates, where they are staying, why they are over here, and so on – even second or third rate celebrities. Searching the CCTV footage of Birmingham for the day the Masri woman arrived in the UK could be a problem but see what you can do. Start by tracing that phone number. See also if we have anyone known by initials NH."

Kingsley, the MI5 liaison officer who had first brought Ritson the deciphered message, spoke, "You could read the message that one group is meeting up with another and that this message is not in itself anything to do with a plot, or at least only indirectly."

Kingsley was sharp, and it was a pertinent observation. Ritson thought on it for a few moments before saying, "I agree, it could be, but we can't afford to assume that until our enquiries prove negative. My bet is we are onto something big here, so let's get going!"

Once more, the ATU office became a site of almost constant activity. People hurried across the floor to confer with others, whilst colleagues were busy either dialling telephones or checking computer screens. What needed to be done now was routine, albeit highly labour intensive, but it did not require the specialist skills of Dongle who was still busily engaged on searching through obscure databases and old computer records. Ritson's briefing had therefore been relayed to those other officers trained at using the basic software that traced telephone numbers or suggested alternate numbers where the target number was unknown or falsified. It was the same for obtaining lists of VIP's in the country. All his officers had clearance to view those screens so Dongle's special skills were deployed on what was thought most appropriate to the furtherance of the investigation.

Ritson spent the afternoon going round all the persons in his team, one by one, encouraging them, urging them to find out more about the message. He had personally studied the computer printouts that listed all known VIP's, politicians, sports stars, Hollywood actors and actresses, and other notable visitors who were likely to be in the UK. None particularly caught his eye. There was a concert by Madonna in London in a couple of days, a new film starring George Clooney was opening in the West End for which the lead actor was over to help publicise it, and a couple of minor European Union delegations were discussing nothing of major importance all week at a Five Star luxury hotel in the centre of London. There was simply no one on the list that he considered merited a deeply disguised and organised terrorist attack.

"Try for events. See if there are any major events coming up"

Ritson asked, desperate to find the reason for the plot. He was certain there was a threat, any doubts now dispelled by the decoded message. Innocent people do not write such messages in code.

A little while later, he read the new listing. His eyes went down each of the hundreds of so-called major events occurring during the next week but, again, none stood out. Dismayed, Ritson went over to the next officer to see what he was doing.

"The message is clearly about a meeting. Are there any known suspects recently arrived in the UK? Kingsley suggested that maybe the buggers are all meeting up somewhere to discuss their next atrocity."

"I don't think so, Sir. There would have been increased communications traffic and Morwenstow and GCHQ would have picked that up. Also, there are no security reports of movements to the UK of known suspects."

Ritson was becoming exasperated.

"There has to be something. What about the phone number?"

"The phone number doesn't make any kind of sense, Sir. The message was encoded. The phone number was also in code originally so now ought to be kosher, but it clearly isn't. We have the computers working on it, but every time the computer changes the numbers, or suggests alternatives, we come up negative or with a perfectly legitimate number. The computer is even adding and subtracting digits to try and make a proper phone number that we can then trace but that takes a hell of a long time and so far everything we've tried has gone belly-up."

Ritson patted him on the shoulder, "Well, keep at it. Thanks."

At 5pm, whilst his team were busy, Ritson went to see Manders and handed him the copied message and excitedly relayed the news.

"Go over this entire case again, Bill, slowly. Just the salient facts but try to get them all in some sort of chronological order."

Ritson spent the next half hour briefing his superior. He mentioned Crossland, the bank account, Styles and his suspicious death. He spoke of Masri, Chalthoum and Hasan as being the same person – referring to her afterwards only as Masri – stressing the conclusiveness of Dongle's statements regarding her computer. He linked Styles and the bank to Masri, the visits of Masri to Britain and the money withdrawals. He briefed Manders on the French police investigations and findings; the mobile phone sudden disuse and the concealed trail of ownership of the French flat and its selective cleaning. At the conclusion of the resumé, Manders was more than satisfied.

"That's great Bill, really good job. I will ask for an emergency meeting of JTAC. We have such little time now if that decoded message is to be believed. We need to be putting more things in place. As head of the ATU, I am going to make a decision I may well regret, but something is going down and we must do what we can to be prepared. As it could be anywhere, notify all our regions of an imminent threat, level one, and to have as many ATU trained personnel on standby as they can muster."

"Sir, you could lose your job if this is a false alarm, but you can count on my support if it comes to that." Ritson knew that Manders was going out on a limb by issuing the order in advance of any instructions from the JTAC but was prepared to stand alongside him.

"Thanks, Bill. I appreciate that. If something happens tomorrow and we haven't issued an alert – what then? Do we tell the public we were having a JTAC meeting to debate it? I'm damned if I do and damned if I don't, but I won't drag the commissioner into it."

Ritson nodded and half smiled before rejoining his team. The officers worked on until 10pm in the desperate hope of tracing something that would crack the case wide open, but to no avail. The tired team headed home, their heads held low. They made no conversation as they left the office. They alone knew that time was running out and they had no idea what was going to be attacked or where, but they knew that they were the only persons likely to be able to stop it.

The members of the JTAC had received formal notification of the following day's emergency meeting at 6pm, the same time as Manders issued his Level 1 notice. As a precaution, the Home Secretary, Cabinet office and members of the Joint Intelligence Committee were placed on warning and notified of the following day's unscheduled meeting of the JTAC.

The Joint Terrorism Analysis Centre, or JTAC, was created as the UK's centre for the analysis and assessment of international terrorism in June 2003. It is situated in a Grade II listed building at the corner of Millbank and Horseferry Road in central London, known as Thames House. The Secret Intelligence Service's distinctive ziggurat building at Vauxhall Cross, which is often mistaken for the Security Service's headquarters, is located on the other side of the Thames near Vauxhall Bridge. JTAC analyses and assesses all intelligence relating to international terrorism, at home and overseas. It sets threat levels, and issues warnings of perceived threats and other terrorist-related matters, for a wide range of government departments and agencies, as well as producing in-depth reports on trends, terrorist networks and capabilities. JTAC brings together counter-terrorist expertise from the police, key government departments and the various intelligence agencies. Collaborating in this way ensures that information is analysed and processed on a shared basis, with the involvement and consensus of all relevant departments. Existing departmental roles and responsibilities are unaffected.

The head of JTAC is accountable to the Director General of the Security Service, who in turn reports to the Government's Joint Intelligence Committee (JIC) on JTAC's activities. JTAC had already received a routine – and very cursory – report on the possible Masri plot, but as the evidence had been sketchy it was never discussed in detail. As JTAC worked especially closely with the International Counter Terrorism (ATU) branch, headed by Manders, in assessing the nature and extent of the threat to the UK, the JTAC had hitherto been content to leave him to continue with his enquiries.

Effective command and control is essential to successfully manage an actual counter-terrorist incident and the UK's approach to emergency response and recovery is founded on a bottom-up approach in which operations and decisions are made at the lowest appropriate level. In the event of a terrorist incident occurring, the Office for Security and Counter-Terrorism (OSCT) is responsible for activating and coordinating the Home Office response. The OSCT provides a crisis response twenty-four hours a day, 365 days of the year and liaises with the Cabinet Office as to whether to activate central government's crisis management arrangements in the Cabinet Office Briefing Rooms (COBR). The aim of COBR, or COBRA as it is more commonly referred to, as meetings are often held in Cabinet Room A, is to provide effective decision-making and rapid coordination of the central government response. The Home Secretary usually chairs COBR meetings, but confusingly COBR also has its own threat assessment levels that grade the severity of the actual attack as opposed to the perceived (JTAC) one. The lowest level of this assessment is one with three being an attack that might threaten national disaster such as that on a nuclear installation. The Prime Minister would almost certainly chair a Level Three incident. It is not until the attack has happened that COBR can accurately assess its likely impact, which is why the early warning (JTAC) system was introduced, and why devolved decision making and initial command and control procedures are in place to initiate a prompt and effective initial response.

60

Donaldson was finding his all-terrain vehicle very much to his liking as he drove towards Loch Arkaig. The vehicle handled the twisting, narrow road with ease and the elevated driving position enabled him to have an excellent view over the tops of the small, but steep, undulations in the road. It was very early morning and without too much effort he had again been able to get close to Mealag Lodge and study the layout of the chalets and other buildings. In fact, the relative ease with which he had been able to operate unnoticed as he followed the perimeter fence caused him to regard the security guards with disdain and contempt. He and a group of his friends from Africa would have no difficulty in completely capturing the lodge and all its occupants, police or no police. Despite his disregard for those charged with protecting Mealag and those within it, Donaldson maintained his thoroughness and professionalism. He wanted to know all he could about the lodge layout, possible ways in, and – more importantly – ways out, so he sketched the location of the buildings and known pathways onto a note pad for reference later. The lodge itself had seemed deserted and he thought it was eerily quiet, until he heard a branch snap about eighty metres directly across from where he was crouched adjacent to the swimming pool flank wall. The sharp noise came from the other side of the pathway that led from the jetty to the lodge and he slowly raised his field glasses to study the forest opposite. As he did so, the merest flick of light reflected back from the lenses and was seen by Fadyar. She quickly dived low and lay perfectly still, cursing that she had carelessly walked onto a dead branch causing it to break loudly. Donaldson saw nothing and within a few minutes he made his way slowly back along the track to the Ford. Feeling far less conspicuous in the 4x4 he spent the next few hours driving along numerous rutted forest roads and tracks in the hope of finding other ways into Mealag but to no avail. He revisited the lodge once again in early afternoon in the hope that Cindy might have returned, but it was still silent so, disappointed, he resolved to try again the next day. He had not planned that killing her would necessitate several days of preparation and he was also acutely aware that this job was significantly more difficult than he had ever envisaged. He had no idea for how long Cindy Crossland would be remaining in Scotland, and as his employer had stressed the urgency of the assignment Donaldson felt honour bound to carry out his task here in the Highlands though he recognised that this was considerably more dangerous for him. He needed therefore to be really careful, not to rush, but also not to delay. Very reluctantly, he was also beginning to contemplate that only assassination might be achievable, his other pleasures may have to be foregone. That really annoyed and frustrated him, and when angry he was doubly dangerous.

★ ★ ★

It was seven in the evening when Chief Inspector Keith Maythorp had his evening meal interrupted by a call from the duty officer at the Fort William constabulary. His wife took the call initially and a very apologetic constable asked to speak to her husband on a matter of some urgency. It was typical of the calls she had grown accustomed to taking throughout most of her marriage. Fortunately their number was far less now than it had been in the early years, when her husband had worked at Glasgow and Leeds, and she was grateful for that, but she also knew that a call from Fort William, out of hours, was always serious. For that reason she immediately called Maythorp to the phone and went to get his coat.

"Aye, you're right, dear" Maythorp said as he put down the receiver, "probably two hours, three at the latest."

He then made two phone calls. Both were to his Area Inspectors, John Curry and Colin MacRae, whom he met in his office an hour later to discuss the implications of the issuing a new Level 1 threat assessment. The procedures that Maythorp and his two subordinates had to follow were well documented, and the sites at which he was required to deploy additional security measures had been identified long ago. Although Maythorp, Curry and MacRae were familiar with the procedures, Maythorp insisted they each read again their copies. Having done so, he turned to them and spoke.

"The threat assessment level is now at one – Critical. An attack somewhere in the UK, as yet unknown, is imminent but it is important to stress it has not yet happened. For that reason neither OSCT nor COBR are yet operational. This is still only an assessment by JTAC which may be revised by the Joint Intelligence Committee. For that reason it is vital that all your men are briefed, know precisely what they should do in the event that such an attack occurs on our patch, but their actions must not over-alarm the public. Unless absolutely critical, all leave is cancelled and you should get back officers that are on leave and are at home or elsewhere in the UK. We have our list of places that will require immediate, additional full-time security. In particular, these will include the ferry terminals and the ferries themselves whilst in port, plus the Ballachuilish and Skye bridges. The ski lifts must be closed to passengers immediately – its only sightseeing tourists that use them at this time of the year anyhow. OK so far?"

Both nodded.

Maythorp continued, "Arm every officer up to the level of their training and in the event of a real terrorist attack on our patch, I do not want heroes. I want information."

"I think we all understand, Keith" commented a rather weary sounding Curry. "But I have a question. Do we continue to use Greaves up at Kinloch Hourn? He's a valuable guy and probably more use elsewhere. He reports that there is nothing untoward up there, a few tourists on the road and a couple out fishing but Mealag Lodge has its own special forces security people so they will be fully aware of this threat assessment. By the way, he briefly glimpsed one of the geeks the other day at the far side of the dam, dressed as a bloody English copper in a flak jacket. To Greaves, of course, he stood out like a sore thumb. We had quite a chuckle about whether he should arrest the guy for impersonating a police officer! This threat level can't be to do with them, can it?"

When Maythorp stopped laughing, he said "Nay, don't think

so. As you say, they have their own intelligence and security. I think the original notification from HQ would have mentioned if anything going on there might ever merit a Level 1 – for a start we would have been instructed to increase patrols and ensure reinforcements were on stand-by. Anyway, no one is going to get in there with all those SF's around. I agree. Pull Greaves off immediately."

★ ★ ★

Nasra Khan's practice at fly fishing was beginning to yield results and he had supplied three more trout that Fadyar had cooked for the group's evening meal at the cottage. His catch had provided a welcome diversion from their thoughts and gentle banter was exchanged across the table instead of serious deliberation. They were in no hurry and Fadyar let everyone enjoy the meal and the camaraderie. It was only later that Fadyar carefully spread the Ordnance Survey map onto the bare wooden table and started to detail the plan for the following day.

"It appears that tomorrow Assiter and his friend will be hunting again. They came down from the hill today with nothing and that is good for us as it will mean they have no reason to change their intentions. The other man is going with his wife to a relative so there will only be four people on the hill – Assiter, Truscott and the two CIA agents. That helps us as well. The other two women at some time will be going over the dam. They might become a problem, it depends where they go and at what time, but they will be unarmed and I am confident they do not present any real threat."

"Suppose they do not go, Fadyar, but stay at the lodge. Also, is it not possible they could raise the alarm if they hear shots? In my experience, women often change their mind. Is that not right Nasra?" Bagheri joked and everyone laughed, but he had made a serious point and one that Fadyar had already fully considered.

"You're right, Sharid. I am grateful to you for pointing that out. Either the lodge communications have to be severed or the women have to be kept out of the way, preferably both. I will see to that."

Khan spoke next. "Talking of communications Fadyar, is it really necessary tomorrow to use fruits as our call signs? What difference can it make now? We know we are not being listened into, but even if we are overheard tomorrow so what? I think it will make everything easier just to use our names. Whatever happens, in twenty-four hours we shall be all over the television screens and on all the news broadcasts. If anything goes wrong I want my family to know I did my duty."

The others murmured their agreement and Fadyar willingly agreed. She spent the next two hours going over the details and crosschecking with each member of her team that they knew exactly what they should be doing and at what time. Her plan was refined and honed; eventualities considered; contingencies worked out.

She stood up and turned to face the others. "We all know what to do. Tomorrow is our day, my Brothers. Our Jihad. Allah is with us. We are ready."

61

Cindy and Paulette returned from Inverness carrying brightly-coloured bags of all shapes and sizes each filled to capacity. They talked and laughed as they unloaded the vehicle and carried their purchases to the small jetty. It was late afternoon and the brightness of the light cloud cover was beginning to fade into greyness, but the loch still retained a glossy appearance, and fish were beginning to feed on flies that had rested on the water.

"This is such an amazing place, Paulette, I have really grown to love it here. It is always the same yet always looks different; the light, the birds, the fish, the water, all of it. It's just magical." Paulette agreed with Cindy. She had realised just what a sacrifice she and her husband were making by continuing to work and live in Washington DC, and remarked to Cindy that she would love to stay longer.

"Well, you must come again. Soon. If necessary, I will talk to your President!"

Cindy parked the Volvo in the garage and walked back to the jetty to join Paulette. The boat was loaded and they crossed to Mealag where Margaret poured them some hot drinks. A short while later they were joined by the stalkers, tired and without even a sight of a deer to report, despite scouring the hills all day. Far from being disappointed, Dean Assiter was even keener to find a stag the following day much to the chagrin of his two exhausted guards. Four hours later and relaxing in the drawing room after another fine meal, the two women were anxious to show off their new purchases. Paulette had an idea.

"I shall organise our own fashion show, we shall call it the Mealag Collection!" Everyone laughed. Gordon offered to provide the commentary until Cindy reminded him that he wouldn't know cashmere from cotton, bringing forth more laughter and ribaldry. All the new clothes, and some others that neither of their partners had yet seen but which had been brought along for the holiday, were placed in a side room near to the lounge from where the changes of apparel could take place. Paulette opened the modelling by entering the room dressed in a pair of tailored, deep blue slacks and a silky black blouse. Poised and graceful, her tallness accentuated the cut of her clothes and she walked up and down to a round of applause from Gordon and Dean. Cindy followed, wearing a fetching country hat, moleskin trousers and a checked shirt loosely tied around her waist instead of being fastened all the way down the front and tucked into the trousers. More applause greeted her amid shouts of "Ride 'em cowboy".

Successively, Cindy and Paulette displayed the clothes to ever greater applause until finally Cindy said, "It is now time for our finale. You will have to give us a few minutes, so be patient."

She and Paulette rushed upstairs, changed, and started applying make-up to their faces. Twenty minutes later, they were ready and standing in the hall. Cindy went to the music control panel, pressed the illuminated blue button, selected the music for the lounge and turned up the volume. Joe Cocker's unmistakeable and unique voice filled the air with his famous rendition of the 1972 Randy Newman classic, *You Can Leave Your Hat On.* The women entered the room slowly and walked provocatively towards their partners, their elbows sticking out as their hands rested on their swaying hips. The large coats they were wearing swayed and swirled as they moved exaggeratedly forwards before they stopped opposite Gordon and Dean, whilst slowly unfastening the coat buttons.

"A striptease! How wonderful!" shouted Dean. Gordon entered into the spirit of it all, laughing and calling out "Get 'em off" and "Show us what you've got then!"

The women let their coats fall to the floor, revealing very short white trousers, long black stockings and a flimsy top which soon became detached. Their heavy make-up and glossy red lips shone in the bright crystal lighting as they mouthed silent obscenities whilst slowly undressing. Shouts of delight filled the room and, in time to the music, most of the remaining clothes were gradually, but purposefully, removed until they were modelling their new swim wear. Very slowly they unpeeled their costumes, the expectation of their audience rising rapidly with Gordon and Dean leaning intently forward on their seats. Exaggerated groans of disappointment mixed with ribald comments followed as the final items worn by Cindy and Paulette were revealed. The women paraded up and down the large room several times before stopping in front of their partners. As each removed their bra in unison, they were careful not to reveal much of their upper body by judicial placement of their hands. Now wearing only a hat and the tiniest G-string imaginable they turned and faced away from their partners. Still dancing in rhythm to the beat of the evocative music they took three steps and slowly eased their G-strings down until they fell to the floor and could step out of them. As the music ended, they flung their arms into the air, took off their hat and placed it over their pubic area. In a grand finale, the two make-believe strippers performed a full 360 degree turn giving their excited audience only a brief glimpse of their bare breasts before they ran out of the room. Everyone dissolved into laughter.

"Encore, encore", came the shouts from the sofas, but Paulette and Cindy declined as they dressed in the hall before coming back to gather up their discarded clothes.

"I think that's quite enough for you at your age," mocked Paulette speaking to her husband. "Too much excitement isn't good for you."

"Weren't they just marvellous, Gordon? Tremendous. Well done!" said Assiter, beaming.

The fun continued with them playing some not too serious games of snooker, before they ended by taking a late night plunge into the pool, splashing each other and generally larking about. It had indeed been a great evening: one to remember; one to savour; one never to be repeated.

62

The first light of dawn brushed across the loch, illuminating the wisps of mist that were gently caressing the surface of the water. The only sound that could be heard was the occasional plop from a fish that had risen to feed or had jumped simply to clean any lice from his scales and for the fun of creating a splash. Fadyar went outside the cottage and breathed in, filling her lungs with the fresh, cold, pure air. As she viewed the mountains, she reflected that they had remained constant over thousands of years and would look, and be, the same tomorrow.

"But will I?" she asked herself, but obtained no reply. She had checked and re-checked all her equipment, especially her firearms. She had again mentally analysed every aspect of her plan, recently amended to ensure that no one would be able to communicate an emergency message from the lodge. Whilst she kept telling herself that Assiter and Truscott might change their intentions to go deer stalking, somehow she just knew they wouldn't. She was calm now and she hoped she could remain that way when later in the day she was going to be called upon to act. For the first time, she felt the real burden of leadership and the onerous responsibility of possibly leading her comrades to their deaths. It had been a long and arduous journey from the ruined streets of Baghdad and the torn bodies of her parents to the calm of this highland paradise, and the irony was not lost on her that she was about to inflict on this place a similar, albeit different, atrocity to that which befell her beloved home. She had not heard Khan as he walked up behind her and was startled when he put his arms around her waist and kissed her gently on the back of her neck.

"You have grown to like this place, haven't you Nasra?" he asked gently.

She didn't give an immediate response but slowly she turned to him and said, "It is beautiful, it really is. I have begun to take notice of it more and more, and each time I look I see it differently.

Truscott must be a wise and clever man. With his fortune he can live anywhere, yet he lives here: where travel is inconvenient; where life, in many ways despite his wealth, is harsh. Why do you think he does that Nasra? I will tell you why. Because he is sensitive to nature and to life itself and values it higher than he does his money."

Nasra stayed silent for a moment, thinking upon what Fadyar had just said.

"And so are you Fadyar." After a pause he added, "I came out to say I am ready but also to tell you something I may not have chance to say later. I love you."

"I know," she said simply, "and I you. I fell asleep last night thinking that it was us in the lodge, not Truscott. How weird is that?" Neither she nor Khan answered, and they jointly loaded up the small boat and prepared to make the long journey towards the dam as the new sunlight began to dissolve the mist.

In contrast to Fadyar, Donaldson had slept little. His contract with Crossland was becoming a burden and a considerably dangerous one. He sweated with nervous energy as he thought about the various ways he could possibly penetrate the lodge defences, but failed to find any that totally satisfied him. Sure, he could get close, but there was no real requirement for him to take such risks. His task was simple: kill Cindy Crossland. He could use his rifle to do this from a safe distance, either when she was crossing over the water in a boat or simply lie in wait for her at a passing place and shoot her through the windscreen of her vehicle as she drove along the road.

There was only one reason why he longed to get inside the lodge and it had little to do with murderous intent. Not being able to sleep he rose very early and had quickly washed and shaved the overnight red stubble from his face. The lure of Cindy Crossland was considerable and he decided to go to the lodge again and simply see what happened in the morning. If no opportunity presented itself, he would have to resort to taking a shot at her later in the day, or if he had to, the following day. He knew he was good at dealing with situations as they arose and he would rely on his instincts and reactions rather than try to devise some elaborate plan to circumvent the security. There was one thing he was certain about.

Delay was not an option, never had been and never would be. To delay means failure and Donaldson knew only success. He carefully packed his suitcase and placed it in his 4x4 alongside his rifle, field glasses and ammunition. He called in at the local store, always open early for the camper and caravan tourists, and bought provisions that filled his rucksack – having first emptied it of some miscellaneous items which included a bundle of long nylon cable ties held together by a thick elastic band. He drove slowly but purposefully around the southern and western shores of Loch Lochy, before turning left for Loch Arkaig and to the Mealag Estate track that he had come to know so well. He hid his vehicle deep into the forest and looked at his watch. 8am. He took his rifle from its case and slung it across his shoulder, checking first that it was loaded and the safety catch secured. He placed his glasses around his neck and made certain his large hunting knife was in its sheath at his side. Finally, he took two bacon sandwiches from his rucksack and put them into his left jacket side pocket before undoing the band from around the ties and stuffing a large handful of them into his right pocket. His last act, before making his way through the trees to the lodge, was to lock his car and place the keys on an inside pocket that he could securely close by its zip. He took several gulps of air and set off to hunt for his human prey.

Sharid Bagheri and Mawdud Mattar had been meticulous in their preparations. The Land Rover was full of fuel, more to aid its stability than for the miles it was expected to travel, and their equipment had also been double-checked. As soon as they left the hotel, they changed into sturdy, studded walking boots and their camouflaged jackets and trousers before Bagheri drove to the passing place a quarter of a mile beyond the garages. They waited there, their shortwave radios switched to the 'on' position. They had an excellent view of the loch and of any comings and goings from the lodge itself, whilst not appearing overly conspicuous themselves. They placed their high powered glasses to their eyes and searched for any activity on the lodge estate, where Fadyar was going to be landed in about thirty minutes time. Fadyar had instructed them that if it was not safe for her, then they should start their vehicle and drive along the road. She would see it and abort her landing. All was still amid the trees and they remained in their position.

Khan skilfully cut the engine and silently brought the small boat onto the opposite shore. Fadyar jumped out, and immediately Khan rowed out towards deeper water before starting his outboard again. The boat had been at the shore for barely ten seconds. Khan made way towards the dam, it being his role to take out the officer patrolling the wall and gate when Fadyar gave the signal. He dropped anchor and prepared to start fishing. Ordinarily either Mattar or Bagheri would have made some light hearted comment upon Khan's fishing, but today such thoughts did not disturb their concentration and they remained silent. Several minutes passed and then the radio came to life.

"In position. Synchronise watches. In ten seconds it will be 8:15am exactly. Nine, eight, seven, six, five, four, three, two, one, mark. Over." It was Fadyar.

Almost simultaneously three voices responded "Affirmative. Out"

63

The previous evening, Chief Inspector Keith Maythorp at Fort William had reasonably assumed the raising of the terrorist threat had been sanctioned by the JTAC, since as far as he was aware that was their responsibility. That was also the very firm view taken by the Chair of the JTAC, the Assistant Director General of the Security Service, Rosalind Craglis – a redoubtable woman of immense experience in intelligence and counter intelligence. She had been a skilled field operative in the days of the cold war where she had demonstrated considerable courage and fortitude in various overseas countries, many of them visited without a valid passport and entered by non-conventional means. She then served in various embassies and UK missions, often masquerading as an Under Secretary for Trade, a euphemism for her real work as a spy. Since taking up a position at Millbank, she had risen steadily to Assistant Director General and she did not take kindly to having her role usurped by someone whom she regarded as a promotion-seeking policeman. Assistant Commissioner Manders was being firmly reminded that his responsibilities did not include unilaterally issuing threat assessments prior to any discussion of the actual facts by the JTAC. Craglis had opened the meeting at 8:30am when the sixteen representatives from government departments were present, but it was now nearing 9am and Manders was becoming impatient. He and Ms Craglis had clashed previously, and it was apparent that the Assistant Director General was now using this opportunity to settle old scores.

"If the Chair would permit, I am finding this lecture time consuming and non-productive. I move that we immediately discuss the main item under review and either confirm or rescind the Assistant Commissioner's threat warning. I cannot imagine he issued it lightly."

Everyone turned to face the interjector, a little known figure with a fresh, round face, who was standing in for the Permanent

Secretary at the Ministry of Defence. Murmurs of assent gathered in volume.

"I should like to second that." John Walters of GCHQ, who had unofficially helped earlier in the investigation, called out. The obvious affront to the Chair inwardly delighted Manders but although Ms Craglis blushed she kept her composure.

"Very well, then," she curtly replied. "Assistant Commissioner, the floor is yours."

She beckoned at Manders to start. Manders then laid out all the evidence. His presentation was flawless as was his mastery of the facts both salient and the less significant. He replied to questions with courtesy and patience and succinctly explained the reasons why he had taken the extraordinary step of pre-emptively raising the threat level.

"With these facts and particularly the decoded message that reveals the dates for such an attack, it was imperative in my view not to lose any time at all in alerting our security and protection forces across the country. To have delayed until this morning, only to find that overnight an attack had occurred on an unprotected installation or, worse, during the London rush hour, would in my humble submission have been tantamount to a dereliction of my duty and obligation to the state." Manders ended his evidence with a flourish that brought wry smiles around the table but which did nothing to harmonise his relationship with Rosalind Craglis.

A further hours debate followed, and then various proposals were put by the Chair and voted upon, the most pertinent being unanimous agreement to endorse the raising of the threat level and to also immediately notify the Joint Intelligence Committee. Craglis closed the meeting at 10:45am, twenty minutes after four persons were either dead or dying 600 miles away.

Manders returned to the office where he saw Ritson leaning over Dongle's shoulder staring intently at a computer screen. Ritson looked up.

"How did it go?" he enquired.

"Fine, apart from that bloody Craglis woman." Then mindful of Dongle's presence added hastily, "I'll tell you about it sometime. God, these meetings can be tiring." Manders threw his file of papers rather too hard onto Dongle's desk and sat back on a vacant chair. The documents spewed out of their protective folder with some going over the desk and others drifting drunkenly to the floor. Dongle and Ritson went to gather them up, when a piece of typescript caught Dongle's eye.

"Can I ask what this is, I haven't seen it before?" He enquired, passing it over to Manders.

"You don't know? That's the decoded message that was the clincher for the raised alert, are you sure you haven't seen it?" Manders asked, as he looked quizzically towards his detective chief superintendent.

Ritson replied, "Dongle wasn't shown it, Sir. His skills are in computer analysis and stuff the rest of us don't understand. We don't want him tied up in doing phone number searches on databases, stuff we can all do!" he chuckled.

Dongle remained serious. "May I look at it again, Sir?"

Manders passed it to him and Dongle studied it in silence for about a minute whilst the others looked at each other, puzzled.

When Dongle spoke again he did so in a hushed, faltering manner. "I, er, I don't think this has any phone numbers on it. In fact... um, I don't think it's got anything to do with a phone number at all."

"*What?*" Ritson shouted, and jumped up from his chair. Manders mouth gaped open but no words came.

"No Sir. You see, I do a lot of walking when I can, holidays and the like, and I use Ordnance Survey maps. This number looks awfully like a grid reference to me. And the initials NH at the end would probably be the actual map. It will be somewhere up north."

Manders grabbed the paper from Dongle's hand and looked at it. He then passed it to Ritson. All three men stood for several more seconds before Ritson broke the silence.

"Oh fuck."

64

A number of persons, each with differing motives, observed the MacLeans drive out of Mealag at 8:45am using the Range Rover. The British protection officer patrolling the lodge waved at them as they passed by and offered to close the gate behind them as they drove out. Donaldson, carefully concealed at the outer edge of the fence, also noted their departure. Fadyar Masri, having taken up her familiar position, glanced at her watch as the MacLeans pulled away. The smell of diesel fumes invaded her nostrils and she fleetingly resented the affront to the usually clean, odourless air. Ten minutes later, Assiter and Truscott appeared. They were carrying their rifles and rucksacks and headed towards the jetty where two boats were moored. They got in the larger one and sat down. A few moments later, the American agents walked smartly down to join them.

"Get in," said Gordon, "You can travel first-class with us today."

Five minutes later, they had drawn up at the jetty, unloaded the boat, and were about to commence their ascent of the hill. Fadyar waited, her telescope firmly focused on the group. As soon as they started the climb she spoke into her radio.

"Sharid. They are on their way, as planned. It's safe to move out. Over."

"OK. Over"

Bagheri started the Land Rover and drove it to the track by the garages where he parked it out of sight of the road. He and Mattar deliberately left the doors unlocked and slid the key under the driver's floor mat. Concealed by their fabric carrying cases and hidden by their loose-fitting camouflage jackets were their CAR-15 sub-machine guns and the Walthur hand guns, holstered at their side. Each wore an ammunition belt, also underneath the jacket, from which hung two grenades, clips for the Walthurs and a large supply of bullets for the SMG's. Mattar wore the field glasses around his neck, whilst Bagheri carried various items in a rucksack. A few minutes later they walked along the road to the dam where they turned off and started to climb the hill. Their ascent attracted the attention of the officer at the dam gate, curious as to why, today, two groups should be deer stalking the same area. He switched on his radio and spoke into the microphone which was pinned to his lapel.

"Bill. It's Nigel at the dam. Are there any others on this deer stalking trip that we know of?"

"Don't think so. I can go and look on the board if you think it's important."

"Yes, can you do that. Two other guys have just followed our party up the hill, about fifteen minutes behind at a guess."

"Will do. Out"

Bill Green, still on his patrol, walked to Ruraich and looked at the board. Nothing was mentioned about more persons joining the party.

"Nigel, I'm outside Ruraich. Nothing on the board – what next?"

"I'm not sure. I'll come over to the house. Can you get Pete from the gate to join us before he goes off duty. No point in waking up Simon, at least not yet. Oh, and can you confirm with the women that no one else is expected on their husbands' trip."

Fadyar watched intently as the three officers gathered outside the house and she moved silently to be in earshot of their conversation. She was just in time to hear them trying to raise their CIA counterparts on the radio.

"Bloody things. You would think that with all those farts in Whitehall and Washington they could at least ensure that the radios we use are the same or at least compatible. The US guys have their own comms and I think theirs must work on a different frequency. I can't get them."

"Well, I think two of us should go across and follow the second lot of walkers. After all Assiter is the priority and if something odd is happening over there we should take a look. Pete and I will go. You and Simon stay here, but wake Simon." It was Bill that was taking charge and a few moments later the two officers started their long walk across the dam wall towards the mountain opposite. The four went their separate ways just as Cindy and Paulette took their usual morning swim and dived into the pool. A few minutes later the phone rang in Ruraich but no one heard it. Then the phone in the hall of the lodge rang and no one heard that either. Eventually the MI5 officer in London hung up and went on to ring the next number on his list of those who should be told of the Level 1 alert.

Fadyar slid herself back into deeper cover until she was well away from the lodge complex, then she spoke quietly into her radio, ensuring the scrambler was on. "Mattar. There are two British police coming over and they will be behind you. You will need to take them out before attempting any attack on our target. Note there are four, repeat four, British police in total. Not three. And some good news, the Americans and British can't communicate via their radios."

"Understood Fadyar. We will let you know the outcome."

She then told Khan to withdraw from his position and make his way back, past Mealag, and anchor a little way beyond so as not to attract any attention from the officers who would be crossing the dam. Fadyar had considered whether she, and perhaps Khan, could have shot the officers as they walked across but dismissed the idea. Although her rifle was silenced and she was an expert shot, the odds did not favour a clean kill on two moving targets at a distance she estimated to be in excess of 700 metres. Also, the muffled noise would still be very audible to anyone close by and any shots would totally compromise her position and probably the mission itself. Khan would have a very difficult shot from a boat bobbing around on the waves. She slowly wriggled on her stomach to return to her original vantage point, pleased that at least severing the communications at the lodge was now going to be a whole lot easier than she first envisaged – though there was still the matter of the two remaining protection officers to resolve, not to mention the two women, but her plan included those challenges.

65

Donaldson, in hiding by the pool, had also overheard the conversation between the officers and he, too, had watched the two disappear from sight only to emerge several minutes later beginning their ascent of the hill. His pleasure at knowing that two of the enemy (a term he used for anyone in opposition to his objectives) had removed themselves from the zone, was only slightly dimmed by his concern at what he had learned. He now understood for the first time that someone named Assiter, an American, was being guarded not Truscott. The name was familiar to him, but he was not interested in politics – so exactly who Assiter was, or what he did, failed to arouse any interest or curiosity. He also realised, like Fadyar, that there were in total six guards of which four were climbing up a mountain half a mile away. That left two at the lodge and one of those had been woken up so presumably would be tired. Donaldson started to get excited, the odds were moving quickly in his favour to achieve all his ambitions. He needed to strike very soon as he might never get a better chance.

Officer Simon Willison joined his colleague on the lawn in front of the lodge. Donaldson started to subconsciously stroke the handle of his knife with his stubby fingers. His blue eyes were wide, clear and alert. His short cropped hair began to stiffen as did the hairs on the nape of his neck, all signs that he was ready for action.

"I'll do the patrol, you take the gate Simon. You can continue to rest up a bit there."

The words were music to Donaldson's ears. *Things just get better and better* he thought. In his lifetime, Donaldson had effected entry at numerous establishments allegedly well protected and guarded, many of them via the main gate. In his experience, it was often the most vulnerable area and where security measures could be at their most lax. The guard or guards were usually tired, bored, drunk or all three. The gatehouse, if there was one, was overstuffed with electronic gadgets and monitors so numerous that the guards didn't bother to look at them, let alone reposition the cameras at frequent intervals, thereby allowing attackers to creep up unseen using the blind spots. The same folly was being repeated here. Instead of putting the freshest, most alert officer at the gate, there was going to be some poor guy named Simon who had not fully rested and would be only half awake. Manning the entrance, he would not have long to wait before he was asleep again. Permanently.

Donaldson now knew exactly how he was going to get inside Mealag Lodge. He just hoped that the two women would still be there when he knocked on the door. For some while, he had concentrated upon the officers and their conversations at the lodge and as he prepared to leave his hideaway he took a quick glance back at the pool building. To his amazement he saw Cindy and Paulette swimming leisurely up and down its length. Any other time such a sight would have delayed him, but not now. He licked his lips, whispered an obscenity under his breath and left. When he reached his hidden vehicle he climbed into the driver's seat, changed out of his new camouflage jacket into his normal one, and started the engine. He leant across the passenger seat, collected up the hire papers from the glove compartment and placed them in his inside pocket. He then drove straight to the gate at Mealag Lodge. As he approached, Police Constable Willison stood more erect. Donaldson gave a brief press of the horn button and waved at the officer to open the gate. The officer responded by an exaggerated wave of his hands clearly indicating "No". Donaldson got out of the car and went up to the gate.

"You're new here, haven't seen you before. Open up mate," said Donaldson pleasantly.

"I'm sorry. No one is allowed in today" replied Willison.

"Don't be bloody daft. It's Friday. I come every Friday to clean and maintain Mr Truscott's pool. Sam Dickens is the name, it's bound to be on that list of yours – if that's what's in your hand." Donaldson had pulled this ruse so many times, most people at gates held lists, another means of their undoing. The officer did indeed hold such a list in his hands that showed the names of authorised, prearranged visitors. He scanned the list carefully but before he reached the end and looked up, Donaldson spoke again.

"Look, here is the authorisation and order signed by Mr Truscott personally". Donaldson moved closer to the wire mesh, producing the papers from his jacket inside pocket and proffered them in his left hand, just far enough from the gate for Willison to have to take a step towards the fence in order to view them. As he neared, Donaldson slightly lowered the papers, and unthinkingly the police officer automatically leant forward to study them. Donaldson instantly pulled his knife from its sheath with his right hand and in one movement plunged it through the large gap in the mesh, deep into the side of the officer's neck. Blood spurted in great profusion as the officer fought for his breath, whilst Donaldson grasped hold of his tunic and held him firm against the wire. As Willison went limp, Donaldson withdrew his knife and wiped it on the nearby grass before calmly replacing the papers in his pocket. The officer fell to the ground, vainly trying to stop the massive flow of blood with his hands. Donaldson had never wasted time watching a man in his death throes, and before Willison died Donaldson had taken out a crowbar from the tool box of the 4x4 and prized open the padlocked chain. He flung back the gate and dragged the almost lifeless body into the nearest undergrowth, out of sight. He used his considerable strength to pull out by the roots a couple of medium-sized bushes and swept them back and forth across the blood that had spilled onto the track. As quickly as the earth dropped from the impromptu brooms, the blood disappeared until none could be seen. Any observer arriving at the gate would notice only the soil.

Donaldson resumed his position behind the wheel of the Ford. Collecting his semi-automatic pistol from his rucksack, he screwed on the silencer before placing the gun on the seat beside him. He pressed the starter and drove into the lodge complex. Officer Nigel Probert was seated at the bench just above the jetty, but he was not taking in the view. He was watching the mountain opposite through high-powered binoculars, straining to see if anything untoward was happening. Assiter and his party were out of his sight, having walked around the hill a little below the summit, but the other two stalkers were still following. Probert heard Donaldson's approaching vehicle, but, thinking it to be the MacLeans returning early for some reason, he didn't trouble to turn around. Anyway he had no reason to investigate who had arrived, as his colleague Simon Willison was manning the gate. Donaldson now knew for certain this was going to be his lucky day. He had overheard all that he needed to plan an easy assault on the house. The two women were still indoors, oblivious to their plight. The guard at the gate was tired and stupid and now the one on the bench was too busy sightseeing to even look round. Donaldson picked up his gun and held it out in front of him as he walked silently on the grass. He stopped, took careful aim and fired. The bullet smashed into the back of Officer Probert's head, blowing half of it away. Donaldson ran forward, roughly grabbed hold of the lifeless body and pulled it into the trees only a few metres from where a shocked and alarmed Fadyar was laying as flat as she possibly could, her own hand gun held rock steady in her right hand, the safety catch off. She need not have been concerned for her own well-being. Donaldson was in triumphant mood. He had successfully stormed Mealag and he thought his ex-army mates would have been proud of him. He recalled their own arrant motto that was embroidered onto the sleeve of his army jacket in Africa: *adepto tantum victorem praemio* – 'only the winner will get the reward'. It was time to collect his.

Fadyar held her breath as Donaldson walked past her, the crunching sound of his heavy boots on the stone pathway gradually fading as he neared the lodge. She hardly dared move and had only managed a fleeting glimpse of the man who alighted from the 4x4. Initially thinking him to be additional security from the army she had laid low anxious not to be detected, but the cold-blooded killing of the British police officer had completely unnerved her. She had pressed herself so hard into the ground, not risking lifting her head, that all she could see was Donaldson taking his final steps before he entered the kitchen door. Her mind was in turmoil. *Who was this man and what was his connection with those at the lodge? Were there others involved? How had he got past the gate? Was he in collusion with one of the guards? Surely not*, she thought, but in those few brief moments nothing made much sense to her.

Yes, there must be others as how else had he got past the gate? She asked herself any number of questions but found no answers.

Was the man after Assiter, too, and would he now lie in wait for him? Again more questions.

She gradually regained her composure and started to think about what had happened more logically, more calmly. She reasoned that the man could not be after Assiter. *Why risk being killed at the gate, or even in the grounds several hours before the American returned. Surely the man, whoever he is, would have been surveying the lodge and watching Assiter's movements so would know he had left earlier to go shooting?* The fact that this intruder must also have been undertaking surveillance was a concern. She had not noticed anyone else near the house and she had spent many hours keeping it under observation. Then she remembered the brief flash of reflected light, across the path and from within the trees behind the building, the day before.

"Him. It was him, had to be", she muttered to herself as she continued her rational analysis of the events she had just witnessed.

The intruder had somehow come through the gate, therefore making it highly probable that the guard positioned there must almost certainly now be dead. Her mind reeled with questions. *What brought this man and his accomplices, if there were any, to Mealag on this day at this time, if not Assiter? Was it perhaps a man with a personal grudge against Truscott or a fanatic against the wealthy?* She kept thinking and trying to make sense of it all. *The man was clinical and bold.* She had spent many months in training camp and only the best graduates could have done what she had just witnessed. *He was unhurried, certain of himself and what he was about to do. Completely detached, unemotional, focused and accomplished; the man was a ruthless killer.*

"That's it," she said to herself, "A hit man, professionally hired. Cold, calculating, fearless and deadly." She knew the job demanded that virtually all professional assassins work alone and in secrecy, and as some time had now passed with no one else appearing, she was becoming more confident that this was a lone killer. She now weighed up the risks the unwelcome visitor presented to her own mission, slowly but inexorably nearing its finale a thousand metres away across the loch. She thought, momentarily, about aborting it entirely for the day but dismissed that almost as instantly. The deaths of the two police would hardly go unnoticed and by tomorrow Mealag Lodge would be cordoned off and sealed tight by numerous other officers. More pertinently, and assuming he was still alive, Assiter would immediately be on his way home to the US surrounded by an armed guard. His kidnap now had to take place today; there would be no other opportunity. Fadyar subconsciously placed her hand on her rifle at the grim realisation that she would quickly have to neutralise the threat to the mission of the red-headed man inside the house.

Red Head. The man had a red head. Her recollections were becoming clearer and she suddenly remembered his short red hair. There was something about him that seemed vaguely familiar and it was the red hair. *Where had she seen red hair? It had to be in England as no one in Iraq or Pakistan had red hair... except... except...* She strained to remember. Somewhere she had seen a person with red hair *but where? And when?* She shook her head, angry with herself for not remembering and, failing to recall any details, she returned to the topic of her mission. That was the most important thing.

"Concentrate. Concentrate," she told herself.

As she was starting to analyse her options, she heard Bagheri call on the radio. "Fadyar. Are you there? Over." She switched to speak and as she did several loud, terrified screams from the house punctured the still air, followed immediately by an eerie silence.

66

Assistant Commissioner Manders had for the first time in his life run to the commissioner's office, but he had already left for the emergency Joint Intelligence Committee's meeting scheduled, according to the Commissioner's secretary, for 11:30am. Manders glanced at his watch. 11:20am. He tried to raise the Commissioner on the emergency mobile number but, as was mandatory at all JIC meetings, no mobile was even allowed into the room, all of them were switched off and safely placed under lock and key. The only telephone allowed in the large oval room was placed immediately in front of the Chairman, in this instance the Home Secretary, who had just arrived having had to cut short a meeting with representatives from the Bar Council. The meeting started a little early as all were present and the factual evidence was being outlined by Rosalind Craglis seated beside her boss, the Director General of the Intelligence Service. She gave an impressive report, brief and well-delivered. The room listened intently. The Home Secretary had made some jottings on a note beside him, but before referring to them he asked for input from any others who might wish to add information. He had stressed he wanted any speaker to provide additional fact, not supposition and certainly not opinion, at least not yet. There were no additions.

"Then I have one point to add which I believe may be highly pertinent" the Home Secretary referred to his notes. "The Assistant Director has just informed us that repeated sweeps of the various computer databases and other information sources have revealed no person of significant standing who may represent a potential terrorist target other than our own governmental and political personnel, but I should inform you that in this country at the moment is the United States Secretary of State, Mr Dean Assiter."

There were several audible gasps from various attendees. Some others, including Rosalind Craglis and her boss, simply shook their heads in disbelief. The Director General of the Intelligence Service hastily scribbled a pencilled note, 'Another government cock up on the way? Mind our backs!' and pushed it in front of his female Deputy, who sniggered slightly just as an Assistant Secretary at the Foreign Office spoke.

"With respect Home Secretary, I believe Mr Assiter flew home last weekend."

"That is where you are wrong, Assistant Secretary. That news was disinformation – I believe that is what it is technically called is it not, Director General?" He looked at the man beside Rosalind Craglis, but continued without waiting for an answer. "It was his specific wish to have only limited protection. We didn't like it, of course, and neither did the Americans, but the Secretary of State was insistent – so to aid his protection, we restricted information on his movements to only a very few people. Very, very few people in fact, and we were meticulous in ensuring that nothing even remotely connected to his visit appeared on any file or computer record."

He smiled thinly, almost seeming appreciative of how clever he and his department had been, before continuing, "That is why his name did not appear on your searches, though the Foreign Secretary and your Permanent Secretary were informed."

The room filled with noise as persons started murmuring to those near to them. The Home Secretary turned to the Commissioner for Police.

"Commissioner, you will of course wish to take immediate measures to reinforce the protection of Mr Assiter now we are aware of an imminent threat, and I also believe the JIC should now officially categorise this threat as our Level One, a threat against an individual. I am sure I have no need to remind you all that although this is our committee's lowest ranking, it represent a most serious and actual threat. As such, I shall be convening COBR immediately and acquainting the Prime Minister. I anticipate he will wish me to chair COBR and given what we know COBR will also issue its own threat level. Any questions?"

The Commissioner spoke, "Does the Home Secretary recollect where Mr Assiter is staying and for how long. Also what protection, if any, does he currently have?"

"I am sorry I cannot recall all the details which were agreed many months ago... I think he was planning to stay with some tycoon or other. The Foreign Secretary and a small planning group with the Foreign Office dealt with most of the detail. To keep it in house, the FO was going to use some of its own operatives and the Americans were going to have a couple of CIA in tow. You, of course, wouldn't know would you Assistant Secretary?"

The fatuous remark, designed as much to demonstrate his superior position as it was to denigrate a subordinate within the department which the Home Secretary was clearly lining up to take the blame if any harm befell Assiter, was typical of the man. Nicknamed The Teflon Kid, since nothing bad ever seemed to stick to him, he could also have been called a number of more colourful epithets. The Assistant Secretary at the Foreign Office reddened, "Regrettably, I, like others here Home Secretary, appear to have been kept very much in the dark. However, if the security on Assiter's whereabouts was so restricted and if, and I stress if, he is the target, then either we or the Americans also have a major breach of security to worry about. The latter could turn out to be more significant even than Mr Assiter."

"Quite so, quite so. We will start an internal investigation at the appropriate time but the commissioner now has to be released to contact the Foreign Secretary."

Sir Neil Roberts rose from his chair and walked to the door.

"Commissioner!" The Home Secretary was shouting. "The people who Assiter was staying with... can't recall much but I remember the wealthy chap had a new girl-friend. She was married and used to work in the Cabinet Office. Maybe that's the leak."

"Crossland," sighed Roberts. "Her name is Crossland. My ATU people came to me months ago with her name, though not as a suspect. Simply that it had come up as part of a routine investigation but her file was so highly classified my staff were unable to access it. Perhaps you could minute my request that any future inquiry on this incident should include in its Terms of Reference file access levels and protocols. We have to get away from turf issues. The government of the day must trust the ATU with everything. It is also now obvious that an attack is underway, rather than probable, and I need to leave immediately."

Roberts was as highly-skilled a political operator as anyone around the table, and he saw no harm in laying down an early marker that might serve to muddy waters or even deflect criticism when the inevitable review of the events took place.

"Quite so. Agreed."

Commissioner Roberts left and collected his phone. Almost immediately it was switched on he saw had an urgent message to phone Manders, but did so from a secretary's desk that had a scrambler built into the land line.

"We think we know where the attack is to take place, the bloody Highlands." Manders was excited and forgot all forms of deference.

"I can equal that, Phillip. I know the target. It's Assiter, the US Secretary of State guy, principal adviser to the President. He never left the UK. See you soon."

Manders replaced the receiver and called in Ritson.

"Everything is falling into place, Bill. We know from Dongle's lead that it's this lodge place in the Highlands and the commissioner thinks the target is Assiter, the US Secretary. Evidently he never left the UK. The lodge is owned by Gordon Truscott, whom Five now confirm is having or had an affair with Cindy Crossland, wife of Alan Crossland of the bank. What a bloody fiasco. Cock up after cock up. We could have stopped all this if that prick Roberts had the balls to access that secret file. Now we have JIC and COBR meetings, plus a probable assassination. Oh, and by the way, the phone line at the Scottish lodge is dead. What would you say were the odds that it's been cut? Don't answer."

"Bloody Hell!" Ritson exclaimed, but Manders was in full flow.

"The Scottish mob are saying that they need confirmation from their executive that they are to take operational instructions from me! Bloody Scottish Nationalism. Anyway, they haven't any option now it's a Level One JIC and COBR is sitting. They have an automatic seat on the JIC so they are in it up to their arses from here on in, like we are."

Ritson stared opened-mouthed at Manders. "Shit".

"Didn't I just say that?" retorted Manders, but his quick wit was lost on Ritson.

It was thirty-four minutes past midday and the forces of law and order had a lot of catching up to do.

67

Dean Assiter and Gordon Truscott were making a slow climb across Gleoraich headed in a broadly Easterly direction. The main part of the mountain reared its huge head to the west but its long eastern flank, also impressively tall, was a lot easier to traverse. The two CIA agents were maintaining a distance of no more than fifteen metres behind the stalkers. Three hundred metres behind them were the two kidnappers, and the two British police were a similar distance behind Bagheri and Mattar. As the flank gradually became less steep, Gordon and Dean changed direction and headed north before doubling back behind the hill in order to continue the climb. The two British protection officers had barely started their walk along the eastern flank as Dean and Gordon disappeared behind the mountain. Bagheri and Mattar, alerted by Fadyar that the two officers behind them represented a threat that had to be dealt with, were also steadily making their way across the hill, but they did not turn behind the mountain.

At the Eastern end of Gleoraich, just slightly away from the path taken by the walkers ahead of them, was the entrance to the surge shaft access tunnel that Gordon had pointed out to Cindy on her first visit to the dam. It was still protected by a padlocked wrought iron grille door and the large DANGER safety notice swayed slightly in the gentle breeze. The entrance was small, permitting only one person to enter at a time and the interior of the tunnel was pitch-black. Being cut deep into the hill, no sunlight ever entered it and daylight only penetrated a few yards into the dank interior. It was an ideal spot from which to spring an ambush, provided Mattar and Bagheri could quickly remove the padlock. Carrying no tools and not wishing to risk the noise their silenced weapons might make, they would have to improvise. Fortunately, as with the dam, cost constraints at the time of construction were severe and there was no money available for clearing the detritus and unwanted or broken machinery. A lot was buried within the massive works but considerable amounts were either submerged by the rising water in the loch as the dam took effect or just left to rot at the shoreline. Similarly, the excavations for the surge access tunnel had not been removed and an ample supply of broken and torn metal, mostly iron and steel, littered the immediate surroundings. Mattar picked up a deformed and twisted iron bar about 2cm thick. It was crusted with bright orange flakes of rust, which fluttered to the ground like sprinkling tea leaves as he wedged it firmly into the padlock's hoop. He twisted the bar round and asked Bagheri to lend his weight and their combined strength soon overcame the lock's resistance. It snapped open and fell to the grass. They opened the door slowly, which much to Bagheri's dismay squeaked and squealed as it moved on the rusted hinges.

"Stop," cried Mattar. "Wait."

He then walked a short distance and started picking the berries, full and ripe, from a nearby large rowan tree. When he had gathered two handfuls he brought them over to the gate and squeezed his hands together, letting the sticky liquid drip over the rusted mounts. He moved the grille very slowly back and forth and it was soon operating silently, much to his partner's admiration.

"Good trick that Mawdud, well done" remarked Bagheri. "Let's get in."

They entered the long, narrow tunnel, pulled the grating closed and waited. Several minutes later, from their secret hideaway they saw the officers come into view, their upright posture indicating that the climb was not demanding much effort from their fit bodies. It was time for Mattar and Bagheri to ready their weapons.

The CAR-15 is a highly versatile submachine gun. Not only is it short barrelled, light and easy to use, but it can also be switched easily from a machine gun to a fast firing single shot repeating rifle, the setting now chosen by both terrorists.

"You take the one on our left, I will take the one on the right. Remember, they have body armour. Go for the head." whispered Bagheri.

A moving target is clearly more difficult to hit than a static one. Normally, any trained killer will aim at the body as it presents a larger target area and does not move quickly in unpredictable directions as does a person's head, but the Kevlar protective vests altered the odds. The officers passed in front of them.

Mattar gave a quick nod to his companion and silently opened the gate. The two stepped out and lay flat on the coarse grass and took aim. The officers were no more than fifteen metres away and Bagheri and Mattar could not miss. Two silenced shots were fired and two bodies fell, both dead before they hit the ground. The sound of the shots, like that of young child trying to imitate the sound of a steam engine, although muffled, was still loud enough to alarm Bagheri.

"Will the CIA hear that?" he asked, but Mattar reassured him.

"No, my friend. They are the other side of this high mountain. We heard it, sure, but it will pass well over their heads. We are safe."

He was right. The two stalkers and the two Agents ahead of them carried on walking and chatting with only the squawk of an occasional buzzard catching its prey to distract them. Bagheri switched on his radio to report to his leader.

"Fadyar, are you there? Over." he whispered into the microphone.

The radio clicked, but instead of hearing Fadyar's calm and reassuring voice, he heard the panicked screams of Cindy and Paulette.

"Fadyar, is that you? Are you alright?"

"Mawdud, I'm fine, but something really odd is going on here. Someone else has arrived and he isn't friendly. I am investigating. Meanwhile, just continue with our mission. If you cannot raise me, remember there is Nasra waiting in reserve."

"OK, if you are sure." For the first time some nervousness crept into Bagheri's voice. "I called to say those following us are now eliminated."

"Well done, my brothers. Keep to our plan. We shall succeed. Out."

Fadyar could not waste more time nor risk exposure from the sound of the radio. She needed to quickly investigate what was happening at the lodge as she had to ensure that the alarm systems were neutralised and the communications severed. The red head now posed a significant risk to her mission. Her hopes that he might be soon gone faded when she heard those awful screams. She tried to remain calm and rational, but she sensed that the terrified women's screams meant only one thing. If she was right, the red head would not be leaving for quite some time – time she didn't have.

68

Donaldson marched quickly up the drive, totally indifferent to the sound his boots made on the gravel, before making his way around the outside of the house. He paused underneath the lobby window. Placing his hands on the stone sill, he leveraged himself just high enough to take a rapid glance inside. No one. He smiled to himself as he silently opened the door and entered the house. Almost immediately, his heart began to pump faster and the sides of his temples visibly pulsated in rhythm to the quickening beat. He walked through into the kitchen. The wooden table had been partly set for breakfast with bowls and plates neatly placed in front of two chairs. Packets of cereal, milk and fruit juices were nearby. Two mugs were placed on the work surface adjacent to the coffee maker and a heavy kettle simmered gently on the hotplate of a cast iron cooking range. The constant heat had made the kitchen extremely warm and that, together with his adrenalin-fuelled excitement at the prospect of soon collecting his prize, caused beads of perspiration to quickly form on Donaldson's forehead. He picked up a small towel hanging from the drying rail of the range, mopped his brow and wiped his rapidly moistening hands before superfluously rubbing them down each trouser leg. He clasped his right hand over the handle of his hunting knife, sheathed at his side, and several times subconsciously gripped and released his short fingers from its shaft. As he moved cautiously towards the hall he could hear some distant voices, the excited chattering of two women. Startled, he walked back through the kitchen to the lobby, closing the internal door behind him.

Since the Assiters had arrived, Cindy and Paulette had drifted into what had become a familiar morning routine. They would rise at a pre-agreed time dependent on their plans and, not bothering to dress after washing, would don a pool robe from the previous day and start each morning with a splash in the pool. After their swim they showered in the changing area, took a fresh robe from the many on the pegs, rinsed out their costumes and hung them to dry in their cubicle before walking back to the inviting warmth of the kitchen for breakfast. Donaldson heard them enter the kitchen, Cindy talking about the dam. He waited. He heard the sound of the coffee machine being started followed by the mugs being slowly filled and the steady scrape of the wooden chairs on the stone floor as the two unsuspecting friends sat at the table. Donaldson turned the handle to release the lock on the internal door and then deliberately kicked hard against it knowing that the loud, sudden sound of his boots against the heavy wood would instil momentary fear, adding to the element of surprise and thereby lessening the risk. Both women screamed loudly and turned their heads.

Donaldson entered the room, his rifle aimed at Cindy.

"Shut up," he shouted. Paulette screamed again. He immediately took his rifle in both hands and used the butt to strike the French model in the mouth. Be ruthless at the outset, minimise opposition. She nearly toppled from her chair, but recovered her balance. Blood was spurting from her smashed lip which she vainly tried to stop with her hand. Red blobs ran down the back of her fingers before dropping onto the fresh white robe. Cindy, too bewildered and confused to speak, gaped open mouthed at Donaldson.

"I said shut your mouth, and meant it."

Menacingly, he slowly withdrew his knife and brandished the point close to their faces.

"Leave her alone!" Cindy raised her voice, "What the hell are you doing here, Donaldson? What do you want?" She was recovering her composure.

It was now time to ensure one hundred per cent compliance. Donaldson leaned closer to Cindy.

"I told you to shut the fuck up. If you don't, you see this knife – it has a real sharp blade and your friend here is going to be skinned little by little."

As he spoke, he very gently ran the point of the blade across Paulette's cheek, being careful not to cut the skin.

"Not my face, please not my face," Paulette started to cry, and the blood on her teeth and lips flowed a little more as she spoke with a heavier French accent than was usual.

"OK. OK. Leave her Donaldson. Why are you here? Does Alan know? Why are you following me? I presume it's me that's brought you here?"

Before Donaldson could answer, Paulette whose mind was gradually clearing from the impact and shock of the blow to her mouth, said hesitantly, "Do you actually know this man, Cindy? Why is he here?"

"He works for Alan but… "

"That's enough! Shut up, both of you. Your husband and I parted company, if you must know so I thought I'd look up a few friends," Donaldson smirked, "those who owe me a favour or two."

Donaldson leant his rifle against the table and once more placed the knife close against Paulette's face. "Now Cindy you do exactly as I say or she gets very badly cut indeed. And no more questions. Got it."

Cindy nodded as a terrified Paulette tried to lean further back into her chair. Donaldson threw Cindy several of the long and wide plastic cable ties.

"Handcuff each wrist to the chair. Place one on each of her wrists and secure them tightly. Then thread another one through the first and hook it round under the arm of the chair and then tighten 'em up."

Cindy hesitated. She had always disliked Donaldson, distrusted him, and now her worst fears were turning into some sort of nightmare.

"Do it!" Donaldson barked out the order, and Cindy slowly fixed the ties to each of Paulette's wrists.

"Now her ankles. Pull her legs back so each ankle is next to a rear chair leg. Then fix them in the same way."

Cindy slowly got down from the chair. Her mind spinning with thoughts of how she might escape, but so much was rushing through her brain she found it difficult to think of anything but carrying out his orders.

After a few minutes Paulette's hands and feet were securely bound to the chair. Donaldson sarcastically praised Cindy, "That's good, Mrs Crossland. You see how real easy it is to please Jack." He laughed, contemptuously at her. "You'll get a reward soon. Bet you can't wait!" he contemptuously spat out the words to her. Cindy felt physically sick. The man always had always been gross and uncouth but now he really terrified her. He had become a monster out of control. He positioned an empty chair a little away from the bound Paulette and looked at Cindy.

"Get back into the chair. Slowly."

As she sat down, Donaldson began threateningly waving his knife around between the two helpless women. He touched the point on Cindy's throat and gradually moved it up to her wide open eyes. There he deliberately kept turning the knife around so that the sharp, shiny blade flashed from the reflection of the bright halogen ceiling lights.

"Now, stay there. One move from you and I'll start cutting her up. Put your arms on the chair". Cindy obeyed and he used one hand to fix the plastic strap into place. The process was repeated for the other arm, but he left her legs unbound.

Cindy was desperately trying to think of how best to escape, or at least minimise the danger she and Paulette now faced. She knew that it was not in their interests to anger him and that it would be better to try and strike up some sort of rapport with their captor.

"Jack, what's this all about? We know each other, surely this isn't necessary? What's gone wrong?" She tried to sound composed and calm, anxious not to upset him.

Donaldson wasn't listening. He returned to Paulette, placed his hand under her chin and lifted up her head. "You are really quite a pretty little thing aren't you Frenchie?"

Paulette didn't answer. Donaldson grabbed the belt around her blood spattered robe and cut it through with his knife. The robe fell apart exposing her naked body.

"Not bad Frenchie, not bad. I'll keep you as my bonus prize for later." He replaced the knife in its sheaf and sniggered as he placed his hand on her breast. Paulette quivered as his thick, coarse fingers touched her smooth soft skin. She leant backwards as far as her shackles allowed but Donaldson only laughed at her futile efforts. She opened her mouth wanting to scream but, too fearful, wept silently when no sound came.

"Leave her alone, Jack," Cindy snapped. Donaldson laughed again, still slowly moving his hand across Paulette's breasts.

"Why? Are you getting jealous, Cindy? Your turn will come. I've something very special lined up for you."

He moved between the two chairs, then said, "I want to know why the police, why all this protection. Is it for her?" He looked at Paulette.

Neither woman replied.

"Answer me!" He barked.

"Mr Truscott is planning a party this weekend. Some important people are arriving today and tomorrow. The police wanted to ensure the area was secure," Cindy hoped she sounded convincing.

"Ugh. Well it wasn't, was it? And they'll sure get a surprise when they come, won't they!" He laughed, then spoke more seriously, "Don't give me a load of crap, Cindy. Your stupid husband might have believed your lies but no one's coming here – if they were, lover boy and his mate wouldn't be halfway up a mountain."

"You are really some sick bastard, Donaldson. Really sick." Forgetting all about trying to appease her captor she spat the words at him. Her lapse was painful for Paulette. Donaldson grabbed her left breast and squeezed hard. Paulette screamed.

"What did you say? What did you say? I think you should apologise to big Jack."

"Sorry, Jack. Let her go please." Cindy mumbled. Donaldson released the pressure of his hand and stepped back.

"OK. But you will have to show me how you grateful you are. I deserve a better apology than just you saying sorry."

He stood directly in front of her, so close he rested his chin on the top of Cindy's head. He cut the shackle from her right wrist.

"Now, Cindy, make me happy." He spoke calmly, without menace.

Cindy raised her hand, shaking slightly, lowered the zip on his trousers. She opened her mouth, then hesitated.

Donaldson quickly walked across to the kettle and held it above Paulette's head. Maintain the terror. Ensure obedience. They always give in.

"You win, Jack, you win," Cindy whispered; defeated, humiliated, submissive. Donaldson now knew that she would offer no more resistance, her fight gone. He calmly replaced the kettle on the Aga, and as he stepped back to the chair Cindy lowered her face in readiness of what was expected of her but surprisingly Donaldson started to talk.

"You remember when I came to see you how you kept bending over, first showing me your tits then deliberately showing off that tight arse to me?"

Cindy stayed silent.

"I'll ask you again. Do you remember?" He raised his voice, threateningly.

"I didn't do that, and never would," but Cindy did immediately recall the day he came round for Alan's papers and she had given him coffee.

"Oh, yes you did, sweetheart. You knew exactly what you were doing, how much I fancied you and played me along. We really could have had some good fun, you and me. It was obvious you wanted to but then you backed off, you silly bitch. I'd have given you what you needed." He stared at her, paused, and said quite gently, "I hoped you'd be different, but you're all the fucking same."

"That's not true Jack, none of its true," Cindy simpered as she began to cry.

"Well it don't matter, 'cos now it's time for you to make amends and let me have a real good look, close-up like." Donaldson sniggered as he began cutting through the remaining nylon restraints holding Cindy to the chair.

The ties pinning her hand fell away and he motioned with the knife for her to stand up.

"Now take off that robe, turn around and rest your arms flat on the table."

The truth of what was about to happen gradually dawned upon Cindy. She wanted to yell at him and run but was too tired, limp and exhausted.

Feebly she managed to say "No Jack. Not that. I'll do anything but that," but Donaldson ignored her.

Cindy stood there, her naked body trembling, as he started fondling her breasts then her buttocks before gently pushing her head down next to her hands. She turned her face and shut her eyes whilst he positioned her exactly where he wanted. As Cindy bent over the table she cried out as he thrust into her. *Adepto tantum victorem praemio.*

69

Fadyar Masri left the protection of the forest and furtively crossed the lawn to the house. She walked slowly around the perimeter and very carefully tried to look inside any window that she could easily peer into. She saw nothing. As she retraced her steps she heard voices coming from what she presumed to be the kitchen, but the windows were just above her head which made it impossible for her to see inside. She waited and listened. Minutes passed. Every now and then she heard the man's voice shout out and she thought she heard crying from at least one of the women. She knew what was going on inside and she was filled with revulsion. She wanted to stop it now, immediately, and save the two women from being forced to perform the man's degrading perversions, but she also had to protect her mission. That, too, demanded she enter the house to cut the phone and alarms, but the presence of the two women now faced her with a very difficult dilemma. What was she to do with them, even assuming she could ensure the man was no longer a threat?

She heard another scream and impulsively pulled at the large lounge patio doors. One moved open and she slipped inside. Staying low she crept across the lounge floor and out into the hall. She could hear the voices more clearly now, and it was obvious that her worst suspicions of what was befalling the two women were confirmed. The kitchen door to the hallway was closed. Fadyar knew that it would be impossible to break into the kitchen without the man having sufficient time to kill or maim one of the women, possibly both. Or he would take one of them hostage. She could not allow events to spiral out of control. Stay calm. Reluctantly, she withdrew to the lounge and crept back into the fresh air. She had to find an alternative means of bringing the situation in the house to an early conclusion. An idea struck her. She ran across the grass into the forest and using the trees as cover, she made her way to the smaller A-frame buildings. She went to the rear of the first chalet which was almost opposite the kitchen of the main house. Removing most of her bulky gear, she slung her rifle across her shoulder and shinned up the drain pipe until she was able to climb onto the roof. Slowly making her way to its apex, she stopped and looked over the ridge tiles. She had a perfect view of part of the kitchen. She could see one naked woman seated in a chair and just the right arm of the second woman. Facing them was the red head. She gasped as she saw him.

The school! The soldier!

As Fadyar sheltered behind the wall from the bombs and guns on the day her parents were killed, she saw an infantryman come out of the school building. Several days later she had learned of the atrocities he had carried out on the schoolgirls. That soldier was the same person as the man now in the kitchen of Mealag Lodge and still committing similar abuses. Her anger rose. She was also confused. *Why should he be here, at this particular time? Was he still a soldier? Was he supposed to be protecting Assiter?* No, she ruled that out. *But neither would he be at Mealag simply by chance. It was too remote a location. He was there because, like her, he had a mission. He was a hired killer, she was sure – but who was he to kill? It had to be Assiter or Truscott and he had probably simply taken advantage of the women being alone, much as he had of the schoolgirls in Iraq. It was another case of being in the wrong place at the wrong time. Whatever, he was a killer and a psychotic abuser of women and he was a threat to her meticulously laid plans. He had to be stopped.*

She carefully slipped the safety catch off her rifle and looked through the Schmidt and Bender scope. She loaded two 0.50 bullets into her AWSM rifle and removed the safety catch. This was going to be a most difficult shot and had many attendant risks. She was perched on top of a roof, not particularly comfortably. Donaldson was not a still target and she would be firing the bullet through a double-glazed window. There was no doubt the bullet would penetrate the window, but the impact would almost certainly cause it to deviate slightly, ever so slightly, and that might be enough to only injure the redhead or, worse, miss him entirely. In her favour was the distance, which she estimated at only about fifty metres. A movement in the kitchen caught her attention. Donaldson had hold of one of the naked women who seemed to be being forced to bend over near the table. She raised her rifle and slowly aimed the crosshairs just above the centre of Donaldson's back. A head shot would be too risky, too much chance of a movement of the head or a deviation causing the bullet to miss entirely. His back presented a broader target but she had to wait. She heard the woman scream but dared not risk a shot whilst he was bent over and almost on top of her. Fadyar kept her aim steady waiting for Donaldson to stand more upright so there was no risk of the bullet passing through him and into his hapless victim. Suddenly he jerked upwards and instinctively Fadyar pulled the trigger. The large bullet smashed through the window, instantly resembling a web of cracks emanating from the punctured hole to the outer edge of the frame. Donaldson fell forward onto Cindy, a large blood stain rapidly appearing below his right shoulder.

"Aaaaagh… Fuckin' bitch… I'm hit." His piercing curse mixed with the simultaneous screams of Cindy and Paulette but it still carried across the kitchen and beyond. Donaldson was not dead but wounded, and probably now even more dangerous.

Fadyar instantly slid down the roof, jumped to the ground and ran to the lodge. She saw Donaldson, now freed from his union with Cindy, staggering around in the kitchen. Fadyar flung open the door and rushed straight through the lobby. The startled and enraged Donaldson turned, and with his left hand swept the kettle from the hot plate towards Fadyar before she had time to aim her hand gun. She stepped out of the way of the spilling boiling water as the kettle crashed to the floor, but his action had delayed her and in those few vital seconds Donaldson had grabbed his rifle and dashed out of the kitchen into the hall. Fadyar drew her automatic and rushed after him, but he was gone, running down towards the loch, the back of his shirt completely covered by a large red stain as more blood pumped out of the wound. Donaldson was raging from both the pain inflicted by the high calibre bullet and at being denied his ultimate prize just at the point of climax. His sexual frustration and dented pride angered him almost as much as the hole in his back. He strained to focus on where he was and what had happened.

Instinctively he knew he needed to escape quickly. His senses, heightened by the searing pain, told him not to go back past the house, so he half ran, half stumbled towards the loch. As he turned the corner at the edge of the lawn, the dam came into sight and spurred him to run faster. He ran across the pebbled shore, heading directly towards the small gate, and stepped straight onto the crusted peat. Initially the ground bore his weight, but as he progressed his footprints began leaving deeper indentations into the dried, flaky surface until without warning his right front leg suddenly sank up to his knee, closely followed by his left leg. He came to such an abrupt halt he almost pitched over but regained his balance, held tight and virtually static. He tried to lever himself up, using his rifle, but his hands and arms simply sank into the thick, sticky soup. Slowly, panic came over him. He knew he was trapped and as his head cleared, and the bog reached his thighs, he realised he was sinking ever so slowly into his grave.

Fadyar did not want to waste time pursuing the mortally wounded Donaldson and she returned to the kitchen. Cindy was shaking and sobbing, still naked, holding onto the chair. Paulette was ashen, shivering with fear, open-mouthed.

"You should sit down" said Fadyar to Cindy. "Please, sit down."

Cindy moved slowly and silently to the chair.

"Thank you, thank you. He was a monster. Is he dead. Where is he? Who, who are you?" Her rambling questions revealed the extent of Cindy's shock and confusion.

"He's gone. A terrible man. He will not come back. The wound was serious and he will be too weak to move very soon. You can consider yourself very lucky for he would have killed you after you had served his purpose. He abused, raped and then killed three schoolgirls in Iraq when he was a soldier with the occupying forces. He cut their throats when he had finished with them."

The colour that had just started to return to Paulette's face disappeared again. Cindy made to stand up but Fadyar pulled her gun.

"I am very sorry, but I cannot allow you to go. Sit down please, I will not hurt you if you do as I ask. Please."

"My God, what is going on here! Who are you? Were you with

him – Donaldson? What is going on?" Cindy demanded answers from Fadyar, but there was also something about the olive skinned woman and her words that was slightly reassuring to Cindy who sat back on the chair.

"I will tell you, if you are patient Mrs Crossland. First, though, put the robe on and I will help your friend, but I cannot untie her."

Cindy was too weary to argue and loosely wrapped herself in her own robe. The ordeal had left her devoid of energy and she needed time to recover her strength and mind. Fadyar turned to Paulette, "Are you hurt?"

Paulette shook her head. Fadyar carefully picked up Paulette's robe and placed it on her before she picked up several of Donaldson's discarded ties.

"I am sorry, really sorry after what you have just gone through, but I must do this."

A semblance of a thin smile spread across Paulette's burst lips, "We have just heard something like that," the note of sarcasm ignored by Fadyar.

Cindy studied Fadyar closely as the straps were applied around her wrists and ankles and secured to the chair in much the same manner as Donaldson had done to Paulette.

"You look familiar, and you said my name. Who are you?"

"I was born Yasmin Hasan, though that is not the name I am known by now. I am here to pursue our Jihad against the imperialist occupying forces that are seeking to destroy Islam."

"We have nothing to do with that!" remarked Cindy, wearily.

"Oh, but you do. Or at least Mrs Assiter's husband does. He is responsible for sending in the soldiers who kill us, take our land and make our children orphans."

Paulette instantly reacted, "My husband is a good and honest man. He works for his country's government, but he would never allow soldiers to do the things you say. He is not an enemy of Islam."

Fadyar then told her of how a soldier with a name label of Briggs sewn onto his tunic came into her family home and killed her parents in September 2004.

"We were peace loving. We did not support Saddam in any way.

We did not help any insurgents. My parents ran a store, that is all. They were shopkeepers. When the bombs and the firing started we stayed in our small room. We had to. Your bombs destroyed our shop but my parents never once criticised your country for that. Then, later, the soldier Briggs came in and machine-gunned them both whilst they sat on the sofa."

Fadyar's eyes began to well with tears, but composing herself, she continued. "I was in the bathroom and had to climb over their bodies, ripped and torn by American bullets, when the soldier had left. I am here to avenge their deaths and the hundreds of thousands of others your husband's government has killed. Saddam was bad, yes. But his killings were never on the scale the coalition forces have inflicted. We continue to be killed in our hundreds every week, sometimes every day, and you say that you are peace-loving and that we are the forces of evil?" The bitterness and force of her words made Paulette wince.

"I will tell my husband. He will investigate, I know he will. This soldier you speak of, Briggs, he will be punished."

"He will not. His parents will not be murdered. I doubt if he will even be arrested. Your armies lie over what they do and both your governments support those lies. Briggs is one of many. That man whom you said was called Donaldson. He also was a soldier in Iraq, for the British Army, and it was their imperialist government that sent him to my country to murder and rape our schoolchildren."

Cindy and Paulette looked blankly at each other. The woman had just saved their life. They did not want to argue with her, but Paulette was fearful.

"So why are you here? It's to do with my husband isn't it? Please don't kill him, he really is a good man."

"I cannot tell you exactly, but I hope he is not killed. He is a brave man. I know that much as he has not surrounded himself with many security people. For what it is worth, I could have killed him by now had that been my wish".

Fadyar paused then said. "I have to go. I have my work to do."

"What have you done with the police guards?" Cindy casually remarked.

"I have done nothing, on that you have my word, but they are dead. The man Donaldson killed them."

"Oh my God," uttered Paulette.

"Did Donaldson tell you why he was here? Was he too after Mr Assiter?" Fadyar asked.

"No!" said Cindy. "He wanted me, though why he should follow me all the way up here and take these risks I really don't know. It doesn't make sense. He worked for my husband. Alan and I amicably divorced some while ago, and he is not the violent type or the sort to seek revenge on Gordon… er, Mr Truscott. Donaldson was always making suggestions to me… horrible man. "

"I see" said Fadyar, slowly.

Fadyar then left the women in the kitchen whilst she went around the house searching for alarms and telephone lines. She studied the main alarm system and the panic circuitry which, whilst unfamiliar to her, she found relatively easy to disarm with her electronics knowledge gained from the training camp. She then went outside the house, aimed her rifle at the pylon that distributed the phone wires to the complex and fired. The shot broke the insulator and plastic connector into a thousand pieces, leaving the end of the wire fluttering helplessly down onto a tree. She checked the line was dead from the house and returned to the kitchen.

"I must go now. Please do not try to escape as I would not want to hurt you. You have both been through enough. But be in no doubt, I have a mission to carry out and I will not be stopped."

For the first time Fadyar had sounded threatening.

As she opened the kitchen door Cindy called out "Yasmin, thank you for what you did for us."

Fadyar turned, smiled and ran down to the jetty just as the grandfather clock in the hall started to strike midday. She sat on the wooden planks dangling her legs over the water, looking but not really seeing. Confused by the events of the morning, she needed some time to recover, to refocus, but for the first time in months she was not able to concentrate on the mission. Images of her parents, her homeland, her early life came flooding back brought to the fore by her conversation with the two captive women. More images, this time of the women in the kitchen standing or seated beneath the vile Donaldson, him walking casually away from the school in the dusty heat of Baghdad. She shook her head, trying to clear her thoughts. She looked up and saw the long, grey dam and slowly moved her head to the left taking in the high massif of Gleoraich, where already two people lay slain and where many more were likely to die shortly, but she continued to turn and gaze upon Gleoraich's brothers and sisters, the almost unending array of peaks until she faced completely away from the dam and looked down the loch towards Kinloch Hourn. She could not see the cottage where she and her friends had stayed, where she and Khan comforted and made love, it being too far away, but she smiled to herself as she recalled their first primitive efforts at casting a fishing line. She took in several deep gulps of the fresh, clean air and stood up. No time for sentimentality, no place for indecision, no second thoughts. The kidnap, her plan, her revenge.

Her brain cleared and her mind was sharp once more. She reasoned that the Donaldson intervention, though unexpected and dangerous, had actually enhanced the probability of its success. All the security personnel with the exception of the two CIA agents protecting Assiter were now dead, the communications and alarms at Mealag were disabled and the two women were restrained. One thing only slightly puzzled her. She recognised Mrs Crossland and wondered why people from her past had today, of all days, reappeared into her life. The banker, Crossland, was obviously not around and Fadyar had an uneasy feeling that perhaps those responsible for telling her to use his bank had lied about him. She had been told that he was not involved or linked in any way to their organisation making it safe to use his bank. Whilst he was perhaps less scrupulous than most bankers in taking on risks, he seemed essentially honest and not likely to arouse interest from the authorities. Yet here, at the remotest of places, was his attractive ex-wife apparently living with Truscott – who just happened to be entertaining the US Secretary of State and his wife. She did not like co-incidences and she liked even less the possibility that her controllers had lied. The whole ethos of the Abu al-Mazan organisation was based on absolute trust. It had to be. Seated on the jetty, engrossed in her thoughts, Fadyar had not noticed the rapid change of weather approaching from the west and was startled when a few heavy drops of rain splashed onto her head. She called Khan on the two-way radio and ordered him to pick her up at the jetty even though she could have taken the last remaining boat that was tied there, but she did not want to fiddle about attempting to start the outboard. She had tried doing that a couple of times on the reconnaissance missions, only to discover that the ageing motors were somewhat temperamental and required a considerable degree of physical strength. However, had she attempted to start the Mealag boat it would have fired up instantly, being better maintained than the rental one she had been used to. Clouds obscured the hill tops which moments earlier Fadyar had been admiring but the loch itself was still flat and calm, its surface haphazardly punctured by the heavy rain falling onto it. As she called up Mattar she watched the approach of Khan's boat slicing through the water, the large trailing wake evidence of its speed.

"Mawdud. All police at the lodge are dead, repeat dead. Communications severed. We now have to get our target. Do you understand?"

"Understood. They are in open country high on the hill, but we are having difficulty in following at a safe distance due to the cloud."

"Mawdud. If it is that bad they will have to soon return. Be very watchful and stay in touch."

"OK. Out."

Ever cautious Fadyar deliberately untied the Mealag boat and secured it to Khan's when he came alongside. Khan opened up the throttle and crossed the loch, towing the Mealag boat behind them. Waiting in the Land Rover, Khan nervously tapped his fingers on the dashboard. Fadyar just stared at the dam wall and watched the water gently lap against the tarred slope. Five minutes elapsed, then ten, then fifteen. The silence was shattered by a sudden loud crack of an un-silenced rifle shot, its echo ringing around the hills for several seconds. Fadyar got out of the vehicle and looked up at the mountain behind her. It was still covered in cloud, if anything it had thickened slightly and was now a greyish colour rather than white. The light was poor, the murkiness acting like a blanket thrown over the hill. She could see nothing, but clearly someone had fired a rifle shot.

Another fifteen minutes passed then her radio crackled into life and an out of breath Mawdud spoke rapidly. "They are coming back! The same way as they went. They have shot a deer and have loaded it onto a pole. We will try and take out the CIA at the tunnel, but if we fail you can get them as they descend."

"Ok Mawdud. Good luck. Out."

Fadyar made a rapid assessment of the situation. Mattar and Bagheri would have the element of surprise, but there were actually four armed persons, not two, now descending the hill carrying a deer. The disciplined stalkers would have broken their gun and removed the bullets for safety, but it would not take long to make them function again.

"Nasra. You start to climb up. Stay just out of sight of the tunnel entrance. They may need help when the shooting starts but remember try not to kill Assiter."

Khan immediately jumped out and quickly started his climb.

"Mawdud. Sharid. Nasra is coming up. He will be below you both, do not fire at him."

"OK. We understand," Bagheri was first to respond.

She watched Khan go, hoping she had not sent him to his death. She had deliberately ordered everyone's assignments to keep him away from the hill until the last possible moment, sending the others to take on the guards, keeping her sweet Nasra safe. There was nothing Fadyar could do now but wait.

70

Assistant Commissioner Manders had not stopped barking out his orders for a full fifteen minutes, whilst officers around him furiously scribbled notes of what he was saying. When he had finished, they scurried like rabbits back to their desks, each picking up their telephone or tapping away at their computer keyboard. Some would be briefing other governmental organisations, some notified the border control so that the ports and airports were on warning to ensure that any suspects could not easily slip out of the country. Others would be notifying all police constabularies across the UK of the incident and what was known of the suspects to ensure that road blocks and searches could be carried out anywhere, quickly and easily, should the need arise. The other emergency services, including every North of Scotland hospital, were placed on full alert via a coded message that told them to expect potentially significant casualties. This was a precaution. Manders knew that the target was not mass destruction, such as the tube attack the previous year, but if terrorists are on the run and desperate, they were capable of doing anything, anywhere. That might include running into a busy shopping precinct and either opening fire with machine guns or using explosives. Once his specialist officers had done all they could to address the immediate priorities, they would then turn their attention to allied investigative work regarding the terrorist plot itself – notably identifying who the terrorists were and, if time permitted, some would start looking into why the plot had not been discovered earlier. The ATU team, headed by Manders, could now do little more. The plot itself was now for other teams to handle and to neutralise if possible.

In the UK, terrorism is regarded as a crime and the police are the only law enforcement agency mandated by Her Majesty's Government to deal with crime, however major. Paradoxically, the UK is almost alone among nations of not having a singular force, such as the FBI in the United States, to take charge of major crime and terrorist incidents. The UK has however been copied by many other states in relation to its command structure for dealing with major incidents, such as terrorism, prison riot, major fires, serious hostage taking and so on. Essentially, when a major incident is underway, three command centres – Gold, Silver and Bronze are immediately set up.

The Gold Commander is in overall control of the logistic resources at the incident. The Commander will not be on site but at a distant control room called Gold Command (or simply 'Gold'), where those present will formulate the strategy for dealing with the incident. The Silver Commander is the tactical commander who manages the strategic direction from Gold and devises sets of actions that are completed by Bronze. Silver Command is rarely located at the scene as it needs to be able to take a step back and review all the different Bronze resourcing. Silver will not become directly involved in dealing with the incident itself. Bronze Command directly controls the resources at the incident and will be very near to, or at, the scene. The Commander is usually under the main control of the police unless it is a fire and rescue-led incident or, sometimes, a prison incident, irrespective of which organization Bronze actually works for. This is to ensure safety and efficiency of all involved as far as possible. If an incident is widespread geographically, different Bronzes may assume responsibility for the different locations and if the incident is of a complex nature the separate Bronzes are given their own tasks or responsibilities at an incident – for example, intelligence gathering, cordon management or survivor management.

Mealag Lodge was now the location of a known terrorist incident. As such all three command centres would be headed by serving police officers but, given the idiosyncrasies of the British police force, the Chief Commissioner of Police for the Metropolis and Britain's highest-ranking police officer, can only advise a regional constabulary despite his superior rank, though any local commander would be wise to listen to the advice and be ready to explain, should the need arise, why he had ignored it. As Manders was briefing his team Sir Neil Roberts was in touch with Peter Duncan, the Northern Area Commander with a reputation for plain-speaking and fierce independence. Usually it is obvious who will head the command centres, but Roberts had voiced concern as to the expertise of some of Duncan's subordinates. All, of course, had received anti-terrorist training and would have passed the demanding training courses in order to be able to act as commander but the Scottish Highlands was not noted for its experience of such serious crime. The word Roberts used to Duncan about the current plot was "challenging".

"Sir, I do of course concede that my two local senior officers, Maythorp and Curry, would not previously have encountered anything on the scale of this outrage, but they have enormous local knowledge and are excellent men. I am not sure if you are aware of the particular area, Chief Commissioner, but that knowledge will be absolutely vital."

Roberts did not know the area.

"Possibly then, Sir, you are worried because Maythorp only carries the rank of chief inspector, not that of commander?"

"Well, it had crossed my mind that given the sort of media exposure these events generate, it might be better for you to request someone of higher rank. I would be happy to facilitate that."

"Thank you, Sir, but with great respect it is not the number of flashes on the jacket that matter. Maythorp is our central area commander, despite having only the rank of chief inspector. He has passed every examination and been recommended for promotion several times, but he will not move outside of his beloved Highlands. It is not his ability that has curtailed his rank, but geography. Despite my personal recommendation, the last appointments review refused to raise his rank for the area he polices."

Roberts was rapidly realising that Duncan's reputation was well-deserved and he was determined not to let the persistent Scottish colleague dictate the command structure. Duncan, also, was becoming concerned at the nature of the conversation. He did not wish to risk a confrontation with the chief commissioner. Roberts mixed in important circles and Duncan was aware that a word dropped in the ear of someone in Whitehall could see him sent on assignment to head up the training of a fledgling police force in some goddam Third-World country that had recently converted to something approaching democracy. Not his idea of fun. Duncan was also cognisant of the longer-term implications of the situation. If he asked for another commander to come in and take over, Duncan himself would be Bronze or Silver commander, when he should rightly be Gold. That could have unfavourable repercussions in any subsequent grading review, but in any event, he reasoned, how would Maythorp and the northernmost constabulary ever receive recognition for higher rankings if he now declined the so called 'challenge' spoken of by Roberts? He had an idea.

"I shall, of course, take on the responsibility of Gold Command and for the reasons I have outlined, Keith Maythorp should head up Silver. John Curry should therefore be Bronze commander but perhaps the chief commissioner could spare a high-ranking ATU officer experienced in real front line situations to assist Curry. After all, Curry will be at the sharp end of all of this. It might be good for the press to know we put a top man there, alongside the expertise of the local chap." Duncan spoke firmly, but not arrogantly.

The chief commissioner smiled thinly, highly appreciative of Duncan's cool assessment of both the tactical situation and the wider political implications and responded positively, "Detective Superintendent Bill Ritson of the ATU would be ideal. He has a lot of knowledge of this case and prior to joining ATU was a highly experienced Serious Crimes officer here in the Met. I will ensure he is tasked with joining up with Curry as soon as practicable. Thank you for the suggestion, Peter." The Commissioner silkily replied, unruffled, charming.

Duncan lost no time in contacting Chief Inspector Keith Maythorp at Fort William, informing him that he would lead Silver command and be responsible for tactical decisions and that Inspector John Curry was to head Bronze command. Curry was therefore the operational Bronze commander, the man in charge on the ground, the man at the scene of the attack. Duncan left the mention of Ritson's appointment until the end of the brief conversation. There was no complaint from Maythorp.

The Home Secretary had already decided to chair the Cabinet

Office Briefing Room (COBR) unless the Prime Minister decided to intervene and do so himself. So far, he had declined. The COBR, sometimes referred to as Platinum command, role was to liaise closely with the Strategic Co-Ordination Group (SCG) headed by the Gold commander. The Home Secretary had gathered around him the chief commissioner of police, the heads of both MI5 and MI6, a senior representative from each of the remaining emergency and rescue services and a few trusted very senior civil servants. The Scottish Secretary from the UK government was in attendance and the Deputy First Minister from the devolved Scottish Government would be arriving within an hour. Two secretaries, whose role would be to ensure the huge white boards were written up with every development and time logged, plus some ancillary administrative help, completed the group. Urgency had been vital in setting up the command structures but it had still taken over an hour before all were in place.

The Emergency Support Unit (ESU) is area-based throughout Great Britain and is always on a high state of readiness to be deployed once Bronze and Silver command have identified what particular resources are required. The ESU principally aims to put in place as much technical support as is needed by the command structure and to provide quality and up-to-date intelligence. It is staffed mainly, but not exclusively, with police officers who have received highly specialised training in a particular function, discipline or skill, and can, in extremis, include experts from outside the force. ESU personnel can be rapidly brought together and carry with them a vast array of technical equipment, often utilising specially adapted vehicles. Their luggage varies according to requirements but routinely will include silent drills for boring through walls into which minute cameras and microphones can be placed enabling the police to see and hear exactly what is happening inside a barricaded or closed room. Mobile cameras, electronic jamming devices and a plethora of other sophisticated gadgetry can also be deployed, along with items such as computers, lighting and noise generators. Trained riot control officers, hostage negotiators, explosive experts and so on, can all be part of an ESU task force.

The TSG (Territorial Support Group) is the manpower

equivalent to the ESU, providing non-technical but highly experienced and specialist personnel that will routinely include qualified firearms officers. Like ESU, the TSG will be called by Bronze when needed. Both ESU and TSG travel to the scene of an incident in unmarked vans and cars, and it has often been assumed that the UK's world famous military SAS force is sometimes deployed at incidents under the guise of the police ESU and TSG units. The local ESU and TSG units were alerted within minutes of Mealag Lodge being identified and confirmed as the location of a terrorist attack.

Gold, Silver and Bronze commanders, and COBR, sit in specially designed and equipped rooms used for no other purpose but for an emergency. One of the very first tasks is to switch on the monitors and sound equipment so that whenever the ESU can supply the link to an incident site, the command centres are ready to receive it. Curry, with a few officers, took over the Eagles Rest Hotel and declared the Bronze command centre operational at 1:45pm. On the way to the hotel, he called in the area ESU with his initial assessment of his requirements. Some travelled at full speed by vehicle from Inverness to the hotel, where they began setting up their satellite broadcasting equipment, whilst the remainder were forming and obtaining other necessities. A helicopter equipped with a surveillance camera and long-range microphones was also despatched. TSG officers started to arrive an hour later. Initially they made the hotel fully secure and safe, clearing it of residents, but later TSG would assist with any possible attack on the terrorists. It was 3pm.

The delay frustrated Curry. As with all commanders faced with the awesome responsibility of dealing with an outrage, he needed quality information and resources. His limited forces were gradually mobilising, but he was desperate for more manpower. Had the incident occurred in a large city, officers for things like traffic management and control could fairly easily be found, but the Scottish Highlands were thinly resourced and geographically were a long way from the big metropolitan forces. Curry did what he could. He set up a road block at the A87 Kinloch Hourn road junction and ensured that the Skye bridge at the Kyle was also closed and blocked. As other traffic units raced to the area, he was able to seal off more roads, limiting and finally closing potential vehicular escape routes. He decided not to risk sending Greaves, or anyone else, along the dam road until he had further intelligence and increased specialist support at his disposal.

71

Cindy and Paulette were so dazed and shocked, it was several minutes before either one of them spoke.

"Can you get free?" Cindy asked.

"No. The straps are too tight, what about you?"

"The same. We must keep trying, though." They struggled to pull themselves free, but the strong nylon restraints dug deep into their flesh and hurt their wrists. Exhaustion and despair gradually overtook them and Paulette was becoming tearful and ever more worried about her husband.

"We must do something, we must. They will kill him, I know they will. Cindy, help me. Please help me," she blurted out amid her sobbing.

Cindy wanted to help but she was unable to move either.

"The woman said that it was not their intention to hurt Dean. We have to trust her. She helped us and had no reason to lie."

Cindy tried to reassure her friend, but inwardly was not confident. Whichever way she looked at it, she and her friends had got caught up in a major terrorist plot and her own experience of being frightened and alone in the dusty swirl after the bomb went off in the train, kept flashing back into her mind. The women began to shout out for help, they painfully tried to lift themselves up, raising the chairs before sitting back on them trying to bang them on the stone floor, but no one heard and no one came.

"Margaret and Sandy might come back soon, let's hope so" said Cindy.

"What time were they planning to return? asked an anxious Paulette.

"About five, but they may be back sooner," Again Cindy tried to inject a positive note, but Paulette started to cry again.

"That will be too late." Her simple words needed no answer. Both women looked at each other and eventually leant back in their chairs, once more defeated and bereft of any ideas.

★ ★ ★

"Have we gotta take this deer all the way down the hill?" Josh Atkins was not accustomed to carrying much weight and the dead beast, albeit shared by his three companions, was causing him to be out of breath.

"I was thinking the same Gordon." Dean Assiter, the eldest of the four clearly needed a rest and they agreed to stop a while. They lowered the deer onto the ground and the four quickly sat back and relaxed on the stubby, wet grass. Mattar and Bagheri were waiting in the tunnel entrance and, as time passed without the shooting party showing, became increasingly anxious.

"Nasra, come in Nasra," whispered Bagheri into his radio.

"You are very faint, I can hardly hear you. Over"

"Can you see them? They have not arrived, yet they should be here by now."

"No. Maybe they have gone a different way."

"We are in the tunnel and we cannot see them, but if we come out at the same time as they appear we will be in real trouble."

Fadyar interrupted, "This is Fadyar. You will all stay where you are until I say so. Do not break your cover."

"Understood. Out."

Five more minutes passed and then distant voices slowly descending the hill were heard by Bagheri, who inched back into the dark recess of the tunnel. Mattar leant up close to the iron grille barred entrance and eyed their quarry, slowly coming into better view.

"An agent is first then Truscott, then Assiter and then an agent at the rear. This is good. As they are carrying the animal, they will not be able to react quickly and raise their weapons. You take the one at the rear, I will deal with those at the front," Mattar started to unleash his grenade from his belt as he spoke.

Oblivious to the danger awaiting them, Assiter's party continued their descent unaware that every step took them a moment nearer their death. As soon as they were level with the tunnel entrance, Mattar threw open the gate, pulled out the firing pin on the grenade and threw it at the feet of Atkins, the agent at the front. The blast killed him outright and Gordon was hurled clean off his feet, landing unconscious twenty feet away. The animal trussed to the pole dropped to the floor, and as Chuck Drew went for his automatic, he was hit by a hail of sub-machine gun fire from Bagheri's Israeli made Galatz. Bagheri had loaded the detachable magazine to its capacity of twenty rounds of 0.308 calibre bullets and half were discharged with frightening force and accuracy into Drew's body and head, his protective vest proving totally inadequate for such a close range and high-powered onslaught.

Assiter yelled "Don't shoot, don't shoot" and held his arms aloft.

Saying nothing, his two assailants quickly held him and removed his rifle, throwing it onto the ground. Bagheri and Mattar each grabbed Assiter by an arm, and half ran, half marched him down the hill where Khan met up with them.

"Well done my brothers, well done. Praise be to Allah."

An excited Khan switched on the radio, "Success, Fadyar, success. We are on our way."

"Excellent. Out."

Fadyar started up the Land Rover and turned it around to face in the direction of Kinloch Hourn.

"What do you want? Who are you?" Assiter gasped out the questions between taking large gulps of air, struggling for breath as he was pulled, half stumbling, down the hill.

"No questions," retorted Bagheri. "Do as we say and you will not be hurt."

The group soon reached the road and the waiting Fadyar. She handcuffed Assiter using some of the nylon straps left by Donaldson and the struggling US Secretary of State was bundled into the rear of the Land Rover, quickly followed by Khan. Mattar jumped into the driver's seat and Fadyar into the seat beside him just as Bronze commander, Curry, made a fateful wrong decision and issued orders to a police traffic observation helicopter. Curry's urgent briefing to the pilot was totally inadequate merely telling him to fly along the Kinloch Hourn road and over the Mealag area on a reconnaissance mission. He needed information quickly, and impatiently exercised his operational command prior to awaiting the arrival of all his specialist units.

72

Paulette Assiter was slowly recovering from her ordeal. The bleeding from her swollen lip had stopped and she was telling herself how much worse it would have been had the foreign woman not intervened. She shivered as she remembered the steely look in Donaldson's eyes as he removed her robe and fondled her breasts. She started to recall the morning's events in more detail and particularly the indignities he inflicted on Cindy.

"Did, did, that horrid man hurt you? I'm sorry Cindy, I should have asked long before now. Are you alright?"

"Yes, I think so." she lied. "I'm sore and bruised, but he was shot just before... he... Thank God." Cindy found it hard to speak of the traumatic experience and started to cry. The ordeal had left her stunned and she also felt ashamed of herself for not putting up more resistance. She kept recalling the morning she had a coffee with Donaldson that had seemed to trigger his assault on her. *Had she been provocative? Should she have changed out of those stretch jeans and that old T-shirt? Was she flirting with him?* She was beginning to doubt herself. Maybe she was to blame and said as much to Paulette.

"No, Cindy. You were not to blame for that... that animal. You did nothing wrong. That woman said he had done terrible things before."

She had forgotten all about what Fadyar had said, and Paulette's words immediately lifted Cindy' spirits.

"Thank you Paulette, but what about you? He hurt you."

"It was only a bit harder than my first encounters with the boys at school. You know, all grab!"

Cindy laughed and then the two of them giggled uncontrollably for several minutes, releasing their tensions. Suddenly Paulette became serious.

"The knife, Cindy. What happened to his knife? The woman didn't have it when she left and I don't remember him holding onto it? Where is it?" Paulette's recollections were proving invaluable.

"You're right! Yes. It might still be here, somewhere." Cindy was now looking about her, straining at the bindings fixing her to the chair.

"It must have dropped on the floor, must have."

Cindy started rocking her chair back and forth until it crashed onto its side, taking Cindy with it.

"Ouch. That bloody well hurt," swore Cindy, but she immediately started manoeuvring across the wet floor using her body to provide the propulsion. As she rounded the table she shouted, "I can see it, it's near to the Aga. He must have dropped it when he hurled the kettle at the woman".

She worked her way over to the stove.

Slowly and painstakingly, she turned the handle of the knife so she could hold it firmly in her hand and she then wriggled her way back to where Paulette was still seated.

"I can't uncut my own straps but I may be able to do yours" Cindy called out.

Carefully, she slid her body so that the hand holding the knife was adjacent to Paulette's right leg. Cindy slipped the knife under the plastic and gently pushed it further forward. The lethally sharp blade instantly cut the tightened nylon strap. She repeated the process for Paulette's left leg and then Paulette was able to move herself easily to where Cindy could cut one of the bonds restraining her wrist. It took less than a minute for both women to be free. They stood up and hugged and kissed each other, tears of joy and relief spreading down their cheeks.

After a few brief moments Cindy said, "Come on. We must get dressed and warn the others."

She picked up the phone, but the line was dead. She then hit the panic alarm, but that too failed to sound.

"Damn. Everything has been knocked out, Paulette. We'll have to go across the loch."

The two had never dressed themselves so quickly. In less than five minutes, Paulette appeared in practical blue jeans and a green sweater having washed away most of the spattered blood from her hair, face and body. Likewise, Cindy had dashed under the shower to thoroughly cleanse her body of Donaldson's odour and removed all traces of his unwelcome intrusion into her body. She too donned a pair of blue jeans, but her top was a hand knitted roll-neck yellow jumper given to her by Mrs MacLean.

They grabbed their anoraks and boots and rushed outside towards the jetty, giving only a momentary glance at the obviously fatally wounded protection officer, as they ran passed by his body.

When they saw that the boat had gone, Cindy called out to Paulette, "Come on, follow me, but don't stray from my footmarks."

She started running towards the dam, making sure that Paulette was closely behind her and staying on the solid ground. As the women rounded the knoll, they were startled by the sight of Donaldson, still alive, and up to his shoulders in the peat bog.

"Help me, Cindy. Please help. I can't move," he wailed weakly.

The pressure on Donaldson's body exerted by the heavy, wet peat had slowed his bleeding, but he was surely and steadily sinking into the deep morass.

"You bloody bastard. That marsh will be your slimy grave. You'll die there and I hope you sink very, very slowly and go to hell." Cindy's anger exploded into venom as she shouted out the words.

"Are you sure he will die, Cindy? He will drown won't he?" Paulette asked nervously.

"Yes. Absolutely, he will."

"Cindy, please. You can't do this. Surely you can't leave me to die, helpless like this?" but Cindy was already hastening onwards to the dam.

"If you won't help, then can you at least tell the police to come and rescue me? Please." Donaldson was desperate. Even the act of talking slightly disturbed the peat enveloping him and had made him sink a further inch.

Cindy turned and shouted, "Jack. I'll give you some good advice. Give that tiny dick you think so much of a rub from me. You'll drown quicker, you bastard." Cindy could not resist mocking the helpless Donaldson and laughed out loud as his face visibly reddened in silent fury.

They reached the dam wall and had just started to run across when the Land Rover, parked on the road opposite them revved up and sped away towards Kinloch Hourn.

"Was that them, Cindy? Did you see Dean or Gordon?"

"I couldn't tell who it was. It might have been the woman or whoever she is with, but it's been a long time since she left us."

A loud regular thudding noise caused them to stop running and to look back across the loch towards the lodge. A small helicopter flying very low and with POLICE markings clearly visible came into view. The women waved their arms excitedly and as the helicopter turned west, the male pilot waved back. He was already transmitting on his radio that he had spotted two females on the dam wall waving at him and that all appeared normal. He was accustomed to members of the public gesturing and signalling as he flew low; there was nothing unusual about it, and a couple of women on their own walking across the dam wall did not arouse his suspicion. Several seconds later, he received information that the dam wall was supposed to be guarded and that no one should therefore be able to walk across it. He was ordered to return to base, the full realisation of the possible consequences of the rushed deployment of the helicopter pilot having become apparent to everyone at Bronze, Silver and Gold commands. It was too late. Immediately after receiving the message, the inadequately briefed pilot began to turn the helicopter around when he spotted a Land Rover travelling along the road. He throttled back, trying to keep the vehicle in view, and reached for the radio switch. Fadyar had noticed the helicopter as it crossed the dam and asked Mattar to stop. She gathered and loaded her trusted rifle, lowered the window and took aim, just as the pilot was about to report. Two massive thuds rocked the helicopter, tearing its skin apart. Fadyar had deliberately aimed her first bullet at the engine block, which on impact shattered into several pieces before exploding, flinging blackened shards of metal in all directions that fell to the ground like confetti thrown at a wedding. The second bullet was aimed at the cockpit. It missed the pilot but ripped through the electronics and short-circuited all the electrics.

The pilot's only words that he managed to relay before the inevitable crash were "I'm hit. Vehicle... "

Devoid of power and leaving a thick black smoke trail, the helicopter spiralled wildly downwards hitting the loch. Large chunks of aluminium, steel and plastic were thrown into the air as the impact broke the helicopter apart. What was left, disappeared into the depths of the loch within seconds, the pilot still strapped to his seat as the water gushed over him. The early loss of a police helicopter and pilot in such inauspicious circumstances forced Maythorp to call Curry and order him to await Ritson's arrival before embarking on any further major initiatives. He should continue to deploy his resources, but unless forced he should not take precipitate action to engage the terrorists until Silver had sufficient intelligence and an adequate plan. Curry's impatience at not awaiting a specialist helicopter to be readied for action, allied with the totally inadequate briefing given to the pilot, had clearly played a major part in what was already being regarded as the unnecessary death of a police officer.

Cindy and Paulette saw the downing of the helicopter. For a few seconds neither spoke, the realisation of the gravity of their situation and that of their respective partners temporarily silencing them. They reached the road and looked about them. Seeing nothing, Cindy said "They cannot all be in the Land Rover, there isn't room. Perhaps some are injured up the hill. Come on."

She started walking and it was not long before they came across the macabre aftermath of the Mattar and Bagheri attack. Blood and body tissue was strewn in a roughly-shaped circle in the centre of which was a dead deer, its feet still neatly bound to a wooden pole but whose flesh had been torn to shreds in parts. The sight resembled more some sort of ritual killing than a kidnap. Cindy searched for Gordon and burst into tears when she spotted him prone on the ground, but at least not cut to pieces by a grenade or high velocity bullets. She ran and cradled him in her arms. Gordon started to mumble incoherently as he recovered consciousness and Cindy burst out, "You're alive. Darling, you're alive," and hugged him closer.

"They have taken Dean. He isn't here." It was a tearful Paulette that focused Cindy's mind back to the general situation. As Gordon recovered, he confirmed he must have been knocked out by the blast but he was otherwise unhurt. He quickly surveyed the carnage that lay spread on the ground before them and reflected how in an instant lives and circumstances change. A few moments earlier he had been talking and laughing with the two CIA agents both of whom now lay dead, mown down by fanatics intent on taking hostage his friend Dean Assiter. By nature Gordon was not easily angered, but he was now furious at the outrage that had been committed upon them all.

"Gather up the agents sub-machine guns and all magazines; we have to go after whoever did this. I know it's not pleasant, but we must do it." He spoke firmly, assuredly confident that he was doing the right thing.

As they hastened down the hill, Cindy tried to tell Gordon all that had happened but skirted over the trouble with Donaldson.

"I'll tell you more of that later," she said to him. "How can we rescue Dean?" Gordon did not reply. Instead, overloaded with miscellaneous thoughts, he asked a question of his own, "Did you not raise the alarm?" Gordon asked.

"Everything was severed at the house, nothing worked." Cindy replied.

"What about the garages? Have you been there? That alarm is on a different circuit."

"God, I'm sorry. I forgot. No, I was so worried about finding you, but a Police helicopter came over and has just been shot down, so they know something is happening here."

They exchanged more information as they headed off the hill towards the garages. As soon as they were inside, Gordon triggered the alarm. The warning was received at both Fort Augustus and Fort William and less than a minute later the scribes in Gold, Silver and Bronze command centres were logging their whiteboards, noting the time and location of the alarm. The Home Secretary and COBR were informed, the alarm being regarded by Gold as a highly significant development.

"Cindy, are you quite sure they headed towards Kinloch Hourn?" Gordon queried.

"Positive."

"In that case, we must go too. The police will wait at the main A87 junction and travel slowly towards the dam expecting to run headlong into the terrorists. They will not be expecting them to go to Kinloch Hourn. They must have a boat there."

As he spoke, he pressed furiously at the digits on his mobile phone, before putting it back into his pocket. "Damn these mobiles. That's another reason to go West. There's a signal at the coast."

Gordon knew that taking a vehicle from the garages and then driving along the tortuous Kinloch Hourn road would necessitate him having to drive slowly. As the road wound its way around the bases of several large mountains, it was also a considerably longer route than going straight down the loch itself. The three ran to the small jetty where the boats were tied up.

"Take the mini cruiser, its faster" yelled Gordon.

They jumped aboard and Gordon pushed the accelerator lever fully forward once he had reversed out into safe water. The engine roared as the throttle widened and the small boat's bow rose up causing a large wake to spread across the loch, scattering the few black-headed divers that were patiently waiting for their meal of a small trout or eel to swim by beneath them.

73

Maythorp and Curry had been discussing the tactical situation. A substantial amount of equipment had already arrived or was nearing its deployment at the hotel. The full complement of electronic resources they required was at least twenty minutes away and it would be some considerable while before the substantial reinforcements of men arrived. However, a lot of equipment was now on site and being installed. The TSG would have to travel from Glasgow and possibly Edinburgh, but the commanders agreed to send two police vehicles, each with four fully armed officers, to drive slowly along the Kinloch Hourn road, keeping one hundred metres apart, until they reached the dam. The convoy was given orders that if the terrorists had not been intercepted they were to set up a road block whilst three officers secured the dam wall access. They were not permitted to cross the dam to the lodge. One vehicle only was permitted to drive slowly along the road towards Kinloch Hourn, but not to intercept or engage the targets unless it was to protect themselves. If they saw anything they were to stay at a safe distance and report it. Another two vehicles of four armed officers each were despatched urgently to enter Mealag Lodge by the Arkaig entrance. There were to be no heroics. If the lodge was occupied by terrorists they were to report back and retreat, setting up road blocks to prevent escape. An ESU unit was readied to be sent to the lodge in case the terrorists were holed up there. If it was unoccupied, and the entire complex could be safely secured, the helipad was to be made ready for a specially equipped helicopter.

Eagles Rest now scarcely resembled a hostelry. Various assorted vehicles, cars, vans and trucks were steadily arriving. One disgorged twelve specially trained and well-armed officers whilst another carried a vast amount of weird looking electronic equipment. Two satellite dishes had been erected; one, a couple of metres high, was affixed to a pole that had been rather unceremoniously banged into the lovingly manicured lawn. The other sat aloft an innocuous looking van, which was slowly making its way around the car park. Inside the hotel, perched in front of a box of electronics that included a monitor from which a green light glowed brightly, was an operative waiting to pick up the signal from the van. As soon he did so, he called out "OK" and the van stopped.

"Full comms and video working whenever it's needed," the operative called out; his message logged and timed, noted by Curry and Maythorp, as it was written up in front of them. Maythorp had also requested a police launch, with armed officers, be sent by sea towards Kinloch Hourn. He was informed it was berthed at Arisaig, where a couple of nights before it had been used to intercept a minor drug running operation organised by local youths from the mainland and the Isle of Skye. The boat was presently moored at least twenty miles away from Kinloch Hourn and its crew of officers were now in Glasgow having escorted the miscreants there the previous day and was therefore discounted by Curry and Maythorp as offering viable assistance. However, as a further precaution the Royal Navy fisheries protection vessel, currently patrolling off the Isle of Rhum, was placed on alert in case the terrorists had a powerful sea going boat moored offshore near Kinloch Hourn. On receiving the signal, Captain Harris of HMS Varsity immediately ordered a change of direction and full speed.

Gold command agreed with Silver that the Special Air Service (SAS) at Hereford be put on alert and provided with all maps and drawings of Mealag Lodge, the estate and surroundings, just in case a serious hostage situation developed there and needed their expertise and intervention. The receiving stations at Menwith Hill and Morwenstow, plus personnel at GCHQ, were tasked with two immediate specific roles. One was to intercept all telephone traffic, electronic signal or other communication emanating from an area of twenty-five square kilometres from grid reference NH0701502488 and to also search their archives for any intercepts as and when names or details became known as the incident unfolded. The significance of the alarm triggered at the garages was actively being considered by several advisers within Silver command, who were liaising by telephone with Curry's deputy at Bronze. The benefit of such a command structure is that calm, rational evaluation leading to better judgement can be made by persons distanced from the pressures of operational minute-by-minute decision taking. Additionally, by virtue of being more remote Silver was totally free of bias and not influenced by the high levels of adrenalin surging through Bronze's veins. Curry was passed a note. On it was Silver's assessment of the current position:-

The alarm proves at least one person is alive.

That person is likely to be an occupant of Mealag Lodge.

The two women seen on the dam wall should be found. Their identities are probably that of Paulette Assiter and Cindy Crossland.

Highly improbable any terrorists are in the vicinity of the garages.

Silver recommend early deployment to garages.

If garages are secured and no visible sign of terrorists consider using any boats at jetty to cross to Mealag Lodge, or use the dam.

Curry read the note and immediately ordered the vehicles slowly making their way to the dam to increase speed and to go to the garages and report. He glanced at the white-board slightly to his left and read the constantly updated status of his resources and their deployment. Directly in front of him was a projected map of the area on which markers had been placed for ease of visually identifying where those resources were located, and at some point, when known, would show where the terrorists were. A computer operator had responsibility for the map generation and projection, electronics having superseded the once laborious manual task. Curry checked the location of the road blocks. He would like to have more but with his current manpower, that was simply not possible. The Bronze commander felt he ought to be doing something, anything, and subconsciously began to whistle a favourite tune whilst he waited for more information.

74

The weather continued to slowly deteriorate. The cloud thickened and Mattar, driving in and out of the mist, had to use the intermittent setting on his windscreen wipers to maintain his visibility. He was about to embark on the most hazardous road journey he had ever undertaken and he, and his compatriots, were fully aware of the danger they faced. He had driven as fast as he was able on the winding road and reached a point where a mile-long finger of the loch passed under a road bridge. This pushed due north whilst the main loch continued its vast spread west towards Kinloch Hourn. Just past the bridge, he swung the vehicle hard right and off the road, progressing along a track that followed the contours of the long inlet. After a few minutes, he turned sharply left and started to climb the massive and dangerous Sgurr a Mhoaraich mountain.

He momentarily stopped the vehicle and engaged four-wheel drive and the low ratio setting for the gears. The powerful Land Rover had made this journey once before, but then Mattar was the only occupant. He was not concerned as to whether the vehicle could climb the unmarked track – he knew it had sufficient power, but he was worried about the grip of the tyres on the uneven, wet grass that was littered with scree and boulders washed down by the torrential rains of numerous winters. The passage, since to describe it as a track was a gross overstatement of its quality, had shown no signs of it having been used for decades and it was only his sharp eyes on their reconnaissance earlier in the year that noticed the slight indentation that ran along the middle of the mountain. At some time, but probably not for a hundred years and never by a vehicle other than Mattar's, the pathway had been used, but Mattar had no time to speculate upon why. At times, the nearside tyres came close to slipping off the edge, and at others it took all his skill to steer the vehicle around the rocks without making heavy contact with the mountain on his offside. As it was, the additional people in the vehicle and full fuel load had made it heavier and therefore slightly compressed its tough suspension system and he regretted not ensuring they had hired a vehicle that had been fitted with an axle clearance height adjustment. At times the sound of rocks hitting the underside of the vehicle alarmed him, but he did not let his fear show. The engine and low gears made a deafening noise inside the Land Rover as it ground its way onwards across the face of the mountain; going in and out of cloud with Mattar wildly turning the steering wheel full lock one way and then the other. The tyres spun, slipped and created deep channels of mud but somehow Mattar kept the vehicle going forward, even if it was haphazardly so at times. It was a highly accomplished piece of true off-road driving and in other circumstances would have been much admired and no doubt earned him, and his tough vehicle, well-deserved accolades. As it was no one, other than his silent and ashen-faced passengers, was a witness to his prowess. Or so he thought.

"Can you see anything of them?" Gordon shouted to Cindy above the roar of the boat's exhaust and the noise of the wake rushing past them as the craft split apart the calm water. Cindy had his powerful field glasses pressed to her eyes and was searching for anything that might reveal Fadyar's whereabouts.

"Not a thing. I don't think they are on the road. Of course it isn't always in view, but I should have thought by now we would have spotted them. Maybe they are already at Kinloch Hourn."

"Mmmm. Maybe, but it's a long, slow road. Here, take the wheel. Keep us headed straight down the loch and pass the glasses to me." Gordon briefly gave her a quick kiss as she handed them to him. He surveyed the road for several minutes and confirmed that she was correct.

"They're definitely not on the road."

More out of curiosity than hope, he started surveying the Munro to his right. The cloud was fairly low down on the hill but suddenly, almost as if appearing out of nowhere, he saw them.

"I've got them. They're on the mountain! My God, the bloody mountain! That's some feat. There isn't even a track there. I've walked every inch of that hill deerstalking and there is definitely no road or track. Some of the locals tell the tale that a century ago a few cattle drovers used that hill as a means of getting their beasts to Glenelg, but is wasn't used much even then as easier passages were found. There must be a hell of a driver at the wheel of that 4x4, the whole area is littered with rocks, loose gravel and scree – to say nothing of the slope itself that he's on."

After his initial euphoria the realisation that the vehicle was not going to Kinloch Hourn struck him. He turned and in a sombre voice spoke to Paulette. "Paulette, almost certainly they have Dean. The fact that they did not kill him at the dam is a good sign, and from what Cindy and you have said that is not their intention anyway. But the bad news is I really have no idea where they can be headed. If they are prepared to risk their lives by driving along the side of the mountain, they must have worked out some sort of route off it, or have something else planned, but what and where? There is nothing in those hills where they can rest up or hide, not even a shelter."

"What do you think we can do then, Gordon?" a nervous Paulette replied. Gordon did not immediately answer, but when he did his reply surprised them.

"They will not be going to Kinloch Hourn. They would have used the road or a boat if that were the case. They may be going to try and get through the hills to somewhere along the main A87 or they may be able to get through the mountains to somewhere beyond Kinloch Hourn, like Corran or Arnisdale."

The trio were silent for a few minutes, deep in their own thoughts.

"What would you do, Gordon – if you were them?" Cindy asked.

"The group who have captured Dean are obviously very skilled and also ruthless. This is not a back of a fag packet operation. It had to be well planned and resourced. Even when unexpected things occur, they remain focused on their task and carry it out with deadly efficiency. Driving on that mountain is what convinces me they will not do the obvious thing and head for the A87. My bet is they have found a way to traverse the next mountain and will come off it somewhere close to Corran or Arnisdale. Corran probably, as it's nearer, and from there they will either have a boat waiting at the coast or drive along the road probably to Skye. Of course they were not expecting anyone to spot them on the mountains."

"Can we stop them?" enquired Paulette.

Gordon laughed. "I don't think *we* can stop them, Paulette. These are professionals and fully armed. All we can do is call the police when we get a damned signal on this phone."

"But we brought all those guns. Surely we can delay them from taking Dean?" persisted Paulettte.

Before he could reply, Cindy spoke, "I thought you had another boat at Kinloch Hourn. Can't we at least use that to see if we spot them at Corran, or wherever?" Cindy was thinking of her friend Paulette, worried, and now sitting in silence nervously tapping her impeccably manicured fingernails on the side panelling of the boat. "At least if we spot them we might be able to tell the police," implored Cindy, who wanted to do all she could to help her friend.

"I suppose there is no harm in that. OK. We'll use the *Greek Dancer.*"

"Is that its name?" giggled Cindy "Don't tell me now, later. But it sounds as if there is a story there!"

"There is, or more accurately, was," a sombre Gordon retorted.

75

Ritson arrived at Inverness Airport and was soon speeding under escort towards Corach. Curry was anxious to receive information of the terrorists' whereabouts and was pacing around the eerily quiet room.

"Where are they? Where are they?" he muttered to himself, but his voice still sounded loud as it broke the silence.

Soon the centre would become a frantic, but disciplined, noisy hub of people talking or writing, phones ringing, pictures bouncing off walls, speakers blaring – but not yet. This was the quiet before the storm. He had hoped that the gang would have been sighted by one of the road blocks established at several key points along the A87, the A887 the A82 and at the Skye (Kyle) Bridge, but he did not yet have the resources to block off every exit from every major road and so had allocated his resources where they could be the most effective.

Many roads that led from the major trunk routes were either long cul-de-sacs (like the Kinloch Hourn road) or simply went in a large semi-circle returning to the major route several miles farther along the highway. These roads were not blocked. Also, as there was no road beyond Kinloch Hourn, Curry did not position any road blocks or patrols along the Glenelg Road, reasoning that the terrorists could not reach there. He had received confirmation that the specially equipped helicopter with camera and an armed crew was only a matter of minutes away.

His yellow phone rang. An officer reported in that Mealag Lodge was secured but it was evident that some sort of struggle had occurred. Blood was spattered onto clothing and around the kitchen. A window was broken, apparently shot through by a high velocity bullet and plastic ties used for handcuffs were scattered onto the kitchen table and floor. The personnel had left in a hurry. Blood spattered bathing robes and a large hunting knife were strewn across the floor and no attempt had been made to secure the property. The phone line and alarm systems had been rendered inoperable. Worse, two SP officers were found dead in close proximity to the lodge, and the search was continuing for other casualties but none was so far apparent. Footprints leading to the loch would indicate that someone may have tried to escape and drowned in a peat bog. The area was being sealed as a crime scene pending detailed forensic examination. The helipad could be used, if required. Realising that little more was likely to be achieved at Mealag in the short-term, Curry recalled most of the officers, leaving two on armed guard.

Even for the experienced police officers and specialist personnel in the three command centres the reports which were being instantly relayed to them, were chilling. It was unusual that terrorists and civilian personnel were missing from a scene, leaving only the murdered special protection officers. Bronze Command started to get busy, and the phones on Curry's desk started ringing. Silver gave an updated assessment that several hostages had probably been taken. The red phone bleeped and an aide answered; the Westland helicopter was only a minute away. The green phone again: Silver once more. Gold had ordered no concessions if terrorists and hostages located. Gold had also sanctioned a shoot to kill policy in the light of the terrorists having already committed murder. Curry heard the rhythmic beat of the helicopter rotor blades as it passed overhead, on its way to scour the loch area. Minutes later, more phones were ringing and more reports, all being written up, almost verbatim, by the shorthand note takers and in précis form by the small team in charge of the whiteboards. The latest entries concerned the garages which had provided additional evidence that someone had left in hurry, its two large doors were swinging open in the breeze and the alarm was sounding but no one was present. A cursory examination around the area had not revealed any bodies and there was no sign of blood. At the Bronze control room a voice came through one of the powerful side speakers hanging by a nail that ESU had recently banged into a wall.

"This is Sky 1. Are you receiving?"

Curry was shown a microphone amongst the vast array of equipment now on his desk and switched it on, "Bronze here, receiving loud and clear."

The helicopter radio operator wasted no time, "Sky 1 here. We can see at least two bodies halfway up the mountain beside the dam. There may be more. Wait. Now a third. Suggest you send a team up or do you want us to winch down? Over."

"Bronze here. We are seeing everything from the camera. Continue flying due west to Kinloch Hourn. We believe that is where target is headed. Follow the road. Do not intercept if sighted and keep out of rifle range. We believe they have at least one high velocity weapon. Over."

"Understood. Out."

Curry dispatched some officers to go up the mountain. As the road was secured and safe, he also sent two ambulances but didn't believe their life-saving equipment would be needed. He was passed a scribbled note. Ritson had arrived and was being briefed in an ante room. Curry rather resented the presence of someone from London sitting on his shoulder but he had to admit, even to himself, that the Met had a lot more experience at handling these situations than he possessed.

He smiled broadly and held out his hand as Ritson entered, "Welcome to Bronze. I understand you've been fully briefed. Anything else you need to know?" He beckoned Ritson to sit beside him.

As he slid easily into the chair Ritson replied, "No, thanks. Its John, isn't it? I'm Bill."

The informality surprised Curry and immediately he felt more at ease. At least the guy didn't appear to swagger about, full of his own self-importance. The two sat back, eagerly watching the monitor pictures emanating from Sky 1. The black, incoming land line telephone on Curry's desk rang and he and Ritson looked at one and other each unsure who should answer.

Curry laughed, and said, "You answer. It's patched through into the loudspeakers anyway"

"Sir, we have caller on the line. Name of Truscott. Says it is to do with Mealag Lodge."

"Good God. Put him through immediately." Ritson said, looking at Curry.

★ ★ ★

Gordon, Cindy and Paulette quickly tied up the boat at the head of the loch and ran as fast as they could the three quarters of a mile to Kinloch Hourn. They saw no one, and rushed to remove the protective canopy tarpaulin covering *Greek Dancer* and slipped the mooring ropes. Crime was unknown in such a small community and Gordon had no qualms about leaving its spare ignition key in a galley drawer. The powerful inboard Volvo engines burst into life at the first press of the electronic starter and Gordon pushed forward on the twin control levers. As he neared the open sea, his mobile flickered into life and the signal bars appeared. Holding the steering wheel with one hand and beckoning Cindy to help him by also taking hold of the large chromed spoke wheel, he pressed 999.

"Emergency. Which service do you require?" a female voice.

Gordon quickly managed to convey a degree of urgency into the operator who dispensed with some of the usual formalities, though insisting that Gordon provide his name and location. Her experience of recognising someone genuine and in trouble was considerable and as the man who called was asking for Chief Inspector Keith Maythorp by name, and also mentioning Mealag Lodge, she transferred the call to her duty supervisor who immediately looked up Maythorp. The computer told him of a suspected terrorist attack and that Maythorp was currently active on that assignment. He wasted no time in making contact with Fort William who instantly patched the call through to Bronze Command, not to Maythorp at Silver.

A breathless sounding Gordon started speaking excitedly down the phone. My name is Gordon Truscott. I own Mealag Lodge. We have been the victims of a terrorist attack. Several officers have been killed. We are… "

Ritson interrupted. In a very calm voice he said, "First things first Mr Truscott, I would prefer to call you Gordon. My name is Bill and we know of the incident. We are currently in pursuit of those responsible. We have considerable resources already deployed. Are you alone and are you hurt?"

"No. Yes. I mean I have my partner Cindy Crossland with me and Paulette Assiter the wife of the US Secretary of State. We are basically unharmed. The terrorists though have taken Dean." Gordon was still having an adrenalin rush.

"You say 'taken', Gordon. Do you know if Mr Assiter is hurt or where his captors are headed?"

"I don't believe he will be hurt. They told Cindy they would not harm him, but take him hostage. We are in a forty foot cabin cruiser, with a black hull and white stripe, heading out of Kinloch Hourn. There is no sign of the terrorists here, but they escaped by going over the mountains towards the coast. The clouds prevented me from keeping them in our sight."

Ritson remained poised, despite the fact that he wanted to ask a hundred questions, he knew that others would already be acting on the information being blurted out from the loudspeakers.

"Can you remember what type of vehicle they had?"

"No. But it had to be a bloody good 4x4. They took a most dangerous route that is not even marked on any map I know of. The driver must be highly skilled, especially in this weather."

"Do you know how many of them there are, Gordon?"

Gordon hadn't considered this until Ritson posed the question. He looked at Cindy and Paulette.

"There was a woman according to Cindy, and there were two men who attacked us on the hill when they killed the US agents. So at least three, possibly more, but there cannot be many unless they have help elsewhere. The escape vehicle wasn't huge, it couldn't be to drive on that mountain."

"What you are telling us is excellent Gordon. Can you give us any more information? We have a helicopter in the vicinity, can you see that?"

"No, I can't. The woman is an excellent shot with a rifle though, Cindy has just told me. Oh, and the men have machine guns. Cindy thinks their vehicle might be a Jeep or Land Rover."

Ritson nodded to Curry. They knew a lot of this detail already from the initial reports at the various scenes of crime, but Truscott was providing vital additional intelligence.

"Gordon?"

"Yes"

"I would hate it if your mobile went dead on us. Do you have a radio on board in case we need it?"

"Yes, of course, I'll give you the details, but my phone should be OK. It's fully charged."

"Where are you headed now Gordon, and can I ask why?" Ritson was showing just how skilled he was at asking probing questions, designed to elicit maximum information.

"I'm heading west at the moment but then I shall turn and head towards Glenelg. The terrorists may come out onto the A876, but if not they have to come out onto the Glenelg road."

The name meant nothing to Ritson, but Curry animatedly pointed to the map where the operator immediately highlighted the small village and the road that runs through it. Ritson nodded, signifying he now understood.

"Gordon. Your help has been most invaluable. Can I suggest you now make your way back to Eagles Rest Hotel, which is where I am talking to you from. We can have you all checked out for injuries etc and you will be safe here. We have all the information we need now to track down these terrorists."

Gordon told his makeshift crew what Ritson had said. It was Paulette who reacted first, "No. No, Gordon we can't just abandon Dean. I want to see him. Please, don't give up now."

Ritson heard the plaintive cries of Paulette and raised his eyebrows at Curry.

"It will be best if you come back. I do not want any more casualties, Gordon. These people are extremely dangerous, please do not try and pursue them."

Gordon looked about the boat and at the faces of Cindy and Paulette. He also felt that having come this far, they should continue, but he was fearful as to what they could possibly achieve.

"Well, we've decided to motor on along the coast. If we see anything, how do I contact you again without going through all the emergency call centres?"

Ritson thought quickly. By giving out a direct line he was almost conceding that Gordon could proceed, and under no circumstances did he want them to become embroiled in something that might easily go out of control. On the other hand, he did not have any boat himself patrolling the coast as the police launch was still miles away and Gordon seemed determined to carry on with or without permission.

"I will give you a number, but I must stress to you that if you see anything you are to stay at a safe distance, at least 1000 metres, and report it. You are to remain in the boat at all times and not land until I give you the all-clear. Is that understood and agreed?"

"Yes. Agreed" said Gordon. Cindy suddenly motioned him to pass her the phone.

"This is Cindy Crossland. There is one thing you should know, because it is very important. The woman of the group saved my and Paulette's life this morning and that was nothing to do with their capture of Dean. She and her group did not kill the police at Mealag Lodge, only the ones on the hill next to the dam."

Ritson was stunned, as was Silver and Gold. For once, no one knew what to say.

It was Curry, who being somewhat detached from the conversation reacted first and replied to Cindy, "Hi. I'm John Curry from Fort William. Say hello to Gordon for me. Can you confirm precisely what happened at Mealag involving you and Paulette, and whether you know who killed the police there."

"I'm sorry" said Cindy, "but I can't... I really don't want to go into detail about this morning. We can talk later about that. It was totally separate from Dean's capture, but I can tell you that the man who attacked us and the police there was named Donaldson. He fled and drowned in the peat bog by the loch. The woman saved our lives."

"Thank you, Mrs Crossland. We will contact you or Gordon if we need any more information, but meanwhile please do not approach the kidnappers. They are clearly very ruthless."

"OK. Bye."

Curry turned to Ritson. "So we have two incidents now, though the one involving this Donaldson bloke at Mealag Lodge seems to be over, thank God. What about Truscott? Do you think he will stay in the boat if he sees those holding Assiter?"

"I hope so. He and his friends seem to have been through a lot already that we know of, and probably a lot more that we don't know. They must be shaken at the very least. The woman with him, Cindy Crossland is very level-headed and the profile we have of her suggests she is not someone to take unnecessary risks."

"The ATU know of her then?" Curry was intrigued.

"Another time for the detail. But yes, I have been on what has turned out to be this case for a long while, and we have quite a lot of knowledge on her and her ex-husband. I think I recall him having a driver named Donaldson," he paused, and absent-mindedly stroked his chin, "strange coincidence. Anyhow, let's focus on the kidnapping."

The loud speaker momentarily crackled and then a clear voice spoke, "This is Sky 1. Are you receiving?"

"Yes, Sky 1 go ahead."

"The cloud cover over the mountains is making it impossible for us to see anything clearly, even with the high intensity and thermal imaging cameras. The mountains are nearly 4,000 feet high and in these conditions it is too dangerous to fly between them, but you ordered us to stay at least at 3,000 feet due to the danger of potential incoming rifle fire. Do you have any fresh information?"

"Sky 1. Maintain your patrol along the A87 and immediate vicinity. Suspects are confirmed as travelling in a 4x4 across the mountains on an uncharted track. We do not know where they are headed, but presume the A87. They have to come off the mountain soon."

76

Mattar was making excellent progress, his skill evident to all his passengers including Assiter. The ground became less rocky as he descended towards the coast enabling him to increase speed. Fadyar was studying her mobile, waiting for the signal bars to appear and was slightly startled when the blue display lit up. She wasted no time in making the call to the same number she had dialled from the public telephone box earlier. It was answered immediately. Fadyar spoke clearly and precisely.

"We will rendezvous at about 5:10pm at location 1." She disconnected the call once the receiver had acknowledged her message.

"We are on our way. All is well, my brothers!" she exclaimed. Her three compatriots smiled and cheered. Assiter said nothing.

Mattar left the mountain two miles south of Arnisdale and turned right onto the small coastal road, engaged two-wheel drive and the high axle ratio and accelerated towards Glenelg, leaving trails of fresh mud on the newly washed tarmac. He was headed for the parked camper van which had been specially adapted internally to conceal Assiter. So far the American had not been a problem, but Fadyar carried a syringe that she could administer if it was necessary to sedate him. As the Land Rover picked up speed, Fadyar allowed herself the luxury of looking across the Sound of Sleat to the mist covered Isle of Skye. As she gazed over the water, an extremely large bird swept low over the water, its fierce talons spread wide. Suddenly it dropped downwards and its feet momentarily entered the water causing a slight splash. When the bird rose into the air a glistening, writhing, silver fish was clamped tight in its grasp and it flew off at tremendous speed.

Assiter saw it too and said to Fadyar, "Impressive isn't it?"

"Yes what a wonderful sight. Do you know what it is?" she inquired.

Assiter was not an ornithologist but he certainly recognised the bird of prey.

"That's a white-tailed sea eagle. I believe it to be the UK's largest bird but we in the States have one or two slightly larger."

"There's a surprise!" Fadyar quipped, and they both shared a brief moment free of tension and a common appreciation of what the natural world had just displayed to them. It was Bagheri that spoke next and he shattered the calmer ambience.

"I can't see that helicopter we heard earlier, but the weather is clearer here on the coast. I suggest we all keep a good look out. We can easily be spotted now."

It was true. The group were now at their most vulnerable. They had lost the protection of the mountains and, more importantly, the cover of the cloudy conditions. They were on an open road that would be easy to seal off leaving them trapped. It was the highest risk element that Fadyar had identified when planning and refining her mission. The next forty-five minutes would be critical.

As Mattar joined the road Gordon was at the helm of his cabin cruiser also travelling towards Glenelg, and only fifteen minutes behind the fleeing assassins. He was thinking hard and asked Cindy to take over the wheel. He pressed a few numbers into his phone and waited a minute until it was answered.

"Is that you Kathleen? It's Gordon."

"Aye. How are you Gordon? I expect you will be wanting to speak with young Sandy here?"

"Indeed, thank you Kathleen. It's a bit urgent I'm afraid, but we'll speak later."

Sandy MacLean took over the phone. Gordon very briefly outlined the terrible situation that had befallen Assiter and explained that he, Cindy and Paulette were approaching Glenelg in the *Greek Dancer*. It was a couple of minutes of rapid exchanges before Sandy, sitting in the chair at his Sister in Law's small lounge, fully appreciated what was being said to him.

"Sandy, have you seen anyone go by at speed in a 4x4? Is anything unusual going on? There's no sign of anyone in Corran at the end of the road and we are just nearing Arnisdale."

"Nay, Gordon. I've seen and heard nothing. Glenelg is its usual tranquil self. A few casual tourists are ambling about and looking at the memorial, but nothing untoward."

"OK. Do me a favour. Keep a look out and ring me if you see anything. If those bastards are on the road now they will easily outpace us and we'll never catch up."

"Shouldn't I phone the police if it's that important?"

"No, phone me. I have direct number of their incident room. It will actually be quicker for you to phone me than dial 999. When we get to Glenelg, I'll tie up and pop in and say hello to Kathleen, but it will have to be quick as we will need to get back to Mealag."

"Right you are, Gordon. Take care."

77

Silver command led by Maythorp had been considering the latest intelligence gleaned principally from Ritson's conversation with Gordon. The evidence had been well examined and considered reliable. The psychologist had confirmed that Truscott was not suffering from any delusional features and was remarkably calm in the circumstances, if understandably somewhat excited. Gold had instructed that whatever incident had occurred in the morning at the lodge involving the two women, investigation into it could wait, but in the light of what Cindy had said they amended the order about sealing off the lodge pending forensic examination to include the area down to the loch and along the shoreline to the dam. COBR were updated and were still insisting that despite the latest major developments, the incident was still to be treated as a hostage incident involving a very eminent foreign statesman by persons who had already committed murder. The Prime Minister had been updated by the Home Secretary and the necessary channels were being opened to the US President. There was a speedy response from the Prime Minister that the President and the British Government affirmed that no deal should be made with terrorists. The instruction was relayed to Gold and Silver commands, the latter passing it on to Curry. Seated three away from Manders was an intelligence analyst coordinating any information received from GCHQ. He turned and passed Maythorp a note.

"GCHQ Morwenstow report several incidents of suspicious mobile phone traffic in the vicinity. We have eliminated Truscott's call to us, but he has made another to a house in Glenelg. There is another made from near Kinloch Hourn to a location on Skye. Its brevity aroused suspicion and it is currently being retrieved."

"How long will that take?" the Silver commander asked.

"Impossible to say, but minutes probably."

They waited. The intelligence officers phone rang and was immediately answered.

"We will rendezvous at about 5:10pm at location 1." The officer spoke as he wrote it down. "Message ends."

"Where was it sent to, do we know that?" Maythorp asked impatiently.

"It's coming through now, Sir" a voice answered. "A mobile phone somewhere on Skye, around Broadford."

"Get me the map up, please" and almost immediately his request was granted. Everyone in the room studied the Broadford area. A brief general discussion followed, expertly chaired by Maythorp who kept comment brief and very much to the point. He then went around the room asking his senior advisers and experts for their assessment. Six favoured Skye as the rendezvous, with four of those opting for the nearby Isle of Skye airport. Three favoured a port or inlet on Skye, with two saying that it was too early to draw any conclusions. The commander addressed the room.

"This is potentially very serious, very serious indeed. Bronze has deployed his available forces widely in order to attempt to cover a vast area. Many of those forces are not anywhere near Skye and certainly not on it. We must stop these people before they get on the island. However, there are two potential crossing points – the Skye bridge and a small ferry at Kyle Rhea, off the Glenelg road. The bridge is effectively sealed, but there are no forces along that other highway. The suspects could simply drive on the ferry and disappear. If we remove forces from the bridge, we leave that exposed. There is, of course, no reason to suppose that they do not have a boat moored up somewhere which can take them across the Straits – it looks a short crossing." Suggestions please."

Another discussion followed at the conclusion of which Maythorp picked up the phone and spoke to Bronze.

"It is our assessment that the suspects are headed for Skye. We recommend immediate deployment of the helicopter to keep watch on the Khyle Rhea ferry area for the suspects' vehicle and also keep a good look out for any boat heading directly across the Straits from the mainland towards Skye. We also believe some ESU and TSG units should be deployed west along the A87 towards the Isle of Skye and to wait at Shiel. The road block currently at the eastern end of the A87 could be manned with less officers, freeing up resources that could be redeployed towards Glenelg and the Kyle Rhea ferry. We consider it a low risk that the terrorists will head east."

Curry and Ritson considered the options. They were still in operational command, but they would have to have compelling reasons to go against the tactical assessment made by Silver.

"Is it a large ferry, this Kyle Rhea one?" asked Ritson, fearing there may be many passengers on board.

"No. It will carry four to six vehicles on an open deck. Occupants normally stay in the car. The crossing only takes a few minutes."

Reassured, Ritson said, "We don't have much option do we? No one has yet really seen this vehicle, though we know roughly where it is. This is such a large area to cover, with our current resources we cannot lock up every road, let alone every track and pass. I say go with it."

"Agreed" a sombre Curry replied and he issued the orders. An ESU unit with its cargo of secret electronic wizardry and other devices and twelve fully kitted out specialist anti- terrorist officers of TSG, were already waiting in a lay-by on the A87, their unmarked white vans attracting little interest from the few passers-by. Curry, using his local knowledge and considerable foresight, had sent the units part way along the A87 half an hour earlier, believing that the terrorists were heading towards the coast and possibly Skye, but it would still take them at least twenty minutes at full speed to reach Shiel – the junction where the unclassified Glenelg / Kyle Rhea mountain road joins the main route A87 to the Kyle of Lochalsh.

Mattar slowed as he approached the large car park at Glenelg and parked in the far left hand corner, close to where they had left the camper van. A few sightseers were gathered around the memorial, reading the inscriptions. Others were milling about, some leaning on the sea wall. No one turned to look at the muddy vehicle that had just pulled in and parked. Bagheri placed a large strip of medical tape on Assiter's mouth and then wrapped a tartan scarf around his head and face to conceal the gag. Bagheri withdrew his pistol from his shoulder holster inside his flak jacket.

"No noise, you understand," he menacingly waved the gun in Assiter's face as he spoke.

Assiter nodded.

Fadyar alighted and quickly entered the camper. She walked through the spacious interior and then unlocked the rear doors and lowered the steps. There was no rush, no noise, nothing that might arouse suspicion. Bagheri was first to leave the rear seat of the Land Rover quickly followed by Assiter who was half pulled by Bagheri and half pushed by Khan. Assiter started to struggle, but was quickly restrained by his two captors and between them they quickly escorted Assiter up the steps of the camper. He stumbled as he climbed and Khan quickly called out.

"Come on. You will feel a lot better when you have slept off all that whisky." Any observer would have immediately turned away convinced the groggy man had imbibed too heavily.

Mattar, slightly saddened to be leaving his 4x4, locked its side doors once all the weapons and equipment had been transferred. He went to the back of the vehicle, opened the rear door and lifted up the floor panel. In the centre well was a small package wrapped in oily brown paper with wires leading to a small device, which became extremely sensitive to movement five minutes after it had been activated. He carefully set the switch, closed the floor panel and locked the door. After a few minutes, the bomb would be charged, and any subsequent vibration would result in it destroying any evidence of their brief, but deadly, occupation of the vehicle. He joined Assiter and his companions inside the camper and sat in the driving seat. He started the engine and moved away from the car park exactly one minute after their arrival, just moments before Gordon telephoned Sandy.

"Remember Mawdud. Drive purposefully, but we are now tourists. Do not attract attention. And by the way, well done on the mountain," Fadyar gave Mattar a deserved compliment.

Twenty minutes later, Gordon quickly secured the boat at the jetty beneath the car park at Glenelg and walked carefully up the slippery concrete steps, green with algae, carrying the two submachine guns taken from the dead agents. He was closely followed by Cindy and Paulette, each carrying a concealed rifle.

Sandy and Margaret, along with Kathleen were at the top of the steps to meet them all.

"I'm really sorry Kathleen, there's no time for proper introductions. Have you seen nothing at all strange Sandy?"

"No, can't say I have. It's all been very, very quiet."

"They must have gone through the hills then onto the A87, goodness knows where though. I don't know of any way through or round The Saddle." The Saddle was yet another Munro that was situated between the Glenelg Road and the A87 and represented a significant obstacle even to walkers, and was utterly impassable for vehicles trying to take a shortcut from one road to the other.

"We will wait here for a few minutes, see what happens. They could still be on the hills or coming from Corran, but the likelihood is that they should be quite a way ahead of us."

They went and sat on the public benches, staring out across the sea to the Isle of Skye. "That camper has gone, of course." Kathleen nonchalantly remarked.

"Camper? What camper? Do you mean a camper van?" Cindy responded.

"Yes, Morag next door said they were nice people. Four of them I think, up here to meet friends, but it has been here a while. It's gone now but it was here at lunch. Over there, by that Land Rover."

Gordon looked to the far corner of the car park. He cursed for not noticing earlier the neatly parked vehicle, but his attention was now drawn to the bay next to it. It was dry, whereas all the other non-occupied bays were darkened by the moisture in the air and from the sea.

"They must have only just gone. Look at the dry areas. Give me your keys Sandy, we're going for a ride." Sandy obliged and handed them over.

"No Gordon, NO!" Cindy shouted at him. "You promised the police."

"Well we don't know it is them, do we? Let's see if we can spot them on the road."

Before Cindy could say more, Paulette shouted "I'm coming too" and, as one, all except Margaret and Kathleen rushed to the Range Rover.

"Don't worry Margaret – we'll be back soon." Gordon called out as he opened the driver's door. "Stay indoors and don't go near that Land Rover. We'll phone the police and tell them what's happened."

Sandy jumped into the front passenger seat, whilst Cindy and Paulette sat in the back. Gordon started the engine and accelerated hard out of the car park, causing the tourists to turn and shake their heads at the unwelcome noise caused by the revving engine. Gordon gave Sandy his mobile phone and the slip of paper with Ritson's direct line written upon it.

"Phone that number and tell them what we are doing, can you Sandy? Thanks."

Seconds later Ritson answered, "I am with Gordon Truscott in a Range Rover travelling on… bugger, the signal's gone" Sandy was not prone to bad language and 'bugger' was about as bad as it got for him.

"Well, I'm not turning back. We may get a signal at the top of Ratagan. We can try at the viewpoint there."

That was several miles away and Cindy wondered if stopping there might waste precious time. The delay at the car park had already cost them several minutes.

"I know they are ahead of us, but not by much, and we will be a lot quicker than a cumbersome camper van, albeit being driven by a pretty able driver" said Gordon "I wonder why they changed from the Land Rover?"

"So they could pass themselves off as tourists, I should think," said Cindy "Also, Dean would be very visible in a Land Rover but not so in a camper van."

Gordon nodded, impressed.

"The trouble with the road ahead is that it's almost impossible to pass anyone, unless they allow you by. Let's hope we don't get stuck behind some selfish tourists". It was Sandy who spoke. He seemed to be treating the pursuit of the terrorists as if it were some sort of surreal adventure on one his courses, but Gordon's next comment swept away any fantasies.

"If we come across the camper, we must decide what we are to do. We will soon be spotted if we follow them. These people are professionals and they may know this vehicle anyway as they must have had us all under observation for quite a while. The terrorists have killed several police already. I think Ritson is right. If we spot them, we should report it and then leave it to the police."

Paulette remained silent. Cindy and Sandy murmured their agreement. Gordon tried to mentally calculate how much quicker their vehicle would be than the camper van around the twists and turns of the road as it climbed Mount Ratagan, but decided that it would probably hinge on how much traffic there was on the road. Even the Range Rover could not risk taking the dangerous bends at speed.

78

Ritson was not best pleased with Gordon. In fact he was very irate. The last thing Ritson needed was a maverick on the loose and he ordered an assistant to keep trying Gordon's phone, the number of which was automatically logged, but there was no response other than the 'number unobtainable' message. There was no response either from the *Greek Dancer's* radio. He sent a message out to all units to keep a look out for Truscott and his boat but emphasised that their attention should remain focussed on sighting the terrorists. They remained the principal targets. Another call came through from Silver.

"The press have got wind of the fact that something big is happening in the Scottish Highlands. Gold has placed an embargo on press helicopters within a fifty mile radius, but in return we have offered a press liaison officer at the Fort William nick. Should anything come through, refer all press there."

"Understood" said Ritson, relieved that the local police station should take the calls. He had known situations where the crafty press had sometimes pretended to be persons with information in order to get through to a command centre and instructed the Bronze team to be very alert to that possibility if they took an incoming call. He also knew that it would not take the press very long before they would start asking some very searching questions.

He and Curry requested a status update on the ancillary emergency services that were also rushing to attend the vicinity. Fire crews, ambulances and Mountain Rescue helicopters (for their on board paramedic facilities) were all approaching the area and ready to be deployed once the terrorists had been located. However, the news from Sky 1 continued to disappoint. They had patrolled the Sound of Sleat and were circling high above the Kyle Rhea ferry, whilst observing the close-up pictures produced by the powerful camera. Nothing. No trace of anything remotely suspicious nor a Land Rover travelling at high speed. They had five minutes flying time remaining before they would have to return to their base for refuelling. That in itself did not cause Bronze a problem as another observer helicopter, Sky 2, would immediately take up the station occupied by Sky 1.

Ritson turned to Curry, "the targets have to surface soon. They have been very lucky so far I think."

"And this has been very well planned," added Curry. "Taking that highly risky mountain pass must have been deliberate and chosen because of the probable weather. That area is the wettest part of the British Isles and on average nearly an inch of rain falls every day. Those mountains are usually shrouded in cloud or mist and when it is not raining only a very few days ever have clear skies above the mountain tops. That was clever."

Ritson was impressed at his colleague's insight and mentally noted how valuable local knowledge can be.

"Actually, John, that's a very astute observation and not picked up by Silver. This is a really, really clever operation. The suspects have not done what we expected at any stage. Mrs Crossland even reported that one of the terrorists, presumably Fadyar Masri, or whatever her name is, saved their lives this morning. That could never have been planned, it had to be spontaneous, yet it showed our kidnappers to have a compassionate side and also to be able to modify their plans. Whoever is in charge, maybe this Masri woman, is certainly very able and adaptable. The whole thing is bloody weird, really strange. I wonder what the odds are that they are not going to do what Silver anticipates now."

"We have little choice though, Bill, but to follow their advice, at least until it proves wrong," said Curry.

"Mmmm. Maybe. I'll think about that one." Ritson was more used to challenging his superiors than Curry and he would not be afraid to take a risky decision if he felt it to be correct. He was effectively joint Bronze commander and he would stretch that brief to the full if he felt it right to do so.

★ ★ ★

Mattar saw the flashing blue lights in the centre grille of the unmarked police Vauxhall as it approached them travelling at high speed on the opposite side of the road.

"Pull over, let them go by. We are tourists remember." Fadyar anxiously called out.

"Calm down Fadyar, I know." Mattar said as he gently pulled into the nearest passing place. As the speeding vehicle was almost level with them, the driver slightly raised his right hand from the steering wheel as a gesture of thanks. The camper had not aroused even a flicker of suspicion, it being a common vehicle seen on the roads in the Highlands.

Five minutes later another police vehicle, a marked 4x4, travelling towards Khyle Rhea or Glenelg, also sped past them with three burly, armed officers clearly visible in the passenger seats. Gordon, travelling several minutes behind the camper van, repeatedly flashed his lights at the approaching police vehicles hoping they would stop, but when they showed no signs of doing so he, too, pulled into a passing place. He waved as they dashed past, dismayed that neither had not stopped.

"Why should they?" he said rhetorically to Cindy. They don't know of us in this vehicle and think we are just trying to be helpful to them. They are also still searching for a Land Rover."

Gordon pulled out of the lay-by and drove as hard as he could to make up time, feeling positive that around the next bend he would catch sight of the camper but at each turn of the wheel he was disappointed.

"Where do you think those police vehicles were going?" Cindy suddenly asked Gordon, but it was Sandy that responded first.

"I've been wondering that. Either someone saw you get off the boat with those weapons and has raised the alarm at Glenelg or they are going to close the small ferry and seal off Khyle Rhea. I don't think Kathleen or Margaret will have raised the alarm – we told them we would do that."

"They will never take Dean to Skye," Gordon ignored Sandy's suppositions and remained thinking about the terrorists. He was adamant.

"Although a large island, Skye is just too easy to completely seal off. No, his captors will stay on the mainland. It is possible, of course, they have somewhere to stay but nothing happens around these parts without someone noticing and commenting. This group know that you hide in a large city, not in remote countryside. Although we haven't sighted them, I still believe they are ahead of us."

At the summit of Mount Ratagan there was still no signal on the mobile. The mist obscured the view down to Shiel three miles away but as they came down the other side of the mountain the cloud disappeared and the fading sun lit the panoramic vista that lay before them.

Gordon stopped the car and reached for his field glasses. Sandy removed the scope from his rifle and also scoured the dozen or so vehicles on the road ahead. Simultaneously they exclaimed, "There! About two miles ahead."

79

"Have we got a fix on that abandoned call from Truscott?" Curry asked to the room.

There was no answer.

"Damn," he uttered almost inaudibly, but it was heard by Ritson and disturbed his thought.

"Can we have a close-up map, please, of that Glenelg road?" Ritson asked.

A large, detailed image of Glenelg appeared before him and Curry.

"Zoom out a bit please, and then follow the road." Ritson again.

"What are you thinking, Bill?" Curry asked.

"Well. Truscott must be headed towards this small ferry," Ritson used his electronic pointer to indicate the Khyle Rhea ferry, "or further along the road towards this place."

He pointed out Shiel on the map.

"That has to be right, doesn't it? Surely he'd still be in contact with us if he was at the coast where there is a mobile signal, so that must make Shiel favourite. No? Yes?"

"Yes, probably. Units Juliet 3 and Papa 1 should be nearly at the ferry area by now, probably sealing it off at this very moment." Curry replied

"If that's the case, and Truscott is going to Shiel, would it not be reasonable to assume that to disobey his undertaking and to take the road, he must have a good reason, a very good reason? He will not simply be enjoying the scenery." Ritson remarked.

Curry was beginning to appreciate the assistance of his colleague up from the smoke. Ritson was right.

"Good point. Absolutely. It can't be the ferry or we would have heard, nor back towards Corran." Curry then pressed a button on a panel of switches and pulled a microphone closer.

"Juliet 3, are you receiving? Report your position please. This is Bronze. Over"

"Juliet 3. We are at the ferry. Over."

"Thank you Juliet 3. On your way did you see any vehicles? Over."

"Obviously negative to the suspects, Bronze. There were probably about twelve other vehicles, maybe fifteen, we passed on our way to Shiel and then onto reaching here and we overtook about the same number. It's quite a popular route with the tourists. All seemed quite normal. Remember, we were only looking out for a Jeep or Land Rover. Over."

"Yes, I guess so. Papa 1 can remain at the ferry. Please return to Shiel immediately as fast as you can. Wait there for other units to rendezvous with you. Over."

"Will do. Over and out."

As the car radio operator of the unmarked Vauxhall put his receiver back into stand-by mode he turned to his driver and both raised their eyebrows, not best pleased at being told to turn round the moment they had arrived at the ferry embarkation jetty.

"Christ. I wish they could make their bloody mind up where they want us, we're running around like headless chickens." The driver swore to his passenger as the tyres squealed from him making a fast U-turn.

Curry next called up the surveillance helicopter which was now on station, and he asked the crew to widen their search pattern.

As he descended, Gordon and his passengers lost the benefit of being able to view the road ahead from an elevated position and again lost sight of the camper van. Even when a section of straight and level tarmac appeared, momentarily raising their hopes, a sharp bend ahead rendered it impossible to locate or even glimpse the camper van ahead. At Shiel there was no sign of Dean's captors, and at the junction with the A87 a frustrated Gordon thumped the steering wheel.

"Which way?" he asked.

"Left" said Sandy. "Has to be. If they turn right they must know that the police will have set up a road block at the junction with the A887 and there is no other road they can take in that van going that way. It must be left."

Gordon made the turn and started to accelerate. "But they

won't be going to the Skye bridge either for the same reason. This doesn't make sense. Maybe they've hidden the van and are on foot."

At that moment a small plane flying fairly low passed over the road ahead of them before it climbed and banked sharply to avoid the hills ahead of it.

"That's very unusual," observed Sandy. "We often get the air force practising low flying between the hills, but not privateers. Wonder what it's up to? Do you think it's a police spotter plane?"

"We've been so stupid!" Gordon shouted out, thumping his hand even harder on the steering wheel. "The plane is for them, don't you see? It's their escape. The plane. That's how they are going to get away."

"But there's no airport here!" Sandy was incredulous. "There's the place over at Broadford, but that would mean them crossing the bridge. The police will definitely be there, and at the airport."

Gordon revved the engine and started to gather speed on the wide, smooth trunk road. "It's not there they're headed for. What about that small landing strip, virtually disused, over at Criannich? That's my bet."

Cindy yelled at him from the rear.

"No, Gordon. No. Please stop. This is a job for the police, not us." She started to cry, "We really have been through enough today. Please."

"But the police are all going the wrong way and we can't communicate. We must follow and hope that a signal comes through soon. Then I'll stop. Promise."

"Oh... Gordon, no." but it was a sigh of resignation. Cindy's stomach suddenly felt very empty and slight shiver of fear passed over her.

Gordon gunned the Range Rover as hard as he dared along the wide, fast A87 before he swung off right at Larnacran, violently throwing his passengers around, despite them being securely held in their belted seats. Once more, they were travelling along a narrow road that undulated through and over high slopes and hills, but with no massive mountains to negotiate. As the terrain softened, the mobile flickered into life again. Almost immediately the ring tones sounded and Sandy answered. As he did so, Ritson pushed a switch down on the loudspeaker phone console in front of him and Curry, whilst simultaneously pressing a button marked 'Sky 2.' The phone call would automatically be patched through to Silver and Gold, and their commanders had similarly enabled simultaneous transmission to their assistants. A lot of people were about to listen in to the ensuing conversation.

After the cursory introductions Sandy started to explain where they were headed. "Dean's kidnappers swapped vehicles at Glenelg car park. For various reasons we assumed they would be driving towards Shiel, and we are now hopefully on their trail having taken the Larnacran road."

This was no time for criticism and Ritson ignored any suggestion of it. The people he was talking to had priceless information which he desperately needed. The map of the Larnacran road appeared on the wall as he spoke.

"What vehicle are they in?" asked Ritson.

"Camper van, grey and white," Sandy's words were noted by everyone listening in, but particularly the radio operator in Sky 2, flying at 3,000 feet above the Khyle Straits. He passed a scribbled pencil message to the pilot.

"We saw a light aircraft flying low a moment ago and we think they are heading for the disused landing strip near Criannich," Sandy spoke into the small phone.

"Affirmative Bronze. We glimpsed it too but it disappeared before we could get a fix," Sky 2 interrupted.

"OK. That's excellent, thank you. Now, we will do the rest. You are to stop immediately and leave the area. Our units are now arriving at Shiel. We will talk later, but you must now leave. Do you understand?" Ritson sounded rather stern.

Sandy turned to Gordon, "He's saying we must stop and leave."

Gordon grabbed the mobile from Sandy's hand and spoke to the Bronze joint commander, "Look. This is how I see it. Several people I got to know quite well were shot to pieces today, and I myself was nearly blown up by a grenade. My best friend is now a hostage, and his wife and Cindy have also been through a terrible ordeal. You guys were nowhere when we needed you, your protection has been proved inadequate, and two of your vehicles have recently passed us going completely the wrong way. Now, level with me. How long will it take you to get to the landing strip?" Gordon could no longer contain the suppressed anger within him and as he delivered his outburst his voice rose in pitch and volume.

"Mr Truscott, please. That is not the point. I am trying to protect you and the occupants in your vehicle and must insist you stop now. We will be on the scene as soon as possible. Now, Sir, Please stop your vehicle."

"He's right, Gordon." Cindy spoke, but Paulette intervened.

"No Cindy, please. I want to go on. I must be there in case they take the plane. These people will kill Dean, I know they will, as our government and the President will never give into the demands they will make for his release. I have to do something. Please. It may be the last time I shall ever be close to him."

Ritson heard the conversation going on in the car. He was also acutely aware that every second that passed Gordon would be gaining on the camper van. He heard Curry giving instructions to all nearby units to head for the airfield and he opened the palm of his hand and extended five fingers three times towards Ritson. Then held up both hands and pointed skywards.

"Mr Truscott..."

"Call me Gordon."

"Gordon, How far away do you estimate the camper van to be from the airstrip?"

"About two minutes, no more."

"And you?" Ritson asked

"About four."

"Then you must stop now. If you haven't yet been spotted by the suspects, you surely soon will be. I cannot take responsibility for your safety unless you stop now."

There was no answer.

"Gordon? Gordon?"

"How long before you get your people here, Bill?" Ritson heaved a sigh of relief that Gordon had not switched the phone off. "Don't bullshit me. I will time you. How long?" he asked Ritson.

Curry had signalled fifteen minutes for the first patrols and ten minutes for the Merlin. "Eight to ten minutes" Ritson replied.

"See you there then," and Gordon switched off the phone.

Gordon half turned his head to Cindy and Paulette.

"The police will not arrive in time to prevent them taking off. They may of course intercept the plane in mid-air but quite what will happen then I dread to think... or we have to delay them a few minutes." Gordon's words hung heavily in the confined cabin of the vehicle.

No one spoke. There was nothing anyone wanted to say. Gordon continued to drive fast. Sandy started inspecting the Heckler and Koch machine guns once carried by the Agents Drew and Atkins. The MP5K-PDW (Personal Defence Weapon) is used by most special force and armed police units around the world. It is short, easily carried and the slightly curved magazines have a thirty round capacity. Sandy checked these were full.

"These are neat," he said. "They have symbols on the firing selector: safe, single burst, three burst or fully auto. Pretty straightforward if we have to use them. I'd prefer not to though, bet they produce quite a kickback."

They rounded a long sweeping curve in the road and caught sight of the camper van ahead, before it disappeared again behind another bend in the road. Gordon immediately eased his foot off the accelerator pedal and slowed so as not to be spotted. As the road straightened out, the van was immediately ahead, no more than 300 metres from them.

"Gordon. Please take care." Cindy pleaded.

"Don't worry. It will be OK. The police must be really close now."

The rear left indicator light on the camper flashed brightly and it left the narrow road opposite a dilapidated, wooden sign with faded black lettering marked 'Criannich Airport.'

Twenty seconds later, Gordon stopped at the turn off.

"The description of 'Airport' is a bit rich. It's only a strip of grass!" He tried to make light of the situation but no one laughed.

Very slowly, he turned onto the track and continued down the slight slope towards the airport entrance in silence. Sandy MacLean slipped his hand onto a MP5 and pulled it across his lap.

The pilot of the twin engine light aircraft had already positioned his plane at the southern end of the strip. The landing had been bumpy and on the slippery grass it had taken considerable skill to slow the plane to a halt, level and straight. Turning 180 degrees, he slowly taxied back to the other end where he performed another 180 degree turn, ready to take off over the sea at the northern end of the so-called runway. As he saw the van, the pilot electronically lowered the access steps and waited for his passengers to climb into the six seater cabin. Fadyar was first out of the camper. She then held open the rear doors whilst Khan and Bagheri pushed Assiter towards the exit. He offered no resistance and walked slowly but purposefully towards the aircraft. Mattar gathered up a bundle of weapons and left them at the steps whilst Assiter climbed into the plane, closely followed by Fadyar. Khan and Bagheri hurried back into the van and brought out bulging rucksacks and ran with them to the foot of the aluminium steps.

Gordon did not risk driving into the entrance. As soon as it came into view, he parked the car off the track, out of sight. The four nervous occupants got out.

"Leave the doors open, they may hear us," instructed Gordon. They started to walk, half stooped, until they were no more than sixty metres from the plane, now clearly visible to them. Gordon beckoned them to lie down behind the rocks and knolls that bounded the muddy track. He and Cindy quickly concealed themselves as they slid their bodies beside a particularly huge boulder. Paulette was hiding within a deep crag where, sheltered from the prevalent strong winds, tufts of grass had grown surprisingly tall. Sandy, like Gordon and Cindy, had taken up position on the opposite side of the track from Paulette, behind a series of large individual rocks that were almost joined together to form a greyish stone ridge a couple of metres tall and several metres wide.

"What are they doing?" Cindy whispered to Gordon.

"Loading the plane. I think Dean must already be on board. I can only see three men, the woman isn't there."

They watched, fascinated. Cindy was willing the police to arrive soon. Paulette became agitated and scurried across the grass, crouching next to Gordon.

"I can't see Dean," she said.

"Nor me. He must be on the plane," Gordon replied.

Suddenly, the eerie silence was broken as the 375 horsepower port engine started up and spluttered into life, quickly followed by the matched starboard engine. The initial slow steady whirr of the propellers began increasing to a whine, and then to a high roar. Mattar and Khan were climbing the steps, each carrying a rucksack in one hand whilst holding onto the rail with their other to maintain their balance.

"Time's up," Gordon shouted above the noise. "We have to act now if we are going to. Whatever you do, stay down behind the rocks."

He passed Cindy a handgun. "Use it only if you have to" and kissed her briefly on the cheek.

Gordon set his machine gun to fire three round bursts. He looked across at Sandy and gave the thumbs up sign. Sandy reciprocated. Carefully, slowly, they raised their MP5's, took aim and fired.

80

"Bronze, are you receiving? Over."

"Go ahead Sky 2. This is Bronze. Over."

"Am one minute from target. Can see light aircraft on the ground... coming into camera range now. Cessna 421 C – the aptly named Golden Eagle. Over."

"We have pictures, Sky 2. Deploy as soon as you can. The ETA of TSG is four minutes."

The news that the support group was three minutes behind them was some comfort to the three armed officers on the helicopter, but not much. The pilot of Sky 2 said that he could land on the airfield but that had obvious risks, otherwise he would have to put down some distance away and by that time the Cessna would probably be airborne.

"Bronze. Sky 2 again. Over."

"Go ahead Sky 2. Over."

"Do I have permission to land on the airfield, in front of the plane? The alternative landing is half a mile away."

The next few seconds seemed like an eternity to the pilot. Curry and Ritson looked at each other. Both knew that sending the helicopter into the airfield was likely to result in the deaths of the crew, even if it did delay the plane's take-off or thwart the kidnap. The joint commanders were spared making the decision.

"Sky 2. This is Silver. Negative. I repeat negative. If the plane takes off, we will follow its course. Land where safe. Over."

"Understood, Silver. And thanks. Sky 2 out."

The helicopter began to circle over the scene seeking a clear area to touch down, when the crew noticed the images coming into view from the camera. The operator immediately switched to high resolution mode and adjusted the zoom.

The initial quick bursts of gunfire spat from Gordon's and Sandy's highly efficient machine guns, taking Fadyar and her three comrades totally by surprise. Mattar, halfway up the aeroplane steps, dropped his baggage and reached for the weapon still slung around his shoulder.

"We're under attack! Fadyar, we are under attack!" the frenetic note in his voice evidence of his alarm.

No sooner had he shouted his warning than he let out a loud scream of pain and fell backwards off the steps, clearly having been hit. He lay still on the grass alongside the plane, blood slowly staining the side of his shirt. Khan dropped his bag and raced up the steps, but a second burst from Sandy felled him on the top rung and he twisted and fell over the side rail smashing his shoulder onto the hard ground. Bagheri was halfway between the plane and the camper van when the shooting started. He immediately grabbed an automatic weapon and fired towards the rocks protecting his pursuers, before taking up a position behind the camper van, using it as cover. Splinters of rock exploded from the boulders that were sheltering the quartet. A hail of bullets zinged and fizzed about their heads as they flattened themselves on the ground, not daring to move.

"Get down, get down" shouted Gordon superfluously.

More incoming fire bounced off the rocks. Gordon and Sandy both switched their guns to auto, allowing them to fire repeatedly all the time they pulled the trigger. Sandy inched his way around his hide and fired in the general direction of the plane, before rolling backwards to the safety of the makeshift shelter. Gordon watched him and did likewise. A fierce gun fight ensued with rapid automatic fire being exchanged by Bagheri and the prone, but not fatally stricken Khan, still sheltering behind the aircraft's large tyres. High velocity bullets were still exploding large chunks of rock around Gordon and Sandy, forcing them to turn their heads away from those firing at them.

"A helicopter has just landed in the field, over on the right," Cindy went to point with her hand but immediately another round of firing started causing her to quickly place her arms by her side, and not notice the two armed police running from the helicopter the moment it touched down. Within a few seconds it was airborne again and rapidly rose into the air where it hovered above the battle being waged below, relaying its pictures. Unnoticed by the officers on the ground, and the four sheltering from the kidnapper's bullets, the aluminium steps were being raised. As soon as they had been fully retracted and inside the plane, the fuselage door was pulled shut and the pilot pushed forward the twin control levers to accelerate the engines to take off speed.

"Shoot at the wheels, the tyres" Gordon shouted to Sandy. Don't aim for the plane we may hit Dean."

The plane moved forward, slowly at first then gathered speed. Sky 2, acting without instructions, aborted his surveillance and approached the airstrip, flying low and fast. Its side door was wide open and, as it passed the plane, the officer who moments before had been operating the radio and camera, fired. Black, smoking holes spread along the Cessna fuselage as it was hit by the volley of shots, but its speed along the grass runway continued to increase. Once the plane moved off, Khan, no longer able to hide behind its tyres, became critically exposed. The officer in the helicopter aimed and fired mercilessly. Clods of earth and grass kicked up from the ground before the bullets seared into Khan's body, causing wisps of blue smoke to rise from the punctured, red hot wounds. His torso was lifted into the air from the battery of bullets striking it and he landed in a grotesquely contorted shape little more than a metre from where he had been sheltering. No one saw a woman's anguished face, pressed hard against the large side window, straining to see what was going on below. If they had, they might have noticed her wipe her eyes as Khan's torn body rolled on the ground.

"Sky 2. This is Bronze. Cease fire. Do not, repeat not, fire at the plane. Do you read me? Over." Ritson understood the pilot's motives in the heat of the moment but his actions could easily lead to Assiter's death, either at the hands of his kidnapper's or, worse, by a police bullet penetrating the fuselage.

"Understood. Bronze. But we are not the only ones firing at it. Looks like Truscott. There's a Range Rover and nearby there appears to be two persons – no three, I think – firing SMG's; moving the camera into position now. Over"

"Yes, I see it" replied Ritson, "but keep the camera on the plane."

The Merlin and Cessna were now rapidly moving apart and

travelling in opposite directions. Assiter would be in the air before the helicopter could turn again. Gordon replaced the magazine and slotted it into position on the MP5. He checked it was still set to fully automatic. He held the trigger as he aimed at the offside tyre. Several bullets hit the grass, kicking up large mounds of earth and stone, which he used as tracer indicators until his last five bullets found their mark. The tyre exploded and lumps of fabric and rubber showered into the air. The plane slewed sideways, the naked rim cutting a trench across the soft grass. The pilot was desperately trying to decelerate and steer the aircraft. A wall of rock ran down part of the side of the airstrip, and as the aircraft continued to turn it looked for a moment as though the wing would crash into it. The pilot and Fadyar held their breath as the wall passed safely underneath and the plane continued to slow under the controlled braking, finally crawling to a halt thirty metres from the camper van.

"You've done it, you've done it. Well done you two." Cindy turned and hugged Gordon.

The relief in Cindy's face was self-evident, but Gordon shouted a warning, "Stay down. Everyone stay down. It's not over yet."

As if to remind them, another burst of machine gun fire hit the rocks around where they were sheltering. It was Bagheri, still hidden behind the camper and obviously with plenty of ammunition in his belt or rucksack. The pilot of the plane cut both engines just before the aircraft had come to a complete stop, the noise of the propellers gradually fading as the speed of their revolutions dropped. The moment the plane came to a halt, the pilot opened the cockpit door, jumped to the ground and started running. Bagheri, angry at seeing the fleeing pilot deserting them, lifted his Galatz and, focusing the man in the centre of the scope's cross hairs, fired a short burst dropping him instantly.

"At last!" shouted Gordon as several police vehicles rushed onto the scene. One car, the unmarked Vauxhall, sped past the van and the plane before turning almost at right angles across the runway. Several officers quickly got out and took up protective positions alongside the edge of the strip, their weapons in hand. Two other vehicles stopped near to Gordon and Cindy, and more armed police emerged and spread themselves amongst the rocks. Bagheri was hopelessly trapped. At the camper van, he was between both sets of armed officers and he knew his position was defenceless. He wriggled underneath the van and lay totally still, waiting, his hand resting gently on his machine gun. An uneasy calm and silence spread across the scene and two officers crawled their way toward the civilians.

"Are any of you hurt?" one asked politely.

"No, we're fine," a relieved Cindy answered.

"Then you have been very fortunate, but I'm pleased. Now, make your way back to the safety of the officers on the track."

"I'm not going," Paulette stated bluntly. "I will not go. My husband is aboard that plane and I want to be here when he comes off."

"He is still in the plane is he?" enquired the officer.

"Yes, and there is a woman terrorist with him."

"OK. Stay here and keep your head down. Everyone stay down." They did as they were told as the officer talked into his radio.

"Bronze. This is Juliet 3. All civilians are safe at the scene but refuse to leave. The area is not yet secured and we have a hostage on the plane. Believed one or more suspects are holding the American. His wife is here. Over."

"This is Bronze. Thank you Juliet 3. Await instructions. Over."

Curry, pleased at the reporting officer's care not to use Assiter's name over the radio, had taken the call, but needed time to confer with Ritson, and if necessary Silver. Although the immediate area had not yet been declared secure, it was clear that the scene was now becoming one of a hostage recovery. Hostage situations can change very rapidly, almost in an instant, giving no time for instructions to be obtained by the usual protocols and niceties of radio messages. Ritson knew from experience that it would be useful to have either himself or John Curry at the scene, able to give immediate orders. He explained his thinking to Curry who agreed his assessment. Ritson switched on the radio to talk to the crime scene officer.

"Juliet 3, this is Bronze. Are you receiving? Over."

"Go ahead Bronze."

"Do not force the civilians to leave until the area is fully secure unless you believe them to be in imminent danger. They have survived very well behind those rocks, where they should remain. If this is prolonged we will have to move them but if it wasn't for them that plane would be in the air. Perhaps you could give my thanks to Mr Truscott and his friends for their assistance today."

Ritson knew he was stretching operational rules to the limit, if not beyond, for the safeguarding of civilian personnel in a hostile environment, but he was genuinely concerned that the area could still be very dangerous for moving them.

"I will, Sir. Could you confirm your order to leave the civilians where they are?" Juliet 3 was ensuring that there would be no misunderstanding as to the instruction he was being told to follow and Ritson repeated the order.

"I take full responsibility, Juliet 3. Over." Ritson added by way of further reassurance.

"Thank you Bronze. I note you take full responsibility." Juliet 3 signed off.

Ritson pressed another switch on the radio. "All units, this is Bronze. Do not attack the plane. Repeat. Do not attack the plane. Do not return fire at the plane. Continue to secure the area. Await the arrival of Bronze."

Ritson turned to Curry. "Good luck, John. It could be a long night."

"Thanks Bill. I'll radio in when I get there." Curry replied before he rose from his chair, stretched his arms above his head and picked up his coat. On his way out of the door he said goodnight to the armed guard, of which at least one is permanently stationed outside the door of every activated Command HQ, despite the general security of an operational centre.

Ritson then spoke to Silver who, after several minutes of what seemed more like debate than discussion, agreed not to countermand his order regarding Truscott and his friends. This was not the same as Silver endorsing or confirming Ritson's instructions, but it was enough for the spirited detective chief superintendent who continued by listing his requirements for the next phase of the police operation.

"We shall need two trained hostage negotiators at the scene as soon as possible".

Silver confirmed they were already on standby at Fort Augustus and would be sent immediately, although it would still take them up to an hour to arrive.

"We shall need additional lighting crews and rigs, it will be getting dark soon." Ritson interjected. Silver confirmed they would be sent but pointed out the ESU did carry some emergency lighting.

While the radio conversations were happening, more and more police units were arriving on the scene. Others were held in reserve, on the tarmac unclassified road near the turn off to the airport. At least six ambulance vehicles of varying types were also parked on the road, away from the airstrip, and they had been joined by three fire tenders. The Territorial Support Group vehicles carrying the specially trained officers arrived at the same time as the Tactical Support Unit with its cargo of various electronic equipment and other gadgetry, both reporting they were at the scene within minutes of Juliet 3's call, their noisy diesel engined vans breaking the uneasy quiet once again. As the number of police increased, several slowly proceeded to move closer to the stricken aircraft, concealing themselves by crawling on all four limbs behind the rocky walls that lined both edges of the airstrip. They moved closer towards the camper. When it finally came into their view, several uniformed police slowly left the protective cover of the outcrop and eased their way forward, still unaware that a member of the terrorist cell was lying close by. Bagheri remained totally still, silently watching and waiting for his moment. Suddenly the loyal fanatic rolled over and shouting, "Praise be to Allah", fired his fully automatic weapon at as many officers as he could see, downing three, before he succumbed to the barrage of return fire.

Moments later, a sombre voice crackled onto the speakers in the command centres.

"Van secured, no occupants. One target down. We have three deceased uniformed casualties being evacuated now."

Slowly, inexorably, the police ringed the plane. An officer made an attempt to move closer to the Cessna, but withdrew as a female face at the window appeared. She shook her head and held up her gun in a gesture that was unmistakeable, indicating she would shoot her hostage unless he left. That message was passed onto the command centres who recalled all officers from anywhere near the aircraft. The targets had been isolated, the area ringed. Escape would be impossible. Bronze Commander Curry, being taken by light helicopter, was less than ten minutes flying time away. He had no qualms about leaving Ritson to man the Bronze room, inwardly relieved Ritson was there to provide a second opinion if needed. It had taken a long time, but Curry and Ritson now had the terrorists contained and the resources needed to end this Scottish outrage.

81

The first priority in the management of any hostage situation is to do nothing that would exacerbate the danger facing the hapless captive. Usually, the captors will make demands and discussions will ensue, sometimes lasting only a few minutes but on occasions may continue for several hours or even days. The declared policy of successive British governments of never conceding to the hostage takers' demands is known throughout the world, but a theoretical stated objective will never be 100% absolute. In practice, there will always be negotiations. The skill is ensuring that any concession appears not to be one, or to be so trivial as to be inconsequential. The task facing the law enforcement agencies is to gain as much intelligence as they can, whilst satisfying their first priority of not endangering the hostage; and it is the intelligence gathering aspect that necessitates deploying the ESU with its electronic wizardry. It is also important to have specially trained hostage negotiators whose task is not just to establish a relationship with the hostage taker, but also to note every detail that might be useful in the event that the police decide to use force.

Fadyar now accepted that her prime mission had failed, but the reasons for it almost incomprehensible as she had been so certain that she had planned properly for all the aspects crucial for a triumphant outcome. She was bitterly upset, blaming her own shortcomings for its lack of success and was deeply affected by the loss of her friends, particularly Nasra Khan. She wept as she saw his torn and crumpled body, reddened with blood, his lifeless eyes gazing unseeing towards her face at the window. She was suddenly very tired. She needed to rest and consider her secondary mission of killing Assiter, but she was in no hurry to carry that out. Fadyar could afford to wait. The person in charge of the swarm of police outside the plane would make an approach soon enough. Until the negotiators arrived, little would happen and Fadyar sat on the floor of the plane, out of sight of those on the ground but in a position where she was able to get a reasonable view of the landing strip through the large windows. She was in contemplative and reflective mood. After several minutes silence, Dean Assiter spoke. What he said amazed her.

"Your brave colleagues, had you known them long?" he inquired gently.

She found herself replying, doing exactly the opposite of what her camp training had tried to drill into her and which she had practised many times in mock situations.

"Not really, several months, but they accepted the risks. We all did." She replied somewhat sombrely.

"The driver was very good. I was more nervous on that mountain than now." He chuckled and Fadyar smiled.

For a few moments neither spoke, then Fadyar said slowly, "They were all good people".

A small tear ran down the side of her cheek and she turned away from Assiter in order to hide her uncontrollable emotion as she thought of Nasra and her expressing their love for each other a few hours earlier at the cottage. The noise of a helicopter overhead drowned out any further exchanges as it hovered only feet above their plane. Assiter looked scared, expecting something to happen but Fadyar was calm. She got closer to him and shouted in his ear.

"Do not worry. They will not attack. This is to prevent us hearing them plant microphones on the plane. They may even be drilling through somewhere to put a camera in."

"You know a lot more about this sort of thing than me, and I'm the goddam US Secretary of State!"

Fadyar nodded, but she was slightly wrong in her assumptions. Three ultra-sensitive microphones had indeed been fitted along the plane's fuselage, but there had been no drilling as the detailed design specification of the plane had not been faxed through to ESU and the precise layout of the fuel tanks and pipes was unknown to the scene of crime officers. Until it was, the enablement of a miniature camera via fibre optics had been postponed. Silver and Bronze had authorised the microphones to be installed not only to overhear any conversations within the plane from which mood swings could, and would, be analysed by the psychological team, but also an accurate placement of the personnel on board could be mapped by analysis of the outputs from all three listening devices.

Fadyar was aware of all of this, and contemplated the counter measures she should be taking, such as frequently changing where she and Assiter sat, turning on the Cessna audio equipment and playing some loud music, or even insisting that she and Assiter communicate only by writing messages to each other. These, and other simple counter actions she had been taught, but she did none of them, indifferent to her plight. Her tiredness was close to overwhelming her and she felt as if her body and mind could work no more. She needed rest, but the last few hours had been so momentous and confusing she knew she must force her brain to keep active. The events of the day spun wildly about in her head, in no order. Haphazard and unrelated to each other, her recollections were both confused and confusing. Her mind kept going back over aspects that troubled her. *Why was the man Donaldson at the lodge and who had sent him?* Fadyar was not convinced the man would act on his own, travelling all the way to the lodge and overcome and kill the police, solely to rape the banker's wife. Fadyar knew men could satisfy their desires easier than that. Donaldson was just a sadistic opportunist who took advantage of the situation when he found himself in the house alone with the two attractive, defenceless women. It was similar with the schoolgirls in Baghdad. No, Mrs Crossland had to be wrong. For Donaldson to take on the risks, and potential consequences of murdering the police, had to mean his agenda was a lot more important than sex. Fadyar quickly reached the conclusion that his prime purpose had to be to murder, probably killing Assiter when he returned, or whilst he was crossing the water by boat. The women needed to be neutralised, but why should he not enjoy himself first?

She kept thinking, worrying and trying to recall events. *Everything at first seemed to be going so well. Truscott and Assiter had started out in the morning accompanied as usual by the two CIA agents and followed by Sharid and Mawdud, but then the two British police appeared – why had they both gone on the hill? Had they spotted her two compatriots or had they received some sort of alert? Whatever, the security forces had been* overcome, and Assiter had been captured essentially to plan. *The journey across the mountain, the pick-up of the camper van, everything went so smoothly. Even the police went by them going the wrong way! Surely if the police presence on the hill was an indication that the security forces had received some advance knowledge or alert they would have been much better prepared and co-ordinated? They would have had time to completely seal off every conceivable route and that didn't happen. In fact the reverse was true and no police arrived at the airstrip for nearly a quarter of an hour. Yet, within a minute of arriving at the plane we came under attack from accurate submachine gunfire. It didn't make sense, unless... unless.*

The eruption of her thoughts started to calm and Fadyar felt that the fragmented pieces were falling into place, albeit with certain details unknown. The more she thought of it, the more convinced she became. *Treachery! We must have been betrayed by our own people, someone who knew the mission but who was not interested in a kidnap, someone who wanted to guarantee only an assassination, and whose agents had very nearly succeeded a few moments earlier as we boarded the plane.*

Her eyes watered at the thought of it. Her companions were dead. Good, young lives just thrown away. She wished she had been on the ground when the shots started. She and her three brothers might have succeeded in eliminating the initial few attackers, or at least she could have helped her brave brothers get to safety. Her mind kept going over what had happened. *Her plan had worked, but the traitor had known sufficient detail to devise an even more cunning dénouement. Those who attacked the aircraft when we arrived were expendable. They would either succeed in killing Assiter by shooting up the plane or, even if they failed to kill Assiter, they would prevent it from taking off. In all probability they would subsequently be overpowered and killed by the police in a shoot-out. Once the kidnap attempt had to be aborted, our instructions were to assassinate Assiter and as soon as we did that the police would be there to storm the plane and we would also be killed. It was clever, very clever. No one would ever know the truth or the identity of the real killers, those faceless people who only ever planned for an assassination. Which left the mysterious Donaldson – how did he fit into it?*

She sub-consciously shook her head and then it struck her. *Of course! If we had failed on the hill to kidnap Assiter, Donaldson needed to be there as a back-up assassin at the dam or lodge. He had simply taken advantage of the women whilst he waited to see the outcome of our own mission. He worked for the apparently respectable Crossland who, it was obvious now, must also be part of Claude Carron's network, and why she had been told to contact him regarding the Chalthoum account.*

It all fitted – or so it seemed to Fadyar. The more thought she gave it the more convinced she became of her theory that they had been cruelly betrayed. Whatever transpired during or after the kidnap, her masters had planned all along that Assiter would be killed. There was one remaining question she needed to answer in order to be certain: Why was Mrs Crossland also at Mealag? Fadyar desperately hoped that Cindy was not involved somehow, too.

Curry was passed a note saying the two hostage negotiators were at the scene. He spoke with them for a full fifteen minutes, briefing them on salient facts which the two noted down on small, wire-spiral, bound notebooks. He listened to their questions, gave the answers and issued the order for officer Christine Fellows to be the first to speak to the terrorist onboard the plane. Fadyar noticed a white flag held aloft in an unarmed officer's right hand as he walked next to another unarmed officer, a female and one dressed in civilian clothing. She held up a large board on which in thick black marker ink was written a phone number. Fadyar picked up her mobile, dialled and listened.

"I'm Christine. How are you?"

"I do not need anything. If any officer attacks the plane, I shall blow it up along with Mr Assiter. Explosives are wired throughout the cabin and I have grenades and automatic weapons." Fadyar assertively replied.

"I understand. What can I call you?"

Fadyar did not reply and several moments passed before Officer Fellows spoke again in a calm, unhurried, reassuring voice. "Is Mr Assiter well?"

"Yes."

"Is it possible for you to give me some certainty of that, please? I should like to sure."

Fadyar beckoned Assiter to stand up by raising her hand gun up and down. He did so and then sat down. Fadyar passed him the phone. Say "Hello," she told him.

"Hello," said a nervous Assiter.

"Are you alright?" Christine asked quickly.

"Fine. Do as she says." Assiter replied, quickly handing the phone back.

"Thank you," said Christine.

"Please go away. If you all stay away and do nothing, Mr Assiter will remain safe and well. I will phone you if I need anything." Fadyar said.

"Can I call you, Fadyar. It is Fadyar isn't it?"

The question temporarily stunned Fadyar, although after a moment's reflection she realised that of course the negotiator would know, either from Mrs Crossland or from the intelligence gathering process. There was nothing sinister in the question, but she gave considerable thought to her reply. She could not get the idea of betrayal out of her mind; it was almost choking her. People she trusted, or had probably met. Thoughts of their duplicity, their cowardice, their ruthlessness burned inside her.

"No, not Fadyar. My name is Yasmin Hasan."

"OK, Yasmin. But I should like to talk to you about how we might resolve this situation. Can we do that?" Christine gently enquired, but Fadyar shouted back.

"Go away, now, please" and brandished her automatic.

"Yasmin, if you or Mr Assiter want anything just give me a call." Christine and the officer returned to the perimeter and waited. The initial contact had been made, carried out by the book. Its brevity was not at all unusual. If this incident followed the norm everyone could now be in for a long wait.

Silver was struggling to keep only one person at a time from talking in the ensuing discussion. Everyone seemed agreed that what had transpired was unexpected. The hostage taker was calm and allowed her victim the phone without making any demands. There was the usual threat which had to be taken seriously, but it appeared Assiter was in no immediate danger.

A small panel of vetted medical experts, notably of psychiatrists and psychologists, will be quickly established as part of the support services the Gold and Silver command can call upon in hostage or similar type situations where knowledge of the mental condition of the suspect is important. The small team is often housed in a specially equipped room that enables secure communication to the various command centres. If it can be arranged a trained psychologist will also be present near to the scene, but not at the face of a hostage negotiation. Within the hastily convened room at a Glasgow hospital, real excitement had been caused by Fadyar Masri giving her real name and the psychologists were considering why she had done so. They were also trying to absorb what information the police had passed onto them about the terrorist and what the appropriate response should be in the light of the threat to the hostage himself and his mental condition.

"We wait" Maythorp said. The command rooms at Gold, Silver and Bronze were now all quiet, activated only by routine messages and updates. An exhaustive weather report for the area was received detailing the anticipated rainfall, wind speed and so on in half-hourly intervals for the next twenty four hours. It would be revised hourly. Coffee, tea and sandwiches were taken. There were no changeovers, even of the more junior personnel. Many decided to walk around the room and stretch their legs. Ten minutes, twenty minutes, forty minutes elapsed before one of the telephones on Maythorp's desk rang. It was from the head of the psychological team.

"We have concluded our initial assessment of the suspect's state of mind. We find her calm and rational. She is lucid. We rule out any drug dependency, though this may become apparent later. The absence of any demand may simply be an oversight, though unlikely as the suspect would have received intense training and exposure to conditioning techniques, including that of hostage negotiation. It would appear therefore, that at this stage the captor has no demand to make. The giving of her real name is highly unusual. The first aspect of the terror camp training is to disassociate the subject from their past, and therefore they are told they are no longer the same person. In other words they receive a new name and a new identity. Her original name will never have been referred to again, and she would have undergone extreme interrogation as part of her training to ensure that she was able to withhold revealing her original name even under duress. The importance of why she did so, willingly and voluntarily, cannot be overstated. It is remarkable. We recommend the negotiators continue to use it, unless it upsets the subject, as it is possible that for some reason she is losing her commitment to the cause in which she once believed. There may be other explanations, but we rule out memory loss or psychological problems as being causative. She would have lost all contact with her parents and relatives as part of her indoctrination and if she now feels her situation is hopeless it is possible she gave her real name so that her family will become aware of her sacrifice."

"She is also polite – you will recall she used the word 'please' at one point. That is also a very positive development. We assess the subject as educated who quite probably has been brought up in a civilized household. The hostage seems to be withstanding his ordeal reasonably well and at this stage we have no concerns regarding his mental stability, though his voice indicates he is understandably nervous. We are of the view that a reasonable relationship already exists between captor and captive. He quickly returned the telephone to Yasmin Hasan, but we do not think that was as a consequence of being forced to do so – in fact almost the reverse. We believe he wanted to say nothing more and was simply endeavouring to maintain relations with her."

Maythorp thanked the doctor and relayed the information to Bronze. As soon as he had finished he received a flash note on his screen saying the detailed drawings of the Cessna were now being examined by the SAS in Hereford who were considering the options for storming the plane, if so ordered, and by Bronze who was arranging for the camera to be installed if circumstances permitted. It was just under an hour later when Silver received a message that a small contingent of the SAS had landed at the scene, having received their final operational briefing on the journey in their unmarked helicopter. They would be given the exclusive use of a TSG van and remain isolated from all other units until needed. Maythorp instructed Bronze that there was to be no action taken at the scene unless Assiter was killed. Then the plane would be stormed, under SAS direction with the assistance of the TSG.

82

The time had passed in silence within the plane. Fadyar had been continuing her reflections as the events of the day continually churned in her mind. For no particular reason, she found herself thinking of Paulette Assiter.

"Your wife said you were a good person."

She had broken the silence and a startled Assiter replied, "She did? When?" He asked anxiously.

"Today," she nonchalantly replied

"You spoke to Paulette today? Is she safe? She's not been hurt, has she?" A note of alarm entered his voice and his concern brought the command centres back to full attention as his words were transmitted into their respective rooms.

"Of course, you don't know, do you? Yes, I spoke to her this morning, and Mrs Crossland. They can tell you all about it, but they were being held captive by a truly evil man who was doing disgusting things, hurting them."

"*What?* Who did this? Was it one of your people? Is she, are they, all right?" Assiter's questions blurted out, panic stricken by what Fadyar had told him.

"Please calm down, Mr Assiter. No one in my team would do such things and I certainly would not tolerate it. Actually, the man used to be a soldier in the British Army but I rescued them, and if they were here they would tell you all about it as they are alive, safe and well. But that is not the point I wanted to make."

Assiter knew there was no reason for Fadyar to lie as her story could all too easily be verified when his ordeal was over and anyway, if his captor was correct about the microphones, the police would be hearing this conversation as they were speaking and no doubt someone would be quickly checking it out.

"If you rescued them I am obviously grateful. Who was this man?"

"I am not sure of his name, but it's possible Mrs Crossland

does. I think she called him Donaldson or something similar. Anyway, I was thinking of what you said earlier about my colleagues and we spoke of them as good people. It was a similar phrase to that used by your wife today, about you."

"Paulette said that? That's typical of her. I suppose we all try to be good people or think we are," Assiter said.

"Well, there's half an army of people out there that probably think I am evil. A wicked, heartless terrorist, but they would be wrong in one important respect. I am not intrinsically an unkind person, nor heinous. It is true that I have planned your kidnap, meticulously I thought. I put so much effort into it day after day, night after night I went to sleep dreaming of nothing else. The man who attacked your wife and Mrs Crossland also planned things. He also defiled and then killed three little girls in Iraq and I suspect a number of others. In my view he is evil, totally evil. He does what he does to satisfy only his own perverted desires. He has no cause, no beliefs, no morals. He is totally selfish and utterly ruthless. I believe we are both better than that." Fadyar angrily spat out her words.

Assiter was stunned and worried, "… did he hurt Paulette or Cindy?"

"Not seriously, they are ok. I give you my word."

"Thank you" said Assiter, still concerned.

"I should like to ask you something though, if you can tell me? Fadyar enquired.

"Anything, go ahead. If I know the answer I will tell it to you truthfully," Assiter wanted to ensure he maintained his captor's confidence.

"How did Mrs Crossland meet Mr Truscott?"

"Oh, that's easy. Cindy was injured in the terror attack when the London Underground got bombed. She happened to be on the same train as Gordon and he looked after her until they were rescued. They stayed in touch and she eventually left her husband to live with him here. In fact it was when they were both here last Christmas that we arranged this holiday of mine."

"Thank you," Fadyar said slowly. She now knew for certain that Cindy Crossland could not be part of any plot and that her presence at Mealag was, after all, just coincidence.

Several minutes again passed in silence before Assiter spoke. "Your plan was obviously a good one, otherwise I wouldn't be here, but why did you think you could get away in a plane? It would be detected on radar, and the military would shoot it down."

Fadyar thought carefully about whether to reply, knowing that she would be overheard by those listening-in.

"I don't think we would have been shot down. The British would certainly not take responsibility for your death, and so would not act on their own, though their jets would shadow us. Your own government would have to make that decision. The political pressure on your President would be such that he would wait. Your kidnap is embarrassing enough – he would not want to explain why he killed you, when he could have waited. He would have hoped to negotiate your release, but at that time we would have landed in a country friendly to our cause and from there I was to hand you over to others. You would still be alive and, whilst you remained so, we would all be safe."

"That's a hell of a gamble," said Assiter, not knowing quite what else to say, then added, "where were we headed?"

"I will not say that, but the plane can cruise at about 250 knots and has a range of more than 1700 miles. I don't think using a plane was any more of a risk than certain other aspects of your kidnap. It *was* a good plan but others…. "

Fadyar was interrupted as a noisy helicopter hovered overhead and shone an intensely bright light into the cabin. Fadyar went to the window but was blinded by the dazzling brightness. She picked up the phone and dialled. Almost instantly, it was answered.

"Hello Yasmin. This is Christine. How can I help you?" spoken very softly and in the same languid but assured voice.

"Get the helicopter away now! Stop putting in your bugging devices unless you want to this to end in thirty seconds." Fadyar threatened menacingly.

Bronze, overhearing the conversation, immediately ordered the helicopter to withdraw.

"That's better. Thank you," said Fadyar politely as the noise of the rotors rapidly receded.

She turned to Assiter, "Why did they do that? Why try and

deliberately upset me? They must be able to listen to us. They know you are unharmed and that I haven't made any demands. Fools. All they are likely to do is make me angry." She found herself explaining the obvious to her captive, but her words were also deliberately meant for the ears of her pursuers.

"I cannot answer you, Fadyar, or if you prefer, Yasmin. They work to orders, procedures, rulebooks, but sometimes all that does is stifle initiative and common sense. We call it the tick box mentality and it pervades all aspects of commercial, political and law enforcement agencies."

Fadyar did not reply, still deeply troubled and absorbed by her own thoughts.

Several minutes elapsed in total quiet before a hesitant Assiter spoke again. "I'm sorry to ask but what is going to happen to me, now your kidnapping mission is over?"

Again Fadyar did not reply directly, "We were talking about evil, weren't we? Before the helicopter flew over."

"Yes, that man" said Assiter.

"Not just him, there are others; those who remain faceless and who commit their evil on a grand scale from plush office chairs." Fadyar corrected her still handcuffed captive. "I look around this mountain area in Scotland and in a strange way it reminds me of what my homeland used to be like. Not the terrain nor the weather of course, but peaceful, beautiful. Nature is in harmony with itself and without the horrid, foul footprints of an evil mankind all over it. Iraq was like that when I was a child, but now there is blood everywhere. Buildings are destroyed daily, people that were once neighbours are fighting each other whilst foreign troops... " she paused and raised her voice, "... seek to impose their will, their beliefs, their politics on everyone. And here, today, in this lovely location facing the islands and the sea in front of us and the big mountains behind us, brave men, good men, yours and mine have died, their flesh torn to ribbons by red hot bullets. A few miles away, a depraved man seeks to violate innocent women. That sort of thing does not belong here – and neither does it belong in my homeland, Mr Assiter, where you and your President send your soldiers whilst you sit in those big chairs."

Assiter was lost for words. He had spent his life serving his country, helping to formulate its most important policies and implementing its global, sometimes, stellar strategies. He believed in them, and truly loved his nation and the supremacy of its doctrines and political systems. The woman sitting across from him was not actually questioning those, yet what she said was troublesome to him as for some considerable time he had found himself increasingly sceptical of the morality of it all. In a few simple words, she had articulated for him how he felt, expressing feelings and emotions he had never before fully analysed.

"You are a remarkably brave and intelligent young woman, Yasmin. And you are also very perceptive. I am glad we met, though it would perhaps have been better in other circumstances." He spoke seriously, but both smiled.

"I need to trust you, Mr Assiter." she replied.

"Trust *me*? How, with what? What can I do?"

"Yasmin Hasan or Fadyar Masri will not be remembered, at least not for long. I will be attacked and vilified by your press and government. What I and my brave comrades have done today will not influence events let alone alter policy. But you, Mr Secretary of State, are in a position where you can change things. Your wife said you are a good person. I believe her. Listen to her, and do what you can to stop this desecration of our beautiful lands and bring to justice those that dishonour them."

Fadyar cut his handcuffs and, looking at him directly, carefully repeated the words "I trust you."

Before Assiter could stop her Fadyar placed her gun to her head and pulled the trigger.

83

"This is Bronze. All units, stay where you are!" Curry's voice rang out and into a hundred radio receivers. No one moved. Several nervous minutes later, Curry asked the hostage negotiator to make a fresh approach to the plane, but as she stepped forward the boarding steps began to lower and a dazed looking Assiter appeared at its door.

"She's dead. There are no explosives." His words were being instantly relayed by the microphone on Officer Fellowes tunic.

"Stay there, Sir. Please. Are you hurt at all?" the negotiator asked.

"No. I'm fine but I shall be glad to be off this goddam plane."

"I understand Sir, but I must ask you to wait a short while longer."

Curry was taking no chances. Assiter might be under all sorts of pressure to walk down the steps and he might be wired with explosives ready to be detonated by the terrorist. He sent two fully protected officers to the plane and withdrew all other personnel.

"Please come slowly down the steps and then turn completely around, very slowly", instructed an officer.

Assiter obeyed and as the officer approached him impatiently explained "It's OK, I tell you. She's dead, killed herself."

"If you don't mind Sir, I have to check you. I'm sure you understand."

He gave Assiter a thorough body search and, satisfied there were no hidden weapons or explosives, spoke into his radio to Curry who immediately ordered four more officers to meet Assiter at the foot of the steps. Paulette Assiter was watching intently. Alongside a few officers, she, Gordon, Cindy and Sandy had taken up position close to a temporarily erected 'DO NOT CROSS' tape that stretched across the landing strip well to the rear of the plane, but she was able to see her husband.

"Thank God, there's Dean," she cried out, relieved to see her husband. "He's alive!" she yelled, hugging Gordon and then Cindy.

The officers arrived and, taking hold of Assiter, started to quickly walk away from the aircraft. Paulette could contain her joy no longer and ran through the tape shouting and waving to her husband.

"Dean. Dean. I'm here."

Her dash across the field had taken everyone by surprise and it took Gordon and several officers a few brief moments to react before they, too, ran after her.

"No, Paulette. Stay here." Gordon shouted as he caught and grabbed her. "Come on Paulette, they need to check Dean first. He will be here soon," and he turned and started to lead her back to the tape.

The injured Mattar had been lying motionless, his body almost totally concealed amidst the pile of abandoned luggage, now some considerable distance from the aircraft which was occupying everyone's attention at the far end of the runway. He was still losing blood from the wound in his side but he had the strength to slowly move his hand over his Golatz. The sound of the commotion caused by Paulette's rush towards her husband enabled him to accurately assess the woman's precise whereabouts on the field. Making a supreme effort to overcome the pain, Mattar rolled on his back and squeezed the trigger. Bullets sprayed in a lethal arc of ninety degrees, bouncing off rocks and the runway before the police were able to silence him firing. Four bodies lay on the grass strip. Two were officers, one badly injured, the other dying. The two others were that of Paulette and Gordon whose arm protectively pinned her slim body to the ground. As the shooting ended and more police ran to them, Paulette tried to raise herself up but screamed, "Oh Gordon... No... No!"

Her cries were heard by Cindy as she and others rushed to Paulette and the injured officers. Gordon was moaning, quietly, and a large wound was evident in his back. Cindy cradled him in her arms.

"Gordon, it's me Cindy. Please be alright. Please."

He did not move. Cindy, oblivious of what was happening around her, kept talking to Gordon. The officers and paramedics that had run to her were now pulling her reluctantly away.

"We have to ma'am. It's for the best," a man in a yellow jacket spoke into her ear as a couple of ambulances screamed onto the airstrip.

"Let us take over. He needs to get hospital quickly."

Cindy was hysterical. Paulette and Assiter were reunited but only briefly as they insisted that they wanted to comfort Cindy. The next few minutes passed as a blur for Cindy. Gordon received two injections and was laid carefully on a stretcher. A hastily erected drip was inserted into his wrist, an ambulance man holding up the bag of saline solution. His mouth and nose were covered by a white, plastic mask from which a narrow tube led to a small canister. Four burly paramedics then carried the stretcher to an ambulance, and Cindy, Paulette and Dean clambered into the other. Both then made a short journey out of the airfield entrance and along the tarmac road to a waiting Mountain Rescue helicopter, already starting up.

"Where are they taking him?" Cindy cried. "I must go with him. Please let me go with him." She struggled free of Paulette's comforting embrace and ran towards the helicopter.

"I must come with him," she pleaded to a crewman who didn't argue and helped her up into the belly of the chopper.

Almost immediately, the rotors increased speed and it lifted off.

"Mr Assiter. You should also be given a medical check. Can you come with us please?" an ambulance woman asked.

"Do you know where they are taking Gordon?" he asked.

"Inverness Hospital. He will be there in only a few minutes flying."

"Then if you want me to have a check-up, that's where I'll be, with my wife"

"I will have to get clearance on that, Sir."

She contacted her superior, who in turn contacted Curry.

"Where is he going?" Curry asked impatiently. He had enough things on his mind to do with sorting out the scene and getting the various forensic teams organised but as Bronze Commander it was another decision for him to make.

"Inverness Hospital. If you are agreeable, Sir."

"OK. He will be accompanied at all times, and I mean all times, by an armed guard of eight officers. Two must travel with him in the ambulance, two will be in a leading police vehicle and four others will follow in a Cat 1 specially equipped vehicle. Both he and his wife will be required to give statements as soon as they are fit to do so," he issued the orders.

Three minutes after he spoke, a white van that had been parked in the midst of others along the perimeter wall of the small airfield drove carefully out onto the narrow tarmac road, later making a rendezvous with a Merlin helicopter at Broadford airport, Isle of Skye. The discreet SAS contingent was on its way back to their Herefordshire base, their expert services not used.

Once Curry was satisfied that the scene was totally secure, the hostage safe and the injured evacuated, he contacted Bill Ritson, manning the room at the Eagles Rest Hotel.

"All secure here, Bill. I'll leave the lads to stay around. Everyone is now off the scene pending forensics and the usual clean up."

"Great, John. Thanks. Excellent job. At least the hostage is safe but the aftermath will be interesting. See you in a while. Would you like me to contact Silver and Gold?"

"Yes please" said Curry.

After a few moments Bill Ritson formally reported that the incident was over and requested Silver and Gold to stand down. They both congratulated Ritson and Curry on a successful outcome. An hour later, the Home Secretary added his own thanks and those of the Prime Minister to all the personnel who had served in Gold, Silver and Bronze commands. When Curry returned, he joined Ritson who had already begun winding down the Bronze command room.

"Time to call everyone in" he said to Ritson, who nodded.

Curry switched on the radio and spoke to all the units involved in the rescue.

"Debrief at the hotel in one hour."

84

Cindy had been waiting anxiously in a side room that the hospital staff had offered for her exclusive use. She had been warned the operation was likely to be lengthy and that she may not be able to see Gordon for several hours. She was desperately tired, exhausted, but her concern for Gordon was keeping her awake and alert. A look in the mirror showed the extent of her anguish, but also revealed to her that she was badly in need of a shower and a change of clothes. The events of the morning, which seemed a distant memory now, had prevented her from using any make-up and she irrationally told herself that she had to look good for when Gordon opened his eyes. She started to cry again. She was often breaking into small bursts of uncontrollable crying and wondered if she had been wise in refusing any medication. She realised she ought to tell someone about the morning, about Donaldson, but she could not face doing so. Not yet. All she could think about now was Gordon, though she knew she must sometime consider her own health and also tell the authorities what had happened.

"Oh God" she sighed. "I can't, I just can't," and she started crying once more.

Images of Gordon flashed in front of her, a miscellany of intense and varied recollections. She saw his smile, his voice, their times together. She sobbed as she remembered how really happy they had all been less than twenty-four hours earlier when she and Paulette performed their mock striptease. Her thoughts reflected on Gordon's tenderness, his always gentle but sometimes urgent love-making, his thoughtful consideration of her such that he ensured she always gained as much pleasure from it as did he. She saw him standing at the dam gate, relaxed, dressed in jeans or his favourite mole skin trousers and a jumper, awaiting his next band of students just as he had for her when she first went to Mealag. She began to cry again and a nurse appeared asking if she needed anything. Cindy shook her head. Unwilling to reveal the events of the morning, she asked simply if there was anywhere she could take a shower and borrow a comb.

"Come with me. I know just the place."

Cindy followed and they entered a large room, beautifully equipped with a bed, television and its own en-suite bathroom.

"We have a few of these for private patients, but you can use it. You will find shampoos and even a small make-up kit including comb."

"That's so kind of you, but I will be happy to pay. It's no problem"

"No need, but anyway we can talk later. If you need anything just ring the buzzer or come and see me. I'm only down the corridor."

"Is there any news of Gordon?"

"No. He is still in theatre. I will let you know as soon as he comes out."

Cindy showered. Refreshed, she sat in the chair and was trying to focus on reading a glossy magazine. She found it hard to concentrate and had just put the book to one side when there was a knock on the door. Several police were surrounding Paulette and Dean, with others stationed along the corridor. Cindy was overjoyed to see her friends and invited them in.

"I am just so sorry. It's all my fault, Cindy. I shall never forgive myself." Paulette was full of remorse.

"It wasn't your fault, Paulette. If it had been Gordon on that plane coming down the steps I would have done the same. Please, don't blame yourself."

"You are so kind, Cindy, a true friend. I have told Dean how brave you were you this morning, and how you kept that monster away from me."

"That must have been terrifying. I learnt a bit about that on the plane, from the woman," Assiter added.

They spent several more minutes whilst he repeated to Cindy what he had already told Paulette about events on the aircraft and the conversation he had engaged in with Fadyar.

"Extraordinary thing to do," said Assiter. "I am amazed she didn't kill me. Paulette tells me that her instructions were to kill me if the kidnap attempt failed."

"Yes, she mentioned something similar to that at the lodge this morning. She would be bound to create world headlines had she done so." Cindy was glad to have the diversion of conversation.

"How would you assess her, Cindy? Was she for real?" Assiter asked.

"I'm not sure I understand quite what you are driving at Dean, but she saved our lives when she didn't have to. She put herself and her mission in danger to prevent something she found abhorrent. I will always be grateful to her for that. Yes, she was 'for real' as you put it. I think she was a very genuine person and I believed her story regarding her parents killing in Iraq."

"What's that then, Paulette, you haven't told me this?" Assiter asked questioningly.

"Dean, you and I have not stopped speaking about today's events. There simply has not been time for everything. Look, Cindy and I can talk to you later about all that. For the moment, we must think only of Gordon."

"Yes, my dear, of course. But for what it is worth I, too, think she was genuine and very courageous. She died for her principles, but actually those were not terrorism. Her beliefs could have been Muslim, Christian, Buddhist or all of them. I think, paradoxically, she believed in the sanctity of life and the right of people across the world to live their life as they want to, not as others wish it. She abhorred evil and wrongdoing. That is why she saved you this morning, even though it might have put her mission to capture me at risk."

They chatted for a while longer, but with no news of Gordon forthcoming Paulette offered to stay with Cindy, for at least a few hours.

"Dean, darling. Cindy must be exhausted, I know I am. I think we need to rest up here now, just us two girls."

"Sure, of course. How thoughtless of me. I'm so sorry Cindy. The police have booked me and Paulette into a hotel in the town, so I will go there now. Call me if there is any news, will you?"

Cindy agreed she would, as she kissed Assiter's cheek at the door.

Paulette was a necessary tower of strength to Cindy. She organised food and asked the police to urgently obtain some clothes of Cindy's and hers from Mealag Lodge which arrived two hours later. Importantly she told the police and the hospital about their ordeal at the lodge. The police agreed to take a full statement later, but the hospital persuaded Cindy that she ought to be examined and a blood test taken. Although unpleasant, it helped to take Cindy's mind away from dwelling on Gordon. Later, Paulette made numerous telephone calls and again enlisted the police help to contact Sandy MacLean, finally catching up with him at his sister-in-law's house. After briefly talking to him, Paulette passed the phone over to Cindy. He explained that in the confusion at the end of the siege he was whisked away by the police. He tried to get back to Mealag but it had already been sealed off and no one was being allowed to enter under any circumstances.

"Crawling with the blue shirts," was how Sandy described it. "They were also at the garages and the boats. Arc lights set up everywhere, looked like a damn pop concert."

He spoke for over half an hour with Cindy. It took up more time, temporarily slightly easing her angst.

As the hours passed by and midnight approached, tiredness overcame them both. Cindy lay on the bed, shut her sore, reddened eyes and was shortly joined by Paulette who comfortingly put her arm over her friends shoulder.

At three in the morning there was a slight knock at the door. Blearily, the two women woke as a doctor in a crisp, white knee-length coat entered the room.

"Mrs Crossland?" he enquired looking at both.

"Yes, that's me." Cindy replied. The doctor glanced at Paulette, then back towards Cindy's pained face.

"It's all right, Doctor. This is my friend. It's about Gordon, isn't it? How is he?"

"He has had major surgery and he remains in a very grave condition. The bullet entered his right side and struck his spinal column where it caused severe injury. It then deviated upwards and came to rest in his neck, below his ear. Another bullet entered his side causing a lot of bleeding but, essentially, that is a flesh wound and not life threatening. He is out of theatre but the next few hours will be critical. His body has received a tremendous shock and we are having to maintain the life support systems."

"Oh my God," said Cindy, dropping to her knees sobbing. Paulette rushed to comfort her and slowly Cindy rose from the floor.

"What are his chances, Doctor, of pulling through this?" Cindy enquired.

"I would be lying to you if I did not say that we are very concerned. He is stable at the moment and sedated. We shall have to keep him that way for some while on the Intensive Care Unit. We may know a little more by morning."

"Can I see him? Please." Cindy pleaded.

"Of course. You can sit by him but I would advise against many visitors. In fact, ideally, probably only you, but if your friend would like to pop in now and then, I'm sure that would be fine."

Cindy was stunned and dazed. She had heard what the surgeon had told her, but did not wish to comprehend its significance.

"I'll go now if I may."

"Certainly. I will inform the ICU staff. Follow me and I will show you where he is."

Cindy opened the door and saw Gordon lying in the bed. He was surrounded with an array of electronic equipment, tubes, three drips and breathing apparatus. The steady beat of the machines, interspersed with irregular high-pitched beeps served only to remind her of the gravity of Gordon's condition. She drew up a chair and sat beside him as the doctor withdrew from the room. Paulette sensed Cindy wanted to be alone and also left.

When she had gone, Cindy broke down, "You stupid, stupid man. Why did we have to do all that? I told you not to," but she was not really angry. She knew that Gordon had felt compelled to help his friend but he was now paying a terrible price. She felt under the sheets for his hand and held it softly. "You held my hand once and saved me," she whispered. "I just hope I can do the same for you now."

The minutes and hours passed without Cindy once releasing his hand from hers. Paulette came in briefly a couple of times and brought in a coffee. Busy, pleasant nurses entered and checked

Gordon every fifteen minutes and were constantly monitoring the equipment from room 275 on the console of their centrally placed desk within the ICU. Cindy spoke to Gordon about her plans for them both when he was out of hospital and how she would look after him whilst he recovered his strength. She talked of Mealag and the dam, and she started chatting to him about when they might next go to the villa – but it was a one-sided conversation. Gordon's laboured breathing was the only sound that emanated from the bed, though Cindy felt he had slightly squeezed her hand when she mentioned the underground bombing.

Although well past daybreak, Cindy was almost asleep in her chair when she was awoken from her slumber by a constant high-pitched tone, accompanied almost instantly by a rapid intermittent alarm sounding in the room. Nurses and doctors rushed in and moved Cindy aside. A doctor gave Gordon another injection and started resuscitation whilst the paddles of the crash trolley were prepared. The medical team tried to resuscitate Gordon three times. Twenty minutes after the alarm was triggered, the doctor slowly stood up and took a small torch from his breast pocket. In turn, he lifted each of Gordon's eyelids and shone the piercing light into them. As he turned off the torch he glanced at the clock, immediately calling out the time and pronounced him dead. Cindy, the tears flowing down her cheeks, went to the bed and placed her arms around Gordon hugging him tightly, not wanting to let him go, crying loudly.

"I am truly very sorry. We did all we could," the doctor said, but his words went unheard.

85

At the time of its purchase, Gordon had issued instructions to his small property company that the cottage should always be made available for Cindy if ever she needed it and was never to be sold whilst she was alive. As she gradually came to terms with her grief, the cottage had proved of immense benefit as she slowly began immersing herself again in the garden, pruning and clearing, but she found more difficult the routine household tasks. She thought constantly of Gordon. She was frequently being reminded of him and the awful events of that September day: the correspondence, the funeral, her own final negative blood test report, and even the songs she would hear on her radio. The days seemed interminably long and she was unable to concentrate on any of her unfinished articles. Evenings were spent sitting alone and usually ended with her crying herself to sleep on the sofa. She rarely spoke to anyone, though she had kept in touch with Paulette. She had had a very brief conversation with Alan, who expressed his relief that she was unharmed in the terrorist incident itself, and his horror and revulsion at the assault upon her by Donaldson. He had sounded genuinely remorseful when he apologised for not listening to her warnings about him.

Now, on a damp, dark November morning, two months since the horrible events leading to Gordon's death, the cold mist clung to the bare branches of the trees and Cindy was picking up the dying twigs of the pruned perennial bushes and gathering the annuals she had dug up. Her thoughts were on Mealag Lodge. She knew she had to visit it again. She had not returned there after Gordon's death, nor even after the service of commemoration and cremation which was the last time she had seen the MacLeans. Gordon had no surviving relatives, or at least none that anyone knew of, his parents having died many years before and he being an only child. No uncles nor aunts seemed to exist and certainly no relative made contact with either Gordon's solicitors nor came to the service which was attended by Dean and Paulette, the

MacLeans, some estate workers, Dimitrius and his family from Monemvasia and several business friends. Chief Inspector Keith Maythorp and Area Inspector John Curry represented the police. Cindy had been given Gordon's ashes and she knew that she must take them to Mealag Lodge and bury or scatter them there. As she was pondering when to go, her telephone rang and she ran inside to answer it.

"Mrs Crossland?"

"Yes."

"Sorry to bother you, Detective Chief Superintendent Ritson speaking. It has now been some while since we last spoke and I was wondering when we could have another chat."

In the immediate aftermath of the terrible events in the Scottish hills, Cindy had given statements about the Donaldson assault and about the kidnapping to a number of different police officers of which Ritson had been the most senior. As the weeks passed, she had forgotten that he had said he would in all probability need to re-interview her dependent upon what his subsequent enquiries revealed about the plot and those who perpetrated it, and so she was startled to hear his voice.

"Oh. Yes. I'd forgotten you said you might want to speak to me again. What about tomorrow?" she asked.

"Saturday? Well, I suppose so if that is convenient to you," he replied, "about eleven?"

"Sorry, I had forgotten it was Saturday tomorrow," said Cindy. "The days seem all the same to me now, I forget which day it is most of the time. Are you sure it is convenient to you?"

"No problem at all. See you tomorrow, then." Ritson rang off.

As she returned to the garden she wondered just what was so important as to merit such a high-ranking officer from London to visit her on a Saturday.

The following day, exactly as her hall clock struck eleven, Ritson arrived and rang the bell. Cindy invited him inside and they sat in her small, cosy lounge. After exchanging pleasantries and enquiring as to how she was getting, along Cindy brought in some coffee and biscuits. Now they were both more relaxed, Ritson brought the conversation around to the main point of his visit.

"Mrs Crossland, we have obviously been investigating all the circumstances regarding the plot that ultimately led to the tragic death of Mr Truscott and I do have some unanswered questions, more akin to loose ends, that I should like your help upon if you feel up to it." Cindy nodded and he continued.

"We have a statement from Mrs Assiter wherein she describes the moment that the female terrorist, let us call her Fadyar, attacked the man Donaldson. Evidently, Fadyar knew your name. Mrs Assiter is positive Fadyar called you Mrs Crossland. Have you any idea why she should recognise you?"

"Did she? Yes, I think she did call my name at least once. I really can't remember it clearly, but I believe she did. She knew Paulette too, of course, as Mrs Assiter."

"Quite so. But Mrs Assiter thought the woman terrorist was surprised to see you." He left it for Cindy to decide if it was a question or a statement of fact.

When Cindy did not respond, Ritson added, "As if she wasn't expecting to, and of course if that is right, that she did not expect to see you, why should she know your name?"

"Well, I can only guess that she had done her homework pretty thoroughly on Dean and Gordon. If she had, she probably knew who I was."

"Mmmm. But then she would not have been surprised, would she? When she saw you in the kitchen," he probed gently but firmly.

Cindy shrugged her shoulders, "I've no idea. Is it important?" she asked somewhat impatiently.

Ritson did not answer but instead decided to change tack.

"How are you getting along? Perhaps there are questions you would like to ask me. If I can help I will." Ritson was anxious to put Cindy at ease. The probing could start again in a minute.

"No, not really. Of course I have hundreds of questions, but none of them matter anymore. Only one is important to me. Why Gordon, why Gordon? He was such a lovely man." She started to cry.

Ritson offered a handkerchief, but Cindy declined and wiped away her tears with a tissue hastily pulled from a box on the table.

"Thanks, I'll be fine in a minute."

"How are you finding life back in Worcestershire? I presume

you have some friends you can see? Didn't you used to live not far away in the Cotswolds?"

For the first time since her return, she momentarily thought of Don and the gun dogs and wondered what they had been up to. The club had not entered her traumatised mind and she resolved to try and summon the courage to make contact again.

"Er, yes, I suppose so, but I haven't felt up to doing much visiting." Cindy answered despondently.

"What about your ex-husband, is he still living in Stillwood?"

Cindy replied instantly, "Oh yes. Well, he was the last time we spoke as he hadn't been able to sell it. Although he has the house there he spends most of his time in London and the South East and only comes to Red Gables on the occasional week-end. He has found someone else and seems very happy. When the news broke about what had happened he was obviously very concerned and supportive, but I haven't seen or spoken to him recently."

Ritson pondered carefully about his next question and a silence filled the air for several seconds before he spoke.

"Were you aware that the funds used to finance the kidnap terror plot were deposited and later withdrawn from his bank?"

Cindy's face fell. "What? Are you saying Alan's bank was involved?"

Then the realisation hit her – *the female terrorist*. No wonder she recognised Cindy and that she, Cindy, found her vaguely familiar. It was the same woman who had visited Alan at home the previous year. Cindy was instantly alarmed at where Ritson's easy style questions were leading. Alan was a lot of things but he was not a terrorist, nor would he ever be involved with terrorism.

"Yes, quite heavily involved. Is it possible you may have met the female, Fadyar, previously? She may have called herself Halima Chalthoum, or possibly Yasmin Hasan."

Cindy's heart was thumping. This was dangerous territory. She had lost one person very, very dear to her and she was not going to stand idly by whilst someone with whom she had been in love with in the past was being implicated of aiding the plot. She just knew that Alan was innocent, but also strongly suspected that any admission of a meeting would be really bad for him.

"Goodness no, Chief Superintendent. I am sure I should remember if I had met her and would have recognised her at Mealag if I had. It's been at least two years since I attended any of the bank's corporate entertainment things where sometimes wives or partners were invited. I can't recall her at any of those I did go to and she certainly never came to Red Gables or our flat in London, if that's what you thinking."

"Are you quite sure, Mrs Crossland? It is very important."

"Certain. I would remember. "

A few minutes later Ritson left. He drove to Red Gables where he knew that Alan Crossland and a smart-looking woman were in residence, having had him tailed when he left his London bank early Friday afternoon. Ritson rang the bell and Crossland answered it.

"My word, it's you again, Superintendent. What brings you here to my home on a Saturday. It must be important. Come in."

"If it's convenient Sir, perhaps we could just stroll around the front lawn. It will not take long."

"As you wish. I'll just grab a coat."

As they started to walk, Ritson explained that he had just finished an interview with Cindy.

"Our enquiries with regard to the bank's involvement, or more specifically your possible personal involvement, in the terrorist activities that led to the assault on Mealag Lodge are now at an end. That is unofficial. It will be made official in due course but as I was passing I just wanted to tell you face-to-face, and off the record, that you have been a very fortunate man."

Crossland gulped, not quite knowing what to say.

"Well, thank you – I think. I appreciate you telling me, but at no time was I involved."

"Sir, I never thought you were knowingly active in funding terrorism, but in my opinion your less than scrupulous actions made it possible to conceal the financing for the attack. Had you been totally truthful at the outset with me our enquiries may have not have been delayed, and it is just possible the terrible business of what happened in Scotland might have been averted. I cannot prove that of course, but I believe it. I also believe you and Mrs Crossland met the female ringleader here at your home or nearby, but you deny it. It is obvious from my enquiries into the plot that Fadyar Masri, or Halima Chalthoum as she was known to you, did know Mrs Crossland as she recognised her and called her by name as the attack unfolded. Despite her grief, Mrs Crossland is a very astute woman and I think – no, I'm certain – that to protect you she is also denying prior knowledge of the terrorist. I can do no more, but I do wish to warn you Mr Crossland. Either get out of banking or stick to the rules. This particular plot has cost a great many lives, probably as far back as your friend Styles. That should remain on your conscience."

Alan was shaken but mightily relieved. He had had been desperately worried for the last two months that Cindy might incriminate him ever since he learned Donaldson had failed. He had no worries now, though he was already realising how hard it was to live racked with the guilt of his own murderous and ill-conceived plot against Cindy.

"Thank you Superintendent, I appreciate all that you say. By the way, did you ever get to the bottom of what Donaldson was doing up there?" Crossland asked innocently.

"He had been following Mrs Crossland around for months, both before but particularly after you dismissed him. We know that much. We are also sure he knew nothing about the visiting American. It seems as though he was fanatically obsessive about your ex-wife and it was just pure coincidence that he was there at the time of the kidnap plot. I have no doubt the unexpected presence of the beautiful Mrs Assiter further inflamed him."

"Cindy was always concerned about him, saying he gave her the creeps and was over familiar, but to my deep regret, I rather dismissed what she was saying as fanciful. If only I had taken more notice and got rid of him earlier." Crossland reflected.

"He was clearly a dangerous psychopath and must have harboured his sexual fantasies regarding your wife for years, really off his head in my view. To get to Mrs Crossland and Mrs Assiter we believe he murdered at least two police officers. Anyway he suffered a horrible, lingering death. I don't know if you have been told, but he took hours to slowly drown in a peat bog. Serve the bastard right." Ritson gave an unusual off-guarded reply.

"At last, something we agree on!" Crossland exclaimed as Ritson turned and walked away to his car.

Alan Crossland went inside and picked up the telephone. "Thank you, Cindy. Thank you."

He then wrote his resignation letter and personally handed it to the chairman on Monday morning. He left the Hannet-Mar International Bank six months later with a tax paid net severance payment in excess of a million pounds and an inflation-proofed final salary pension of around half a million pounds a year. Chloe was finally persuaded to leave her teaching job and they spent the next two years travelling the world together.

86

Mealag Lodge had been boarded and shut since Gordon's death, but the MacLeans still lived in their bungalow and the estate still functioned. Gordon's solicitors had indicated to them that that they would be well provided for when the will was finally proved and the estate was properly safeguarded to ensure its continuance. Much to Cindy's surprise, she had received a phone call saying she would become a very wealthy woman. She hadn't appreciated just how meticulous a man Gordon was until the solicitors contacted her, and it was a surprise that Gordon should have altered his will when he had known Cindy for only a short while. It was only later when speaking with Dean that she learned of Gordon's intention to propose to her. Although overjoyed at what Assiter had said, his comment had really upset Cindy. It reminded her of what might have been; what she had hoped and wished for. *God, how she missed Gordon.* Even now, months later, she could almost imagine he was still there in the room with her, talking together, laughing, kissing. Christmas was nearing and all around her people were getting ready for the festive season. It was the most poignant reminder of the excitement, joy and love she and Gordon had shared twelve months previously, when they talked of a fantastic life together. Now, she was unable to foresee her future, and desperately unhappy. She realised she had to visit the dam and Mealag once more, one last time – she had outstanding business there. She owed it to Gordon, to herself and the MacLeans. It was the only way she would obtain closure.

The journey to Scotland was so unpleasant and heartbreaking she failed to notice the scenery in the early winter sun. The tops of the hills were showing the first heavy snows of winter and the brackens were still retaining their pigments of burnt gold, brown and red. It was probably the most colourful of all seasons in the Highlands but she drove on without a glance. She had reached and passed Corach when her frayed nerves shuddered involuntarily as the dam came into view. All her previous experiences came flooding back, but one particularly was etched on her mind, that first morning Gordon met her. She stopped on the rough ground next to the switchgear building and cried for several minutes.

She had not contacted the MacLeans, deliberately, as she was not sure she wanted to meet anyone but she had written them a letter which she posted en route. She needed time alone, here at the dam and around Mealag. She put on a thick waxed jacket to keep out the chill air and the drizzle away, and walked across the dam wall. In her hand she held a tiny engraved brass urn, and at the gate where Gordon had so often waited she knelt down and laid it on the damp grass. From her pocket she produced a small trowel and, with tears running down her cheeks, she buried the casket. She stood up, wiping her eyes with the back of her hand and walked to the shore, picking up a collection of large stones to place upon the sepulture. She did this several times until she had erected a small cairn.

She stood over it and whispered, "Goodbye my love, my Gordon. Thank you for the dream. I will always love you."

She stood for a few more minutes reflecting on the joys they had shared together and started to cry again. She wandered along the shore, past the peat bog where Donaldson had drowned, and stood on the jetty looking at the empty Mealag Lodge and the deserted chalets. The silence overwhelmed her. She turned, retraced her steps, climbed back over the gate and walked slowly over the dam wall. At the car, she raised the tail gate and put on her gum boots. She climbed the hill where Dean and Gordon had been attacked and passed the grilled entrance to the tunnel where the assailants had hidden, a shiny new padlock securing the same rusting chain. There was no reminder of the four murders that took place here, no markings to indicate the grenade attack, and Cindy did not stop. She climbed onwards and reached the surge shaft protected by the forty-six feet diameter circular fence of nearly three hundred close spaced steel stakes, each one having a sharpened trisection at its top. She stood at the railings and looked into the vastness of the expansion chamber. The autumn rains had swelled the level of the loch and deep below her she could clearly see the rushing water as it sped across the surge shaft and into the start of the high pressure tunnel. Cindy took off her thick jacket and placed it over several of the protective stakes. Holding onto the horizontal bars that held the stanchions in place, she levered herself up and over and stood on the narrow concrete apron inside the barrier. She closed her eyes and stepped forward.

87

It is normal procedure after the activation of the command centres, indeed any large police or prison operation, to hold an initial debrief as soon as practicable afterwards. Everyone, from secretaries in the command office to the Bronze commander himself, has to give their initial thoughts, reactions and comments on the day. The truth is sought and constructive criticism, even if it is about a colleague or superior, is encouraged. These early recollections are followed up later, in depth, but statements made whilst events are still vivid in the mind tend to reveal the most important aspects and are a vital component of any post-operation analysis. Those who took part, whether at the frontline or not, would be tired but none complained. Those who were still on active deployment, at the scene for instance, would have their initial debriefing as soon as they were off-duty. Debriefing is part of the job, however painful some of the facts to emerge might be, and this debriefing was not going to be pleasant for anyone. It never is when fatalities have occurred. Gold and Silver Command went through the same process of winding down, and also their own debriefing. In due course all the debriefing reports would be merged and cross-referenced with an in-depth, subsequent, debrief. An exhaustive set of further questions is asked about the interfaces between the command structures to ensure that they always operate smoothly and effectively. Finally, after several weeks or even months, the full internal report will be made available to the Home Secretary and COBR, and if necessary further detailed reviews will take place involving all the principal agencies in order to determine and implement improvements.

The debriefing of the command and operational personnel had highlighted several major weaknesses in the initial investigations, liaison and the cross-discipline sharing of information plus serious errors in tactical and deployment when bringing the kidnap to an end. All would be actioned; lessons learnt; and the new measures incorporated into the next revised procedural manual. Computer access codes were overhauled and updated. Sharing of information was deemed essential. No one was disciplined; no one was commended. The twenty-four hour TV news stations had exhausted the story within two days and then it was supplanted in their bulletins with news of major floods and landslides in China that had caused significant devastation and loss of life. The serious Sunday papers examined and scrutinised such facts as they had gleaned or had been made available to them, but they too ceased making any further investigations after a couple of weeks. Unsurprisingly, the tabloids had sensationalised the success of the police in defusing the bomb inside the abandoned Land Rover and several alleged eyewitnesses filled more column inches with stories of their lucky escape. The factual aspects of the plot itself were only barely mentioned and nothing of Cindy's and Paulette's ordeal with Donaldson became public. Several years later, due to other factors, the various Scottish constabularies were amalgamated into one unitary force – Police Scotland – though still retaining regional commanders, one of which has responsibility for the Highlands.

GCHQ had spent hours trolling through all the data available to it and after several weeks had found what they were looking for, a lead as to who leaked the holiday plans of the US Secretary of State. Any euphoria was short lived. Sadly for the British, it was not the Americans who slipped up. GCHQ had traced past intercept messages made from a mobile phone user in the Islington area of London to a known organisation long suspected of terrorist sympathies. The information was relayed to the ATU who made the subsequent investigations and enquiries that ultimately led to Detective Chief Superintendent Bill Ritson to be given the job of interviewing Stephen Baker, the boyfriend of Peter Knowles. Baker confessed almost immediately.

It transpired that a couple of years previously he had embarked on a sordid assignation on Hampstead Heath with a young Middle-Eastern teenage boy. Baker became obsessed with the lad and a steamy relationship ensued with both going back to the flat owned by the teenager's wealthy absentee parents. Unknown to Baker, he had been specifically targeted due to his close relationship with Peter

Knowles, and when intimate photographs of him and the boy were pushed under the windscreen wipers of his car one day he realised he was in serious trouble. His blackmailers pressured him to obtain information about the British Government's foreign policy towards Middle-Eastern affairs but Baker knew of none, Peter Knowles never revealing state secrets. Baker had to resort to paying the blackmailers considerable sums of cash. Deeply worried and ever more in debt, Baker had reached desperation point when one day Knowles and he were discussing who to invite to their next party.

"We must of course get Cindy along, she simply makes the whole thing go with such a swing. I suppose we shall also have to invite her rather boring husband." Baker remarked to Knowles.

Without a moment's thought, Knowles replied, "Oh, of course you don't know do you? Well, I think our lovely Cindy is being a rather naughty little girl. I met her the other week and she confirmed to me that she is madly in love with… guess who? My dear, none other than that dishy Gordon Truscott, you know the bachelor millionaire who lives in Scotland."

"Well, shall we invite Cindy and Truscott to our little do in September? It could be fun if she brings her handsome new man!" Baker mischievously laughed.

"Oh they won't be able to. What a pity. Dean Assiter has already agreed to holiday with them in September. Aren't you just so thrilled for her, Stephen? Truscott must be so much better than the banker."

It was Baker's opportunity to get back the negatives of the photos and be rid of the blackmailers, and he took it. It was easy for him to ascertain the precise dates. Assiter's public movements were published well in advance and he therefore knew he would be in the UK on official business until September 11th. It was pretty certain where he would be on the 12th and he had to attend a Presidential Address in Washington on the 25th. Baker fully cooperated with Ritson. He supplied the police with all the names, addresses and phone numbers of those he knew. Peter Knowles retired early without receiving the MBE that was customary for his civil service Foreign Office rank. Baker spent several years in jail, but those whom he had implicated had fled the country.

Several families from Birmingham were interrogated for hours in various police stations, but after careful consideration all were released without charge. The same was true of the friends of the three British-based terrorists; none had any inkling of their acquaintances' radical fundamentalist beliefs. The French police had to endure a similar frustration when they eventually identified Claude Carron and other members of his network. Several simultaneous dawn raids across Paris and the suburbs captured no one. The quarry had fled, appearing to have done so immediately prior to Assiter's visit to Mealag.

88

When Dean Assiter arrived back in Washington DC, the first instruction he gave was to order an internal inquiry into the September 2004 attacks in Haifa Street which had led to many civilian deaths, among which were the parents of Yasmin Hasan. It was a month before the military issued the report and it said little more than the original notes taken at the time.

"Bullshit! This is bullshit," Assiter shouted down the phone. "I want you to find that goddam soldier Briggs and whoever was his platoon commander in Haifa, the one who signed the papers that said it was a bomb blast. When you find them, you haul their asses in and phone me. I wanna see them face-to-face."

The general at the end of the line was not going to argue with the Secretary of State, though why there was all this fuss over what happened several years ago baffled him. Two days later, Assiter got the call.

"We have them both at Maryland. Now what are we to do with them?"

"Hold them. Behind bars if you have to. I'm on my way."

Assiter marched into the detention block of the military base accompanied by two generals, one a four-star and the other a five-star. He had already fully briefed both on the part they should play. Briggs, and his then platoon leader Jacobson were still fortunately in the army. Jacobson had risen to sergeant but Briggs still languished in the rank of private. Both were very nervous about being detained and interrogated by such high-ranking generals. Initially, Jacobson denied that anything but a bomb blast had caused the deaths of Yasmin's parents. The five-star general started to get tough.

"Well you see son, I just don't fuckin' believe you and I take great exception to being lied to. Now, unless you start by telling me how it really was, I'm going to send you to Guantanamo on an extended tour of duty looking after some of the most dangerous bastards God ever placed on this earth. And, you see son, I might just let it be known why I have sent you there."

He let the words sink in. A nervous twitch appeared over the Sergeant's left eyebrow which he tried unsuccessfully to swat away. A trickle of sweat ran down his forehead and onto his cheek. The general continued, "If I do that you ain't coming back son, 'cept draped in the Stars and Stripes and I wouldn't want your mama and papa to see your face. They are a real mean bunch of nutters over there."

The mention of the notorious detention centre made an already nervous Jacobson even more ill at ease but he summoned enough courage to suggest that the general could not do as he threatened. The general walked close up to him and putting his face almost against that of the soldier snarled menacingly, "Sonny boy, don't try and get clever with me. I can do what the fuck I want with you. You are in my army and you signed up to go where I fucking tell you to go. Now stop the crap and tell me like it was, not how it's written on this arse wipe paper."

He waved the official report. Jacobson remained silent.

The general left for the cell down the corridor where Briggs was huddled in a corner. He stood to attention as the general walked in.

"Seems you're being hung out to dry, boy. Your platoon leader says you just lost it and he had to cover for you with the story of the bomb blasts," drawled the general.

"It wasn't like that, Sir." The private stated loudly.

"Then what was it like, soldier boy?"

"Well, there were lots of bombs going off and we didn't know who was shooting at us, so we had to be very careful. We couldn't take risks, Sir."

The General laughed, "Where'd ya dream that load of crap up, Private Briggs? If you didn't know who the fuck was shooting at you, or where they were, you'd all be fuckin' dead. No, I'll tell you what happened and you tell me if I'm wrong. Haifa Street was a bomb alley and you were all pissed off by it. Day after day the same bloody carnage: insurgents fighting insurgents; natives fighting natives; bombing each other, blaming each other – and all of 'em fighting us. Day after fuckin' day. You were understandably pissin' your pants when you walked down it. No shame in that 'cos someone has to go in, at some time. That's our job, see. The army goes where no one else will; to clean up the crap; to sweep up the blood and guts; to reopen the road. Then someone – not you, Private – gave the order to totally clear out the place. Friend or foe, no distinction, just fuckin' wipe 'em out. And you, boy, went in firing your weapon even at innocent people, people who actually might have helped us. Think carefully boy, 'cos your mate up the corridor says you acted alone and he had to cover for you, but I don't believe him."

"OK. OK. It wasn't Jacobsen either. The order came from higher up than him. We were told to go in and it would all be put down as bomb blasts or some such. Anyway, covered up; only enemy in there; no survivors. We were told, totally clear the street. We were green lighted, Sir. Told."

Assiter had heard enough on the relayed speaker system. He went in to the cell, shaking with rage, "Do you know what you did, you mother fucker? You didn't just kill innocent people. You made a terrorist out of one of their children, someone who saw you kill her parents who had nothing to do with the insurgency against us. You made her into a terrorist. That woman has subsequently been responsible for the deaths of several more innocent people and she also captured and could have killed me. That she didn't is down to her ultimate humanity. You make me sick. If I could, I would put you on trial. As it is I shall have to leave that to the army but I hope you remember all your life just what you have done."

Assiter left the room, disgusted. He heard three months later that Briggs and Jacobson were but two of twelve soldiers of varying rank who were charged with dishonourable conduct, found guilty and discharged from the army without benefits. When Assiter learnt that the army hierarchy decided not to prosecute them on more serious charges he picked up the phone and spoke to the generals who had interviewed the soldiers.

"It wasn't us, Secretary of State. The order not to prosecute came from the President's Office."

Assiter was furious and dismayed. In his position within the

Administration, the Secretary of State is entitled to ask for an immediate meeting with the President, who customarily never refuses. As the situation was not one of impending national security it was the following morning when Assiter made his way to the West Wing and to the Oval Office, where the President was standing looking out over the magnificent South Lawn. An aide brought in refreshments just after the pleasant introductions had been exchanged. Assiter and the President had a regular schedule of meetings already planned in their diary, and so the request for a further meeting implied something serious. The President gestured Assiter to sit alongside him on one of the easy chairs at the opposite end of the room from the famous Resolute desk, given to the presidency by Queen Victoria.

"What's up, Dean? Something happened?"

"More accurately not happened, Mr President. You will recall my kidnap and the suicide of the terrorist leader. I investigated her story and found that in fact her parents were murdered, exactly as she said, by our troops. The army eventually conducted a proper investigation and twelve of our guys were found culpable. General Stanway and I were firmly of the view that those involved would be prosecuted for these war crimes. In the event, I learn that all they received was a rap on the knuckles. Those that were still serving were kicked out with a dishonourable conduct charge, those that had left have lost their army benefits."

"What are you suggesting should have happened to these soldiers, Dean?" the President asked.

I believe they should have been put on trial for war crimes or murder. That is what they committed."

"That's a little over the top, Dean, surely? These boys were serving their country, things happen in a war. Collateral is always regretted, but it happens." The President's deep voice was soft, even toned.

"What actually occurred Mr President was not collateral, not some by-product of an operation that went bad. It was deliberate and planned. We have the facts, we know they are guilty," Assiter was becoming exasperated.

"Dean. What good would a murder prosecution serve? Can you

imagine the mileage that would give our enemies? And think of the impact back here with our own folks. It will be a long time before we get out of Iraq and we are already fighting another damned conflict in Afghanistan. It would not be good for public morale, you know, to see their heroes being prosecuted by their own side. Look at the numbers of our war dead. The American people want to believe, Dean – no, they have to believe – that ours is a just cause, and that our boys act properly and honourably. We are trying to bring peace and democracy to troubled lands, all a trial would do is undermine our efforts and sap the army's and the nation's confidence. God, that's shaky enough as it is. No, Dean. A trial is out of the question."

"If that is your view Mr President there is nothing more I can say."

"Thank you, Dean."

As Assiter rose and turned to go out of the door, the President added, "Dean, you have been outstanding in the service of this great nation and to me, personally. I value your wise counsel and your contribution to this administration and I do understand how you feel, especially given the circumstances of your horrific ordeal and the comments made to you by the woman that held you hostage. Believe me, Dean, I studied this case very carefully, and I sincerely wish I could have done as you ask."

★ ★ ★

A month later Assiter, to the delight of his wife, resigned his post citing health reasons and shortly after retired from public life disillusioned with politics. He was a fairly wealthy man having made his money from oil, and used a large slice of it to start a foundation to help finance Iraqi and Middle-Eastern students through American colleges and universities. At the White House farewell dinner in his honour the President gave his Secretary of State a personal thank you letter for his services and presented him with a gift, a copy of the Gettysburg Address enclosed in a silver and gold case.

As he relaxed at home later that evening, and although familiar with the words, Assiter unfurled the scroll and read:

Four score and seven years ago our fathers brought forth on this continent a new nation, conceived in liberty, and dedicated to the proposition that all men are created equal.

Now we are engaged in a great civil war, testing whether that nation, or any nation, so conceived and so dedicated, can long endure. We are met on a great battle-field of that war. We have come to dedicate a portion of that field, as a final resting place for those who here gave their lives that that nation might live. It is altogether fitting and proper that we should do this.

But, in a larger sense, we can not dedicate, we can not consecrate, we can not hallow this ground. The brave men, living and dead, who struggled here, have consecrated it, far above our poor power to add or detract. The world will little note, nor long remember what we say here, but it can never forget what they did here. It is for us the living, rather, to be dedicated here to the unfinished work which they who fought here have thus far so nobly advanced. It is rather for us to be here dedicated to the great task remaining before us — that from these honored dead we take increased devotion to that cause for which they gave the last full measure of devotion — that we here highly resolve that these dead shall not have died in vain — that this nation, under God, shall have a new birth of freedom — and that government of the people, by the people, for the people, shall not perish from the earth.

Assiter carefully replaced the scroll inside its casing, walked over to a cabinet and placed it in a drawer before returning to his chair.

"Paulette. I need a large whisky".